D1228343

The HERO of A HUNDRED FIGHTS

The HERO of a HUNDRED FIGHTS

★ ★ ★ ★ ★ ★

COLLECTED STORIES FROM THE DIME NOVEL KING,

FROM BUFFALO BILL to WILD BILL HICKOK

NED BUNTLINE

☞ EDITED AND INTRODUCED BY
CLAY REYNOLDS

UNION SQUARE
New York

UNION SQUARE
New York
An Imprint of Sterling Publishing
387 Park Avenue South
New York, NY 10016

© 2011 by Clay Reynolds

Library of Congress Cataloging-in-Publication Data

Buntline, Ned, 1822 or 3-1886.
 The hero of a hundred fights : collected stories from the dime novel king, from Buffalo Bill to
Wild Bill Hickok / edited and introduced by Clay Reynolds.
    p. cm.
 Includes bibliographical references.
 ISBN 978-1-4027-5842-3
 1. Buffalo Bill, 1846-1917–Fiction. 2. Hickok, Wild Bill, 1837-1876.–Fiction. I. Reynolds, Clay, 1949-
II. Title.
 PS2156.J2H47 2011
 813'.3–dc22

                    2010034423

Distributed in Canada by Sterling Publishing
c/o Canadian Manda Group, 165 Dufferin Street
Toronto, Ontario, Canada M6K 3H6
Distributed in the United Kingdom by GMC Distribution Services
Castle Place, 166 High Street, Lewes, East Sussex, England BN7 1XU
Distributed in Australia by Capricorn Link (Australia) Pty. Ltd.
P.O. Box 704, Windsor, NSW 2756, Australia

Book Design: Rachel Maloney

Sterling ISBN 978-1-4027-5842-3

For information about custom editions, special sales, premium and
corporate purchases, please contact Sterling Special Sales
Department at 800-805-5489 or specialsales@sterlingpublishing.com.

For Michael, David & Theresa; or, Friends Indeed.

—"HOLY MOSES AND MAPLE SYRUP!"

"He was the hero of a hundred fights and the victim of a hundred wrongs."

—Richard J. Walsh, *The Making of Buffalo Bill*

CONTENTS

INTRODUCTION
The Great Rascal

ON A BRIGHT LATE SUMMER'S DAY IN **1869,** a locomotive pulled up to the depot of the tiny station at North Platte, Nebraska. Passengers with business in the small town or at nearby Fort McPherson stepped onto the platform and began making inquiries about transportation and accommodations. The occasion was momentous, as this was one of the first cross-country excursions since the completion of the Transcontinental Railroad at Promontory Summit, Utah, on May 10 of that year. The singularity of the experience meant it was still new, still exciting, even to read about; people lucky enough to experience it had a sense that they were part of history. The overland journey from San Francisco to Council Bluffs, Iowa, had previously taken months and entailed enormous hardship and danger. Now, the trip required only a few days, and—apart from the nominal discomfort of the rail coaches and uneven quality of the cuisine—it was a pleasurable outing by comparison.

Among the disembarking passengers was a stocky figure of a man wearing a frock coat festooned with about twenty gold medals and badges of membership, honor, and rank, representing a variety of fraternal, sectarian, semi-political, and quasi-secret organizations. As he blinked into the bright sunlight of the Nebraska plains, he likely weighed the options of hiring a buggy or taking a horse of his own for a ride out to Fort McPherson. Which option he chose is not recorded, but it would not have been in character for him to arrive at the fort perched on a wagon seat with the hoi polloi. He was a man who knew the importance of making an entrance. He most probably hired his own conveyance. He could, as it happened, well afford to do so.

The man's name was Edward Zane Carroll Judson, but anyone aboard the train who made his acquaintance had most likely learned that he was "Colonel" Ned Buntline—Son of Temperance, political organizer, social reformer, raconteur, orator, publisher and editor of literary periodicals, and, most famously, a nationally known author of arguably more publications than any living writer. Indeed, he had recently claimed he was one of the best-paid writers in the country, pointing to his $15,000 yearly income, derived from his pen. In an era when twenty-five dollars a week was considered a princely wage for a skilled laborer or well-educated businessman, the amount was stupendous. That Judson was also a bigamist, a slanderer and blackmailer and notorious scoundrel, an inciter of riots and a fugitive from justice, and very possibly a murderer, an ex-convict, deadbeat, philanderer, and one of the world's greatest liars likely did not come up in conversation.

To Judson, such alarming details of his past were distracting slanders collected and ascribed to him by personal enemies and political and professional rivals—the pettily jealous and desperately envious. Had he been accused of such to his face, he might well have decided the matter with pistols or cutlasses. Alternatively, he might have invited his accuser to join him for a drink. Insofar as he was concerned, he was a socially conscious gentleman, a celebrity of the first order, an amiable and dependable companion, and as solid a patriotic citizen as the United States had thus far produced. He was also, and not incidentally, one of the most widely read authors in America.

Ned Buntline, as he preferred to be known in public and as he was referred to in the press, was not, apparently, a particularly imposing figure. Never an especially handsome man, his face, which usually sported a thick mustache, was creased and scarred by worry and wounds that had stalked him through forty-six years of incredible adventure; but he owned a confident smile and an affable manner. Slightly shorter than average, he had red hair and bright eyes, a booming voice, and a tongue glib enough to win strangers over quickly and, from all accounts, permanently. Few men with such a nefarious past could boast so many loyal friends, eager to come to his side at the slightest hint of trouble, ready to vouch for him or provide money when it was called for, even though he had bilked some out of large amounts of cash and left others holding an embarrassing bag of trouble when he skipped town. He seems to have been one of the most personally charming individuals of his era, capable of wooing the hearts of beautiful women and of reconciling them not only to his rambunctious lifestyle and bombastic manner, but also to accepting and apparently forgiving his chronic bigamy and reprehensible escapades.

Temperance man though he was, he was no stranger to strong drink, and he had a reputation for indulgence. He was in the habit of lecturing on the evils of liquor so effectively as to collect hundreds of signatures on The Pledge; then he would invite the crowd to join him at the nearest saloon for a celebratory libation. One observer at Fort McPherson reported that Judson appeared to walk as if he were drunk. He may well have been, but in this instance, it's doubtful that alcohol caused the uneven gait. Judson's pronounced limp was not the result of war wounds, as he often averred, any more than the ugly scars on his chest were the results of Seminole arrows or Mexican lances or Confederate bullets, as he also sometimes claimed. His stuttering step was more likely caused by chronic sciatica and periodic arthritis, complicated by an imperfectly healed broken leg, sustained as he leapt from a three-story window while trying (unsuccessfully) to escape a Nashville lynch mob.

If the term "live large" had been part of the argot of his time, it would have applied to Judson more than to anyone else. He probably would have preferred the Latin admonition *carpe diem* (seize the day), for more than anything else, Judson was an avid opportunist. He was no more than twelve years old when he impulsively jumped aboard a merchant ship pulling away from the Philadelphia docks and launched a five- or six-year nautical career that provided him not only with a stockpile of stories of pirate kings and Latin American revolutionaries, but also with his pseudonym, Ned Buntline. A buntline is the straight rope at the bottom of a square sail.

By the age of thirty, he had seen more, done more, suffered more, and accomplished more than any dozen other men might. He was the founder of a half-dozen magazines and a celebrated author of stories, novelettes, articles, broadsides, scandal sheets, political diatribes, temperance lectures, reformist oratory, poetry, and at least one hymn. Yet none of it seemed to him remarkable enough to be recounted without the adornment of hyperbole or an outright lie. In a literary epoch when the tall tale would form the basis for the publishing efforts of Mark Twain, Artemus Ward, and Bret Harte, Judson outdid them all. The facts of any matter merely formed a starting point, although he always claimed that the stories he told were true in every detail. The trick was to tell them before anyone else could and to be well paid for the exercise. In this, perhaps, more than any other endeavor, he was an unrivaled master. Later admirers would call him "The King of the Dime Novel," and while such a coronation might be open to challenge, no other writer so completely made the form his own as did Ned Buntline.

In the words of his chief biographer, Jay Monaghan, Judson was a "great rascal," and, in the parlance of the time, both a mountebank and humbug. Almost nothing he said about his life was strictly true. He frequently lied about his birth date; even the exact place of his birth isn't known for sure. But for all his flaws of character, he had a pronounced and demonstrable sense of integrity. He championed no cause he did not fervently believe in, and he was quick to put his life and safety on the line to support a principle. He was also a philanthropist, a bibliophile, a naturalist, and a politically active citizen of his hometown. Part confidence man and part swindler, he was also a proponent of law and order and supporter of civic institutions. He was a doting father, a loving husband to no fewer than six and possibly seven wives and, allegedly, a dozen mistresses. He was as comfortable among the wealthy and famous as he was among political radicals, unwashed sailors, bums, gangsters, and other habitués of the Bowery saloons of New York and the back-alley brothels of Philadelphia and Cincinnati. He was seemingly as content to take a simple meal at a riverport inn as he was dining at Delmonico's in Manhattan.

A difficult man to discourage, he was familiar with the inside of jails, prisons, and military stockades, and had, from time to time, been accosted in the street and beaten badly. Once, he was hanged by a mob, but was cut down before he choked to death. He'd been chased out of New York on a yacht that he effectively stole, using the boat to help him jump bail posted against charges of slander, spousal abandonment, and incitement to riot. He once fired a broadside with a cannon loaded with wadded-up Union Jacks at a British man o'war, and on another occasion he led a posse to run down murderers. He knew the gnawing hunger of being totally without prospects and the exhilaration of organizing a street mob into military formations and sending them forth into battle against well-armed state militias. He also was, somehow, an expert horseman, a crack shot, an accomplished swordsman, and an inveterate hunter and fisherman. He was a veteran sailor of the high seas and, as a proclaimed hero, the youngest commissioned midshipman in the U.S. Navy. He had field experience (albeit dubious) in the Seminole Wars in Florida and with the Mosquito Fleet patrolling the Mexican coast and had tasted the blandishments of Caribbean ports and fought numerous duels to protect his honor.

Exceedingly erudite and rhetorically astute, he had a remarkable knack for prose style, especially for a man with no formal education. He had an impressive vocabulary and a way with words that could provoke as often as they persuaded. He wrote exposés about crime and indecency and railed against sweatshops and slums, but he also was a denizen of the lowest haunts and dens of iniquity and worked his own people hard for low wages as they produced his magazines. He was a public moralist and self-proclaimed "America first" patriot who named and possibly founded The American or Know-Nothing Party, which campaigned actively against foreign immigration, especially from the British Isles; yet he determinedly married and fathered a child by an English-born daughter of a British immigrant.

Judson's ambition to be a writer was apparently born out of his youthful reading. His goals were high. Initially, he despaired of writers such as "Professor" Joseph Holt Ingraham, the eminent author of historical novels, who claimed to be able to write a book per year. Judson averred that it was impossible to generate quality at such a rate. Later, though, he would be producing as many as six stories and novelettes a week, along with multiple articles, essays, and books, often working so frenziedly that characters and plots bled over from one to the other. Always eager for contention, he wrote letters under a variety of pseudonyms to his own publishers, attacking himself and his own position on various matters. He never revised or corrected his work, but seemed merely to lie down on the floor and write, from start to finish, seldom taking a break until the piece was done.

Judson's publications were almost always imbued with ego and unbridled self-confidence; they also were often shamelessly self-promoting, full of bombast and brag. Still, as a publisher, he attracted work by some of the most celebrated poets and critics of the times and caught the flattering eye of such distinguished New York editors as Lewis Gaylord Clark of the *Knickerbocker,* one of the most influential antebellum journals. Judson's life was a landscape littered with contradictions. He disdained the theater as a hotbed of elitism, crime, and immorality, but he collaborated on plays and even appeared in them. He despaired of social injustice but only reluctantly spoke or wrote against slavery. He admired strong and independent women, but he held suffragists in nearly satiric contempt. He was apparently areligious but treated the faithful (including Indians and their pagan beliefs) with respect, and once tried to embrace spiritualism. He proclaimed the virtues of the public peace, but was a chief organizer of the most violent street demonstrations in antebellum New York (the Astor Place Riot) and was also indicted for inciting a riot in St. Louis. He loved disguises and costumes, role-playing and *outré* behavior, but he insisted that his private life—and especially his wives and children—be protected from public inquiry. He was a Union Army veteran who never rose above the rank of sergeant and saw but one minor skirmish before being jailed for desertion. He was subsequently charged with being drunk and causing a public disturbance; then he was stripped of his insignia and left disgraced and bereft on the streets of Baltimore. Undaunted, he entered a photographer's studio and had his portrait made in a full colonel's uniform, then adopted the honorific for the rest of his life.

For Judson, the line between fiction and fact was always blurred, just as the line between Edward Z. C. Judson and Ned Buntline was always blurred. Judson didn't lie pathologically or maliciously, only to enhance the entertainment value of the yarn he was spinning or to get himself out of trouble. He was fond of ripping open his shirt to display his scars to anyone who challenged his character; he would swear that his wounds were the result of whatever evil force he felt might arouse the most sympathy in his auditors. So convincing a storyteller was he that in most cases only a close examination of the relevant or contextual facts—such as could be established—could reveal the falsehoods. Astonishingly, most people who were victims of his antics were apparently quick to forgive and to accept his flaws wholesale. In an age that would spawn such larger-than-life luminaries as Victoria Woodhull and Tennessee Claflin, P. T. Barnum and Henry Ward Beecher, J. P. Morgan and George Armstrong Custer, Judson was unique; only a handful of Americans, before or since, could match him for conspicuous audacity, utter outrage, or sheer gall.

The King of Border Men

Judson's detraining at North Platte, Nebraska, in 1869 was no accident. Some time before he had boarded the train in California, he had learned of a skirmish involving elements of the United States 5th Cavalry, commanded by General Eugene A. Carr, and a small band of Sioux and Cheyenne. The Indians had left the reservation and were raiding and hunting along the North Platte River. A company under the command of Lieutenant Frank North, was detailed out of Fort McPherson to locate and round them up or kill them. The troopers located the Indian camp, and, learning that two white women were being held captive in the village, mounted an attack. The warriors immediately scattered, and Frank North and his brother Lute, a subordinate officer, gave chase. Eventually, they ran the band's leader, Sioux chief Tall Bull, to ground and, by means of trickery, managed to shoot and kill him.

The soldiers found one of the white women dead from a tomahawk blow. The other, a German immigrant by the name of Weichel, who spoke almost no English, was rescued. Some four hours later, Pawnee and white scouts arrived and joined the troopers in a typical destruction of an Indian village. Troubles with Sioux and Northern Cheyenne bands were, at that point on the plains, growing more intense—the result of the completion of the railroad and the rumors of gold being discovered in the sacred Black Hills of what would become South Dakota and in what would become Montana, so the event created a sensation. The transcontinental telegraph flashed the details of what came to be called "The Battle of Summit Springs, and it was soon published in newspapers across the country, with the usual editorial flourishes.

As the preeminent dime novelist of his time, Judson was always alert to exciting stories that might interest his readers. He determined to interview North for a firsthand account of the affair, which he was sure would make a sterling dime novel. Actually, he was in need of something solid to send to his publishers in New York, as his sojourn in California had not proved to be as useful or profitable as he had anticipated. He had arrived in San Francisco some time in the summer or early fall of 1868 and was welcomed as "the official guest" of the Sons and Daughters of Temperance. Initially intending to be on the first west-to-east Transcontinental Railroad train across the country, and planning to write about the adventure, he awaited the line's completion and the first embarkation by giving temperance lectures, calling on notable writers, and founding *The Golden Era*, a magazine that would later publish Mark Twain and Bret Harte. He also was distracted by excursions to the gold fields around Sacramento and by other ventures, as well as by the rough-and-tumble politics of San Francisco. At any rate, he missed the train.

Finally en route on a later train and with a fresh Indian battle on the horizon, he abandoned the notion of a travelogue. There was genuine adventure to write about, and from the very beginning of his career, Judson had found his stock in trade in stories of intrepid heroism and swashbuckling stories of derring-do. This, though, was something new. It was a tale drawn out of the newly accessible West, and with a deft sense of timing, he understood that the eyes and the imagination of his readers would eagerly turn to a "true" story of the frontier.

In a sense, the story already had everything it needed: a young, bold heroic military leader, a rescued captive female, a chase, a slain Indian chief, and the suppression of renegades who threatened the peaceful march of civilization.

After a possible brief detour into Colorado, Judson made his way via the new railroad line to North Platte and nearby Fort McPherson, where Lieutenant North was posted. Frank North may well have been a modest officer who viewed the skirmish and his role in it as nothing worthy of further publicity, or he might have been contemptuous of the potboiler fiction for which Ned Buntline was known. He wanted nothing to do with the brassy writer. Apparently unimpressed by either Judson's person or the proffered reputation, North reportedly told him that if he wanted a man "to fill that bill," he could be found asleep, and probably drunk, under a nearby wagon.

Judson immediately went over to the figure and roused him to his feet. He was confronted by the person of William F. Cody, an heroic ideal, an in-the-flesh symbol of the American frontiersman, the perfect protagonist of a dime novel. Tall and muscular, dressed in greasy buckskins and a broad plainsman's hat, his long curly hair flowing down to his shoulders and his piercing blue eyes revealing both intelligence and wit, Cody was almost too good to be true. To Judson, it must have seemed that the army scout and forager had stepped off the pages of a Sir Walter Scott or James Fenimore Cooper novel, removed to the high plains, where he was waiting to be transformed—with Judson's help, of course—into "Buffalo Bill, the King of Border Men."

Thus began a new chapter of Judson's literary life, one that would, ironically, never be that satisfying. In many ways, it was something of a footnote to a far more complex and expansive career, one that would, insofar as Judson's assessment of it was concerned, prove to be somewhat disappointing. Nevertheless, the encounter and the novelette that resulted from it would tie Ned Buntline's name directly to the western dime novel; he would be remembered more for that than for anything else he ever did.

Literary Rubbish

The first dime novel, so-called, was written by Ann Sophia Stephens. *Malaeska; The Indian Wife of the White Hunter* was published by the firm of Beadle and Adams in 1860. It was an unrivaled success and a publishing phenomenon, selling more than 300,000 copies. In a nation of only about thirty million, where less than twenty percent of the population was more than functionally literate, that was an incredible number. Ann Sophia Winterbotham Stephens, though, was not unknown. Very likely part of "that damned mob of scribbling women" Nathaniel Hawthorne complained of in 1855, she had a reputation as the author of several cloth-bound romances and as editor of *Portland Magazine*, *The Ladies' Companion*, and *Ladies' World*. She had also achieved some fame with a poem, "The Polish Boy," and had entertained William Makepeace Thackeray and Charles Dickens, among other distinguished writers, in her New York salon, reputedly the first ever in the city.

In 1860, E. S. Ellis's *Seth Jones; or The Captives of the Frontier*, also a ten-cent book, was published and rivaled Stephens' volume for sales, and the dime novel as a form was successfully launched. Although no one was aware of it at the time, a whole new trend in publishing had just begun, one that would see the first profitable production of literature in the country.

Beadle and Adams, Stephens' publishers, had earlier found success publishing *The Dime Song Book*; they had moved from Buffalo to New York City about two years before and had begun casting about for another successful venture. With the success of *Malaeska* and *Seth Jones,* they were positioned to turn what had been a chaotic and haphazard publication market into the source of a well-defined commodity that would offer inexpensive and often sensational publications to a great mass of people.

Prior to 1860, the field of popular fiction had been crowded and, to a great extent, disorganized and reactionary. Since the introduction of the steam rotary press in the 1830s, rapid mass printing had become extremely cheap, and specialized periodicals of all sorts emerged and disappeared with rapidity. Canny editors sought the most alluring or controversial copy and sometimes ran competitions with cash prizes to attract the best possible work. Principally dominated by inexpensively produced romances, sentimental melodrama, and lurid adventure fiction, the periodicals of the day exploited the formulas and structures of stories ranging back to Sir Walter Scott and imitative of the much lauded "Leatherstocking Tales" by James Fenimore Cooper. Particularly in demand were historical settings with stories of thrilling exploits on the high seas, during major wars, or in exotic climes.

Among the most successful of publications was an imitation of a form that had emerged in England, called "penny dreadfuls." In the U. S., they were casually referred to as "shilling shockers"; they were coverless pamphlets offering sometimes garish stories of thrilling action, courtly love, and melodramatic adventure. Initially selling for 12.5 cents, they eventually were priced for as much as a quarter and sometimes carried more than one author's work between the pages.

These unique publications were produced under such titles as *Flag of Our Union*, *The New York Ledger*, or *The Youth's Companion*. Several New York newspapers such as *The New York Herald* also carried the same kind of material. Some periodicals were issued weekly or bimonthly and sold for anywhere from 5¢ to 25¢; they might offer one or more serialized stories. Standards varied, but generally they appeared in a two- to three-column format of small font print and were often fronted with lavish woodcut illustrations. They contained fiction, articles on various matters of interest, "letters" written from corresponding travelers, satiric political observations, essays on morality or social reform, the text of hymns, and doggerel selected from thousands of submissions by aspiring poets. One of the most successful of these periodicals—one that would survive until the mid-twentieth century—was *Street & Smith's New York Weekly*, which began publication in 1858, with Ned Buntline as one of their premiere authors.

The fiction in these story papers was usually broken up into serialized format and offered short, digestible chapters, each headed by a summarizing title, all part of an ongoing serial that would run over a number of issues. On average, the stories ran between 30,000 and 50,000 words and were characterized by lavish description and action scenes punctuated by inflated dialogue and theatrical posturing. Episodes frequently ended with a "cliff-hanger" to encourage readers to snap up the next number as soon as it emerged, or, better, to purchase a regular subscription so they wouldn't miss an installment. Subscriptions were difficult to sell, though, because of postal regulations that required the recipient of a periodical to pay postage on receipt. The Post Office Act of 1852 ultimately permitted a less expensive and less cumbersome method of collecting postage from the mail source. For the rest of the century, story paper publishers and dime novel publishers would take great pains to ensure that their publications looked more like periodicals than like individually published books, as they competed for readers' subscriptions as well as for prominence on street-corner newsstands.

A number of publishing firms were actively engaged in this type of publishing during the antebellum period. They ranged from well-established concerns that would grow into major houses to fly-by-night organizations that put out only few numbers before folding for lack of capital. Derisively called "yellow backs" by highbrow detractors, the books were regarded as utter trash, prosaic pandering to the lowest common denominator of the literate public. But, in truth, almost everyone read them. Competition was fierce, and advertising was so highly prized that some publications would actually take out ads in rival papers to promote their next number.

Because the rights to any given piece were assigned wholesale to the publisher, the editors could reprint any story at will and could do so for years, sometimes marketing it under a different title (a "house title") or even under the name of a different author. Plagiarism was common; some writers, including Judson, would often recast a previously published story, give it a different title, and then market it elsewhere, sometimes under a different name. At the same time, more prestigious journals and magazines of a more artistic bent—the *Knickerbocker*, for example—carried the higher-brow reading market and offered material by writers acknowledged to be more "artistic," a market that would in the years following the Civil War come to be dominated by such organs as *Harper's Magazine* and the *Atlantic Review*, among others.

Initially, the *Knickerbocker* and like organs were the market young Edward Judson sought to enter. His efforts to start his own literary magazines during this period indicate that, in spite of his more or less ham-handed editorializing and jingoistic patriotic diatribes, he longed for recognition. Lewis Gaylord Clark, editor of the *Knickerbocker*, gave Judson's sporadically produced journals favorable reviews; this inspired him. When his story "Running the Blockade" appeared in the *Knickerbocker* in 1844, Judson believed he was launched; by 1847, he had added three prize-winning novelettes, published by well-known publishing houses in New York, and had become, he said, "a literary man."

Judson initially agreed with Nathaniel Hawthorne that mass-produced, cheap fictional forms were rubbish, and they pretty much were. The high cost of books put quality fiction out of reach of the average American, but here was escapist entertainment aplenty for the common man in an accessible and affordable form. The cheap story papers could be easily folded into a pocket, read as time permitted, and then discarded or merely left on a train or park bench for someone else to find. The fiction was sensational, sentimental, and moralistic; much of it was unoriginal; the prose was smoky and heavy, burdened by inflated vocabulary. Virtual oratory often took the place of dialogue. Nevertheless, it was extremely popular, and after 1860, it would become even more so. Hundreds of writers—thousands by the end of the century—were actively engaged in producing it. Most used pseudonyms to protect their reputation, should they ever achieve some more respectable fame, but a large number of them, judging from the list of their fates, were merely desperate individuals with a modicum of talent, seeking to make a few dollars.

This wasn't the kind of writing Judson wanted to do. Still, his editorial ambitions had not led him to prosperity, and he found that he couldn't compete with such writers as William T. Porter and Frank Forester in producing sporting stories. His desire was to be accepted in the first rank of American authors. So, armed with copies of *Ned Buntline's* and *The Western Literary Journal*, Judson made his way to Boston, where he believed the seat of American literary art resided. Once there, he attempted to secure introductions to Nathaniel Hawthorne, Washington Irving, and others; none would see him. But when he returned to New York, he observed the common people—laborers, factory workers, domestics, store clerks, and even policemen whiling away time spent waiting for a train, an omnibus, or in some waiting room—reading the same cheaply produced fiction of which he had despaired. From so small an investment as a "bit," or half a quarter, he noticed, people were deriving hours of entertainment, and they were enthusiastic about it. He also had to acknowledge that among the most loyal audience for his own work were the soldiers bound for Mexico and the Southwest and sailors aboard U. S. warships, men who sometimes found time heavy on their hands and uplifting amusement hard to come by. Never one to overlook an opportunity, Judson ignored the snub of the bookish elite and embraced his fate by producing stories as well as the same cheap novelettes for the story papers by the dozens, selling them wherever he could.

In 1847, he decided to exploit his interest in social reform and to build on his rapidly growing celebrity. He began working on a series of books he entitled *The Mysteries and Miseries of New York: A Story of Real Life.* Part exposé, part diatribe, but mostly melodramatic hyperbole loosely based on facts, his announced intention was to warn the general public about the deadly pitfalls of various gambling and drinking establishments in Manhattan. He modeled the idea on a French volume, *The Miseries of Paris;* nothing quite like it had ever been seen in America. At first, he found no takers for the manuscript, so he published it himself. So successful was the book—it sold more than 100,000 copies and was translated for sales in Europe—that people clamored for him to add a promised second volume. But he had exhausted his funds. Berford and Company, recognizing a good thing when they saw it, offered a deal, and the series eventually ran to five full volumes. Ultimately, he would join forces with Benjamin Baker to produce an amalgamation with Baker's earlier melodrama, *A Glance at New York,* which Judson believed Baker initially had plagiarized from him. Together, they mounted a co-authored production, *New York as It Is,* and then a second production under the booklet's original title. He extended the series to include *The B'hoys of New York* and *The G'hals of New York* over the next few years.

Whatever money Judson made from the publications and productions, though, was supplemented by his practice of visiting the same sorts of places he sought to expose. He would offer to keep their names and the names of the propri-etors out of print—for a fee. Most were happy to pay it, although a few who were not happy sought Judson out for personal revenge. On at least one occasion he was badly beaten and thrown into the street by an outraged proprietor, and another encounter lead to his arrest for public brawling.

Regardless of the personal danger he brought down on himself, he made a good deal of money from the books and also established the name of Ned Buntline in the world of inexpensively published, sensational literature.

By 1861, Judson was in the army, serving with the 1st New York Mounted Rifles. The unit saw almost no action, and Judson, who had lied about his age in order to be accepted as a recruit, rose to the rank of sergeant before being busted down to private. Called "Uncle Ned" by his messmates, he was known to be a grand storyteller and reliable purveyor of whiskey for the camp. He had been writing regularly for Street & Smith's story paper, and he had a following for his independently produced novelettes and booklets, but he now became familiar with the possibilities of the dime novel. He observed that the cheaply wrapped volumes arrived in the military camps in bales and that the men read and traded them until they fell apart. It was easy to imagine that the same sort of thing was going on aboard ships, in logging and railroad and mining camps, around factories and mills—anywhere people gathered and were hungry for inexpensive reading matter. Here, again, was an opportunity. By 1863, Ned Buntline was officially included in Beadle and Adams' Ten-Cent series, but he continued to contribute regularly to *Street & Smith's New York Weekly* as well as other publications. By the late 1860s, he had become a significant name in the dime-novel writing world, better known and more widely read than many of the literary giants who had snubbed him in Boston.

The emergence of the dime novel was perhaps the most astonishing publishing phenomenon in United States history. After the incredible success of *Malaeska*, Beadle and Adams moved quickly to the forefront of the market, although they were by no means without competitors. By 1865, more than four million ten-cent volumes had been published, with sales of individual titles ranging from 35,000 to 80,000 each. The story papers would continue to flourish, but now there was a natural reprint outlet for the completed serials, and they, too, would come to be sold by subscription. The impact of the dime novel was felt nowhere more than on an emerging category of fiction, one that had barely been touched on before the Civil War: the western.

Going West

Although Judson is sometimes credited with more that 400 titles, only twenty-five known novelettes are set west of the Mississippi or in any way involve western themes or settings. That he had a fascination with the West is well documented by several biographers, but Judson's idea of the West in the antebellum period extended no farther than St. Louis. By reading his western fiction, one learns that he was familiar with the published work of Lewis and Clark and knew of the exploits of John C. Frémont, but his personal experience in the West seems to have been exceptionally limited.

This wasn't atypical. James Fenimore Cooper's detractors (including Mark Twain) would aver that Cooper not only knew nothing of the West (defined as western New York State, Pennsylvania, and Ohio, primarily), but also that he'd never met a woodsman such as Natty Bumppo or encountered any Indian, outside of a cigar store carving. Edmund Pearson writes, "Some of the most popular of the Wild West stories were written by authors whose nearest acquaintance with the great plains was in White Plains, New York."

Still, Fred E. Pond asserts in his biography that Judson had always been fascinated with the West and had ventured there following his resignation from the

U. S. Navy. This advances what was apparently Judson's claim that he worked for the North West Fur Company, trapping around the headwaters of the Yellowstone River in Montana between 1842 and 1844. This seems plausible, as Judson disappeared entirely during these two years; but Jay Monaghan notes that Judson's name appears nowhere in the company's records.

It's also possible that during an 1851 visit to New Orleans, Judson might well have taken a packet or excursion to Galveston Island, by then a thriving commercial center and home to one of the largest cities on the Gulf Coast. But apart from a brief reference to the island in an authorial intrusion in one novelette, there's no record that he did so. Moreover, in several novelettes, his flawed sense of geography about the terrain of the Lone Star State indicates that he had no firsthand knowledge of it.

Prior to his 1868 trip to California, Judson had probably never ventured west of the Mississippi; nor, apparently, did he ever return after that trip. The celebrated account of his traveling to Dodge City to present Wyatt Earp and Bat Masterson, among others, with the storied Buntline Specials (Colt .45 revolvers with 12" barrels and specially designed grips that featured the letters NED in ornate carving) was apparently a pure fabrication, advanced mainly by Stuart Lake in his biography of Earp; it was based on an obtuse reference by Pond and has been fairly thoroughly discredited. And even though Judson did subsequently invest in the Cheyenne Gold Mine Company in Deadwood, South Dakota, a venture that made him truly wealthy, there's no record of his ever visiting it.

Nevertheless, when the name Ned Buntline is mentioned and anyone recognizes it at all, his association with what would in a later era be called western pulp fiction is nearly automatic. To a large extent, that connection is predicated on the events that followed that late summer meeting in 1869 with William Cody, a man Judson would identify in the minds of millions as Buffalo Bill.

Buffalo Bill, The King of Border Men; The Wildest and Truest Tale I've Ever Told, the novelette Judson produced following his meeting with William F. Cody, appeared in *Street & Smith's New York Weekly* between December 23, 1869 and March 10, 1870. It came at a watershed moment in the development of American culture, a point in time when it seemed that every eye in the newly restored Union was on the Wild Wild West. Following the Civil War, disillusionment came hard on the heels of four years of bloody fighting that ripped the nation in two; a healing force was needed. Horace Greeley's famous 1865 admonition, "Go West, Young Man," never had seemed more applicable to the national spirit than at this time. The completion of the Transcontinental Railroad in May 1869 marked an astounding achievement. It not only was a demonstration of an incredible feat of engineering and human determination, it also, for the first time, made the concept of the American West a concrete reality in the minds of millions.

It would have been unnatural for Judson, opportunist that he was, not to have taken notice of this national trend. He may have been a New Yorker and more experienced in seafaring adventures, Latin American exploits, and Floridian Indian warfare, but he understood the appeal of an exciting frontier, filled with unknown danger and rife with unimaginable possibility. By the late 1860s, people were going west in droves. Between new discoveries of gold and silver in the Dakotas and Montana and Nevada and the prospect of arable farm and ranchland aplenty in a vast territory that had previously been regarded only as "The Great American Desert," prospects were bright. Manifest Destiny was becoming manifest reality, and it was only a matter of time before the civilizing influences of the East would conquer the plains, mountains, and deserts; tame or push back the Indians and wild beasts; and adapt to the harsh climate of the continent. There was an overwhelming sense that the West was the place where the future of America would be found.

Prior to the Civil War, Western American fiction had lost much of its luster. Cooper's novels of the frontier focused on a geography that had, by then, been pretty well settled. The tales inspired by Daniel Boone and Davy Crockett involved Kentucky and Tennessee, now well known to Americans. The category was marked by the works of such writers as Robert Montgomery Bird with his *Nick of the Woods* (1837), William Gilmore Simms with *The Yemassee: Romance of Carolina* (1835) and Border Romances series (1834–1840). Emerson Bennett's *The Prairie Flower* (1849) was hugely popular and sold more than 100,000 copies, and Judson's own *Norwood; or, Life on the Prairie* appeared that same year. But almost all of these were imitative of past masters whose West was actually *east* of the Mississippi. Moreover, their themes and ideas had degenerated into a stale sameness. In 1858, William T. Coggeshall, State Librarian of Ohio, author of *Poets and Poetry of the West* (1860), described the western American fiction of his day: "Tomahawks and wigwams, sharp-shooting and hard fights, log cabins, rough speech, dark-devil boldness, bear-hunting and cornhusking, prairie flowers, bandits, lynch-law and no-law-at-all miscellaneously mixed into 25 cent novels." To Coggeshall and others, the West as a subject for fiction had become little more than a sorry mixture of wild imagination, hackneyed plots, and cliché.

Ten years before Coggeshall's castigation of the western, though, novelists had paid some attention to the greater western territory. In 1849, Kit Carson became the model for the plainsman, a completion, in a way, of the alliterative nicknames given to Cooper's intrepid Natty Bummpo: pathfinder, pioneer. As an actual figure, Carson loomed large in the American culture. As a fictional character, he was given heroic status in such novels as Emerson Bennett's *The Prairie Flower*, and shades of his nature—particularly his physical description—can be found in Buntline's character Norwood. Unlike other western heroes then or later, Carson seemed to combine the qualities of explorer and intrepid adventurer into a single image. He extended the ideal of Cooper's Leatherstocking toward a new horizon and into a new geography and, along the way, transformed him into a different sort of hero. The transition from pathfinder to plainsman, however gradual, is visible in the postwar westerns. Tomahawk, musket, coonskin cap, and moccasins are traded for Bowie knife, six-gun, sombrero, and high-heeled boots. Intricate woodsmanship is exchanged for expert equestrian talents and a practical knowledge of featureless prairies and their special signs and tracks. The staunch defender of democratic principles against monarchical tyranny is replaced by an avid exponent of progress and civilization who pushes back savagery and wilderness. Carson, or the character he would inspire, would be cast in more than seventy fictional works before the end of the century; other than Buffalo Bill, he was possibly the most often characterized historical figure of the West. In his manifestation lies the beginning of a more significant evolution in the western protagonist that would emerge full-blown in the cowboy hero, fully realized in Owen Wister's *The Virginian: A Horseman of the Plains (1902)*.

Between the intrepid Carson and Wister's steel-jawed hero, though, there was a gap, and it was Ned Buntline and his twenty-five western dime novels that would almost accidentally fill it. "Buffalo Bill," Richard Etulain claims, "more than any other figure, is responsible for what has become known as the myth of the American West." Certainly, Cody and his fame grew steadily from the moment Ned Buntline wrote about him in what Street & Smith called "The Greatest Romance of Our Age." By 1900, Kit Carson's name had faded, but Buffalo Bill Cody's name would be synonymous with the western hero. Buffalo Bill's associates, particularly Wild Bill Hickok, Texas Jack Omohundro, Annie Oakley, and Buck Taylor, would be household words, real-life role models and heroes to people who would never travel farther west than the Jersey meadows. For the last thirty years of the nineteenth century and beyond, Cody, his western landscape, and the denizens of the frontier would rise to dominate the popular culture. Of the 1500 novels published by Beadle and Adams from 1860 on, more than three-quarters dealt with settings west of the Mississippi. To a very large extent Ned Buntline played midwife to the birth of a mythos that is a persistent force in American culture up until the present day.

At the time, though, this was hardly evident. Indications are that Judson did not regard his essay into the West or his tale of Cody and Wild Bill "Hitchcock" (he misunderstood James Butler Hickok's name, initially; in later volumes, he got it right) as being anything terribly significant beyond the moment and the immediate opportunity it presented. "The Buffalo Bill incident," Jay Monaghan claims, "never loomed as large in [Judson's] life as the subsequent fame of Cody made it appear." The two apparently hit it off famously that day at Fort McPherson. Judson impressed Cody with his horsemanship by taking a jog on Cody's infamously difficult horse, Powder Face, and with his marksmanship and enthusiasm for adventure. Though Cody had a notable appetite for both strong drink and fiery women, his moral compass, however compromised by temptation, was always active. It might well be that he found in Judson something of a kindred spirit, a flawed but essentially good-hearted individual who understood the value of exploiting a chance when it presented itself.

Over the three years following the publication of *The King of Border Men*, Cody's reputation would rise. He and Judson would astound the American public with their touring play, *Scouts of the Plains,* a thoroughly disreputable piece of melodrama based largely on the novelette that, for some reason, had huge appeal. Eventually, they would part ways because of a dispute over money. That Judson did not embrace Cody or the West entirely or devote the remainder of his writing days and energy to either topic indicates that while he did not dismiss the importance of western fiction to his career, he also did not see it as his primary interest. He made some efforts to capitalize on his "discovery" of Buffalo Bill by producing four more Buffalo Bill stories in 1872 and 1873, the same period of time in which the play was flourishing. Then, for more than a decade, he abandoned the sensational character he created, not returning to him until 1881.

Oddly, even though the name Ned Buntline is more closely associated with the western dime novel than the name of any other writer of the same period, he was still not the most prolific, the most committed, or even the best known writer of the form. His rapid establishment as an author of ten-cent novels of any sort is attributable to the fact that, among those who immediately began producing them in the early 1860s, he was one of the few who already had an established reputation. His titles always sold extremely well; but if his biographers can be relied on, he never devoted himself more to any one theme or idea than he did to anything else. Essentially, then, his identity as a western writer would seem to rest more on the happenstance meeting with William Cody and his brief but sensational effort to exploit it and parlay it into an enhancement of his celebrity and his fortune, than on any spiritual longing for the frontier.

During the fifteen years between his meeting with Cody and Judson's death in 1886, he wrote voluminously: sea adventures, stories about the Seminoles and the late war, hunting and fishing articles, historical novels of the American Revolution, travel guides, interviews with Civil War generals, and other pieces. Judson followed the same diverse path he always had, capriciously seizing on whatever attracted his attention or imagination and always testing the waters of taste and trend while developing his own interests. Capable of producing multiple works in a very short time, he exploited whatever idea or inspiration came his way—between juggling wives, dabbling in both local and national politics, going on fishing expeditions, touring the Eastern seaboard, and arguing with his neighbors. At the same time, though, Judson somehow managed to establish himself as one of four most important western writers of his time and truly the only one whose name is still remembered. (The other three were Edward Ellis, Edward Wheeler, and Prentiss Ingraham.) He may not have invented the dime novel western, but he defined it. The elements, devices, plot points, and character types that appear first in Ned Buntline's novels grew into literary icons that would survive for more than 150 years.

The King of Border Men was not Judson's first western. He initially tried his hand at the category in 1849 with the publication of *Norwood; or, Life on the Prairie.* This rambling story of a Kit Carson style hero accompanied by a crusty mountain man, a rustic Missourian, and a pair of greenhorns as they ventured down the Santa Fe Trail is typical of the western fiction of that period. But it also bespeaks of a primitive interest in and, all things considered, an astounding particular knowledge of the frontier. As with most of his western fiction, the geography is absurdly wrong and the Indians (Comanche in this instance) seem to be taken directly from Cooper's pages. The novel was apparently highly successful, as it was reprinted widely by several different publishers under at least three different titles over the next forty years. Still, Judson didn't return to western themes until 1859 when he offered *Stella Delorme; or, The Comanche's Dream,* to the *New York Mercury.* This novelette, though plagued with the same factual flaws and plausibility issues that worry all of Judson's work, shows a good deal more sophistication about the western frontier, and it seeks to employ more historical accuracy in placement, if not in plot. That it was reprinted by Beadle and Adams in June of 1869, shortly after the well-received run of Judson's successful serial about Buffalo Bill, suggests that its potential appeal was high. It is neither the number of volumes nor their immediate impact on the reading public that elevates Ned Buntline's name to the top of the western dime novelist's charts. It's more that Judson, trend-spotter that he always was, never seemed content to slavishly reproduce a prescribed formula, even when he had had a hand in establishing it. One of the marks of the work of a professional in any category is the writer's ability to take the conventional template and convert it into something that's recognizably his own, not by straying from the perimeters of the formula, but rather by developing it within its own confines and deepening its value within its own context. Each of the twenty-five known novelettes of the West that Judson wrote is unique among the group of Judson's westerns and also among dime novel westerns in general. This, actually, may be the substance of his significance to the category.

King of the Dime Novel

Reading a Ned Buntline novel today is not an easy task. Most modern readers will automatically wince at his casual displays of sexism, racism, and xenophobia. His near-evangelical admonitions against strong drink and immoral behavior seem archaic and naïve. Further, Judson's narrative technique reflects the very best of the heady rhetoric and overblown theatrical style that characterizes the popular fiction of the period. He was a virtual master of the dramatic point of view, allowing dialogue to carry the burden of description, holding exposition to a minimum, and focusing always on action. In places, one can envision the characters striking poses and delivering speeches that would alert the audience to what the characters can see, or how they're feeling, or what they suspect may be about to happen. He borrowed liberally from Elizabethan stage devices, as well, frequently allowing characters to offer long soliloquies summarizing their thoughts, actions, emotional states, or plans (revelations that sometimes lead to trouble if they are overheard) or having them invite a companion to walk or ride along with them so they can explain at length matters or situations the reader already knows. Often, the narrative passages are reduced to bridges between long exchanges of dialogue, broken up principally by a summary of plot points that took place earlier in the narrative but which might have been forgotten by the readers during the lapse of time between published episodes.

Judson relies on the two mainstays of the action/adventure writer that are typical of this type of fiction: contrivance and coincidence. It's a strange situation indeed when a character doesn't have a handy piece of rope tied around his waist, a trusty knife, or some other implement that proves to be just the thing to get him out of a scrape. It also seems to strike no one as odd that in a place as big as the West, people who have been separated for decades run into one another in remote locations and under the strangest of circumstances. Language differences pose no significant barrier to communication; initially, Indians and whites may have to speak in Indian dialect, but as the plot thickens, the matter is soon forgotten, and everyone speaks almost perfect English. Even rustic idioms or pidgin English are rendered in grammatically correct forms. Signals and signs, tracks, and codified indicators are everywhere visible to the trained eye. To Judson, apparently, the West was merely one large place that was more or less the same throughout. No matter where a character found himself, he was intensely aware of what was going on elsewhere, although there was no means by which information could be transmitted.

In all, Judson confined his western settings to six areas, focusing primarily on the high plains of Nebraska and eastern Montana, but occasionally including Kansas. Eight of his western novelettes are set in the high plains region, including all of the Buffalo Bill series. Second in frequency was Texas, with five novelettes set there; then the Mountain West, California, and the Pacific Northwest, New Mexico and Arizona, and the Black Hills of South Dakota. The specific setting didn't truly matter, though, as realistic geography is never a primary concern to Judson. Although most of the stories commence in a named location with precise topographic features—prairie, mountains, forest, etc.—the action of the narrative will ordinarily, and in only a few hours' time, take the characters across deserts, through swamps, into groves of trees or densely forested areas, across dusty prairie, and up into high craggy mountain tors where further dangers may be found in deep abysses or behind impassable mounds of rock. That such geographic phenomena would not always occur in close proximity—or in some settings would not occur at all—never seems to bother Judson. His interpretation of the West, gathered as it was from a rail car's window, assumed these singular accidents of nature not only to be commonly located but also to be more or less constant from the northernmost territories to the deep Southwest. To Judson, it seems, the West looked pretty much as it did along the route between San Francisco and Council Bluffs, Iowa. He had no real reason to think otherwise.

Rivers and streams are plentiful in Judson's West, many too fast or too deep to cross except at fords, and a fast-flowing one is always available when someone needs to hide a trail from pursuers or when a natural bridge needs to be washed away. No matter where the characters find themselves, they can be assured that a tall tree will be handy for someone to scramble up and reconnoiter or from which they may drop onto the back of a horse or eavesdrop on some speech being given by an adversary as he or she passes underneath. Vast canyons and insurmountable passes occur with regularity, but down on the plains, mounted parties can race at full gallop for hours on end without encountering a single natural impediment—unless, of course, some obstacle is needed to advance the tension.

Weather also plays a principal role in the typical Ned Buntline dime novel. A full array of flooding thunderstorms, complete with thunder and lightning, are juxtaposed against long periods of hot, dry conditions conducive to prairie fires, and both can occur in a day's time. Notably, inclement weather is inclined to show up whenever tracks need to be erased or some villainy needs to be masked; and just as remarkably, the thoroughly soused ground beneath hoof or foot seems to dry out completely and almost immediately once the storm passes.

In Ned Buntline's West, wild game is plentiful enough that only a few moments' hunting no more than a casual stroll from any campsite can produce sufficient antelope, elk, deer, or even bear to feed two to ten people. Fishing, though rare, is also dependably productive, and it's a sure bet that whatever characters are awaiting food to prepare are well provisioned with utensils and any necessary condiments the meal might require. Firewood is available for the gathering almost anywhere, and if seasoned wood is wanted to prevent telltale smoke, it can be as easily found as a greener variety. At the same time, vicious beasts—usually bears—lurk constantly. Snakes and large cats also play minor roles in some adventures.

Incongruously, Judson is meticulous in his treatment of horses, firearms, and other equipment. He understands that a horse can go only so far without rest, grass, and water, and there are numerous incidents of mounts being ridden to death in a chase. He also knows weaponry, both caliber and type, and even though he sometimes makes mistakes and requires a powder horn for a cartridge rifle, he elsewhere takes the time to have characters change primers on their cap-and-ball pistols and change their powder when wet conditions prevail.

Towns in a Ned Buntline novelette are seemingly small affairs and are minimally described. Most have the necessary establishments: a saloon or two, sometimes attached to "rooms," although the suggestion of an operating brothel is too subtle to remark; a café or restaurant, sometimes connected to a hotel or to the saloon; and a livery or stable where mounts are available for purchase. There often is a bank, a freight office, and sometimes the home of some positive figure, generally a prosperous businessman, eager to befriend the honest and bankroll a promising enterprise. Most of his stories use town settings as conveniences—sometimes for secret assignations or as headquarters for some operation, generally nefarious, to be planned—not as harbingers of an advancing threat to the natural wildness of the frontier.

Judson's imagination ranged wide in his depictions of the West, and somehow, if one is not experienced or has no other knowledge of the territory, it all seems completely plausible. In an era before modern photography, when the only graphic representations of the West were rendered in woodcuts, lithographs, paintings, and crude tintypes, it was next to impossible for the average American to comprehend the vastness and variation of the American frontier landscape. Corny stage presentations, including Judson's own theatrical effort, provided tactile details of costume and an approximation of frontier conflicts, many based on the tall-tale-inspired journalistic literature of the day, but verbal descriptions were limited to individual experience. Judson's personal view of as much of the West as he saw, augmented by all he could find to read about it, were both credible and consistent with some of the more hyperbolic treatments widely published in his time.

Background and setting may have provided a unique appeal, but audiences also demanded action. Thus, the formula for the dime novel plot was well established before the western rose to dominate the market. Essentially, stories followed a familiar melodramatic pattern. Action ordinarily begins with an abduction, then a flight, followed by a chase, a fight, and then a rescue. Although there are variations on that theme—principally, the addition of a re-abduction, a renewed chase, and a second fight, and rescue, possibly nothing more than a ploy to add more episodes or chapters and thereby lengthen a story's run—this pattern would remain the bedrock of the American western for the next century and a half. As in the melodrama proper, the person abducted is most often a woman, specifically a young and virginal ingénue whose beauty is often matched only by her courage and moral certitude; she always prefers an untimely death rather than the unspeakable fate of remaining in the power of some unscrupulous villain. But from time to time, objects of a familiar nature substitute for a damsel in distress: a safe or strongbox, important legal papers, the claim on a mine, gold or money, or some combination of these.

One common twist on this theme is the hidden or unknown identity of one character that, when revealed, results in the reunion of long-lost siblings or of parents and children. More often than not, a family fortune is involved in such revelations. Generally, the audience is let in on the secret early, so anxiety, not only about the prevention of justice but also about the possibility that the characters might die ignorant of their fortunes, contributes to the suspense. Things always turn out for the best; most often, the stories end happily, usually with a marriage.

Judson's treatment of women expanded the formulaic depiction of females on the frontier and in some ways exceeded the standard social boundaries. Almost all of his young female characters are innocent, in possession of beautiful hair, skin, and eyes; they also tend to be resilient, determined, physically strong, and far less helpless than the average melodrama heroine. Many of his contemporary writers presented women who had the uncanny ability to faint on cue—especially when their conscious presence was not wanted in a scene—and to be simpering weaklings in the face of danger. A Ned Buntline heroine is tougher than that. Although his women are often at the mercy of larger, stronger, or quicker and more ruthless men, and although they are capable of demonstrating emotional distress and terror, they never lose their spirit or give up hope of escape or rescue. Indeed, many extricate themselves through trickery and cunning from some villain's containment, and some few prove proficient enough with firearms or other weapons to defend themselves, at least up to a point. From time to time, Judson casts a woman in the role of villain, not precisely as a *femme fatale*, but often as the catalyst or instigator of some evil, frequently because she perceives that she has been wronged and wants her revenge.

His female characters are never in danger of being called "liberated." As a rule, if they don't understand their place as daughters, mothers, or wives, they're ultimately undone. Overall, though, a refreshing independence about them suggests that they know their own minds and are not shy about asserting their will and maintaining their individuality.

At the same time, an undercurrent of restraint informs the entire spectrum of the dime novel. Long before the passage of the Comstock Act of 1873, producers of story papers and other popular fiction were sensitive to the moral content of the material they shipped through the U. S. Mail. Nothing salacious or even suggestive was allowed. Even official government documents relied on euphemisms and polite phrasing to avoid unsavory details; military reports about Indian depredations would make such substitutions as "outraged" for "raped" and "unmanned" for "castrated." In the dime novel, not even that much of a suggestion could be allowed. Instead, the "fate worse than death" for most of Judson's heroines is to be forced to marry some villain—quite often an Indian chief. The assertion seems to be that if the young woman is forced to go through some sort of ceremony, she would be ruined forever. Even the blackest of knaves treats his female captives with decorum, threatening harm, perhaps, but never actually assaulting them.

Thus, only suggestions of less than scrupulous behavior dominate the form. The roughest and toughest characters certainly never stoop to profanity or verbal vulgarity. Curse word substitutes such as "dod-durn it," and oaths such as "Moses and maple syrup!" or "By Jupiter and all attendant moons" substitute for stronger language, even in the direst circumstances. Viler cursing is sometimes alluded to, and from time to time, a character might announce that if he had a less strident conscience, he would utter an oath, but none ever appears. To some extent, this was a reflection of the forced gentility of what some would call "The Sentimental Age." On another plane, however, it was a recognition that a large part of the market for the dime novel was youngsters, and impolite language of any sort, if discovered by curious parents reading over their children's shoulders, could have a devastating effect on sales. Hence, even the most evil of bad men and roughest of frontier rustics speaks with a sensitivity to correctness that extends to their most emotionally laden utterances.

Judson's male villains also tend to reflect the moral climate and antisocial traits of his age. Mainly, his western villains can be divided into three groups: Indians, renegade white men, and outlaws. The distinction between the second and third is important, for the implication in his works seems to be that the renegades (often half-breeds or individuals who have for one reason or another "gone native") who align themselves with evil forces against the greater good of society are far more dangerous than mere malefactors. Outlaws may well have been driven to a life of crime as the result of greed or, in some cases, as a result of perceived injustice; they tend to run the gamut from thieves and gang leaders to men whose criminal inclinations are the result of the irresistible temptation to enrich themselves at the expense of others. Frequently, both types appear in a single plot. This offers an opportunity to contrast the types against each other; it also affords an extension of the plot, as the hero must battle them both evil forces, one at a time and together.

A common feature of many of Judson's westerns is the attempt on the part of some villain to seize a hero's or heroine's birthright and to remove its owner from the scene, either by arranging for his or her capture or demise at the hands of others (especially Indians) or by killing him or her outright. Even within this category, though, he makes distinctions between those villains who have cunning and wit enough to evolve intricate plots and schemes and those who are mere brutes, dangerous individuals whose ruthlessness and capacity for violence knows no subtlety.

Renegade white men villains appear with less frequency in Ned Buntline's work. Generally, these individuals are former soldiers of fortune who have turned their backs on institutionalized civilization and aligned themselves with hostile Indian tribes. They usually have taught the Indians the white man's strategies and combat tactics. Additionally, the renegades introduce the savages to modern arms and teach them to avoid the pitfalls of drunkenness and disease which, Ned

Buntline constantly proclaims, are the bane of the red man's existence. From time to time, the renegades are redeemed, sometimes by the restoration of that which they believe they have lost, and sometimes by the expressed nobility of the hero or heroine. More often, though, they are regarded as particularly dangerous, because they combine the sophistication of a civilized life with the primitive hostility of the savage Indian to form a deadly and conscienceless combination.

It is with the Indians, however, that Ned Buntline's dime novels depart from the norm most obviously. A casual glance might suggest that Judson knew very little about the American Indian and that he was responding completely to period stereotypes, but a closer reading of his works reveals a subtle difference in the way he treated Native Americans and the manner in which they were depicted by many of his contemporaries.

Indians in these Ned Buntline western stories divide typically into two groups: "good Indians" and "bad Indians." But the line between the two groups is not particularly distinct. Bad Indians are almost always drawn from tribes that were, during the period, notably engaged in hostilities against white encroachment: the Sioux, Cheyenne, Blackfoot, Comanche, Lipan, and Apache. Good Indians, as a rule, are Pawnee, Arapaho, and occasionally Kiowa. That Judson had only the most rudimentary knowledge about these native peoples is obvious, particularly when he has traditional and bitter enemies (Comanche and Lipan, for example) forging alliances against the local whites and combining forces for their mutual benefit.

He also pays no particular attention to a band's geographic locale, sometimes admitting Sioux to Texas and Comanche to the High Plains. Finally, he seems to make little distinction among tribes in their dress, language, religion, or culture, assuming—as, indeed, did most whites of his era—that they all subscribed to the same social structures, practices, and beliefs. He generally assumes that plains Indians would not fight at night and that when they do go into battle, they form skirmish lines and put out flankers, as any quality military strategy would dictate. He indicates that they always require tobacco for any ceremony, that they place some sort of monetary value on scalps (often using them as currency), that their strongest desire is to marry white women, although they would never capture or molest a married woman, and that their war parties routinely number in the hundreds or even thousands. Although a Ned Buntline Indian—good or bad—is fiercely brave (and therefore a grand adversary for the hero) and devoted to principles and integrity, he almost always is sufficiently flawed in intelligence and sophistication, so he can be more easily defeated by stealth and wit than by outright assault.

Not all western novels turned on the conflict between whites and Indians as civilization pushed forward. Working within the limitations of that formula, Judson developed complications based on betrayal or apparent betrayal of a man's word and on the corrupting influences of civilization on the more primitive but well-established cultural philosophy of what he clearly viewed as the "noble savage." Even the worst of his Indian villains mix threats of mayhem and acts of terror with expressions of reasonable justification for their actions. They almost always display a sensitivity to their role in the universe and to their relationship to the "Great Spirit," and they place a premium on courage and bold action, even in the name of villainy. Curiously, when an act of treachery occurs in one of these novels, it's almost always by one white man against another; when a Ned Buntline Indian makes a promise, he tends to keep it.

In a way, this attitude reflects Judson's reading of Cooper and others who depicted Indians as being more reactive than proactive in their violent rejection of white civilization, but Judson took the matter further. His understanding of the American Indian was, in places, laughably naïve and poorly informed. In several of his novels, characters hold forth at length about their personal antipathy to Indians and about their view of them as hopeless savages who ought to be exterminated. But apart from several isolated exceptions, Judson seemed years ahead of his time in his depiction of a people more sinned against than sinning. His Indians' savagery is encouraged by the approach of a white civilization that had no appreciation of the Edenic purity represented in the Native American, a civilization that either wanted them pushed back even farther into the wilderness or dead.

Such an attitude represented no new direction for Judson, who had been lecturing on the wrongs done to the Seminoles in Florida since the early 1850s, but it did cut against the grain of public opinion in the United States. In the 1870s, as conflicts with the Sioux and Cheyenne heated up on the Great Plains and murderous stories involving Comanche and Apache came regularly out of the Southwest, to raise sympathy for the Indians' plight was an uphill struggle, even for those most committed to doing so. Either way, Judson used the Indians as tools, elements in his fictional West that served an exciting purpose and represented a pagan evil that only a civilizing hand could vanquish. He never made a political issue of the Indians' plight, nor did he exploit them. Even after news of the Little Bighorn debacle reached Judson, he never used it as a background or subject for a dime novel, although the commercial advantages of doing so had to be tempting.

Finally, though, and most importantly, there's the Ned Buntline hero, the protagonist of his novels. Once again, a surface analysis of these western novels would seem to reveal that a Ned Buntline hero is pretty much like any other dime novel hero. Taken directly from the tradition that had spawned Natty Bummpo, and the fictional creations that were based on the real-life figures of Daniel Boone, Davy Crockett, and Kit Carson, the hero of the new Wild Wild West seemed to differ only in armament and accoutrement from the traditional frontiersman. The similarities are striking, even on other levels. To the antebellum audience, the frontier hero was generally one of two types. The first was a man who had suffered some severe loss, usually to the Indians. Adopting the ways and learning the wisdom of Native Americans, this individual would spend his life seeking revenge on those who had caused his pain. By direct or indirect action, he would aid the cause of civilization as it crept into the impenetrable forest, timidly searching out a path for the rest of civilization to follow.

Alternatively, the hero was a well-educated, well brought up, well-mannered gentleman of the East, both a product of and a representative of institutionalized civilization. He brought to the frontier not only a high sense of nobility and personal courage but also a refining spirit and genteel civility that would ultimately prevail against the savagery and primitiveness of the wilderness, sometimes by joining forces with those who had come before and found the path, and sometimes by being tutored by them in the ways of the West.

From time to time in the literary tradition of the nineteenth century, both of these hero character types appear in the same work—as they do in Cooper's novels, for example. But their distinctions became increasingly distinctive and archetypical over time and came to serve more didactic purposes. The rustic Indian-hater character in early western fiction was principally based on the historical figure, Lew Wetzel, dramatized sensationally by Edward Ellis in *Frontier Angel; or, A Romance of Kentucky*, in 1861. The rustic hero's role was to teach the lessons of the frontier to the young and inexperienced sophisticate, who also provided a love interest for the heroine. Gradually, the former devolved into a consistently subordinate role, often paternal, sometimes providing comic relief, but also supplying the measure of violence required to subdue evil and make the West safe for the honest and the sincere. Just as gradually, the latter took on a natural understanding of the frontier sufficient for him to survive and ultimately to transform and civilize it; and he would, also naturally, get the girl in the end.

The dime novel structure refined this ideal even further, and under Ned Buntline's pen, the two individual types were sometimes combined into a single hero who possessed both sets of characteristics. The rustic role, for Buntline, was relegated to a more avuncular position, developed out of his notion of Fritz, the plainsman of *Norwood,* who ultimately morphs into a rustic heroic ideal. Eventually, he becomes Cale Durg, a character Judson created for the stage, and ultimately Judson's—or perhaps, Ned Buntline's—alter-ego. In each of these cases, the hero was a native of his own land, suddenly thrust into the position of caring for and protecting the innocent pioneers and adventurers who had arrived in the wilderness, singularly ill-equipped to survive. Christine Bold notes, "When Buntline put the native Westerner into the heroic role previously reserved for an Eastern gentleman, he did not break sharply with the other conventions of the romantic hero." But Daryl Jones points out, "Such traits as humility, self-reliance, and moral insight found expression in the hero's plain speech, his functional backwoods attire, his marksmanship, and his keen woodcraft. An agent of civilization, he was equipped to function in a wilderness setting. Yet the refined Western hero who also appeared in the middle 1870s was defined in terms decidedly social. His natural nobility found expression in youth and physical attractiveness, polished speech, drawing room *savoir faire,* and marriageability." Thus, the foolish naiveté of the Eastern sophisticate and the brutal harshness of the Indian-hater became less polarized. Ultimately, over the course of Judson's western dime novels, they were combined into a single character. He distilled the hero's role and developed him into the kind of individual who would bridge the gap between Cooper's intrepid Leatherstocking and Owen Wister's cowboy hero, who would emerge in full flower at the end of the century.

As before in the shift from the woodsman to the plainsman, the change was not sudden or immediate. Following the tradition as he came to it (and to some extent, as he had helped to develop it through his previous writing), Judson's first essay into western fiction, *Norwood; or, Life on the Prairie* (1849), handles the matter gently. In *Stella Delorme* * (1859), he casts the role of white avenger against red mayhem in the form of Ben McCulloch, the famed Texas Ranger who ultimately died a hero's death fighting for the Confederacy in 1862 at Pea Ridge in Arkansas. (Judson spells his name McCullouch or McCullough.) The heroic love interest in the novel is a somewhat ineffective but still brave young man, schooled by the veteran westerner whose admirable nobility of character is balanced against his protégé's honorable innocence. In *Buffalo Bill, The King of Border Men,* which appeared from December 1869 to March 1870, Judson follows the same pattern, never exposing his more civilized hero, Buffalo Bill, to blood revenge and slaughter, but leaving that task to Bill's more volatile sidekick, Wild Bill Hickok. As the

---

* *Stella Delorme* is not included in this version of *The Hero of a Hundred Fights,* but can be found in the e-book version.

novels developed, though, Judson began reshaping his idea of the hero, gradually evolving figures such as Dashing Charlie and Tombstone Dick, a hero who could, with impunity, massacre a half dozen or more bad guys without a flicker of remorse, while risking his life to save even the least worthy of the party he was protecting. In several of the novelettes, *Big Foot Wallace*, for example, whole groups of villains are laid waste in gory scenes that border on summary execution, but the moral justification for the action seems always to override any outrage at excess that might arise.

A fully evolved Ned Buntline hero contains all the ordinary virtues required of the period. Handsome, athletic, capable, and daring, his heroes are expert marksmen who can break wild horses in a few moments' time, find game on a barren landscape, and locate groves of trees surrounded by good grazing and plentiful grass in which to camp without trouble. They can go days at a time without sleep, never drink liquor, and they are always well spoken, grammatically correct, and oratorically gifted. They spit in the eye of danger, laugh at threats, and can endure the most torturous conditions while exuding practical wisdom about the need to rest horses or themselves. They can fall in love at a glance with women they've barely spoken to and then risk their lives to obtain their ladies' favor. Their honesty is beyond reproach, their integrity beyond question, and a promise, even rendered to the most villainous of enemies, is worth their life to keep. And, without fail, they always get the girl.

That Judson saw himself in these roles seems likely; or perhaps it was not so much Edward Z. C. Judson he saw, but rather Ned Buntline, the public image he created and always advanced into the fray. As Jay Monaghan put it, referring to Judson's early account of his adventures, "Always he told the reader that his story was going to be true, and then he told a whopper that nobody could believe." But in the western dime novels, he suddenly had an audience that was ready not only to believe but also to embrace this new brand of heroics; and in his discovery of Buffalo Bill, Judson had a real, living and breathing apotheosis of the western hero in buckskins and sombrero to provide the evidence that such truly existed.

Hence, all of the heroes in Judson's dime novels are, in one way or another, part Buffalo Bill, part Judson. Had he not stumbled upon William Cody lying asleep, and possibly drunk, under a wagon on a late summer's day in 1869, chances are good that the handsome young man with greasy buckskins and long flowing curls would have merely continued his work foraging and scouting for the army. Eventually he would have faded into the anonymity of western history, along with hundreds of others who were doing the same thing, many of whom had also been called "Buffalo Bill." Instead, he became a living symbol of the western hero, and in his projected character and public image, he came to represent all that was possible in the utopian ideal that the West seemed to offer.

Judson himself must have seen this and must have been sensitive to it, for all the while he was promoting Cody in print and on stage, pushing the initially shy and awkward plainsman out into the limelight, he also was creating his own fictional image. It would emerge as the nameless narrator of *The Miner Detective*, then more boldly as Cale Durg, sort of a stage name for Ned Buntline, who would figure as the avuncular but intrepid hero of *Hazel-Eye, The Girl Trapper*. But more often, it would appear in the authorial voice with which, in the style of narrative pose so common at the time, Ned Buntline's persona would intrude into the narrative to verify the accuracy of some detail, sustain the correctness of some testimony, or merely to illuminate the story with an avowal that what the reader was vicariously experiencing actually happened.

In a way, on that day at Fort McPherson when Judson and Cody met, the more sustained meeting was between Ned Buntline and Buffalo Bill, the public images and perceived personalities that were utterly created out of the mind of one of the most remarkable men and one of the most imaginative writers of his time. That Cody would go on to become the archetypal western hero, whose name resonates more than a century after his death, while Judson would fade into philological obscurity in almost the same amount of time is ironic.

Another irony resides in the fact Judson probably never fully appreciated the impact of what he had done. The amount of time between the initial serialization of *The King of Border Men* and its first reprint ten years later suggests that whatever sensation the original novelette created was not immediately apprehended. It would take time and the contributions of writers such as Edward Wheeler, Prentiss Ingraham, and hundreds of others to augment, develop, and shape the western mythos into the form it would take in the next century, long after the frontier closed and the nation looked elsewhere for both adventure and utopia. In time, the western hero Judson molded out of the raw clay of the frontiersman left him by Cooper and others would be shaped into the cowboy hero, and names like Calamity Jane, Belle Starr, Billy the Kid, and Butch Cassidy would join those of Buffalo Bill and Wild Bill Hickok as part of the fabric of the nation's iconographic past. When Owen Wister's *The Virginian* came onto the scene some thirty years after *The King of Border Men* appeared, the new archetype was fully realized; but few, if any, acknowledged the role that Edward Z. C. Judson played in building it.

A Literary Man

In his own time, Judson fought the elitism that condemned the work he produced to the negative category of "popular." In effect, the books were seen as "boy's books," simple, unsophisticated stories of frontier adventure that offered the added benefit of an elementary lesson in life. They confirmed the notion that good always triumphed over evil if the agents of good remained true to high moral values and sustained the positive influences of civilization. They *couldn't* truly be literature, not in any sense that such a term had meaning in the salons and drawing rooms of the educated and worldly. That they made money, that they had wide appeal among the common people were not perceived as virtues; such attributes were actually signs that they were indeed as lowbrow and simple as they appeared to be.

But their influence, not only on the western novel but on shaping the form of the modern novel, cannot be denied. In their transition from story paper to dime novels, then ultimately to pulp fiction and mass-market paperbacks, these works gave a distinctive shape and design to modern fiction. Their influence can be found in writers of no less stature than Stephen Crane, Theodore Dreiser, Jack London, and Upton Sinclair. They certainly can be found in the works of Zane Gray, Walter Van Tilburg Clark, Louis L'Amour, Elmore Leonard, Larry McMurtry, and Cormac McCarthy. Beyond the western, they are recognizable in the works of John Le Carré, Ken Follett, Tom Clancy, and even Stephen King. To some extent, their structures and expectations inform the best of American popular fiction today, for we still see the central struggle in modern fiction to be between a lone hero, standing for noble principles and objective justice, against a savage foe and the corruption of civilization, bent on their destruction; and more often than not, whatever else is at stake seems less important in the moment than does the girl.

In retrospect, then, it may well be that Ned Buntline's sensational tale of western adventure not only rejuvenated a category of fiction, but that it set a pattern, established a new formula that continues to flourish nearly a century and a half later. It's probably not too much to say that he set a standard and, hackneyed and trite as the formula might appear to contemporary readers, it remains the measure of what a good novel, western or otherwise, aspires to be.

—Clay Reynolds
The University of Texas at Dallas
2011

Editorial Note

THE TEXTS OF THE FOLLOWING SELECTIONS have been digitally scanned from microfilm. The original publications, where available, are not in a condition to permit reproduction via photocopier or digital scanner; in most cases, they cannot even be handled without risk of severe damage or destruction.

The best information available suggests that usually the original serialized novelettes appeared in story papers such as *Street & Smith's New York Weekly*. Then they were reissued or reprinted as independent pamphlet-style publications known as dime novels, with only slight re-editing or no re-editing whatsoever; exceptions have generally been noted. Chapter headings have been preserved where they were used, but without more specific examination, it's not possible to tell where serial breaks or caesura occurred. These must be inferred in some cases at any event, because the original serialized version cannot be located or safely examined.

It's important to bear in mind that the term "dime novel" applies generally to all inexpensively produced, mass-market fiction that appeared from 1860 until about 1910. Not all of these sold for ten cents; indeed, they sold variously for a nickel or a quarter or two-for-a-quarter or at other price points throughout the period. Some, such as *The King of Border Men,* were reprinted in full volume form in later issues. The term, therefore, has become a generic indicator of a type of fiction, rather than a particular series of publications that sold for a specific price. Although Beadle and Adams were the originators of the dime novel in 1860 and issued only 631 titles as either "Dime Novels" or "New Dime Novels" between 1860 and 1885, it's estimated that as many as eleven million titles in numerous formats for a variety of cover prices were issued by multiple publishing houses in the fifty-year period from 1860 to 1910. Even a more realistic estimate of 4 million titles is still a phenomenal lot of popular fiction to emerge from any period.

The chief literary value of these stories lies in the historical development not only of the novel in general but of the western American novel, specifically.

Conventions established in these works would continue to appear as virtual requirements in the western for a good long while. Such clichés as "head 'em off at the pass," "white man speaks with forked tongue," and "shootin' iron," were propagated if not coined in this form. Stereotypical heroes and villains were established here more as archetypes than as flat, undeveloped stock characters, and the vagaries and caprices of the western American landscape were established as fixed entities. In that sense these works provide a bridge and a foundation for literary efforts to come in all categories, not merely in the western. Their importance is vital, and, as one reads them and discovers, their entertainment value, though often archaic and somewhat overcooked, is obvious to the objective eye.

A Cautionary Note on Language

IN MOST ALL OF THE SELECTIONS IN THIS VOLUME, as in most of the material published for public consumption during the nineteenth century, there appear words and phrases that, by modern standards, are decidedly offensive to the eye and ear. Epithets and expressions regarding race, ethnicity, and gender used during the period of the mid-to-late nineteenth century were not restrained by any sense of political or social sensitivity. Difficult as it may be to accept by twenty-first century readers, and tragic as it may be to admit in our more enlightened and tolerant age, the use of such language in that era was not intended to provoke or incite or especially to insult, denigrate, or disparage any group. In most cases, such phrasings were part of the average American's standard vernacular, the common parlance of the common man, in sum. Such terminology was regularly used by people whose political, social, and philosophical sensibilities ran counter to the practices of discrimination and subjugation of the very groups the terms refer to. As a matter of social relevancy, it was the tone of voice and accompanying gestures to such language that defined them as being deliberately insulting, not the words themselves.

Edward Z. C. Judson (aka Ned Buntline) was no different in this regard from any other American or any other writer of his time. Terms that are today deemed to be defamatory as they applied not only to ethnic and racially defined groups but also as references to national origin or religious preference were so much a part of the acceptable vocabulary of his world that he would never have regarded them to be particularly noteworthy. Like most writers of the time, he saw himself, correctly, as a member of the American mainstream. He championed the causes of Native American rights and refused to agree to a political platform plank endorsing the continuation of slavery.

Other writers of the era—James Fenimore Cooper, Herman Melville, Louisa May Alcott, Mark Twain, Bret Harte, William De Forest, to name a few— routinely incorporated such phrasings into both their narratives and characters' dialogue. The practice would continue well into the twentieth century, indeed up to and even beyond the era of a raised social consciousness that has emerged in the last four decades. The intent was not to do harm, but to produce authentic dialogue. For authors to have substituted polite euphemisms or politically correct phrases would have struck their contemporary readers as more than odd. They would have seen it as affected and false.

Accordingly, the works of Ned Buntline here presented are offered intact, as they were originally printed. To excise or edit certain words or phrases or alter editorially the expressions of either narrators or characters would be a betrayal of the historical integrity of the originals. Such changes would damage them by trying to force them to conform to a level of social sensibility that neither their authors nor their original readers could comprehend.

It's important to note that such language as might be deemed to be offensive that appears here appears only in the context of the Ned Buntline novelettes. It is not elsewhere repeated, or even cited. It is not the intention of the editor or the publisher to sensationalize such expressions or to promote them. They are merely part of the fabric of the literature of the past, and, as such, they serve as reminders of the distance we have come from that time of ignorance and intolerance into a more enlightened and accepting world.

∾ I ∾

Buffalo Bill, the King of Border Men; or, The Wildest and Truest Tale I've Ever Told

Editor's Note

Originally published over a period of three months between December 1869 and March 1870, this story has become the signature Ned Buntline tale of the West. Edward Z. C. Judson's discovery of William F. Cody and his immediate exploitation of him created a western hero unparalleled in his era. It's likely that neither Judson nor his publisher, *Street & Smith's New York Weekly,* had an appreciation of the magnitude of what they actually were doing. Although Judson would go on to produce five more dime novels based on Buffalo Bill's exploits—mostly imagined—and although he would certainly predicate his traveling road show, *Scouts of the Plains,* upon material he clearly had gathered from Cody, neither Buffalo Bill nor any western idea seemed to dominate his writing career either before or after 1869.

The story follows a standard plot formula, one that would become something of a Ned Buntline trademark: abduction, pursuit, rescue, re-abduction, re-pursuit, re-rescue, with a multiple set of villains (in this case, four distinct groups). It is, by comparison, much bloodier and more violent than most of his other westerns (*Big Foot Wallace* being a notable exception), with dozens and dozens of villains being slain at a time and even the bodies of innocents left littering the prairie and mountain landscape. In this version, Buffalo Bill is a vengeful and deliberate killer, a trait that would be softened in subsequent tales. Here, the action ranges from somewhere near the Missouri/Kansas line, near the valley of the Republican River, up to the Platte River, and out to the Colorado River. Characters traverse these great distances in a matter of days, or sometimes hours. Mountain crags and deep abysses, rushing streams and waterfalls, broad prairies and heavy woods are spread akimbo throughout the narrative. There is also the more or less requisite timely thunderstorm and constant attention to the needs of horses, as well as several temperance lectures, many of which are ascribed to Buffalo Bill, probably to Cody's surprise when he read it.

Buffalo Bill and his erstwhile sidekick and boon companion Wild Bill Hickok are at the center of the story, which begins with the brutal murder of Buffalo Bill's father by the chief villain, Jake M'Kandlas, a pro-slaver and Missouri bushwhacker. After swearing revenge, growing to manhood, and developing extraordinary frontier skills, Buffalo Bill and his horse Powder Face join ranks with Wild Bill and his equally talented mount, Black Nell, to recapture Lottie, Buffalo Bill's sister, who has been kidnapped by Dave Tutt, one of the M'Kandlas gang. Other villains, including Alf Coye, Ma-no-tee, a Sioux warrior queen, and ultimately Ben Mc-Culloch, in a reprise role from *Stella Delorme,* challenge the pair, and the action is virtually nonstop.

The story breaks in two; after Chapter XXX, the action shifts from the high plains to St. Louis; the focus also changes from dealing with frontier bushwhackers and hostile Indians to the opening days of the Civil War. The climax occurs at the Battle of Pea Ridge (or Elkhorn Tavern), which actually took place in March 1862, in which William Cody was insignificantly involved. Ben McCulloch, however, was killed in the fray in what was regarded by his troops as a highly heroic manner. Even though McCulloch is a serious threat to Buffalo Bill and his security in the Ned Buntline tale, Judson is careful not to make him out to be too much the villain and redeems him in an offhanded way.

Historical facts are mostly adverse to the story itself. William Cody did shoot it out with the M'Kandlas gang (actually spelled McCandlas or McCandless), but the encounter took place in Nebraska, not in Missouri. Cody met James Butler ("Wild Bill") Hickok much later than the early 1860s, and the pair never particularly partnered up or rode together for any length of time. Typically, Judson seldom stopped in his composition to check facts or verify much of anything. He again uses "McCullough" for "McCulloch," misspells Hickok's name as "Hitch-cock" throughout, calls William Clarke Quantrell "Cantrell," assigns a mythical sister named Lottie to Cody, and gives Cody a true love and eventually a wife, Louisa La Valliere, even though Cody was already married to Louisa Frederici. The battle scene that brings the story to its climax and close is ludicrously inaccurate in detail. Nevertheless, the story establishes a remarkable number of precedents and leaves matters open for a sequel, which Judson would provide in *Buffalo Bill's Best Shot; or, The Heart of Spotted Tail. A Story of Life on the Plains* in 1872.

Judson completed the Buffalo Bill cycle with: *Buffalo Bill's Last Victory; or, Dove-Eye, the Lodge Queen; Dashing Charlie, the Texan Whirlwind; Texas Jack, the White King of the Pawnees; A Mate to Buffalo Bill;* and *Will Cody, the Pony Express Rider; or, Buffalo Bill's First Trail.* The last of these appeared in 1885 and possibly was the last dime novel Judson published under the name Ned Buntline. His conclusion of the Wild Bill Hickok adventures appeared in *On the Death Trail; or, the Last of Wild Bill.* Buffalo Bill, though, would be frequently referenced and lauded in many of Ned Buntline's tales, as would be Wild Bill himself.

The version of the original Buffalo Bill serial presented here is taken from an 1886 reprint of the first complete edition, which was issued by J. S. Ogilvie & Company in 1881. Insofar as is known, Street & Smith never issued any reprint of the original serial as a separate piece, but they did reprint the serial in some fashion or other during the time in between its original appearance and the 1881 Ogilvie edition. Ogilvie offered another reprint in 1887, and P. O. Vickery published an edition of the story in 1896. Subsequent editions continued to appear for the next century, including an expurgated version from Arno Press in 1974 that only includes the first thirty chapters. The Ogilvie edition is believed to be taken directly from the Street & Smith plates, a conjecture that is more or less verified by the preservation of such errors as the misspellings "McCullogh," "Hitchcock," and "Cantrell."

BUFFALO BILL,

THE

KING *of* BORDER MEN,

---

or,

THE

WILDEST

AND

TRUEST TALE

I'VE EVER TOLD

CHAPTER I.

An oasis of green wood on Kansas prairie—a bright stream shining like liquid silver in the moonlight—a log house built under the limbs of great trees—within this humble home a happy group. This is my first picture.

Look well on the leading figure in that group. You will see him but this once, yet on his sad fate hinges all the wild and fearful realities which are to follow, drawn, to a very great extent, not from imagination, but from life itself.

A noble-looking, white-haired man sits by a rough table, reading the Bible aloud. On stools by his feet sit two beautiful little girls—his twin daughters—not more than ten years of age, while a noble boy, twelve or thirteen, stands by the back of the chair where sits the handsome, yet matronly-looking mother.

It is the hour for family prayer before retiring for the night, and Mr. Cody, the Christian as well as patriot, always remembers it in the heart of his dear home.

He closes the holy book, and is about to kneel and ask Heaven to bless and protect him and his dear ones.

Hark! The sound of horses galloping with mad speed towards his house falls upon his ear.

"Is it possible there is another Indian alarm?" he says, inquiringly.

Alas! worse than red savages are riding in hot haste toward that door.

"Hallo—the house!" is shouted loudly, as a large cavalcade of horsemen halt before the door.

"What is wanted, and who are ye?" asked the good man, as he threw wide open the door and stood upon its threshold.

"You are wanted, you black-hearted nigger-worshipper, and I—Colonel M'Kandlas—have come to fetch you! And there's the warrant!"

As the ruffian leader of the band shouted these words, the pistol already in his hands was raised, levelled, fired, and the father, husband and Christian fell dead before his horror-stricken family.

"If them gals was a little older—but never mind, boys, this will be a lesson for the sneaks that come upon the Border—let's be off, for there's plenty more work to do before daylight!" continued the wretch, turning the head of his horse to ride away.

"Stop!"

It was but a single word—spoken, too, by a boy whose blue eyes shone wildly in a face as white as new-fallen snow, and full as cold—spoken as he stood erect over the body of his dead father, weaponless and alone. Yet that ruffian—and all of his mad, reckless crew—stopped as if a mighty spell was laid upon them.

"*You*, Jake M'Kandlas, have murdered my father! You, base cowards, who saw him do this dark deed, spoke no word to restrain him. I am only little Bill, his son, but as God in heaven hears me now, I will kill every father's son of you before the beard grows on my face!"

"Hear the little rooster crow. He'll fight when his spurs grow, if we don't cut his comb now," cried the leader, with a mocking laugh, and he raised his pistol once more.

"Monster, you have robbed me of a husband; you shall not kill my boy," shrieked the mother, as she sprang forward and drew her son up to her bosom.

"Colonel, there's a big gang of men comin' over the prairie. We'd better git," cried a scout, riding in at this moment.

"Aye! For I don't want to kill a woman if I can help it. Column to the right, boys, and follow me."

In a minute, at full speed, the party dashed away after their leader, and the wretched family were left alone with the dead.

Frozen with terror and awe, the beautiful twins, Lillie and Lottie, crept out to the doorway, where their mother and brother knelt over the stiffening form of him who had been so good and kind—their dear father.

Oh, what a picture! Grief was still. Nor sob, nor tear, not even a moan arose. They were dumb with agony—paralyzed with a sense of utter bereavement.

They scarcely raised their heads as a noble-looking officer, in the United States uniform, rode up, followed by a body of cavalry.

"Who has done this foul murder?" he cried, as, springing from his horse, he advanced to the mournful group.

"Jake M'Kandlas, and may God, in His just vengeance spare him for *my* hand!" said that pale boy, in a tone so low, so deep, and with a look so wildly stern, that the officer looked at him in wonder.

"Heavens, how savage!" muttered the officer, as he marked the look of ferocity which accompanied the words.

"Tell me, madam, if you please, how this occurred, and which way the murderer or murderers went. My name is Sumner, and I serve a government which will avenge, if it cannot always prevent outrage," continued the officer, addressing the poor widow.

Tears and sobs now came to her relief, and amid them the sad tale was told.

The officer detailed a small party to assist her in the last sad offices for the dead; but himself, heading the rest, dashed away over the prairie, in the hope to catch and punish the murderers. Vain hope!

Mounted on the best stock in the land—the most of it stolen—Kandlas and his party were already miles away, speeding to coverts known to but few, and those few of their own kind.

All this occurred in those dark days when the struggles on the border were the theme of conversation and dispute all over our land, and it was but one of a thousand, or even more, such cases—real, terrible, and unnatural as it may seem.

"Mother, don't cry any more," said little Bill, when, with his two young sisters, he stood beside new-made grave. "Tears will not bring him to life. You have these to look out for at home. You need all your strength now."

"You are not going away, William?"

"Not far, mother—not far. But there were thirty of them beside old M'Kandlas, and it may take me time to kill them *all*."

So quietly, almost gently, did the boy speak, that one would hardly think his young mind capable of studying out, his small hand of doing such deeds as he contemplated.

Ah! little do the thoughtless know how character is formed, how destiny shapes our course, how circumstances forces us, as it were, upon a tide from which we may not turn.

In years a boy, in mind, in a preparation for a wild, desperate, eventful life, already a man.

Such was the hero of our story then, and now our prefatory chapter ended, we must leap over a lapse of years and spring into the full interest of our story.

CHAPTER II.

It is now 1861. The old log house has disappeared, but in the same noble grove a pretty white cottage is seen. Around it trellised bowers of vines and climbing roses, a lovely flower garden, and in the foreground not far away, are fine grain fields, broad acres, well stocked with sheep, cattle, and horses. Barns and haystacks all tell a story of good farming and profitable results.

On the embowered porch of this cottage sits the widow, still in her mourning garb, worn for him whose death we pictured in the first chapter, and near her stand two lovely girls—the twin sisters, Lillie and Lottie, now in the early bloom of beautiful womanhood.

They look alike, are dressed alike, and are exceedingly beautiful.

I will not waste time in description—just imagine hazel eyes, dark brown hair, slightly brunette complexion, figure of perfect symmetry, and you have them before you.

Lillie held a letter in her hand which the mounted mail carrier had left as he swept by, adding in hurried words: "The war is begun—the rebels are fortifying posts all over the South and threaten Washington from Manassas."

Lillie's loving eyes sparkled as she read the letter, and she cried out: "Oh, mamma, mamma! brother is coming home! He says he will be here before the sun sets on the twenty-fifth! The letter is from Fort Kearney, and has been long in coming." "Is not to-day the twenty-fifth?" asked Lottie. "To be sure it is, and he will be here. Our William is wild, but he never tells a falsehood. He is too proud for that! Heaven bless him!" said the mother, in a low, earnest tone.

"He is not coming alone," said Lillie. "One whom he calls 'Wild Bill'—I wonder if he has become tame himself—he speaks of as a very dear friend, one who has three times saved his life. The other one he calls Dave Tutt, says he is handsome and brave, but I know he doesn't like him, for he doesn't speak of him as being good at heart and true as steel, as he does of the other."

"It lacks scarce a half hour of sunset," said the mother. "Tell our good Kitty Muldoon to put on the tea-kettle and hasten preparations for supper. Tell her how many will be here, and to let nothing be lacking. Thanks to my good son and that Providence which has smiled on his efforts, our home is ready to welcome him to comfort when he comes!" Lottie called out in her clear, ringing voice: "Kitty Muldoon!"

"Here, miss, here fresh as a daisy and three times as natural," cried a-plump, cherry-cheeked young girl, with just enough of the brogue on her tongue to tell most likely that sweet Erin's Isle was her birthplace. Dressed as well as the sisters, she looked more like a companion than a servant.

"And what is it, me darling Miss Lottie, that Kitty can be after doing to plase you?"

"Mamma wants you to hurry and get the supper, good Kitty, for my brother and two of his friends are coming here to-night."

"The young master and two of his friends?"

"Yes, Kitty—so make haste!"

"Are they young men, Miss Lottie?"

"Yes, to be sure they are."

"And are they half as handsome as the young master and as tinder of heart as he is."

"Oh! botheration, I expect so. What is it to you, Kitty."

"Sure, miss, to me 'tis nothing. But to you and swate Miss Lillie, it may be something, since it's a beau apiece for yez, if they're but worth the looking at and spaking wid."

"Oh you good-for-nothing—"

Kitty did not wait to hear the rest of the not angry expletive, but ran laughing away to carry out the wishes of her mistress.

At the same instant Lillie, who had been glancing through an avenue which led westward in the grove, cried out: "They are coming! They are coming!"

And three minutes later, their horses frothy and hot, three riders at full speed dashed up to the gate fronting the cottage.

"Oh brother! brother!" cried the two sisters, joyously, and all heedless of the stranger eyes now looking on them, they rushed out to embrace and kiss him.

Buffalo Bill, for this was he, had learned to hide all his feelings, but with a gentle tenderness he shook himself out of their embraces, and, presenting his two friends by name, hurried on to meet the dear mother, who, with glistening eyes, waited to greet her idol and her pride.

"My good mother!" was all he said, as he pressed his manly lips to her white forehead. "My dear son!" was all she said, but pages would not describe the reverence in her tone, or the undying love in her look.

Bill now presented his friends in more form to his mother than he had deemed it necessary in the case of his sisters.

"This, mother," said he, presenting a young man who, in form and appearance, resembled himself very closely, though he was an inch taller, and hardly so muscular, "this is my mate—this is Bill Hitchcock, the best friend I ever had, or ever will have, out-side of our own family. Three times has he saved me from being wiped out. Once by the Ogallalas, once when I was taken with the cramps in the ice-cold Platte, last winter, and once when old Jake M'Kandlas and his gang had a sure set on me. He and I will sink or swim in the same river, and that's a safe bet. Bill, that's my mother, and a better never trod the footstool!"

Wild Bill, with a natural grace, bent his proud head, and took the hand of the lady, saying, in a tremulous tone: "I'm glad to see you, ma'am, for I've a good old mother that I haven't seen this many a day, and this rayther brings her up afore me!"

"And this other," continued Bill, "is Dave Tutt. He is good on a hunt, death on the reds, and as smart as bordermen are made now-a-days. Now, boys, you're all acquainted, make yourselves at home. The darkey out there has got the horses, and he'll see them all right. I know that mother will soon have a good old supper for us."

"Yes, Kitty is getting it ready as fast as she can, and I'll go and help her," said Lillie, who did not like the wild, passionate gaze which Dave Tutt seemed to fix upon her.

I don't like to use time or space for description, but as the three men now before us are *real*, not fictitious characters, I think it due to them and the reader to paint pen-portraits of the trio.

Three more perfect men, in point of personal beauty, never trod the earth.

Wild Bill, six feet and one inch in height, straight as an ash, broad in shoulder, round and full in chest, slender in the waist, swelling out in muscular proportions at hips and thighs, with tapering limbs, small hands and feet, his form was a study. His face, open and clean, had regular features, the nose slightly aquiline. His large bright eyes, now soft and tender in expression, were a bluish gray in color, shaded by lashes which often dropped over his bronzed cheek as he looked down, somewhat confused in female society, to which he was unused. His long brown hair fell in wavy masses over his shoulders, but it was fine, soft and glossy as silk.

The same picture will do for Buffalo Bill, only this difference noted. The eyes of the latter were nearly a blue in color, his height one inch less, and his hair a little more wavy and a shade lighter.

Dave Tutt, nearly of the same height, was equally well formed, but here the resemblance ceased.

His eyes were black as jet and deeply set, though his features were perfect, and, when he chose, his expression soft and winning. His hair, curling slightly, was black and glossy. But with all his beauty, there was a sensual expression about his mouth so utterly different from that in the other two, and a fierce, passionate longing in his eyes, which made the two girls, instinctive in their purity, shrink from him.

Lillie, toward whom his glances seemed from the first to be directed, especially felt, and scarcely could conceal, an aversion.

Now this most unpleasant picturing duty is over, and I can heave ahead on my story.

Pretty Kitty Muldoon was busy setting the table in the dining-room when Buffalo Bill, unobserved, came slyly in and, bending his tall form over her shoulder, suddenly touched his lips to hers.

Bounding aside, quick as a fawn with a bullet in its heart, she wheeled and brought the palm of her fat, chubby hand into contact with his cheek with a force that made him see stars, and brought unbidden tears into his laughing eyes.

"Bad'cess to yez, Master Bill, and it's at yer ould thricks ye are!" cried Kitty, laughing at the woful look he put on. "Sure haven't ye sisters as swate as honey, purtier than the wild roses, to be kissin' wid, instead of slobberin' over a bit of a wild Irish girl like meself!"

"Why, Kitty, I hadn't seen you for so long, I couldn't help it. Thunder and whip-stalks, but you hit hard! My cheek tingles yet!"

"Faith, then, it'll make your memory better, sir, but maybe I did hit a little harder than I had razon for, sir, for you're a good son and brother, and I know you'd cut your right hand off before you'd harm a poor girl like me, or see harm come to her."

"That is so, Kitty, that is so, and now here's something to wear I brought from the traders. It's a new dress, and if it isn't just like those I brought for mother and sisters, it is just as good and cost as much."

"Thank ye, Master Bill—thank ye for your kind thought of the poor girl that has no one to think after her but you and yours. Sure the angels sent me here when I came, and I hope they'll keep me here till I die, for it's like heaven to work for them that's so good to me. But call your friends, Master Bill, for the supper is all ready, and it's nice enough for a king and a king's people, sure!"

CHAPTER III.

There was no piano in that Kansas cottage, but two sweeter voices, alto and soprano, never thrilled a human ear than filled the sitting-room with melody as Lillie and Lottie sang song after song to please their brother and his guests after night set in.

The good mother with her knitting, and Kitty already engaged in sewing on her new dress, listened while they worked. The young men smoked, for in the Far West the pipe seems *apropos* everywhere, and from time to time expressed themselves warmly in praise of the treat they were receiving.

The night was lovely. A gentle breeze rustled through the leafy trees, the moon shone out brightly, though passing clouds at times obscured it for a minute or two, the air was soft and balmy. In through the open window came the delicious perfume of rose and honeysuckle, taking away at least a part of the tobacco-taint in the atmosphere.

That sweetest of all songs, more dear to the writer than any song ever sung, "Thy bright smile haunts me still," had just been sung by the twins, when Mrs. Cody, whose face was toward the window, screamed out in sudden terror, and rose to her feet with a face so deathly pale that it seemed as if she was death-stricken.

"What is it, mother?" cried Bill, springing to her side.

"The window—*he* was there!" she gasped, and then swooned away.

"He? Girls, look out for mother! I'll see what *he* was at the window!" cried Bill, and he sprang to the open casement.

As he did so a bullet whistled passed his ear, and struck the opposite wall, while a hundred wild yells proclaimed that Indians had surrounded the house.

Wild Bill, cool and collected, instantly blew out both the lights, exclaiming: "Darkness here and moonlight out thar! We'll be all right in a shake. Jump for your tools, boys; mine's handy! Gals, lay down out o'range; we'll soon let the reds know old hands are here."

The three young men, reinforced by three negroes and one white man, the farm hands, were ready for work in less than a minute, and as the Indians did not seem disposed to make a rush for the inside of the house, crept quickly to points where from the doors and windows they could pick the fiends out from their coverts among the trees around.

Meantime the twins, aided by Kitty Muldoon with a pitcher of water, had succeeded in restoring the mother to consciousness, and to the hurried inquiry of her son as to whom she had seen at the window, replied that she had recognized the face of Jake M'Kandlas, the murderer of her husband, glaring in with a look so full of hate and vindictive cruelty that she was completely horror-stricken.

"There's too many reds out there, or I'd rush out and settle his hash!" said her son. "If he'll only stay till we thin 'em down a few, I'll accommodate him with a private entertainment. Look out for yourselves, girls—the boys are giving 'em Jessie, and it's about time my hand was in."

A rapid fire had been going on from the moment Wild Bill got to the door, the Indians shooting at random, for all in the house was dark except the flash of the guns, but every now and then a yell of agony told that the attacking party were not going unpunished.

They could only be seen as they sprang from tree to tree for cover, but their terrible yells ringing through the air told that in numbers they were at least ten to one of the attacking party. "Whar's the stock? Won't they try to run that off?" asked Wild Bill, as his mate, standing by his side, sent a red to eternity with a shot from his favorite long rifle.

"I expect they will. I would almost as soon lose my hair as to lose Powder Face, for the insect* has carried me through more bad scrapes than I've time to count," said Buffalo Bill, referring to his favorite horse.

"And I will lose my hair afore I'll lose Black Nell, for she never deserted me.

---

* "Insect" was colloquial for horse."

She'll kick the head off any red that tries to mount her. But can't we get to the horses? If I was on Nell, I know I'd be good for a dozen out there where I'm getting one a skulkin' in here. If the mare is where she could hear me, I could have here in half a minute."

"Yes, and they'd plant a dozen arrows in her hide, or pepper her with lead as she came through 'em. Wait till I give Dave and the boys in here their orders, and then you an' me will get to the horses and come in on 'em like as if we were fresh hands in the fight."

"That's the talk, Bill—that's the talk. Only let me and Black Nell and you and Powder Face give 'em a charge in the rear and they're gone in."

"Pepper into 'em, then, till I tell the boys here where we're goin', so they'll be keerful how to shoot when we're a comin."

Buffalo Bill now hurriedly told Dave Tutt and the men, who were firing at everything they saw among the trees, what he and Wild Bill intended to do. The girls and his mother were to know nothing of it till it was all over, for the two Bills felt as sure of driving off the foe by their plan as if they were already in full chase of them.

Dave Tutt did not express any wish to go along, which rather surprised Buffalo Bill, for it was a duty that brave men would surely court. But there was a reason for this, as there is indeed for everything, as the reader will learn by and by.

According to instructions, Dave and the other white man, with the negroes, now increased the rapidity of their fire, moving from window to window, but firing high and avoiding one direction —that which the two brave bordermen had taken.

The two friends, carrying their arms and bending low in the shadow of the garden bushes, crept away from the house until they reached a grain-field beyond the trees, into which they moved swiftly. They had but a little distance now to go to reach stock pasture, and they got to the last in the very nick of time.

A half-dozen dusky figures were already there, and the horses, disturbed by the firing, were very uneasy as these advanced.

Two shrill calls, understood well by the animals for which they were intended, brought two noble animals, "Black Nell" and "Powder Face," to the edge of the grain-field. The next instant, needing neither saddle nor bridle, the two men were mounted, and, without a word, both dashed forward upon the Indians who were after the stock.

So suddenly and unexpectedly were they over-whelmed—not a shot being fired, only the tomahawk used—that there was no alarm in the grove. Then the two men sped on, not noiselessly now, but whooping and yelling in wild concert, and urging their steeds faster by their cries, till they were upon the rear of the astonished redskins, pouring out shot after shot with deadly effect on the enemy.

Wheeling and circling here and there, never missing a shot—it seemed as if there were twenty, rather than two—Wild Bill and our hero dashed on, carrying death at every leap.

The Indians, who were Cheyennes, supposing this to be a reinforcement to those who had defended the house so well, soon gave way and fled in every direction, but not before full half their number had fallen.

"Curse them, why do they shoot so careless from the house—this is the second graze I have had from there!" cried Wild Bill, as he wiped the blood from a wound grazing his cheek.

"There's a hole in my hat from the same quarter," said Buffalo Bill. "I'd like to know what they mean. It can't be but they know where we are. Never mind—I must hunt up old M'Kandlas now, for if mother saw him he must be here. Let's chase them, Bill, as long as we can."

The two men dashed away, and again a bullet, evidently from the house, passed so close to Buffalo Bill's head that he felt the wind.

The Indians scattered far and wide, but the two men succeeded in knocking over a half-a-dozen more, when the thought struck them that it was better not to go far from the house lest some lurking behind would continue the attack, and they rode back.

The search for a white man among the bodies of the slain was unsuccessful, so Bill decided in his mind that if M'Kandlas had been in the party he had escaped this time.

As they approached the house they took pains to make their individuality known by signals which could not be misunderstood, therefore they were spared the perils which it seemed friends rather than their foes had cast upon them during the charge.

In a short time, their horses left close in the shadow of the house, the two brave friends were in it once more.

"You can light up, I reckon, cried Buffalo Bill, when he entered. "The reds, or what's left of 'em, are off to their tribes on the run. But I'd like to know who in thunder it was that was shootin' so careless from here while we was wipin' 'em out in the grove. Me and my mate both got grazed, and it wasn't from none of them close by. It was long shootin', and as close as if 'twas done on purpose."

"I don't see how it was. I shot for Indian, and nothin' shorter than Indian," said Dave.

"Well, it's no matter; we're here now, and our hair is on. I reckon there's a pretty good lot o' reds lying around loose for crow-bait, as we'll see when day comes again."

"Thank Heaven, you are safe!" said Mrs. Cody, as she heard the voice of her son. "I hope you and your brave friend are unharmed?"

"All right, mother, but a scratch or two that cold water will heal; but are you sure you saw the face of Jake M'Kandlas at the window?"

"Yes, my son—I never can forget his face. I purely saw it."

"Then he has got off this time. I knew most of his gang had gone under, but I didn't think he had taken up with the Cheyennes. They say that every tribe in the West but the Pawnees are going with the South. If they are, we border folks will have our hands full. But we're good for 'em, aren't we, Bill?"

I reckon we are, if we know ourselves," said Wild Bill. "Was the gals much frightened, ma'am?"

"No. They were so busy at first in getting me out of my faint they forgot to be scared, and after that they had to think who was here to take care of 'em, and they'd blush to be his sisters if a few Indians could scare them," said Mrs. Cody.

"That's the kind of grit for me. Oh, but they're game!" cried Buffalo Bill, as his eyes glanced proudly at the sweet girls. "And here's Kitty Muldoon, as fearless as they, I'll bet a horse. Isn't it so, Kitty?"

"Faith, sir, it's not meself that'll tell a lie. I was scared out of a night slape, I'm sure, and that's some-thin', when one is sure to drame swate drames, as I do. But what do you think, sir, one of them red haythens has shot forty holes in my new dress, that I'd folded up and put on the window-sill when I run for water for the mistress in her faint."

"Never mind, Kitty; there's more where it came from, and so long as the dress wasn't on your own body it's small harm that is done. And now all hands of you be off to bed, but us men that are used to watching. It isn't likely any of the reds will come back to-night, but we'll keep our eyes peeled and be ready for 'em if they do. When morning comes we'll see about their trail."

"I thought you was in such a hurry to get to St. Louis to join Fremont and his men," said Dave Tutt, his tone quiet, but the slightest gleam of sarcasm in his eye.

"Not while there's any danger hangin' about them I love, if I know myself," said Bill. "If you're so hard put for whisky that you can't wait, why you can start as soon as you like. I told you that my dear old mother never would have the pisen in the house, nor cards either, so them that want to drink or play must keep a fast while they're here, or go where they can get served more to their likin'."

"I neither wish to drink or play," said Dave, blushing, for the keen eyes of both the girls had been fixed upon him while their brother spoke. "And I reckon when there's danger about, I'll be as loth to leave the helpless as any one that wears shootin' irons in his belt."

"Well, that's right. I didn't mean to hurt your feelings, Dave, but I'm more touchy here than I be out on the prairie or on the hills."

CHAPTER IV.

The moon had gone down before day dawned, but the repulsed Cheyennes never bated in their headlong speed until a couple of hours after sunrise, when they had reached a thick cottonwood grove on the south bank of the Republican River.

Here, at the call of their chief, they dismounted and gathered around him. By his side, with a scowl of anger, and some show of distrust, too, in his face, stood Jake M'Kandlas, the white ruffian who had planned this foray.

Looking sternly at him, after counting the warriors left, the old chief said: "There will be a great cry among the squaws in the lodges of the Cheyennes. Many warriors have gone down—their scalps are in the belts of our enemies, and we have not a scalp to show that has been taken in return for ours. What has the Hawk of the Hills to say to this?"

"That which the Great Spirit wills to be, will be!" said M'Kandlas in reply. "Two nights ago I went to the cottage on the plains, looked in, and saw only women there. There was stock, meat, plenty of goods.

I told Big Maple, the chief of the Cheyennes, that he could get these and not lose a man. But while I was gone the fighting men came—we know not how many—I saw but three. If we had fought as white men fight and charged right in on them, we would now have their scalps in our belts. Big Maple would not listen to my words. He fought his way and lost half his warriors. It is not my fault. I have spoken."

The old chief knew that so far as the advice was concerned M'Kandlas had spoken the truth. He had overruled the wish of the latter to charge, when it was found men were there who would fight to defend the women. For he said: "We can kill them in our way best, and then the women and the plunder will be easy to take."

"The Hawk of the Hills has spoken with a single tongue. His words are true. But the faces of the tribes will be black when we go back without scalps. What has my brother to say to that?" asked the chief.

"That if we go back without scalps we are fools!" said M'Kandlas quietly. "If the gun of Big Maple misses fire, does he throw it away, or pick the flint and try it again? There are more days and nights than one, and plenty of palefaces are scattered about the plains. The Hawk of the Hills knows other settlements which we can reach in two or three days' journey. We can go there for plunder and scalps, and then come back here, and when the fighting men are not here, or are asleep, we can sprinkle the bones of our dead with the blood of vengeance where they fell."

"The Hawk of the Hills speaks like a man. The heart of Big Maple was weak. It is strong again. The warriors will cook meat and eat while their horses rest and feed. Then we will take the war-path, and the Hawk of the Hills shall lead the way. Big Maple is his brother, and will follow where he leads."

Light blazing fires, emitting scarcely any smoke, were now made from dry twigs, and the warriors made a hearty meal, the first for twenty-four hours. It was not finished when an alarm was given by a scout. White men mounted and armed were coming in from the south.

"They are not those we fought last night!" said M'Kandlas. "They have not had time to get to this side of the river. I will ride out alone and see who they are. Let my red brothers remain where they are, ready to fight or to flee if they see that I am among their enemies."

"The Hawk of the Hills is a great brave. His words are good and his deeds go with them," said the Cheyenne chief.

M'Kandlas now mounted his horse, put a bit of white cloth on the ramrod of his rifle, and rode out from the shelter of the grove toward the group of advancing horsemen, some ten or a dozen in number.

They halted as soon as he was observed, and seemed to look to their arms.

He rode boldly on until within two or three hundred yards, when a shout of recognition rose on both sides, and men rode rapidly to meet him.

They were his own men from the Black Hills, whom he had left there to carry on his business of pillaging emigrant trains, while he came down on an expedition on his own private account.

"Why are you here?" he asked, as they rode up.

"What did you leave Cave Canyon for?"

"Because we got sarched out, and scorched out, and whipped out!" said one, who seemed to head the party. "That gal you took from the Mormon train, and made so much of cause she was likelier than most gals in face and figure, got away and went down to Laramie in the night. The next thing we knew the troops was right in amongst us, and we got away—that is, half of us, for the rest went under in the fight. We got off afoot, and had to go clear down to the Border for horses, and we were on the look for you, when here you turn up."

"Well, we'll make the blue-coats pay for this. A war has begun. I heard 'em talkin' about it when I was on a scout last night, and we'll have every Indian on the plains and in the hills with us in it. We'll sweep the borders, and have no end of plunder. I'm glad you are here, for now I'll do the work I failed in last night. That infernal fiend, Buffalo Bill, with Wild Bill and Dave Tutt, wiped out over twenty Cheyennes that I piloted down to the Cody place last night."

"Dave Tutt? Why he is one of us—one of our sort at any rate!" said Frank Stark, the one who had spoken first.

"Yes—he used to be, but he's with them now. I couldn't get no chance to see him alone, or I would have known what it meant. I had my own idea that he was after one of the gals, for they're purtier than any picture that was ever painted, and I know he's death after that kind of game. But ride on, boys, and get something to eat, and then we'll plan for a nice bit of work to-night. There's between twenty and thirty Cheyennes left, and they'll fight like blazes for revenge."

M'Kandlas now turned and rode back with his men to the grove, so busy in talking with them that he did not notice a single person on a hill beyond the river, who had evidently seen all his movements, and who rode off swiftly when the ruffian leader entered the grove.

"These are warriors from my band in the Black Hills, come to fight by the side of their chief!" said M'Kandlas to the Cheyenne chief, as he and his men rode up among the camp-fires.

"They are welcome as the rain when the earth is dry. Big Maple is glad to see them here. There is meat, let them eat. There is water, let them drink."

"Here's something better than water, boss. Take a pull out of that and it'll make your eyes snap. It is prime old whisky—I got it from the last train we took," cried Stark.

"Whisky is not better than water," said the old chief, as he pushed back the proffered bottle. "The Great Spirit made water for good. The Bad Spirit made whisky for evil. In every bottle there is one song and a hundred fights. It is the enemy of the red man, and he is a fool if he shakes hands with it."

"Well, there'll be the more left for me and the colonel," said Frank Stark, as he proffered the bottle to M'Kandlas, who did not refuse it.

"Now cook and eat, boys, and let your horses rest and feed till we are right. We'll then wipe out Buffalo Bill and his party, and make a raid down the river as far as we can, and then strike for the Platte for a rest."

CHAPTER V.

After breakfast the morning following the attack, while the negroes were burying the dead Indians, Buffalo Bill and his companions held a consultation in regard to what they had best do.

It did not, in their judgment, seem likely that the Indians, especially if under the influence of a bad white man, would rest submissive under defeat, and this being the case, they would return reinforced, bent on destruction of both life and property.

There were no settlers very near them, though scattered farms and houses could be met all around in a day's ride—no fortified place to which sudden retreat could be made. Only in the villages where numbers insured safety could they find refuge if the red men made a determined raid over the borders.

"They may have got enough last night to sicken them of coming again," said Buffalo Bill. "I believe the best way is to find out what kind of a humor they're in, and whether they're mad enough to try for our hair again or not. I believe I'll get on my insect, Powder Face, and follow their trail and see what they're about. You boys stay here on the watch, and mother and the girls can pack what they need for moving with, if I find that it will be best to move. And you may be sure the old place won't be given up without good reason."

"Why can't I go along?" asked Wild Bill.

"For this, Bill; I'd rayther you'd stay here to look out for the gals. One is as good on a scout as twenty, 'specially when he has got such an insect as my Powder Face under him, for that pony can out-smell, out-see and out-hear any livin' thing, be it man, dog, or catamount, that ever yelped. Look at him standing there, one eye open and t'other one shut—but see how his ears pint. He knows I'm talking about him. Come here, Powder Face, and let the folks look at you."

The horse, a rather large-sized pony of full Indian breed, in color a regular light buckskin, with long black mane and tail, walked up to the porch and rested his nose on the shoulder of his young master.

Clean-limbed, deep in the chest, heavy in the arms and quarters, full of muscle, he was a splendid specimen of that breed.

"Isn't he a rare insect? He can run ten hours and never flag, swim any current this side of the big hills, and he knows as much as I do about hide and seek. Powder Face, go bring your saddle and bridle—we're going on a scout."

Just as if he really understood human speech, rather than the slap which Bill laid gently on his back as he spoke, the pony turned and trotted away, but soon came back with the saddle and bridle in his mouth.

"Isn't that gumption?" said Bill, as he patted the animal's head and proceeded to saddle and bridle him. "I only put these on because it's easier to him and to me, and in the fashion. But when I hunt buffalo I toss them out of the way, and him and me go in light, just to kill, and we do kill, don't we, Powder Face?"

The pony nodded with a look of intelligence, which made the sisters smile and Kitty Muldoon roar with laughter.

Mrs. Cody came out at this moment with a spyglass slung in a leather case, which her husband formerly owned.

"Take this with you, my son," she said, "and you can reconnoitre parties at a distance before they can see you with the naked eye."

"That's a fact, mother, and I'll take it along with thanks to you for thinking of it. Kitty, put me a bite to eat in my saddle-bags while I belt on my arms. And mother, I'm thinking you may as well have all ready for moving down to where the settlements are thicker. If the Indians and Missouri men go in on the Southern side in this war there will be no safety here for you and the girls till it is all over. I'd have to stay here all the time if you did, and I want to be where men are needed, if the war does go on. So be ready, if what I see while I'm gone makes me think we'd better shift our quarters."

Bill said no more, but sprung on his pony and was off at a gallop in a moment.

"Better son never blessed a mother, wild as he is," said Mrs. Cody, with love in every tone, as her glance followed his form. "Rough he may be to others, but to us he is kind and gentle as the breeze of a summer eve."

"Yes, ma'am, Buffalo Bill is just as good as was ever made, no matter whar you find him. I've been his mate now goin' on three year, and I've tried him in all kinds of weather," said Wild Bill. "There isn't a bit of white in his liver, nor no black in his heart. What he says and does is as open as day, and when he goes in for a fight he don't ask to see the hand he has got to play against, but he makes 'em show afore he's through. Bill is ahead of wild cats, twenty to one, and I'm jist the man to bet my pile on proving it."

And Wild Bill looked around as if he would really like to have some one try to disprove it. His eyes fell on Dave Tutt, who sat on a corner of the porch, grave and gloomy, studying with his eyes the graces and beauties of form and face as exhibited by Lillie, for upon her he seemed to have bent all his regards.

"What makes *you* so dull here, Dave?" he asked, in a bantering tone. "In the hills or out on the prairie, you're as full of fun as a squirrel in nutting time. What's up—if you wanted to go along with Bill, why didn't you say so?"

"I did not want to go with him. I'm sure it's no harm for me to be quiet in a little haven like this, such as our sort isn't used to. I'm always still when I hear the birds singing, and we hear better than bird-music here."

"That's so, Dave—but there's sort of game out there—antelope, sure's yer born! Let's have a couple, what d'ye say?"

"I'm ripe for that, for we will not have to go out of sight of the house!" cried Dave.

Wild Bill gave a chirrup—it sounded like the call of a bird to its mate, and his beautiful black mare galloped up and stood with gazelle-like eyes, looking; her pleasure at being needed.

"That's my Nell. Oh, isn't she a treasure," he cried, as he seized his gun, and sprung on her back without saddle or bridle.

Dave had a noble horse, but he was not trained like the "insect" of Buffalo Bill, or like "Black Nell," to come at his call.

But he was soon mounted, and the two rode off side by side at full speed toward the herd of antelope that had just shown their slender forms a mile or two away.

"What a handsome man that Mr. Tutt is!" said Lottie, as the two men rode off.

"Handsome in face and form, but oh *so* ugly in his heart and soul, something tells me!" said Lillie. "He looks at me and my spirit shrinks from him, as if I could see a fiend instead of a man before me. I cannot say why, but I fear him and I hate him!"

"It is wrong for us to hate any one, especially wrong to hate those that do no harm to us!" said the mother, gravely.

"Please, ma'am, if I'm not too bould, will ye answer me one question?" asked Kitty Muldoon.

"Certainly, my good girl; I never refused to answer you any question, I am sure!"

"But, ma'am, maybe I'm not mindin' my own business by askin' the like, but I mane no harm, sure. Don't ye think if Misthress Eve, in the garden of Aden, had hated the purty snake that tould her to ate the apple of badness, she'd been a hape better off, for she'd have tould the decavin' sarpint to thravel his way and she'd take hers!"

"That would have been better surely, my good Kitty."

"Well, ma'am, I'm jist like Miss Lillie in belavin' that there's a hape o' badness in that man, forbye all his good looks. Sure when his eyes are set on me, I shiver all over. And last night when the young master said that bullets from the house went all too nigh him and his friend, I saw a shadow come on that man's face, and there was no good in it!"

"Then must we watch him closely after this, my dear girls. For one traitor or enemy in the house is more dangerous than fifty outside. But see—they have dismounted and left their horses. They will creep up within shot of the antelope."

"No, mother. Wild Bill is too good a hunter for that!" said Lillie. "Now both the men sink out of sight the grass. But see! there is a red handkerchief gently waving in the air. Bill has taken it from his neck and tied it to his ramrod. Notice how the antelope watch it. They begin to come closer and closer. Caution is strong, but curiosity is stronger. They will come until in easy range, and then two of them will surely fall. Brother has often told me about this way of hunting. See!—nearer and nearer the poor things keep coming, and will come till the fatal bullet ends life and curiosity at once."

In silence the family now watched the little herd of animals as they came on toward the decoy, pausing at times, and seeming to yield to fear and turn aside, but again coming on, until at last the flag went out of sight.

Then two puffs of smoke were seen, and long before the reports of the rifles reached the ears of the watchers, two antelopes were seen to leap high in the air and fall to the earth in the death-struggle, while the rest sped away swiftly over the prairie.

The two hunters now mounted their horses, which had dropped from sight as well as themselves, and riding up to their game prepared it for bringing in.

This, as they were in no haste, took them several minutes, and when they were on the way back to the house, a third rider was in sight beyond them.

CHAPTER VI.

The two hunters came on leisurely, each with the slain antelope before him on his horse, but the third horseman—first visible in the distance when they started for the cottage—came so fast that before they reached the house the females had recognized son and brother.

"Hurry and have the men put the teams to our wagons, and help me pack clothing and provisions!" cried Mrs. Cody to her daughters and to Kitty. "My son is riding at full speed, and he would not do so without he had good cause."

All was bustle, therefore, about the house when Wild Bill and Dave Tutt returned with their game. But the preparations were made without excitement, and carefully, so that when Buffalo Bill came in and sprang from his horse, if he had said the word, the family could have moved in a very few minutes.

"I'm glad to see you getting ready to start, mother!" said he, as he met her at the door. "Me and the insect have traveled fast for a couple of hours, not that we had good news to bring, but for fear bad news might get here afore we was ready to start. Your spy-glass did me some service this day, you can bet your bottom dollar on that. I saw Jake M'Kandlas more than three miles off, as plain as if he was right afore me. He has got a reinforcement of eleven hang-dog wretches, white men like himself, and I've no doubt intends to try us again to-night. If we stay here we can hold the house, maybe, but he'll get all our stock, and then we can't move. I reckon the sooner we are away the safer our hair will be. For myself or the boys I've no fear; but for you, mother, and the gals, there's more to consider. You'd better all be dead than in *his* power."

"Oh, yes—indeed, yes!" murmured the mother.

"We are nearly ready, my son. Bedding and clothes, and the money, and what provisions we can carry, are ready in the wagons. I was afraid to put the powder in till you came; it is in the cellar."

"How much, mother?"

"Four twenty-five pound kegs, my son, that have never been opened."

"Good! Two of those kegs we will take with us. The other two will do for a present for Jake M'Kandlas and his friends."

"A present, my son! Are you crazy?"

"Not quite, mother. But I have an idea that they will be so mad when they get here and find we've left our castle, that they'll set fire to it and dance around it while it burns. At least that is one of their ways. Now, if they do, and this powder is hid where the fire will find it before they do, it will make some of 'em dance the hornpipe on the downward road."

"Well, my son, do as you think best. The men are driving in the stock, the teams are ready, and so are we."

"Have you packed all you can carry that you need, mother. They may leave things alone, but it isn't likely."

"Yes, my son, all but the powder."

"I'll see to that, mother."

It took but a short time to make final preparations, and in a half-hour after Bill's arrival, the cottage home was deserted, and the cavalcade of horsemen, wagons, and stock was moving eastward over the prairie.

The first wagon, with the white laborer driving it, contained Mrs. Cody and the three girls, and Dave Tutt, without being told to take the post, rode near it. A negro was driving each of the other wagons, and the horses and cattle were driven up by Buffalo Bill and his mate, who closed the rear, having given directions for the course.

It was late in the day when they got away, and they could not make very rapid progress through the tall grass; therefore, when night came on, they were just passing a low range of sandy hills not more than ten or twelve miles from the farm.

They were slow in getting over these, but after a couple of tedious hours they reached the summit.

Buffalo Bill, just as they were starting down the opposite decline, looked back, and instantly saw a bright light, which indicated too plainly the fate of their recent home.

"One more debt for Jake M'Kandlas to pay before I am done with him!" he muttered in a low tone, for he did not wish his mother to know the work of destruction was going on.

But her eyes had noted the direction of his glance, and she looked back, just as a vivid flash lighted up the whole country in the rear.

"The powder has exploded!" she exclaimed.

"Yes," said Bill, after listening till a heavy report came booming through the air. "I reckon if they were anywhere near the house, they got more powder than they wanted all at once. But we must move on lively. We haven't got any too much start, and we're a good way from help yet. Drive up rapid, boy—drive up rapid. The reds can follow a trail as broad as ours by such a moon almost as well as by day."

"We shall not have a moon to see by long. Look yonder—there's the wildest kind of a storm brewing!" said Wild Bill, pointing to a range of black clouds swiftly rising in the northwest.

"Yes—yes, and I'm glad it is coming," said Buffalo Bill. "It will be nasty for us outdoors, but the women will be all right under the wagon covers, and the rain will wash our trail so the reds can't follow. Old Jake is as good as a hound, but he can't smell a trail in the track of a Kansas thunder shower, or see it either. Let the wind and the rain come, and the sooner the better. We'll keep going while we can, and then park the wagons and corral the loose stock inside."

"That's the idea, mate—that's the idea for a match game!" cried Wild Bill, putting a water-proof blanket over his shoulders more to shield the arms than his person.

The wind now came sharp and spitefully in blasts, over the hills and plains, and as the clouds rushed up from the far-away horizon, they rapidly overspread the sky, until at last the moon and stars were so nearly obscured that the travelers could see but little around them.

Hastily the wagons were parked—that is, drawn into a square so as to leave a space in the quadrangle. Then the cattle were put inside, the harnessed horses hitched around outside and secured as well as they could be in the now utter darkness.

The three border men agreed to remain mounted and to ride slowly around outside the wagons in turn, so as to keep a continual guard against any hostile approach, although any one not used to the deviltry of Indians would not appre-hend an attack from them in such weather.

The females in the covered wagon conversed cheerfully with their protec-tors, for the storm, instead of being a terror, was looked upon as a Providential thing, calculated to favor them.

Louder and more fiercely blew the wind—none but those who have been on the prairie or on the ocean know how it can blow.

The darkness was so intense that only by the sense of hearing could the young men know where the train was, as in their turn each made his regular circuit.

At last the rain came pouring down in torrents, and every now and then a vivid flash of lightning lit up for a brief second the entire group of wagons, men, horses, and cattle.

Then would follow deafening peals of thunder, almost shaking the earth, causing occasional cries of alarm from the twins and poor Kitty, for there are few women who can quietly stand the excitement of such storms as one meets on the prairies of our Far West.

Crashing thunder, hissing lightning, and pouring rain seemed to have dead-ened the wind for a time, but it was only a lull, for once in a while its shrill diapa-son rung wildly in the watchers' ears.

But suddenly a fearful scream rose from one of the girls in the wagon—one wild cry for help, that fairly rent the air as well as the hearts and ears of those who heard it.

Buffalo Bill was on the circuit, Wild Bill was on his return, and both by the same lightning flash got a bare glimpse of a girl struggling in the arms of a man on horseback, and then all was darkness.

Both dashed toward the spot where they had seen the man—another flash lit up their own forms and faces, but nothing else could they see.

"Lillie! Oh, Heaven, where is our Lillie?" screamed Mrs. Cody.

"Lillie—swate Miss Lillie is gone!" cried poor Kitty Muldoon, at the top of her voice.

"Dave Tutt—where is he?" shrieked Lottie.

"He was here and asked how we were, not a minute ago, and Lillie answered him."

"Dave Tutt!" shouted Buffalo Bill. "Dave Tutt, where are you?"

No answer came.

"The curse has carried Miss Lillie off!" cried Wild Bill. "It was him we saw with her in his arms."

"Oh, my child—my child!" moaned the unhappy mother. "You had indeed reason to hate and fear that man!"

"Do not try to move the wagons while we are gone," said Buffalo Bill, in a hoarse tone, to his mother. "Wild Bill and me must go after Lillie. We will keep between you and harm if we can. I never should have trusted that man. I knew he was a gambler, and out here *they're* always close kin to a robber. Lillie, Lillie darling, we'll save you yet. Come, Bill—keep in hearing of me—come!"

And the speaker dashed off over the hills.

CHAPTER VII.

Out into the utter darkness—on in the pelting storm, only knowing his course by feeling that he was going up hill, the maddened brother led the way, and Wild Bill, giving his mare head, followed, knowing she would by her keen hearing follow the other.

On until the crest of the hill was gained, and then faintly, for it was far off, could be seen the light of the yet burning cottage.

"Come on," shouted Bill, "his horse is as fast if not faster than ours, and he will go to them, I know. Come on, mate, and ride as you never rode before."

Wild Bill made no reply, but each lightning flash showed one to the other, close and near, and on they went at a speed which no horses but those used to the prairie could have kept up in the gloom.

Soon the rain ceased, the thunder was heard no more, the lightning did not flash. The wind again swept wild and unrestrained over the plains.

The light of the fire became plainer as they neared the old farm, though it was actually going down. This told them how swiftly they cleared the way. On—on until they were so near that they could see men grouped close to timbers and rails that had been heaped on the fire for fuel.

"Let us creep up and see who and what is there," said Wild Bill, as he rode up alongside of his mate.

"No—no!" thundered the other, completely maddened by his feelings. "The murderer of my father is there! My poor sister, too. Ride on as I do, and let your revolver do your talking!"

Wild Bill saw that argument would be lost and used no more. Setting his teeth, his revolver in hand, and his eyes fixed on the group not now a hundred yards off, he urged Black Nell up to the side of Powder Face, and both horsemen at the same instant dashed into the circle of light.

Jake M'Kandlas sprang to his feet as a hoarse voice shouted his name, and fell the next instant with a bullet through his body, while dashing on and over them, firing as they came, the two riders swept, shooting down Indians and white men side by side as they passed on. In an instant, wheeling, with fearful yells, back they came, but found few either of the white or red men waiting for the onslaught, for all but three or four had already fled away into the protecting darkness.

These fired only two or three random shots before the surer aim of the bordermen sent them to death, and then there were none to resist.

"Oh, Heaven, where is Lillie—where is Lillie?" shouted Bill. "She is not here—back to the prairie, mate—back to the prairie—the moon is coming out, and we'll find her yet. Follow me—she is not here—waste no time on the dead, but follow me!"

Away again, swift as the driving clouds, the brother and his wild prairie horse sped, and Wild Bill kept faithfully on the track.

Away over the plains, now in shadow, then in light, as the moon looked down through breaking clouds—away once more toward the wagons where the other dear ones had been left.

"Have you found Lillie?" was the cry of the mother, as her son rode up to her side.

"Not yet, but I have slain the murderer of my father!" he cried, sternly. "His dead body lies roasting by the embers of our ruined home. Go on due east when day dawns—Bill and me will be scouting the prairie for the trail of Dave Tutt. We will not rest till our Lillie is found and his body left to sicken wolves!"

And again he and Wild Bill rode off.

He urged Black Nell up to the side of Powder Face.

CHAPTER VIII.

But a few moments after the two bordermen rode away from the ruins of the cottage, where their reckless charge had produced a panic as well as a fearful carnage, another horseman rode within the circle of light.

It was Dave Tutt, and on his saddle before him, limp and lifeless in appearance, he held poor Lillie.

Leaping from his horse he lifted her down, and drawing near the fire, looked in her face anxiously, as if he really feared she was dead.

A tremor in her pale lips, a long faint sigh, told him that this was not the case.

"The swoon was so like death!" he muttered, "She would soon come too if

I had any restoratives. Hallo—where are you all! Some dead and the rest all run away from only two men. If I hadn't had the gal to bother with, I'd have fought 'em alone. They went by within twenty feet of me in the dark. Hallo—here! Jake M'Kandlas, or Frank Stark, where are you!"

"Who calls Jake M'Kandlas. Here's what's left of him, and that's pretty much run out. I reckon!" said the ruffian himself, as he tried to rise from among three or four bodies that lay stretched on the ground, but failing, sunk back with a groan.

"It is me, Dave Tutt, colonel—are you hurt bad?"

"Yes—I've got a heavy dose, Dave, but draw me away from the fire. I don't want to roast till my time comes, and then I'll have no choice in the matter."

Dave laid his helpless burden down with her head on a saddle, and hurried to place the wounded man in a more comfortable position.

As this was done the eye of M'Kandlas fell on Lillie.

"Who have you got there, Dave!" he asked hastily. Isn't it one of the twins?"

"Yes, it is Lillie, and her destiny is to be a robber's bride. She turned the cold shoulder on me, or I'd have been less rough in my courting—but the storm came up and I lifted her, and here she is."

"Then it was her them two, Wild Bill and her brother, were after when they charged on us here?"

"Of course it was, and as they found she wasn't here they didn't wait to be particular and lift hair, but put out to scour the prairie after me. They passed me twice within half pistol shot, and if she hadn't been still in her faint, I would have had to have stilled her. But where's all your men? There's not over half dozen, red and white, stretched here."

"No, there's more, but they've scattered. Blow this whistle, Dave, I'm too weak."

Tutt took a large whistle from the neck of the wounded man and blew a long, shrill call. It was answered a second later by another whistle.

"That is Frank Stark," said the robber chief. He will be here soon, and he carries what I need now, for I'm as weak as a sick chicken. There's a bad hole in my carcass. I've stuffed a bit of my hunting shirt in to stop the bleeding, but I'm afraid from the feeling it bleeds inside."

"We'll soon see—here come the boys."

"Hi, here's Dave Tutt and a gal too, by the Big Elk. Snakes and reptiles, what a beauty!" cried Frank Stark, as he strode in from the darkness, followed by a half dozen more white men and a few Indians.

"Never you mind the gal—tote out your whisky flask and 'tend to the colonel, for he is pretty nigh gone under. She is my property, and I reckon I can take care of her without help," said Dave Tutt, moving to the side of poor Lillie, who began to show signs of reviving consciousness.

"I reckon it won't spile her to be looked at," said Frank snappishly, as he went to the assistance of M'KandIas. "Are you hurt bad, colonel?"

"Give me a pull at that flask of yours, and I'll soon know!" said the chief. "I've bled a good deal, but if the shot has dodged my lung, I reckon I'll crow again. The ball went clean through, and it's a close call if it is no worse!"

A draught of liquor stimulated the wounded man so that he rose to a sitting position and was able to have his wound examined. It was a bad one, but without internal hemorrhage not necessarily fatal. A bandage on and another stimulating draught and he felt much better than a dying man.

"Frank," said he to Stark, "count noses and see how many of us is left! Them two Bills are the boys on quick work!"

Stark looked around, questioned the living, and soon found that four white men and five Indians, among the latter Big Maple the chief, had been killed, and two more beside the colonel wounded.

"Bad, by thunder, bad, and only them two to do it all!" muttered the colonel. "But we'll pay him for it. One of the gals is here, and that's worse than death to him. And I'll have the other yet. I'll wring the core of his heart out in that way. How is it over there, Dave, is your prairie rose coming to?"

"Yes—her eyes are open—but she does not speak!" said Dave, who gazed almost in alarm on the wild, stony look of horror with which poor Lillie gazed on him and the scene before her.

"Give her a drop of bourbon—that will start her tongue!" said Frank Stark, tossing over his liquor flask.

"Try a little—it will take the damp chill off!" said Dave, as he uncorked the flask and offered it to the girl, who now sat upright.

"Wretch! Take me back to my mother!" she said, in a low, angry tone, as she pushed the flask away.

"Not yet—not before our honeymoon is over, my pretty wife that is to be!" said Dave, trying to smile into the face of her look of scorn and hate.

"*Your* wife? Fiend! I will die a thousand deaths first. I hated you from the first moment I saw you! And now, coward, dog, I loathe and despise you!"

"Go on—go on, my beauty. Spit your spite while you're before folks, and you'll be more tender when we are alone. That's the way with women, I've heard. But you'd better take a drink from this flask to keep your courage up."

"You'll need it, Dave Tutt, more than I. My brother will soon find me, and then your life will pay for this cruel, unmanly act!"

"Your brother has been here, gal—there's some of his marks left layin' around, and if these red Indians find out you are kin to him that killed their chief, it may be more than I can do to keep them from roasting you!"

"I don't care. I had rather die at their hands than to live in yours. You say my brother has been here?"

"Yes, he and Wild Bill rode in here in the search for you, and laid out nine of the party. They couldn't find you, so they took the back track. I had you snug in my arms, and they passed close by without knowing it. So, my beauty, you are all safe for a home in the Black Hills with one that will treat you well if you behave yourself. If you don't—"

"Will you only kill me?"

"Kill you, gal? Kill you with such a face and form? I reckon not. No—you'd be worth too much in an Indian trade to make the killing profitable. I could get fifty head of horses for such a gal as you any day among the Sioux. It's getting to be a fashion for a big chief to have a white wife to set up over his red ones. I'll find offers enough if you don't keep quiet and take your fate easy."

Poor Lillie shuddered and looked around upon the rough faces of the other men, to see if there was even one that looked humanely upon her. Alas, there was not, and her heart sunk as she thought that perhaps she had gazed on her mother, sister, and brother for the last time.

Until now she had not recognized the place to which she had been brought, but the fire-light glaring strongly against a great elm tree near by, made her think she had seen it before. Glancing around she saw tree after tree with whose gnarled limbs she was familiar, and she now knew that the cottage was in ashes.

The storm was over, and a consultation was held as to the next movements of the party. Frank Stark wanted to follow up the wagons. But Jake M'Kandlas could not, and Dave Tutt would not go. M'Kandlas could only be moved slowly and with care, so it would take a part of the force to attend to him.

Therefore a pursuit which would be attended with the certainty of a hard fight was given up, and as soon as day dawned the route for the Black Hills was taken up.

Lillie was placed in a light wagon which had been saved from the flames, and the wounded colonel and his two injured men were also laid on a heap of straw in the same vehicle.

With their usual disregard for the decencies of humanity, the robbers and Indians left their dead to the tender mercies of the wolf and buzzard, without a thought of burial, careful, however, to bring away their arms and ammunition, for these were valuable. Dead men were worthless.

Before sunrise they were miles away, Dave Tutt now taking the leadership of the party and hurrying them on, for he dreaded pursuit from the two men whom he knew but too well, once on his track, would not leave it while he lived.

CHAPTER IX.

To and fro, making wide circles over the prairie and hills, rode the two bordermen, until the day dawned, and yet they found no sign of the lost one.

When the red sun threw its light upon the earth, they found it so washed with the heavy rains of the night that had ten thousand buffaloes marched over it the night before, not a track could now be seen.

Rapidly on, one circling here and the other there, meeting only to communicate, they rode all the morning, but found not a single track.

"What can we do? She is somewhere, and in the power of that fiend, Dave Tutt!" said Buffalo Bill. "He did not make back to the M'Kandlas party, for he would have been there ahead of us. Where can he have gone?"

"He has most likely made for the Black Hills. I've heard him brag how he knew every canyon and rock in 'em, and tell how friendly him and the Ogallala Sioux were who live in that section," said Wild Bill.

"Then we will follow him there. If a hundred tribes, instead of one, were at his back, I'd have her from him and my knife in his heart! It maddens me to think she is in his power. If he wrongs her by an insulting word, much less a rude touch, I'll kill him by inches! Bill, let's bear for the Black Hills."

"Hold on a bit," said the other. "I'm just as hot for her rescue as you can be, Bill. But there's reason in the worst of cases, as well as the best. We are but two, and though we could ride over and through twenty, red and white, in the dark, we two couldn't get to the Black Hills and back, no way, let alone bringing her off. We must have help. And there's your other sister, your good mother, and Kitty Muldoon. Would you leave them till they're safe?"

"No—it isn't right. But my poor Lillie! It drives me wild to think how she may suffer. But what do you propose, Bill?"

"That we hurry the train into the nearest settlement where we can leave the family safe. Then gather as many men as we can and start for the Black Hills. If we move fast he'll not have over a couple or three days' start, and we'll be sure to find his trail. His horse has a good mark—shoes forward and none behind. That I noticed when he first jined us, and I kept still about it, for I never did trust him fully. And now I feel just life-sure that I'm the man picked out to put him under. And when I feel that way about a man, he's dead sure to come to me when I want him. I felt so about Dick Hawley, and you remember that he rode up and picked a quarrel with me when I no more expected it than I did to go up in a balloon. He came after his gruel, and he got it. Now what do you say, Bill—shall we make for the wagons?"

"Yes; your plan is the best," said Buffalo Bill. "Though were I on his trail, nothing on earth should take me off from it till my hands were on his throat. I'll try to wait, Bill—I'll try to wait."

The two friends now rode eastward rapidly, and before the sun reached its meridian were once more with the wagons.

"Have you given up the search for your sister?" asked Mrs. Cody, when she saw her son and his mate ride up.

"No, mother, no, nor will we until she is found. But we can strike no trail— the rain has washed it away. We know this, however, that Dave Tutt has friends among the fighting Sioux in the Black Hills and he's most likely making for them. We must have more force than us two to go there with any chance to get her away—so our plan is to get you all in safety to the nearest post, then collect a party and start for the hills. Dead or alive, we'll find her."

"Better dead than alive if she is his victim, or in the hands of the heartless Indians," said the mother bitterly. "But why wait for us—we go too slow. Ride on and raise men—ride on, and do not mind us."

"Mother—your life, that of Lottie and poor Kitty too, must be thought of. We do not know who is moving about the border. Missouri is close by, and a thousand—yes, ten thousand such men as Jack M'Kandlas will swarm into Kansas on the least pretense to fight out old quarrels. We must see you safe first, and then we will take the back track."

"Then get up the riding horses and put on saddles for me and the girls. The wagons go too slow. We can reach the settlements by night if we ride."

"That is true, mother, if you can stand it."

"I *will* stand it, my son—I will stand it. Hasten and saddle the best horses. The wagons can follow at the best rate they may."

In a short time the mother, Lottie, and Kitty Muldoon were mounted on good horses, and soon the wagons were left far behind. For, like nearly all of the hardy, noble women of the West, they were not only used to the saddle, but to swift and fearless riding, and had no need of that tender care which some of our more delicate equestriennes on the Boulevard or Central Park drive require.

Before the setting sun had sunk behind the western horizon a settlement was reached, and soon, on fresh horses, to let their own rest, Buffalo Bill and his mate were riding from house to house gathering men for the expedition to rescue Lillie.

CHAPTER X.

It was a sickening ride for poor Lillie, with no music but the groans of the wounded men, as the wagon, driven so fast, jolted over the uneven prairie. And yet hope was in her heart, for often did she strain her eyes looking back to see if help was not coming.

This was noticed by Dave Tutt, who kept urging his party to its utmost speed, and a sarcastic smile would now and then light his face.

"They're but two that would follow," said he, "and when they've had time for a second thought they'll not leave the other women till they get to a safe place. That is what took 'em back so quick last night. Now, it'll take 'em at least two days to drive to the settlements, and a full day if they get men and start right back, before they can by any chance get on our trail. Then we will have from three to four days' start, and by the time they're where we are now I'll be close to the Black Hills, where I've red warriors enough, who are *my* friends, to wipe out a hundred such men as they. Yes, a thousand braves will jump on their horses at the call of the Eagle-Eye of the Hills. So, gal, dismiss all hope, and make up your mind to be mine willingly. It will be your fault if I'm rough."

A bitter answer was at Lillie's lips, but at that instant she caught a glance from the eye of Frank Stark, who rode along on the other side of Dave Tutt—a glance expressing his admiration so plainly that a new idea entered her mind.

Could she not use this man against the other? Through him might she not effect her escape? She would try it. It would be hard to assume what she could not feel, but life and that which was even yet more dear—her honor—was at stake. She would try.

A look—ah! how much a look can say!—told the lesser ruffian of the two that the captive liked him better than she did her captor, if no more. His eyes met hers again and again, and a glow of strange pleasure flushed his face, for he certainly saw in her look an encouragement of hopes which were but too pleasing.

"By all the reptiles that ever crawled, Dave Tutt goes under if she says I can take his place," he muttered to himself. "And if I can read eyes, that is what she means."

Lillie saw that her plan was beginning to work, and the air of deep despondency which she had been wearing passed away.

Tutt did not penetrate the cause; but he noticed that she was more cheerful, and it rather pleased him, for he had feared she would in her desperation try to take her own life.

Their route now tended more to the north; for, leaving the Valley of the Republican, the leader wished to strike the South Platte, and follow it up to the region where his friends were thickest.

When night came on a halt was made on the open prairie by a pond made by the rainfall in a buffalo-wallow. But only a couple of hours were allowed for the men and animals to get food and rest, when they again moved on by moonlight.

Lillie saw and rejoiced at the thought that Dave Tutt anticipated pursuit, and she believed it would be more eager than he dreamed, and that they would surely be overtaken by her friends before he could reach his allies.

Frank Stark, encouraged by her glances, had made several attempts to get a word with her, but Dave Tutt, while they were stopping, remained near her all the time, and when they moved on rode continually where his eye was upon her.

Once, when his attention seemed drawn away, she made a sign as if she was writing, and Frank answered it by an understanding nod, but neither sign nor nod had missed the keen eye that was on them.

"Look here, Frank Stark," said Tutt, in a savage tone, "if you've lived long enough, try, just *try* to cross my path. You know me, and I'm in no humor just now for trifling. Come within twenty feet of this wagon again till I give you permission, and I'll put six ragged holes in your carcass with my revolver. Now to the rear, and stay there."

Stark, physically, was no coward, but there was something in Dave's eye just then which told him that silence and obedience would be politic, if nothing more.

So, with but a single angry glance, he fell back, and poor Lillie thought that he was too much of a coward to help her, and felt ashamed of herself for, even by a look, having tried to encourage him.

Hers was a very expressive face, for Tutt read her feelings in the glance of contempt which followed Stark as he fell back, and a bitter smile illuminated his own countenance in place of the cloud of anger which had darkened it.

"If you want to coquette, find a *man* and not a sneak to try the game with," he said, in a low tone. "You'll find *me* worth a hundred such cowards if you are but half kind. As to your ever getting away from me alive, don't think of it. I wouldn't like to hurt you, but I'd kill and scalp you before another should glory in possessing you, or them get you back from whom I've taken you."

Lillie made no answer. She was weak and weary. Hope was indeed faint in her sad heart. Yielding to fatigue, she leaned back against the curtained side of the wagon and slept.

How long she slumbered she did not know, but she was wakened by the sound of rushing water, and looking out, saw that it was light and they were fording a river, broad but shallow, and full of willow-covered islands.

"Oh, had it been night," she thought, "what a place for concealment, if I could only have slipped out of the wagon unseen!"

Dave Tutt was ahead testing the depth of the water before the wagon followed, and on looking out she saw Frank Stark riding close by the hinder wheel.

A glance from his eyes told her that he was yet her friend and meant to do something for her, what it might be she could not comprehend.

As Tutt neared the opposite bank of the river, it became deeper, and it was evident that the team would have all it could do to get the wagon through over the quicksand bottom, for the water would reach to the wagon-bed, if not higher.

"Put your whip to your horses and make them drag through here lively!" shouted Dave to the driver, and the latter obeying, urged the team on.

But a heavy lurch of the wagon while it was in the deepest part told that something had given way, and the next second nearly half the hinder end was submerged, and the team came to a complete standstill. One of the wheels had come off, most probably from a lost linch-pin. Lillie in an instant thought how the linch-pin was lost, and repented of her precipitate condemnation of Frank Stark.

Delay was everything, and this must cause delay.

Dave Tutt rode back, cursing awfully. The four horses ahead of the wagon plunged fearfully. The treacherous quicksand washing from under their feet terrified them. The wagon itself began visibly to settle deeper and deeper into the water.

In vain the driver, assisted by Tutt, who lashed the horses until it seemed as if they must break from the harness, tried to move the wagon on.

Deeper and deeper, until the wounded men shrieked out for help to save them from drowning.

Then, and not till then, did Dave Tutt give up a hope of getting the wagon out.

Now he took Lillie on his own powerful horse, and called upon Frank Stark and others to get the helpless men to the land in the same way.

The harness was then cut, the team got to the shore, and the wagon abandoned.

To M'Kandlas, the rough removal was terrible. His wound bled externally afresh, and blood coming from his mouth made matters appear even yet worse for him.

A halt was now imperative. The colonel could not be moved at all in his present condition, and when moved it must be on a litter, or another wagon must be procured; for this, within a half-hour, went entirely out of sight.

Stark proposed that the whole party should camp, throw up a cotton-wood stockade, and be ready to fight it out if their pursuers came up.

"I, for one, will never desert my old leader while life is in him," he said. "The colonel has been true as steel to us, and we're worse than cowards if we desert him."

This was loudly applauded by the men, and Dave Tutt, who, in his own utter selfishness, would have gladly gone on with all the able men, leaving the helpless behind, did not dare propose the measure.

But he did not like to remain there, even for a short time, for he dreaded the pursuit of two such men as Buffalo Bill and his mate. He knew that death, worse than mere death, beside the loss of his prize, would be his fate.

"Yes," said he, deeming it best to chime in with the man whom he had hated in all the bitterness of his heart from the instant he saw him exchanging glances with Lillie—"Yes, I think we'd better make a stand here until we can move our wounded. I go in for it. So, Frank Stark, you take all the men that can be spared from horse, guard and fit up as good a stockade as you can with the tools we have. There's some drift-wood around, and sod can be cut with a hatchet as well as a spade. And as them who may come can't overtake us for a day or two yet, why I'll ride on and get the gal out of the way, so that they can't get her no way, and then if they find out she isn't here, why, maybe, they'll take another track and let us alone. I can do this and be back before there's any fighting."

"I don't like Dave's plan a bit," cried Frank Stark.

"Who was it asked you to like it? I didn't expect you would!" said Dave, grinding his white teeth ferociously together.

"We can't afford to lose a single rifle when such men as Wild Bill and his mate are after us. And we don't know what minute they may heave in sight. As for the gal, she can be hid right here—put on one of them islands where she can't git away, and where bullets won't hit her in the fight, and when we've whipped the enemy, Dave can go and fetch her and tote her off to the hills."

If Dave Tutt could have killed Frank Stark with a look while this was being said, Frank would never have finished his speech. But he got through, and was rewarded by a really grateful look from poor Lillie, who trembled lest she should indeed be carried on alone by her ruffianly abductor.

This glance, detected by Dave, almost set him wild with angry jealousy. But his was one of those, not human, but almost infernal natures, which can conceal its hottest passion—just as the tiger is stillest ere it leaps. His white face wore a ghastly smile, as he said: "Since Frank Stark seems to have so much to say, I will yield up the leadership of the party entirely to him. I only took it because the colonel here asked me to, but I now resign. So, Mr. Stark, you are now captain! I hope you'll prove your ability to take care of this party and get them off to the hills in safety."

"I will, with your help," said Frank, coolly.

"You'll not have much of my help, my brave fellow. I'm going on my own hook, and the gal is going with me."

"What! Desert your comrades in the hour of peril? You dare not, and you shall not. You say I am captain. Then, by the Big Elk of all elks. I'll show you that I am. Offer to leave us now, and half a dozen bullets shall pierce your carcass. Am I not right, men?"

"Aye, aye—hurrah for Frank Stark; he carries a full hand with every ace in the pack!" shouted one, and his words were applauded and echoed on every side.

"Scoundrel, I'll cut your heart out for this!" cried Dave, no longer able to restrain himself.

"Wait till I get this party to the Black Hills and I'll give you the best chance you ever had," said Frank, who, encouraged every instant by the approving eyes of Lillie, began to feel every inch a hero.

Talk of magic—talk of power. The approval of a woman whom he loves will do more to make a man manly, or even a coward brave, than anything else that can be named between heaven and earth.

"It may be a long time, but, curse you. I'll wait. And now build your camp and its defenses. I suppose your captainship has no objection to my taking the young lady, in whom you seem to take so much interest, over to one of the islands, and after I build a brush house to keep her from the night dews and the day breezes, standing guard to see that she does not run away? I can shoot as well from an island, if our enemies try to cross, as from here."

"The young lady will be quite as safe inside of the stockade as on an island under your *gentle* care," said Frank, urged by an appealing glance from her eyes to prevent the plan which Dave now laid to have her alone in his power. The companionship of ruffians was more safe than solitude with him.

"Well, have everything your own way now. But remember, Frank Stark, when we get to the hills, it is you or me and with *knives!*"

"All right, Mr. Tutt—I'm your man then, but now we've got work to do."

CHAPTER XI.

All night long, without a thought of sleep or even a sign of fatigue, Buffalo Bill and his mate rode around, gathering men and making preparations for the expedition in search of his lost sister.

By sunrise they were all assembled, had breakfasted and were ready for a start.

Not uniformed, scarce one dressed or armed alike; some mounted on noble thoroughbreds, others on hardy, wild-eyed mustangs; some young and slender; others tall, weather-bronzed, all bone and muscle—they looked like *true* fighting men, but no more like the holiday soldier of the city than a painted Grecian-bender on Broadway looks like a whole-souled, rosy, bright-eyed, full-formed country lass whose very glance makes you *dream* that angels drift along life's dark tide some time.

There was a slight pause after these men, some thirty in number, were ranged in the line ready to take column of march.

It was when Bill's mother and sister stepped forward to say good-by.

"Heaven bless and aid you and your friends, my dear boy!" said the good, Christian mother. "We women can only pray for your safety and success. A mother's prayers and hopes go with you!"

"And a sister's too, dear brother!" said Lottie, tears in her eyes as she spoke.

"And Kitty Muldoon says the good-luck be wid yez all, and bad luck to the wicked 'uns, that's got Miss Lillie wid 'em. Bring wan home wid ye jist, so I may scratch the eyes out of his ugly head!"

A shout of laughter followed this outburst from Kitty, and before it fairly subsided, Buffalo Bill, who had a good deal of the soldier in him, sung out: "By fours—column right and forward at a trot!"

There was no sound of bugle—no gay pennant fluttered in the air, but there was material for deadly work in that small, compact body of men.

The red men of the plains dread such men more, even in small bodies, than they do an army of thousands, moving with pomp and show—parks of artillery used only for noise, wagon trains and fluttering banners.

They know by many a sudden onslaught, many a brief, wild fight, how bordermen fight, and their dread of them—is wholesome.

Away at a sweeping trot, changing to a walk only when they ascended some steep pitch, and frequently a gallop as they went down, steering as true by the sun as if he had a compass, Buffalo Bill now headed for the farm where his mother's home had been.

It was almost night when they reached the spot, but there was plenty of light and time left before darkness to examine the unburied bodies of whites and Indians.

That of Jake M'Kandlas could not be found.

"He either is not dead or else they have carried his body along to bury it," said Buffalo Bill.

"They've got a wagon—here's the tracks," cried Wild Bill, whose eye had been more on signs than on the bodies.

"There was one in the old barn that wasn't burned," said Bill, riding to the spot where the wagon had been loaded.

"And here's more, mate—she, your sister, is with them. Look at that track," cried Wild Bill, as he sprang from Black Nell and examined a small footprint in the soil.

"Yes, yes, it was her foot did that," cried the brother. "Look for the track of Dave Tutt's horse further on, Bill."

"I've found it right here," cried Wild Bill. "We're on the right track now, and it is only a matter of time to get to 'em. We've got to reach 'em careful, or they may kill poor Miss Lillie for spite. Jake M'Kandlas, if he is alive, is mean enough for that, and I don't believe Dave Tutt is a bit better."

"Yes," said Buffalo Bill, "we must be fast and careful too. Loosen girths, boys, and feed your horses. There's corn and oats in the old barn, and hay in the stacks. We'll all get a bite and rest for two hours, and then go ahead by moonlight. The wagon trail will be easy to follow in the grass or over the sand."

The men now put their horses out to feed and then went to getting supper, while the two Bills for the first time in sixty hours dropped on the ground to get a little sleep before starting again.

CHAPTER XII.

With no tools but their camp-axes and tomahawks, the men under Frank Stark built for themselves a really formidable stockade from drift-wood and the trunks of small cotton-wood trees which grew along the banks of the Platte.

It was built on a kind of point which jutted out into the river with bold, precipitous banks, so that it was only assailable practically from the rear, for if horsemen should ford the river in front, or approach it on either flank, they could not get up the bank or over the walls of the stockade.

These were lined inside with rods cut from the prairie, where the coarse blue grass grew thick and matted near the water. Holes left for use by the marksmen were plentiful.

To enter it a rude ladder had been made, so that without an appliance not to be expected or easily made on the plains, it could scarcely be scaled.

Inside, for the comfort of the wounded, and with a special apartment for poor Lillie, a house sheltered with thatch of grass, and walled with willow twigs, had been made.

Near the stockade, and completely under rifle cover, was a corral of stakes, into which the stock could be driven at night, or on the approach of danger.

These arrangements showed that Frank Stark was capable, to say the least, of taking the command which Dave Tutt, more from spite than any other cause, had resigned into his hands.

Dave had assisted in the work, but took particular pains never to go out of sight of Lillie, and to keep such a watch on her that she could not hold an interview unobserved by him with Frank Stark.

But the latter had seen from glances of Lillie what he believed to be an encouragement, not to improper advances, but to a friendly understanding; for amid those lawless men she was in look and act pure as a lily fresh blown on the wave.

He determined to have an unobserved interview with her, and to effect it called off a regular stock and picket guard for the night, assigning to each man a special post. That farthest from the stockade—and it was a six-hour watch—was given to Dave Tutt.

The latter was about to moodily refuse the duty, but on second thought, realizing that it would be best for the present to yield to authority he had been instrumental in creating, he expressed his readiness to do the duty.

Hunters who had taken a ride of scarce a mile from the camp brought in several fat antelopes; and had there been no anticipation of attack there would have been nothing but hilarity among the men.

The night set in not quite as clear as on the preceding one, for floating clouds frequently swept athwart the sky, and shut out the moonlight. The sentinels were all posted, the reliefs had turned in to sleep till their time came on, and all was still inside the stockade.

Now Frank Stark determined if possible to find out how Lillie regarded him, and if, as he hoped, his conduct in regard to Dave Tutt had pleased her, to avow something more than a mere interest in her.

Approaching the separate apartment which he had built for her, and seeing her seated near the door on an improvised bench he had himself made for her use, he asked, in a low tone, if she would not like to look out on the river.

"Thank you, sir, you have been kind to me; I will be glad to do so," was her reply.

And she followed him to a part of the stockade where, from a bench of turf, they could look out on the river and its bush-covered islands.

Frank was silent for two or three minutes after they reached this spot, allowing her to look out on the water and the prairie beyond without disturbing her reverie. Even in his rude nature, lawless and full of evil, there was a reverence for the purity which made him silent, until she chose to speak. At last her voice fell on his ear.

"I ought to be very grateful to you, Mr. Stark," she said, "for interfering with that wretch to keep him from carrying me off to the hills. And I am. From my heart I thank you."

"Lord bless your sweet face, Miss Lillie, I haven't done half what I'd like to do for you!" he said, eagerly. "I have never in all my life seen any one half so good or half so pretty as you, and it makes me feel wild and wicked to think any harm should come to you, and I'll die before I see you wronged."

"Oh—thank you, thank you, Mr. Stark. You do not know how your words comfort me. If you only *could* get me back to my poor, broken-hearted mother, I believe you *would*! Wouldn't you?"

And her dark hazel eyes turned on him with a look which thrilled every nerve in his frame.

"Wouldn't I? Miss Lillie—I—I don't know what to say. I hate to leave them that trust in me, but since I have met you, I don't want to lead a wicked life any more. Them that I serve with now are determined to fight against the old flag that I was born under, and to entice the red fiends of the plains to do the same, and to carry fire and carnage along the border. I don't want to do it. If I can manage to get you off and back to your friends, will you try to have them receive me, not as a robber and a bad man, but as a soldier who will fight for his country?"

"I will—I will, and my brother—but forgive me, sir, if I ask one question. Were you one of the men who were with Colonel M'Kandlas when my poor father was murdered?"

"No; I have only been with the band for two years."

"Then I can promise for my brother. He has sworn never to touch hands with one of those men but to kill him."

"I don't blame him, for I've heard old Jake boast how the cowardly deed was done. Miss Lillie, I will help you, because I love you better than life. I don't ask you to love me, but when you see how I am ready to risk all, and, if need be, to die for you, I know you will not despise me."

"No; I shall honor and respect you, Mr. Stark, and hold you as a dear and noble friend. In such a time, and in such a situation as I now am in, you can expect no more than this."

"No, Miss Lillie, and it is more than I deserve. But, now that we understand each other, you had better go back to your quarters and rest all you can. I will lay my plans to get you away from here either to-night or to-morrow night, and, when they are laid, I will carry them through. Rest while you can, for when I call on you all your strength and courage will be needed."

"I will be ready, and I will pray for the good Father above to help you in all your good intentions, and to frustrate those whose thoughts are evil. Good-night, Mr. Stark."

"Good-night, Miss Lillie."

"She is an angel, if ever one walks the earth!" murmured Stark, as he watched her gliding away toward her quarters. "I never meant to leave the boys, but for her I'd die twenty deaths. She may love me for it yet. A woman who knows a true heart beats only for her, must think of it some time, not unkindly, either."

CHAPTER XIII.

With only a couple of hours rest, the party under Buffalo Bill started on from the ruins of the cottage home, the trail made by the wagon being quite easy to follow.

While it led toward the valley of the Republican the two leading bordermen were rather surprised, for the sinuous windings of that stream led far away from the direct route to the Black Hills, in which it was known the M'Kandlas gang had their secret haunts and hiding places.

But when it made a sudden turn toward the north-west, leading toward the valley of the Platte, then Wild Bill exclaimed: "I know now the very spot the varmints are heading for. If they wasn't so rascally tricky and might change their course after taking it. I could take a nigh cut and head em off."

"They've got Cheyennes with em, and there's no knowin' what bend they might take," said his mate. "We had better follow the trail. They can't reach the hills ahead of us—not with a wagon to drag; and till they do, we're enough for twice their number."

"That's so; but we mustn't wear out our horses," said Wild Bill. "A man without a good horse isn't half a man in a fight on the plains, and that we all know."

"That is so; but I hate to think how my darling sister must feel as she goes further and further away from those she loves. But she knows I'll be on the trail. I'll not fret any more, but hold my spite till I can draw a bead on Dave Tutt."

When the party reached the first halting-place on the plains, where the robbers had made a temporary rest, they looked in vain for the foot-tracks of Lillie.

But Lillie had not been allowed to descend from the wagon here.

They had now come so far and so fast that a halt for the entire night was necessary, or their stock would be used up too much for active service.

No fires were made—they had cooked provisions sufficient; therefore the buffalo-chips that lay thick around the little pond were undisturbed.

The dawn of another day found men and horses fresh and ready for a vigorous start. The trail freshened as they went on, and the bordermen felt sure that unless the wagon was abandoned, they would overtake those whom they pursued inside of thirty or forty hours.

They moved at a steady, sweeping gait until after-noon, and then Buffalo Bill brought them down to a slower pace. He saw trees which grew along the Platte rising on the horizon, and he deemed it best, lest he might be ambuscaded, to approach that river in the night.

For over the plains the eye can detect objects at an immense distance, while concealed among the tall grass, bushes and trees that skirt the river banks, hundreds might lurk unseen, their vicinity unknown until it was felt.

Halting in sight of the river-growth, the party had another long rest. When night with its shadows came on, they moved again. The moonlight enabled them to see the trail and yet it was not sufficiently vivid for the party to be discovered at any great distance.

It is doubtful if any discovery of the rovers would have been made by our bordermen, had not one of those incidents occurred which no camp with animals in it can be guarded from. The neigh of a horse or the braying of a mule can be heard as far as a trumpet, and the latter sound, reaching the ears of the bordermen as they approached the river on their third night out, put them at once on their guard.

There had been no fires lighted by the M'Kandlas party at night, but they could not keep their animals still.

When this sound was heard, the party at once came to a halt and dismounted, while Buffalo Bill rode on to reconnoiter. They left orders for their party not to move till they returned, without they heard firing, and if they did, then to hurry in and take a share in what might be going on.

The two bordermen rode swiftly on toward the river, during a brief time of comparative darkness while a cloud bank obscured the moon, then as the clouds moved by they dropped with their well-trained horses to the earth, for with the coming light they saw that they were very near the river.

"It was well for them to do so, for when the moon came out clearly, they distinctly saw the stockade looming up on the other side of the river.

What it meant they could not understand. Why a party like that of which they were in pursuit should halt and fortify a defensive position was something they could not comprehend.

Buffalo Bill was the first to speak.

"That's a fort—and by the way it rises from the bank, a pretty strong one I'm thinking," said he.

"Yes, but have they had time to build it, or are they in it?" said Wild Bill. "If it is their work, and they are there, they mean fight, and to do it with all the advantages. We could charge 'em on the plains, but charging a fort won't pay without we know we can get into it on a jump."

"That's so, Bill. And we must know all about that place before we go any further—that is with the party. You stay here till I cross and see what's there."

"No—you stay, and I will go. It's a risk and your life's worth more than mine," said Wild Bill.

"That's no such thing, Bill—your life is as dear to me as my own, and where's the risk it's my right to go, for I've got more at stake in this game than you. My poor Lillie is over there in the power of Dave Tutt. I couldn't stay here if you went."

"Then let us both go."

"No, Bill; and I'll tell ye why. If by any accident they should get us both, our party without one or other of us to lead would never do anything in a fight with such scoundrels fenced in. So now stay till I come back, or you know by hearing a shooting that they've got me. Do it, Bill, if you love me!"

"It is about as hard as drawin' sound teeth, mate, but if you say so. I suppose I must. But be careful and get back. We haven't got a great deal more of night ahead of us, so you'll have to be lively."

"I'll be all that. Keep Powder Face and Black Nell out of sight, for I'll foot it over."

Buffalo Bill now in a crouching position passed on toward the river, while his mate with the two horses lying down waited for what might turn up.

Wild Bill watched his friend as long as he could see him, until he was lost in a thick clump of bushes on the edge of the river.

Shortly after he saw quite a log of drift-wood moving slowly down the current, but as it neared the other shore very fast while it went down, he comprehended the plan of Buffalo Bill to get across unobserved, if they were on the watch in the stockade.

When the log stranded near a steep bush-crowned bank on the other side of the river, he knew that his friend was safety on the other side, and that now the most dangerous part of his work was to be done.

Anxiously he watched the stockade—hardly breathing aloud lest he should lose a sound, he looked and listened for some token of Buffalo Bill.

A full hour passed in this way. He began to glance often toward the east, for he knew that the dawn could not be far off.

"What can Bill be about?" he muttered. "He has had time to scout all around there and get back. I don't like this layin' here like a fool and doing nothing, a bit. But he'd make a noise if they'd got him. I can't make it out. Ah! there's the log in the stream again. He is coming at last."

CHAPTER XIV.

In the settlement where Mrs. Cody, Lottie, and Kitty Muldoon were left for protection, there was much anxiety after the departure of so many of the men with Buffalo Bill. For it was too near two borders, the Missouri and Indian, to be considered safe, if all the fearful rumors regarding rebellion and war were true which had been reaching them through various sources for weeks.

In truth there was not ten men capable of bearing arms left in the place, though there were full a hundred women and children.

The widow and her daughter were quartered at the small and only tavern in the place, kept by a crippled octogenarian, whose constant boast was that he had "fit" the British in 1812, and could do it "again," if they'd only come where he was. As his only weapon of defense was a crutch, there was not much danger of his injuring anybody in his exhibition of the manual of arms, which were frequent when the war humor was on him.

The tavern only contained four rooms and a garret, so that what occurred in one part was pretty sure to be soon known in another.

The first floor rooms were the bar and general smoking-room, the dining-room, and kitchen all in one—the landlord's family room, and the best bed-room—the last of which, with two beds, was occupied by Mrs. Cody, her daughter, and the irrepressible Kitty Muldoon.

The presiding genius of the bar-room was Major Williams, the landlord—the presiding genius of the kitchen and boss of the whole house was Molly Williams, his young wife—that is, young compared with him, for she was only five and thirty, while he was eighty years old, if a day.

Late on the afternoon of the same day on which Buffalo Bill left with his party, two smart-looking strangers, well mounted, but with no arms visible, arrived at the tavern. They carried saddle-bags on their horses, as western travellers generally do, wore rather superior clothes, and carried themselves as men do who think themselves above the "common herd" of humanity.

Directing that their horses should be well fed and well groomed, they ordered supper, and stated that they should remain all night.

Major Williams hobbled about on his crutch, quite delighted at this acquisition of custom, especially as the strangers patronized the tincture of aqua-fortis which was labelled "old rye," in his decanters, and to a very quiet system of careless questioning gave a perfect statement of everything regarding the population of the place, absence of the men, even to the presence of the mother and sister of the famous scout and Indian hunter, Buffalo Bill.

The two men, both young and stalwart in form, keen-eyed, and with rather a military look, exchanged meaning glances from time to time as the garrulous old man chatted on, but his eyes were dim, smoke-clouded too from his ever active pipe, and he did not notice it.

Supper was served for them with the whole family, and the widow, with her beautiful daughter and Kitty Muldoon, occupied one part of the table.

The eyes of the elder of the two strangers, a dark-complexioned man of probably twenty-eight or thirty, flashed with a wild, passionate glance as it fell upon the perfect form and lovely face of Lottie, while his companion seemed more impressed with the less soulful look but plump proportions and rosy face of bright-eyed Kitty Muldoon.

The widow, ever reticent to strangers, took scarcely any notice of these persons, though the elder, very conversationally inclined, sought to introduce several topics of interest to attract her notice.

From his talk it appeared that he and his companion had been up the Missouri river purchasing a large tract of land with the intention of settling.

When the major asked questions about the coming war they appeared to be very poorly informed, but Mrs. Cody, with that quickness of perception peculiar to her sex, made up her mind that they knew more than they cared to disclose. Also, that when they chose sides, if they had not already done so, the Southern, and not the Northern, was where they would be found.

As soon as the supper was over, the widow and her child retired to the bedroom, followed by Kitty Muldoon, while the strangers returned to the barroom, into which, with the coming of night, the most of the male population of the place found its way.

To make themselves popular with these people, the strangers were quite liberal in treating, and it was not long before nearly all were more or less under the influence of the vile beverage which was vended at the bar.

The strangers pretended to drink quite as freely as those whom they treated so often, but they poured out scarcely anything for themselves, and so diluted what they did take with water that they felt none of the effects which they were producing on others.

Poor Mrs. Cody trembled while she listened to the foolish speeches and maudlin songs which proclaimed that the few men left to protect the settlement were becoming each moment less and still less capable of doing service. She almost felt relieved when the night wore on and comparative silence told that those who were not helpless from drink had staggered away to their homes.

The old major hung out as long as he could, but at last sank down helpless in his chair behind the bar, and then the two strangers were alone.

An eye was on them, however, for Mrs. Molly Williams, though perfectly willing to see the money come into the drawer did not believe in its going but again, so when she saw her old husband sink down into helplessness, as she did through a crack in the kitchen door, she took post where she could observe the actions of her guests.

She saw that, with their heads close together, they were talking low and quite earnestly, and she tried hard to catch some idea of what they said. But this was not possible, though she once heard the elder say "*the girls,*" as he glanced toward the interior of the house.

She felt confident that they were planning some mischief, for now that they believed themselves unmolested, they exhibited a brace of revolvers and two huge knives, which hitherto had been hidden under their clothing.

She was not a woman of timidity—few border women are—and she was thinking how she should act to secure the money in the drawer, inform them that it was bed-time, and drag her drunken old husband to his nest, when the tramp of horses' hoofs reached her ears.

"The boys are coming—we're all right now!" said the elder of the strangers, springing to his feet at this sound. "The plunder and the girls first, and a big blaze afterward!"

CHAPTER XV.

It was almost daylight when Buffalo Bill got back to where Wild Bill and the two horses had been left.

"Quick, Bill," said the former—"quick, mate, and get out of sight. We've got work to do over there, but we can't do it by daylight. They're too well fixed. Mount and let's get back to the boys and out of sight and then I'll tell you all I've seen."

The two men mounted and sped away swiftly, and in a few minutes had rejoined their party. These were also put in motion, and when day dawned they halted behind a low range of pebbly hills, about seven or eight miles from the river.

Here the first act of Buffalo Bill was to post a dismounted man where he could just look over the crest of the hills and see the river and bushy growth along its margin, without exposing his own person to observation from that direction.

The horses, picketed with a guard to look out for them, were put among the low ravines where the buffalo grass was finest, and a half dozen men taking turns with a spade which had been brought along set out in the lowest place to dig a well so that they might have water. No fire was allowed, and silence was enjoined—at least so far as loud talk or halloing was concerned.

All this was seen to by Buffalo Bill before he would relate anything to his mate or to any of the party of what he had seen over the river. In truth, there was enough of the Indian in his nature to enable him to conceal even in his looks as well as in his silence all information until he thought fit to impart it.

This time came when the party was properly settled and concealed.

Then calling Bill and the others to his side, he said: "I was right in among the cussed varmints over there. They're fixed up in a strong stockade, with a good corral for their stock, and playing an open game wouldn't pay for us. They're fixed to stay till they can move their wounded men, for they lost their wagon some way in crossing the river. Old Jake M'Kandlas is alive, with a hole through his body from my revolver, and there are two or three more as bad off as he is that can't be moved!"

"Your sister—you havn't said a word about her," said Wild Bill anxiously.

"No—but I'm coming to that. She has made a friend there some way, and Dave Tutt has got his master. Frank Stark bosses the crowd and I heard him tell Dave Tutt that he should not disturb her. She has her own room in a house they've built inside of the stockade, and I heard Frank Stark tell Dave that neither he or any other man should intrude on her. Dave was fighting mad, but it seems that Frank has got the men with him, and Dave has to bottle his mad for a while. I tried to get a word with her but it was too risky, so I gave it up for then, satisfied no harm would come to her before they move from there. And if you'll all stand by me to-night, we'll get inside of their works before they know it, and then good-by to every one of the cusses but Frank Stark. I'll save him for the good turn he has done for Lillie. So take things easy to-day, boys, and rest—we can't do anything till night comes on."

"What do you suppose makes Frank Stark take the part of Lillie?" asked Wild Bill. "Thought he was as bad as the worst of the gang?"

"I can't tell. He spoke as respectfully of her as you would, and talked as if he meant what he said. It seemed to me that he had been quarreling with Dave about her before, for Dave reminded him that it wasn't the first time he'd promised to cut his heart out on her account, and he would keep his promise, if it was the last act of his life."

"Well, I'm glad she isn't no worse off; but this is going to be a long day, waiting for night to come to go in and wipe 'em out. Is there many reds among 'em?"

"No—not over eight or ten, if so many. I couldn't get to count noses, for it was ticklish work creeping over the walls and in among 'em when a good part of 'em were awake. The quarrel between Dave and Frank helped me some, because they made so much noise. I took a good look at the corral where they put their stock at night, because that must be stampeded at the same time we pitch in to save Lillie and wipe them out so not a cuss out of the crowd can get away. I don't mean to kill old Jake if I can help it. I want to take him back to the spot where he murdered my father, and roast him there over a slow fire. Death—a mere man's death—is too good for him. He wants, and shall have, a taste here of what he'll get when he is dead!"

"Mate, you're as bad as the reds, by thunder you are!" said Wild Bill.

"Yes, when I think of him and his gang, I am. Why should I not be? Can the memory of my good father, butchered in cold blood before his poor wife and helpless children, ever pass away? No, Bill, never—never! I will never feel that he rests easy in his grave while one of them is alive to boast of the black deed he has done. I have with my own hand killed two-thirds of them, and until all are gone—and by my hand, too, I will not feel content. I heard the wretch groaning from pain this morning. It was music to my soul. Oh, how I wanted to whisper in his ear, '*Fiend*, the pursuer is at hand! Your time is drawing near; the spirit of the murdered hovers near to exult over your tortured end!' Bill, I could glory in every pain that racked his frame. I could see his eyeballs start in agony from his head—the beaded sweat, blood-colored, ooze from his clammy skin—each nerve and tendon quivering like the strings of a harp struck by a maniac hand. Oh, how I could gloat over his howling misery! And it is coming, it is coming—his time. When it *does*, mercy need not plead to me—not a throe, not a pulsation would spare for the wealth of all the world!"

CHAPTER XVI.

Molly Williams stood still and trembled when she heard those ominous words from the lips of the eldest of the two strangers, and saw the fiendish look which accompanied the expression.

She trembled yet the more as she knew by the thunder of the hoofs that a large body of horsemen had galloped to the front of the house.

"Open the door, Hubert, and tell the boys that I, Alf Coye, am here!" cried the elder stranger.

"There's nothing to fear. Every man in the place is drunk or asleep."

The younger man threw open the door wide, and when the men outside saw him and his companion, their cheers rang out clear and hearty on the night air.

"Hurrah for Captain Alf!" yelled one.

"Hurrah for the Southern Confederacy!" cried another.

"Down with the Yankee interlopers!" shouted a third.

"Dismount, men, and come in. Eat, drink and be merry. The best in the land is not good enough for you, but it is free as you are free."

"There's neither free drink nor free provisions here, I'd have you to know, sir," cried Mollie Williams, now thinking it time to assert her rights. "You've made my poor old husband drunk and helpless, but he isn't me, and I'll soon show you that!"

"Whew! Our pretty hostess is getting warm in the cool of the evening," cried the captain.

"Warm enough to scald you if you don't keep your ruffians out of my house," screamed Mrs. Molly, as she sprang behind the bar, and, first securing the money from the drawer, gave her old husband a sound box on the ear which partially awoke him.

"Surround the house—let no one leave or enter besides our own men, without my permission," cried the captain.

This order was given because, fully dressed and ready for departure, Mrs. Cody, her daughter Lottie, and Kittie Muldoon made their appearance in the back room.

"What does this mean?" asked the widow, pale, but not terrified.

She addressed the question to Mrs. Williams, but was answered by the man who called himself Captain Alf Coye.

"It means, madam, that a part and parcel of the Southern Confederacy has made a raid over the Kansas border, and as one Buffalo Bill is arrayed on the Union side, we shall deem it a good policy to hold his mother and sister in our hands as hostages for his future good behavior. I am glad to see you are dressed, ready for travelling, for my men will only remain here long enough to collect what plunder they want and to make a bonfire of the rest. We will then head for Missouri, and you will accompany us."

"Never, monster, never!"

"Oh yes you will, madam, and I would advise you to spare such opprobrious terms, lest I be tempted to deserve the name by some act which your own rudeness may provoke."

"Fiend, I defy you and your vile followers!"

"Madam, the beauty of your daughter may tempt me to deserve the name. Beware! I am not a man to pause or trifle if I make up my mind to any course, good or bad!"

The poor lady sunk with a shudder into a chair, while Lottie, weeping, knelt by her side. That threat, so quickly understood, was more terrible than the thought of death.

But there was one yet left to face the bold, bad man, who had no such thing as fear in her composition, and but little care for the anger she might excite.

It was pretty, brave-hearted, good Kitty Muldoon.

"You are a dirty big blackguard, you are, to thry to scare a poor lone widdy woman, when the son is away who'd bate the very sowl out of ye, big as ye are, wid one hand tied behind him and a glove on the other!"

Kitty stood with her arms akimbo, looking him square in the face as she said this. Her eyes flashed like sparks of fire and her cheeks were all aglow with passion.

"By the gods of war, girl, you're almost as pretty as your young mistress. If my lieutenant, Hubert Stanley, hadn't taken a fancy to you and spoken first, I believe I'd have had you for my sweetheart."

"Divil the one, you or your liftenant, will make a swateheart of me!" cried Kitty, madder than before. "I'll be a sour and bitter pill for the best of ye to swallow. Lay but the weight of a dirty finger on me, or on them I serve and love, and I'll scratch the eyes from yer heads."

"We'll see by-and-by," said Coye, coolly. "My men will soon get through with their work, for they understand it. Hubert, find a good carriage or wagon to put these women in. I shall carry them over the border, and if Buffalo Bill comes after them I'll have a rope for his neck!"

"Sure an' 'twill fit yer own better," said the indignant and unterrified Kitty. "I could make a better man out o' mud than you are, wid all yer fine clothes on yer crooked back. You're not fit to kiss the ground that young master Bill treads over. It is him that will pay you for this—not in silver or in gould, but in cold lead and blue steel. Worra the day that the likes of yes came up from below, to bother good Christians like them that's before you."

"Girl, you have said about as much as I want to hear. If you care for the comfort of your mistress and her daughter, get their clothes and blankets together. For they are about to start on a long and hard journey, with little chance for getting comforts after they leave here. No more impudence now, or I'll turn you over to those who know no mercy and never dream of pity."

"Yes—hush, my good Kitty," said the poor widow. "You only excite his anger without bettering our situation. Heaven will not desert us, child, and though it is very, very dark now, light will come by-and-by. We are in the power of these men now, but I trust will not be so for a great while. They will not dare to wrong us, for a fearful retribution will follow as surely as light follows darkness when day succeeds night."

"I'll do yer bidding, ma'am, but these haythens had better sing small if they don't want to know what a bit of an Irish girl can do wid her nails and her teeth."

CHAPTER XVII.

Buffalo Bill and the men whom he led noticed with pleasure as night drew near, while they almost counted the minutes which must elapse before they could with prudence attack the robber stockade, that the clouds began to overspread the sky, indicative of an approaching storm.

This, while it would tend to lessen the vigilance of the enemy, would conceal their movements and be likely to save them men and trouble.

As soon as night came on, every man was mounted, his arms having been carefully inspected and loaded while there was light. The wind, coming from the west, fresh and fitfully, was favorable in two points of consideration.

First, if there were dogs with the Indians or white wretches, they could not scent the approach of the pursuers. Next, the wind, sweeping in mad blasts over the prairie, made sufficient noise to drown all other sounds.

The leader of the bordermen had carefully laid out his plan of attack, and explained it to his followers, detailing the men for the two points of action, so there should be no error when the work began.

Wild Bill, with five picked men, was to shoot down the stock-guard and to stampede the animals from the corral.

Buffalo Bill, with the rest, only two men being left with the horses on the east side of the Platte, was to enter the stockade, and, at a signal given by himself, the attack was to commence.

Every precaution was taken, even to the wearing of a white mark around the left arm, made from white shirts torn in strips, that the party might distinguish their own people in the fray.

Moving up to the river with silent caution, it took the party full two hours after they started to reach the fording-place. And when they did so, the moon was completely hidden by the black clouds which flew like lost spirits overhead.

The rumble of distant thunder, and a kind of heavy dampness in the air, indicated the approach of rain.

"Boys," said Bill, in a low tone, to the men close grouped around him, "when we take to the water to cross I shall lead the way. You might follow in single file, careful to keep so close to your file leader that you can touch him. Take care of your arms and ammunition, and keep perfect silence."

A low murmur of assent told him that the orders were heard and understood, and then he moved on.

The ford was only deep in mid-channel, and to footmen the quicksand was not so bad as it was to heavy animals. The current was rather rapid, especially in the channel, but in about half an hour every man of the party was on the west side of the Platte, about two or three hundred yards above the stockade.

The louder sounds of thunder, as well as now and then flashes of distant lightning, told them they had but little time to wait for the outburst of the storm, so the order for the stampeding party to move to their post was at once given.

Away in the darkness went Wild Bill and his men, taking a course from the river-bank.

Two or three minutes after, Buffalo Bill, with his men, carefully followed the river down to reach the walls of the stockade.

It was an exciting moment, for it was yet so early that the enemy could be heard talking in their camp. Now and then a coarse laugh, following some jest, would reach the ears of the bordermen, thus assuring them that their close proximity was a thing un-dreamed of.

On, until at last the stockade was reached, kept Buffalo Bill and his party. And now the young leader, before getting over the wall at the only assailable spot which he had discovered the night before, gave the signal agreed upon, which was to inform Wild Bill of his readiness to begin.

This signal was the peculiar cry of a small owl which is found all over the Western prairies, and is heard only at night.

Bill was an adept in imitation, and the cry came so natural from his lips that the oldest bordermen of the party would have believed it came from the bird itself had they not known differently.

At the same moment that Bill gave the signal there was an alarm at the corral—a loud challenge—first a single shot, and then several more, followed by the sound, not of a general stampede, but of one, or at most two, horses making at full speed toward the river.

Buffalo Bill was puzzled at this, for Wild Bill had a return signal to make, which had not yet been heard, and he was not to fire a gun until the attack inside of the stockade commenced.

But he had no time for thought now. The garrison of the stockade was alarmed, and the hoarse voice of Dave Tutt was heard shouting: "Where is Frank Stark?"

CHAPTER XVIII.

"Where is Frank Stark? Where is the girl prisoner?" shouted Dave Tutt, with an angry voice from inside the stockade. "Now who is the traitor—who deserts you now? Your famous captain is gone, and that is what the row at the corral is about. I hope they've got him there. I'm going to see!"

And Dave sprang upon the wall of the stockade.

As he did so a vivid flash of lightning, followed by an instantaneous crash of thunder, lighted up the whole place, and he saw at a glance that a body of armed men were on the point of entering the stockade, while just entering the river at the ford was a man mounted on his own horse, close followed by a female on another animal.

A dozen shots were fired at him at the same instant, and he fell back wounded into the interior of the stockade, as he shouted: "They're here, men—they're here. Fight as you never fought before, or we're all wiped out."

There was no further hope for concealment, no use now in a second of delay, and though Buffalo Bill felt sure that his sister had escaped from that gang, he was not now the less inclined to punish them.

"Over the works, boys, and let your revolvers and knives tell the tale!" he shouted, and sprang up the ladder which was kept for general use by the garrison.

Up and over, as speedily as thought, close followed by his men, into the darkness, soon to be made light by the firing of a tent, went Buffalo Bill, and hand to hand, with revolver and knife, amid the yells and whoops of white men and Indians, the fearful work went on.

It could not last long, for with the blaze of the tent the brave bordermen could see where to shoot and strike, and now the victorious shouts of Wild Bill and his men, with the thunder of the stampede, reached the ears of the terror-stricken defenders of the stockade.

"Mercy—we surrender!" shouted a huge villain, already down with a bullet in his brawny breast.

"Take the mercy your gang gave my father!" shouted Buffalo Bill, and his knife clove through the villain's skull.

A minute more and Wild Bill was over the wall, another minute and, except a few wounded wretches on the earth, not one of the Indians or robbers was left.

These would have been at once dispatched, had not Wild Bill sung out with a chivalrous generosity peculiar to men of his class: "Boys, it's a shame to butcher them that can't raise a hand to defend themselves. Let's hold up—let's hold up! We've our own wounded to look to!"

"It is poor policy, but excepting old Jake M'Kandlas, the rest may live for all me," cried Buffalo Bill. "As for him, he shall live until I can hang him over the grave of my murdered father, or roast him to ashes on the ground stained by his blood. But my sister—she is safe from here, but is Frank Stark to be *trusted*?"

"Yes, just as you could have trusted me, if I had got her off," said Dave Tutt, with a feeble voice; for, terribly hurt, he lay yet living among the wounded. "He is off for the Black Hills with her."

"That's a lie, for I saw him and her crossing the river by the light of the same flash which revealed you to us, and us to you, you mean sneak," cried Buffalo Bill. "If I wasn't sure you'd suffer more by being let alone, I'd cut your throat where you are, you infernal spy and deceiving cuss! Look out for him, men, and for old Jake M'Kandlas—I am going across the river to find my Lillie."

"You need not cross the river to find her, for she is here," cried Frank Stark, coming over the wall, followed by the fair girl. "We met the guard on the other side of the river, and nearly lost my number, too, for one of 'em shot my horse. But we found out you were here and knew you'd be all right, too, so here we are."

Lillie was already in the arms of her noble brother, while Frank Stark stood looking at the pale, angry face of Dave Tutt, who gnashed his teeth in impotent rage.

"Oh, curse you, you traitorous dog. If I could only live to cross knives with you, I would ask no more," cried the wounded robber.

"Gentlemen, do doctor that poor thief up. I want him to live till I can show him how good I am at carving," said Frank Stark in a tone of bitter sarcasm. "But I suppose I'm a prisoner myself, and have no right to talk."

"You are not a prisoner! Your kindness to my sister entitles you to my friendship," cried Buffalo Bill. "And if, as she says, you wish to join the Union men in the work just commenced, you shall have the best of chances. I was on my way to join the Union army at St. Louis when Dave Tutt, like a black-hearted scoundrel that he is, tore my sister away from her mother's side."

"I will go wherever you lead, and fight to death for the dear old flag I was born under," cried Frank.

"Good on your head! There's my hand, and my heart is as free as it for one of the right sort," cried Wild Bill.

"Heap up a bonfire—there's no danger now—and let us have light," cried the happy brother. "When day comes we'll be on the back-track, for my poor mother will sleep little until she hears from Lillie. Hallo! where have you come from? You look as white as a ghost, man! Speak out—what is the matter in Corinne?"

"Matter, Bill?" gasped the new-comer, as he sank exhausted to the earth. "There's matter enough to drive us all mad. There's not a house left standing in town—all are in ashes. Worse yet, every man but myself, I think, is killed, with some of the women, too—and the youngest and fairest carried off. I crept away, ran miles on foot, then caught a loose horse, got on your trail, and am here. I've neither eaten nor drank since the massacre."

The man was well known to them all. He had been one of those left to take care of the settlement.

"Who did this?" asked Buffalo Bill, hoarsely.

"One Alf Coye, at the head of a hundred bush-whackers from Missouri."

"My mother and Lottie," gasped Bill.

"I saw them in a wagon under guard as I crept away," said the man. "For mercy's sake, give me some food and drink—I am almost dead."

"Attend to him, some of you," said Buffalo Bill. "And now, men, we have work to do. Frank Stark, for the good heart you have shown, I am going to trust you as I'd trust no other man on such short acquaintance. I shall take all but five of my men and the best horses, and make after the party that have carried off my mother and sister, and we know not how many more. With those five and this man here, guard my sister Lillie and get her to St. Louis just as quickly as you can. I will meet you there if I live. Not a word, my dear sister. You never could stand the mad riding that me and Wild Bill must do now. I feel that I can trust you with this man, for he risked his life to get you out of the clutches of Dave Tutt. Heaven bless you, darling—trust him and be my own brave sister until we meet. Come, men, all but the five who have no families in Corinne. Come: we must over the river and to horse like kinked lightning on a tear."

One brief embrace between brother and sister and our hero was off on his new course to endeavor to rescue his mother and Lottie.

CHAPTER XIX.

By the time Buffalo Bill and his men had made their hasty preparations for starting in chase of Alf Coye and his gang, the storm fairly broke over them. The rain came down in torrents, while the rolling thunder and flashing lightning added wild grandeur to its weird effect in the midnight darkness.

This forced a delay until the dawn of day, for in the wind, rain and utter gloom the keenest scout and most accomplished guide could not have kept a true course over the plains.

The time flew swiftly by, for the brother and sister had a brief opportunity for conversation, and the messenger from the settlement, revived by food and drink, was able to give a partial account of the fearful outrage which had left most of his hearers homeless, and even worse off, if their fears were verified as to the loss of loved ones.

When the dawn came, though the storm had not abated, a course could be laid, and the young leader at once called his men to horse.

The animals had all been brought over, and now the men mounting, the cavalcade was put in motion, the two bordermen leading the way at a gait which only the literally tireless steeds of the prairie can keep up, swept over the stream and far away toward the southeast.

Lillie, not heeding the pouring rain or chilling wind, stood by the side of Frank Stark on the parapet of the stockade, and watched her dear brother, as he rode away with his companions, sad that he must leave her, but feeling that it was *his* duty to fly to the rescue of her mother and sister, and hers to be brave and hopeful, trusting in Him who is strength to the weak, for her own safe delivery from impending perils.

She watched her handsome, noble brother, until his form was out of sight, beyond the grassy hills, and then with a sigh she turned and asked her companion how soon they could start upon their journey.

"Were it only ourselves to go on we could start at once," said Frank Stark. "But your brother wished me to carry Jake M'Kandlas and Dave Tutt in as prisoners, that they may swing from the gallows tree in the presence of a multitude, as they should, for to die as men who are soldiers or brave frontiersmen die will be no punishment to them. To carry out his desire and to keep them alive until the proper hour of doom arises, they must be moved with care. I shall have litters made, and when they are ready, move on."

"You surely will not fatigue brave men by carrying the worthless bodies of such men?" said Lillie, in surprise.

"Oh, no—we will collect the animals that were stampeded, for they have not gone far, and will I swing each litter between two mules. It will be rough travel for the wounded wretches, but as they never knew mercy for any one else, I think they have no right to expect it from others. Go beneath the shelter, for we will be ready in a little while to travel. I do not wish to stay here a moment longer than can be helped, for the Sioux and the Cheyenne hunt along this stream, and the force left by your brother is too small to resist a large party of them with any hope of success. I will have a talk with Jake M'Kandlas and Dave Tutt while the rest are getting the litters ready."

Lillie at once went into her little room and began to make preparations for her journey, while Stark went into the place where M'Kandlas and Dave Tutt were lying.

Both men eyed him with a bitterness of expression far more speaking than words. They were powerless to do more than look their hate, but if looks could kill, his life had not been worth a thought.

"Traitor!" hissed M'Kandlas at last.

"Treason to the devil is duty to God," said Stark, quietly. "There is no use for either of you men to put on airs—you are down, and you'll never get up in this world until you are lifted up by a rope."

"Dog! down or up, we're higher than you are!" cried Dave Tutt.

"That is a matter of opinion," said Stark, smiling. "But I've no words to waste. I came in to see how you looked, and if you required any fixing up before we started."

"Started? What do you mean?" asked M'Kandlas.

"That we start in a little while for the settlements. I am having mule-lifters fixed for you and Dave. It will be rather rough, but I reckon you can stand it. It's only a short delay, for you'll swing when Buffalo Bill gets back from punishing Al Coye."

"He'll never get back from that bit of business," said Dave Tutt, scornfully. "Alf Coye is not the man to get away from, and Buffalo Bill will learn that if he crosses his path. Ah! your new sweet-heart is in trouble, Mr. Frank Stark—and so are you! Here is Raven Feather—the Ogallala, and my friend."

Even as these last words passed the lips of Dave Tutt, caused as they were by a wild scream from Lillie, the opening in the brush house that served as a door was darkened by the presence of several Indians, hideous in their war paint.

Foremost of these was a tall warrior of most ferocious look, with a cap composed of black raven feathers on his head. The silver crescents, three in number, on his breast, proclaimed his rank as a great chief, even had not his haughty, commanding look done so.

"What is the matter with my brother, the Eagle-Eye of the Black Hills?" asked the Ogallala chief, as he looked on the reclining form of Tutt.

"My body has eaten too much lead. A false friend brought the enemies of the red man and of the Eagle-Eye upon him, and he is weak from many wounds," replied Tutt.

"It shall be well with Eagle-Eye. Raven Feather will bind up his wounds and punish his enemies," said the chief.

"There is one—the worst of all. Let him be bound!" said Dave, pointing to Frank Stark, who had stood till now almost paralyzed with surprise at this sudden appearance of an enemy which had stolen in unseen by his sentinels, or at least without an alarm reaching his ears.

But now, life and liberty both endangered, his native courage came back, and quicker than thought his revolver was drawn from his belt.

Twice had he discharged it, a death among his dusky foes following each report, when with a bound Raven Feather sprang to his rear, and hurled him to the ground before he could turn his weapon on him.

In a second his arms and feet were secured with hide lariats, and then in agony he was forced to listen to the taunts of Jake M'Kandlas and Dave Tutt.

But even this was not his deepest trial.

Poor Lillie was brought in, her white arms clutched on either side by a grim and hideous warrior, while with reeking scalps uplifted, others pressed forward to tell Raven Feather that the other pale-faces had been slain.

"Ugh! A pale-face squaw. Heap handsome, like the wild rose of the valley. Raven Feather will make her his wife! She shall bead his mocasins and cook his meat. His other squaws are old and ugly in his eyes since he looks upon the face of the prisoner!" said the chief, as his eye rested eagerly on Lillie!

"Will Raven Feather listen to the words of his brother, the Eagle-Eye of the Black Hills?" asked Tutt, anxiously.

He did not wish to lose the prize for whose possession he had risked much and suffered also.

"The ears of Raven Feather are always open when his brother speaks. Let the Eagle-Eye talk."

"The pale-face squaw belongs to me. I brought her from among the pale-faces. In trying to get her back they wounded me—made me their prisoner. My red brother will not be unjust. He will not take from Eagle-Eye his property which has cost him these wounds!"

Dave Tutt knew who he had to deal with in talking thus to Raven Feather. Justice in an Indian is less a name than a fact. Would we Christian people could say as much.

And to render impartial and strict justice in a chief, is held as the highest virtue. To render justice the chief of a red tribe will order the death of his nearest friend, his own son, father, or brother. Claim from him a favor, he will deny it, without his inclination is for it. Claim from him justice in the name of right, and he will yield it.

His wild, fierce eyes looked lovingly on the beautiful, trembling girl, but he said: "Raven Feather will not rob his brother. The Pale Rose is very beautiful. The eyes of the chief feed upon her loveliness, but he will shut them up. He will not look at her again. She shall be kept safely for my brother until he is strong and able to take care of her himself, and my brother, Eagle-Eye, and the old chief of the pale-faced warriors of the hills shall be lifted up and carried back to the village of the Ogallalas, where the swift river that is red* with the golden earth runs its race toward the great waters in which the sun sleeps. But this paleface who has slain two of my warriors must now die."

And drawing his hatchet from his belt he turned toward Frank Stark, his face gleaming with fiendish ferocity.

"Let Raven Feather hold his hand till he hears the word of Eagle-Eye," said Dave Tutt, who now sat upright on the ground, so much had the change in affairs strengthened him. "There is no pain when by a single blow the spirit of a warrior is set free. The pale-faced prisoner is not a warrior, that he should die a warrior's death. He is a dog who tried to steal the squaw of Eagle-Eye from his arms. Keep him bound, so that Eagle-Eye may punish him when he gets strong, and after Eagle-Eye has had his fill of vengeance, then let the warriors of the Ogallala dance around the fire which shall drink up his blood and reduce his bones to ashes."

The chief returned his tomahawk to his belt.

"The words of Eagle-Eye are wise. The Raven Feather will wait; his warriors will keep the prisoner until it is time to sing his death-song."

All this time poor Lillie stood silent, her eyes dry from excess of terror, her cheeks white and cold with fear. Frank Stark, fearless for himself, careless of his own fate, thinking of her whom he had so quickly learned to love with a love which made him hate his past wickedness and his vile associates, stood also still as a marble statue, trying to hope against hope—for there was no light now for either of them.

---

*The Colorado River.

Buffalo Bill and his companions were already far away, each minute increasing the distance between them—and it surely would be long before he could hear of their fate—indeed it might be never.

Poor Lillie, silent with her lips, even speechless in the stony gaze of eyes that oft had spoken in their swift glances, was so hopeless that she had even forgot to pray.

Dave Tutt, with malignant joy in his face and look, said: "Let the red warriors put the pale-face squaw here on the ground beside Eagle-Eye—he will watch her himself. And let the dog of a white man be taken out where the rain will wash the dirt from his coward face and show how white fear makes him."

"It is not fear of you—no, nor of them, which will ever blanch my face, Dave Tutt," said Frank, proudly. "I hate and defy you and them. You fear me and that poor helpless girl, and must keep us bound because you fear us!"

"I do not ask to be unbound," said Lillie; "but take me where I cannot have *his* serpent-eyes burning into my very soul, for I loathe and hate the very sight of the dastard wretch who fed at my mother's board, drank from my brother's cup, and then forgot even what an Arab would remember, the due that the receiver of hospitality owes to the giver. Chief of the brigands, I would rather die than live among you, or belong even in thought to the enemies of my people. But the man whom you call Eagle-Eye, like the other wounded wretch beside him, is a thief and a murderer. Their hands are red with the blood of my father and his people. I would rather be your slave than his. Take me from his sight!"

Lillie uttered those words with a wild vehemence of tone, a look of fierce hate, an expression of utter abhorrence of Tutt, which fairly maddened the latter.

"Girl," he cried, "I will soon be strong, and for every word you have now uttered you shall suffer. Raven Feather will not interfere between you and me. You are mine—*mine* as I will, and no fiend from the shades below will rejoice as I in my power, and no one could use it more mercilessly than will I. I loved you once—now I hate you; but I own you, body and soul, and you shall—as the fawn in the hands of the panther—be toyed with, that in the end you may perish miserably. Let the pale-faced dog of a man be cast out in the rain, and there watched over; but place the squaw here by my side!"

The Indians, after a glance from their chief indicating obedience, took Frank Stark away, while poor Lillie, with hands and feet both bound, was placed in a sitting posture on the ground near Tutt and M'Kandlas.

The pelting rain, the bleak wind, told how the storm yet raged without, but it was not headed—nor aught else now—by poor Lillie. Tears had come to her eyes at last, and prayer to her lips.

CHAPTER XX.

For four days after having struck it, across the Missouri border, Buffalo Bill, with a force increased by volunteers to about fifty men, had followed the trail of Alf Coye, and he was again in Kansas, the route of pursued and pursuers tending toward the Rocky Mountains, or that part of them known as the Black Hills.

His force was small in numbers, but it was composed of men whose hearts were filled with hate of the fiends who had burned their houses, insulted and outraged—and in some cases slain—their friends and relatives. The strength of such a force need never be judged by its numbers.

Men fighting for vengeance or justice, and armed with right, are a hundred times stronger than those who, steeped in villainy, have nothing but villainy behind them.

It was not a company with gay uniforms, burnished arms and bright guidons, riding over those grassy plains. No—with plain, dust-covered clothes, arms ready for service but not for show, stern faces and forms that scorned to show fatigue—those men rode on, determined to die or to sweep from the face of the earth the wretches they were after, and to rescue the helpless ones whom they were dragging off to a fate worse than death.

Erect in his saddle, his eyes as bright, clear and strong as those in the head of his wild prairie steed, Powder Face, Buffalo Bill led the way, while here and there, with many a wild jest on his lip, and fun enough in his composition for all hands, rode Wild Bill, sometimes in front and then in the rear, with his Black Nell fully as playful as himself, though for days neither he nor she had had more than four hours' rest out of twenty-four.

The horses of most of the men were those clean-limbed, wiry mustangs, which will tire a rider far sooner than they tire themselves, but, with few exceptions, the most had been going for the eight days which had elapsed since the party left the stockade on the South Platte, with only about four hours in a day and night for feed and rest, and they began to show it.

Of all the cavalcade there were two horses which seemed, like their riders, to be literally proof against fatigue. Black Nell and Powder Face were the two.

It was late in the afternoon and the trail was freshening, though at least two days, and perhaps three of them, had elapsed since Coye had gone along. But trees, the sure sign of water, were in sight not far ahead, and Bill frequently lifted his glass and scanned the country ahead, for he did not know when his enemy would halt to give his party rest.

He knew well that Coye must be confident of pursuit, for he had done too much damage not to merit it and the most deadly punishment.

All that the bordermen feared was that he would not halt until he got fairly into the mountain range, where defense would not only be more easy, but he would be among the Indians, who, as allies, would fearfully strengthen him against attack.

The distant mountains, snow-crowned, in which the Platte and Republican find their source, were in sight, and well-known peaks whose base was washed by the swift Colorado were within reach of the eye.

"I'd give all the gold I ever had or ever expect to have for a fresh mount of horses," said Buffalo Bill, as his mate rode up by his side. "You and I are the only two well-mounted men, if we had a race for life before us. Our men are game yet, but I can see their horses beginning to flag. We'll have to rest all night when we get to water. If we don't, we'll not be able to charge out of a walk when we overtake that black-muzzled wretch, Alf Coye."

"What is that glass of yours good for, Bill?" asked his mate, with a quiet smile on his face.

"Good for a great deal, Bill. I can see the trunks of trees ahead through it, while with the naked eye we can just detect that timber is there," replied Bill. "My father used to own it, and I wish I had known its value sooner."

"Thunder! I can see more with my naked eyes than you can through it."

"Well, think so, if that will do you any good."

"I can prove it. You are wishing for fresh horses, and yet can't see 'em though they are close under your nose, for all you are peeking around with your old tell-lie-scope."

"Where's your horses?" exclaimed the leader, looking around eagerly.

"Over there to the southward—don't you see 'em in that hollow plain, this side of the rise?"

"I see buffalo," said Bill. "There's no sign of horseflesh among them black humps."

"Well, shoot your eyes at 'em through the glass," said Wild Bill, laughing. "Maybe you'll change your tune. I've been looking at 'em this ten minutes."

Buffalo Bill carelessly raised his glass, more to satisfy his friend than in a belief there was anything more than game to look at.

But once there he held it, while a flush came over his face, and an exclamation of surprise broke from his lips.

"They *are* horses," he said, "and we are not yet in the range for wild horses. I don't understand it."

"I do," said Wild Bill. "The Cheyennes or Ogallala Sioux have been down to the Texas range or somewhere over the border for a drove, and there they are. Those are not wild horses; they're too quiet and too much together."

"You're right, Bill, and we must have 'em, or at least a fresh horse for every man, and we've got to be tricky to do it. The Indians have seen us, for they are keeping back in that hollow, so they can't be very strong."

"You are right there, mate. But it isn't likely they've run their stock very hard this far from the settlement, and if we tried to go on and take what we wanted, they'd git and go where we couldn't overtake em."

"Yes, our way is to creep along slow, so as not to get far from them before dark, and then get back and surprise 'em. By keen work we can get their stock, or what we want of it, and with fresh horses, so we can lead our others, we'll double our speed."

"That's so. Slacken down your pace, and I'll caution the rest."

This was done, and when night came on the horses of the party were much rested, for they had crept on at a snail's gait for the past two hours.

As the moon did not rise till late, Bill had an excellent chance for getting back unobserved with his party, and they were materially assisted as well as encouraged in their movements by the light of camp fires.

For the Indians, supposing the passing party had not observed them, but had gone on where they could get water and good feed, had camped quietly for the night in the bowlders among the low hills.

By a cautious approach, dismounting his men and only leaving a small guard with his tired horses, Bill was enabled, after a couple of hours or more of maneuvering, to completely surround the horses and the Indians taking care of them.

There were only about a dozen of these, it being a mere thieving expedition, and not a war party.

Slowly and still as the panther creeps before it springs, they kept on, until at last, without even a yell, they bounded upon the astonished red men, slaying all, without the loss of a man themselves, or giving scarce any alarm. The surprise was complete. It did not even have the effect of stampeding the horses, and now without difficulty a fresh horse was secured for every man of the party.

The brands on most of them told that they had been stolen, and old saddle galls marked with white hair enabled them to pick those which had already been broken for riding.

With their fresh horses and a led horse for each man, when the day dawned again, the party dashed forward at full speed.

It was such a sight as city men never see, scarcely realize—the close column of stern, sun-browned men speeding over the plains and ridges, halting for nothing, but sweeping forward, with the hot breath of vengeance steaming from their lips.

CHAPTER XXI.

A wild, a grand, a beautiful scene. Mountains, great ragged peaks, covered with stunted foliage, like battered and war-torn giants breathing angry defiance to Heaven, lift their heads up among the clouds—heads whitened with snows which never disappear beneath the genial touch of summer's hand.

Winding down through deep gulches, bounding in reddish foam over huge bowlders, whirling and circling in shadowed eddies, rushes a mighty river—the Colorado, the great red river of the West.

And close beside it, approached from the east by one of those long, winding canyons, or natural roadways, which seem to have been made only as approaches to the little Edens few and far between to which they reach, was a plain of perhaps a mile in length by half that breadth, as level as a floor, covered with short blue-grass interspersed with miriads of brilliant flowers.

A fringe of trees, mostly willow and cottonwood, grew along the river bank, and up the mountain sides the nut-pine and cedar predominated.

Scattered over this lovely plain was a large herd of horses with a few cattle, while close along the river stretched the lodges of a large Indian village.

Around these were many squaws and children, and a few warriors. The numerous disproportion of the latter could be accounted for in but one way. A great war party was absent on some foray. Only a guard for stock and hunters to keep the village in meat had been left behind.

The village was completely shut in by the mountains, which seemed to be almost if not utterly impassable, though mountain-men who know how to creep along the dark ravine or scale the rugged steep know not what impossibility is in the way of travel.

The one narrow passageway in and out could be defended by a few against the approach of thousands.

And for this reason had Raven Feather, the great war chief of the Ogallala Sioux, chosen it for the chief village of his tribe. For thither their ever-enemies, the brave and warlike Pawnees, would never dare to come. The Apaches of the South, or the Snakes and Shoshones of the North, nor the Utes and Piutes of the West would never risk their warriors in an attack on such a defensive spot as this.

His own lodge, conspicuous for its size, was in the front center of the line, with a tall pole in the front of it to designate the circle where the great councils should be held when the braves met to celebrate a victory or decide upon taking the war-path.

In front of this lodge was seated Ma-no-tee, the Turtle Dove, his favorite wife, to whom all the rest were subservient, and around her at a distance were five other squaws, each of whom called the Raven Feather husband.

But to Ma-no-tee alone did the passing warriors speak or show respect, and she, full as haughty as the proudest of them, received their respect as if it was her due, and not a mere compliment.

Shadows began to lengthen in the valley, for the sun was swiftly moving toward its western cradle, when two Indian warriors were seen coming at full speed up the canyon toward the village.

Ma-no-tee, keen-eyed and vigilant, was the first to see and recognize that they came from the sentinel-post at the further end of the long canyon.

With a wild cry she summoned every warrior in hearing to her side.

Rushing to the chief lodge with their arms in hand, they waited to know the cause of alarm.

"If the enemies of our tribe are near there are not many of the warriors of Ogallala to meet them; but they must not be weak because they are few. Ma-no-tee is a woman, but a man's heart beats in her breast. She has a rifle and a hatchet, a knife and war club, and she knows how to use them. We will die, if we must, but we will not turn our backs."

The warriors gave a wild yell of approval and turned to hear what the messengers had to say who were coming so fast across the plain.

Halting their horses, white with foam, at the very feet of Ma-no-tee, one of the Indians spoke: "There is a friend to Raven Feather? Is he known to the Little Elk?"

"He is—he is a friend of Eagle-Eye, the great brave of the Black Hills," replied the warrior, Little Elk. "His name is Captain Alf."

"Then bid him welcome, and let him pass the jaw of the canyon, where the braves of Raven Feather keep their watch. Tell the pale-faced chief that Raven Feather is out on the war-path, but he trusts Ma-no-tee, because she has a warrior's heart in her bosom, and knows no fear. She will build fires to cook meat for his people; let them come. If they are the friends of Raven Feather they may come and go as they will. If they are his enemies there is room for them in the deep waters of the great river. Ma-no-tee, the Turtle Dove, has spoken. Bear her words to the chief of the pale-faces, and tell him to come."

The warrior messengers mounted their horses again, and swept back through the canyon as fast as they had come.

The warriors who had gathered at the call of Ma-no-tee, now by her orders built great camp-fires and slew several fat cattle, which in some of his forays had been taken from emigrant trains passing the plains, kept for a time when they had not leisure or inclination to hunt the buffalo.

The sun was fast sinking behind the hills, but the great blazing fires sent out the red light far and near, making the grand old hills and rocks look weird and picturesque in their bold outlines and dense shadows.

CHAPTER XXII.

Ma-no-tee, to set off her tall form to the best advantage, that the guests of Raven Feather might see in his queen something of his own dignity, donned a dress made almost entirely of feathers of the pink flamingo. Upon her head she wore a coronet of gold, rich with rough rubies and opals, brilliant even though uncut.

Over it a single black feather drooped, to show to whom she owed allegiance. She was, for an Indian woman, very handsome. Her features were classical, her form fine, her eyes large and expressive.

In age she was about thirty, but having never been exposed to that drudgery which breaks down Indian women while they are yet young, she did not seem near so old.

Her warriors and attendants were also ordered to put on their best apparel, and make the welcome as imposing as possible when the main strength of the village was absent.

The sun was down, and the shadows of night were black in the ravines, and the gray robe of passing twilight rested on the peaks, when Alf Coye, handsome in his half Indian garb, rode into the valley at the head of his weary column.

It was a long cavalcade, for beside his men, one hundred in number, he had nearly as many poor, unhappy women, mostly young and beautiful, who had been dragged from desolate homes by the wretches whom he commanded.

It was a sad sight to see those pale, drooping captives mourning over their own dreaded fate, weary with long, forced marches, hopeless of rescue, terrified as they look at the mountain gorges through which they were led, uncertain of the doom before them. Oh! it was sad, very sad!

Handsomely mounted, splendidly armed, Captain Alf Coye made a splendid appearance as he dashed forward at the head of his command to make his obeisance to the favorite wife of the great Raven Feather. For he had heard often of her power over that chief and with the tribe, and knew that it was policy to impress her at first sight in his favor.

He addressed her in her own language, which he spoke fluently, but for fear my readers may not be able to read *Sioux*, I will be their medium to *anglicise* the conversation.

"The chief of the pale-faces from the river that is muddy thanks Ma-no-tee, the beautiful wife of the great Raven Feather for her welcome. He is glad that she has lighted fires, for he has heard of the great Queen of the Ogallalas, and wished to look upon her face and form!"

"The brave chief of pale-faces speaks pleasant words, and the ear of Ma-no-tee drinks them, even as the notes of a singing bird or the sound of happy waters. Let the great chief choose a camping ground for his people. For himself and his wives, Ma-no-tee has had a new lodge set up near her own."

And she pointed to a large circular tent made of the gaudily-painted tanned hides of buffalo, with pennons of tufted hair, bright-colored, waving from the lodge poles.

"Ma-no-tee has a big heart. The pale-face chief hopes to hold a little corner in it, for he loves to see a woman who is not a slave, but is brave and free and proud and beautiful. Will the wife of Raven Feather wear a gift from the hand of her husband's friend, which will tell her what all others may see, that she is very, *very*, beautiful?"

Alf Coye, as he said this, took from his own neck a golden chain to which was suspended a small, circular mirror, framed in gold, and threw the massive chain over the neck of the Indian woman.

Her bright eyes flashed as she raised the mirror and looked in it. And she threw on him a glance which told him that from thence on she would be his friend, if not indeed more affectionate than mere friendship would evince.

The party of Coye had now all come up, and waited his orders in regard to camping.

These were speedily given. They were to pitch their tents, or the few tents they had, directly in front of his own lodge and but a hundred yards away. The camp-fires already built were to serve for their cooking, and meat in abundance already hung around them on poles set by the warriors of Ma-no-tee.

"Where are the wives of the great captain, whom I shall call Silver-Voice from this time forward?" asked Ma-no-tee, addressing Coye.

"Silver-Voice, as you kindly call him, has never taken a wife," replied Coye.

The eyes of Ma-no-tee gleamed pleasantly as she heard those words. But a cloud came over their brightness as he added: "But he has some fair prisoners, and among them there is one whom he means to make his bride. He has had no time to woo her since she has been in his power, and it is not likely he will stand on much ceremony now. Here is his choice."

And he pointed to poor Lottie, who, clinging to her mother, stood where both had dismounted from their horses.

Kitty Muldoon, looking as if she would like to do some scratching and biting, stood just behind her.

"There is your home for the present. Take your child in there and remain until I make a change, if you would not suffer more than you have already," said Coye, addressing Lottie's mother, and pointing to the new lodge.

Without a reply the latter moved toward the lodge. Kitty Muldoon also followed.

"Stop, girl! You belong to my lieutenant, Hubert Stanley, and he must find quarters for you," cried Coye roughly, to Kitty.

"May the divil take wings and fly away wid you and your liftenant, you big bla'guard. It's not meself that will be parted from me mistress, an' now you hear it."

And Kitty bravely strode on after those whom she loved so faithfully.

"Halt! when I bid you, or it will be the worse for you!" said Coye angrily, and he clutched her by the shoulder and jerked her fairly around facing him.

"Is that ye gave, ye big coward? I tould ye once before not to lay the weight of yer dirty fist on me. Take that, you mane spalpeen!"

And Kitty with a strength that seemed wonderful, struck him two fearful blows directly between the eyes. The first staggered him, the second sent him reeling and senseless to the ground.

The eyes of Ma-no-tee flashed with anger, as well as surprise.

"The white squaw shall lose her life, for she struck the face of Silver-Voice."

And she called to a warrior near by to step forward and carry out her will.

But as the Indian but too willingly sprung toward the poor girl, Hubert Stanley interfered, and hurling the warrior back, cried out:

"The girl is *mine*, and no one shall harm her. Captain Coye had no business to lay hands on her, and if he wants a mutiny in camp, just let him try to interfere with the rights of others."

Stanley was angry, for he had really become attached to the girl, though he had been but little in her company since they had been on the march, and had learned to look upon her as his own, or to be so whenever the party came to a resting place.

"Sure, sir, if ye value the life ye'd save the worth of a bawbee, let me go wid the mistress!" pleaded poor Kitty, looking at Stanley with streaming eyes.

"Go with her for the present. I have no fitting place fixed up to take you to at any rate, just now," said the lieutenant.

And as the three females passed out of sight into the lodge, the lieutenant turned and lifted his captain to his feet.

The eyes of the latter, fearfully swelling, were already "in mourning," for no pugilist hitting straight from the shoulder could have done the work better than Kitty in her fierce indignation had done it.

"Silver-Voice has been struck in the camp of Ma-no-tee. The squaw who struck him should have died. But the friend of Silver-Voice put back the warrior when Ma-no-tee told him to take vengeance for the blow."

Alf Coye heard the words of Ma-no-tee, but he could not see her, for his vision was closed.

"It was not necessary that she should die. Death is for men," said he. "There is a harder fate than death for her to meet. He whom you call Silver-Voice never forgives, nor does he ever forget. Let not Ma-no-tee feel bad because I have met this insult in her camp, for it did not come from her people. Hubert, take me into the lodge, get some raw meat and put over my eyes, and I will soon have my sight back again. That girl of yours needs taming, and if you don't tame her I will."

"I'd advise you to keep your hands off from her in the trial," said Hubert quietly, as he led Coye into the lodge and showed him a pile of buffalo robes on which to recline; "for she handles herself about as well as the best man I ever saw. Two blows laid you on the grass, and if I had been within ten feet instead of three rods off, they were given so quick I could never have stopped her."

"Well, she shall pay for it yet. Now go and see to the camp. There is no need of posting sentinels here. The outpost at the mouth of the great canyon through which we came is enough. Let the men eat and drink and rest. I shall not move out of here for a month. I am going to rest and to enjoy a honeymoon, and you can do the same."

"Suppose our trail is followed? We have done enough work in the settlements to rouse the whole section along the borders."

"Let them follow. We are here in the very heart of the Rocky Mountains. The passes through which we came are known to few of the best scouts on the plains, and with twenty men we can hold these passes against a thousand. Our Indian allies are on the alert, and no foe can approach without our being made aware of it long before they are near. Let nothing trouble your mind, Hubert. Here we are safe, and here I mean to revel as I have never done before. It is a grand old place, this nest among the eternal hills and deep gorges. What music in the rush of mad waters as they sweep through the wild glens and over the great cliffs. With that and the gentler tones of fair women, whom we will soon tame down to quiet obedience, we can enjoy ourselves as the free lords of forests and plains and of hills and valleys should. Where is your flask, Hubert? I am hot and thirsty."

"Water, cool from the rushing river, is far better for you now, captain, than a draught from my flask."

"Fury, man; do you think I need water now? No—give me something stronger than that to feel instead of cooling the fire that runs through every vein as I think of the future. Water will do when I can't get anything else."

The lieutenant handed him his flask and left the lodge.

CHAPTER XXIII.

The red sun sank behind the cold, white peaks of the mountains which overhang the Colorado, and with it almost sank the hopes of Buffalo Bill—the hope, I mean, of rescuing his dear mother and his sister Lottie.

Little did he dream that Lillie was again in the hands of his enemies, much less that, even then, one twin was almost as near to him as the other.

Though, by the exceeding freshness of the trail, he knew he was very close to the party of Alf Coye, he saw that they must have gained the mountain range, for the set of sun found him within three or four leagues of their base.

There, with rocks, sheltering ravines, a thousand ramparts everywhere, the wretches could make easy defense. Only stratagem could dislodge them; only cunning could release their unhappy captives.

Most likely, too, they were among Indian allies, for well did the young borderman know that in these hills were their secure retreats, their villages and camps, to which they retreated when they left the hunt or the war-path.

"Men," said he, as he ordered a halt, "we must rest a bit somewhere before we go in where blood has got to run like water, and it may as well be here. We've water in our canteens for ourselves, and the dewy grass will help our animals. And, while you rest, I will ride on and see how things look ahead. One thing is sure, they can't go beyond the Colorado, and our journey westward is nigh to an end."

"Mate, it's me that is goin' in there on a scout!" said Wild Bill. "You needn't fix for a jaw now, for I *will* go. And we shouldn't both leave the party at once, for we two are the only ones of 'em all who know the country hereabouts. I know every inch of the ground ahead of us. Raven Feather, the big Ogallala chief, has his haunt in there. I know pretty nigh where it is, and I'll be cool. You can't, if you see them that is dearer than life to you, in their trouble. Come now, I must go."

"Can't we both go?" said Buffalo Bill. "I know there's peril, and we've swam the same stream too long to be parted when danger's about."

"No. As I said before, it isn't right for us both to be away from the party," said Bill. "Me and Black Nell can do the work. So, good-night, mate. I'll be back long afore it's time for you to stir."

The gallant fellow did not wait for any more argument, but calling his horse to his side with a shrill whistle, sprang on her back and darted away.

He had been gone but a little while when Buffalo Bill, who had wandered thoughtfully away from the place of bivouac a short distance, heard faintly, but distinctly, the sound of a bugle. His heart bounded wildly in his breast, for he recognized the well-known notes of the "Tattoo," or the turning-in call of the United States cavalry. And he knew that no small party would use bugle-calls and the forms of regular marches and camps.

"There's help nigh!" he cried, in wild, exuberant joy, as he bounded back to his party. "We'll wipe out the enemy and their red friends now. I heard a call that none but the United States troops use, and there's a camp not far away. I must go and see who is in it, and if they'll help us. If they will, we'll root the devils out of yon mountain range, if there are a thousand of 'em. Stay here in quiet, and if Wild Bill comes back before I do, tell him where I've gone, and to hold on till I get back. Here, Powder Face! Here, you insect-lightnin', you're wanted."

The Insect, at the call of his name, trotted up to his master, who, without waiting for saddle or bridle, sprang on his back, and dashed away at full speed to the north, for from that direction the bugle sounds had come.

The men, with both leaders gone, huddled together and talked anxiously about the situation. They knew that a crisis was at hand, and that a struggle for life and the rescue of loved ones must take place before many hours went by.

Their tired animals fed from the rich dewy grass which grew around and rested for long, forced marches, even with frequent changes on the extra animals, had told on their powers.

The men ate sparingly of their cooked meat, for even that was getting short. They had not had time to hunt.

CHAPTER XXIV.

Unerring in all natural instincts, as keen in hearing as in sight, Buffalo Bill knew to a mile almost in the gentle breeze of that evening how far away the bugler was who blew the notes that reached his ear; also, the precise direction. In this he rode swiftly for nearly half an hour, and then, checking his horse, he listened. He thought that he might catch some sound from the camp; and he did so. The clear notes of "Benny Haven, O!" a song as dear to our army officers as the Marseillaise to a Frenchman reached his ears, and he knew that some West Pointer was giving the air, while a ringing chorus following told that a lively set of officers were making the welkin ring.

Bill rode on more cautiously now, for he did not know where their sentinels and pickets might be posted, and he knew from experience that soldiers throw lead as if it cost nothing when they fancy Indians are about.

Rising over a small ridge he came in sight of the encampment, and from the number of tents and baggage wagons, knew that there was a full battalion, if not more, in the party.

And now Bill thought he would show them what could be done by a white man, and what Indians, if around, would be very apt to do.

Dismounting, he led Powder Face into a little hollow.

"Stay there, little lightnin', stay there, my insect, till I come back," said he, and Powder Face nodded his head knowingly, proof, of course, that he would obey orders.

Bill now turned toward the camp-fires of the detachment again, and stooping low in the tall grass, holding his long rifle at a trail, he moved swiftly, silently on.

Soon he came in sight of a picket guard of two men, with horses picketed close by them. By a short detour he passed them, and then another guard, and in a few minutes was inside of all the sentinels.

Approaching a fire in front of a large marquee, but crouching low in the grass and keeping in the shade of some wagons, he came so near that he recognized several of the officers, and knew them to belong to the gallant Fifth cavalry. The principal singer was Captain Brown (now a major), and with him Bill had enjoyed many a lively ride and hunt over the plains.

The captain was a noble, fine-looking soldier, and by the respect paid him, was evidently in command of the battalion.

Bill crept on till he could hear every word said by ten or a dozen young officers seated around him.

"Cap, suppose the noise we've made should bring down some of the Sioux or Cheyennes on us, for we're in their range?" old Sim Geary said.

"Well, if they came down on us, we'd come down on them with a dose of blue pills from our carbines, and that would be all. A good Indian fight here would give us an appetite for the enemy we shall meet when we get over the Missouri border. I'm sick of garrison life outside of all creation, where a stray squaw is a luxury to look at, and a white angel only a thing to dream of."

"Do you ever dream of angels, cap?" asked Dr. Nettles, a young surgeon, who had been engaged in looking over and wiping dry a set of instruments.

"Yes, often," said the captain. "There was a golden-hair divinity at the Academy who so wove herself into my life that I find myself dreaming of her very often. I promised her when I came out West to take and save a scalp for her, and if I don't take the scalp of a red man, I mean to save my own for her."

"Cap'n, do them Southerners do any scalpin'?"

It was old Sim Geary, the guide and scout, who asked the question, as he half raised his buckskin-clad form from before the fire.

The captain had no time to answer, for at that instant, right in their ears, so close that it seemed to be among them, rang a wild, frightful war-whoop. Not one alone, but a dozen terrible yells, which brought every man and officer in the camp to his feet but one.

That one was old Geary, the guide and scout, who never moved, but lay with a grim smile relaxing the generally stern features of his sun-browned *face*.

"To arms! Indians! To arms, every man!" shouted the young captain, drawing the saber that lay at his feet. "Geary, what the devil are you laughing at?"

"Nothin' much, cap, only such an Injun as gave that yell never made me nervous. It is good imitation, though, and it would make anybody but an old mountaineer hop as you did just now."

"An imitation? I might have known it, for an Indian's blow would have come as soon as his yell," said Brown.

"That is a fact, cap'n, but if your boys in blue don't keep a better look-out, reds *will* come in on you and wipe you out while you're dreaming of that golden-haired angel at West Point!" cried Buffalo Bill, stepping boldly forth into the circle of light.

"Buffalo Bill, by the chances of war!" cried the captain. "I'm glad to see you."

"Not half so glad as I am to see you, cap, with all these boys about you, if so be you'll help me in a little matter of work that I've got close at hand."

"*Work*—what is it, Bill?"

"The whole story is too long to tell, cap, but the short of it is this. We are within two or three hours' ride of a hundred Missouri bushwhackers, who have got many helpless women prisoners, among them my own dear mother and one of my sisters. Alone, I should have tried to rescue them, if I went under while try-ing. But if you'll help me, I know I can succeed. Yes, sir, united—for I have fifty as good men, regular rangers, as ever drew trigger—we can rid the earth of every rascal of the lot. Will you help me, sir?"

"Of course I will, Bill. You know I never turn from friendship's call, or allow an enemy to cast a shadow on my path without resenting it."

"That's so, cap. And now, since I've seen you, I'll ride back to my men, about five or six miles south of here, and let them know where you are. By that time maybe Wild Bill will be back from his scout, and we'll know what to do."

"Is Wild Bill with you? Then you and him are worth fifty men," cried the captain.

"We are but two, but we know how to throw lead," was Bill's quiet reply, as he gave a sharp, low whistle.

In an instant Powder Face came galloping into camp, and at a second call halted in front of his master.

"Cap," said Bill, as he shouldered his long rifle and leaped on the animal's back, "in all the kingdom of horses, above or below or all around, you can't find a match for this *insect*. He is lightnin' after buffalo, two gales of wind biled down into one on a race, and he don't like niggers, red nor black. He knows more'n most men, and does better than them, for he keeps it all to himself. But—there's Wild Bill's yell—cau-tion your pickets not to fire; he's coming with news, or he wouldn't yell that way."

Orders were instantly sent out, and only in time, for the next moment Wild Bill dashed into camp, with Black Nell snowy with foam-flakes.

CHAPTER XXV.

Black Nell, with her wild rider, dashed up so close to the grouped officers that most of them sprang back, thinking she would go right over them; but, at a word, without even the touch of a bridle-rein, she stopped, rearing so that, with her fore feet in the air, she was settled back on her haunches. Her rider slipped to the ground, and looking about him saw many faces that he recognized among the officers, and one that he seemed better pleased with than all the others, except the brother of his heart—Buffalo Bill.

That one was Geary, the scout and guide.

"Sim," he cried, before uttering a word to any one else, "have you ever been in the village of old Raven Feather?"

"Yes, twice—both times as a prisoner, when they had only saved my life and hair for a roastin scrape. I never want to go there again. I got away, they never knew how, but they thought the devil helped me, I suppose, for they've got a name for me. They call me 'the Man with Wings.' We're not twenty miles from the village now."

"Not *twenty*? No—fifteen will measure the distance if you don't stretch it. But that is neither here nor there. We've got to get to that village, and that as sudden as springin' a trap. And if Cap'n Brown backs out helpin' his old friends in this scrape, I'll turn Injun and take soft hair every chance I get as long as I live."

"What have you seen, Bill—what have you *seen*?" asked Buffalo Bill; and his pale face, tremulous lip, with the earnest, almost imploring look of his full blue eye, told how anxiously he waited for the answer.

"I've not seen your mother, nor Lottie, and Kitty Muldoon," said Bill. "But they are in there, for Alf Coye has gone through the big canyon to the village. But I *did* see poor Lillie, riding behind old Raven Feather himself, and Jake M'Kandlas and Dave Tutt are in the party. So is poor Frank Stark, painted with black streaks— and you know what *that* means."*

"Yes, they will burn him if we don't hinder it. And that I'd do, if I had to go alone to put a bullet through his heart from my rifle and die myself. Captain Brown, will you let my mother and sisters suffer worse than death at the hands of those fiends incarnate?"

And Buffalo Bill's face was white as snow when he spoke, not with fear, for that has never entered his system.

"No, Bill," cried the brave officer, "no. I will risk everything for their rescue. You scouts must plan now, and plan quick, too, for we have no time to lose. If they do not know we are near we may surprise them. A surprise is equal to a defeat, were they treble our number—for Indians never stand in such a case, if they can get away."

"They mustn't get away; they must be wiped out. I owe 'em a big bill, and it has got to be canceled, as you folks with larnin' say," cried Sim Geary, now on his feet in earnest.

"How are we to do it?" asked Wild Bill. "The mouth of the canyon, with a big guard already there, is so narrow that not more than three can ride in abreast. The cliffs either side are a thousand feet high."

"Yes, nearer two thousand," said Sim, "and that will be all the better for us."

"As how?" asked Wild Bill.

"Because, when we've got them packed in that canyon, as we will have 'em by-and-by, ten or fifteen men up there, rolling down rocks as the Mormon saints used to with Johnson's army, when you and I scouted to Echo canyon, will do more damage than all these men can with their carbines!"

---

* A prisoner destined to die at the stake.

"But how will you get 'em there?" asked Buffalo Bill.

"As easy as eatin' rattlesnake when you've nothin' better to chaw on. Captain Brown must make an open attack in front, keeping his men back far enough not to lose while he makes a heap of noise about it. A picked party of men must get to the top of the hill overhangin' the canyon before daylight, and not be seen when daylight comes till it is time to roll rocks. Out on the plains they'll not come to attack the troops, for you'll corral your horse-stock with the wagons, and have the last ready for a breastwork, and they'll be careful not to come too nigh. While all this is goin' on, and it don't need any of us in front, we three old bordermen, with the party that Buffalo Bill bosses, will get behind 'em, come down on their rear after we've got their captives safe; and, if we don't finish 'em then, I'm willin' to eat dirt!"

"But how are we to get to their rear?" asked Buffalo Bill.

"No one but the 'Man with Wings' knows, and he will lead the way," said Sim, quietly. "And now, Captain Brown, if you'll understand the thing and move your command to the front of the canyon—you'll know it by two great red cliffs jutting right up two thousand feet in the air from the plains—we scouts will do the rest."

"When shall I show myself in front and open fire?" asked Brown.

"Just as soon as you have light to see to do it. We don't want to give the devils in there any time to do any deviltry after day comes on; and if you attract their attention, we will soon give 'em all they want to do. Pick your men for the heights, and let Sergeant Hill lead 'em, for I've seen him in the hills before. He is an old hand; he was with Sumner's Rifles at Ash Hollow when we wiped out three hundred Cheyennes in thirty minutes! Life on that day wasn't worth a drink o' whiskey to a red!"

"We will move at once," said Captain Brown.

"And without sound of bugle. Remember, gentlemen, and be quick in mounting your commands."

"Make as much noise after daylight in front as you like," said Geary, starting for his own horse. "Come, Bill, you and your men have got to ride fast to reach the point where we will leave our horses. I know that no plan but mine can save the captives, for they'd kill them at any rate, whether we conquered or not, if we didn't get them in our hands before they've time to do it."

The two border leaders required no urging to make haste, but the moment he was mounted, sped away with him at the top speed of their horses.

And in less than half an hour, with all the Kansas men in close column, the spare horses now left behind, they swept away to another gorge in the hills north of the Great Canyon, which led to the village of Raven Feather.

CHAPTER XXVI.

A painter of the Salvator Rosa school, fond of black shadows contrasting with glaring lights, could have found a "study" inside the lodge which had been erected by Ma-no-tee, for the use of Alf Coye, or "Silver Voice," as she called him.

When the night's dense darkness came on, a huge lamp, stuck on a post in the center of the lodge, filled with fish-oil, which sent out a sickening odor, was lighted. It flickered and flashed, but revealed the three hapless women crouched in one corner, pale, wretched beyond the power of words to paint, and Alf Coye stretched out in the other with a great bandage over the eyes which brave Kitty Muldoon had so effectually closed.

In low whispers, Mrs. Cody and her daughter and Kitty talked, but low as they spoke, some of their words reached the keen ears of the fiend in human shape in the other corner.

They were talking of self-destruction, for hope had left their poor hearts, and death is not, to a brave woman, the worst fate in life or the hardest to endure.

A harsh laugh grated on their ears. It came from the lips of Alf Coye.

"If you're so anxious to die, death shall come soon enough," he cried; "but not in your own way. My red friends like tragic amusements, but they want to share in them and to afford the music. I will see that you wait for death until the proper time comes."

"You'll see, will you, ye dirty bla'guard," cried Kitty. "Faith, it'll be eyes you'll have to borry to do it with, if I get at you again. I'll have 'em out instead of shuttin' 'em up, if you don't kape your ugly mouth shut. It's my belafe that you were niver born at all, at all, but was dug out from among Satan's castaways below."

"I'll pay you for this, you she-devil," cried Coye, grinding his teeth together in his anger. "You shall dance on hot coals to the music of a hundred warriors."

"Sure an' that'll not be like the chance that's waitin' for you, you ugly haythen. It's ould Satan will give you the *cead mil failthe* down below, wid all for a ball-room and yer own groans for music. An' maybe he's comin' for ye now—it sounds like it."

Several wild, shrill yells heard from outside caused the last remark of Kitty.

And while they were yet ringing through the night air, Ma-no-tee, queenly in her wild finery and lofty stature, came into the lodge.

"Let the heart of Silver Voice be glad," she said.

"His friend, the great Raven Feather, is close at hand. He comes with many scalps and with prisoners. When the sun looks down to-morrow it will see a good sight. The braves of our tribe are all here. Their squaws will be glad. The great fires will be lighted, and the dance of victory and the scalp-dance will be danced. And if any of our braves have been sent to the happy hunting grounds by the hands of the pale-faces, we will send pale-faces there on the wings of fire to wait on them and serve them as their slaves. Are the words of Ma-no-tee pleasant to the ears of Silver Voice?"

"Her words are as the music of a sweet singing bird in his ears," said Coye. "When Raven Feather comes, ask him to enter the lodge of his guest, who is sorry he cannot see him with his eyes to-night. But he will talk with him."

"It is well. Ma-no-tee will meet Raven Feather and carry to him the words of Silver Voice."

The Indian woman cast one scornful, haughty glance on the poor prisoners, and, turning, strode away.

In her heart there was not one womanly instinct of tenderness and sympathy—in truth, much as the writer has been among the "noble aboriginals," he has not been able to find anything of that nature except in books regarding them. He hopes the Quaker commission may bring about a millennium among the Red men, but his faith on that point is very weak indeed.

But a few moments passed, and the shouting and yelling grew louder all the time, when Raven Feather entered the lodge.

He did not come alone. Clutched by the arm he led poor Lillie as if he feared that, escaping from his grasp, she might rush to destruction in the water of the river so near at hand—the waters that spoke so loudly in their angry rush through the confining channel of the rock-bound gorge.

One wild, glad cry, and tearing herself from his grasp she was in the arms of her mother.

"Mother, daughter, sister."

These were the holy words sobbed out in what may be called the glad agony of their suffering hearts, for with death and misery before and around them, they were at least *together* once more to meet it.

Even that cold, murderous Indian, who could smile while he wrenched the quivering heart from the breast of a yet living enemy—even that cowardly, murderous white man who could burn peaceful homes and drag into captivity worse than death innocent and helpless women—even they were for a moment silent—dumb. Heaven alone knows from what impulse, for Heaven gives impulses which mortal nature cannot fathom.

Weeping and sobbing, murmuring low words meant for comfort where comfort could not come, the four women now clung together, while Raven Feather, who did not at first understand it, now began to comprehend that he had brought a daughter to a mother and a sister to a sister in captivity—that he had three of the nearest relatives of the dreaded Buffalo Bill in his power.

"My friend, Captain Alf, heap sick! Pale-face squaw hurt his eyes. Is it so? For Ma-no-tee, who calls him Silver Voice, has spoken to Raven Feather."

"It is. I am blind. But by to-morrow it will have passed away. A still night with my medicine, and I shall be well," replied Coye to the chief.

"Then Raven Feather will leave him to his rest. To-morrow will be a big day in the village of Raven Feather. When the sun looks up over the hill-tops, he will call his braves together, and our pale-faced friends shall see the scalp-dance, and hear the songs of victory. We have a prisoner whom Eagle-Eye wishes to torture. The pale-faces shall see the red fire drink his blood while he weeps like a woman! It will be a great day in the village of Raven Feather, and the heart of my brother will be glad."

"Yes; for I too have a work of vengeance to carry out," said Coye, bitterly. "Let me rest, that I may regain my sight and be strong once more. And let these women talk together this night, for it is their last night of peace and quiet on earth."

"Raven Feather has heard, and the wish of his brother shall be done. Good-night."

CHAPTER XXVII.

The sun rises alike for the rich and the poor, and with its great glaring eye, views the wicked as well as the good, the hideous as well as the beautiful things of earth.

And rising over the white cliffs which to the east overhung the village of Raven Feather, it looked down on a wild, strange scene.

From the gray of dawn "life" had been moving about the valley, and in the camp of the white as well as the red men.

Hasty was the meal that was taken, for there was something more gratifying to savage minds in preparation; something to come off which aroused their wild passions to a frenzy of anticipation.

The Indians gloated in imagination over the pleasure of dancing around the stake of torture and seeing victims writhe in the death-agony unmercifully prolonged. The white men, full of hate and malice, were worse a thousand times than the red fiends, for they had known good through civilization, and were evil from their own wicked inclinations and not through ignorance.

When the sun rose, the preparations for torturing the chief victim were almost completed. In front of the lodge of Alf Coye a large post had been set, and near it dry fuel lay in a huge heap, ready to ignite when all was arranged.

The warriors of Raven Feather in their war-paint, gaudiest robes, wildest guise, gathered near. The white men, filthy and repulsive to a greater degree than the red men, lounged around, for they were not under that discipline which insures neatness of attire and cleanliness of person as in the army.

The beating of the great war drum of the camp by the prophet of the tribe was the signal for assembly, and when it sounded there was a hurrying from all quarters toward the great circle.

Foremost came Raven Feather, carrying a lance, ornamented with the many scalps taken by himself in battle. Then, assisted by a stout warrior on either side, Jake M'Kandlas, grim, gaunt and grizzly, and Dave Tutt, pale and thin, but fierce and hateful in every glance.

The frequent application of raw meat to the eyes Alf Coye during the night had so lessened the inflammation that he could see out of them, though hideous dark rings encircled them yet. He, too, strode forth, ready to enjoy the horrible work in contemplation.

At a shrill yell from the lips of Raven Feather, another of our characters was brought to view.

It was Frank Stark, with his hands securely bound, but his feet free, so that he walked erect between the two warriors selected to guard him.

His face was flushed, and a look of angry defiance marked it. He felt that he was to die—he had no earthly hope of deliverance now, no chance for escape, but he did not mean that they should triumph over any weakness in him. He would endure turture without a groan, die without a single weak, useless plea for mercy.

His eye flashed as he was led past the white leaders, but he did not speak. He walked without guidance directly to the stake which by its paint and preparations around it he well knew was meant for him.

Quickly he was bound to it, and then a few loose fagots were cast about his feet. They did not mean to hurry his death.

The great drum again sounded, first in slow beats and then faster, as, led by Raven Feather, the red warriors began to make the circuit of the circle.

Faster and faster beat the drum—yell after yell now pealed out from the lips of the red fiends, who boasting of their deeds, rushed wildly around the captive, brandishing their spears and knives and flashing the weapons before his eyes as if at each pass they meant to bury them in his body.

"See the pale-face tremble," cried Raven Feather. "He has the shape of a man, but the heart of a squaw. We will roast his body and feed our dogs with his heart. See how he trembles."

"Raven Feather is a *liar!*" thundered Frank, determined, if possible, to excite him so that by an angry blow he would save him from torture. "The captive scorns and spits at him. It is Raven Feather who is a coward. He takes prisoners when they sleep and have no strength to resist him. His captive defies him and his slaves, both red and white, and will not tremble."

"He shall. He shall cry like a baby that is whipped. Light the fires and warm the feet of the pale-face!" shouted the chief, his eyes glaring red with anger.

A warrior brought a blazing brand and threw it among the dry fagots at the feet of poor Frank.

Again the drum beat fast and loud, and the dance of doom went on. The fagots caught and the blaze began to curl up about the straight limbs of the victim.

"Ha! The fire laughs at the feet of the pale-face. Now see him tremble," shouted Raven Feather in wicked glee.

A defiant smile was on the face of Frank Stark, when a piercing scream broke on every ear, and the next instant, Lillie, her face white as snow, her hair all loose over her shoulders and flying out on the wind, rushed through the yelling circle, closely followed by her mother, Lottie, and Kitty Muldoon.

With her own hands, Lillie tore away the burning fagots from about the prisoner's form, while the Indians, silent for the instant, stood aghast at her frenzied look.

What Raven Feather or the rest would have done to her or those by her side for this interruption may not be known, for suddenly, with no warning, a sound came rolling up the canyon which in a second changed everything.

Not like the roll of pealing thunder, but sharp, quick and crashing, leaping in loud echoes from cliff to cliff, and peak to peak of the everlasting hills, came the report of a cannon. It was the field-piece belonging to the cavalry train.

For a few seconds every warrior was dumb, still as a bronze statue, in surprise. Not even the hand with the uplifted hatchet fell—not a man moved.

Alf Coye was first to break the spell of silence. And before he spoke, the rattle of small arms and the yells of fighting men far down the gorge were heard.

"To the mouth of the canyon," he shouted. "To the mouth of the canyon, every man, red and white. There are regulars in that attack, or there wouldn't be cannon. If they get through the gorge we're whipped. Follow, men—follow!"

And with his saber drawn he rushed to his horse picketed close by, mounted without waiting to saddle, and rode away.

In less than a minute every white man and every warrior, except alone Dave Tutt and Jake M'Kandlas, was speeding off toward the sound of battle.

And now, quick as thought, Lillie turned to un-bind Frank Stark, that he might be free for flight or defence, for weak as they were, and fortunately unarmed, she knew not what the two white renegades might do to him.

But there was another fiend there to hinder her angel-hand in its work of mercy.

It was Ma-no-tee, who, rushing forward, hurled her away from his side, as she cried:

"The captive of Raven Feather shall stay there till the chief comes back to finish his work. Let the white squaw go back with her mother and sister to her lodge, or it will be worse for her! Ma-no-tee has spoken. Her warriors are gone, but the rifle, the knife and the war-club are playthings in her hand. Let the white squaw obey, or Ma-no-tee will dip her hands in her heart's blood!"

"Not yet—she has got to live for *my* vengeance, good Ma-no-tee," cried Dave Tutt. "Call your squaws and drive these women back to their lodge, and my friend and I will guard the pale-face at the fire-post till Raven Feather comes back."

"The words of my white brother are good. Ma-no-tee will bend to them as the tall reed bends to the soft night-wind."

And the wife of Raven Feather called her women to her, while Lillie, Lottie, Kitty Muldoon and the poor widow gathered close to each other, not knowing what to do.

"Make no efforts for *me*—for your own safety go back to the lodge, kindest of friends," cried Frank Stark. "Our friends are fighting for our deliverance—go and pray to Heaven to help them."

"Pray to the—"

Dave Tutt had no chance to finish the derisive words he commenced, for, coming no one could tell whence, but as if they had dropped from the sky or sprung up from the earth, fifty riflemen, with Buffalo Bill, his mate, and Sim Geary at their head, rushed upon them.

Every squaw dropped in terror to the earth, Ma-no-tee alone excepted, for superstition added to their fear. They thought they were not mortal, for "the Man with Wings" was recognized by all.

While Buffalo Bill was embracing his loved ones, Wild Bill was cutting the thongs which bound Frank Stark to the post of torture, and Sim Geary, first knocking them down to make the work easier, was tying Jake M'Kandlas and Dave Tutt.

Meanwhile the firing outside grew sharper and heavier and the yells of the fierce combatants louder and more loud.

"We've no time to spend here!" cried Sim Geary. "There's a heap of warriors out there, beside Alf Coye's gang. Brown will have too much to do, if I don't close in on the enemy's rear. Not a rock will roll till we've opened fire. And we'll have time enough to attend to matters here when we've wiped them out that's in front."

"That is so—we must help our friends there. Mother, sisters, you are safe now. I will leave a half-dozen men, however. But I must go and help to exterminate the wretches. Boys, six of you release every prisoner here, and stay to keep the she-fiends of squaws quiet. The rest follow me!"

Buffalo Bill waited not to hear an objection, but, followed by his men, and Frank Stark also, who had armed himself from a lodge close at hand, bounded away toward the gorge.

Ma-no-tee eyed the women and the prisoners whom Alf Coye had taken, as the guard hurried to release them, for a few moments in silence, and then, turning to her own lodge, disappeared, followed in a body by the squaws of her tribe.

Dave Tutt and M'Kandlas, bound hand and foot, lay helpless on the ground, and listened to the sounds of battle in the distance. Their faces, which had been flushed with the joy of success in their black wickedness, were now pale and troubled, and they trembled as they listened to the cannon, the rattle of heavy musketry and, soon after, the sharper fire of the riflemen.

Then came sounds which they could not understand. It was not like the report of cannonry, though all as loud. It was not thunder nor the sweep of the tempest; nor yet the rush of charging horsemen or the heavy tramp of advancing columns.

It was a rumbling, rushing, crashing sound, and a shaking of the ground, as if an earthquake was upheaving.

What could it be?

Louder and louder, drowning the yells of the warriors and the rattle of fire-arms.

"What can it be?" asked Jake M'Kandlas, turning his head with startled look toward Dave Tutt.

"It sounds as if the very mountains were falling. I feel the earth shake," said Dave.

"Yes, yes, that is it. There has been an attack in front to draw the Indians and Alf Coye there, and while now their rear is cut off by Buffalo Bill and his men, some of their men are above, heaving down rocks. That is it. Our chance to swing is sure now, for Alf Coye can't get himself out of the scrape, let alone helping us."

"It looks dark. I wish they'd cut every woman's throat before they went," cried Dave. "If I had only killed Frank Stark, instead of waiting to see him roasted, it would have been some satisfaction."

"It is no time to think of what we haven't done!" said the other. "Can't we do something to get away from here? If I was untied I'd roll into the river, and run my risk of getting out below before I'd wait for such mercy as I'd get from Buffalo Bill now!"

"No use—but look! Ma-no-tee and her women are up to some dodge!"

CHAPTER XXVIII.

Moving with all possible celerity, it took Captain Brown until daylight to get to a position in front of the canyon, for his wagons, laden with stores and ammunition, and his heavy field-piece, could not be moved at a gallop, nor was it safe to leave them behind.

The Indian guard, whom Wild Bill had described as laying behind a natural rampart of rocks in the mouth of the Great Canyon, did not seem to be on the alert, for he moved slowly and cautiously on until quite near without seeing any of them.

But at last, a little after sunrise, when quite as near as he desired to go with his men, while uncertain as to the force before him, he had the satisfaction of knowing that he was observed by the enemy, for a band of fifteen or twenty warriors, mounted on fine horses, galloped out on the plain, and circling around for a few hundred yards, reconnoitered his party.

"It is time to make a noise now to attract the main body from the interior camp," said he to the officer in charge of the field-piece. "Send a shell in among those fellows, and then we will give them some pepper from the carbines to settle their opinion concerning us."

The piece was quickly unlimbered to the front, ranged, and while its thunder went rattling in among the hills, the shell went with a shriek just over the heads of the startled redmen.

The next instant, a couple of platoons of cavalrymen sent in a volley from their carbines, which dropped two of the Indians from their horses and seemed to have touched more.

Quickly dragging their fallen men after them to save their scalps from falling into the hands of the foe, the Indians fell back into the gorge.

Now, placing his piece so as to throw an occasional shell in there, but ready with grape should a charge be made on his position, with the wagons placed en corral, so that the teams and loose stock were all inside, Captain Brown threw forward his skirmishers, and commenced the attack in earnest. Riding to and fro, Indian fashion, and firing whenever they saw a red to fire at, his men moved forward, while the Indians, shouting and yelling like fiends let loose from down below, kept up from their side a quick but not a dangerous fire.

In a short time, however, the latter were evidently increased in numbers, and the brave officer in command of the regulars took a fresh position, just at the crest of a low hill, which completely covered the mouth of the gorge, and planting his piece so as to throw shell fairly into the faces of those who might attempt a charge from there, he poured in his fire more rapidly than at first, while his carbine range was excellent.

That white men were also in his front was soon apparent, for the sound of heavier guns and hoarser shouts fell on his ear.

In a little while the fire on his front lessened, though the yells in the gorge were louder than ever. The sharp crack of rifles could be heard as his own fire was suspended now and then.

"Buffalo Bill is at them!" he shouted. "Now is our time to close up and hold the mouth of the canyon. Limber up your piece to the front, and forward! Charge with me, men—charge!"

And away on his gallant bay the brave captain rode, followed by officers and men in good order, but at full speed.

Only a few scattering shots annoyed them as they swept into the narrow mouth of the gorge, for both Indians and white men, startled by the attack in the rear, which told that their village was in the hands of the enemy, had turned to meet that onset.

Now, with his large gun commanding the defile, the gallant captain felt that the enemy was doomed to annihilation, for he knew that the bordermen would never let one return alive, and he was sure none could pass him.

The Indians and their white allies, after charging back on Buffalo Bill and his party with immense loss, and an utter failure to drive back men as well protected by rocks as themselves, better armed and quite as desperate, now once more faced the regulars, evidently hoping to get out on the plains, where their numbers would give them an advantage. Followed by Buffalo Bill and his party, quickly as they fell back, when they had to halt in the face of the grape and canister that met them, they were huddled all up in a disorderly heap.

And now came the most terrible work of all. Suddenly huge rocks came bounding down, with a noise louder than thunder, from the cliffs above, which no man could climb. Down, with clouds of dust, came ton after ton of rock, crushing and mangling men and horses in a dreadful mass.

Nothing now reigned but confusion, despair—death. They threw down weapons which were of no avail. They rode over each other, trampled and even hewed each other down with their knives and hatchets in their mad endeavors to get out of the way of the terrible avalanche which rained down the mountain steeps.

Backward and forward, to and fro, reeling and staggering worse than drunken men in their dread of this horrible death, mad in fears worse than madness, they tried to break through the regulars in front or the bordermen in the rear.

"I surrender! In the name of mercy stop this butchery!" shouted Alf Coye to Buffalo Bill.

The rebel bushwhacker was bare-headed—his right arm hung broken and useless by his side—his face was a mass of dirt and blood, he was almost alone, only a few wounded wretches around him were left alive.

"Mercy is a name not fit for your lips, you woman-killing fiend!" shouted Bill.

"There is the mercy he showed my gray-haired father in Kansas!" cried a boy not over eighteen, as he raised his rifle and sent a ball through the heart of the murderous man.

A dozen more shots and not one of Alf Coye's party were left in sight alive.

But now came a rush which even Buffalo Bill, brave and confident ever, thought might break his lines. Leaving their horses, dropping their guns, coming with knives and hatchets only, Raven Feather and near twenty of his braves dashed toward the bordermen. Not a yell broke from their set lips. That alone told how desperate they were. With eyes flashing red, every muscle swollen with fierce energy, like tigers they came. And as tigers leaping against bars they cannot break, they were met.

Face to face, knee to knee, and hand to hand, Raven Feather and Buffalo Bill met. Twice the borderman parried the deadly thrusts of the wily chief—twice again the steel of the savage drank his blood, but weak from twenty wounds, the Indian's eyes were not sure, and soon the knife of the brave borderman reached his body with a fearful thrust.

There was despair in the eye of Raven Feather, for nearly all his warriors had fallen around him, taking some pale-faces to death as they fell, but he made one more mighty effort. He struck down wildly, heavily, and broke away the guard of Buffalo Bill, but the latter, closing, grappled him with his strong arms, and then both fell among the dying and the dead, the Indian undermost. But lithe, with the strength of the death agony, the savage turned his opponent, and while his eyes glared with fury, he clutched his throat with a strangling grasp.

In vain did the borderman strive to tear himself away—his knife was gone—his breath was going—his doom seemed certain.

But now Wild Bill, released victoriously from a similar struggle, sprang to his aid, and quick as thought his keen knife set his mate free from the Indian's deadly clutch, for again and again it pierced his quivering heart.

Sullenly, hate glaring even as his eyes glazed in death, Raven Feather sank down among his fallen braves—the last of them in the vain struggle for life and life's liberties.

A glad shout of victory rose from the lips of Wild Bill—it was echoed from cliff to cliff, while he looked around for a single living foe. Not one could be seen.

The gory dead—friend and foe, white and red, lay thick about him—mute proofs of a conflict which could know no other ending.

It was over.

Forced to leave their horses behind, for only with difficulty could men climb over the debris of rocks and earth which had filled up a portion of the canyon, destroying and burying the murderous foe came the regulars, led by their gallant young commander. With them came the surgeon, ready to aid the wounded, and his services were needed in many a case.

Even Buffalo Bill, anxious as he was to hurry back to his loved ones, had to delay to have the blood staunched which poured from many a sad gash in his noble frame.

But the delay was brief. In a little while the force moved on, and debouching from the close canyon on the beautiful plain, hurried forward to the Indian village.

The two border heroes, our hero and his mate, led the van, while by their side Frank Stark, who had fought as bravely as the bravest, hurried on, eager once more to rest his eyes on the noble girl who dared the fierce wrath of the fiendish warriors to save him from torture.

On they all sped to the lodges, but, wondering, they looked in vain to see the dear ones hurrying out to meet and welcome them.

Not a human being was in sight. From lodge to lodge the bordermen and their Kansas followers rushed, but not one of the loved ones could be seen—not a voice answered to their calls.

Buffalo Bill was in agony. What had become of the guard he had left behind him—where were his mother, sisters, and the rest of the captives? What new foe had swooped down and gathered them up?

A cry from one of the men who had gone further than the rest in the search was heard down near the river-side, and instantly all hands hurried to where this man was standing.

And then they saw a sight which froze the hot blood in every heart in a brief breath—a sight which struck them, for no power of theirs could save if one will was carried out!

CHAPTER XXIX.

On a great square rock, inaccessible except by a single narrow path, but where one could ascend at a time, and this path overhung with a rock which her women stood ready to hurl down if the ascent was attempted, stood all the prisoners, also the Indian women of the village, the widow of Raven Feather, and the two wounded white renegades.

The rock overhung the foaming torrent of the river where it was widest and roughest, and where no hope for life could exist if one were cast into the terrible yeast of foam. Foremost of all was this terrible tableau.

Holding poor Lillie, who was bound and helpless, as were all the captives, so before him that her form shielded his body, stood Dave Tutt, with a keen knife pointing to her heart, requiring but a motion to sink it there.

And Jake M'Kandlas stood in the same position, holding the poor widow as his shield and at his mercy.

Lottie was in the hands of the Indian queen, and each of the other captives were in a similar position, at the mercy of the squaws who held them.

"Pale-faces, raise but a hand against us and we strike!" cried Ma-no-tee. "We have sworn by the Great Spirit, and we will not lie. The waters of the Red River of the west will save us from your hands, and when they are dead we will carry our captives with us! Raise not a hand, but hear the words which Eagle-Eye will speak."

The hand of Buffalo Bill clenched his long rifle so hard that the blood seemed ready to start from beneath the nails. Yet he read death in that fierce woman's eye—death to those who were part of himself, and he dared not raise a hand.

"Let him speak! Our ears are open!" was all that he *could* utter.

Dave Tutt, while a sardonic light gleamed from his dark eyes, raised his voice so that it could be heard by every man of the command.

"We know that you are victors, that our friends are dead, and we can expect no help from them. Yet we are not in your power. We can die. But it will be by our own choice. Ma-no-tee has spoken truly. Every captive shall die at our hands if a weapon is raised against us. And with them we will bury ourselves in the river that rushes madly on below. We have sworn it! But we have terms—terms which you can grant."

"Name them, fiend in human shape, name them!" cried Captain Brown, shuddering as he spoke, for it seemed as if the savage fiends would slay their victims even while the talk went on.

"Hear them!" continued Dave Tutt, "and we will give five minutes for their acceptance after they are offered. It is that you promise on your honor as men and soldiers, and swear on your oath as believers in a hereafter, that you will allow every one on this rock, red and white, their free, unrestrained liberty to leave this plain, with provisions and stock to carry them away; that you will not harm them in any way, or check their departure, nor follow them when they depart. On this condition, and this alone, we will surrender these captives unharmed into your hands. Speak quick, for if your answer is not yes, so help me high Heaven, I strike the first blow *here!*"

And the broad blade of his knife quivered over the heart of Lillie, who did not speak though her face, white as snow itself, and her great, mournful eyes looking hopelessly down, spoke more than words could say.

"Yes,—in Heaven's name, *yes!*" cried Captain Brown, in an agony of excitement.

"Let Buffalo Bill, Wild Bill, Frank Stark—let all say yes, and swear it!" cried Dave, his hand still upheld.

"Yes—yes, *yes*, YES!" gasped the men, one and all, for they were almost palsied with the position of the captives.

"*Swear* it, and we ask no more."

"We swear it!" came solemnly from every lip.

In an instant every prisoner stood free—their bonds were cut at a signal from Ma-no-tee, with the knives that threatened their existence.

And those who would have slain them, even the widowed squaws, now helped them in the perilous descent to rejoin their friends.

Soon all that party but one stood on the plain. The relatives, clasped in each other's arms, sobbing out their joy, forgot that they had suffered, forgot their past peril in the depth of this new happiness.

All but *one*, I said. It was Ma-no-tee.

Lofty in stature, regal in face and form, there she stood on the verge of the rock, the wind blowing back the long black hair from her shoulders and toying with the folds of her scarlet robe.

"Raven Feather is dead and Silver Voice has gone with him to the happy hunting grounds," she cried. "The braves who would have died to defend Ma-no-tee from the rifles of the pale-faces have all fallen. The hunters who slew the fat buffalo and killed the swift antelope as it ran have perished. Ma-no-tee only sees the squaws of her people and the little children. She has no one left to hunt for her or to serve her. She will not stay alone. She hates the pale-faces, and will not accept life as a gift from their hands. She goes to join Raven Feather and Silver Voice. The River Spirits shall bury her in the caves of the deep waters!"

She ceased her wild harangue, drew her scarlet robe over her head, and, with a fearless step approached the brink, looked not, paused not, but sprang off, and went down into the mad current which swept in foam along.

A mournful cry rose from the squaws of the tribe, then all was still.

Shunned by the soldiers, and by the Kansas men, who, but for their plighted word, would have rended them limb from limb, the two white renegades tottered feebly off with the Indian women to where their horses were grazing, and made preparations for leaving.

And now the troops took possession of the lodges, and began to kill and cook meat, for hunger spoke loud words among them all.

And while the widowed squaws, with their ponies laden down with their camp equipage, were mournfully moving away from their desolate homes, great fires were sending smoke and light aloft to the cloudless sky, at which hungry men were roasting the meat fatted under the care of their slain enemies.

Little did the soldiers care for their sorrows, as little, indeed, as they had cared for people murdered, homes destroyed, or captives brought to torture by the warriors whose deeds were now forever ended.

Such is life. As night follows day, and day succeeds night, so do our fortunes vary. It is well! For doth not He order it who doeth all things well?

CHAPTER XXX.

Busy months have passed since that wild day of hot carnage, when the spirits of Raven Feather and his band of warriors sped on blood-tipped wings away to the happy hunting-grounds of their fathers gone before. Busy months, and over the flowery South, over the fertile West, through the cities of the North, and along the Atlantic's rock-bound coast, the tocsin of war, ringing fearful and loud, has brought out a nation's strength and a nation's chivalry.

In the streets of St. Louis, that great city of the West, whose future can only be measured by the strength and enterprise of her men of mind and means, all is life—busy, noisy, martial life. The rolling drum, the pealing bugle, the glitter of gay uniforms, the flash of burnished weapons, the dash of steel-shod steeds, falls upon the ear and meets the eye wherever you go.

In the streets of the great city you meet men of every class; hunters in buckskin and fur; Indians in the panoply of the plains; soldiers in the uniforms of their corps; countrymen in butternut and jeans, and citizens in broadcloth and patent leather.

And, alas! for the humanity that smiles on the all-destroying *traffic*, among these busy men you see the fell effects of that demon of rum, which, degrading humanity, makes man fiendish. Reeling and staggering on, cursing and blaspheming, groups of rum-maddened soldiers are seen here and there, licensed in excitement to liberties that, in times of peace, would soon lodge them in a prison cell.

A wild throng of such men—a mixed party, in which the colored trappings told that cavalry, artillery, and infantry men were all on a debauch together—swept along Fourth street, singing Bacchanalian songs at the top of their voices.

A young girl, not over sixteen, very, very beautiful, with great dreamy eyes, hair hanging in loose manes all over her white shoulders, drew back at the corner to let them pass. On her arm hung her satchel of books, for she was a schoolgirl.

The eye of a great bearded sergeant of artillery fell upon her shrinking form. Excited with strong drink, he forgot his manhood, and shouted: "Halt, boys! Here's a girl that turns up her nose at a Union soldier."

The poor girl grew lily-white as she saw every rude eye turn upon her, and she would have fled, but the grasp of the drunken speaker was on her round arm already, and she could not tear herself from it.

"Say, is it not true, isn't your dad a Confederate?" cried the brute, his rum-laden breath throwing its sickening odor in her fair face.

"No, sir; my father's name is too well known as a Union man to have that epithet applied to him. He is—"

And the young girl gave the name of a wealthy Union banker in the city, and then added: "Let me pass on, sir; I am going to school."

"You don't pass here until you prove you love Union soldiers by kissing every man of the party," shouted the sergeant. "That's the tune, isn't it, boys?"

"Aye, aye—that's the ticket!" cried one and all of the drunken crowd.

"So, stand still—it's my turn first, my beauty, and so put out those rosebud lips of yours."

"Coward! I'll die before I submit to this insult," cried the brave girl.

The coarse wretch laughed, and bent his shaggy head down as he threw his rude arms about her slender waist.

Wildly arose her shrill scream upon the air, as she dashed her small hands into his eyes, for the moment delaying his purpose.

"Girl, mind what you're about, or this shall be the worse for you," shouted the sergeant, hoarsely, and he raised her form in his arms as if she had been but a doll.

But before he could again bend his hot, sensual face toward her pure lips, a horse and rider came rushing down the street with the speed of a winged bird.

It was Buffalo Bill on his wild Powder Face, and he dashed into and over that crowd as if they were only bags of down in his way.

With one blow of his clenched hand he dashed the bulky miscreant to the earth, with his other arm he encircled the waist of the lovely girl, and, lifting her to his saddle-bow, gave the word "on" to his noble horse, and dashed through and over the crowd before a hand could be raised to check him.

On for a block, until he was out of range of any shot which might, in their mad excitement, be sent after him, and then he halted, and looked down into the lovely, confiding face which beamed up with a look of glad wonder into his own.

"If you'll tell me where to leave you, miss, so you'll be safe, I'll go back and give them drunken chaps satisfaction if they want it," said Bill, as he drew his horse to a stop.

"Oh, sir, you are so brave and so good! I was frightened almost to death, for they would have killed me. I would have died before they should kiss me," cried the lovely girl.

"Dying would come cheap for a willing kiss from such lips, but the brute that would force it is too mean to die—he ought to be wedged in a swamp and fed on raw porcupine skins, shells thrown in. But where do you live, miss? People will stare to see you here; and I'm rather bashful when I'm in such good company."

"You have stopped right before my father's house, and—oh, I am so glad! he is coming down the steps—for he can reward you better than I."

And the young girl pointed to a fine-looking, middle-aged gentleman descending the stone steps of a handsome mansion.

Bill reined his horse up to the sidewalk, and lifted the girl lightly down; then, as she hurriedly told her father of the insult, her peril, and her gallant rescue, he remounted to ride away.

But a word from the father and daughter stopped him.

"Young man, your name, if you please?" asked the banker.

The borderman gave it, also with his sobriquet of "Buffalo Bill."

"I have heard of you, young man, and all I have heard tends to your credit. But what is better still, I knew your brave, Union father, and I honored him in his life and mourned him in his death. For your rescue of my daughter, were you any other man, I would offer you a full purse, in addition to my gratitude. Not a word—I know you would refuse it, and therefore do *not* offer it. But Louisa shall thank you, and as I know you are already in the ranks of our country's defenders, I will use my influence to lift you to a position which you will honor. Make my house your home while you are in town."

"I dare not, sir!" said Bill, and his voice trembled as he spoke.

"Dare not? What is the reason?" asked the banker in astonishment.

"If I see *her* any more, I shall love her, and love above my station would be madness and folly," said Bill, bluntly, and with that honor which was part of his nature.

"*Love* her, man? Why, what if you do? If she loves the man who has saved her from wrong, and protected her from insult, and is able do it again, she has a father who will honor her for it, and never by word or deed of his stand between her and her heart's choice. I say again, make my house your home, and if love comes from that, so much the better. Take him right in, Lou, and introduce him to your mother, and I'll go to General Fremont and get him commissioned."

"Hold on about that, sir, if you please," said Bill. "As you were a dear friend of my dear father, I will thankfully accept your hospitality, even at the risk of losing my heart. But I do not want a commission. I command a party of noble, brave, tried friends—scouts who are fearless and true—able to do good and efficient service. But the moment I put on shoulder-straps, I've got to have other shoulder-straps over me, who'll be ordering me about, and the first I know, they'll say something I don't like, and then I'll buck, as Powder Face would do if anybody else tried to ride him. No sir; let me remain independent, as I am, and I will do more service ten times over than I would with a U. S. commission inside my haversack.

"And now I'll go in and see your lady, and then, if Miss Louise will go, I will take her to see my own dear mother and my twin sisters, who've had hard times out among the redskins and bushwhackers, but are here safe at last, where I hope they will be contented until we've squelched through this trouble.

Then I'll build up the farm-house again, and set things to rights once more."

"And I'll help you, my brave boy. I must go now, but I'll meet you at dinner time."

CHAPTER XXXI.

In a neat cottage in the old or French part of the city, where even yet, amid grassy mounds and old forest trees, dwell the descendants of the first settlers, the old *voyageurs*, such as the Sublettes, Choteaus, Vallees, etc., etc., close by the bank of the great river, with the moonlight playing in the windows through trellised honeysuckles and climbing roses, was a cheerful, happy scene.

The good mother of Buffalo Bill sat there with her knitting in her hand. Close by the twin sisters were seated, while Kitty Muldoon, in one corner, was diligently engaged in paring potatoes for the morning meal, for early rising was a virtue never forgotten in that family.

The females were not alone in the neat little sitting-room.

Wild Bill, in an agony of uneasiness, sat there, for he had got boots on his feet and a citizen's suit of clothes on his body, and he was like a fish out of water in them. Frank Stark, handsome even in store clothes, and happy in the thought of being a reformed man and a Union soldier, was also there, looking a love which he dared not speak, for the pure young girl whom he had saved from wrong, and who had saved him from the cruel death by torture to which he had been doomed.

It was a noble group, worthy of better pen-painting than my stiff hand can give.

The door opened, for Buffalo Bill was not one to stand on the ceremony of knocking at his own home, and the son and brother came hurriedly in with a young and blooming girl on his arm.

"Louisa, here is my dear mother, there are my twin sisters, Lillie and Lottie, there is good Kitty Muldoon, and last but not least, here are Frank Stark and Wild Bill, rough diamonds of the hills, brave as the bravest and true as the truest. Mother, girls and all hands, here is Louisa La Valliere, the daughter of an old friend of our father, and if you'll love her half as much as I do, you'll try to make her as happy as a beaver among young cottonwoods!"

This was rather a long speech for Bill, but as he led Louisa forward to his mother and sisters while he was talking, hands clasped hands, and speaking eyes made them know each other before he was through.

Then came a narration of the adventure which had made him acquainted with the sweet girl and her parents, and an invitation through Louisa from her parents for the whole family to come and make La Valliere mansion their home while in St. Louis.

Though not instantly accepted, the offer was gratefully listened to, and then work was all laid aside, for Bill, proud of his sisters and their natural accomplishments, insisted on having some music. Both sisters sung sweetly, Lillie accompanied finely with the guitar, and with Louisa joining in their songs, the little cottage was literally flooded with melody.

But a sudden interruption chased the thought of harmony away.

While Mrs. Cody was sitting wrapped in pleasant thought near the window, a hissing voice—a low muttered curse reached her ear, and turning she saw the wicked face of Jake M'Kandlas glaring through the window.

Wildly she shrieked his name, and the villain, seeing he was recognized, fired his pistol with deadly aim at her and fled away. In an instant Wild Bill and Frank Stark sprang from their seats, one through the open window, the other out of the door in pursuit of the wretch. But Buffalo Bill, groaning out the words, "My poor mother!" leaped forward as she fell from her chair and caught her falling form.

The blood, gushing from a wound in her temple, seemed to tell the screaming girls, who rushed to her side, that it was a death wound.

Kitty Muldoon, whose outcries were piercing, had yet presence of mind to run for some water. A part of this, applied to the lips of the widow, revived her, and then Bill, to his joy, examining the wound, found that it was only a graze, plowing a furrow in the temple, severing a small artery, but doing no serious damage.

Oh, how thankful they all were when they found that the wound was so slight—how full of joy when, by simple appliances, the hemorrhage was stopped and the wound properly dressed.

And now, the excitement over, Buffalo Bill wished to go after the villain whom his mother had distinctly recognized. But he knew that if by that time either Frank Stark or Wild Bill had not overhauled him, he had got to some hiding-place where for the time at least he might be safe.

And soon the return of both Frank and Bill, unsuccessful, from their pursuit, convinced him of the fact. It was now for them all to be on a constant watch. For where M'Kandlas was, Dave Tutt could not be far distant, and they were men who would never be without confederates in crime, if bad men could be found to join their ranks.

The incident broke up all the pleasure of the evening, and Buffalo Bill soon escorted his newfound friend back to her father's house.

CHAPTER XXXII.

It had been known for some time to the commanding general at St. Louis that the Confederates were recruiting men for their armies from the secession sympathizers in the city. He knew that with so much money floating among them, prominent leaders must be likewise there—men to be trusted with money, and possessed of both talent and influence.

But when he heard from the lips of Buffalo Bill that Jake M'Kandlas, the great guerrilla leader, his right-hand man, Dave Tutt, and several other notoriously desperate men had been seen in town, he began to look on the matter with a serious eye, though until then he had scouted the thought that Confederate audacity would go so far as to recruit disunion soldiers under "his very nose," to use a common, but not a very refined phrase.

"It must be stopped—nipped in the bud, sir," said he to the chief of scouts, for that was now the position of our hero. "I give you every authority, call for men and means as you need them, but hunt these men down without mercy. They are spies and murderers, and if *you* spare them till they reach my hands, the nearest tree will be their gallows."

"Not much danger of my sparing them, sir," said Bill. "But I wish you would offer a reward for their arrest, or any information that leads to it—not that I or one of my men wants the reward, but because money may induce some of their followers to turn traitor to them, and let us know where we can find them."

"You are right," said the General. "I will issue a proclamation to that effect immediately. By the way, sir, a valued friend of mine called on me this morning, who is much interested in you—Mr. La Valliere. If you will accept it, you shall have an eagle on your shoulder and a full regiment to command."

"Thank you, General; Mr. La Valliere knows my mind on that subject. I am not fitted for that position, and have just sense enough to know it. In the place I now hold I can do my work, and do it well. In the other I'd be as helpless as a beaver without a tail, and—*what's the matter, Bill, what's up?*"

This last question broke excitedly from his lips as Wild Bill, closely followed by Frank Stark, rushed into the parlor where the General held his receptions.

"Jake M'Kandlas, Dave Tutt, and sixty men left here before the break of day to join Price down beyond Pilot Knob. They are all armed and mounted on good horses. I have it from a poor wretch who owed me a life, and wanted to pay a part of the debt, and I know he wouldn't lie!"

Wild Bill spoke fast, and every word was distinct and to the point.

"Have every one of our boys in the saddle and here in fifteen minutes," cried our hero. "Bring Powder Face along with *you*, Bill."

Not a word or questioning look, but away hurried Wild Bill and Frank Stark to mount the scouts.

"General," said Buffalo Bill, "please send an order to the cavalry barracks, and have forty-three saddled and bridled cavalry horses sent here for my use. With fresh horses to change and relieve our own, I will overtake the men before ten o'clock to-night, though they have at least seven hours the start. And when they are overtaken, I think I can take care of them. They'll travel no further, or else my journey is over."

The General rang for an orderly, wrote out the order, and sent him in all haste to execute it. Then he turned to the chief of scouts and asked: "Do you not want more men, sir? With forty-three, including yourself, you are to follow over sixty men."

"Yes, sir, to follow and to wipe them out, too. My men know me, and I know them, and two to one of this trash is poor odds for us to take. More men would be in my way. And now, General, if you please, a favor."

"Anything, sir, that I can grant will not be refused."

"It is only this—you know Mr. La Valliere well."

"Yes, sir, he is a bosom friend of mine."

"Then please tell him yourself, sir, where I have gone, and ask him to let little Lou run down and tell my mother and sisters that I'll be back tomorrow."

"I will do it with pleasure, sir; but I beg you not to risk too much, or too rashly expose a life which I feel will be of great value to the country in this crisis. I am not one who believes good men are scarce—I believe they are plenty of them when they are roused up, but the nation needs them all now. We have too many bad men to oppose and defeat, to spare any good ones who can be saved."

"Don't fear for me, sir. It will never be my fate to die by such hands. Some red warrior, in time, may lift my hair, but no white renegade to his race and his country shall do it. I'll come back to report them used up, sir—but hark, I hear the clatter of horsemen. They are my boys, for you hear no bugles, no jingling sabres—their rifles, knives, and revolvers don't reach your ears with their noises till they're needed."

"True—for such service as you perform they are the best fitted of all men. I will see you off."

And the General with the stars on his shoulder walked out side by side with the scout in buckskin, and saw him leap upon his fiery horse without touching foot to stirrup, and run his keen eye along the line to see if every man was there. A quiet smile on his fine face and all was right. Then the led cavalry horses coming up a gallop, each man took the halter of a spare horse, and at the word away they went like leaves on the swift autumnal winds.

CHAPTER XXXIII.

Many an eye followed the swift cavalcade that passed at a gallop through the crowded streets of St. Louis, and out on the road which led to the wild mountain region where in the far distance Iron Mountain and Pilot Knob rested their towering heads.

Well they *might* look. Three nobler-looking men, three finer horsemen never sat in a saddle than the trio who led that compact body of plain-clad, well-armed, stern-visaged, silent men.

In that swift-passing column, riding in ranks of four, no jests were passed, no loud, hilarious laughter rose on the air to make the observer think that soldiering with them was mere amusement—every look and action, every motion as well as that stern, thoughtful silence, told that "deeds not words" would mark their career. Three "sons of liberty" were they.

On, at a gallop, only pausing here and there after they had passed some way on the route to inquire if a body of horsemen, easily described from their numbers and the appearance of their grizzled leader, had passed. They soon found the trail, and after that no questions were asked, none necessary indeed, for those men had trailed the wily red men over sterile plains, through boundless prairies, among the rocks and shelves of the great mountains, too long not to follow easily the tracks made on beaten roads.

On—swiftly on, changing horses every eight or ten miles, they kept, until, when night fell, they were coursing along the banks of the swift Gasconade river and enveloped in the wooded hills and thickly settled valleys of that region.

It was moonlight, and though dark, where the trees rose thickly on either hand and the road almost invisible in some of the dark ravines, they never checked their speed, for they knew they were rapidly closing on the enemy whose horses must be well nigh given out, for already had that party passed over ninety miles of ground—perhaps even more, with their relief of horses.

It was probably ten o'clock when they rode silently through a small settlement, where the few inhabitants seemed to have gone to rest, for in but one house was a light seen.

Our hero had adopted the old army precaution of throwing out an advance and rear-guard—Wild Bill, with two men, rode two hundred yards in advance— Frank Stark, with two men, as far in the rear, while he led the main body.

Shortly after passing this little settlement, a rocket was seen to ascend high in the air, and then another until five had been counted.

Buffalo Bill checked his men at once, and calling in his officers, Wild Bill and Frank Stark, held a hurried consultation.

"We're spotted, boys," said he. "The party ahead has friends in the settlement back and they were writing news to 'em with their rockets."

"Yes—and it is received and *answered!*" said Wild Bill, as he pointed to a rocket rising in the sky directly ahead of the party and not more than two or three miles ahead. "They're warned of our coming now, and we'll have harder work than we would have had if we had come upon 'em unawares. But never mind, boys, we could whip five times their number. Remember one thing—we must do all on the dash. They're used up in horse-flesh and we are not. We must go through 'em like a winter sleet-storm, cutting and tearing 'em all to pieces as we go."

"I'll take the lead now, and we'll all close up except one man to scout three hundred yards ahead to see the first glimpse of them and then get back to us. Little

Joe Bevins, there's just enough Injun in you to do that work well. Put out! You know what to do!"

It was but a boy to whom he spoke, in years not over eighteen, but his little frame was wiry as steel, his eyes sharp and active, his heart as fearless as that of a panther, and his nature just suited for the work he was in.

Checking their speed a very little, to breathe their horses, they rode on for twenty minutes more, passing in that time over four miles of ground, but nothing was seen or heard to indicate the near presence of the enemy.

But suddenly a half dozen rifle-shots were heard in front. Then for a minute or more all was still.

"I'm afraid they've got little Joe," said Bill, who had halted his party to receive news from the front.

A few seconds more, and more rifle-shots were heard; then followed the rapid reports of a revolver, and a second after little Joe came tearing back, firing as he rode upon a half dozen horsemen who were following him up.

The bordermen had halted in a dense shadow where trees on both sides obscured the moonlight, and the pursuers out in the light did not see them as little Joe dashed back into the ranks of his friends.

But they felt them, for a volley from the foremost rank took every man out of his saddle, and as they fell Buffalo Bill received the report of the young scout.

He had ridden right into the face of the enemy, who, mounted and drawn up in good order, waited in an open cornfield among the stubble for the onset of their pursuers.

"Drop the horses you are riding—leave them in the road and mount the fresh ones—form by eights, till we reach the open field, and then spread to a line and charge when I yell. Frank Stark takes the right, I take the center and Wild Bill the left. Let your pistols work first and your knives next. When we get into it, every man for himself and Heaven for us all. Remember your homes, wives, and your sisters, and don't let a shot be wasted, but sweep the villains from the footstool."

These were the brief orders, plainly given, of one who speaks quick as he thinks and acts even yet more rapidly.

The formation by eights just filled the road, and with horses well in hand, yet ready for the burst, the party dashed on.

A minute only passed, the open field was before them, and in the clear moonlight, not sixty, but more than two hundred men waited for them, for several parties had joined Jake M'Kandlas on the route.

Not an instant did the bordermen hesitate, not a second did they wait to count numbers, not even for an order did they pause, but riding into line, right and left in a gallop, swept forward as their leader gave his wild yell—forward like an avalanche, firing as they went, upon the enemy.

A volley from the latter emptied only four or five saddles, and then face to face and hand to hand the parties met.

On through the mass dashed Buffalo Bill, a revolver in each hand, and shot after shot, in the very face of his opponents, dropped a man at every fire. In a minute he was through, and his trained horse wheeling at but a touch of the leg, brought him right back into the broken, confused mass. Every shot had been fired from his revolver, but now his great knife-blade flashed in the air and came sweeping down here and there, as he saw foes to strike, while Wild Bill, Frank Stark and all the rest were at the same kind of work.

It could not last long—scarce the time I take to describe it elapsed before the foe, beaten and whipped from their stand, made for a dense thicket bordering the river.

All who could gain this left their horses, and plunging into the river, either perished in its rapids or, gaining the other shore, crept away into the mountain fastnesses where, at that time, they could not be followed.

The victory was complete. Dead men and horses lay all around—a few wounded lay groaning on the ground.

Bill now ordered the bivouac fires to be lighted. Full two-thirds of the enemy were past doing harm, and the rest were scattered. Their arms had been dropped and horses left, so he had no fear of any resumption of the attack.

His men were counted and looked to, as soon as the fires were blazing.

Only four had been killed, but full half the number had been wounded, some severely, others but slightly. There was no surgeon in the party, but half of those bordermen were worth more than five-tenths of the volunteer surgeons of the army, who, until the war had progressed some time, knew no more about wounds than a cow knows about the manufacture of cheese, though she is a material aid in the matter.

Of the enemy one hundred and fifty lay on the field when daylight enabled our heroes to examine the vicinity with care.

Buffalo Bill looked at every dead man anxiously.

There were faces—several, indeed—which he recognized, but he could not find the bodies of those whom he wished to see.

"Satan must help his own," he said, as he looked at the last of the party. "Jake M'Kandlas and Dave Tutt and Cantrell have got away. I expect, coward-like, they ran when we charged, for I did not get a glimpse of either in the fight. I would rather have had those three men than all the rest who are stretched out here."

"We'll have 'em yet, mate; don't fret. This has been a big night's work though, hasn't it?" said Wild Bill.

"It has, indeed," replied our hero. "Where's little Joe? I hope he isn't hurt, for he brought their scouts back so nicely for us to wipe out, that he deserves a big credit mark. Is he hurt?"

"No, cap," cried the young hero. "I got a scratch from one of their pistols and a hole in my jacket. But if you'll speak a good word for me to that rosy-cheeked gal that lives at your house, she'll mend the jacket and a bit of a hole in my heart that she made her own self, when you sent me there with a message the other day."

"What? Kitty Muldoon, you mean?"

"Yes, sir; that's the gal."

"She is pretty and good, Joe; and if you'll fight this war through and come out all right, if she don't cook your meat and wash your clothes for the rest of your life, it shall not be my fault."

"Thank you, cap. Just put me where there's work to do, and see if I don't do it up brown, after this."

"I will, boy; and I know you'll do well. And now ride back, a half dozen of you men, to the nearest farm-house and get spades and shovels, and all the men you can find. We'll be decent, if we have been rough. We'll bury the dead, and that is more than they would have done for us. They would have left the wolf and the buzzard to take care of our bodies."

Leaving these men to the work of humanity, we will now look elsewhere.

CHAPTER XXXIV.

Jake M'Kandlas, Dave Tutt, and Cantrell, the guerrilla, escaped, when so many of their vile confederates took water in the River of Death. They saw defeat in the terrible rush made by the bordermen—defeat in the instant confusion and panic in their own ranks, and rode out of the melee into the woods, and away by a side-path well known to Cantrell, before their presence was detected by any of the attacking party.

When the fight was finished, and the Kansas men lighted their bivouac fires, the three ruffians were safe and secure in a mountain cave some six or seven miles beyond and above them—an old place of refuge for these men when, in former days, they had followed the pleasant occupation of horse and negro stealing.

Until they had reached this almost inaccessible point, and had stabled their horses so far inside the extensive cave that no sound from them would attract the attention of pursuers, they scarcely paused to draw a long breath, or enter into conversation.

But now, refreshed from their whisky flasks, and out of fear of bullets for the time, they opened their mouths and let out volleys of abuse against the men from whom their flight had alone saved them.

"Buffalo Bill, Frank Stark, and Wild Bill have done a big thing to-night," growled Jake M'Kandlas, adding an oath.

"They have, and the whole country will ring with their fame, while we poor wretches will only hear how we've been whipped by less than a quarter of our number. We may as well dry up and keep away from the borders after this," said Dave Tutt.

"Away from the borders, for *this*? No!" cried Cantrell. "I'll haunt the borders now worse than ever. We've lost men—but there are more where they came from. I'm neither beaten nor disheartened. I shall take the back track and raise more men. And then let Mr. Buffalo Bill look out. He'll find that though I'm in his debt now, I know how to pay up old scores."

"Well, I'm glad to see you so hopeful. I am as bitter as the best of you, but luck has run against me so long, I'm sick of the deal."

"Satan isn't sick of you yet, or you'd have been called home to-night, colonel," said Dave, with a laugh.

"You'd have your joke if he had you by the neck, I suppose," growled the colonel.

"Yes, but it would be a black joke. But the question now is—what are we to do next?"

"I've said my say," said Cantrell. "I'm going back to St. Louis for more men."

"And I'll go with you—not for men, but for a woman, for I've sworn to humble that girl Lillie, and I'll do it, if it costs me my life!"

"The bigger fool you. There isn't a woman on earth that I'd put in the balance against my life," said M'Kandlas, with a sneer. "You, boys, may risk the city if you like, but I shall not put myself in the way of the great Pathfinder. The open country for me hereafter. I can raise a few men, I reckon, and I'll bushwhack it for awhile. I can make my grub and transportation, if nothing more."

"Where'll you make headquarters, so a fellow can find you when he gets back?" asked Dave.

"At Rolla, or thereabout. Black Jake, the Cherokee half-breed, will know where I am, for he is my 'fence' in that region. He's Union in talk, but that's a blind. He's right side up for the South."

"When are you going to start for the city, Cantrell!" asked Dave.

"Just as soon to-morrow as we see them fellows take the back track. From here we can see the road forty miles with a glass, and I have a good one. We've got to go in careful, for when they don't find us with the dead, they'll know what to expect when our chance comes."

"Yes, about as little mercy, as far as I'm concerned, as a wild cat gives a rabbit. But I'm going to turn in," said Dave. "I'm as hungry as a cub wolf, and sleep is all that will help it, till we get to where there's something eatable to be had."

The ruffian drew his blanket around him, and dropped to the ground. The others followed his example.

CHAPTER XXXV.

"Och! Isn't he a darlint, the bowld boy-soje!" cried Kitty Muldoon, as Joe Bevins rode up the street at full speed, the day after the return of Buffalo Bill and his party to the city.

For Joe had just ridden down with a message from the chief of scouts for the young ladies, and had taken this opportunity to put a big ring on Kitty's fore-finger, and to tell her it should be her fault if it wasn't a wedding-ring when "the cruel war was over."

"Sure, and he rides aqual to the best hunter that iver broke his neck among the hills of Tipperary. He's not very big, that's true, but sure all that there is of him is worth the havin', and that's more than we can spake of everybody. An' what's wantin' wid you, ould man?"

Her last words were addressed to an old white-haired man, whose thick mat-ted hair almost covered his face. His clothes were scanty and ragged, his form bent, and he leaned upon a staff with shaking hands as if afflicted with palsied weakness.

"Bread! I'm so hungry, and so weary!" said the old man in a low, husky voice.

"Wouldn't meat be better than bread, sure. Stay here and I'll get you a bite to ate, for it's not hunger should ever be denied." And the good-hearted girl went into the house to procure the food.

In an instant the old man approached the door and quickly examined the lock. From among his rags he procured several keys and soon found one that fit-ted the lock of the door after he had returned the other key. Returning the regular key to its place in the lock, he pocketed its duplicate and took a hasty survey of all the surroundings.

When Kitty came back with a large plate of bread and meat, however, he was seated on the doorstep with his head bowed in his hands, as if from excess of weakness.

"Here, ould man, here's what'll drive the hunger out," said Kitty, as she put the plate down by his side. "And there's a dollar apiece from the young ladies I serve—two bits of angels all but the wings, d'ye see, and I'll put another dollar wid it, so you can have some mendin' and washin' done: for sure you nade it bad enough."

"I thank you—the people of the world are not often so good as you are," said the old man.

"Faith, that's their business and not mine, then. But I don't see what we're put here for, if it isn't to do a bit of good when the chance runs in our way. But ate away, and I'll get a mug of pure water from the pump for yes to wash it down wid."

"Water! Haven't you any whisky?" asked the old man.

"Whisky! The drunkard's own drink, that. No, faith, and it's a shame for an ould man like you to be askin' afther it. Sure, it's bad enough, and too bad, too, to see a young man seekin' after the crater, let alone an old man like you, wid one foot in the grave and the other close behind it. If ye'll have water I'll get it, but if I'd an ocean of whisky to dip a bucket into if I'd the choice, I'd put a brand of fire there instead. There's a bit of a gossoon of a soldier lad that says he loves me, and I love him by the same token, but let me smell whisky on his breath, and he'll never come again where I'll smell it."

The old man made no reply, but ate a little of the food, then rose and leaving the rest, hobbled away.

"Mad because I would't get whisky for him," muttered Kitty, as she took up the half-emptied plate. "Well, bedad, when the next comes I'll ax him will he have champagne wid his mate before I bring it. But what he ate did him good, I reckon, for he walks away twice as fast as he came. Maybe he knows where there's whisky, and it's that he's afther in such a hurry. If it is, it's sorry I am he got any money from us, for it's a sin and shame to feed men wid that which makes bastes of 'em here and fiends hereafter. But there comes the young master and the bit of an angel too under his wing. Sure they say she's a rich man's daughter, but for all that she spakes as soft to me as if I was born a lady instead of in a cabin on a bog."

CHAPTER XXXVI.

"How long are you goin' to stay here amongst this noise, mate?" asked Wild Bill of our hero, when they had been back three or four days after the chase and defeat of the M'Kandlas party.

They were both standing on the porch of the house held as "Headquarters" by the general in command.

"I don't know. The General wants me here to tell him about the country they've got to operate in very soon. Old Price is raising the old Harry among the few Union folks out towards the borders, and he has got to leave. The General is going to send a force that way, and when he is ready there will be work enough for us. For the scouts are to have the advance. I have bargained for that."

"Good on your head, mate. But what are we to do in the meantime, that's what I want to know. I'll *rust* laying around here. I go down to your mother's to see the girls, but I'm nothing on the talking trail, and I look like a fool sitting there watching their pretty fingers come and go with the needle. Frank Stark has got tongue and can enjoy himself as he deserves to, but I'm a dumb fool and I know it."

"Bill, that is no discredit to you. A man can't have every gift all to his own self. You can take a squirrel's head off at forty yards with your revolver, or at two hundred with your rifle. Frank Stark can't do it. You can outride any Comanche that ever swung over or under a horse. Not one man in a million can ride up to you, and no one can beat you. As to fear, if you feel it you don't know how to show it. And for love—there's your good old mother in Illinois, and Black Nell, your pet mare, and *me*, your mate—why, you love us all enough to die for any one of us."

"That's so, mate—that's so, and I love one of my enemies a little too much, too."

"Who is that?" asked Buffalo Bill, in surprise.

"His name is *whisky*, but I'm going to kick him out of my company. If I don't he'll spoil my shooting—if he don't do worse."

"That's a fact—and now I've thought of something. I saw my darling 'Lou' turn her head away when my lips came mighty close to hers, this morning, and I don't wonder. I'd been swallowing some barreled lightning, and she smelled it. I'll not give her reason to turn her dear head away again. It weakens the strongest, unnerves the coolest, and befools the wisest. I'm done with fire-water, mate."

"So am I, and there's my hand upon it. And now, Bill, I'm dying for a hunt. As you will not move out of here for a week at least, suppose I take a run up into the Gasconade hills and knock over a deer or two. Maybe I may trail out something, too, that will pay. Frank will go along for company, and we two will be able to take care of ourselves."

"I've no objections, mate, if so be you feel like exercising yourselves and them creepin' insects that can't go over a mile in two minutes without you use a spur. If you go, don't be gone over three or four days, and if you hear heavy guns anywhere, you'll know the army is on the move, and you'll know where to find me."

"All right, Bill; me and Frank will be off in two or three hours, for I told him I'd ask you about the trip."

Buffalo Bill was looking at the same old man who had begged for food and been answered by Kitty Muldoon on the day before. He stood just below them, near enough, indeed, to have heard what they said, if he had been listening.

"Oh, he's one of those curiosities that grows in cities, I reckon, for I never saw one on the plains or in the mountains. He's a beggar by his rags and wrinkles, and when he's as old as that and has to beg, we young 'uns ought to help him."

Wild Bill took a couple of dollars from his pocket and tossed them down at the feet of the old man.

The latter looked his thanks out of a pair of glittering black eyes, and bowing his head, picked up the money and moved away just as Buffalo Bill was drawing out his bag of buckskin.

"Hold on there, old boy—here's something to get better clothes. It will be cold by-and-by, and you need 'em bad enough now."

Bill followed his words with a twenty-dollar gold piece, which the old man caught ere it touched the ground with an agility which made the two bordermen laugh heartily.

The old man muttered something—they supposed it was thanks, but had they *heard* his words they would not have let him go on unquestioned.

For he said: "Laugh now—laugh now, but it will be somebody's turn to cry before many hours go by. It's a long road that hasn't got a turn, and the one you travel has got a short turn, just ahead."

They did not hear it, however, and when their laugh had died away, he was out of sight around the corner.

The two bordermen now walked to the stable where their horses were kept, and Wild Bill had his Black Nell saddled, also the horse of Frank Stark, for he intended to lead the latter around to the cottage, for he knew that Frank would be there.

CHAPTER XXXVII.

Just below a succession of wild rapids, where the cascade, rushing through a gorge in the hills, came boiling and foaming into a broad eddy, there was one of those open groves which, if near a village, would have been "run down" with picnic parties and promenading lovers.

For beneath the great limbs of old trees the green sward was level and soft, the road passed just to the right, while the deep river, calming down from the rush above, purled and whirled along the low bank as quietly as if it hadn't been torn all to pieces among the jagged rocks in the hills beyond.

In this grove their horses, too well-trained to move away from their masters on such good grass, Wild Bill and Frank Stark camped on their second night out.

Their saddles and blankets were at the foot of a big tree. In front a fire blazed up cheerily, and before it hung a haunch of venison and a couple of wild turkeys, roasting nicely and browning from side to side, as one or the other of the men gave them a turn before the red heat of the hard wood coals.

Hunters don't take the trouble to slice and cook sparingly when they're in a game country. They cook as they kill, by "wholesale," and what they don't eat is left for the fox, the wolf, or the raven.

The two men were happy. They had bright water close at hand, plenty of meat, and bread too, though the last was a luxury rather than a necessity; fuel, and warm, bold hearts.

Their arms and horses were tried, trusty, and near. Their friends, though absent, were yet in their hearts, and that was a joy forever.

Oh! it is a blessed link, that of memory, even though it has shadows as well as its lights. There are none so soulless, none so utterly without heart, that they have not some cherished memory to dwell upon—something in the vista of the past ever dear, which will come up to the vision, making the good happier, the bad better.

The two men sat and talked about those they loved and cared for—the mother of one far distant, the sisters also of the other, and the dear friends yet nearer in St. Louis.

After awhile the well-browned venison and juicy turkey claimed their attention, and while from their tin cups they sipped the warm, pleasant coffee, rudely made, but all as fragrant as if it came from a silver urn, they sliced off pieces of meat or fowl, and ate with that keen appetite which perfect health, exercise, and pure air always carries.

They had fasted since morning and ridden fast; therefore a hearty meal was easy to take, and natural.

After supper the inevitable pipe made its appearance, and while circles of smoke came whirling from their mouths and nostrils, for your borderman smokes as only he and the Indians do—as much through his nostrils as his mouth—they talked about those who were left behind.

All at once, however, a sound reached their ears which caused them to spring to their feet and seize their rifles, standing within reach.

It was the swift clatter of hoofs coming up the road.

And the next instant, on a powerful bay horse, a man dashed into the circle of light made by the fire, and before him, held in his arms, and apparently insensible, was a female.

One glance at the man and at the white face of the girl was enough.

"Lillie!" shouted Frank Stark.

"Dave Tutt!" cried Wild Bill, as the horseman dashed madly past them with his helpless prize.

Both rifles were raised and fired at the same instant; and just as the bay horse bounded into the darkness beyond the glimmer made by the fire-light, he fell with two balls through him.

The bordermen did not wait to mount their own horses, but both rushed on to overtake the dismounted rider.

The horse, struggling in his death-agony, was on the ground.

A scream from Lillie told where she was, for the villain was carrying her to the river. After her, with a wild shout, to assure her help was near, rushed the two bordermen.

Another shriek and a pistol shot froze their hearts.

Fearing the worst, they rushed on, and in a second more came to Lillie where Tutt had dropped her on the earth, firing at her as he wheeled away to plunge into the river, with deadly intent, of course.

"Lillie—oh, my poor Lillie—are you hurt?" cried Frank Stark, as discovering her by the light color of her dress, he raised her in his arms.

"No; he fired almost in my face, but missed me," she cried, as she recognized by his voice the person who had lifted her up.

"Thank Heaven for that! Bill, Lillie is safe!"

"Yes, and I expect Dave Tutt is, too, for he is across the river here where it is dark, and nobody but his master, Satan, could find him now. Is Miss Lillie hurt?"

"No, thank you," she answered, "but terribly frightened. That man tore me from our home in the dead of night, and changing horses I know not how often, for he had horses and friends all along the road, brought me here. We were pursued more than once, fired at two or three times, but he never stopped. Oh, it was horrible, horrible! Such a ride, such wild threats and curses! I could not have lived to see the light of another day, had not kind Heaven placed you where you could save me."

"Dave Tutt shall be hunted for this, as the hound follows the trail, till he dies!" said Wild Bill, in that low, solemn tone which means even more than it says. "As soon as the light comes I will find his track, for I heard the stones rattle where he went up the other bank. He shall not rest, for he has no horse, and Black Nell can climb where he can go."

"It is my work—the hunting him down," said Frank Stark, eagerly. "You take Miss Lillie home, Bill, on my horse, and I can follow him afoot—and I will, till I lift his hair and leave his carcass for the wolves!"

"No, Frank. Lillie would rather go with you, and I want her to. I think as much of her as any man on earth ought to, but I'm not company for any sweet pearl of a woman like her—I'm too rough, you see. Take her, Frank, on your own horse—it's more than likely you'll meet Buffalo Bill and his men on the trail, though if that fiend changed horses so often, he has got well ahead."

"But, Bill, I don't like to have you go alone after that villain."

"You make me laugh, Frank. Dave Tutt is smart, I know that; but if he were ten times the man he is, when I get sight of him, and think that this is third time he has had Lillie in his hands, and that it isn't his fault that she is not now cold and dead in your arms, I'll use him up as easy as I would a bear cub. I will not hear a word against it—take Miss Lillie back, after we've given her a bite to eat and a cup of coffee, and let her rest awhile, and as soon as a gleam of day opens to let me go on his trail, I am there, to stay till I find him, and then he goes under."

"Well, Bill, I know it is no use to argue with you, and as one of us must see Lillie back safe, it will have to be me—not that I don't like the job, but I feel as if I ought to be the one to give Dave Tutt his ticket of leave."

The men had now got back to the camp, for Lillie, strengthened by the glad presence of dear and true friends, was able to walk, though her wan face bore evidence of the fearful suffering she had known within the past few hours.

CHAPTER XXXVIII.

Before day dawned, Frank was on his way toward St. Louis, with Lillie seated on a blanket behind his saddle, for one horse had to carry both until he could get another.

And when day dawned, Wild Bill, swimming the river where it ran slow in an eddy, on his petted Black Nell, took the trail of Dave Tutt where he had climbed up the bank after swimming the river in the night.

The trail was easily found, for the ruffian had been too much hurried to be careful, and the instant that the eye of Bill rested on it, he said to Black Nell, even as if she was human:

"Old gal, there's the track of the ongainliest reptile that ever trod the airth! Keep your eye on it, for we don't leave it till it's maker is found, and then him and me has got to *settle*. You know what that means, don't you, beauty?"

The small, sharp ears on Nell's head had been pointed forward, as if she was listening to every word he spoke, and now she nodded her head as if she understood it all.

Then as he dropped the bridle reins, she turned up the bank, following the place where loosened rocks had made small furrows as they tumbled down—on through grass bent only slightly, yet enough to show that something had recently gone through—on among trees and bushes, only now and then hesitating as she came to a hard, rocky place, where no trace could be seen. Here Wild Bill, bringing his judgment into play, would guide her until in some softer spot the trail would again become visible.

Where it was possible, Bill rode rapidly, but the chase had a good start, and the route was over lofty hills, through rough gorges and tangled ravines, and hours passed swiftly by without bringing the fugitive in sight.

Bill, however, did not hesitate or falter, and when night with its darkness came, he was satisfied that he must be very near, within three or four miles, perhaps, of Tutt. He also knew, by the course he had come, as well as by the lay of the land, that he was near a small village in that part of Missouri supposed to be most southern.

When it became too dark for him to see the trail, he loosened the saddle girths and removed the bridle from Nell's mouth, when he dropped into his blanket under a tree to sleep. He well knew that Nell would wake him,* as she had often done before, if danger approached, and rest was needed.

When morning came, the mare refreshed on good grass during the night was ready for the bit and tightened saddle, and with a hasty lunch on dried vension, washed down by cold water, he mounted and struck the trail again.

Within three miles he struck the spot where Dave Tutt had dropped his frame in the grass to rest, for the bed was plain to view. But the latter had undoubtedly started the instant he could see, and started much refreshed by rest, for where his steps could be tracked the stride seemed a great deal longer than before.

The country, though much broken yet, was easier to travel than that traversed the day before, and Bill got over it quite rapidly.

---

* A historical fact, well known.

At noon he was close to a small village in which the one tavern was made conspicuous by a huge sign as well as by a crowd congregated about its doors.

Toward this, after resting his horse for at least a half hour to give her breath, Wild Bill galloped.

The village contained probably a hundred or more houses, mostly on one broad street, with the county court house nearly opposite the tavern.

Wild Bill rode directly up to the tavern, and leaping from his mare, left her untied at the door, and walked boldly into the bar-room, which was crowded with people. Of these he knew some, and some knew him, and he knew that most of them were Southerners.

But his quick eye caught sight of the only man he wanted *then*. Dave Tutt, flushed and heated, stood at the bar, raising a glass of whisky to his lips, as he saw Bill enter.

The color left his face, and with trembling hand he set the liquor down untasted.

"Drink it, Dave Tutt, drink it, for you'll need it now more than you ever did in your life!" said Bill, sternly, as he strode up within two feet of him, the crowd parting to right and left as he advanced. "Drink it, I say, and then go to the opposite side of the street with your revolver, and remember, it is *you* or *me!*"

David Tutt, reassured, when he found that work was not to commence instantly, swallowed the fiery liquid, and the color came back in his face.

"You've followed me sharp, Bill," said he, and I can't blame you. But I'd rather it would have been Frank Stark than you, for he is an infernal turn-coat, and—"

"Look here, Dave Tutt, you've got neither time or breath to spare in talkin'. Just cross the street and be ready to take care of yourself, or I'll rip your heart out where you stand!"

Bill's look as well as his low, determined tone told Tutt there was no chance of evading the combat or of delay which might be of advantage where friends on his side were so plenty.

So he at once put his hand on the butt of his revolver and slowly passed from the bar-room into the street, and on across it to the front of the court-house.

"A fight! A fight! Stand clear!" shouted the landlord of the hotel.

"A fight! A fight!" screamed a hundred delighted men, and all drew off on one hand or the other to arrange a free line of fire between the two men.

"Are you ready, Dave?" asked Wild Bill, as the other reached the path fronting the court-house and faced about.

"One question and I am!" cried Dave.

"Speak it quick, then, for my arm aches keeping it down so long!" replied Bill.

"Did I kill Lillie last night?" asked Dave.

"No!" thundered Bill. "She is too much of an angel to die by such a fiend's hand as yours. You never even scratched her!"

"Then I'll kill *you* now and go for her on your black mare. I'm *ready*," yelled Dave, and he raised his pistol.

Both men fired at the same time, and for an instant it seem as if both had missed, for both stood erect, calm apparently, looking at each other.

Only a second, and with a death-yell on his whitening lips, Dave Tutt essayed to fire again, but his pistol exploded harmlessly as he fell forward on his face, dead.

Then Bill raised the hat from his head and looked at a hole in it where the ball had passed through, actually cutting away the hair on his head as it grazed the skull.

"There's one debt paid!" said Bill, as he glared fiercely on the crowd. "If any of you cared enough for him to stand in his place, I'll wait just one minute to see it done!"

Bill calmly waited the minute. Not a man stirred or spoke.

Then he whistled to Black Nell, sprang on her back as she trotted up, and rode off without hearing one word from those who stood around. They knew him too well to *talk* then.

CHAPTER XXXIX.

When Wild Bill rode away from the village where Dave Tutt met but too honorable a death, there was not a man among all the people assembled, and nine-tenths were Southerners, to raise a hand to stay him, or speak a word to rouse his anger.

But as he rode away to the westward there were fifty who cried out: "Why did we let him go? We should have hung him up on the spot."

"I reckon the talking would have had to lead the swinging!" said a rough-looking customer, who with revolvers and knife belted around him, looked as if *talking* would not be mere talk if it was tried on *him*.

"Are you a friend of his?" asked half a dozen of men, frowning on the stranger.

"Not if I know myself, and I reckon I do. But I know him, and the man that tackles Wild Bill single-handed has got his winter's work paid for in advance. I thought I'd see if you all would let him go before you'd speak or raise a hand—so I kept still and saw you do it. Now I'm going to fix him, or start them that will. I want a gal that's smart as lightning on-hitched, who can ride a race-horse and tell a smooth lie without blushing."

"Mister, I'm one that can do all that if 'twill *pay*," said a small but well-formed girl of eighteen or twenty years—the landlord's daughter—a brunette, with a good deal of mischief in her dark eyes, and a firm, cruel look about her thin, close-drawn lips.

"It shall pay—his purse and gold watch, the one is full, I reckon, and the other worth two hundred dollars, for 'twas a gift from General Harney," said the man, in a quiet, business way.

"Well, I'd go for half that, but what am I to do?" asked the girl.

"Come in the back room and I'll tell you. You'll have to ride my led horse out there, he's a thoroughbred, and will take you over the ground as quick as you ever went, if he don't histe you out of the saddle."

"I'll risk that," said the girl, laughing, as she followed the man in to hear what he had to say.

This did not appear to take long, for she came out soon dressed for a ride, and as soon as he had put a side-saddle of hers on the horse, a magnificent chestnut gelding, clean-limbed, deep-chested, and with all the points of a thoroughbred visible, she sprang into her seat as the horse was led up to the tavern steps.

The animal was not used to a female rider, and bounded into the air with a wild spring which would have unseated many a *man*, not to speak of a woman.

"Let him have his head, and take the trail of you know whom. The story you tell will take him where he'll meet his match and get his gruel!" cried the stranger, as he saw the girl keep her seat in the saddle with a coolness which told him as well as the horse that she was mistress of the situation and able to remain so.

She made no reply, but gave the horse the reins and sped away at a gallop.

"That gal is fit to command a regiment, and worth the whole caboodle of you men," said the stranger, with a sneer, as he turned and faced the loungers at the bar. "Landlord, give me a slug of your best brandy to drink her health in. If I come out of this war a major-general I'll take her off your hands, as sure as my name is—*what it is*."

The crowd, eager to know his name, looked their disappointment as he ended thus, and asked, speaking unusually respectfully:

"What mought that name be, stranger?"

"It might be Smith, or Brown, or Jones, or Jenkins, but it isn't," said the stranger, showing his white teeth in an icy smile. "Landlord, is this the best brandy you've got?"

"Yes, I paid eight dollars a gallon for it in Pilot Knob," said the landlord, not pleased with the way the stranger tasted it and then tossed the contents of his glass on the floor.

"It was good whisky, I expect, before they put burned sugar, oil of bitter almonds, and oil of vitriol in it and called it *brandy*," said the man, with a mocking laugh. "Never mind, there's your money for it, whether it is drank or not. And now, if any of you men are for the South enough to fight for her, starve when you can't get food, go wet when you can't keep dry, and die when your time comes, why there's a muster roll for you to sign. My name is at the head of it, and if you don't know me now, you will when I take any of you under fire, for you'll see *me* in front."

The men went one after the other and looked at the name which headed the muster roll, and more than one hat went off as the whisper passed from lip to lip—"It is Ben McCullough, the great Texan ranger!"

CHAPTER XL.

Wild Bill did not ride very fast after he left the village. He did not know but some of the bush-whackers would feel inclined to follow him, and if they did, knowing well that he could keep his own range with Black Nell under him, he felt no desire to get away until he had given them a chance.

He had gone four or five miles, perhaps, when he saw a woman coming on behind him at an easy gallop.

"That don't mean fight, but it may be a trick," he muttered, as he checked his speed a little to allow her to come up.

She was soon nearly alongside, and turning carelessly in his saddle, he glanced, first curiously, and then admiringly at her.

For not only was she dashingly pretty, but she sat that horse in a way to captivate the fancy of any one like Bill—a good horseman himself, and a judge not only of animals, but how they should be ridden.

"That's a stunnin' animal you're on, miss," said he.

"It ought to be. Aunt Sally gave two hundred for him when he was a yearlin' colt," said the fair rider. "Uncle Jake M'Kandlas wants to buy him, but I don't mean to let Aunt Sally sell him, for he just suits *me*."

The girl spoke in a careless way, and did not *appear* to observe the sudden start which Wild Bill involuntarily gave as that last name left her lips.

"Who is Uncle Jake M'Kandlas? Is he Aunt Sally's husband?" asked Bill with well-assumed carelessness, recovering his self-possession in a minute or less.

"Oh, no—we call him *Uncle* Jake because he's old. He isn't well; he got hurt among the Indians not long ago, and he's stayin' at our house to get well," said the girl, speaking as easily and natural as if she had not learned a lesson. "Aunt Sally knowed him years ago, I've heard her say, when I was a little girl. Aren't you the man that shot a chap a while ago back there?"

And she pointed with her thumb over her shoulder toward the now distant village.

"Yes, he was my enemy. I gave him an equal chance, but he wasn't quite as sure as I. That drink of whisky kind of outsteadied him, I reckon."

"I heard 'em say you shot him to kill. But I must get on, or it'll be plum dark afore I get to Aunt Sally's."

And the girl urged her horse on faster and diverged more to the southwest, over the rolling prairie land.

"Hold on a minute, please," said Bill, letting Black Nell "slide" a little faster. "How far do you live from here?"

"About ten or twelve mile, I reckon—it's just over that range of hills there."

"You wouldn't mind if I rode home with you, would you?" continued Bill. "Jake M'Kandlas is an old friend of mine, and I'd like to see him, and sleepin' in a house is nicer than campin' out when a chap is all alone. I've got plenty of money to pay my way, and I reckon your Aunt Sally won't object to my giving you the price of a new dress."

"No, indeed, she wouldn't say nothin' agin that, not if you're a friend of Uncle Jake's; but you shoot careless, they say, and it makes me kind of fearsome of you."

"Oh, you needn't fear me. I never spoke a cross word or did a mean thing to a woman in all my life, and I'm not goin' to begin now. So, if you'll let me ride home alongside of you, you may let that chestnut beauty of yours skim, and I'll try to keep up."

"All right, stranger—I'll trust you."

The girl, whose artless manner had won away all feeling of distrust from Bill, rode along rapidly, and Bill, chattering as they galloped, tried to make himself agreeable.

CHAPTER XLI.

Frank Stark, securing a second horse for Lillie at the first settlement after leaving camp in the morning, made a rapid journey toward the city, but even as Wild Bill had anticipated, before night he met Buffalo Bill with a party on the trail of Dave Tutt.

The story of the rescue was soon related, and when Buffalo Bill was told that his mate had kept on after Dave, he took two of his men with him and pushed forward to overtake Wild Bill, sending the rest back in charge of Frank Stark with his sister.

He knew that Wild Bill would not now leave the chase until he had run his game down, and he determined to be "in at the death" himself, if he could.

But as we have seen this was impossible, for Wild Bill had been fast, and Dave Tutt had been dead long before Buffalo Bill had reached the spot where Lillie was rescued.

It was so dark after they crossed the river and found the trail of Wild Bill and the man he had followed, that they had to lay over until morning.

But when dawn came they started without any delay, and pushed on at a rapid rate for the next two hours.

But now, while crossing a valley of some extent, between two hill ranges, where all was level, and there was neither bush, tree or rock to serve as concealment, they saw that which would have chilled the hearts of any man less fearless and less careless of odds than these bordermen.

Yelling wildly, full a hundred Sioux Indians came dashing over the hill in front of them, charging fairly down upon them.

Flight seemed to be the only policy. But to retreat is not in the tactics of Buffalo Bill.

His plan was formed in an instant, and acted on as quickly. Powder Face, trained to a hundred tricks, was made to lay down by a single word. The other horses were *thrown*, and tied so they could not rise, and then all were sheltered as far as possible with their saddles and blankets.

The animals were so arranged as to form a triangular breast-work, and inside of this, each man facing an angle, with his breech-loading rifle and revolvers ready for use, they waited the onset.

Yelling, as if *yells* could kill, the Indians came into range, and the moment Buffalo Bill knew his fire would tell, he and his companions began to blaze away. He knew that only an effective fire in the start, checking the enemy and throwing them into confusion, would save him and his two men, and not a shot was wasted.

Indian after Indian tumbled headlong from his horse, and soon circling away further and further, the red warriors rode out of range. In less than five minutes they had lost full twenty warriors, one of them a chief.

Wild yells for vengeance rose from their lips, and after a pow-wow of half an hours' duration, they again prepared to attack.

This time, dividing off into different squads, they charged all at once from various points, laying down on their horses, and shielding their bodies from fire with all conceivable cunning.

"Shoot the horses if you can't get a bead on the men," said Bill. "Fire sure and fast, and when a warrior is dismounted, put him out of the way of mounting again."

His men, cool as himself, poured in a steady fire with their long range guns, and though the Indians, firing as they charged, repeatedly came within a hundred yards before losing many, they wheeled away. Not a single shot of theirs did any serious injury, though some of their balls struck the saddles, and two of the horses were slightly wounded.

The Indians lost more in the second than on the first attack.

Another pow-wow was held among them and a change in the mode of attack made.

Buffalo Bill was the first to discover a small smoke rise where the Indians had huddled together.

"They are going to try to fire the prairie," said he. "But it is foolishness. The grass is too green to burn. They must try some other game. If I only had twenty men here I'd charge and whip the crowd. As it is, I'll try it before I stay cooped up here till after dark, when they'll be sure to creep in upon us and use us up. Ah! there they come again. Now I'll show 'em another trick. Don't fire this time as soon as they get in range, but lay as low as you can. They'll think we're out of ammunition."

Again the Indians swept in a wide circle, whooping and yelling, and keeping under cover of their horses as usual.

They seemed astonished when no shot was fired from the novel barricade.

And then, when Bill hoisted a white handkerchief on the barrel of his gun, their exultant yells came wildly down on the wind. Not that for an instant would they respect a flag of truce or accept a surrender, but they thought the poor men, without ammunition, were at their mercy.

They held a hurried pow-wow, and then, in dense column, rode, yelling and tearing, directly toward their supposed victims.

Bill and his companions, with their rifles pointed and two revolvers to each, loaded in their belts, waited until the Indians, who did not now think it necessary to fire, were within a hundred yards, and then, like flashing lightning, poured in their deadly fire.

Through that confused, headlong mass the rifle balls tore, killing and maiming them in line, and, as they could not check themselves before they were in revolver range, those swift, deadly weapons rained in a leaden hail with terrible effect.

Confused, huddled up, terror-stricken, the red men turned in every way to flee from that shower of death.

"Now, up and follow me!" cried Bill, and, without waiting to saddle, he sprang on Powder Face, and, with a fearful yell, charged right in among the enemy, brandishing his heavy rifle as a club, and striking down the warriors as if they were but playthings in his hand.

Oh, it was a grand as well as a fearful sight, to see him, bare-headed and bespattered with blood and brains, dash here and there, Powder Face kicking, plunging and snorting as he dashed his red hoofs into the dead and dying, while the Indians, utterly terror-mad, sought only to escape.

Bill was well supported by his two brave companions, and as long as there was an Indian left within reach of blow or bullet, they fought on.

It was a gallant fight.

Kit Carson, or Ben McCullough in his glory among the Comanches, could not have asked to see a better.

To the Indians it was a bitter, a terrible lesson. A few only fled far away, to tell that demons, instead of men, had been met, and their party had been swept away as the strong winds of November strip the sere leaves from the forest tree. They had fled to tell another story of the prowess of the "Long-haired Chief," whom none of them could kill; who was shielded by the hand of the Great Spirit.

When the fight was all over, and the mere scratches got in the last melee by Bill and his men had been looked to, the saddles were again put upon the horses, a little food eaten, and a drink of pure water from their canteens, and then the route was resumed.

Night was approaching when Bill, observing the smoke rise from a distant house on the prairie, remarked that they would go to it to camp, for possibly there they might hear from Wild Bill.

CHAPTER XLII.

When the sun was just dipping to the crest of the farthest western hills, the fair brunette showed Wild Bill smoke rising from a house half hidden in a little grove of locust trees.

"There's where Aunt Sally lives," said she; "now for a race to see who'll get there first."

And even as the words left her lips she touched her horse with the slack of the reins and he started at his wildest speed.

He had thus two or three rods the lead of Black Nell, but she began to slowly close the gap, and when they reached the door the two horses were side by side.

As Wild Bill leaped from his horse he turned to help the girl down, but laughing, with a fiendish light in her eyes, she cried out:

"Your *friend*, Jake M'Kandlas, comes yonder—I'll go to tell him Wild Bill is here!"

And she pointed to a group of men, eleven in all, who were slowly riding that way, and instantly rode at full speed toward them.

A woman came to the door—an old woman whom Bill had met years before, but who knew him instantly.

"Oh, merciful Heaven, Mr. Hitchcock,* what will become of you?" she cried. "Jake M'Kandlas and his gang will murder you under my roof! Oh, what brought you here?"

"Your precious niece there," said Bill, as he turned Nell loose and shouted: "Go for help, old gal—find Buffalo Bill and bring him here to bury me."

"My niece? I have no niece—I do not know that girl," said the woman, looking in wonder to see the black mare speed away as if she flew.

"Then I'm sold and the money paid in," cried Bill. "She has told Jake M'Kandlas, and there he and his tigers come. Old woman, if you ever do any prayin', get into your cellar, if you have one, out of the way, and pray your tallest, for there's going to be just the toughest fight here that ever was fought. Go quick, I want a clear range and no squalling to bother me."

There was a cellar and a trap-door leading to it, and through this the weeping woman fled for safety, perhaps to pray, as Bill asked her to do.

The next moment, throwing aside his hunting shirt and putting knife-hilt and revolver-butt where his hand would reach them easiest, Bill stood firm, fronting the door with his rifle cocked and ready.

A rush of horsemen, the sound of heavy feet leaping from the saddle to the ground, and then the burly form of Jake M'Kandlas loomed up before the door.

"Surrender, Yank!" shouted the renegade.

He never spoke again.

An ounce ball from Bill's rifle tore away the very tongue that spoke, and took half the head with it, for he was on the threshold and the muzzle of the gun was in his face.

As he fell back dead, the gang rushed in on Bill, and firing as he backed to a corner—one, two, three, four, five, six successive shots sent a man down in less time than I can write. Four more were left, and now, knives in hand, they were on him. One clutched him by the throat with a strangling grasp, while the others hewed and mangled him as he struggled to free himself.

*His real name.

One fearful blow with his clenched fist sent one combatant stunned out of the way, then he clutched the arm which was extended to his throat, and broke it as if it had been rotten wood instead of flesh and bone—and now his own knife was out. Oh—fearful for an instant—sickening was the work. Like tigers mad for blood, with flashing, clashing knives, silent only that their breathing could be heard for rods, they sprang and leaped at each other, parrying and thrusting, until the last man of the crowd lay dead before the hero.*

He, a mass of blood from head to foot, staggered out of the door, where the brunette yet sat on her horse to await the issue.

She saw him, and with a wild scream gave her horse the rein and fled away in the thickening twilight.

Bill staggered to the well, and bending his head down to a trough full of water by it, drank a few drops and then dropped senseless to the earth.

The widow, who had been frightened from the cellar by the blood which dripped down in streams upon her through the cracks in the floor, now came up, found the state he was in, and, carrying him in her arms into the house, laid him on her bed and dressed his wounds as well as she was able—stanching them with ice-cold water and lint hastily scraped from the bed linen.

She had the joy to see his eyes open after a long death-like swoon, and to hear his husky whisper as he asked: "Have I wiped 'em all out?"

"Yes, all but the girl, and she fled away. Oh, I do believe there's good in prayer!" said the old woman. "I prayed and I cried, and I cried and prayed all the time I heard the terrible work go on—and I stayed there where the blood ran down on me, until I thought I should die myself. The good God must have heard me, for though you are hacked and slashed all over, there isn't a wound that has reached your vitals. You'll live—Heaven be praised, you'll live!"

"Yes—it is to Him I owe it all!" said Bill, solemnly. "Nothing else could have saved me, for every man of 'em was a fighter! I reckon my old mother in Illinois must have been prayin' too, for 'twould take a heap of it to carry me through such a scrape. Are you sure all of them cusses are dead?"

"Yes—there is not a breath in any of 'em. I'll drag 'em out of the house—it's an awful job, but I can't bear to see 'em lie here after I light up. Their dead eyes would stare so awful like, for there isn't one that shut 'em afore he went out."

"I wish I could help you," said Bill, in his low whisper. "But I'm weak as a babe now. There will be help though afore long. I sent Black Nell after it, and she'll never rest till she brings it."

---

* A historical fact.

CHAPTER XLIII.

All the long night the widow watched poor Bill. He was so weak that the flutter-ing breath, the low pulse, scarce told that he lived; but she prepared a mild stimu-lant—not alcoholic, but a home preparation of roots and herbs—and by noon of the next day he was, through its effects, able to take a little broth.

While she was holding up his head to feed him, a shrill neigh was heard, and Bill at once recognized from whence it came.

"Black Nell is back, and she has friends with her!" he said. "You'll not have to bother with me much longer, my good, kind friend."

Almost as soon as the words left his mouth, Buffalo Bill rushed into the room.

He, almost always cool and calm, was white as snow now in the face, and trembled like a dry leaf in the winter wind.

"Bill, is life left in you?" he gasped.

"Yes; lots of life, but not much blood," whispered Wild Bill.

"And you killed 'em all—old Jake and ten more—for I saw and counted 'em as I ran by."

"Yes, mate—I wiped 'em *all* out, but 'twas just the hardest job I ever tackled," said Bill, his bright eyes telling how sure he was of the work.

"Mate, I loved you before better than I loved my own life—I don't know how I can love you more. But if I ever have a chance to *die* for you, I'll laugh while I'm going. I should like to have given old Jake his dose, but it came just as good from your hand. He knew you and me were one. This has been the biggest single-handed fight I ever knew; for every man of them was a fighting man, a desperado. Me and two of the boys have had a big tussle with the reds while we was hunting you up; but our fight isn't anything compared with yours. But can you stand moving?"

"I'll have to. A gal that led me into this scrape got away, and I expect more of Dave Tutt's friends will be after my hair when she gets back to tell 'em I haven't gone under."

"Dave Tutt! Have you seen him?"

"Yes, and for the last time. He was fool enough to exchange lead with me at thirty paces. There is a hole in my hat and one through his heart. So *he* is settled with."

"Thunder, Bill—you don't leave nothin' for me to do."

"Yes, I do, mate. You've got to get me back where they can put the blood into my veins once more, and make me strong, so that I can follow the scout as before. Did you see Miss Lillie?"

"Yes—Frank is with her. I sent all the men back but two, so I could move fast and quiet to join you. Do you think, if I sling a bed into the wagon out here, that you can stand the ride back?"

"I *must* stand it, mate, whether I can get through or not. It won't do for us to stay here. Just the hardest man on the trail in the Southern army knows of this last scrimmage by this time. I saw him in the little town where I killed Dave Tutt. He and Van Dorn hunt in the same claim, and they are both men whom you know to be hard to get away from."

"Who is this other man, Bill?"

"Ben McCullough, the old ranger. I saw by his eye that he wouldn't interfere between me and Dave, for he is one that never would prevent fair play in a personal matter; but as soon as that was over I made tracks out of that, for I knew he'd overhaul me, and if he found I wasn't on his side in what is going on in the States, I must go under. But, by the way the landlord's daughter acted in showing me where Jake M'Kandlas and his gang were, I feel satisfied that he sent her. And she is back with him by this time, and has most likely told him that his friends were too few to put me under, and took the down track themselves. That being the case, it is more than likely he'll come or send to look after my welfare with anything but a friendly interest."

"You're right, Bill—you're right. I'll rig up the wagon outside and have the horses harnessed to it, and we'll fix you as comfortable as we can, and start right away."

"That's the talk, mate. The more start we have, if we're to be followed, the better. But look here—don't take a thing from this old woman without paying for it. There's not far from three hundred dollars in my pouch, and there's the watch old Harney gave me. If it hadn't been for her I should have gone under, sure. When I got through I was too near gone to stop the bleeding myself, but she did it, and I live."

"All right, my mate—I'll do the clean thing by her; and if she'll come along and nurse you as we go, I'll make it worth her while out of my own pocket. Indeed, I reckon it'll be best for her anyway, for they that will come after you will not be likely to treat her well for having befriended you."

The widow had overheard the colloquy, for she stood near.

"I will go gladly, asking no recompense, and not willing to accept any," she said. "Take my wagon and mules, pile in the feather beds and clothing, and he'll lay soft and easy on 'em. As for me, I'm a lone widow. My two boys have been carried off to serve with them that you do not like; and I'm sure if I stay here I'll see rougher times than I have seen. Get ready as quickly as you please; take what you need, and I'll go with you."

"You're just as true and good hearted as women-folks can be when they try," said Bill. "Go with us and we'll stick by you to the last, and see that every comfort we can command comes to your share. We're rough, but we never forget our own mothers, and while we remember them we can't be unkind to you."

It took but a little time for the party to get ready, and when the widow's wagon was all arranged, it was far ahead of the usual ambulance used in the army for comfort.

Wild Bill was lifted into it, the widow seated near his head, with a canteen of water, and then they drove on, taking a course which Bill believed would soonest bring him to where Union forces were stationed.

It was a painful ride for the wounded man, but he was too much of a hero to show by any complaint what he suffered.

CHAPTER XLIV

Back with all the speed of which her thoroughbred horse was capable sped the traitorous beauty who had led Wild Bill into his fearful peril with the M'Kandlas gang—back over the plains toward the village where her father lived.

"What will the great Ranger say," she asked herself, "when I tell him his friends have been slain, single-handed by the man whom he sent me to betray into their hands."

For before he had dismissed her, he had told Ruby Blazes, the landlord's daughter, his name and rank, and that, as well as her natural proclivities, had made her so willing to serve him and the cause in which he was engaged. He had told her also where his camp was situated, so that, if not still in the village on her return, she might know where to send the noble animal which he had loaned her.

But when she reached her father's house, he was there, and not alone. In the large sitting-room, generally used as a family room, she found him and Van Dorn, who, with all his faults, was the bravest of the brave, with a few more kindred spirits, engaged in a friendly game of euchre, while her father, delighted at the occupation, was very frequently called upon to replenish their toddy glasses, for they were at leisure now and could afford their grog with sugar fixings.

The room was blue with smoke, and long before she reached the house, Ruby had heard the laughter of those within.

But when the door opened and McCullough saw her flushed but weary-looking face, he dashed down the cards he held in his hand and rising, cried: "Ah, here comes my Prairie Queen. How is it, my little fairy? Have you seen a little bit of tragedy since you left?"

"If the hardest and wildest fight that was ever fought single-handed is a tragedy, I have seen it!" she said, and a shudder ran through her fine form.

"What—that man was not fool enough to fight such a party as Jake M'Kandlas had around him?"

"He was fool enough to fight them, and man enough to whip them. There is not much of him left that hasn't got a hole or a gash—but of them not one man lives!"

"Girl, you surely do not speak this in earnest?"

"I do—it is the truth—neither more or less, and Jake M'Kandlas with ten more lay dead, for I saw them myself. I might have killed him, when it was over, for he had just life enough left to stagger out for water, but I hadn't the heart to do it. He is all man, if he isn't on our side."

"Yes, too much of a man to be on the other side. He must be made a prisoner. As a guide, what he knows of the country is invaluable. I do not blame you for anything that has miscarried, but that man has done us too much damage now, and can do too much yet to be permitted to escape. He must be made a prisoner, or else he must die."

"Who is it?" asked Van Dorn.

"The man Hitchcock, generally known as Wild Bill. You know him well."

"I reckon I do. No better shot ever fired a rifle or pistol. And is it he that has wiped out old M'Kandlas and his gang?"

"Yes, so Miss Ruby says, and she saw it. But you've had a hard ride, my brave girl, and need rest. You found the horse true, did you not?"

"Yes, general; a better never skimmed the prairie."

"Then keep him hereafter for my sake, my little beauty. One who rides so well as you deserves a good horse to ride on, and you'll not find many to beat him, especially with your weight on."

"Oh, you do not mean that I shall keep that noble horse as my own?" cried the pleased as well as astonished girl.

"I do. You deserve some recompense for your trouble. I may want you to go on another errand for me some time."

"I'd die for you!" cried Ruby, her dark eyes flashing as she spoke. "Oh, if I were only a man, I'd ride where you ride, and fight where you fight, as brave as the best of them all. I wish I was a man."

"Some may; I'm rather glad you're not, and if I live to come out of this war, my beauty, I'll tell you why. If I *don't*, there's no use in your knowing."

Ruby blushed with pleasure, for the bold speaker was one of those dashing, handsome men whose kind attentions are seldom displeasing to the fair sex.

"What is to be done about that man, Wild Bill?" she asked. "He is pretty badly hurt, but if he is left alone, he'll get over it, and get back where he can do work against our side."

"Yes," said McCullough, thoughtfully. "That will not do. He must be taken care of. I'll send a party, or go after him myself to-night, or early in the morning."

"There needn't be much hurry," said the girl. "It'll be a good while before he is fit to travel, if I'm any judge. He was terribly used up. They fought awful, I tell you."

"I should think so, with such odds. That man is a human wild cat. There is no use in talking. For *one* man, he hasn't got his match on earth. Couldn't you win him over to our side, Ruby? You've a mighty taking way with you."

"It wouldn't take with *him*," said Ruby, with a sigh. "All that did take was the way I rode. He liked my horse a heap more than he did me."

"Pshaw! I thought he had more taste. But never mind, my beauty. You shall see him dance on nothing yet."

"I'm not anxious for that. When a brave man goes under I'd rather he'd die like one than to be choked like a dog. He was polite to me, and I don't owe him any grudge. The chaps he wiped out you know were mean as sneaks, even if they were on our side!"

"You're right, Ruby—but be off to rest, for you need it. I'll see you before I start in the morning. I've got something I want you to take care of for me, for one don't know how soon he'll be beyond care in this skrimmage. I've led a pretty swift sort of a life, and have looked old Death in the face about as often as any other man, but I never felt before as I do now, that I've got pretty near the end of my grazing-ground. I've never made a will yet, but I think I shall before I get out of this settlement."

McCullough said this in a low, serious tone, and a gentle pressure of the hand told Ruby that he meant all he said, perhaps even more.

CHAPTER XLV.

Dreary in its loneliness stood the cabin home of the widow after its owner departed with her wounded guest and his friends, but the unburied corpses of Jake M'Kandlas and his gang made the picture terrible.

It must have seemed so to a party of men who reached it just as the sun was going down on the eve of the day when it was deserted. For the leader of these— they were but half a dozen, dressed as hunters and trappers usually went, and armed like them—drew back as he glanced at the bodies, and, with a shudder, said: "Mates, we've come to a poor place for food or rest either, by the looks of matters here. Nothing living in sight, and dead men strewed around as if life cost nothing."

"Don't you know who that is, cap?" asked the man next to him, pointing down at the ghastly face of M'Kandlas.

"Bears and wild cats! It is the old colonel—the very man we've come to meet!"

"Yes, cap, and do you know who has been here?"

"Buffalo Bill, of course. I've heard of his oath, and you are one of the gang that he has sworn to kill? Isn't it so, Rackensack?"

"Yes, cap, it is; and I'd rather meet any other ten men all at once than him alone. Not that I'm afeard of any man as a man, or afraid to die when my time comes, but there's luck goes with him. Colonel Jake has shot at him twenty times, and he never missed any other man. We've all tried to put him under, public and private, with lead, steel, and pison, but he lives, and he lives and swears he will live till we're all gone. There's but two or three left of the original lot—for truth, I don't know *positive* of any but me and Ginger-blue, the Texas Boy. But let's go inside—maybe we'll see something living in there."

The man who was called "cap" pushed open the unlatched door, and only saw the marks and stains of the terrible fight which had occurred in there. Bill and his companions had laid all the bodies outside while they were there.

"There are but few of our boys left now," said the captain. "All of Alf Coye's men are gone; but Dave Tutt must be left, for his body isn't among these, and he generally hunted in mighty close company to the old colonel."

"Yes, most likely he was off when this fight came on. Dave would go a hundred miles any day to see a lump of money in the shape of a pretty girl, and most likely that took him off. Hark! what is that?"

"It's a voice singing—some girl. Like as not Dave coming back with a prize."

"She has a horse under her, and is alone," said one of the party, who glanced out of the door.

"Young, too—why, cap, haven't you seen her before?"

"Yes; it looks like that gal the colonel took from the Mormon train at Ash Hollow one time," said the captain, looking out.

"It is her," said Rackensack, "and she is as crazy as a loon with a ball through both eyes! She is coming right here, too!"

The men all had entered the cabin, but they now hurried to the door to see the female, whose shrill, plaintive voice rose louder and louder as she approached, chanting a wild improvisation like this:

> *"Over the prairie, lonely and cheerless,*
> *Wanders poor Mary, eyes dry and fearless—*
> *Why should she weep?*
> *See the birds flying home to their nests,*
> *Daylight is dying away in the west,*
> *And Mary must sleep."*

She did not seem to heed the presence of any one, but let her horse take its own course until it halted where the others were standing near the cabin door.

Then she raised her pale, haggard face, and, with a look as cold and meaningless as if it had been marble instead of plastic flesh, saw the men before her.

"Why are you here?" she cried. "Mary does not belong to you. Her people are lost, and she is looking for them."

"Does Mormon Mary know that man?" asked the captain, pointing to the dead body of M'Kandlas.

"Yes; it is the colonel. Don't wake him up, or he'll beat you terribly. He is worse than a tiger when he is mad," she said.

"He'll not wake again in this world," said the captain. "But come in the house, poor girl—come in. There's no one of us will hurt you."

"Mary is hungry. The red Indians are afraid of her because she is a spirit, and she cannot get food from any one," said the girl, plaintively.

"We will find something for you. The man who wronged you most is past wronging you or any one else. Old Jake is dead."

"Dead—there are no dead!" said the girl, in a low, sad tone. "They only sleep when they do not move any more. I shall sleep by and by, and the winds will sing wild songs over me. The flowers will nod their heads and go to sleep, too. But we will all awake when God's daylight comes."

"Crazy or not, the girl speaks bright ideas," said the captain. "Stir about, men, and find something for supper—if you can't do better, kill a mule, for we've got to eat!"

"There's meat and potatoes in the cellar!" cried a man who had just made the discovery.

"Good! We'll have supper and a night's rest. When morning comes it will be time enough for us to decide what to do."

Soon a bright fire roared in the great chimney; a huge pot full of potatoes was hung over the fireplace, and a great pan of bacon was set on to fry.

One of the men attended to all this, for the poor, crazed girl had seated herself on a stool in one corner, and there sat rocking to and fro, singing low wild strains to herself, and not seeming to heed the presence of any other.

The widow had not taken away her housekeeping utensils, so these visitors found articles for setting the table in her cupboard, and in a little while the volunteer cook announced that supper was ready.

"Come, Mary; come, poor girl, and get something to eat," said the captain to the female, whose tangled hair and scanty, ragged garments made her look so pitiful.

And she, without a word, took the seat to which he led her, and ate ravenously of the food which he placed before with a bounteous hand.

All the men sat down and ate as if long abstinence had given them good appetites, conversing but little during the meal.

"Mary, have you ever seen me before?" asked the captain, when the woman at last drew back as if her hunger was fully appeased.

"Yes, you ride on the clouds when it storms. I have seen you at night when the owls sing, and I have listened to you when you told the red men to go back to the hills. You are the spirit of the hunting grounds, and the red men fear you."

"Poor girl! her brain is indeed gone wild," said the man. "Hallo! look outside, one of you, quick! I hear horses at a gallop. Be ready with your tools, boys, for we don't know what is coming."

One of the men sprang to the door, but had those who approached done so with hostile intent, he would have been too late for resistance, for at the same moment that he opened the door, a dozen armed men stood before him, ready to enter.

At their head was the dashing-looking stranger who had lent Ruby Blazes his horse when he sent her to act as guide to Wild Bill, and who, on her return, had made her a present of the animal.

"Who are you here?" cried the man, as, with a cocked revolver in his hand, followed first by the little brunette who had guided him there, and next by several of his own men, he entered the warm cabin.

"None of us are enemies to Major Ben McCullough," cried the captain. "I've too good a memory of hot times on the Brazos, when the Mexicans were throwing *escopette** balls like hail among a few of us, to travel with them that do not like a Texan Ranger now."

"Why, it is old Cap Lewis, or I'm short of memory," cried the Ranger, extending his hand.

"It is me, of what is left of me, Major," cried the man; "and I'm glad to see you here. I got word the other day up in the hills from Jake M'Kandlas to meet him

---

* French for blunderbuss.

down here with what boys I had. I got here just as night came on, and found Jake and his gang, but they're done work for this world. Some one has wiped 'em out with rough and bloody hands."

"Yes; I know who did it, and I came here after him."

"Him? You don't mean one man did all the killing that lays outside of this cabin?"

"Yes, it was all the work of one man—Wild Bill; and here is a girl who saw it, Miss Ruby Blazes, who has just guided me and my party here."

"Where is he? Wasn't he hurt?"

"Yes," said Ruby; "he was all shot and all cut up—bleeding from head to foot when I saw him last. He couldn't have got away from here without help. Where is the widow? That isn't her."

"No; that poor girl is a victim of old Jake, who lays dead outside. She came in since we did, and there was no live man or woman here when we came."

"Then the widow has carried him toward a settlement for help, most likely," said McCullough. "When day comes so we can find a trail, we'll see to it. There seems to be plenty to eat here, so my party will have supper, and we'll smoke a pipe and talk over old times. Ruby may do something to comfort that poor girl."

"I don't like women folks," said Ruby, with a careless glance at poor Mary—"not without they're like me, saucy, able to take care of themselves at any rate. But I'd like to know what has become of Wild Bill."

"We'll find out soon enough in the morning, my little humming-bird," said McCullough, with a smile. "Our horses will be fresh and rested then. You must rig up a place for yourself and yon poor girl to sleep to-night—we men can tumble down on our blankets anywhere."

"Supper, major, supper," cried the temporary cook, for the second table was now ready.

CHAPTER XLVI.

All the first day and well on in the night, Buffalo Bill hurried on with his small party, after leaving the widow's cabin, for he realized how impossible it would be to defend Wild Bill from capture, if not death, if such a man as McCullough should institute pursuit, and with anything like an escort overtake him.

Brave himself, he knew how to estimate bravery in others—untiring in pursuit, determined in under-takings, he knew what his own peril was when one like him might have taken his trail.

Therefore, he did not camp until the exhaustion of the wagon train made it a matter of actual necessity, and then he chose a position in a ravine which was not only defensible, but well calculated for concealment if any scouts should pass near.

Wild Bill, though suffering intensely from the jar of transportation, in his mangled condition, had borne up bravely, not a groan escaping his lips, but his spirits never flagged.

When asked by the widow if he suffered, his only answer was a smile, and a look of well-assumed indifference, with a quiet "not much"—but one who *knows* what suffering is could have told from the transient flush which would occupy the ashy paleness of the face once in a while, the wild feverish glance of the eyes moving to and fro and the set lip, that he was in physical agony hard for any but such as he to endure without complaint.

Buffalo Bill had a small fire built and supper cooked, and then made his men lay down to rest, but with his usual disregard for self he kept guard, seeing that the horses did not stray from the feed near camp and that no danger of surprise should occur.

He knew the importance of this watchfulness, for he was yet some distance from a part of the country where he could expect help, and he could not move with a wagon either with the speed or concealment of trail which would make escape practicable if pursuit was earnest.

The gray dawn, therefore, through his watchfulness and care, found the little party again ready to move forward, and another day of rapid travel followed. But the end of it found the wagon mules so nearly used up that he knew others must be had, or the progress of the party reduced to at least half of its former rate of speed.

Therefore, when camped on the second night, after selecting the feeding ground for the stock, and leaving orders for a strict watch to be kept until his return, he mounted Powder Face and rode off in search of other stock. He was somewhat acquainted with the country, and knew enough of it to be aware that if he and his real character were known there would be but one way for him to get fresh stock, and that would be by force.

He rode out from the blind old river road which he had followed during the day, to another more traveled, and along which an occasional farm-house might be seen, for on this route, if anywhere, he felt stock might be secured.

He had money with him, and if he could but purchase a team of smart mules, he could go on with a speed which would soon place him among friends where safety would be no longer a matter of doubt.

He was about four or five miles from his camp, riding westward along the road, when the baying of dogs told him that he was approaching habitations, and soon in the dim, uncertain starlight, shadowed by passing clouds, he saw a clump of buildings, such as are generally huddled up with the well-to-do farmers—the dwelling, corn-cribs and stables all near each other.

There was no light visible as he rode up, but the furious baying of half-a-dozen fierce dogs soon aroused some one within the dwelling house, and a door flew open, revealing a man half-dressed, with a light in his hand, who shouted roughly: "What's goin' on out thar? Has Satan got into the dogs, or is there some one out thar?"

"Satan may be in your dogs, for they make noise enough, stranger," said Bill. "But there is a chap out here who calls himself half white, who is rather tired of a long day's ride, and wouldn't suffer by a little rest and a bite to eat, which he is willing to pay for."

"Who ar ye and whar ar ye from?" asked the stranger, raising his light so that its rays fell on Bill, who now rode close up to the door.

A sudden thought struck Bill—by a single name he might know whether he was with friends or foes to the "cause" which he loved, and thereafter act accordingly.

"Have you ever heard of Jake M'Kandlas?" he asked.

"What, the old dare-devil colonel? I reckon I have and seen him, too—but you're not he! He is a brick, though, and I like him."

"I'm glad of that," said Bill, now knowing how to act. "He isn't a great ways off. My name is Tutt!"

"Tutt—Dave Tutt? Why one of my gals met you over in Liberty—my Sal—my name is Nat Perkins. My darter Sal will be crazy to see you. She is over at Bill Done's, a mile from here, tonight; but she'll be back in the morning. I've heard her talk about you a hundred times. Why don't you 'light and come in? We'll have some redeye and the old woman will have bacon on the fire in a minute—'light and come in."

"I would," said Bill, "but I left the colonel in a bad fix and must go back to him. Our wagon is bagged and we want a couple of span of mules or horses to drag it out. If you could spare them, why I'd have him here in an hour or two and all will be as right as an open sight and a hair-trigger with game before you."

"Why didn't you say so on the first?"

"Because I didn't know whether you was friendly to our side or not. These are times when one doesn't know who is *who*, till he tries."

"That's so, and I don't blame you. How far away is the colonel?"

"About four miles back, up the road."

"All right—here, Jim, Ben—tumble out, you curs, and harness the six-mule team. Be in a hurry while me and the stranger takes a swash of red-eye. I'll start the niggers and we'll soon overhaul them," cried Mr. Perkins.

"You needn't take the trouble to go. In fact, as we'll not make much of a stay after day, for we're hurrying on to join Price. After you and me take a drink, if you'll just ride over and tell your gal I'll be here soon, you'll do me a favor. Because I've got a present for her that I promised her at Liberty, but I didn't think I'd see her so soon. She is a powerful smart gal, is Sallie!"

"You'd better believe that, Dave, and says you're just about as smart as they make 'em now a-days!"

"Well, she is a good judge. So I'm rather flattered!"

Bill had now dismounted, and entering the house was soon engaged in a social glass, in which Mrs. Perkins and two of her grown daughters joined, for they were all up in the house now, anxious to see the man whom "Sal" had made famous in her talk about him.

In a very few minutes the mules were harnessed, and Bill, going in a direction just opposite to that which he must take to reach his own camp, started.

The old man Perkins at the same time mounted his horse and rode away to bring his daughter home, so that she might meet her lover.

For such in reality Dave Tutt had been, though of this Bill knew nothing when the thought struck him to assume the character.

Starting at a sharp trot he rode on with the mule teams about half a mile, then riding alongside of the negro who had them in charge, he spoke to him by the same name which his master had used when he told him to go along with Cap'n Tutt.

"Ben!" said he, "how far is it across to the old river road?"

"'Bout a mile, mas'r capn'—bout a mile I reckon! Your wagon isn't ober thar, is it?"

"Yes—I left it there and got out here some way. But no matter, we can get there, can't we?"

"Yes, mas'r cap'n—dere's an old field here on de left, but it's kind o' over-flowed now, de water is high from dem late rains!"

"No danger of missing it?"

"No, mas'r cap'n—all hard ground. Only jess de water in de way!"

"It is just where I want it," thought Bill, as he knew the water would hide his trail.

And at once, by his direction, the negro guided his team from the main road across the flooded field into a piece of wood which he well knew extended to the other road.

Not until he was on this road did he again speak to the negro, but now when he urged him down instead of up the river, the man exhibited a surprise which made an explanation and an understanding necessary.

"Ben," said he, "do you know there is a war going on?"

"Yes, mas'r cap'n—I've hearn 'em tell 'bout dat. But I doesn't know nuffin about it. I spec you do!"

"Yes, a good deal, and you'll know more about it before long. For you're in the service now!"

"Me, mas'r cap'n? De Lor' I doesn't know what you mean!"

"I mean this. I have appropriated you and these mules for the benefit of Uncle Sam, and you'll be wise if you mind me and ask no questions, but hurry on them mules. They'll never see Nat Perkins's stables again."

"De Lor', mas'r cap'n, you isn't a hoss thief?"

"No, Ben, I am not, and if your master had been a Union man I should have bought his mules. But as he was not, I knew I couldn't get them for love or money in any way but as I have. So they're mine till he can get them back from me, and I shall *hire* you to drive them and take care of them, if you will go with me willingly. If you don't I shall have to tie you up in the swamp somewhere, even if you should starve, till I get out of the country."

"I doesn't want you to do that, mas'r cap'n; but sposin' old master gets hold of this nigger if I goes off with you!"

"He'll not have the chance, Ben. In another day or two you will be free among free men, and never again be in his power."

"Did you say dat for true, mas'r cap'n?"

"Yes, Ben. I need you and these mules—will you go on willingly?"

"I s'pose I'd better, mas'r cap'n; but by the big gum tree, I doesn't see what it all means! But I is only a nigger, and me isn't expected to know much. So I'll jess do what you tell me, mas'r cap'n."

"Do it, Ben, and I'll see you through it all. The route we've taken will keep them from finding out our course, and I'll be many a mile away from this section before I camp again."

Bill was in high glee when he reached his camp with six fresh, strong mules to take the place of the four worn-out ones in front of his wagon.

CHAPTER XLVII.

Day dawned over the crowded cabin in which we left McCullough and his party a couple of chapters back, and with the coming of the light all hands were astir.

One of the first to greet the rosy smile of the eastern day-god was Ruby Blazes, coming from the little bedroom, as bright and fresh as a flower bathed in dew.

She met the Texan ranger with a cheerful look, bidding him good morning, as she extended her little hand to meet his.

"Where is the poor crazy girl? Was she quiet last night?" he asked.

"I reckon so. She was too proud, or to ugly to share the bed with me, and tumbled down in a corner on a pile of blankets. I did not notice whether she was awake or not when I came out—in fact, it was rather dark in there, and I had no candle. She is big enough to look out for herself; and as to being crazy—that's all bosh! Women don't get crazy so easy, though some of 'em can put it on, when they think it will *pay*."

"What is the reason you women never have any sympathy for each other?" asked McCullough.

"Because it is a dead waste. The sympathy of one true man is worth that of fifty—to *me* at least!

But excuse me, major—I must look to my horse. He is too good an animal to be neglected!"

"Never mind—one of my men shall groom him."

"But where is he? I picketed him here last night and put the saddle and bridle close by the picket-pin under this tree. All are gone! The horse might have strayed off, but the saddle and bridle could not."

"No. This must be looked to. Boys, where is the horse Miss Ruby rode—the bay that I gave her?"

No one could answer.

A search was vainly made; every other animal belonging to the party, even the pony which Mormon Mary had ridden, was there. The horse belonging to Ruby, with all its trappings, was gone—and it was the best horse of the whole lot.

"Count noses here inside the house and out!" cried the ranger. "Horses don't go off alone, with the harness on, very often!"

Lewis counted his men.

They were all right. So were those in McCullough's party.

Ruby rushed into the bedroom, and found the corner vacant where she had last seen Mormon Mary. There was no sign of her around the house.

"There's where my horse has gone!" cried the girl, with flashing eyes. "She *was* crazy, wasn't she? Yet she knew enough to get away from this camp without waking me or any of you up. That is craziness for you! How am I ever to get my horse, I'd like to know. It will not be well for her if I get my hands in her hair."

"Never mind, Ruby—we will take her trail and get the horse back. We'll have some coffee, and then take the trail, if it can be found. We've got Wild Bill to follow and capture."

"Yes, sir; and more than him," cried the old ranger, who had been out examining the trails leading to and from the place. "There's a wagon mark leading east from here, and quite a lot of shod-horse tracks, Wild Bill has been carried off in a wagon, and he has an escort of some kind with him."

"There was nobody with him here!" said Ruby.

"Not when you left, Miss Ruby," said McCullough. "But he has friends, who most likely have come across him and are trying to get him back to the Federal lines. But we'll block that game. We can go two miles on horseback to their one with a wagon and we'll overhaul them long before they can reach a point where we cannot go."

"But my horse? It is no way likely this crazy woman has followed the trail of Wild Bill."

"She could not have done so in the dark—did you see a *single* trail—a shod horse? You ought to know the track of my bay," McCullough asked.

"Yes, sir, it is fresher than the rest," replied the ranger.

"Then we are all right. Hurry, all hands, and get breakfast, and we'll then follow the trail."

"What am I to ride?" asked Ruby, pouting. "That crazy girl has left her pony, but he isn't worth shucks."

"You had better remain here—if you wish, I will leave a guard with you," said McCullough. "We shall ride fast, and as they have a long start, it will be hard work to come up with them. You could not endure the fatigue."

"Major, you don't know me—but you will before I'm through. I can stand as much fatigue as the best man you have here, and where you go I'm going. It is a sorry bit of horseflesh, that pony of hers, but I'll ride it until I get a better one."

"I'll do better than that. One of my men has got to go back with a message to General Van Dorn—he shall ride the pony, for there is not much haste required, and you shall have his horse."

"Oh, thank you, major. I'm happy now, for I never, never wish to leave your side."

"Ah, Ruby, with a long and bloody war before me, it will be very foolish for you to try to follow *my* fortunes."

"Foolish! Will any woman with a woman's heart in her believe it is folly to follow the ideal of heroism, in a cause to which her very soul is wedded? I may be young in years, but I am old in thought, and when I resolve, I am firm as the mountains are. Get me the horse, while I make coffee, for I will be so useful to you that you cannot do without me."

The ranger smiled, and turned away with a low sigh to give orders about the horse.

"Had I nothing else to do, I'd surely fall in love," he murmured, as he saw the girl hasten away to assist in getting breakfast.

CHAPTER XLVIII.

When Buffalo Bill got to his camp, and the negro, Ben, found out in real earnest who he was, and that it was a matter of life and death with them all to reach the Federal lines speedily, he proved himself an auxiliary worth having.

The fresh mules hitched to the wagon were put forward at a rapid trot, for the new driver was well acquainted with the road, and at several points he not only gained by making cuts across the country, but he crossed water often, so as to make the trail more difficult to follow.

Another day of travel was nearly ended, and Bill was already looking out ahead for a good camping-place, when the clatter of hoofs in their rear attracted his attention.

A momentary alarm passed from his breast as he saw that it was a woman who followed—a wan-faced but wild-eyed creature, whose hair floated out in disheveled tresses over her bare, sun-browned shoulders. She was mounted on a magnificent horse, which showed signs of having been ridden very hard.

Bill reined in his horse as she came up, deeming it best to question her, though there was nothing in her appearance to denote danger to him or his party.

"Where from, my friend, where from?" he asked kindly, as with a sad, wistful gaze she looked at him.

"Mary has ridden far, over the hills and over the plains. She is hungry!" said the woman, in a pitiful tone.

"We shall camp soon, and will have plenty to eat there; but here is a chunk of bread and meat to last till then."

And Bill instantly took some food from his well-filled haversack and handed it to her.

She ate a little, and then, in the same wild tone, said: "Mary saw them lying asleep all around her—the bad and the bloody. She could not stay there, so she rose and took the best horse and came away. They will follow, and they will kill us all!"

"Who—who do you mean?"

"Colonel M'Kandlas, Captain Lewis, and all."

"Why, M'Kandlas is dead!"

"No, he sleeps; I saw him. He was asleep, and men slept all around him. Then others came, and they fed Mary, and wanted her to sleep. She could not, and she took a horse and came away."

"*Others* came!" Bill muttered; for though he felt sure that she was insane, he began to gather something from what she said.

His eye accidentally fell on the silver front-piece of the bridle on her horse. He saw a name engraved on it—the name of one whom he knew but too well. It was that of BEN McCullough.

In an instant the thought came to him as to who had fed the girl, and from whom she had taken the horse.

A few questions adroitly put drew from her a nearly coherent story—enough, at any rate, to satisfy him that she had seen McCullough with a party at the deserted cabin of the widow, had taken one of his horses, and would, without a doubt, be followed.

To go on without stopping would be his best policy, if it could be done, but his horses and mules were too nearly used up to think of it.

He could do no more than to select as he had done the night before a defensible position for his camp and take a night to rest stock and men.

Yes—a second thought came to him—he could get the woman, Mary, as she called herself, to go into the wagon with the widow, and on her horse, which yet had plenty of vitality, send one of his men on to a point where Union troops might possibly be met.

He would do that. She was so weary with her long long ride that Mary made no dissent when he proposed to her to ride in the wagon.

The moment this change was made, he started his lightest man forward with a message for the first Union man or officer he could meet, and then, as night was close at hand, looked out for a good camping-place.

He found one even better than he hoped for. It was under a lofty ledge which overhung the stream, with a little level ravine running back close by, where there was plenty of grass for the stock.

A cave, not large or very deep, ran back a little way in the great cliff, and a fire built here could only be seen after entering it.

In truth, it was as good as a fort.

As the wagon could not be brought in there, Bill carried his wounded mate in, and had his bed made near a cheerful fire within.

The widow had succeeded in making Mormon Mary quite contented with her situation, and after night set in, and supper had been cooked and eaten, Bill felt very well satisfied with his position, for even if McCullough did follow up the trail, he thought he must have start enough to keep ahead of him some ways yet.

Wearied out at last, he knew that he must get some sleep or he could not much longer keep about, so posting his single sentinel out on the road by which they came, and bidding Ben look out for the stock, he laid down near the fire.

Wild Bill, worn out with continual suffering, also slept, an uneasy, dreamy slumber, while the widow and Mormon Mary alone kept awake.

The latter, with strange, incoherent, and rambling complaints, told so much of her sad story that the widow, listening with many a shudder, learned what fearful wrongs she had endured ere her brain became crazed. And it seemed to her as if retribution was but partial in the mere death of such a wretch as M'Kandlas.

Suddenly the girl paused, listened, and then starting to her feet, cried wildly: "They come! they come! I hear the tramp of horses!"

Buffalo Bill, aroused by her cry, started up, rifle in hand, just as the sharp crack from his sentinel's gun told that he was on the alert, and that enemies were approaching.

The next second the man himself rushed in, announcing a body of horsemen and two women as being close at hand.

He had hailed and halted them, and satisfied by one expression from the leader's lips of what they were, had fired at the other and dashed in, as he had been directed to do, to alarm the camp.

"Put out the fire, mate—put out the fire, and you've all the advantage," said Wild Bill, in a husky whisper. "Then put my revolver where I can reach it. I'm good for six if they'll stand between me and the star-light out there."

CHAPTER XLIX.

Instantly, on the suggestion of Wild Bill, at the moment that the negro, Ben, came rushing into the cave to aid the defense, water was dashed on the fire, and all inside were left in darkness.

Our hero had an instant now for thought, and in which to direct his only two able-bodied assistants how to act, for it was a matter of the sternest necessity to keep ready with reserved loads, and not to give their enemy an opportunity to rush in among them empty-handed.

He knew well that if Ben McCullough was himself in command, and had not been injured by the hasty shot of his sentinel, he had one to deal with who in strategy as well as courage was more to be dreaded than any man in the country.

The very fact that after the alarm was given the outside party did not at once rush on to the attack satisfied Bill that he had old hands to deal with.

They would reconnoiter carefully before they risked life in the work before them.

Bill placed the bed of Wild Bill behind a point of rock where it would be out of the range of fire, and made the widow take Mormon Mary with her into the same place.

He also arranged himself, the negro, and his other man in different parts of the cave, where, while using their own weapons effectively, they would be out of range to some extent from an outside fire, and so far apart as to make their force appear larger than it really was.

All this was the work of not more than two or three minutes at the utmost, and it was done before any demonstration was seen or heard from outside.

But the quiet did not last long. The intense darkness made even the dim starlight outside capable of revealing the first movement.

A creeping form was seen to approach the wagon, raise, look in, then pass on, return, and listening, as if by sound to endeavor to discover the whereabouts of the party.

Unsatisfied—for Bill and all with him were silent—this person crept away.

A minute more and he returned, walking boldly, and with him came two women.

Wild Bill whispered to his mate: "That's the gal who lured me into the hands of Jake M'Kandlas—the smallest of the two!"

"Then I expect the other is Sal Perkins after Dave Tutt," said Buffalo Bill, with a low laugh.

Neither had spoken above their breath, it seemed to them; but the sound evidently reached those outside, for they turned, and seemed to discover the entrance to the cave.

A whispered consultation was held, and the man hurried away.

A minute elapsed, and then Bill saw such odds coming forward that even his brave heart began to tremble—not for the fear of death, but the thought that he would not again see his dear twin sisters, his noble mother, his darling "Lou!"

One by one, silently and yet boldly, they came forward, until he counted in all twenty-three men beside the two women.

All were armed with rifles and pistols, and some bore sabres.

Even yet no word had been spoken aloud on either side. But when his men were formed so as to cut off egress from the cave, then McCullough himself spoke in a tone loud and clear as a bugle note.

"Men—you who are hid away in yonder! Listen to a man who never makes long speeches, but generally lets powder and lead talk for him. I know who you are, and that we are full five out here to one in there! If you will surrender, I will treat you well as prisoners of war. If you do not I will butcher you as we would so many grizzlies. We know your condition. Wild Bill is too near dead to fight."

"You lie, you cuss! I could put a ball through your heart as easy as I did through that of Dave Tutt, if I chose!" cried Wild Bill, forgetting all prudence.

"He killed Dave Tutt—*my* Dave!" screamed the largest of the two women. "Into 'em, men—into 'em, and wipe 'em out this minute!"

The maddened woman was on the point of rushing forward herself, but McCullough held her back.

The very fact that words instead of lead came from the concealed party gave him hope of a surrender.

He told the woman to keep still, and though his men held their weapons ready to fire, told them to wait for orders.

"I could dash in there and maybe lose a man or two, but it would be the last of you," he cried. "I do not wish to see useless bloodshed. I had rather hold prisoners than fill graves. So listen to reason, or it will be the worse for you."

"Ben McCullough, you know me and I know you. Together we had a time once in the Smoky Hills which you ought to remember, and you know what my grit is," cried Bill.

"Buffalo Bill, by thunder," cried the ranger.

"Yes, it *is* me, and for old times' sake I don't want to hurt you. If I had, you know what my needle-gun, now cocked in my hand, could and would do. There are more of us here than you expect, and we're fixed to stay. So, instead of bothering about us, go while you can, without getting hurt. All I'm trying to do is to get my mate back where his wounds can be attended to. Let us go in peace, and this will be the end of it."

"I can't do it, Bill. You must surrender as prisoners of war. You two men are worth too much to the other side to be allowed to slide when you're in my power. Just say you'll give up, and I'll draw my men back, and you can come out."

"I don't want to be impolite, Ben; but I'll see you and all with you in Jericho first. And, now, do *you* move, or I'll throw lead, for I'm tired of talking. There, ready! Pick each a man, and ten of them are dead!"

"Fire! There's no use in fooling—fire!" shouted McCullough.

The words scarcely left his lips, when he felt the graze of a ball along his temple, which, while it staggered him, killed a man just behind him; and then, as his own men fired, shot after shot came from different parts of the cavern, and several men falling, made him believe that the force in there was, indeed, larger than he expected.

"Back to cover, men! back to cover till we get light on the subject, for they can see us now, and we can't see them!" he shouted.

And, leaving a half-dozen men on the ground, he got the rest out of sight.

"Pretty well for a starter! Try again!" shouted Bill, in derision.

"We will! Your doom is sealed, if I have to stay here a year!" cried Ben, angrily.

"We've plenty of grub and powder. You can camp, and take it easy, if you like," said Bill.

Ben made no reply. He was revolving a new plan in his mind. What it was a few moments sufficed to reveal.

Glimpses of men flitting to cover behind the trees on the river bank could be seen, and then all was quiet for several minutes.

"I don't like this. He is Indian enough for anything, and is most dangerous when stillest," said Buffalo Bill to his mate.

"Keep under cover! He is going to try and light up in here so they'll have bullet range of us, I reckon," said Wild Bill.

"Yes, there it comes!" cried Bill, as a fire-ball made of clothing and soaked in whisky came bounding into the cavern, thrown by a strong and skillful hand.

Bill and the white borderman had got out of sight before the ball, all ablaze, rolled in. But Ben, the negro, was too slow, and half a dozen rifle shots rung out, and the balls came singing in about him. One only struck him, and that hit him fairly between the eyes on the thickest part of his skull. The bullet was flattened, and so was he for a moment; but he crept away under cover in a few seconds more, for the blazing ball made him a complete target to the concealed enemy.

"Ki!" he exclaimed, as he crept in among some large, loose rocks. "If dat ar had hit this chile anywhar but on de head I spec' he'd have been hurt."

The fire-ball blazed a little while, and a cap which Buffalo Bill held up on a ramrod got several holes in it, but no other damage was done.

The first plan of the great ranger had not met with the success he hoped for.

His continued quiet after the ball had burned out and all was dark again told Bill that some other dodge was in contemplation. He knew that now McCullough would permit no let up, that even a surrender would not for an instant be listened to.

"Be still and be ready!" he said, in a low tone. "Have knives and revolvers ready if they make a rush."

Creeping forms were again seen moving here and there, and though Bill fired four or five times, he was not sure of any shot.

Suddenly again a fire-ball rolled in, and then, springing up from the ground at the very mouth of the cavern where they had crept, McCullough and his men were seen rushing forward with fearful shouts.

Bullets for a second only could be used, and but two men were down, when Bill, the negro, and the borderman were forced to rise and face the music with their knives.

McCullough, singling out Buffalo Bill, closed with his huge bowie-knife uplifted, and as it came down, Bill met and parried the deadly blow, then with a counter-thrust nearly reached the heart at which he aimed, but the ranger, with a bound on one side, avoided the skillful lunge.

Then, with his keen eyes fixed tiger-like on his enemy, he made another bound, and again the knives flashed fire as they clashed together.

"Down with him! Here's for Dave Tutt!" shouted the Amazonian Sal Perkins, as with a large club she dashed in and struck down the uplifted arm of our hero.

Dark—dark seemed his chances now, though an instant of generous thought seemed to hold back the ranger's hand.

That delay of scarce a second was life to Bill, yes, and salvation to his party.

For the clatter of hoofs and sabres, the sight of blue uniforms, and a wild charging cry was heard outside, and the ranger, almost entrapped, had only time to shout: "Fall back, men, or we're lost!" when the Federal soldiers were seen rushing in.

Kicking the fire-ball far out of his range, McCullough managed to break through the incoming crowd, literally hewing his way out with his knife, and with him escaped a few of his men.

Light was now made, and then investigation showed that while Buffalo Bill and his men had been only slightly hurt, two-thirds of McCullough's men had paid for their assault with their lives.

The leader, with the rest and the two women, had got entirely away.

A pursuit was made—but a man who knew the country so well was not to be overtaken.

Buffalo Bill, whose forethought in sending on a messenger for help had undoubtedly saved him from destruction, was now safe with his partner and party, and with proud satisfaction took his course under a strong escort back toward the lines where he knew he would soon meet his loved ones.

CHAPTER L.

In ten days, by slow and easy stages, carefully nursed by the widow and by Mormon Mary, who, if not sane, had become quite calm under their treatment, Wild Bill reached St. Louis. A regular surgeon had attended to his wounds when the party halted each night, and when he and his noble mate were once more under the home-roof in the great city, he was a happy man.

Lillie had arrived safely under the care of Frank Stark, and the good mother of our hero was once more happy with her children all around her.

Kitty Muldoon was wild in the exuberance of her joy, and when she heard that Dave Tutt and colonel M'Kandlas had been slain, she fairly danced for joy.

"The big bla'guards," she cried. "Is it dead for sure they are? I wonder what has become of their souls? Sure its purgatory is too dacent a place for em, and ould Nick is too much of a gentleman for such company, bad as he is. Sure, I'm thinking they'll wander and wander around outside all through eternity, wantin' the bit to ate and the drop to drink, and never a hope of getting aither! Sure an' isn't starvin' in the midst o' plenty the worst of troubles?"

"How is my little friend, Joe Bevins, Kitty?" asked Bill, with a sly wink, expecting to see the tell-tale blush rise on her rosy face.

"How is he, sir? why he is purty as a saint's picture and as brave as a game chicken wid new spurs on!" cried Kitty, as proudly as if the words had been spoken that would give her a right to comb her loved one's hair with a three-legged stool, if she chose.

"And now, if ye plaze, Mister Bill, will ye be after teilin' me wan thing, and that isn't two?"

"What is it, Kitty?"

"Did you think I'd be after denying an interest in me bould little sojer boy, that has a heart like a lion and a mouth like a cherry, and is the most illegant dancer just that ever flung a leg!"

"No, Kitty, no—it is not the nature of your countrywomen to be ashamed of the one they give their heart to. I know that. And as to the dancing, I hope to see that day not far distant when I may dance at your wedding!"

"Sure that'll not be till the cruel war is over," said Kitty, with a laugh. "And thin, maybe there'll be more of yez sailing in the same ship wid poor little Kitty, and good luck be wid us all?"

Frank Stark came in a few moments after this conversation was over, and with a bright smile on his manly face, told Bill he had just had a fine offer.

"What is it?" asked Bill.

"A commission in the general's body guard!" said Frank.

"You took it, of course?"

"Of course I *didn't* take it!"

"Why not—you'll have big pay and a pair of shoulder straps!"

"Bill, what have I done that you talk this way to me?"

"Why, Frank, I talk nothing, mean nothing, but kindness. We scouts get less pay and meet a thousand more perils than those who hold higher rank. You are a brave, true man, loyal to the heart's core, and I owe you a great deal for the kind, brave acts you have done for me and my family. I wish to see you do well!"

"Then keep me where you can see it. I shall serve as a scout, and under your eye or nowhere. I wouldn't take the stars of a general and serve away from you!"

"Brother, never try to urge such friends to leave you," said Lottie, gently. "We feel that you are safe when brave and devoted men cling to you, for where your daring leads you they will follow to shield."

"Or to avenge," said Wild Bill, gloomily. "For my part I want to be out and doing, though I know I shall go under before long. I feel it, and have since I had a dream the other night."

"Dreams are the sleeping shadow only of the thought that was in your mind when slumber stole over your senses. No man should be so weak as to be influenced by his dreams," said Lillie with grave earnestness.

"I can't help it; but when a man dreams that he dies by the hand of a woman, and knows that he never thought of a woman except with kindness, it is something to worry about!"

"Did you dream that a woman killed ye for sure, Mr. Bill?" asked Kitty.

"Yes, I did."

"Then, sure, sir, it'll be a man that does it, for drames always go by *contraries*."

Wild Bill shook his head and then said: "If you'll all listen, I'll tell the dream exactly as it was. Then, maybe you'll not wonder at the hold it has upon me."

Every one drew near the easy-chair which Bill as an invalid yet used, and he went on to relate his dream.

"I thought that Buffalo Bill and me, with about forty or fifty of our sort—all scouts—were in camp in one of the sweetest spots in all Missouri, down on the Saint Francis, with our horses picketed, supper on the fire, and me just ready to eat it, when in rode one of the boys in blue as fast as he could come, and told us General Carr was in an all fired pickle down toward the Ozark range and wanted all the help he could get.

"I thought we didn't wait to eat supper, or ask questions, but were up and off in less time than it would take a Dutchman to bolt a bologna.

"We went on at a gallop, for we could hear cannon from the start, and after awhile we got into the hill country, and then we heard the crack of the rifles.

"We went no slower for this, but soon came where there was a chance to take a hand in. Sure enough, our folks were getting whipped awful. The batteries over on some hills across were mowing our men down by hundreds.

"Buffalo Bill, says he to me: "Mate, we can't stand this. Their guns must be taken or capsized!"

"I said *yes*, and we went for 'em! Oh, it was glorious! the way we went in, over and through rank after rank, till we got to the guns! We had a fight there, you'd better believe, for it was revolver to revolver, and knife to sabre; but we got the guns.

"I'd just taken off my hat to give one hurrah, when a hand clutched my throat, a knife came hissing down hot into my heart, and, as I felt the blood spout, I looked up and saw the face of a woman. *She* had done it.

"'There's your pay for killing Dave Tutt!' she cried. 'Go where he is, and tell him Sal Perkins sent you there!'

"I choked; I tried to say something to Bill about Lillie and Lottie, but I couldn', for the blood was all in my throat.

"The woman laughed at me like a devil, and it made me so mad that I struggled to rise, and strike her, for I was down, I thought, and I hit my head such an awful thump against the wall that it woke me up. It was a dream—I know that; but it is a warning, and I feel that I shall die soon, and by a woman's hand."

"Oh, nonsense, Bill! Don't talk that way; it is foolish! Lillie, cheer him up with a song, or we'll all get the blues, for they're as catching as the measles."

Lillie laughed, seized her guitar, and in a clear, ringing voice, sung:

A BATTLE SONG.

The tempest is breaking
In wrath o'er the land,
The firm earth is shaking.
Like a storm-beaten strand;
Proud armies are moving
Like clouds on the blast,
And patriots proving
Their manhood at last.
Then up in array,
And on to the fray—
Yes, up and away,
Where the war lightnings play!

Bill forgot his dream in a moment, and his dark eyes flashed proudly as she closed the verse, and he said: "That is the music to get well on. I'll be in the saddle in a week—see if I'm not."

The good girl would have sung another verse for him, but at that instant, the noble banker, Mr. La Valliere, entered with his bright-eyed "Lou," her hair floating in soft waves down her fair neck and shoulders, and the music was for a time interrupted.

For where little "Lou" came, there was music without singing, one may be sure.

CHAPTER LI.

Mounting on the best horse, for there were plenty to pick among now, Ben Mc-Cullough and the remnant of his party, on breaking through the disordered ranks of the charging soldiers, sped away at the swiftest rate, never drawing a rein until they reached the house of Nat Perkins.

Day had dawned before they got there, and the old man was at the door, surrounded by his family, when the party dashed up.

"Hallo! Here you are!" he shouted. "That's the way to ride—lickity-rip! lickity-rip! Wiped 'em all out, hey? Sal, did you take the hair of the he that killed yer lover?"

"Hold yer gab, you old carbuncle!" cried the girl, bitterly. "Mother, you and the gal get us something to eat quicker than ever you did before in your lives. Dad, roll out a keg of whisky—these folks need it more now than ever they did before."

"What's the matter? You uns haven't been whipped back?" gasped the old man.

"We just have, and the sooner you raise fresh horses for us in the neighborhood, the better it will be for you," said McCullough. "For if the soldiers follow us up and find us here, your houses and barns will be apt to go up in smoke and blaze."

"Wild-cats alive! General Ben McCullough whipped!"

And the old Missouri-man looked ghastly in his astonishment.

"Come, dad, there's no use in making faces. This crowd has got to be fed and to have fresh horses. Two-thirds of the party that went from here will never eat again. So the world is saved that much provender—but never mind that. Hurry up—hurry up, or I'll burn the whole caboodle out myself."

"Wild-cats alive—the gal has gone mad!" exclaimed the old man.

"You'll think so, old catamount, if you stand there much longer, for I'll pitch into *you*, sure as I live."

"Well, well, I'll go get the red-eye. But I say, did any of you see my nigger, Ben, and my six-mule team?"

"Yes; I sent a ball into Ben's head, for I don't like a nigger namesake," said McCullough, with a laugh. "As to your mules, you'll most likely see a U. S. brand on them if you ever see them again. I suppose they're contraband, according to the new code of Ben Butler."

"Well, if Ben can't be mine, I'd rather he would be dead than theirs," said the old man as he went down into his cellar.

There were lively times for the next two hours about that ranch. Food was cooked, eaten, and put in haversacks, and messengers sent to the neighbors for fresh horses. These came in rapidly, for the entire neighborhood sided with McCullough and his cause, so he had no trouble in obtaining a fresh remount.

At the end of two hours the ranger was ready. And now came the strangest episode of all.

Sallie Perkins, dressed completely in a suit belonging to her absent brother, Gus, made her appearance on as good a horse as could be found in the whole cavalcade. In the belt which fastened the fringed hunting-coat to her waist, a pair of revolvers and a large bowie-knife rested, while in her hand she carried a useful as well as a dangerous weapon in guerilla hands, a fine double-barreled shot-gun, at once light, yet serviceable.

Her hair, long, curling, and red as a fire-blaze seen in the darkness of night, hung down over her graceful shoulders. That alone, with her fair, smooth face, revealed her sex. Her features were rather masculine, her eye bold and fierce, her voice strong and full.

"Where are you going, Sal?" asked her father, as he saw his daughter thus accoutred and mounted.

"I'm going to have revenge for the death of Dave Tutt!" she cried. "I liked him as well as I ever liked any man that traveled. If he had lived, we would have been harnessed some time. I'm about as good as a widow now that he has gone, and I don't care to live any longer than to meet Wild Bill in a fair, square fight. It will be him or me then, and I don't think it will be *me!* So good-by, dad—keep your hair on as long as you can, and if you have to lose it, be gritty while it is going."

"Wild-cats alive, but this beats me!" muttered the old man. "Gus'll swear when he finds his new trouserloons* and Sunday coat gone."

"Let me hear him swear, and I'll knock his two eyes into one—that is, if he swears about me."

"Go it!" cried Ruby Blazes. "I like your spunk. You've got something to fight for, and so have I."

* Colloquial for trousers.

"I'd like to know what. You haven't had a sweetheart wiped out!" cried Sallie.

"Never mind if I haven't. There is one that I do love going in, and I'll fight by his side all through, and if he falls avenge him!"

Her dark eyes were fixed on McCullough as she said this, and a quick, bright glance from him made her face flush till it was fairly radiant.

"We must have luck when the women feel this way," he murmured. Then glancing his eye along the slender line of his followers to see if they were all right in arms and equipment, he gave his order in a sharp, quick tone:

"By *twos*, right turn, and follow me!"

There was no bugle call, but his men knew their duty, and though he dashed away at a gallop, every man in his place followed at the same pace.

"He's gone, and my best horses with him," sighed Nat Perkins, as the column vanished from sight. "And Sal rode on the best one I had. Wild-cats alive, if I lost that horse for good, it would well near break my heart. I hope I'll not lose him, but that gal is fearful reckless."

He now turned away with a sigh, not for the daughter whom he might nevermore see, but the stock that was gone, and could be but poorly replaced by the used-up animals left behind.

"If them Yanks do come, they musn't know Ben McCullough has been here and got fed, or we'll not have a hair left," he said, warningly, to the family and servants who stood grouped around. "We must be Union up to the handle in our talk, or they'll go through us lickity-rip, like water through a sieve. This war is going to be ruination to honest folks like me."

And the old man sighed again.

CHAPTER LII.

Already the armies of the West were in motion. Lyon, Curtis, Sigel, and, though last named, not least in military skill or bravery, General Carr, were out in Kansas and Missouri, moving to retard at one point or intercept in another the forces rallying under Price, Van Dorn, McCullough and Pike. The general in command of the Western Department, making his headquarters at St. Louis, had for a long time directed matters entirely from there, issuing proclamation after proclamation, but now he began to get ready to take the field in person.

Much against their will, he had kept back the scouts which had mustered under the leadership of Buffalo Bill, assigning as a principal reason that he could make them more useful to the country under his own immediate eye when *he* took the field.

It was to them a happy moment when, late one afternoon, Buffalo Bill received notice that he must prepare to start at dawn next morning for the front.

In his company quarters the news was received with cheer after cheer, and every man began to fix for the start.

If ordered, they would have been ready to move in twenty minutes instead of near as many hours, such was their discipline and the temperate habits which kept them always ready. And it was the discipline of choice inculcated more by example than rule in and by their leader.

There was not much hilarity in the cottage home when the news reached there that the scouts would depart with the rising of another sun. But warm as were the hearts of the widow and her family with love for those who must leave, there was not one of them all who would lift a restraining voice. Patriotism had grown with their growth, and was a part of their very lives.

Silently, though sadly, each had something to do to help fit out those who were to leave, and it was understood that the last evening should be spent by all in whom the family had an interest at home.

Thus at the supper-table there were gathered the mother, her son and twin daughters. "Lou" La Valliere was there also with her good father, and Kitty Muldoon, with no eyes for anybody but brave little Joe, was nestled away as near to him as she could get.

Wild Bill once more in the glory of a full buckskin suit—Frank Stark, genteel and quiet, as modest as he was brave—it was a circle to admire and be proud of.

After supper, when Kitty with volunteer help had cleared the table away, the parties paired off, and a general quiet conversation opened.

Lou and our hero had their talk in one corner, Frank Stark and Lillie in another, while good, sweet little Lottie tried to make Wild Bill laugh at the dream which had taken such serious root in his mind.

Kitty was more than usually silent, though Joe was trying to be just as funny as he could, to hide the real sadness which filled his heart.

For I care not how brave and loyal, how true and patriotic he may have been, there was never yet the loving man who could rush from his home to the battlefield without leaving the best and warmest thoughts of his heart behind him with the dear one who last whispered out, or perchance sobbed the word—farewell!

Many a thought is framed on such occasions, many a word is uttered, which will come to the dying man amid the din of battle, softening his last agony—which will hallow the tears which may yet water the sod above his honorable grave.

But truce to this moralizing—my readers will grow sleepy over it.

Mr. La Valliere and the widow had planned out the whole campaign as they would carry it through if in power, and the rest talked themselves almost into silence when the iron tongue of time spoke out the hour of midnight in syllables of twelve.

This was a signal that could not be disregarded, for men who must mount early and ride all the day and for many days to come needed rest.

"We may as well all say good-by to-night!" said Bill. "For before the light of day is spread out for the eyes of those who stay, we who are to travel will be on our route. For my part, I'm not much on the good-by—it is a shocking sort of word, and I don't like it. All I can say is—we are going where we are needed, and when there is no more need of us at the front, we'll, if the good Father above permits it, be back here to make home look cheerful again. So don't spill any water out of your eyes, but give us cheery looks to make our hearts strong, and hope and pray that we'll all be men, do our duty while we are away, and come back safe to say so."

"Bravo! A member of Congress could not have made a better speech," cried Mr. La Valliere.

"I don't know, sir, why you should link me with a member of Congress," said Bill, laughing. "I have never done anything very bad to deserve it. As to speeches— I'm rough, I know, but Lou will give me lessons by and by, and then I'll improve."

The banker now rose to leave, and Bill whispered a word or two to the darling of his heart, which checked the tears that rose in her beautiful eyes—for hope, brave hope is powerful to check the flood of grief when it is brought home to the heart.

The parting words were soon spoken, and with the solemn matronly blessing of that good mother floating like a wave of comfort after them, the young men filed away to take their accustomed rest before being called to the saddle.

It was a touching scene—one worthy of an artist's pencil rather than the too tame pen-paintings with which I lay it before the reader's eyes.

CHAPTER LIII.

It may interest the female portion of the readers hereof (though they are not expected to have a great deal of curiosity in such matters) if I say that before parting, betrothal vows had been exchanged between at least three couples in whom we are interested in this story. I will not insult the reader by naming them, for she surely knows long before this who is heart-mated in the party; and I don't believe in the linking of hands where the heart does not throb assent.

There is a great deal too much misery in this world produced by mismating to have any sign of approval from me at least.

The sun just began to gild the spires and domes of St. Louis when Bill and his scouts turned at the Five Mile House to give a parting look to the town.

There was little said; but doubtless many a one of the party, realizing what was before him, thought he was very likely taking his last glance at the busy town.

"Forward at a trot, boys; we've no train to bother us, and, now we're off, the sooner we are where there is work to do, the better for us. There is nothing like work to drive the blues away."

"Except whisky," said Wild Bill, with a forced laugh.

"There's where you're a mile outside the mark," said Buffalo Bill, seriously. "I'm not much on a temperance lecture—I wish I was; but you know, and you all know, that there is more fight, more headache—aye, more heart-ache in one rum-bottle than there is in all the water that ever sparkled in God's bright sunlight. And I, for the sake of my dear brothers and sisters, and for the sweet, trusting heart that throbs alone for me, intend to let the rum go where it belongs, and that is not down my throat, at any rate."

"Good for you, Bill! You've got something to live for, and can afford to steer clear of pison," said his mate. "It is all true that drink carries misery with it to us who take it and to those who love us; but as I'm bound to go down before many days slip by, I think I'll take my bitters till I go."

Nothing more was said for a time, for the pace was too rapid for pleasant conversation.

At noon there was a halt to water and loosen girths and breathe the horses, while the men took a bite from the three days' rations in their haversacks.

But half an hour covered the delay, and they again dashed on at a rapid rate.

They frequently passed slow, ponderous wagon trains, carrying provisions and ammunition to the front and occasionally overtook and went by some volunteer infantry regiments on the way to join the brigades ahead.

Officers and men get proud of their new uniforms and burnished arms, for it takes time and service to make one careless of show and alive only to the use and efficiency of arms and equipage.

"Fifty good miles to-day, and the horses ready for as much more to-morrow," said Bill, as he lighted his pipe at the camp-fire when they bivouacked. "That would just suit old Harney, wouldn't it, mate."

"Not much, without he was after reds; then anything would suit him that had go in it. He cares neither for man nor horse when his blood is hot, and that is always the case when he smells Indians. He'll never forget his Carloosahatchie scare while he lives. It is the only scare he ever had, I've heard him say a hundred times, and the only time he ever forgot how to swear and took to praying."

"Look to your horses, boys, the first thing. Give them a rub down, and then, when supper is over, you'll have nothing to do and plenty of time to do it in," said Bill.

The men needed no second order, but at once took care of the good animals which were so useful and necessary to them—a care which always brings its own reward in the condition and readiness for service in which it leaves the animal on which it is bestowed.

CHAPTER LIV.

No one is less fond of alluding to the events in which they were by necessity engaged than those who did the fighting and not the talking during the late civil war, and none are more anxious than those, on either side, who actively participated, to now see the hatchet buried and past animosities forgotten, past errors blotted out.

Yet in a story founded entirely on fact, with *real* characters for its actors, it is impossible to avoid some allusion, descriptively, to the past.

So, within two weeks after he left St. Louis, the hero of this story, with his company of scouts, held the advance of the great army which was destined to play such a conspicuous part in the long contested and fearful battle of Pea Ridge.

For days before this battle came on, Bill and his men were engaged in continual skirmishes, but owing to the nature of the country, and the skill of the bordermen in taking cover, he met with no important losses.

Ever by his side, Wild Bill and Frank Stark particularly distinguished themselves, while Little Joe, who had began to cultivate a mustache, did honor to the devotion of sweet Kitty Muldoon so far away.

Bill had enough to do as leader of scouts. He had McCullough and his Texans to watch—Pike was out with the Indian allies in their war-paint and feathers—and Van Dorn, as stubborn, if not near so morally *good* as Stonewall Jackson, was moving with lightning speed at every chance and opening.

To keep the Federal generals posted in every movement was a hard task, but that Bill did it, and did it well, history proves.

For three days preceding the final struggle—the fifth, sixth, and seventh of March, almost without eating, certainly without sleep—the noble scouts kept the front.

On the last decisive day, when General Carr was so nearly borne down by the combined weight thrown on his command alone by Van Dorn and McCullough, when hoped-for reinforcements seemed delayed beyond the hour of hope, while a hill crested with batteries so commanded his position that to remain was destruction, while to retreat was nearly as bad, then the Kansas scouts reaped a harvest of glory which will remain theirs as long as history lives.

Buffalo Bill, riding up from a distant point where he and his men had been hotly engaged since daylight, saw what havoc the batteries were making—saw, too, that the headquarter flags of the opposite army were on the hill by the batteries.

"Boys," he cried, "I'm going to stop this butchery. Those guns must be taken or silenced, or we're a whipped crowd."

"They will be taken—that is the very spot I saw in my dream!" cried Wild Bill, while a gleam of exultation flashed from his dark eyes. "We'll take the guns—but I shall go under. *My time has come!*"

"To charge, but not to die!" cried his mate. "Men, dismount, tighten every girth, look to your weapons, and be ready for the best piece of work you ever did. We must and *will* take the batteries over there and save General Carr and his command!"

The "boys" dismounted in silence. Noise was not in their line. Their girths tightened, revolvers fresh capped, rifles slung, and then they were ready.

Buffalo Bill waited for no superior orders. His eagle eye had seen what was needed, and now, rising in his stirrups, he shook his long rifle in the air and shouted: "CHARGE!"

Merciful Heaven, what a sight! Not fifty men of them all—yet like one swift cloud in a mottled sky, driving fiend-like before a gale, on—on they dashed!

No bugle note—no wild yell—but on—on to kill and to be killed!

Over the plain, through the sulphurous smoke, up on the ascent, amid bursting hail and rain of iron and of lead—on they swept!

The Federal fire slackened in their rear, though it increased to the right and left, for the charge was looked on by many an eye, and now they were facing the iron hail of the batteries.

Talk not to me of the Light Brigade, famed at Balaklava—talk not to me of Lodi or Austerlitz. On a hundred fields in this, our dear native land, have charges been made and battles fought which were as far beyond them as light is superior to darkness.

On—into and over the lines—through and through, a sheet of fire blazing from their revolvers, and then the clubbed rifle crashing down sabre guard and parrying arm—crashing in skulls and felling stalwart forms, on with their trained horses they swept—those heroic scouts!

Ben McCullough saw them coming—he saw the eye of Wild Bill single him out and the hand raised that never missed.

A smile, a defiant look, and he pressed his hand to his heart. He had got his summons and he knew it. Bitter and defiant to the last, he reeled from his saddle, and as he went down and the Kansas men swept like a destroying whirlwind over his body and the corpses of a hundred more, a yell for vengeance rose on every hand.

Wedged in by foes, it seemed as if these heroes, now fighting hand-to-hand, almost all with their knives alone, must now perish.

But hark to a shout which makes the air tremble!

Curtis is up, and with a wild cry, the Federals rush to the charge.

Wild Bill, for the first time in all the day, raises his voice in a glad, defiant, ringing shout.

Alas! it is his last. His cry has brought an eye upon him—yes, more than one—for Ruby Blazes, who had been in mute despair over the body of the hero of her heart, raised her wild voice as Sallie Perkins, still in male attire, dashed in on the bold scout.

Wild Bill did not see the uplifted hand until the knife came down swiftly to the very hilt in his breast, and he heard her shriek:

"Take that for Dave Tutt! Go, tell him that I did it!"

"My dream is up!" was all he said. "Good-by mate! Tell Lillie—"

He never closed the sentence. Death had him in his grasp, and he sank down helpless to the earth.

The next instant, as Curtis swept forward with fresh men, a bullet sent the brave Van Dorn to his last account, and then for an instant a fearful desperate charge was made by the Confederate forces to hold the guns, while they carried off the bodies of their leaders.

Till now, Buffalo Bill was unscathed; but those two women, fighting like demons, seemed to single him out, and in the few terrible seconds that followed, he went down, with nearly every man of his command. Not all slain, but most of them were terribly wounded.

It was like many another scene that never has been, or will be, faithfully described, where the courage and desperation that immortalized the Spartans at Thermopylae was more than equaled.

When Generals Curtis and Carr stood by the captured batteries and battle-flags on the hill, they found Black Nell laying dead beside her brave master, while Powder Face, with his ears set back, stood defiantly over the body of his wounded rider, ready to bite or kick the first who approached him with unfriendly motive.

Frank Stark and Little Joe both lay near by, wounded, but not fatally.

The shouts of victory now rang far and wide. The hard-fought battle was over, and friend and foe were alike sought out to receive surgical care.

Wild, fearful as had been the fray, terrible as the passions excited during its frenzied continuance, humanity had not perished in the hearts of the survivors, and now tenderly, carefully, many a mangled form was lifted by the very hand that had helped to shatter it.

And this is war—war among brothers!

Oh, God of Mercy spare our land from a sad renewal of calamities so dire!

CHAPTER LV.

After the battle, the army moved forward, but the main portion of the wounded were sent back. Not with the hospital train, but in selected ambulances, with a special escort, and with orders that their own wishes as to destination should be consulted.

Our wounded heroes of the Kansas scouts were retired to the rear.

The news of their glorious conduct, as well as of their condition, reached their friends in St. Louis, over the wires, before the sun had set on the field of carnage.

Was it then to be wondered at, when they reached the pleasant town of De Soto, on a south fork of the Osage, that a kindly face beamed into the end of the ambulance containing three of the most noted of our heroes—Buffalo Bill, Frank Stark, and little Joe Bevins.

It was that of Mr. La Valliere the banker.

"How are you, my brave boys—how are you?" he cried, as he saw their faces brighten on recognition of his own.

"Fifty per cent better than dead men, sir!" cried our hero.

"What do you know of per cent, my boy?" cried the banker, laughing. "Are you not tired of jolting along in this old ambulance?"

"Rather, sir—rather, but there's no use in saying you're tired when it is best to go on!"

"You'll not go any further for the present," said Mr. La Valliere. "You are under my charge until you are able to be out once more. I have engaged a house and some nurses for you. Nurses are scarce out here, but if those I've engaged don't suit, we'll try and improve on them. Driver, you see that large house with the old flag flying over it?"

"Yes, sir."

"Drive to that. It is my private hospital till I get these reckless boys made over again."

In a few moments the ambulance halted before the door of the largest building in the place.

Servants trooped out to carry the wounded in, and soon every man found himself in the best quarters he had seen since the opening of the war.

After each man of the first three named had been placed on cots which occupied a large room into which the sun, now on its western slope, threw soft, rosy rays, Mr. La Valliere looked at them pleasantly and asked if there was anything else they required just then.

"Your nurses will come when you call them—there is a bell on the table in reach of each one of you," said he, as he went out.

"To thunder with the nurses when we've got so much comfort as this around us!" said Buffalo Bill, when Mr. La Valliere quietly walked out of the room.

"I'm going to ring for mine," said little Joe, "just to see if he is white or black."

Tingle, tingle, went his bell.

"Och, you blissid little darlint—is it your own Kitty Muldoon you're wantin'?" cried a familiar voice, and the buxom little body rushed to the bedside and half smothered him with kisses, not caring "a bawbee" for the witnesses to this outpouring of her heart's love.

It was surprising how quickly every bell in that room rung for a nurse then.

And never were bells answered more promptly.

Little Lou, beautiful as a rose and pure as the dew which gems it in the still breath of morning, was quickly at the bedside of her young love's first dream.

Lillie, all blushes and tremulous with joy, was bending tearfully over Frank Stark, while Lottie, more bashful than all the rest, sweet May flower as she was, came in as a kind of supernumerary, ready to help where help was most needed.

Another came in, led by the good banker, and Buffalo Bill turned even from his idolized Lou to give vent to the love and reverence that he felt for his mother.

Her white hand was so soft and cooling to his brow—her words of low praise and thankfulness that while he had done his duty, he had been spared—all, all was like magic medicine to his bruised and gashed body.

Mr. La Valliere looked at this scene a few moments and then made a very singular, but, under the circumstances, a not very inappropriate speech.

He coughed a little to clear his voice and then proceeded thusly:

"My friends, the recollections of a busy lifetime, as H. G. would say, throng in upon me just now and suggest various eventful experiences of my own.

"First, a penny saved counts as much in bank as a penny earned. Second, persons interested in the ownership of property are always more careful of it than those who are merely hired to take care of it. These and a few other considerations have caused me to call in the services of my friend here, Chaplain Danner, for the purpose of making this nurse business a 'joint-stock' affair, technically speaking.

"Lou, my darling, take that pallid looking hero of yours by the hand, while this gentleman speaks the words which I hope will make you both happy."

Tears of joy as well as wonder filled the eyes of the brave scout, when that trusting little hand was placed in his own. His voice grew strong as he responded to the questions, and when he uttered the vow to "love, protect, and cherish," it came up from the inner depths of as true a heart as ever beat for woman! Heaven bless him and her.

"Your turn next, my pretty Lillie," said the banker, as he approached the thrice perilled and thrice rescued heroine and the brave man who for her sake had turned from evil ways and was striving for the good.

Soon that ceremony was over—none were there who could or would object.

For base indeed is the heart which will turn from him who has left the darkness, of his own free will, and come out into the light.

Foul and most ungenerous is the nature which will not rejoice to grasp the hand of him who has been redeemed from error, and who in the strength of redeemed manhood has honorably proven himself worthy of a good cause and pure, ennobling associations.

There was more to be done. Little Kitty stood open-mouthed, blushing and turning white by turns as the marriages went on, and now she trembled like a leaf when Mr. La Valliere approached her.

"There will be no objections here I hope!" said the banker, with a smile as he approached the bedside of Joe Bevins. "What do you say, Kitty; do you love Joe well enough to take him for better or for worse?"

"Faith, sir, I don't believe I'll find a better, and if I waited, I might find a worse, and if he's willin' I'm not the big fool to say no. But sure there's one thing—he mustn't take me away from missis, for I've promised in me heart never to lave her that has been so good to the poor lone girl I was when she found me."

"I'll never take you from them you love, Kitty, for I hope always to be near Bill myself, and he'll never lose sight of his mother, I know."

"Then let his riverence go ahead as soon as he plases," said Kitty, as she put her chubby little hand into that of Joe.

This last ceremony was soon over, and our story is in such a happy stopping place, that I believe it must be closed.

It is enough to say that Buffalo Bill, Joe Bevins, and Frank Stark yet live—that ever since they were linked to live-candy framed *en statuette*, they've led lives of wild adventure on the far western plains, which may yet be worked up into another exciting border tale by your very much obliged friend—The Author.

℃꙳ **II** ℃꙳

Hazel-Eye, the Girl Trapper. A Tale of Strange Young Life

Editor's Note

What makes Hazel-Eye especially interesting is its differences from many other Ned Buntline titles. First of all, it has a unique setting. No other known Ned Buntline dime novel takes place at the headwaters of the Yellowstone River. According to Edward Z. C. Judson's biographer Fred E. Pond, Judson spent about two years around 1842 working with a fur company, trapping this very area. There is no evidence to support Pond's assertion, and Judson's subsequent biographer, Jay Monaghan, states that the records of the fur company have no listing for a Judson or any of his several pseudonyms in that time frame. A second remarkable point about this particular tale is that Judson took great care with geography and paid particular attention to topographic detail and features of the terrain. Whether he drew on personal experience or actually conducted research on the setting, this is one of only a handful of Ned Buntline westerns where he got the lay of the land correct.

A third remarkable point about this story is the use of a character that Judson actually created for himself to play on stage when he was touring in *Scouts of the Plains* with Buffalo Bill. Filling out the tripartite heroic structure of the melodrama was Texas Jack Omohundo and a fanciful old mountain man, Cale Durg, played by Judson himself. Judson frequently posed for photos in the buckskin costume from the play and also appeared in public to lecture or perform in that guise. After his break-up with Cody, he tried to revive the Cale Durg character as the main feature of a second touring production, which ultimately failed.

In essence, Cale Durg, a wise and experienced frontiersman, mountain man, and devotee of justice and morality, is the alter ego of Ned Buntline, who is the alter ego of Edward Z. C. Judson. That Judson would make Cale Durg a principal character—indeed *the* principal character—in a dime novel is indicative of the egocentric bent of Judson's personality.

The story is also unique because, unlike so many of the Ned Buntline dime novel westerns, Hazel-Eye does not involve a long chase or series of chases; nor is there a leap-frogging from one bloody battle scene to the next, although there is a fair amount of gore and there are plenty of bodies scattered around from time to time. Although there is an abduction at the center of the story, it is, in a way, a kind of afterthought; the central issue here uses another typical melodramatic device, a purloined strongbox containing papers that have secrets to reveal. Although none of Ned Buntline's plots is simple, Hazel-Eye is particularly intricate and seems less contrived, better thought-out, and more carefully planned than average, and there's less blustering, posturing, and speech-making here than is typically found in a Ned Buntline novelette.

The heroine, Anna Mauricenne, "Hazel-Eye," as Cale Durg calls her, is very likely modeled on Anna Fuller, a poetess Judson became enamored of in the summer of 1871 and married in October of that year. He openly called Anna Fuller his "Hazel-Eye" and was clearly smitten by her. As a heroine, Anna Mauricenne is particularly interesting because she is no simpering victim of some villain's malice and desire; rather, she is a strong, fiercely independent young woman who is very nearly (although not entirely) capable of fending for herself in a wilderness environment. A crack shot and handy with a knife, she faces down grizzly bears and evil men with equal feistiness, a trait that constantly wins Cale Durg's admiration. Curiously, though, the love interest in the story is not between Cale Durg and Anna "Hazel-Eye" Mauricenne. The heroine of this tale falls for the son of the tale's apparent villain, while Cale becomes taken with Medora Norcross, a relative of the interloping family.

Overall, this is one of the most straightforward of Judson's western adventures, and it generally holds up well for a modern audience, but the familiar elements of the traditional western melodramatic form remain intact. This version is from *The Log Cabin Library* 1890 reprint of the original story, issued by *Street & Smith's New York Weekly* in 1871.

HAZEL-EYE.

THE GIRL TRAPPER

CHAPTER I

The Iron Chest.

Standing by the slab door of a log cabin with a lofty cliff at its back, a wild mountain stream on the right, and a forest to the left and front, a young girl in an attitude of unstudied but picturesque beauty leaned on a rifle, while she appeared to listen for some sound or signal.

In age she could not be less than seventeen or over twenty years.

A large hound stood near her, looking, as she was, down the hill in the direction which the stream ran.

"I heard his gun and shout—father will soon be here with his game," she said in a pleasant tone. "Why don't you go to meet him, Rollo?"

The dog looked up wistfully at her, but did not stir.

"Ah! I remember!" she added. "Father told you to stay and watch over his hazel-eyed child. You're a noble dog, good Rollo; a true friend and a dangerous foe! Ah! there comes father, but he brings no game. His step is quick, his face is white, he bleeds! Oh, Heaven! he is wounded!"

A man yet in the prime of life, near its meridian in years, of noble face and form, armed and garbed as a hunter, came swiftly up from the tangled forest in the foreground.

He came fast but feebly, for blood was oozing through the fingers, which were pressed over a wound in his breast, and his face was ashen white in hue.

"Father! dear father! you are wounded!" cried the girl, rushing forward, while the great Siberian hound gave a mournful howl.

"Yes—Anna—my enemy has triumphed at last! I bleed from a death wound! There is no use to check the outward flow; I bleed internally; have but a few brief moments to live!"

"Oh, father! father! what shall I do?"

"Live, live, idol of my soul, to yet regain your rights and take vengeance for my wrongs and death!"

"Father, who has done this?—whose hand has been raised to take your precious life?"

"*The enemy of my life!*—he who drove me to these wilds, who broke your angel mother's heart; he whose wealth and power were all combined to crush me in my name, my fame, my present, and my future!"

"His name, father, his name?"

"Child—'tis in the iron chest—records, all, all—all are there! Ah! the key— have I lost it?"

The man clutched at a string about his neck. Two ends hung loose—no key was there!

"Lost, lost!" he moaned. "Anna, water—I am dying, child!"

She sprang to the dashing stream but a few yards off and brought a cup of water, but it was almost too late. She placed the crystal beverage to his lips—he could not swallow.

"My rifle—quick! Oh! for one shot more—vengeance—it is your heritage, my Anna—and the—chest!"

The last word came out with his dying gasp, and as she held his head against her throbbing bosom, tearless in her agony, she felt his spirit pass away.

"Father! father!" she screamed, as his full weight fell hard against her. No reply—no look of love from the glassy eyes—he was *dead!*

Again the hound howled mournfully, and then as the sounding steps of an approaching man reached his ears, he turned fiercely to confront him who approached.

"Down, Rollo, and be still! It is Cale Durg—my father's friend."

A giant in stature, dressed from head to foot in the skins of panthers, with the hair outside, his face covered with a rough shaggy beard, his hair long, and like his beard, fiery red—this man hardly looked human. His eyes, a dark gray, had an icy glitter, and even his tone was harsh and rough. But his words were not unkind.

"What's up, little 'un—what's up? I've seen signs of a tussel down the trail, and a trickle of blood leadin' this way! earthquakes and hurricanes! That isn't Guy, your father, and on his back?"

"*Dead!* Cale Durg—*dead!*" she sobbed, and now tears came to the relief of her heavy, heavy heart.

"Dead—a bullet hole in his breast, and a stab, besides!" said the giant, as he quickly bent over the body and examined it. "Who on earth has done this work? I'll foller him to the jumpin' off place, and lift his h'ar. Who did it, Hazel-Eye—who did it?"

"Alas, I know not. He had not time to tell me. It was the enemy he had dreaded for years! I expect his name is in the iron chest which stands in the cabin!"

"Open it quick, gal—open it quick, and let me know. There aren't ten men in all the great Nor'-west that Cale Durg doesn't know—let me know who killed Trapper Guy, and he is my meat!"

"The key is gone—father felt for it while he was dying. The string was broken, perhaps in the death-struggle!"

"Ay—he has been robbed! Where is the old gold watch with the strange marks on the back which he always carried there!"

The hunter pointed to a pocket in the dead man's hunting shirt.

"The watch is gone. Oh, Cale—you are good on the trail. Take Rollo, and trace the murderer up! Do—do, and then come back and help me to bury him!"

"I will take the trail if I can find it, gal. But I don't want the dog. Keep him by you. The reds are gittin' ugly. You need company and the dog is better than half a dozen men for watch and guard, too. But first I'll lift him inside and cover him up!

Tenderly, with his great brawny hand, the man closed the eyes of the dead trapper; then he lifted up the body and carried it inside the cabin.

Taking up the long rifle which he had put down while attending the body, Carl Durg hurried off on the trail by which he came.

The young girl followed him to the door and watched his receding form until it was out of sight. Then she came back and knelt down by the bed on which lay the body of her father, her protector, her best and truest friend.

She knelt there in silence, though from time to time a sigh would shake her from head to foot, until an angry growl from the great Siberian hound at the door told her some one was approaching:

"Strangers!" she murmured, even before she rose, for the sharp, harsh bark of the dog told her so. And she hurried to the door.

Two men, an old one and a young, had stopped in the trail, and the oldest was raising a gun as if he intended to shoot the dog which so fiercely barred their progress. The girl, alarmed for the safety of her dog, sprang forward and cried out:

"Do not fire on that dog, sir. He will not harm those who come hither with friendly motive."

"Our motives are good enough—we're strangers in these parts, but the dog is an ugly customer!" said the eldest of the two men.

"Down, Rollo, and let them pass!" said the girl. "They come at a sad time, but my father never refused hospitality to strangers. Even now his daughter will not neglect his example."

The dog, still looking with a menacing eye on the strangers, lay down near the threshold of the door and allowed the men to enter the house into which the girl invited them.

Till now, she had scarcely noticed their appearance, except that they wore such clothing as persons wear who come from the settlements far away, and that they looked like father and son.

Now that they took the seats she proffered, she saw that the elder was a man of full fifty, or fifty-five years of age—the other at least thirty years his junior. The first had a cold, stern face, haughty in expression, with eyes of jetty blackness, sharp and piercing—she fancied almost malignant in their glance.

The younger person resembled him only in general features. His face was mild in expression, his eyes soft, rather mournful in their look, his figure tall but slender and far less muscular than that of the elder.

The eyes of the elder swept strangely around the room, seeming to take in all its appearance at a glance, but when that glance reached a rusty iron chest in one corner, it rested there with a look so singular that the girl noticed it; and his face flushed a little, she thought, as he caught her gaze fixed on him at this moment.

"Rupert!" said he, addressing the younger, "we little expected to see signs of civilization in this wild region, yet here are evidences of refinement which, apart from this young lady's words of welcome, are surprising."

"Yes, father, and perhaps we intrude," said the young man in a tone at once manly and gentle, and with a look which made her feel as kindly toward him as, by contrast, she felt repugnant to the one whom he called father.

Then, turning to the girl, the young man added, by way of explanation: "We belong to an exploring and prospecting expedition that is camped a few miles away, and in our hunt to-day came upon this trail, and from curiosity followed it up."

The young girl bowed her head, but made no response.

She was thinking what could make that elder stranger look so intently on that iron chest.

The latter, noticing her eyes fixed on him, seemed rather amazed by her look of scrutiny, and asked abruptly: "Do you live alone here?"

"I did not until two sad hours ago. I had a dear and noble father, who brought me, an infant, to these wilds, some sixteen years ago—"

"Sixteen years?" said the elder stranger, abruptly, and with a nervousness which caused the younger to look on him with surprise.

"Yes, sir; and since then, reared, educated, and cared for by him, I have known no sorrow until to-day. And now—now—oh! Heaven! what shall I do? He is there! "He is *there!*"

She pointed to the bed, where a blanket hid her cause of grief from their view.

The young man sprang toward the bed, raised the blanket, and, as he saw the corpse, recoiled with a cry of horror.

The old man rose when he heard the cry which broke from the lips of his son. He, too, looked at the corpse. Could it be—was she mistaken, or did the daughter really see a sign of cold satisfaction in that old man's face as he looked down upon her dead parent? Yet he spoke first. "What does this mean? This man has been murdered!" he said.

"Yes, my father has been cruelly, foully murdered!" said the young girl, vehemently. "And may God's awful curse fall on him who did the cruel deed! Let me but learn whose hand sent him to death, and, woman as I am, I *will revenge the act!*"

Her eyes flashed and her form towered up as she spoke, until she seemed indeed filled with a spirit of vengeance.

"Have you no suspicions which will point to the perpetrator?" asked the young man.

"Indians, without a doubt! The hostile Black feet swarm around here!" said the elder hastily.

"No—the red men were friendly to us. My father spoke their language well, and has done them many a favor when the agents sought to rob and wrong them. He was not killed by an Indian."

"Hazel-Eye speaks the word that is true. Indians do not carry knives like this!"

An Indian, a noble-looking warrior he was, stood in the open doorway and spoke these words. As he spoke, he raised a large white-handled bowie-knife, with a hilt of silver in the shape of a templar's cross. "This, I found, where the Red Panther took the trail—this knife drank the life of her father!"

And the Indian pointed to the young girl.

A look of horror blanched the face of the young man as his eyes rested on the knife, a look which for an instant only, settled on his father, and then with an effort he seemed to stifle a desire to speak, as he drew the blanket once more over the face of the dead man.

"Then Cale Durg is on the murderer's track!" cried the girl, addressing the Indian.

"Yes, Red Panther is on the trail. He met Mad Eagle and told him to bring the knife to Hazel-Eye and bid her keep it till he came!"

"Thank you, Mad Eagle. You, like him, are good to Hazel-Eye in her hour of sorrow!" said the girl, receiving the knife.

"Ah!" she exclaimed, as her eye rested on the silver hilt of the yet ensanguined weapon, "the same device is here that was engraved upon my father's watch! A sword crossing an olive branch! What can it mean—this strange coincidence?"

Again the eyes of the young man went searchingly to the face of his father. They could read nothing now in that cold, stern face.

"Come in and sit down, Mad Eagle. You were my father's true friend, and will ever be welcome in the cabin where he dwelt," said the young girl, kindly.

"No! Mad Eagle will stay here and watch for the coming of Red Panther!" said the Indian, and he threw his tall, stately form down on a mossy rock near the door.

The hound, which had not even growled as he came to the cabin, now rose and, going to his side, nestled his great head upon the Indian's broad chest.

The Indian looked kindly on the noble animal and said: "Rollo knows his friend! He is brave and true. Hazel-Eye may sleep while Rollo keeps watch over her wigwam."

The dog seemed to understand, for his eyes looked toward his young mistress when the Indian spoke. But meeting the glance of the older stranger, he again growled.

"Rollo knows enemies, too," said the Indian in a low tone. "That pale-face has a bad heart. The dog reads it in his eyes. Mad Eagle reads it, too. The pale-face shall be watched. If he means harm to Hazel-Eye, his days are few in the forest of life."

The dog rose, and gave a quick, sharp bark, while his look evinced pleasure rather than anger.

"It is Red Panther who comes," said the Indian.

The next moment Cale Durg came in sight.

CHAPTER II.
A Startling Question.

Cale Durg came up the trail with long, rapid strides, his heavy rifle grasped nervously in his hand, his eyes looking wild and fierce.

As he came, the Indian rose to his feet and bent an inquiring look upon him, while the girl rushed to the door and cried, quickly: "What news, good Cale Durg? Have you tracked the murderer down, and punished him with your own true hand?"

"Who are these?" asked the hunter, looking on the two strangers fiercely, without answering her question.

"I do not know—they are strangers who came soon after you went away," she answered. "I have not asked."

"I will," said he, abruptly. And turning full on the elder man, he asked:"Who and what are you?"

"You question rather rudely; nevertheless, you shall be answered," said the stranger. "My name is Norcross, that is my son Rupert. We belong to an exploring party from the States, camped a short ways down the mountain, and conceive we have as good a right to roam through these wilds as any other men."

"Ay, if you do no wrong to others," said the hunter, looking first from one to the other of the men as if he would strive to read them through and through.

"Have you looked on him?" he asked, speaking to the elder, and pointing to the dead.

"Yes."

"And have you also gazed upon that body?" he asked of the younger.

"I have," responded the young man, and his eye firmly and fearlessly met the glance of the questioner.

"And it did not *bleed?*" asked Cale Durg.

"It did *not* bleed!" said the elder, and his voice had a tinge of sarcastic mockery in it. "Surely, you are not going to charge us with murder!" he added.

"No—not without proof," said the hunter, and his eye again scanned that cold, haughty face closely.

"The trail—you were on it!" said the girl. "Did you lose it?"

"Yes. The murderer was cunning. He went but a little way before he took to the water to hide his tracks. I could not find where he left the water."

"There was but one, you say?" asked the old man.

"But one whom I could track," said the hunter.

"And we are two; have hunted in company all the day," said Norcross the elder, quickly.

The eyes of the young man were cast down when his father said this, but a nervous spasm made his slender form quiver. It was noticed by the girl! A strange suspicion began to creep over her mind. While she felt prepossessed with the appearance of the young man, an aversion fast growing into a horror for the father grew upon her.

"There was but the track of one. That one has left something by which I'll trace him yet," said Cale Durg.

"What was it?" asked the elder Norcross.

"That is my business, stranger. I'm on the hunt for that murderer, and when I find him—"

"Well, what then?"Again it was the senior Norcross who spoke.

"With my hand upon his shoulder I'll lead him to her for his punishment!" said the hunter, fiercely, pointing to the girl.

"And I will show that murderer less mercy than the she bear would show to the slayer of its young!" said the girl, all as fiercely as the hunter spoke.

A strange look, it was not a sarcastic smile, but very like one, passed over the face of Mr. Norcross.

"Father," said his son, "if we can be of no service here, let us return to the camp. If our absence is prolonged, we will cause anxiety there."

"We can aid in burying the dead—that is, if it is desired," said the father, throwing an inquiring look upon the young girl.

"I have old and tried friends to aid in the last offices to him!" said the girl.

As she spoke she looked gratefully on Cale Durg and Mad Eagle.

"Then, Rupert, we will go," said the senior Norcross.

"Hold, stranger!" said Cale Durg, suddenly. "Where is the camp of which you have spoken?"

"On the stream that dashes on to our right—just below a large cataract, a fall over which no boat could pass without wreck and death to any in it," said the old man.

"I *thought* your camp was there. I'll not bid you good-by as you go, for we shall meet again, and soon."

"I care not *how* soon!" said the old man, looking sternly from his dark, wild eyes. "I am not given to avoiding—friend or foe. Lady, adieu—should it ever be in the power of myself or son to serve you, it will be to us a pleasure to render service where 'tis needed."

The son did not speak, but he bowed low and almost reverentially.

Then he turned away and followed his father down the trail.

Once only did he look back. He saw the Indian and Cale Durg watching their retreating steps, but she whom he looked back to see was not in sight.

He kept on till the log-cabin could not be seen, until they were in an open space where no one could lurk within hearing distance. Then he, called upon the father to stop.

"Sir!" said he, "before I go one yard farther in your company, I must know whether I am, or am not, walking with a murderer!"

CHAPTER III.
Hazel-Eye's Thanks.

When the two strangers had passed from view, Cale Durg and Mad Eagle returned into the cabin, where the girl stood in a dreamy, thoughtful way, appearing to ponder over some memory.

Cale Durg stood a moment in silence, and then said to the girl: "Were you ever in the saltpeter-cave, Hazel-Eye?"

"Yes," she answered. "Our line of sable traps runs close by it. I went in there once with father. He showed me the petrified lizards and the deer which had turned to stone."

"Will you let us bear your father's body there? I don't like to put it under-ground, and we may want to see it by and by. It will not rot there, as it would underground."

"Oh, thank you, thank you, good Cale Durg, for the thought. It is a comfort to me, in this dark and terrible hour, to think he will not go to dust. Do as you will!"

"Then it shall be so. Mad Eagle will help me. We will place the brave trapper there in his best dress, with his weapons by his side.

"Good! Then he ready for the happy hunting-grounds!" said the Indian, pleased with the idea.

CHAPTER IV.
On the Alert.

An encampment of twenty tents made a lively scene below the rapids of the beau-tiful Yellowstone, for some seventy or eighty people, with the animals for a pack-train, as well as their own riding-horses, were scattered about in the lovely valley which spread out between the picturesque hills of the region.

One tent was larger than the rest, and in front of this a cheerful camp-fire threw up a ruddy blaze.

Seated, on a camp-stool, near this fire, was a portly, red-faced man of rather more than middle-age, while grouped about him stood several others, middle-aged and young men, whose superior style of dress, as well as the handsome weap-ons in their hands and belts, signified them to be the upper men, or superiors of the party. The pack-men, guides, and hunters, dressed more roughly, could be seen about other fires, and engaged in various ways.

"Any new specimens to-day, doctor, to garnish the glorious scientific record of our expedition?" asked a young man of the portly, red-faced man whom we just alluded to.

"Nothing," said the doctor, with a sigh. "The unlucky sprain I got in my ankle yesterday has kept me in from my usual wanderings!"

"It may be a lucky instead of an unlucky sprain, doctor," said a military-looking man, who approached the group at that moment. "Garnier, the guide and interpreter, tells me the Black-Feet are assuming a very hostile attitude toward us. They have called a council, and he thinks they mean to talk war. I have forbidden any more hunters going out singly, for we cannot afford to lose a single man so far away from a chance for help!"

"War, eh, major? Then my surgery, which has had no opportunity for practice as yet, will come to play. My instruments are all in order. I have time to oil them now."

"And I suppose you itch for a chance to use them, doctor. I hope I shall not become a subject."

"You'd make a good one, major. Spare in frame and plenty of muscle. No fat to bother one, you see. But where is Norcross? I have not seen him to-day."

"He and his son went out early, to prospect for minerals and hunt for game. I feel anxious for their return, since hearing this news about the Indians. I have sent Garnier, and a couple more old hunters, in search of him, to warn him there is danger in the forest. Well, Morgan, what now?"

A hunter approached and saluted the major, who then waited for what he had to say.

"There's somethin' hot brewin' among the reds, sir. Do you see them four straight columns of smoke on the big hill away to the south'ard, sir?"

"Ay. You are used to their signs. What does it mean?"

"It is a signal for a general gatherin' sir; the warriors are warned to rally from the four quarters of the wind, to their place of council."

"Then we must be on the alert. The object of our expedition is not half accomplished; in truth our explorations are only fairly entered on. We will not be driven from our purpose, if it be possible to maintain it. Let the animals be brought into a closer range and the guard doubled. Reiterate the orders that no hunters go out without my consent. I wish Captain Norcross were back."

"He is coming in, sir—I saw him descending the trail near the main waterfall as I rode down from our lookout-station just now."

"His son was with him, I suppose?"

"No, sir—he was alone."

"Strange, very strange! And, Garnier, with those I sent with him, were they not in company?"

"No, sir; nor in sight."

"Most singular! I fear hostilities have already commenced. Was he on foot?"

"Yes, sir; as he went out. He seldom rides, except when on the march."

"He didn't walk as if he were wounded, did he?" asked the doctor, eagerly.

"No, sir, I could see no sign of that."

"What a pity!" sighed the doctor.

"Be comforted, my dear Bugle, there is something the matter with Norcross!" cried the major. "Here he comes, with his face as white as a sheet!"

CHAPTER V.

"This From You?"

"A murderer, Rupert Norcross! Do you dare to charge me, your father, with murder?"

The old man, or rather the elder Norcross, for he might not be properly called an old man while yet in life's full vigor, eyed his son sternly as he spoke.

The latter did not shrink from his gaze, or quail under the angry tone of interrogation.

"Where is the knife which belongs in that scabbard!" asked Rupert Norcross, pointing to the empty sheath in his father's belt.

"I lost it to-day," said the elder, without the slightest hesitation or confusion.

"Yes, sir, and the hunter, whom, the Indian called Red Panther, found it—you heard him say where!"

"Rupert, I am not inclined to bend down in humility, even to my son, to make explanations. But this I will say: The knife which the hunter picked up was not mine."

"Father, have I not seen and examined it a thousand times? Its peculiar mark; the sword crossed with the olive branch, indicative, as you have told me of the legend, 'war or peace, ready for either,' has been commented on by me time and time again. There is no other knife like it, and it, blood-stained, was picked up where that man received his death-blow!"

"It was not my knife!" said the father, firmly.

"And you said to that hunter that we two had been together on the hunt all day, when you know we took different routes above the cateract and were apart full three hours, and only met a little while before we found the trail leading to the cabin. And not ten minutes before we met I heard the report of a rifle. You told me you had fired and wounded an elk, which escaped you and fell into the river as you were about to cut its throat."

"I told the truth in that. I saw that an unjust suspicion might fall on us, and when the hunter said he had seen but one track, I hastily said what I did to throw that suspicion off."

"Yes, sir; and told a falsehood, which I dared not, for your sake, contradict. Oh, my father! it is hard, it is crushing, to think that one whom I have loved and honored so long should be—must I speak it—should be a murderer!"

"Rupert! This from you?"

"Yes, Sir—this from me. And now farewell! Henceforth our paths lie far apart. What can have induced you to slay that man, to make that fair girl an orphan, and leave her unprotected in these fearful wilds, it is not for me to judge!"

"She will not be unprotected while she has you for a champion!" said the father with a little sneer, his passion mastering his hitherto restraint.

"Enough, sir; we will not bandy words. Farewell, and forever!"

The young man turned abruptly from the trail and walked off toward the bank of the rushing river, which could be heard in the distance.

"Rupert! Rupert!" cried the father, while his white face wore a look of agony.

The young man did not heed the cry, but walked hurriedly on.

"Rupert—Rupert, come back and hear me! I will explain!"

There was agony in the tone of that stern man, but if it even reached the ears of the son, one hundred yards away, he did not turn.

"Oh, Heaven, what shall I do? He believes me guilty of that crime! He thinks my hand sent Guy Mauricenne to death!" moaned the father, and he clasped his hand upon his brow as if to keep the hot blood of misery down which swelled every vein almost to bursting. "He will not leave me. Oh, no! he will come back!"

And Mr. Norcross staggered on down the trail, weak from excitement and overwrought feeling. He went a little way, and then turned back, saying: "I will follow him and humble myself to an explanation!"

Sternly, with no fixed purpose in his mind, Rupert Norcross had turned away from his father's side. He believed him guilty of murder, he knew him to be guilty of falsehood.

High-souled and noble in his every principle, he turned in horror even from his parent. He could not become his accuser, but he would not remain in his company. To do so, and to be silent, would make him an accessory after the act, to a cruel murder.

What could he do? He wandered on, he knew not, cared not whither he went, until the river rushing through a gorge foamed and thundered far below him.

He stood on the cliff which overhung the waters and gazed into the rushing current while many a wild, mad thought ran through his half-frenzied brain.

Perhaps he thought of suicide, for such thoughts more often enter into the minds of soulful, noble thinking men, who shrink from the world's impurities, its wrongs and its censures, than into the minds of worldly, sordid, or selfish persons. He paused here, and lifted the felt hat from his hot brow, that the fresh air which rushed down the gorge might cool the fever of his brain.

As he thus stood, he heard a shriek, a shrill cry from a woman's voice, as if one in deadly peril cried for help.

It sounded far away up the stream, where huge rocks interspersed with trees, bounded his view. Not even waiting to lift the hat which he had laid upon a mossy rock, or to grasp the rifle which he had rested against the same rock, he rushed in the direction from which the sound came.

And as he ran he heard the scream again, but it seemed even more distant than at first, though still so distinct he could not mistake its import.

He was scarcely hidden from the spot where his rifle and his hat were left, when the elder Norcross came hurriedly on, following the tracks the son had made here and there where the sand was laying amid the rocks.

On, on came the father to the river's verge, and there his eyes fell upon the hat and rifle where they lay upon the rock.

"Oh, Heaven!" he groaned, as he looked at them, and from them into the river far below. "Oh, Heaven! Now I am a murderer!" and he staggered back, horror-stricken, from the place, then turned and fled from the spot.

CHAPTER VI.

Rescued.

Rupert Norcross rushed swiftly on among the rocks and trees in the direction from whence the shrieks came, and though for several minutes he did not again hear them, he rode on, looking for some sign of her whose lips had uttered them.

He saw nothing, and the thought came upon him that he had heard some animal, and in his excitement fancied that it was the scream of a woman in distress.

He paused to listen, and then he heard, and the voice seemed very near, a man in a harsh, brutal tone cry out:

"Keep still, now, or I'll stop your breath forever. I mean no harm to you, what I'm doin' is cording to orders, and so you've got to come along. Say you'll be still, nod your head to that effect, and I'll take my hand from your mouth."

Rupert did not pause a second longer. Springing lightly forward, over a mossy platform, he burst through a thicket of nut pine, and saw a tall, brawny man, dressed as a hunter, with a female form in his grasp.

The man turned as he heard the dash of Rupert's form through the bushes, and received a well-directed stunning blow fairly in the face, from the clenched hand of the young man, which forced him to loose his hold upon the female.

Again her scream rang wildly out on the air, and a sharp, fierce bark as from a hound bounding through the forest, reached the ears of Rupert as well as herself.

With a bitter curse breathing from his lips, the ruffian rushed away in the direction of the river, while the female turned with grateful looks and words to thank him who had come thus timely to her rescue.

To his astonishment, we will not say gratification, Rupert Norcross saw that it was the trapper's daughter, the girl whom he believed his father's hand had made an orphan.

"Lady, I know not by what name to address you, for the name, Hazel-Eye, which I have heard used, was more descriptive of your eyes, than a stranger might dare to use. I thank Heaven that I was where your cry for help reached my ear, and that I was enabled to overtake the ruffian as I did. I would follow to punish him, but he may have companions near, and you would still be in peril."

"I thank you, sir, for your timely aid. Had you not come, I shudder to think what might have become of me. For once, in my deep sorrow, I wandered away from the cabin where you saw me without the arms I generally carry, and left my faithful Rollo with his dead master and two friends who were preparing to bear him to his grave. I had come down here to a spot where I often used to linger near the water, when the ruffian whom you drove away sprang upon me and bore me struggling to this spot. Here, tired of my struggles and alarmed by my screams, he set me on my feet, and stifled voice and almost breath with his hand. You know the rest, and there comes Rollo—my faithful, brave Rollo!"

The eyes of the great blood-hound gleamed like fire as it came bounding on, but they softened when the animal saw by the looks and attitude of his mistress that Rupert was not her enemy.

"Now, if you please, I will try to follow that wretch," said Rupert.

"No, no, sir; I will not permit you to imperil yourself further for me. Again accept my thanks. Were mine other than a house of sorrow, with my poor father yet unburied, I would ask you to accept its hospitality; but—"

"Kind lady, I would not intrude upon you. It has been Heaven's favor which has granted me the opportunity to serve you thus slightly, and I will only ask to be permitted to see you in safety within sight of your home, and then I will go— Heaven only knows where!"

"Why, have you not a father and friends in the camp not far away?"

"Lady, I have parted with my father in anger and forever. The friends who are in that camp will see me no more!"

They were walking on as Rupert said this, in a tone both sad and earnest.

"Heavens! you will not remain alone here in this wilderness land! The Indians are savage and hostile—you will surely perish!" said the lady.

"It matters but little. I have this day received a shock which leaves my life of little value!"

"Am I connected with it?"

"No, lady, no; yet to you more than all others must I refuse explanation. Farewell! May Heaven bless and guard you!"

The cabin was in sight as he spoke these words, and he turned to hurry away.

"Stay, kind stranger!" the young girl cried. "Stay one moment, and hear me. I may not bid you find a home under the roof where I have lived so long, but there is one who will for my sake shelter and protect you—do more for you than any other man can in all the North-west. I mean Cale Durg, whom the Indians have named Red Panther. He has cabins and trapping shelters all through the mountains. If you come to my cabin I will ask him to receive you as a companion and friend until you choose to return to the settlements."

"You are most kind, fair lady, and thankfully I will accept your commendation to the brave man. A true soul looks out from his clear and fearless eye. I honor a brave, true man, no matter what may be his condition in life. If he will join me here in half an hour I will meet him."

"Why will you not go on with me?" she asked, in an almost reproachful tone.

"Because I must return down the river nearly a mile to get my hat and rifle. When I heard you scream, I sprang forward, forgetful of them. They are on a rock by which I stood to cool my wild brain and reflect on what course to pursue after leaving my father."

"I will tell him to meet you here," she said, observing what she had not noticed before, that he was bare-headed and without his rifle.

The young man bowed low and reverently, and turned off down the stream while she hurried on toward the cabin, where Cale Durg and the Indian stood gazing in surprise at the re-appearance of the young stranger, in her company.

She noticed the look of that tall hunter and a flush darkened her cheek that he should by a look imply that her course was wrong, especially at that hour.

"Cale Durg, you have been too good a friend to my father these long, long years, to look coldly now on his child," she said, warmly.

"Hazel-Eye, if you knew how strongly my suspicions have bent toward one of those strangers, the elder of the two, as the *murderer* of your father, you would not be seen in the company of the younger, speaking as if you and he were friends, before your father's body is out of sight."

"Had it not been for that young stranger, I would now be helpless and at the mercy of a ruffian who had me in his power. I owe most likely life and honor to him whom you condemn," she answered.

"I am in the dark as to what you mean, Hazel-Eye."

"Then I will explain."And she told of the perilous adventure through which she had passed, just as it occurred.

"Was this a white man?" asked Cale Durg.

"Yes, a tall, fierce-looking wretch."

"And the young man did not know him?"

"No—he did not appear to."

"Then he did not belong to his camp. I've seen strange tracks in the hills lately. I'll hunt this chap up after we've laid your father in his resting-place."

"And you will do me a favor, good Cale Durg?"

"What is it, Hazel-Eye? I never do anything with my eyes shut!"

"It is this. That young man has quarreled with his father. He says he will not see him any more, neither will he return to the camp where the rest of his friends are. You know, as well as I, what will be his fate if he is left alone and friendless in these wilds. It is not proper for me to give him shelter here. But you can take him with you and protect him till he can return to the settlement from whence he came. Do this for my sake, Cale Durg."

"I will talk to him," said the hunter, after a thoughtful pause. "If he speaks the truth and tells a straight story, I will be his friend. I think I know why he has left his father. I read truth in *his* eyes, and that was more than I saw on the face of his father. I will see him and hear what he has to say."

"Pale-faces talk with forked tongues," said the Indian, gravely. "Mad Eagle hates the pale-faces. Since Trapper Guy has gone to the happy hunting-grounds, there are but two pale-faces with whom Mad Eagle will clasp hands. One is Hazel-Eye, the other Red Panther."

"We'll see—we'll see," said Cale Durg. "The young stranger may have a white heart. He does not look down when he speaks to you. His eyes take a clear sight over the barrel of his thoughts when he shoots out the few words he speaks. He isn't given to much talk either, and that is a good sign."

"I am glad you seem disposed in his favor," said Hazel-Eye, "for I believe he is worthy of your confidence."

"Hazel-Eye is young. Her heart speaks before her head thinks," said Mad Eagle.

"Ay—'tis the way with the young and innocent, and we old cusses mustn't blame 'em, Mad Eagle," said the hunter. "The Great Spirit makes their hearts like clean snow and a touch marks it. It is only when rain, and sleet, and dust, and cold make it dark and hard, you can make no mark there. So when our hearts are old, and hard, and dark with trouble or with crime, you look on our faces and see no sign, no matter what we think or feel. But come—we will do our work, and then I will meet this stranger and talk with him."

CHAPTER VII.
Under Guard.

Captain Norcross was indeed ghastly white in his face when he approached the group in front of the camp headquarters. His eyes looked wild, his expression more that of a maniac than a sane man.

"What is the matter, captain? Has anything happened to your son?" cried Major Whelpley.

"I never expect to see him again, sir, in this world! Ask me no questions now—I am not fit to answer them!"

And he passed into the tent.

Captain Norcross remained inside of the tent only a few moments, and when he came out his face was flushed. Its ghastly pallor was gone. He had been taking a fiery draught of liquor to settle his nervousness, which even yet he could not conceal.

"You asked me where my son was?" he said, as he walked up to Major Whelpley. "I should have told you at once, but I was overcome with horror. My soul was wild with agony. For I fear he has committed suicide. We had some words on a trivial subject—I spoke harshly to him, and he left me angry. His nerves are fine strung—he was ever too sensitive for an everyday world like this. Struck by the wild manner of his looks as he rushed away, I followed him. Close by the edge of the cliff, overhanging the river, I found his hat and rifle on a rock. But he was nowhere in sight. I called his name and listened for a reply in vain. The ground was too hard to leave a track, but I have no doubt he threw himself in the river. Now, sir, you may not wonder that I passed you without a proper answer."

"Captain Norcross, I feel deeply for you, if your son is indeed lost, and in the way you mention, for it would be doubly hard to think he met death in that way. He was steady, brave, and ever ready for duty."

Then turning to Garnier, who had returned, he said: "As you are already mounted, and it is but a short ride, I wish you would go and get my son's hat and rifle. You see yonder peak where an umbrella-shaped tree stands out prominently? The rock where I saw them is just below the peak. And, my good Garnier, take a careful survey of the ground in the vicinity—he may have wandered off, leaving the articles there. You are better on a trail than I, and my eyes are dimmed with the clouds of trouble."

"I'll go, sir, for Master Rupert is as fine a man as ever drew a rifle up. We all like him. Come, boys—we who are mounted will soon attend to this duty!"

The hunter wheeled his horse and rode away with his companions, while Major Whelpley, to distract the mind of the captain from his trouble, exhibited to him some mineral specimens in his hand, and told him of a discovery made by Garnier and his party.

The captain, however, took little interest either in the news or the specimens, though he remarked that they were rich in comparison to others he had seen.

In a short time Gamier was seen riding in with his companions.

The face of the former was very grave, and it wore a strange look as he glanced at the captain, who looked eagerly for what information he could give.

"Where are the articles I sent for—the rifle and the hat?" cried the captain, not seeing them in Garnier's hands.

"We could find none, though we found the rock you spoke of. But we saw something else a few hundred yards down the river, sir—something very singular."

"What was it? Make your report at once, sir!" cried the major.

"We saw evidences of a bloody struggle, sir—the grass and shrubs torn up, and the ground stained with blood! It was near the water, and though this struggle was on soft-ground, leaving plain marks there, the ground near by was hard, and the tracks were lost."

The major looked earnestly at the captain, as if he would read in his face whether he knew ought of what had occurred at the spot described.

The latter did not notice the look, but he said to Gamier: "If you had followed a trail which led due west up the stream into the hills, you would have found the body of one of the men engaged in the struggle, in a cabin at the foot of a tall cliff, for I saw it there!"

"Was it the body of your son?" asked the major, sternly.

"No, sir; my son was with me, alive and well, when I saw it," said the captain. "You can easily satisfy yourself by riding to the cabin which I have spoken of. The murdered man was a trapper, living in that cabin with his daughter."

"Do you know who the murdered man was, as you say the trapper was murdered?" asked the major, still eying the captain closely.

The latter was about to make an angry reply, and his face was dark with passion; but with an effort he seemed to check himself, and said: "As I did not see the struggle, and only heard what the daughter of the dead trapper said her dying father told her, I have no information to give in the matter."

"Where is your knife, Captain Norcross?" asked the major, glancing at the empty scabbard in the captain's belt.

"I wounded an elk with my rifle; it fell close by the brink of the river, and I ran up to cut its throat. As I drove the knife into the animal, it made a sudden plunge forward into the river, carrying the knife with it as the current swept away."

"Strange! Was your son with you then?"

The captain sprang back as if a serpent had bitten him, for the man who asked this question was Cale Durg, who had come into the camp so quickly and so still that no one noticed him till he spoke.

"Begone! You have no right to question me!" said the captain, angrily.

"I shall take the right," said Cale Durg, coolly. "Trapper Guy was my friend. His orphan child is as dear to me as if she were my own daughter; and, if I knew you were the murderer, I would lead you into her presence, and then hang on like a dog. You have told more than one falsehood to-day—"

"Villain, by the foul fiends I shall not stand this! I'll send you to the doom your friend has met."

The captain drew a revolver as he spoke, and, as scarce a yard in distance separated him and the bold hunter, the fate of the latter seemed certain.

But Cale Durg, before any one else could interfere, seized the up-raised hand, and shook the weapon from the grasp of its angry owner.

"Keep your shootin' irons down for the present. When it is time, if you want to use 'em, I'll not balk you, but give shot for shot, and Heaven help the innocent. Now while I hold your wrist, I will have an answer to one question. Before I ask it, I will tell you where you have told two lies. First, at the cabin, you said before me, and Hazel-Eye, and Mad Eagle, that you and your son had not separated from the time you left this camp until you reached the cabin. That was a lie—I can prove it! He was not with you when you fired your, rifle, you say, at an elk!"

"That is true—he was not!" gasped the captain, trembling from head to foot.

"Good! One lie acknowledged. Now for the second. A knife, with a silver hilt, in the shape of a cross, with a sword crossing an olive branch engraved on that hilt, was found where Trapper Guy received his death-wound!"

"It was not mine—it was not mine!" cried the captain, trembling from head to foot.

"That knife is here!" continued Cale Durg, and he drew the weapon, still red with blood and without a scabbard, from beneath his hunting-shirt.

"It is his knife—I have seen it too often to be mistaken!" cried Major Whelpley, drawing back in horror, as did the other men; for they looked upon Captain Norcross now as a murderer, and perhaps the slayer of his own son.

"As God is the Judge of all, I never used that knife, and I am guiltless of murder, unless my harsh words drove my poor son to destruction!" groaned the captain.

"You said you lost that knife in the body of an elk, which leaped into the river," said the major.

"Yes; and my finding the knife which you all know to be his where Trapper Guy received his death-wound carries this lie home to him," said the hunter. "You may as well own up."

"I have nothing to own. I have not seen the man whom you call Trapper Guy for years until I saw him dead in his cabin."

"Then you have seen him before? Ay—and you are the enemy who drove him to the wilderness, as I have heard him say an enemy did. You are the enemy who has followed him even here, and killed him at last," cried Durg.

"No—no—as Heaven is the hope of the good—no! I have never been his enemy, and had no hand in his death!"

"Captain Norcross, it is painful for me to say it, but every circumstance is against you!" said Major Whelpley. "Before a jury of common intelligence, without a clear alibi, you could never be acquitted of the charge of murder."

"Let him give me the key of the iron chest. In his dying breath Trapper Guy said the name of his murderer would be found there. Captain, if that's your title, hand over the key."

"I have no key—have not had any."

"It was torn from a string which Trapper Guy wore around his neck," continued the hunter. "He missed it when he was dying. And I've come for it!" he added—fiercely to the captain.

"I have it not—never had it!"

"Then why did you eye the chest so closely when you were in the cabin?"

"Because I thought then, and still think, I had seen it before."

"The whole matter darkens," said the hunter. "Will you promise to keep this man in charge until to-morrow?" he asked, addressing the major. "I've got a little job to do yet to-night, and I'll look up more proof maybe in the morning, for I'm going over all the trail again then, with an Indian who can read tracks better than a white man can read books. There's one thing staggers me all the while, and that's in favor of the captain. Trapper Guy and the one he fought with wore moccasins— and this man wears boots!"

"True," said the major. "I never saw moccasins on his feet, and I have known him for years. But he shall be kept under guard till morning."

"Thankee, major. I'm rough, but I try to keep about right, so as to be ready to go when my time comes."

The tall hunter turned, and merely saying he would be there again when the sun was an hour high; walked rapidly off toward the hills.

"Captain, it pains me, but my word is given, and I must put you under guard," said the major.

"Guard, or no guard, I will not leave the tent, sir," said the captain, mournfully. "Unless my son returns, life is of no value to me, though I am innocent of shedding human blood. I knew that man, Guy Mauricenne, many, many years ago, when he was wedded to one of the loveliest women I ever saw. Some dark misfortune fell on him when I was away on a Southern journey, and when I returned I heard that his wife was dead, and he had fled to avoid the penalty of some crime. It is long since, and I do not remember the particulars."

"It matters not. Retire to your quarters now."

CHAPTER VIII.

Giving an Alarm.

"Well, my good Cale Durg, what have you done?"

It was Hazel-Eye who asked this question, as the tall hunter entered the cabin where she sat alone in front of a fire which burned on the stone hearth.

He entered without knocking, for there is little ceremony used in the wilderness or beyond the border. "I have given Rupert Norcross a shelter in my cabin. He talks like a man. He left his father because he believed that he had done murder. I believe it, too. Yet I am bothered. The son says his father never wore a moccasin to his knowledge—surely did not wear any to-day. The man with whom your father quarreled did wear moccasins. In a dozen places, the mark of both men's feet are deeply indented in the sand. And I never saw a guilty man so firm in eye and voice as he is, while he says he is innocent."

"Then you have seen the father?"

"Yes; I confronted him with the knife, which was recognized by all his comrades as his own. There it is. Keep it, girl, till this deed is proved. If I were you I would keep it always. He did not claim it—he denied that it was his, and told a strange tale about sticking his knife into a wounded elk which leaped into the river, carrying it away. But that tale flashed in the pan when I showed the knife and told where I got it."

"What is to be done in the matter?"

"Nothing until to-morrow. He—this Captain Norcross—is under guard, and will be kept so till we know sure whether he is guilty or not. If he is, he swings. That is sworn to."

"I am sorry for his son. He has a noble look, and I know he is brave."

"Ay; but looks lie sometimes. We can't trust anything that comes of bad stock. I'll have an eye to the youngster. If he proves fair, well and good. If he doesn't he has a tough road to travel with nary a tree blazed to show him how to go. But good-night, Hazel-Eye—I must go to the cabin and take some rest, for I've got to be on the trail by daylight."

"Good-night, true friend—good-night."

Cale Durg shut the door as he passed out, and then the girl threw some fresh fuel on the fire, and with a sigh entered the inner room where her neatly curtained bed was placed.

"I cannot sleep; but I, too, must rest," she murmured, and without disrobing, she threw herself upon the bed. "There is no danger, for Rollo is on watch."

Weariness will still the senses, even if the mind is in agony, sometimes, and in this case, though the orphaned girl did not feel as if she could sleep, her eyes soon closed, and she was wrapped in an uneasy slumber.

From it, how long after, she did not know, she was startled by what seemed to her to be the cry of the hound—Rollo.

She was about to spring to her feet, when, with a fearful tremor at her heart, she checked the impulse, for she saw between her and the fire the form of Captain Norcross—not dressed as he had been when there before, but clad in buckskin from head to foot, like the hunters of the region.

She was sure it was he, for the same dark, piercing eyes, the haughty, pale face, the straight, manly form, were unmistakable.

He did not glance even toward her, but moved swiftly across the front apartment to the corner where the iron chest stood. On that chest she had laid the blood-stained knife.

The captain seemed to give an exultant chuckle when he saw the knife, and he instantly took it up and put it into the empty scabbard at his belt. Then he bent over the iron chest, and she heard him say:

"The records are here, and at last, at last they are mine!"

He thrust his hand into a pouch by his side, as if in search of something, then an oath broke from his lips.

"I've either lost the key, or left it behind. The plates are triple, I must have the key. I will have to come again. Ah, the girl?"

It did not seem as if he had seen her until then, and now, when she knew his dark eyes were on her, every power in her seemed to die. She could not move—even if a cry would bring her help, she could not have uttered it.

"She sleeps," said the captain. "Much as I hate him, I cannot harm her. It will be enough that I take all she has, leave her in poverty here. She sleeps and she may live. I will go and look for the key, and then return. How like her mother was she now is!"

While he thus soliloquized, though her own eyes were closed, she felt that his gaze was upon her, and had she been able, she dared not move. Not that she was cowardly. Her life spent in the perilous region where we find her, made her naturally brave. She was skilled through her father's teachings in the use of arms, used to all the perils and excitements of a trapping life, but at that moment a spell seemed to bind every energy.

Yet until the last moment she had watched his every action, and when she closed her eyes she heard each step of his feet, each muttered word that fell from his lips.

Not until he had left the cabin, and she heard the door softly closed, did the power of motion come back to her.

Then she sprang to her feet, wondering what had become of the dog upon whose watch she depended for protection thinking it strange that after making the alarm which woke her, he did not fight the intruder off.

Seizing a revolver in her hand, one of the largest kind, she stepped toward the threshold and, first listening to hear if any one yet lingered near, then opened the door.

The first thing she saw was the noble hound, stretched, as she supposed, in death, before the door, for its head seemed to be cloven open with a sharp weapon.

"Cale Durg's cabin is within hearing of this," she said, and quickly the girl fired three shots in the air.

CHAPTER IX.
Waiting.

The three shots fired by Hazel-Eye rang out sharp and clear on the still night air, and, as this had been an established signal between her father and Cale Durg, she felt sure the latter would hasten to the cabin if he heard it. When her last shot was fired there were yet three loads in the revolver, so if Captain Norcross returned and was alone, the brave girl felt herself fully a match for him.

A whining moan from the poor dog, Rollo, now attracted her attention, and, hastening in for a lamp, she returned and found the animal, though fearfully gashed in the head with some sharp instrument, was not fatally injured.

With a cry of joy she dragged the hound in on the cabin floor, and proceeded to wash away the clotting blood and to dress the wound, while the animal, with a feeble light in its almost human eyes, regarded her gratefully as she labored.

"Airthquakes and hurricanes! What's up, Hazel-Eye?" came from one whom she was but too glad to recognize, a few minutes later, and, raising her eyes, she saw not only Cale Durg, but young Rupert Norcross standing in the door-way. "Who hurt the dog? Speak quick, gal! Has that chap whom our friend knocked over been here? Have you shot any one?"

"No, no. I could not have shot *him!*" she said, and she glanced at Rupert Norcross when she spoke.

"*Him?* You mean our friend here? Why, him and me were sittin' cozy over the fire, smokin' kinnikinic and spinning tongue tackling, when we heard you fire."

"It was not him that I alluded to. But for *his* sake, had I been prepared, I would not have shot the one who was here," said Hazel-Eye, earnestly.

"For Heaven's sake, lady, tell me who was here! I dread the worst! Was it *my* father?"

"It was—the elderly man who was here with you this morning."

"By all that is wicked, this is fearful! I will go to the camp this instant, and myself bring him to account!"

"No, no! We can do better than that," said Cale Durg. "He evidently thinks you have committed suicide—jumped off the cliff into the river. Let him think so. I will go to the camp in the morning, and see what is best to be done. I think that the major who bosses the crowd is a square man."

"As true a man as ever wore steel!" said Rupert, warmly.

"As to the other—I don't like to talk, but I think he stole you when you were a baby. I don't believe you're his child. You don't seem of the same breed."

Rupert sighed. He could not, bad as he believed him to be, deny his father.

"You are *sure* it was my father, Robert Norcross, who hurt the dog, and who was here?" he asked, addressing Anna, or Hazel-Eye.

"Yes, sir. I saw him distinctly. He entered this room, crossed it quickly to the iron chest, took from it the knife which *you* found, Cale Durg, and placed it in the empty scabbard in his belt. Then he looked for the key, which he seemed to think he had in his hunting-pouch. He could not find it, and cursed bitterly because he could not. Talking to himself, he said he had lost it or left it behind; he would go look for it and return. Then he turned and saw me. I closed my eyes and pretended to sleep. In truth, I dared not stir. A palsying terror lay cold upon me. I thought he would murder me if I moved, and I lay still. I could not bear to die at his hands after you had saved me from death, or worse than death."

And the hazel eyes of the lovely girl beamed out such a grateful light that Rupert Norcross, even with his heart full of agony, trembled with an indefinable pleasure.

"So he has got his knife back again. I wonder how he'll account for his elk story now!" said Cale Durg, thoughtfully. Then he added: "I guess he took it only to throw it away and keep it out o' sight. But it is too late to do any good by that, for too many have seen the knife and recognized it, and taking it would hurt his case rather than to help it."

"True—true. If you please, fair lady, describe my father's dress, particularly."

"Hereafter, Mr. Norcross, please call me by the name my father always used—Anna—and I will."

"Thank you, Miss Anna, for the permission. Now please tell me, how he was dressed."

"In buckskin, fringed as hunters have it done, from head to foot. A buckskin hunting-shirt reaching nearly to the knee, and leggins of the same. Moccasins, plain and high, and a cap of black sable fur, which lay close down on his white forehead."

"My father bought such a suit from a trader when we crossed the borders, excepting only the moccasins. The pair he bought was beaded and low quartered. But I have never seen him put the dress on."

"He said he would look for the key and return, you say, Hazel-Eye?" said Cale Durg, at this moment.

"Yes; he said this in soliloquy, while bending over the chest."

"Then go you to bed in your room, and get some sleep. Drop your curtain, and we two will keep watch here until it is light. Then I must go with Mad Eagle, who is to meet me to study out the trail, and look to the trail of the chap that laid hands on you when our friend here interfered to save you. No words, but go in, my good gal, as I bid ye."

Hazel-Eye smiled sadly and bowed a gentle good-night. Then taking a lamp with her, she let the thick curtain of canvas fall, and she was hidden from their view.

"Lie you down before the fire, Rupert, and sleep. I'm used to watchin'," said the hunter. "I'll sit up."

"Were I to lie down I could not sleep," said Rupert. "My mind is all ajar with excitement. I have too much to think of to feel sleepy."

"Well, as you will. We can light our pipes, but we've got to keep still or he'd hear us if he indeed returns. I hardly think he will. He must have heard the firing signal as well as we. If so, he will know his presence or his departure was discovered and help had been called for."

"True; we will smoke and wait."

CHAPTER X.
Again Puzzled.

"You are on hand early, my friend," said Major Whelpley, as Cale Durg and the Indian, Mad Eagle, approached him where he sat before the camp-fire with a cup of coffee in hand.

"Yes, sir; when the gray of dawn lifted the weight of night we were on the trail, Mad Eagle and me. I've been bothered afore in studyin' out deviltry, but I'm more than usual out in this case. But where's the captain?"

"In the tent asleep. If he is guilty he sleeps well."

"Was he under guard last night, sir?"

"Yes; a sentinel, relieved every two hours, was on post in front of the tent all night."

"Yet Captain Norcross was out, and went to the cabin on the hill and took the knife away, which was one of the proofs of his guilt."

"Impossible!" exclaimed the major. "He sleeps within a yard of me, and if a mouse stirs I am sure to hear it. He disturbed me much with his sighs all the fore part of the night, so much so I could not sleep; but after a time be dropped into a slumber, and then I slept. When I woke, half an hour ago, he lay as quiet as a child."

"He must have been out. Hazel-Eye was too certain in her recognition to be mistaken," said the hunter.

"Hazel-Eye is too good to speak a lie," said Mad Eagle.

"Please explain, for I am in a mist as to what you two speak of," said the major.

"Why, it is as I say. The cap'n, all rigged up in a buckskin huntin' suit, was up to the cabin. He wanted to get into the iron chest, but had lost the key. He took the knife and went away, and the trapper's daughter, who saw him, made a signal, and I and a friend went there. We know she told the truth, for the hound, that was as good a watch as ever was set, had its head split open and was nearly killed by him."

"We'll go in and wake the captain and see what he says," said the major. "I cannot believe he could have risen and dressed without my waking. But we will see."

The major led the way into the tent. Captain Norcross, partially undressed, lay on a buffalo robe, with a blanket half drawn over his form. His face, wearing a sad but quiet look, gave no sign of unrest. His breathing was slow and regular. It was no simulated sleep which they looked upon.

"Captain, wake up. You have visitors," said the major, in a loud tone.

The captain turned, opened his eyes drowsily, but they brightened when he saw Cale Durg and the Indian.

"Have you got a buckskin suit, captain?" asked the major.

"Yes; one which I have never worn."

"Can I see it?"

"Certainly, sir; it is in that pack."

And the captain pointed to a package, securely bound as it had been when taken from the back of the pack-mule.

"It is with other goods I bought at the last trading-post we passed on the borders. I have never had occasion to open the pack."

The major looked at Cale Durg, and the latter seemed to be surprised.

The captain was as calm as possible, much more so than he was the night before. He did not notice the exchanged glances.

He was cutting the cords on the package, finding it difficult to untie the knots.

The package was opened, and from amid other goods which had not a crease broken, showing no stain, or mark, or any sign that it had even been tried on, a full suit of buckskin was taken by the captain.

"Have you no other suit than this?" asked the major.

"No, sir; it is the only suit of the kind that I ever owned."

"What do you think now?" asked the major, addressing Cale Durg.

"I'm cussed all of a heap if I know what to think. There isn't no knife there, and she said she saw him put the knife back in its scabbard."

The hunter was pointing to the empty sheath in the captain's belt which hung on the tent-pole.

"Bad spirit take up same shape and walk in the night!" said Mad Eagle, gravely, looking at the captain.

"The devil *must* have something to do with it!" said Cale Durg. "I don't know what to say or do. The trail from where that tussle of death took place is a plain moccasin track, and it is lost on the rocks by the river. There was a moccasin trail to and from the cabin made last night, and it too is lost on the hard rocks near the river. I'd have been glad to hang *him* for the murder yesterday, for I felt sure he did it. Now I'm not sure I don't know what to think."

"Wait and keep sharp eyes!" said Mad Eagle. "Great Spirit is good and wise. When He is ready He will, and we will know who killed Trapper Guy."

The Indian then turned on his heel, drew his buffalo robe about his stalwart form, and strode away without looking to the right or left.

Cale Durg said no more, but he walked swiftly off in the direction where Mad Eagle had halted to wait his coming.

CHAPTER XI.

"White Pine."

At the request of both Hazel-Eye and Cale Durg, Rupert Norcross consented to remain at the cabin on the hill, while the hunter and Mad Eagle paid their visit to the camp and examined the trails as they intended.

But soon after the breakfast which Hazel-Eye had prepared was eaten and cleared away, and the hunter and the chief had left, Rupert was surprised at seeing the young girl place a belt containing pistols and a knife around her waist, and take a short rifle in her hand.

"Are you going abroad, Miss Anna?" he asked, in astonishment.

"I am. The traps which my father set, and which together we have constantly attended, must now be seen to by me. I know where they are, and can soon run over the line. I ask you to remain, for it seems that there is something in that iron chest which is of value to others as well as to me. Until it can be opened and a knowledge of its contents gained, I am anxious it should be constantly guarded. My poor Rollo is hardly fit to watch it now, and I take the chance while you are kindly here to go to my traps."

"Of course I cannot oppose such reasoning, fair friend; but I would rather perform the duty for you—that is, if I understood it."

"Not being a trapper yet, you would not know how to set the traps, even if you could take the animals out. Have no fear for me. I am well armed and know how to use the weapons I carry. Do you see that fish-eagle on that limb? He is fully one hundred yards away. I intended to punish him before, for I saw him rob a little kingfisher that had caught a fish almost as big as itself yesterday."

She raised her rifle with the quickness of thought and fired. As she did so Rupert Norcross saw the bird drop from the limb to the ground so suddenly that it did not even flutter a wing.

"Go and examine it, if you please," she said, "while I load again. If the head was not pierced by my bullet I will give you my rifle."

Rupert gallantly went for the bird. He found that the bullet had pierced its head, and he felt no further doubt that when armed that brave and lovely girl was competent to protect herself.

She quickly reloaded her rifle, put a haversack of fresh meat for bait over her shoulder, and with a smiling good-by started on her errand.

It now occurred to Rupert to look at the iron chest, which had already been repeatedly brought under his notice. It was not very large, yet it seemed very strong, and could not have weighed less than two hundred pounds. It must have been worth much to have been transported thus far, over many a river and hill, into the interior. It bore no mark, no name, and yet it looked very old. It had been painted, but the paint was worn or rusted away, and it was all over one dingy hue.

"Would that she could get it open," he said, "for I would like to know if the name of Robert Norcross is on the record within. If so, the last doubt as to his being the murderer will be disposed of. The dying trapper told his daughter that his murderer's name was there. Ah! Cale Durg and the Indian come."

"Where's Hazel-Eye?" asked the hunter, finding Rupert alone.

"She went to look to her traps," said Rupert. "She asked me to remain till she returned, for she does not wish to leave that chest unguarded. But my father—did you see him?"

"Yes. He has never worn his buckskin suit. We saw it without a crease altered or a stain upon it."

"Yet she was certain she saw him here."

"It could not have been him, though someone was here. We found the trail to and from the cabin, but lost it on the rocks by the river-side. She must, in her excitement, have *fancied* that she recognized your father in the visitor. He never left the tent last night."

"The knife—has he got it? for it was taken hence. Of that she was sure."

"The scabbard in the belt of your father is still empty."

"What are we to think?"

"I don't know. If he hadn't told any falsehood, I would believe him innocent. But innocence never lies. Truth goes hand in hand with it. The story of the elk *might* be true, but it doesn't look so. But, as Mad Eagle says, all we can do is to wait and watch. The Great Spirit in His own good time will reveal guilt—ay, and punish it."

"Until I *know* my father to be innocent, I will never look upon his face."

"I don't blame you, young man. I like you for it, and, till you choose to leave it, my cabin is your home, and what I know of woodcraft, trappin', and huntin' you shall l'arn. That's the most I can say. And Mad Eagle here will be your friend."

"Mad Eagle hates pale-faces. But the hand which Red Panther draws to his heart shall not lie cold in the hand of Mad Eagle. He will look with a good face on the young chief, and he will give him a name, so his people shall know him when Mad Eagle tells them to pass him by if they go on the war-path."

"What shall it be?" asked Cale Durg.

"The White Pine, and let him always wear this, or a branch like it, in his cap," said the Indian, plucking a small branch from a pine tree close at hand and putting it in the front band of Rupert's cap.

The Indian said no more, but, turning on his heel, strode away.

"I'll go up the line and see how Hazel-Eye gets along. She's not been over it alone before, I'm thinkin'," said Cale Durg, and he passed on in the direction which the girl trapper had taken.

"White Pine! There is romance in the name, and somewhat of ornament in the emblem," said Rupert Norcross, as he took off his cap and glanced at the small branch of evergreen placed there; "and as it is to be a protective emblem from hostile red men, it has a double value in my eyes."

The young man now glanced at his own rifle, and, noticing that it was rusty about the lock, took from his pouch oil, rags, screw-driver, etc., and prepared to put it in order; for he had long since learned the necessity of taking care of his weapons and how to do it.

While thus engaged his attention was suddenly drawn by the sound of men talking. As he was inside the door and had not been seen, these men, whoever they were, approached carelessly, and his first thought was that they were from the camp he had left.

Rising, he looked out, but the first glance told him they were strangers to him, not from the company to which he had belonged. Neither were they prepossessing in looks. They were three in number, armed with rifles, knives, and revolvers.

CHAPTER XII.
"It Is He!"

When Cale Durg left the cabin, with his long, heavy rifle over his shoulder, he did not cast his glance down to look for the trail made by the light feet of Hazel-Eye. He knew the direction in which the line of traps ran, and also that he would find her somewhere on that line. So he strode swiftly on, his eye, hunter-like, glancing from side to side to catch a glimpse of game if any came within rifle range, or of an enemy, should one be near.

Here and there, as he went on, the hunter passed an animal which Hazel-Eye had taken from the trap and hung upon a branch as high as she could reach, where she might find it on her return, leaving the trap fresh baited as she went on.

Cale had gone a couple of miles at least, when he heard the sharp crack of her rifle not far away, and he smiled.

"The gal thinks Cale Durg will have enough to do without huntin' for her, and so drops game for herself," he muttered. "She is foolish. I'll hunt for her and care for her as if she was my own child just as long as I live. Ah! it isn't *game* she's shootin' at."

The last expression broke from his lips as the quick, successive reports of a revolver reached his ears, and the hunter rushed up the steep hill at the utmost speed he could make.

On, on he ran, for he heard not only the six shots of one revolver fired, but the remaining six of the second which he knew she carried; and when he heard the last shot of that he was near enough to see her.

Oh, Heaven! what a peril! And how grandly she was meeting it! A huge bear, one of those great gray monsters which *will* terrify the bravest hunter, evidently wounded, was reared on its hind legs and open-mouthed staggering in upon her, where she could not retreat, for a perpendicular wall of rock was behind her.

She did not look as if a thought of flight or even a sense of fear was in her mind. With her rifle clubbed she waited but a second, and as the bear came fairly into reach she brought its butt down upon the head of the animal with a force which shattered the stock, while it staggered the animal, though it did no more.

Again the barrel rose in her hand, and it came swiftly with all her might upon the head of the beast, which stretched out its huge paws to clasp her in a death-hug.

"Gal, I'm here!" shouted Cale Durg at this dread moment, and with a bound he reached the spot, the muzzle of his rifle against the monster's head.

He fired, and the girl stepped one side as the bear rolled forward in the quivering death-throe.

"What a bed her hide will make for Rollo!" exclaimed Hazel-Eye, as she pointed to the thick, shaggy fur of the monstrous beast.

"Cuss it, gal, what did ye run that risk for? You know what a she bear is when the cubs are around."

"Yes; I killed one because I wanted its hide for a mat. There it lies," she answered, pointing to it calmly. "I'm sorry I have spoiled my rifle; I'll have to use father's now, and it is much heavier."

"Nary a shake or a quiver! Gal, you're a notch ahead of all created humans!" said the surprised and yet delighted hunter. "The chap is a fool who thinks you can't take care of yourself. But you was gittin' into close quarters for one of your weight, wasn't you?"

"Yes, good Cale Durg, you came in the nick of time. I was just going to drop my rifle and use my knife, though, when you made it unnecessary."

"You're a queen, Hazel-Eye. Chaw me into rags and spit me out, if you aren't! I'll skin these critters, and we'll take the back track."

"Thanks for your help. You take the old one and I'll soon fix the cub," said the girl quietly, and she proceeded to work as artistically as he did.

In a short time the skins were taken and rolled up, and then, while Cale Durg shouldered them, Hazel-Eye took up her broken rifle, the skins of the animals she had so far taken from the traps on her return, and together the two retraced their steps.

As they had to stop at each trap, it took them some time to get over the route, and the sun was past its meridian when they again reached the cabin.

To their surprise Rupert Norcross was not there to meet and greet them.

A feeble, pitiful whine from the hound, which had dragged itself nearly to the door, told them something had occurred that was startling.

An overturned table, Rupert's rifle left on the floor as if it had been dropped or thrown down, and a broken chair, one of the rude home-made seats prepared by Guy the Trapper in his hours of leisure, gave signs of a struggle having taken place. And, outside the door lay his hat, with the pine branch still in it.

"He has met with foul play," were the first words spoken, and they were uttered by Cale Durg.

Hazel-Eye, pale as snow, almost breathless, stood and looked around. She was searching for his body. She thought surely he must be murdered.

"The iron chest is there and unopened," said Cale, glancing at it in the corner; "and I see no sign of blood. He can't be killed, or if so it hasn't been done here."

"Look for tracks! look for tracks!" said Hazel-Eye, and she pointed to a belt of sand not far from the cabin door. "We may know if Indians or white men have been here."

Cale hurried to the sand and she followed him.

"White men, wearing moccasins, not old hunters either. Their toes turn out. Three of 'em. They came in light; they've gone out heavy. They've either stunned him with a blow, or tied him hand and foot, for he has been carried. The tracks going back sink full a half-inch more in the sand than they did in coming in."

"Wait till I go and get father's rifle, and we'll track them up. I'll not be a minute!" cried the girl.

"But the iron chest—it must be looked to," said Cale.

"Oh, I care not for that. His life is in peril, even if it is not taken. It is more than a hundred iron chests to me."

The girl hurried off as fast as she could go.

"In love, or I am blind," said Cale Durg, thoughtfully. "Well, it's natural, I s'pose, though I don't know nothin' about it or how it feels. They say gals take to lovin' airly and easy, and I s'pose it's so. The more the pity, for it must be hard on the constitution, pinin' and frettin' as I've heard tell lovers do."

His soliloquy was cut short by the return of the girl trapper, rifle in hand.

"Lead the way, good Cale Durg; go as fast as you can and not lose the trail!" she cried.

The hunter nodded his head and moved on toward the river. As they got into hard and occasionally rocky ground the tracks became more and more indistinct, and it was only one of that class who mark each bruised shrub, each bent blade of grass, each fresh-turned leaf, each broken twig they pass, who could trace a sign of those they followed.

Even with his knowledge, Cale Durg had to pause very often, and, moving to and fro, recover the trail almost lost; and thus fully an hour was passed before they reached a point on the river very near where Hazel-Eye had been seized by the strange man on the preceding day.

She remembered the locality, and pointed out to the hunter the spot where Rupert Norcross had overtaken and rescued her.

"Yes," said he, "I was here yesterday. It is a rough spot here, full of cliffs and gorges, ledges and gullies. I lost the track over there close to the water, and never got another sign of it. I and Mad Eagle got all at fault, and that's a new thing to either of us. Ah! I hear some one a-comin' through the brush. Look to your gun, gal—look to your gun!"

"It is he! It is Rupert Norcross—alive, but Heavens! how white!" cried the girl, as the young man came from amid a thicket toward them.

"White Pine! Lookin' as if he'd seen a ghost, or else lost his senses!" exclaimed Carl Durg. "Airthquakes and hurricanes! He's whiter than snow itself! He reels on as if he was blind. Can he be crazed?"

"Heaven only knows! Something fearful must have happened to him!" said Hazel-Eye. "Let us hurry to meet him!"

And she rushed forward, followed by the hunter.

CHAPTER XIII.

More Mystery.

When Rupert Norcross saw Hazel-Eye approaching him and Cale Durg close behind, he halted and, leaning against a rock, as if sick near to death, or too weak to stand without support, he waited for them.

"Have you been wounded or are you ill? What is the matter?" exclaimed the girl trapper, hastily, as she came near.

"Speak up, White Pine! What has hurt ye, or are ye skeered?" added Cale Durg.

"I *am* hurt! Not in body, but in that which, once hurt, will not recover. My heart is breaking!" said Rupert, mournfully.

"Thank goodness there isn't no bones in it, if that's all!" said Cale Durg.

"Explain, sir, if you please. Do you not see that we are painfully alarmed?" cried Hazel-Eye.

"My father! oh, my father!" moaned young Norcross.

"Oh, you've seen him again, have you? Was he after the iron chest?" asked Cale Durg.

"Would that I had seen him dead than as I did! He is in league with if not in command of desperadoes and robbers!" groaned the young man.

"Sit down and I will tell you. I am uninjured in body, but fearfully weak from excitement."

"Sit down, you. We can listen standin' as well as sittin' down."

The young man sat down, and, facing Hazel-Eye and Cale, said: "When Miss Anna left the cabin, I saw that the dog required some attention, and attended to it, and then looked to my arms and put them in order. Then, as you remember, Cale, you and Mad Eagle came back, and we had a talk, and he named me White Pine. After that he went one way and you the other, and I took the lock from my rifle and cleaned it, for I had forgotten to do it before—at least so it seems to me, for I'm dreadfully confused yet. While thus engaged I heard men talking, and went to the cabin door to see who approached. I saw three white men, utter strangers, dressed roughly and fully armed. Supposing them to be only ordinary hunters and trappers, though I did not like their looks, I stood in the door of the cabin, determined that they should not pass in, at least before one or both of you returned to give your consent, and, when, they came within three or four paces, asked their business.

"'We'd like a drop o' something hot and strong, stranger,' said one of them.

"I pointed to the spring close by, and told him that was the beverage used by all who dwelt under that roof.

"'Lend us a cup, then, to get a drink out of?' said one of them.

"This request seemed so natural, I thought nothing wrong of it, and turned to reach a cup. As I did so I must have been struck down from behind by the fist of one of them or some blunt weapon, for there is no wound except a bruise on the back of my head, which I feel. At any rate I was senseless I know not how long, and, when I next know what was occurring about me, I found that I was bound hand and foot and being carried along.

"From what I could gather by the low, muttered talk of the men, I learned that they were robbers, if not murderers, by trade—that they were well acquainted with the vicinity of the camp and party I had lately left, and seemed to think through my capture they'd make a ransom. They seemed to be struck with and commented upon my singular likeness to one whom they called the 'old man.' I did not understand this at first, but, alas! too soon knew what it meant. I felt so weak from the effects of the blow, near the spinal termination at the neck, that I could make no resistance now, and did not speak until they were close by the river and near a wall of rock which juts out beside a waterfall. Thinking it time to learn their intentions if I could, when they halted I spoke and asked what was meant by the outrage.

"'You'll know fast enough when the old man sees you!' said one, as they placed me on my feet and cut the thongs which had bound my limbs.

"And when he spoke another blew a shrill whistle.

"At the same instant, in what looked like a door or narrow passage in the rock, a man wrapped in a large buffalo robe showed himself.

"I saw—my heart sank in me as I looked—but I saw *my own father!* His face so pale, his eyes so dark and fiery—heavens! to think of him thus and there! I never saw his face flush so quick as it did when he saw and recognized me; and then, in tones hardly recognizable from his choking anger, he shouted out: 'What do you mean, villains, by bringing a prisoner here? Take that man out of sight of this place and leave him, or there will be three of you serving your master in the next world instead of this. Not a word—Begone!'

"They seemed to fear him very much, for they rushed me away from the spot, and after hurrying me a few hundred yards, left me by myself. I have just come from that spot. Now do you wonder at my excitement—my agony?"

"Heavens, no! I do not!" said Hazel-Eye. "Are you sure that it was your father whom you saw, whose voice you heard?"

"So sure, lady, that if this were my dying declaration it would not be altered."

CHAPTER XIV.

Pitching Tents.

Breaking up camp and shifting base are not much in expeditionary parties well organized, and in half an hour after the order was given "to strike tents" by Major Whelpley, his command was ready to move—every horse in and saddled, the mules packed and in column ready for the march. "Am I to consider myself under restraint, sir?" asked Captain Norcross, rising from a rock where he had been sitting in gloomy thought during the time the men were engaged in breaking camp.

"No, sir, I for one do not deem you guilty of the charge made by the strange hunter. If you were, the trapper was outside of our party, and it would not be for me to pass judgment upon you. Indeed I acted without thought and hastily in placing a guard over you last night."

"Thank you, major. You only do me justice. I am innocent of the death of that unfortunate man. But I feel as if the blood of my dear son was on my hands. I could have explained to him enough to satisfy his doubts, but my haughty spirit would not stoop to explanations, even to him. It galled me to think he could believe me guilty of crime. But I see my servant bringing my horse. I will tell you more as we ride along."

The command was soon in motion. Garnier, the guide, and four old scouts led the van, while flankers were thrown out right and left, and a rear guard covered the column as it moved on.

The major, long used to military service in past days, omitted no precaution to render his party safe from surprise.

After about two hours had been occupied in the march, the command reached the brow of a ridge which overhung a small but exceedingly beautiful valley, covered with luxuriant grass, and surrounded on all sides but one with thickly wooded hills. That side was bounded by the river, which rushed along between two lofty bluffs of volcanic rock, in a narrow channel. A small stream of clear water meandered through the valley, rising from amid the hills, falling into the river within sight of the spot where the command halted for a moment, that the party, which had straggled apart in some degree, might close up.

Garnier now moved rapidly on, and, descending the hill at a trot, followed by the major, speedily reached the place selected for a camp.

Here the column halted; the order to pitch tent and unpack was given, and in a little while the white canvas village once more dotted the green of the valley. The stock, almost hidden in the luxuriant grass, was turned out under guard, while gangs of men made the woods on the hill-side ring with sounds of their axes, as they cut timber for the corral into which the stock would be gathered at night, and for the stockade which Major Whelpley meant to build, as well as for needful camp-fires.

CHAPTER XV.
The War Council.

While Major Whelpley was changing base, and putting his new camp in order, the warriors of the Black-Feet were gathered in council in vast numbers but a few leagues away, to consult on the manner in which they should unite to drive him and his party from their country.

Their great war-chief, Howling Wolf, had called this council, and now, with Mad Eagle, Falling Water, Dry Stick, Young Buffalo, and other leading men, he was holding a brief talk, while the rest were gathering into the circle, marked by red stakes as the war council.

This circle was in a round plain of perhaps three or four acres, dotted with trees here and there.

When every Indian had taken his seat, Howling Wolf gravely lighted his pipe, and, drawing a whiff of smoke, looked reverently toward the sky and blew it up, as an offering to the Great Spirit. It circled in a white ring above his head until lost in the air.

Then he laid down the pipe. This was a war council, and there was no need to pass the pipe around that circle.

Howling Wolf threw back the buffalo robe from over his broad chest, raised his knotted arm and big, horny palm, and the tom-tom of the prophet was still, for the chief was about to speak.

"Chiefs and warriors! The rifle of the pale-face hunter rings through our forests and echoes over our hills. The pale-faces have not come as a few to look for fur, or to get food—they come in a tribe to look out land to dig up, places to build their villages, and to make roads for their big wagons. They come to build forts for their warriors and to put the big thunder guns in. They come to drive away our game. To cut down our trees. To trample on the graves of our fathers! To feed our young men with fire-water, and to take away their strength. They come to make our women foolish with beads and looking glasses and bright cloths. Shall the red man fold his arms and see all this? Shall he sit down and see the game all killed, or driven away, and then beg of the pale-face for a hoe to dig for roots? No! Howling Wolf will die where his fathers died, with his spear red with the blood of the pale-faces, before they shall see him dig for roots! What is the will of my people who hear me?"

"War! war!" cried Single-Eye the Prophet, and he beat his magic drum furiously.

"WAR! WAR!" came from the lips of every warrior present, until it was one united, terrible cry.

"War! war!" came back in echoes from the seven hills.

Again the great war-chief raised his hand, a signal for silence.

In an instant all was still.

"One brother, Mad Eagle, will speak. He has been among the pale-faces. He told their chief that we would not let them drive away our game. Listen to him, and he will tell you what the pale-face said."

Howling Wolf now sat down, and Mad Eagle rose.

"The words of Howling Wolf are strong!" he said. "But not too strong for the hearts of the red warriors of our tribe. We will not dig for roots, neither will we go away and give place to the pale-face. Howling Wolf told the warriors I had talked to the chief of the pale-faces, who is in camp by the bright river that comes from the land of Yellow Rocks. It is so. I told him he must not hunt on our grounds. I spoke plain words which went right into his ears, like the talk of a father to his child. He did not laugh. But he said his people had found gold, and would stay to dig it. Then I came away. My face was black with anger. I have done!"

Mad Eagle sat down, and at a signal from Howling Wolf, Young Buffalo rose in his place.

"We do not want words!" he said. "Our knives, our hatchets, our spears are dry. They must drink the blood of our enemies. The Great Spirit gave us a home. We are worse than dogs if we give up that home to the stranger. War! war! Let that fall from every mouth—let it come from every hand. War! war! WAR!"

Again the terrible cry rose on every side—rose and rolled off to the wild hills, and came back in echoes all as startling.

Then Howling Wolf, with a smile more terrible than a look of anger said: "It is war! We who are to lead will make our plans for battle. Let the warriors go and cook their meat and sharpen their weapons, and get their guns and bows ready. We will then lead them to battle. I have spoken. The days of the pale-face are counted. The raven croaks for his flesh. It shall lie upon the hills where he hunts, in the valley where he camps, in the hollow where he digs for the gold he loves. Howling Wolf is done. Prepare to fight—prepare to drive the pale-face to death or back to his own land, if he will not stay to fight!"

The chief now turned, and with the other chiefs marched from the circle, which broke up soon as he had left it.

Then away out of this council ground filed the great army of red men, passing through the narrow gorges in the hills, swiftly and silently.

They were leaving sacred ground.

Outside fires were all ablaze in a hundred places, and busy squaws were cooking meat for the braves to feast upon; and, while they were eating, the color of the smoke was darkened by burning wet moss gathered from the dripping rooks over the hot flame made by dry branches, and thus all who were in sight of the smoke, no matter where they were, knew that the Black-Feet had decided to take the war path.

CHAPTER XVI.
Hostile Indications.

"Look at that, sir—look at that!" cried the guide, Garnier, to Major Whelpley, as the latter stood with Captain Norcross near his tent by the water-side, where timber was already beginning to arrive in drift from the chopper's hands.

The major glanced away to the south-west, beyond the river, and saw seven distinct columns of smoke, densely black, rising like pillars against the blue of the cloudless sky.

"I've seen smokes all day in that direction," said the major, quietly.

"Yes, sir; white almost, which merely called a council of warriors to their sacred council ground. "Now, if you notice, that smoke is thick and back."

"Yes. Has it any indicative meaning?"

"Yes, sir; it means *war*. Every Indian who sees it is warned to take the war-path."

"Well, let it come. By the time another day's sun is set we will be ready for it, for the corral and stockade will be done. We will do nothing else until they are finished. Let it come."

"Yes, yes—for then my *surgery* will come in play," said the doctor, eagerly. "Let it come—the sooner the better!"

"It may come before we are ready," said Garnier, quietly.

"No; my instruments are in perfect order—lint and bandages, too—are they not, Jean Burte?"

"*Oui, Monsieur Doctaire*—all is prepare," replied Jean, with the inevitable shoulder-shrug.

"If you please, sir, had not I and a half-dozen of us old hands better set out to scout the hills there away?" said Garnier, pointing to the south-west. "If they see us on the lookout, it may keep them back from an attack long enough for you to finish your preparations."

"You are right, Garnier. Select your men and go. Do not take any of the ax-men, though—we need them too much."

"I will only take the hunters, sir—four men besides myself are enough. More would be in the way."

The guide instantly started to fulfill his duty, and the major, turning to Captain Norcross, asked him what he thought of the matter.

"My mind is so full, or rather so entirely clouded by the agony which fills it— the uncertainty as to the fate of my son—that I can think of nothing else. The men who went back to look for his rifle and hat could not find them. They were gone. If, then, he has not committed suicide, he is wandering alone in this wilderness land full of hostile savages. He will be taken, and then—oh! agony, he will die by torture. Major, I may have seemed harsh and stern to him. It is in my nature to be so to all around me, I believe. But, oh! I loved that boy with all the power of my soul—with all the hidden depth of my nature. He was more than life to me. I am hopeless, I am literally dead without him, though I move and breathe as others do."

"Captain, from my heart I pity you. But be manly. Nerve yourself to the exigencies around us. That we are environed with enemies determined on hostility is certain, but we have arrived at a point from which we cannot turn back without showing moral as well as physical cowardice. We have made a discovery of immense importance, not only to us, but to those who originated the expedition in which we have engaged. The world will ring with the news of our discovery, and how would it sound if that news was followed with the statement that a tribe of poorly armed, half-naked savages had forced eighty well-armed and disciplined men to leave the rich field they had found, but dared not stay to operate in. Would it not mortify every one of us?"

"Yes," sighed the captain.

"Then we will stay and work up our discovery, and fight if we have to do so!" cried the major, enthusiastically. "We will gain credit for our courage and our firmness, as well as for the importance of our discoveries."

"Yes, I suppose so," said the captain, with a sigh. "Oh, if my son yet lives, I hope the scouts will find him and bring him in."

"Jean Burte—you rascal, Jean Burte!" cried the doctor.

"Yes, sare—I am here, doctaire."

"Have you found me a specimen snake—green, with the copper head, such as you threw in the fire yesterday, like a fool?"

"No, doctaire—I hate not had ze time to look."

"*Take* the time. Go find one or I'll dose you to death with ipecac."

"Oh, doctaire—I like not zat. I will try to discovaire one snake!"

And Jean trembled, while he hurried away.

CHAPTER XVII.
In Peril.

When, at the cabin on the hill, Rupert Norcross saw the hide of the monstrous bear stretched out, and heard Cale Durg detail the manner in which Hazel-Eye had invoked and then met the peril, his astonishment made him for a time forget his own agony of mind. Could it be possible that one like her—so slender in form, so tender in her nature, so lady-like in her ways, could have a nature to meet and nerve to face such a horrible death as it seemed must have been hers, had not Cale Durg reached her in time to end the life of the infuriated and dangerous beast? It did not seem possible, yet it was true. Cale Durg would not utter a falsehood, and *she* could not.

He could not find words to express his admiration of her courage, or his joy that she had escaped the danger.

"You will not, I hope, expose yourself again in the same way," he cried.

"No," she answered, naively, "there will be no occasion for it. I wanted the cub-skin for a door mat, and now Rollo will have a fine bed as soon as the large skin is dry. Have I not taken a nice lot of fur this morning?"

"You have, indeed," and the young man looked at the skins she had brought.

"You shall help me stretch them. I will be your teacher in that part of the art of a trapper's life," she said, and she brought from a cupboard a bundle of the thin, shoe-sole shaped slabs, or shingles used to draw the skins over, fur in, until they could be cured and smoke dried so as to keep off the moths.

Cale Durg watched the two as they pursued this labor, with a quiet and rather pleased look.

"I reckon she's taken the disease, nat'ral and about as bad as he," he murmured, in low tones. "That lovin' fever is a sing'lar sickness, catchin' like the measles and shown in blushes, trembling, and sighs. There's but one good doctor to it, I've heard say, and that's the preacher or the squire. They tie a knot, and then the love gets into matrimony, and it isn't always even blankets can keep it warm. For when folks knows they're tied and harnessed, they begin to squirm and kick in the traces, and some of 'em would give a heap to git unharnessed agin. That's what they call 'divorcing' in grammar talk. It's a pity that sich couldn't keep on a lovin' in single harness all their lives—but hark—I heard a yell! Rollo heard it too—the old dog is gittin' life, for his ears are up and he is listenin'!"

The young people were too busy at their work, their hands very often touching, as one helped the other, to notice what had attracted the attention of Cale Durg, and even when he turned, rifle in hand, and went to the door and passed out, they did not seem sensible of his having left them.

"You are learning very fast, Rupert," said the girl trapper, as the young man turned a mink-skin over its proper cap*. "I think you will soon make a skillful trapper, instructed as you will be by Cale Durg, who knows all that a man can know, red or white, of a hunter's and a trapper's work."

"It seems to me that you would make almost as good a teacher as he, judging from your skill with the rifle, your courage in danger, and your aptness at collecting the skins as well as preserving them."

"Far from it. My father, it is true, took me with him along his line, and often on his hunts, but he made me devote a good portion of my time to study, to music, and to sewing. For he ever impressed on my mind that the time would come when he would take me back to the world from which he had been exiled and he has often said he would, before he died, see me, shine as a queen in the sphere to which he said I belonged. There is some secret in that old iron chest. Oh, I wish I could get it open. I never felt any curiosity about it while he lived—but now I yearn to know all I can know."

Rupert Norcross shuddered. What might not that iron chest reveal. The murderer's name? Oh, if it was Robert Norcross, then death to every wild hope which began to rise in his warm, impulsive heart as he looked into those dark hazel eyes, on that face so beautiful, so full of girlish innocence, yet so full of intellect—that form bursting into an unconscious, but, oh! what a voluptuous womanhood.

"Can we not get it open in some way without the key?" she continued.

"Burglars would make short work," he answered; "but I do not understand their arts. They use gunpowder in some way, but how I do not know, to open large safes. Had we files, or crowbars, we might do something. But the largest instrument here that I see is an ax."

"There is my rifle barrel," said Hazel-Eye. "Can it be used as a bar?"

"If we had a place to insert its point we might do something," said Norcross. "But there is none. The chest shows no seam except the slight one in the lid and at the hinges. I fear without the key we will make but a poor attempt if we try our hand at opening it. Where is Cale Durg? He was here a moment ago."

---

* That part of the animal's skin that covers its head.

"Yes—he must have slipped out. He is a true and noble man, to whom my father was much attached. I wonder where he has gone. He would not leave without letting you know. Ah! there is the crack of his rifle—I would know it anywhere—and—was not that a shout or a yell?"

"It was—it was! He may need help!" cried Rupert, bounding to his feet and grasping his own rifle.

The next second both he and Hazel-Eye were at the door, and their hearts throbbed wildly as they saw the giant hunter engaged in a hand-to-hand encounter with four or five men about a hundred yards away, while one lay stretched on the ground near where the struggle was going on.

"Quick! quick to his help!" cried the girl trapper, and with Rupert Norcross she sprang forward.

CHAPTER XVIII.
Mad Eagle's Warning.

Though Rupert Norcross and Hazel-Eye ran as fast as possible toward Cale Durg, he would have fared ill indeed against such odds even with his gigantic strength and fierce will, for he was stricken down almost at the instant their eyes fell upon him.

But at that same moment a band of fifteen or twenty mounted Indians was seen speeding down the hill, and their wild yells rung through the forest and over the hills as they dashed toward the spot.

It changed matters for Cale Durg in a second, for the men whose weapons were raised to end his life sprung away in hot haste and evident terror, and before Rupert and the girl could reach the fallen hunter, they were lost to sight among the thickets in the direction of the river.

"Are you badly hurt?" cried Rupert, as he knelt by the side of the hunter and raised his head in his arms.

"Oh, yes! See how he bleeds from this cruel gash in the breast!" said Hazel-Eye. "Oh, must I lose my best friend?"

"Hush, gal, I'm not on the die this time. I don't choke and there's no bleedin' inside. Just shove something in that hole to check the bleedin' afore I get too weak," said the hunter, cheerfully. "Look, there's Mad Eagle and his friends. He'll know what to do."

"Who has drawn the blood of Red Panther?" cried Mad Eagle, who rode at the head of the Indian band, as he sprang from his horse. "Whose knife is red with this?"

And he touched the blood which Hazel-Eye was now endeavoring to stanch with her handkerchief.

"Are the pale-faces from the camp already striking at you because you are the red man's friend?" he continued, as he took the handkerchief, and, with a hand used to such work, pressed it into the gaping wound effectually.

"It was a different gang from them we saw below. There was but one man from the camp," said Cale Durg.

"Is this he? I will take his scalp!" said Mad Eagle, spurning with his foot a dead white man with a bullet hole in his head.

"No; I laid that chap out in the start and the rest piled in on me," said Durg. "If it hadn't been for your comin' with a yell, Mad Eagle, I reckon my venison would have been cooked this time, though White Pine and Hazel-Eye were doin' their level best to get to me."

"Who was the *one* from the camp?" asked Rupert Norcross.

Cale Durg did not answer.

"I know by your silence. It was he whom I have called *father!*" said Rupert, mournfully. "Oh, that your bullet had ended his crimes. I feel no kindred sympathy with him now."

"Don't bother about it, boy! Old Nick is in him as big as a prairie dog, and he can't help it, I suppose. He headed the gang, and I might have shot him instead of the other—but I *couldn't* draw for him, someway. Help me to my feet—why, I'm not hurt much. It is only a bad scratch—the chap's knife wasn't worth much, for it glanced at my breast bone."

The hunter was able to walk after getting to his feet, though rather feeble, for he had lost much blood.

"Where were you going?" he asked of Mad Eagle, as the Indian, bidding his warriors remain by the body he had scalped, went with him and the girl and Rupert toward the cabin.

"We go to give the pale-face chief his last warning to leave our hunting-grounds!" said Mad Eagle. "The council has spoken, and the black war-smoke has gone up!"

"Ay, I saw it at noontime, or there about. I knew I'd see you soon. Don't let me keep you back. When you see the father of White Pine, tell him Red Panther owes him a debt, and he'll pay it when we meet again."

"I will. But now Mad Eagle wants Red Panther and White Pine and Hazel-Eye to keep near their cabins. The red men will not come here. But when the war-cloud is dark over them, they do not see plain, and every pale-face will fall upon whom their eyes rest. Mad Eagle has told his people to look on White Pine as they have long looked on Red Panther and Trapper Guy and Hazel-Eye. But when their blood is hot, they may only see a white face and not remember whose it is."

"Ay, you're right. And we'll keep out of your road all we can," said the hunter. "I've lost blood enough to make me feel quiet for a while. But if them devils who just left are a hangin' 'round here, I'll lose more or they'll go under!"

"I will trail them now to their death!" said Mad Eagle. "Before I go to the camp of the pale-faces, this shall be done. They shall not live to do more harm to the friends of Mad Eagle!"

The Indian turned, went back to his people, mounted his horse, and rode off on the track of the men who had fled on his approach.

CHAPTER XIX.
Throwing Down the Gauntlet.

It was the morning of the second day of the new camp in what Major Whelpley had named the "Valley of Gold," and the major, with Captain Norcross, was superintending the erection of a stout stockade from timbers floated down the stream to the beaver dam by which the camp was pitched. There had been no disturbance or alarm during the night, though the animals had been picketed close to the camp for fear of it, and the guards doubled in number. The scouts, out till dark the night before, reported the Indians collected in great numbers south of the stream, but not showing any open intention of *immediate attack*, though evidently making ready for it.

The sun was perhaps two hours high, when one of Garnier's scouts rode furiously into camp and reported that the guide had halted a small band of Indians who were coming in with a flag of truce to hold talk with the chief of the pale-faces. The guide, with great wisdom, had halted them out of sight of the camp, over a ridge a mile or thereabout away, until the major could come out there to hold the talk. For it would have been sheer folly to let the Indians see what was being done at camp if it could be helped.

"Come, captain, ride out with me and my escort, and let me see what those red fiends have to say. If we can buy peace with a few gallons of whisky and a pack or two of tobacco, it will be better than war, and we may as well give them the talk they ask!"

Captain Norcross bowed assent to the invitation of the major, and when his horse was brought with the rest, he mounted, and in a short time the party were in sight of the Indians held back by the prudence of Garnier.

Major Whelpley at once recognized his previous visitor, Mad Eagle, and addressed him kindly, as he was evidently the leading chief present, and as such to be mollified if it was possible.

"My red brother has had a short ride!" he said. "His horses have not turned a hair, I see!"

Mad Eagle did not reply. His eyes were fixed upon the pale, sad face of Captain Norcross. He seemed to be in a state of perplexed thought.

"Is the chief, Mad Eagle, deaf—or has he not come to talk?" said the major, rather vexed that no attention was paid to his advances.

"Mad Eagle is not deaf. And he would rather strike than talk. But Howling Wolf, the great war chief of the Black-Feet, does not want to take from the great Master of Life any men, if he can leave them to His hand instead of to the hands of his warriors. He is not hungry for blood. He would rather see the pale-faces go in peace from his hunting grounds, and save powder and lead for game to feed his own people with. What says the chief of the pale-faces? If we will be still for three suns, will he then go away and never come back?"

"We will not go in three suns, nor seven suns, not yet for twenty, if we are not ready!" said the major, firmly. "The Great Spirit made the land for all his people, red, white, and black, and as we are here we will stay here till we choose to go! What has Mad Eagle to say now?"

"That!" cried the chief, with eyes all ablaze, and he drew the hatchet from his belt and cast it at the feet of the major.

Oh, what a picture for a sculptor! His tall form drawn to its fullest height, his head thrown back, his weight resting on his left leg, while the right was thrust forward in the attitude of defiance, his extended right hand pointing to the hatchet.

"War!" he cried. "The Black-Feet will talk no more. The pale-faces shall hear the crack of the rifle, and grow sick at heart. The twang of the bow-string shall whisper death, and the red knife shall open their way to the hunting grounds of lost spirits. Mad Eagle has no more to say to *you;* but to *him!*" Mad Eagle turned fiercely on Captain Norcross now, adding: "To *him* Mad Eagle will speak. You, who are a robber, a murderer, and a coward, to creep up on single men and slay, with your robbers at your back and the Evil spirit to hide you when your work is done—to *you* Mad Eagle gives warning! The red men will not slay you in battle, but they will take you alive, and their prophet shall blacken your face, and you shall die at the torture-post."

"What does he mean?" asked the captain, bewildered at the strange language, as well as the vindictive looks which accompanied the hot-spoken words.

The Indian offered no explanation—no one else could give it—but mounting his horse, with his grim and silent warriors following, Mad Eagle rode away, leaving the hatchet on the ground where he had cast it in defiance, as knights of the olden time used to throw down the gauntlet.

CHAPTER XX.

Eluding Pursuit.

After leaving the cabin to follow the trail of the men with whom Cale Durg had been so recently engaged in the death-struggle, Mad Eagle and his people were gone for a long time. That they had found them, the occupants of the cabin almost felt sure, for the ringing yell of discovery, made when an enemy is in sight, was heard distinctly, and recognized by the hunter, who, with his wound properly dressed, and revived by a stimulating tea made from potent herbs by Hazel-Eye, sat listening near the cabin door to hear each sound.

But no sound of conflict reached the ears of the hunter and his friends, following the cry first heard. Yet the absence of Mad Eagle, prolonged until the night-shadow fell on the earth, made the hunter think they were on the trail, and would follow it up until the men were found.

It was dark when Mad Eagle came back. He turned his horses loose on a grassy spot near the cabin, and his warriors built their camp-fire. After this was done, and he had set a watch for his camp and animals, Mad Eagle came to the door of the cabin from which the three occupants had watched his motions.

Cale Durg asked no questions. He knew Indian nature too well. Mad Eagle would speak when he got ready, and questions would not make him speak any sooner.

The chief came up, entered the cabin, and threw some pine knots from the pile, near the hearth, on the fire, to make it blaze up. Then, as the red light fell on each face and revealed his own striking face and figure in weird beauty, he looked long and earnestly on the face of Rupert Norcross.

"White Pine must make prayers to the Great Spirit for himself," said the chief. "The Evil Spirit holds to the form of his father in his hand, and makes him strong to do bad things. The great rocks open at the touch of the Evil Spirit, and the father of White Pine and the fiends who do his work are hidden from the warriors that follow. We try everywhere to find a trail to follow. But it is lost in the rocks we cannot go through."

"Then you saw my father?" cried Rupert.

"Yes. He laughed in the face of Mad Eagle, he shook before my eyes the knife which killed the father of Hazel-Eye, and then, when Mad Eagle threw his hatchet to strike him down, it rung against the rocks, for the pale-face captain was gone."

"Where was this?" asked Cale Durg.

"By the leaping water and the white rock that goes straight, higher than the pine trees at its foot."

"At the same waterfall where I lost the track of him who laid hands on Hazel-Eye," said Cale Durg.

"And I expect the same whither I was carried by the ruffians who knocked me senseless," said Rupert.

"This is a wild mystery," said Hazel-Eye. "How they can thus escape is wonderful!"

CHAPTER XXI.
Good Wishes.

Two days went by after Mad Eagle had cast the war-hatchet at the feet of Major Whelpley—busy days for the command—and a strong corral for the animals, and a stockade at one corner of it to hold his men, had been built with the skill of men used to defenses on the frontier. The hunters had been kept busy in killing all the game which was within safe vicinity of the post, and now men were engaged in drying the meat for preservation, so as to be ready for a siege, if one was to come. Garnier and his scouts had kept watch night and day upon the massing Indians, and they reported active preparations for battle being made by the latter. They, too, were collecting and drying large quantities of food, so that not a warrior would be forced to hunt while the war went on; and the young warriors were put to the terrible test of self-torture, which would fit them to battle for fame in the coming contest.

"We'll have 'em on us afore another day dawns, major," said Garnier as he rode in, just at sunset of the second day. "They've caught up their horses and have 'em at the lariat, so they're sure to move in the night. If you'd not get mad at a man like me advisin', I think I could tell you how to dishearten 'em on the start, sir."

"I shall be glad to listen to you, Garnier. You've been reared in the West and know more of Indians than I do, though I've fought them in Florida, Texas, and on the plains a good many times. What is your plan?"

"They're south of the river, and have got to cross it to get here. They have three or four crossing places, but at all but one they'll have to swim their horses, and that's risky to rifles and powder. So it is likely they'll take a ford—hardly girth deep, where the river spreads and widens above the Big Falls. It's a couple of hours sharp riding from here. I think they'll start to cross there, as soon as the moon is up, and that comes not far from midnight. I've set two men to watch there. Now the crossin' is wide and easy, but the gettin' out place is rough. They have to come up a pretty steep bank into a kind of canyon which leads out to the level, and then over the roll of hills and valleys it is all plain riding till you get here."

"So you think they might be met and opposed at the crossing, and we begin the war instead of them?"

"Yes, sir; it will be where we can meet them at the most advantage. I can hold this side of the crossing with twenty men as long as powder and lead will last, and not expose my men either. There is good cover such as rocks and stunted trees on the bank."

"Suppose they cross above and below, and come on your rear?"

"Then we'd have to git. But we could keep down the river under good cover till we could reach you here!"

"Your plan is good. Detail twenty such men as you want, with rations and plenty of ammunition. I will leave you to command the party."

"Thank you, major, I'll do my level best, and if I go under I hope you'll remember them that I left behind at Fort Sully and see they get my pay. "

"Your wife and children shall be cared for, Garnier, but I hope you will live to see and care for them yourself. I hope to get my command back, hale and hearty with wealth enough to make them, and those dependent upon them, happy."

"I hope so, sir—but hope can't stop bullets nor turn arrows to one side. Good-night, sir. I'll gather my men and be off. If I'm not here, or a messenger doesn't reach you at daylight, it will be because I'm too busy with the red cusses to come or to spare a scout."

CHAPTER XXII.
Defeated.

The moon was but a little way above the trees, when, from the south, silent as shadows, but, ah, how real, though spectral-looking, a horde of mounted Indians rode steadily toward the river. Not a cry from a single lip, not even a low-muttered order could be heard, and the unshod feet of their horses made but slight sound as they came slowly, steadily on.

Young Buffalo, on a coal-black horse, whose mane and tail dipped in the water when it scarcely reached his pasterns*, rode at the head of the column, his

---

*The portion of the leg of a horse between the fetlock and the hoof.

shield of dried buffalo hide over hardened wood upon his left arm, and his long spear, with a scalp lock for a pennon, in his right hand. Other chiefs and warriors pressed on in a mass close behind, and soon the ford was hidden with forms moving forward in the unbroken march. Yet more were pressing from the rear as far as the eye could reach.

Garnier had spoken truly when he said they numbered thousands. Hungering for blood, grim and silent, they moved on, hoping to surprise the whites in their slumber, intending to attack them just before the dawn, an hour when men almost always slumber soundly, deeming the night almost gone, and danger gone with it.

Young Buffalo had almost reached the northern bank, and he was glancing back with a proud look at the armed host which followed, when a single rifle broke the stillness with its sharp crack.

He straightened on his coal-black horse, shook his spear wildly in the air, then with a gasping yell fell from his horse into the stream, which swiftly carried him toward the cataract. It was a death-shot, and while his horse plunged forward to reach the bank, there came down among the astonished warriors a withering volley, which emptied twenty saddles more and threw the massed column into fearful confusion—for the horses of slain and wounded riders, without control, reared and plunged, or dashed this way and that, keeping back those who strove to press on.

Now came volley after volley from the repeating rifles of a foe so hidden that not a form was seen, and the Indians were awe-stricken, hearing no cry, for the whites were utterly silent, except with their sharp, rapid fire, which was carrying swift death to scores upon scores of the red men.

In vain these strove to press forward. A barrier of dead and of wounded men and horses blocked the way. The river ran dark with blood and full of floating bodies, while the roar of the cataract for once was drowned by the yells of anger and the cries of excited warriors.

Howling Wolf, though he could not get to the front, was madly striving to do so, while Mad Eagle in the front seemed to bear a charmed life, for though nearly all about him were shot down, he was yet unhurt.

While this was going on in front, the Indians in the rear pressed on to join the battle, not knowing how all one-sided it was going, and that their enemies, completely covered, had naught to do but slay, slay, as fast as they pressed forward.

Dismounted, Mad Eagle pressed on amid the dead and dying, and at last, with a yell of triumph, he reached the northern bank.

"Come on—come on, they are but a handful!" he yelled back, as he scrambled up the steep bank and glanced within the ambuscade.

At the same instant a crushing blow sent him bleeding, reeling down the bank again, and he did not hear the shrill cry break from the lips of Howling Wolf, the cry an Indian hates to give or hear—the order to retreat.

The war chief saw that he must lose all who tried to cross—that hundreds of his best warriors were already down—and he knew if he crossed at all it could not be there. It must be by other crossings.

And now he could not surprise his enemy. The surprise, indeed, had fallen upon him and upon his men.

Back went the surging host—back to count their fearful loss and ponder over a wild and hot revenge—back, until once more the river ran on in the still moonlight, unvexed by struggling form or stiffening corpse.

Then from the defenders of the ford rose a cheer so loud and wild that it was heard for miles away and in the camp below, where Major Whelpley and his garrison had listened in anxious fear for the result, there was loud rejoicing. They had heard the long-continued fire—the Indian yells, and now came the shout of victory while many a body went past upon the swift current of the river to tell how the victory went. For those who watched told only of Indian forms being seen.

The Indians gave back the yell, but their throats wore choked with sorrow and with anger, for they had lost almost a fourth of all who reached the river side. Among these were at least four leading chiefs. Mad Eagle was not one of these— he yet lived!

Wounded sorely, he clung to a projecting branch in the edge of the cold river, which served to chill the hemorrhage and save him from bleeding to death. Here he lay while he saw his people falling slowly back from the river, unable to follow them, or to drag himself out of the water in which he lay half immersed. He waited for death, for he believed the victorious whites would descend the bank either to scalp such as might be in reach or to finish any who lay wounded as he did.

He heard the shout of victory, he heard the cries of joy uttered by the victors, and he ground his teeth together in impotent rage because he was too weak to breathe back a yell of hate and defiance.

Then he heard Garnier say: "They will not attempt this ford again. They've learned a lesson here they'll not forget. We must look to the other crossing places now."

All was silent after that, and he knew that the defenders of the pass were gone. Oh! if he could now recall Howling Wolf and the retreating red men, how quickly would the tide of fell revenge roll back upon the conquerors!

It could not be. Weak, and growing chill, as if with the ice of approaching death, he counted his end as very near.

Suddenly voices again reached his ear. The language was that of the hated pale-face.

Nearer and louder, and a thrill ran through his veins when he heard a voice like that of Hazel-Eye—low, sweet, and soft—to his ear a flood of harmony just then.

CHAPTER XXIII.

Losing Consciousness.

Mad Eagle trembled with delight when he heard the voice, for he felt sure his friend, Red Panther, had recovered strength enough to come out, and, if he could see him, would aid him in his hour of need. He knew that with timely help his wounds might be cured, and he [would] once more be strong to walk the warpath. In agony of suspense he listened, for his head was growing dizzy with weakness, and he felt as if he could not long live and sustain his grasp upon the limb which held him from the embrace of the current, which could sweep him, mangled and lifeless, down the fearful cataract.

Again he heard the voice—lower, sweeter, more musical than it had ever sounded to him before. She was talking to some one. It must be Red Panther or White Pine—perhaps both.

How the weakness seemed to overcome him! He longed to cry out—to call their names—but he could not. Yet his hearing was painfully distinct. Nearer and nearer came her voice, and she was asking her companions to look and see if those who had been engaged in battle were in sight.

"Perchance," she said, "we may find some poor wounded creature, and help him in his agony."

"What are their dead or their wounded to us?" said a stern, harsh voice. "We may have our own to care for!"

Mad Eagle was amazed. He had heard that voice before. It was not that of Red Panther or of White Pine, but it was the voice of Captain Norcross—of the father of White Pine.

What could she, the noble Hazel-Eye, be saying in such a friendly tone to the murderer of her father—to the enemy of her best friends? Why was she in his company? He would crawl up the bank—he would confront her, if he died in the struggle!

He made a mighty effort—the blood gushed fresh from his wounds; but he was on shore, in under the fringe of bushes, and he would yet creep up the bank. But he must rest and check that blood, or he would die ere it could be done.

Weaker and weaker as the blood ran fast—his eyes were dim—when with his belt he checked the flow at last. And now she paused upon the very verge of the bank above his head. He could hear her light footfall—her sighs, he fancied—as she looked down on some bodies lodged against the rocks in the stream.

"There seems to be no one living in sight," she said, after a pause.

"I am glad of it. There is no need for you to exercise your sickly humanity."

It was the cold, harsh voice of Captain Norcross, which fell upon his ear now as before.

"Father, the time was when you were not yourself so cruel. Your whole nature has undergone a change. To me alone you yet are kind—for me alone show human feeling!"

What more could Mad Eagle hear to amaze him? She, Hazel-Eye, was calling the man father, whom he fully believed to be the murderer of her *father.*

"The Great Spirit has taken sense, before He takes my life into his hands," thought the warrior. "I am in a dream. I have lost my mind, and hear sounds which are not!"

She spoke again. Trembling in the dizziness which too often precedes death, he clung to life that he might yet listen to her voice.

"Let us go back!" she said. "The day will soon be here, and then we may be discovered."

She rose, and as he looked up he saw a face bending over the bank—a face of utter loveliness, wreathed by curling hair as bright as sunlight falling on the shadowy rock—eyes like stars in all their splendor—but the eyes, the face, the hair, all belonged to a stranger. He had never seen that angelic face before! It was but a glimpse—he saw, and then his consciousness was lost.

CHAPTER XXIV.
The Chest Gone.

After the recent strange visit of Captain Norcross to the cabin at midnight to view the iron chest, and the attack by the desperadoes on Rupert Norcross first and Cale Durg afterward, it need not be wondered at that Hazel-Eye very gladly heard the hunter propose that he and Rupert should remain at her cabin until the Indian trouble with the white intruders was over, and until they were satisfied that the dangerous characters recently seen in their vicinity had gone away.

Thus it happened that on the night of that fearful combat at the ford—I might better term it massacre—all three were listeners to the distant sounds of battle, anxious, but as non-combatants in that quarrel, non-interfering listeners.

Cale Durg sat near the cabin door, from time to time commenting on the sounds by which he seemed to read the fate of the battle, for he was one to form a sure judgment from many an indication which men not used to frontier or wilderness life would pass unnoticed.

At last the firing ceased altogether, and then came the wild, joyous cheer which Garnier and his men gave when the Indians were in full retreat. It came faintly, of course, in the long distance, but Cale Durg knew what it meant, and he said: "The Indians have tried to cross at the ford above the Big Falls to attack the camp below, and have been driven back. They must have suffered fearfully from those heavy volleys, or they would not retreat. There are no Indians on all the Western plains or in the Big Rockies half so stubborn as these Black-Feet are. I hope our good friend Mad Eagle is not slain. Of all the Indians I ever ate meat with, he is the best, most honorable and true. He is brave as the bravest, without being as cruel as some. I hope he has lived to tell us how the fight was fought."

"Can we not go down to the battle-ground, cautiously, and learn what has been the result there?" asked Rupert Norcross. "We might find Mad Eagle wounded and in need of help."

"Just so. I could go alone," said the hunter.

"Oh, no—let us all three go. Rollo is now able to watch here, though not strong enough to follow us," said Hazel-Eye.

"As you will, girl—as you will. Day is breaking and we can see to travel," said Cale, as he looked to his rifle and belted on his knife and pistols.

When the first blush of coming day lay soft as an infant's roseate smile upon the blue of the eastern sky, the three, well armed, were moving silently with rapid steps down along the river-bank toward the recent battle-ground. The roar of the great waterfall came more and more plain to their ears as they passed from hill to hill, now winding through some deep and dark ravine; then skirting a steep cliff, and then walking on the very brink of the rushing river.

"We are at the ford," said Cale Durg, at last, as they emerged on the river-side from a gorge through which they had passed for a quarter of a mile or more; "and look at yonder rocks in the stream. The ravens will feast there before nightfall. It is red meat, too—nary a white man there."

"Here is where they stood, all under cover," said Hazel-Eye, pointing to a spot where the twigs and flowers were all trodden down behind a wall of rock, well hedged by bushes.

"Yes; they rested their rifles on the moss here and here, see the marks," said Cale. "What are you looking at, White Pine?"

"A dead Indian down by the water-side who resembles our friend, Mad Eagle," said the young man.

"It *is* Mad Eagle!" cried Cale Durg, and he hurried down to the spot where the warrior lay, with upturned face, his hand still clasping his empty rifle.

"Is he dead?" asked Hazel-Eye, hurrying to reach the spot.

"No, no—the breath of life is yet here, but that is all," said the hunter, who had his hand on the red chieftain's breast. "The blood has been well-nigh drained out of his carcass. Look at the frozen pool under him. A white man would have caved with half the loss."

"Can we not get him to the cabin, and there nurse him into life?" asked Rupert, who was now bending over him.

"We not only can, but must," said Cale Durg. "It will be a heavy drag, but we must do it, or he will perish. Nothing but tender care and stimulating draughts can raise him now. He is senseless; he neither sees or hears us."

It was a long and a weary journey back to the cabin on the hill, for Cale Durg had not yet regained full strength, and the warrior had a giant form. But when the sun was a little past meridian, they were at the cabin door, and Hazel-Eye hurried in to prepare a draught of stimulating herbs, such as she had learned to make when no other stimulant could be had, but those which the God of Nature places on the earth with His beneficient hand.

A cry broke from her lips as she went in—a cry of alarm so shrill and sudden, that Rupert nearly let his end of the litter drop, but cautioned by Cale Durg, he held it up, and the two passed quickly in with their still unconscious burden.

The hunter did not need to ask what was the cause of the girl's outcry, for at a glance he saw reason enough for it. Rollo, the noble hound, was now indeed dead, and the manner of his death was plainly to be seen. The blade of a large knife, broken short at the hilt, as if in striving to wrench it from the spinal bone, in which it was buried, still protruded from the thick neck of the noble animal, while in its mouth was a portion of buckskin legging, smeared with blood, showing that it had seized an intruder before it met its death.

Rupert Norcross groaned aloud as he looked at the silver-hilted handle of the knife upon the floor, where it had been dropped when parted from the blade. He recognized again his father's knife, the accursed weapon which had given *her* father his death-wound.

All three cast one quick glance to the corner where the iron chest had been kept so long. It was gone!

Hazel-Eye stood for an instant, pale and hesitating; then, forgetful of the safe, murmuring "Brave Rollo—he died protecting my property," she hurried to prepare the draught for Mad Eagle, for she knew as well as Cale Durg could tell her that lethargy with him would be death. Life and pulsation must be brought back speedily, or both were gone beyond the reach of human aid.

While Cale Durg and Rupert laid him carefully on the bed once occupied by Trapper Guy, and, removing the clotted blood, washed his gaping wounds, the noble-hearted girl was busy in her skillful way, and soon as they raised the warrior's head, she poured between the lips and teeth they pressed apart, a potion so warm and fiery in its nature that it forced an electric thrill to pass through his stiffened frame.

"It would burn like fire, were he fully conscious," she said. "I have made it very strong."

"It is what he needs. His pulse can be felt," said Cale Durg. "Get water, White Pine, for the draught is indeed like liquid fire. I have tried it, and I know its power."

The effect of the medicine was wonderful. It caused a flush to follow the pallor which sat like a death-pall on the countenance of the wounded brave, then there was a tremor in the nerves and muscles, and after perhaps ten or twelve minutes the eyes of the warrior unclosed.

He could not yet speak, but a grateful look told that he was conscious of the presence of his friends, and their efforts to revive him.

All that afternoon and all through the long night, the three patient, kind-hearted creatures worked over the form of Mad Eagle, coaxing back life into it. With gentle care, a few drops at a time, invigorating drinks were passed between his lips, then as he gained more strength, he was lulled to slumber by the magnetic soothing of the fair girl's gentle hand. It was a long and patient struggle, but the good Samaritans were victorious at last and when another day dawned, Mad Eagle was not only living, but able to say a few words.

Hazel-Eye soon made a sleeping draught ready, and from its speedy effect, hoped for the best results to their patient. When Mad Eagle was sleeping naturally, they for the first time took leisure to speak of the iron chest, and the slaying of the faithful hound.

"Without a doubt, my father and the mysterious band over which he seems to hold control, separated, too, as they were from the party with which he and I came out, have taken the chest away," said Rupert, with gloom upon his brow. "What its value may be to him I do not know, but that it is not rightfully his, nor whatever is within it, I do know. It and its contents shall be recovered if I live."

"You must not risk life for it," said Hazel-Eye, earnestly. "I do not know what was in it. I only care to know when I think of my father's dying words. His *murderer's name* was there!"

"And to keep that name hidden from human eyes, and yours more than all, he has stolen the chest," said Rupert. "Oh! it is enough to madden me! But I will terrify him into its surrender! He believes that I am dead. He shall see my spirit; and if I can get into the camp unseen, then he may in terror give it up."

"You'll make a healthy-lookin' ghost," said Cale Durg, in his dry way. "I've half a mind to see if I can't trail them that carried it. Mad Eagle will sleep now a long time, and you two will get along without me."

The hunter said no more, but took his arms and left at once, while Hazel-Eye and Rupert turned to their duty as watchers again.

CHAPTER XXV.
To Work the Mines.

When Garnier and his men reached the stockade in the Valley of Gold, black with smoke and wet with the perspiration of swift travel, not a man scathed by a weapon from the hand of an enemy, there was but one unhappy visage seen to greet them.

When Dr. Bugle heard they had fought a fierce battle, slaying scores on scores of their enemies, and that not a single one was marked with bullet, spear, or arrow, he was indignant.

"Do not be angry with him, my brave Garnier," said the major. "Science has carried his knowledge into unknown depths, and his humanity is lost in his professional desire to reach new discoveries."

"Well, sir, I suppose he is to be excused. He is about half crazy, I reckon. And now, sir, we will talk of what has to be done. The Indians have had enough of the ford. I did not leave a single man there, for they have a horror of a battle-field where they have been beaten. They think that the spirits of their dead warriors wander over it, shrieking for revenge, and they will not even pass it in their travels. But Howling Wolf is not a chief who will let his repulse dishearten him. Like Red Cloud, he is a great warrior; like him he has vast influence and an unconquerable energy. He will rally his braves and attack us very soon, crossing from some other point. I will move with two parties, and stationing one with Dion at one point where they may cross, go with the other to the place I think most apt to be used."

"As you deem best, Garnier. But your men, occupied as they have been, need rest."

"We will take rest in turn, sir, when we reach our watching ground. This is no time to study comfort. Our party will never get away from here unless we whip the Indians at points where we have a great advantage. They may be so weakened and disheartened that they'll let us alone here, and give you time to finish what you propose to do, and then to get away."

"Your views are correct, Garnier."

"Where is Captain Norcross, sir?"

"I do not know. He asked my permission to go on a short hunt, and cautioning him not to go far, I permitted him to go."

"He will be in danger, if he is out of sight of camp alone," said Garnier. "For the Indian scouts are undoubtedly around us, and he was ever careless."

"By the way, did you see Mad Eagle in the fight?" asked the major of Garnier.

"Yes, sir; and he is done for. He was in the lead, or near it, but he escaped our fire, and actually reached the bank where we were posted. He clambered up to our barricade, but there he received a death-blow which sent him toppling back into the river. He undoubtedly went over the falls where they were swept by scores as we shot the red fiends down."

"I am almost sorry. He was the most manly Indian I ever saw. I liked him for his undaunted courage and his open hate. But it is better for us that such an enemy is out of our way."

"Better for Captain Norcross, whom, as you remember, he had marked for the torture-post. Those reds never lie when they swear a particular revenge."

"There comes Captain Norcross now, riding as if he saw nothing, cared for nothing. The poor man is nearly crazed about his son," said the major.

The captain, mounted on a favorite hunting-horse, came in on a sweeping trot, and did not draw rein until he was on the spot where Garnier and the major stood.

"Well, sir, any new discoveries? Have you seen signs of the enemy?" asked the major, kindly.

"Enemies? No, sir. I saw no enemy; I saw an angel; a bright creature from the upper world. I would have asked her for my son, but she stood far above me on a cliff, and I could not reach her. When I sought to gain the spot on foot, she was gone—she was gone!"

The tone of the captain was low and mournful as he spoke these words, and he alighted from his horse and went slowly to his quarters.

"He has seen that beautiful girl trapper," said the major, "and he fancies her to be a spirit. His mind is surely wandering."

The major now took occasion to congratulate the companions of Garnier upon their gallant defense of the ford, and to assure them that in the produce of the mines, when he got to work, they should share equally with those whom they were defending, fully as much as if they were themselves at work. He concluded by saying sluices had been dug and rifle boxes made, and a gang would begin to work the gold dirt on the ensuing morning.

CHAPTER XXVI.

Cale's Misstep.

When Cale Durg shouldered his rifle and strode forth to follow the trail of the robbers who had stolen the chest, he made up his mind to penetrate their haunts if it were possible for man to do so, and to capture their leader.

He soon struck a trail which he believed to be that of the men who had been to the cabin, but to his surprise it did not lead in the direction whither they had been tracked on former occasions, toward the Great Falls.

About a mile farther on, a cry of joy broke from his lips. There, on a ledge of gray rock he saw the iron chest. Too heavy, he thought, to be carried, they had given up the job. But this joy was blasted when he reached the spot. The iron chest was open, and the key, which he had so often seen attached to a string on Trapper Guy's neck, was in the lock. The chest was entirely empty. Not a paper was in it. But on the ground close by, there was a fragment of an old letter with only two or three words legible on it. These were a part of the superscription, and it ran thus:

Norcross, Esq.,
Ridge,
Va.

Cale Durg secured the slip of paper in a pouch he carried next his heart, for it held some relics of a dear mother and two sisters whom he had not seen for many, many years, and then with a new energy he struck upon the track again.

He was going for the papers and vengeance now.

On up among the rugged hills the hunter sped for full four hours.

Suddenly the trail swerved away from the river-course, tending toward the forest on his right. And to his joy he saw a long way ahead, yet distinct, a clear column of smoke rising in the edge of the woods.

An hour and he was near the edge of the forest, and the smoke from the camp-fire beyond rose clear and plain in view, though the fire was hidden in the thick forest growth below.

"I will soon be where I can see what they are doing!" he cried, and he rushed on.

Haste was imprudent, even in one so sure-footed as he, for stumbling over a pointed rock at a short turn, with a cry of horror breaking from his lips, he went over the fearful ledge.

Wildly he grasped a stunted bush as he felt that he was falling, and it swung him in upon a slender point jutting from the wall-like cliff, where, breathless and trembling in every joint, he found a bare footing, though it only saved him from instant death.

"Heaven help me!" he murmured. "I reckon I must go under now. I would like to live till dear Hazel-Eye had got the papers, but God's holy will be done!"

Mercy! What did he see? Was it an angel from heaven sent to aid him in his fearful strait? For he saw, with eyes all a-glimmer with mingled surprise and fear, he saw a woman's face, so fair, so lovely, framed with hair of golden hue, bending over the rock above, with a look of pity beaming out from azure eyes.

Yes, the fair face gazing down upon the hunter, in his terrible extremity, with a pitying look, seemed to him to be more than mortal—to be the face of an angel. Almost breathless, he looked at her, and he thought that her voice was heavenly music when he heard these words: "Can I help you?"

"I hardly know, blue-eyed angel; but there's one thing sure: if I've got to die, I'll die a better man for havin' seen your face. You've carried me back to my boy-hood's home—ay, to the only happy days of all my life."

"Do not talk or think of me. Plan some way in which I can help you. You are too far down for me to reach your hand, or I would try to draw you up."

"You'd have a heavier draw than you could stand, I'm fearin', beautiful! But if you had a lariat, or a bit of rope a few yards long, and some place to hitch it to, I could haul myself out of here."

"Will this do?" she cried, and as she bent a lithe and graceful form over the rock, clinging to a small tree to sustain herself, he saw her unwind a long sash from about her slender waist.

"I reckon it will, if you can fasten one end to something solid up there," he answered. "It is silk, and that is strong."

The young female made no reply, but she seemed busy fixing the end of the scarf to the tree by which she steadied herself as she looked over the verge. This was done in a few seconds; then, as she seemed about to lower the scarf to his reach, she said: "You will make me a promise, in return for what I am doing, will you not?"

"I'll promise anything *you* ask, for I know, by your eyes, you'll not ask me to do a wrong," he answered.

"Thank you. I will trust, and save you first. I will ask a favor afterward."

She threw down the end of the scarf, which he could just reach with his extended hands.

"It is securely fastened to this tree, which is firmly rooted in crevices of rock," she said. "Trust your weight to it, and fear not."

"Heaven bless you, beautiful, whether it holds or not!" he cried, and commenced, to draw himself up hand over hand.

In a few seconds he was up to the edge of the cliff, and her small white hands were grasping the stout collar of his hunting-shirt to aid him in the yet perilous task of getting upon the level of the cliff.

With her help the feat was soon accomplished, and, breathing short and quick, he stood upon the narrow ledge, gazing into her face gratefully, with such feelings, too, as he had never known before.

"I am so glad you are safe! Now for your promise."

"I said I'd promise anything to you, and so I will. Ask me to jump down there, and off I go, like a wolf blind after an antelope."

"I ask nothing which will hurt you—I *could* not. You look so noble and so manly."

"Me! Why, I've never seen much of myself except in a still bit of bright water now and then. But I'm not much when good looks are counted."

"You *do* look good, and true, and brave, and—but the promise. You must pledge your honor not to go any farther along this path, but to return as you came."

"Beautiful! Don't, don't ask that! If you knew what I was after!"

"Perhaps I do," she said, and a mournful look clouded her lovely face.

"The papers out of the iron chest, and the old cuss that stole them?"

"I knew, almost, at least I felt sure you were in pursuit of him, and yet I saved you," she said.

"*You* wouldn't protect a fiend like him—you who are a livin' angel of light and beauty!"

"Alas! you know not what *he* is to *me* and I must not, dare not now explain. But you would not cause my death?"

"No, never! I would die at the torture-stake before I'd harm you, lady."

"It would be death to me—death to you also to go on. They who are now where yonder smoke is rising are merciless. They have not seen you, or your life would be taken, in spite of all that I could do to save it."

"You are not with them—oh, it cannot be, or, if so, not willingly?"

"It is not my will, but my fate, which for a time, keeps me in company which I abhor," she answered. "You will keep your promise, and accede to my wish to return?"

"I must—but the papers which were in the iron chest?"

"I will *try* to get them for you—indeed I will. I will risk all to obtain them, even as he seems to have risked so much, and left the bounds of civilization to find them."

"I believe you, lady. Please tell me some name by which I may call you. For I would like to speak it over and over all the time."

"My name? I dare not give it all—*that* has been forbidden by him. But you may call me—Medora."

"Medora! It is a sweet name, and it will fall from my lips in whispers by day and by night, wherever I may be," said the hunter.

"And you—what may I call you brave, *honest* stranger?"

"My name is Caleb Durg. The Indians, who are all friendly to me call me Red Panther, because I dress as you see I do, I think."

"It is a romantic name—but may I call you Caleb?"

"Oh! if—if you will! It is too much honor for you to speak to me as if I were an equal."

"Ah, Caleb! you are my superior in many things. You are a brave, a great, strong, noble man. And you are honorable, I know—do not ever have to hide and shun the faces of your fellow-men."

"Never!" said Cale Durg, proudly; and he drew his massive frame to his fullest height, shaking back his nut-brown curling hair, and looking at her with a loving light from his expressive eyes.

"Oh, if I dared to tell you *all!*" she continued. "Perhaps I may before long. Do you know what the papers are which were in the iron chest? For I see you know where they came from!"

"No; but I know they are of deep value to as good a girl as ever trod the face of earth—exceptin' you. Don't start—she is like a sister, or a child to me, for I was her father's friend."

"*Was?*"

"Yes; for her father was murdered a few days ago."

"*Murdered?* Was it in an attempt to get these papers—these terrible papers?" asked the girl, trembling from head to foot.

"I do not know, but I think they were connected with the cause of his death. When dying, he said the name of his murderer was in the chest."

"I know it, then. Alas! I feared as much! I *know* the name!"

"So do I, Medora, I believe."

"And you do not hate me? Do not shrink from me?"

"*Hate* you, beautiful? I never knew what it was to love till I hung on the rock down there, with but a step between me and death, and looked up into your face. Then it flashed down into my heart, as a bright dew-drop falls into the cup of a dying flower. I am awakened into a life so new, so glorious, that I can hardly realize it."

"And it is I who have awakened you to life?"

"Yes, sweet Medora—*yes*."

"And will you love me enough, Caleb, to extricate me from the power of one whom I fear, and must obey, and whom I now look on with horror, for I fear his hands are red with the cruel stains of murder!"

"You mean—"

"Hush! Do not breathe his name—do not, for my sake!"

"Beautiful, I will not!"

"Now, Caleb, we must part for a time. It will not do for me to linger too long here, or he or some of his band will return to look for me. Impelled by some strange impulse, I lingered in this wild, romantic spot to gaze on yon wondrous scene of beauty, while they went on to build a camp. For some reason, a change of location for the party was decided on last night. When and where can I meet you again?"

"When and where you will appoint, most beautiful. I would like to return, and tell Hazel-Eye that I have not found, but hope to find the papers."

"Do so, do so, and then come back to this vicinity, and make some signal, so that I may come to you."

"I will. I think, from the lay of the land, that I know a shorter, better route to the vicinity of the camp yonder—one directly over the mountain—an old trail, long unused, for a fallen tree, which bridged a chasm, rotted down some time ago. With an ax I can drop another bridge, and make the trail of use once more."

"Then you will come to me again?"

"Yes, as sure as the sun will rise, I will come to-morrow. Do you see that peak, just within the line of forest, rising alone, almost like the dome of some great building?"

"Yes, I see it, Caleb." "Do you see a blasted pine on the western side?"

"I do; it has been lightning-riven, I think."

"You are right, bright eyes! Look for a green branch stuck in cleft, about the height of my form, to-morrow, and when you see it, walk that way. Should you hear the note of a whip-poor-will, come on fearlessly to where it sounds, for it will be me. That bird does not come into this altitude, though it is found in the valleys not far away."

"I will come for a signal, and I will rejoice when I see it."

"Thank you, good and beautiful Medora. Now, farewell. I will return, and, so far as I can, explain what I hope to do."

"Do not say farewell, dear Caleb. It sounds as if we were not to meet again. And I would rather die here now than to think that would be the case."

And thus they parted.

CHAPTER XXVII.
"Who Was This Woman?"

"What success, Cale?" asked Rupert. "Could you keep the trail?"

"Ay, lad. The iron chest is not more than a mile or two west of here. There is the key, Hazel-Eye."

"And the papers?"

"They're gone, but I hope soon to get them. I found the chest open and empty, and I followed the trail till I came as near going under as I ever did before, and yet come through."

"How—were you attacked?"

"No; but I was hurrying along on the trail over a narrow ledge, and I stumbled at a short turn. Over I went, clinging, in my desperation, to a bush, which swung me in on a ledge ten or fifteen feet below the top of the cliff. There I clung for dear life, expecting to go every minute, for I could feel the slender footing crumble while I stood there. Then an angel with golden hair and blue eyes came to my rescue. With a scarf from her waist, fastened to the trunk of a small tree, I got up to the trail again, and looked once more on life as my own."

"Who was this woman?"

"I cannot tell, only, not even barring you, sweet Hazel-Eye, she is the loveliest creature I ever saw or even dreamed of."

"What is she doing in this wilderness?"

"Even that I do not know for certain. She is not here of her own will."

"She must be free, or she could not have been there alone to help you."

"She is free to some extent, but yet under fear and restraint. Ask no more now. Through her I hope to recover the papers taken from the chest. And I yet hope to bring her to you to be a sister and a companion, such as you need in this lonely place."

"I do not seek other companionship. What is this woman, or girl, to me?" said Hazel-Eye. "I am sure I have company enough."

And she glanced far from unkindly at Rupert Norcross.

"Well, as you will. She will not force herself into your company. Were you to see her, you would love her."

"Perhaps so. Love is but a small part of my composition. But see, the eyes of Mad Eagle open. I must give him some nourishing broth now."

"How does my red brother feel?" asked Cale, as he approached the Indian, and laid his hand on his nerveless arm.

"Like one standing on the edge of the Happy Hunting-Grounds, not knowing if it be the will of The Great Spirit he should go on, or turn back. My breath is short and weak, like that of the papoose in its mother's arms."

"You will live. You've had a close shave; were nearly stove, but you're in the channel yet, and will get through."

"Mad Eagle will get up again. He will be strong to strike his enemies. Many of his braves have gone to death. Falling Water, and Dry Stick, and Young Buffalo have gone before him. The water ran red before Mad Eagle, and behind him, and all around. He was like a wounded buffalo turning on the hunters, and he tried to die with his braves. But he is here. Red Panther, and Hazel-Eye, and White Pine are good. They are taking the life of Mad Eagle in their hands and building it up strong again."

"Mad Eagle must not talk much. He must drink this, and then sleep. When he wakes he will have more blood in his veins—more life in his limbs," said Hazel-Eye, as she came with ministering hand to give him nourishment and medicine.

The Indian made no objection, and while he took what she had prepared, murmured out brief words of gratitude.

In a little while he was again in an easy, natural sleep, and now Hazel-Eye sought to learn something more of his recent adventures from the hunter.

But Cale Durg was strangely silent on this subject. He said he had no more to reveal then, but that if he succeeded, as he hoped to do, in recovering the papers, and got her permission, he would tell all he knew of the blue-eyed maiden with the golden hair.

CHAPTER XXVIII.

"He Is On My Track."

A night of rest, with nourishment given whenever he was awake for a few minutes, made a favorable change in Mad Eagle, and he was able to talk coherently and for a long time with Caleb Durg in his own language, which the hunter spoke fluently. Neither Hazel-Eye nor Rupert understood the drift of their conversation. In truth, they were now generally so much engaged with their own talk, they were not often troubled with that of others.

After this long and earnest conversation with the wounded chief, Caleb Durg discharged and reloaded his rifle and revolvers, put some dried meat in his hunting-pouch, and made ready for departure.

"How long will you be absent?" asked Hazel-Eye, noticing the careful preparation of the hunter; also that he made what she had never seen him do before, quite an elaborate toilet, combing out his fine hair and beard very carefully, and arranging his dress with unusual care.

"I hardly know. Look for me when I come. I'm after the papers, you know."

"Are you going to build a new cabin?" asked Hazel-Eye, seeing the hunter take a large ax in his hand, in addition to his usual weapons.

"No, gal, but I've got a bridge to make over about as nice a tumblin'-in place as you can find in all the nor'-west."

The hunter made no further explanation, but, with a cheering word to Mad Eagle, passed out.

On, for over an hour, at a rapid gait, he sped, and then he halted on the verge of the terrible chasm which had been named Roaring Brook.

It was about five or six yards wide, from verge to verge—a yawing cleft in the mountain, through which a stream rushed with never-ceasing roar, fully five hundred feet below the upper edge.

Cale looked around an instant to select a proper tree for his purpose, and then picked out a small pine, with no branches on its trunk except near the top.

This he speedily felled, in such a manner that its bushy top lay across the stream in the center of the old trail, leaving its trunk, not much thicker than his thigh, as a bridge over the fearful chasm.

A slender bridge, truly, but one which a son of the forest would trust his life upon as quickly as if it were ten times as large.

For some prudent reason, the hunter now concealed the ax, which, not needing it more, he did not wish to carry farther. He hid it carefully beneath the butt-end of the fallen tree, and then stepped fearlessly on the bridge which he had made.

The slender log bent and trembled under his weight as he went on, but with three or four firm, rapid steps, he was over it.

On the other side he stepped off, and passed around the top, careful not to break down any limbs, so as to expose to persons from that side the bridge which the green top hid from view, should some one come that way.

He now pressed swiftly on for another hour or more and then he stood upon a stony ridge, from which the wild scene of loveliness met his view which had charmed his eyes on the day before.

A rapid walk of half an hour carried him to the foot of the blasted pine, which he approached from the east, in a stooping posture, lest he might be seen by some prying eye whose glance he did not wish to meet.

Tearing a green trailing vine from the earth, he raised it to a knot about eight feet from the ground on the western side of the whitened, barkless trunk, and fastened it there.

He had not long to sigh in silence over the tardiness of the "angel of his thoughts."

A glimpse of a fairy figure, dressed far different from Hazel-Eye—for Medora wore the garb of civilization even there—soon made his heart throb with mighty pulsations under his tight fitting garments, and he gave out the cry of the whip-poor-will so loud and clear, that the maiden stopped and looked up into some of the neighboring trees, as if she thought it was a bird indeed.

Then, with a smile on her lovely face, she hurried on, remembering the promised signal-cry, and soon after it had been repeated, she was standing before him, her small right hand clasped between both of his hands, while he looked the love he felt from his large, earnest eyes.

"I have watched since the day began," she said, "for the green branch on the blasted pine. Oh, how glad I was when it appeared! Are you glad to see me, Caleb?"

"Is the infant glad when it wakes with its mother's loving eyes looking down upon it? Is the lost and benighted traveler glad when he finds a beaten path? Oh, sweet angel—savior of my life—I cannot speak my joy! It will be your fault if we ever part!"

"Oh, do not say that. I cannot leave *him* now—and it would be worse than death to see you where he is. Besides, I have promised to get the papers for you, and I will. I have seen them. He keeps them concealed from the eyes of the men whom he will not trust, but he has no fear of me, and I have seen him hide, and at his leisure bring them out, and ponder strangely over some of them."

"He destroys none?"

"No; he seems to take great care of them, for he has wrapped them in oil-cloth, to keep them from the dampness of the place in which he lays them."

"And you can get them for me?"

"Yes, I will. I do not feel that he is right in taking them—you must be right in wishing to give them back to her who owns them, as you told me."

"I am, sweet Medora. And I will wait till you can get them for me without danger to yourself—wait in patience, so long as they are safe. If I can only meet you, look in your precious eyes, hear your dear voice—what care I for delay?"

"Why do you love me, Caleb?"

"Why? Ah! who could help it that has eyes to see, ears to hear, or a heart to feel? Angel, I do not ask my heart—I only know that you and you alone fill its every depth. My eyes look upon you, and my soul whispers—I am all thine—forever thine!"

"Ah, heavens! look, dear Caleb! He is on my track. *He is following me!*"

The hunter raised his eyes, and saw Captain Norcross, not four hundred yards away.

CHAPTER XXIX.
"I Will Charge Him with His Crime."

The hunter reached for the rifle that he had lain down, and a look of fierce determination changed the expression of his face in a second.

"Oh! fly—fly! Quick, Caleb!" Medora exclaimed, as she pressed her hand to her bosom. "You can gain the forest over the hill long before he can reach this spot."

Her look, her tone of agonized entreaty, her piteous eyes, all pleaded against his stern nature.

"One word, and quick! You surely do not love that man?"

"Love him? No—a thousand times no—even though he is my—Oh! go—go—and at this time to-morrow I will steal out from the camp to meet you! Go—in mercy to *me*, go!"

"I'll go, Medora, for your sake; but if I hear his voice raised in a harsh tone to you, he dies! Remember, angel, tomorrow."

"To-morrow, darling, if I live! Fear not—he will not abuse *me!*"

The hunter rose, and with a light and noiseless step glided out of sight, while the fair girl, singing in a cheery tone, as if amusing herself in solitude, went to forming a bouquet from the wild flowers all around her.

Cale Durg, as soon as he gained a position where, unseen, he could look back, saw the girl move forward a little way from where he and she had been standing together, and thus meet the captain before he reached the spot where a double track might have been discovered by a keen eye.

There the latter seemed to be addressing her in an earnest and he thought exerted way; but she seemed to soothe him by some gentle words of explanation, and directly she walked back in his company toward the smoke of the camp beyond.

When Medora and the captain were out of sight, Cale started on his return to the cabin on the hill. He would have to leave its occupants yet longer, like himself, in ignorance of what the papers were, but he would now show to Hazel-Eye and Rupert the scrap of paper which he had found and tell them also that he had again seen Captain Norcross, and had spared him, when in easy rifle range.

He moved on slowly and thoughtfully until he was so near the bridged chasm that he could hear the dull roar of the stream which ran through the gorge.

He returned a little way, where a shelving rock almost overhung the narrow pathway. Near it was a huge dry tree, or rather the stump of one, lying loose on it in a manner which made it not difficult to one of gigantic strength to move. This, first at one end and then at the other, he rolled on until it fell directly in the path, blocking it nearly at that point, so if a person happened to come that way, they would naturally turn aside from that obstruction, and thus avoid the discovery of his bridge.

He now passed on over and soon reached the cabin on the hill, where he found Rupert Norcross busy dressing a mountain sheep which he had slain not long before, while Hazel-Eye was watching his rather inexperienced hand, as he went on, encouraging him with the remark that he was a fair hunter, and would make a trapper, too, if he only lived long enough.

Cale produced the paper he had found and handed it to Hazel-Eye, while Rupert Norcross cast his eye upon it.

"Norcross, Esq.,
"Ridge,
"Va."

"Yes; it but adds certainty to my suspicions!" cried Rupert. "The old family homestead is at Rolling Ridge, Virginia. That letter, without a doubt, was once directed to my father. Oh, Heaven! to think that my father is a thief and a murderer!"

"It does not make you criminal, nor lessen you in my eyes," said Hazel-Eye, sadly, but kindly. "I feel for your sorrow, and will do all I can to lessen it."

"The rest of the papers—why did you not get them?" asked Rupert.

"The angel with the golden hair has not yet been able to obtain them," replied Cale. "My interview was brief with her today. It was cut short by the appearance of your father, who was seeking her, it seems."

"What has he to do with one so beautiful, so good as you seem sure she is?"

"I know not. She does not love, but fears him. She begged me to fly and avoid him for her sake. Much against my will I did so."

"I will go and face him, and charge him with his crime."

"No, no, Rupert Norcross—let Heaven avenge my wrongs!" cried Hazel-Eye, earnestly. "You shall not incur any peril for me. It is enough that our brave Cale Durg has risked so much. Even you shall let the papers go, Cale—I do not want them now."

"Gal, for your dead father's sake, you *shall* have 'em! That is just as good as sworn to."

"Well, kind, true friend, I know how useless it will be for me argue against your will. What you say you will do, that will be done."

"You're right, Hazel-Eye. I despise a man who says he'll do a thing and then backs out for a little trouble. I'll break up that rascally gang before I'm done. If 'twasn't for my golden-haired angel, I'd slip over to the Black-Feet camp, and get a score of warriors at my back, and go through them like a hurricane through pine woods. But I'll not talk now. I'm as hungry as a trapped wolf a week in the steel."

"That can soon be changed," said Hazel-Eye, smiling.

CHAPTER XXX.

A Private Reconnoissance.

As Garnier anticipated, a warrior so renowned as Howling Wolf could not remain quiet under the repulse which his tribe had met at the ford, nor rest until he struck another blow for vengeance. The loss of almost all his leading war-chiefs made it necessary for him to select new leaders and to form new plans. Thus it was that on the third day after the fight at the ford, marshaling his men in two large columns, he approached the river at the same hour, just after sunrise, where the slack water of two eddies made swimming an easy matter to horses and men used to taking water.

Garnier had ordered one of his best mounted men—for all were mounted now—to ride at full speed to the Valley of Gold, and to report to Major Whelpley that this time the Indians would undoubtedly be able to cross in spite of him, and that he must be ready for work at the stockade. He told the messenger to say that he would defend the crossing as long as possible, and then fall back fighting. He would stay as long as he could without danger of being flanked and surrounded.

Not until this messenger rode off was Howling Wolf sure that he would have to fight at the crossing, though he expected it, in consequence of the vigilance shown in defending the fort.

With the sagacity of a good general, he now adopted the Sheridan style of movement—dash!—and at once both columns broke for the river in a swift gallop, at a signal given.

And even now no yell was heard. Dark, swift, and silent, the hideous painted demons came on their small, lithe horses, their spears erect, and as they reached the river they broke into line, right and left, so as to take the water abreast as much as possible, and to expose a scattered and distracting fire to the enemy.

Garnier knew in an instant that he could only hope to empty a few saddles, unless he began early at long range, for the river was wide here, and he at once opened fire.

The Spencer rifles, as good almost at eight hundred yards as at half the distance, rang out sharp and clear, and warriors began to drop. But without one answering yell, or one return shot with guns they knew would not throw lead so far, the stern, vindictive warriors kept on, and soon the river was black with the coming foe.

The whites fired fast, and with good effect, until the Indians, coming with over a mile of front, were almost to the shore.

Then Garnier, pained to do it, gave the signal to rally on the center and retreat; for it was his only chance. Two thousand Indians would be upon his flanks and all around him, if he delayed.

It was a gallant sight to see those brave scouts, men of the plains, in their dress almost as Indian as their foes, only twenty all told, gallop along in company, wheeling their horses every few rods to get a shot at the leading warriors of the pursuing foe, who began to so dread their unerring aim and the long range of their heavy balls that they slacked their speed when the scouts slacked theirs.

But the flanks of the Indians closed when the scouts lessened their speed, and though Garnier had not yet lost a man, two were wounded ere he gave the order to fire no more, but to keep on at full speed till the stockade was reached.

It was soon in sight, and Garnier saw at a glance that his messenger had got in in time, for the stock was corraled, the miners called in, and the stockade, in a state of defense.

But he was followed close, for when the gate of the corral opened for him to ride in, three or four hundred Black-Feet were so near that they made a wild effort to enter with him, wounding him and six of his men with arrows, badly but not mortally.

A discharge from a small mountain howitzer in an angle of the stockade now sent this gang back howling, or all that could get back, for fully twenty of them were shot from or with their own horses by the rattling shower of grape.

A few volleys from unerring rifles, and a half-dozen discharges from the terrible howitzer, taught the Indians a severe lesson for their rashness in venturing so near to men under cover, and those who could got quickly out of range.

Scattered about, on the bluffs and among the trees on the hills they could be seen and heard whooping and yelling, but they had received a lesson, and knew that it was not policy for them "in the open" to fight men under cover.

When night was approaching, the major could see by the camp and watch fires dotting every hill and ridge in sight that his enemies were even more numerous than he had at first believed them to be.

Knowing the necessity of extreme watchfulness, he very early set about designating new posts for extra sentinels and preparing to more than double his guards.

While this was being done, Captain Norcross, who seemed now to be actually insane, started out on what he termed a private reconnoissance. The major would not forbid it, but as a fearful storm seemed to be coming up, he fancied he would soon return. He did not think, crazed as he seemed to be, that he would go out of sight of the stockade, or out of howitzer range, and the Indians would not come inside of that range while light would exhibit them as targets.

CHAPTER XXXI.

Cale Durg's Mission.

When the firing at the fort was heard, Mad Eagle was awake.

"Hark! 'Tis the thunder gun of the hated pale-faces!" he cried. "Howling Wolf has crossed the water—he fights the pale-face in his camp! He will take their scalps now—for his warriors are many as the buffalo on the plains, while the pale-faces are few as the hunters that look for meat."

"When the thunder gun sends out its lightning, if the red men are thick like buffalo in the herd, they will fall as trees before a hurricane!" said Cale Durg.

"Yes; but Howling Wolf can count many braves! There are plenty to stand up where many go down. Mad Eagle must get up and go to the fight."

234 ★ THE HERO OF A HUNDRED FIGHTS

"No, you are too weak. Be still until I can make you strong," said Hazel-Eye. "Howling Wolf has braves enough without you now."

"Mad Eagle is weak. He is a child!" sighed the warrior, and he dropped back feebly on the couch from which he had tried to rise. "Will Red Panther go to Howling Wolf and tell him that Mad Eagle lives, and will take the war-path as soon as he is able?"

"I will!" said Cale Durg. "Howling Wolf shall know that Mad Eagle lives."

"Then Mad Eagle will sleep and try to grow strong. He will dream that he is in battle, and that the pale-faces fall where he rides!"

The warrior took a draught from the hand of Hazel-Eye, drew the blanket over his face, and soon his broad chest rose and fell with the breath of quiet slumber.

"I will now go to the Indian chief, for I must keep my promise to Mad Eagle," said Cale. "I will return as soon as I can, for I have got to visit the angel of the golden hair, before the sun goes down. She is striving to fulfill her promise in regard to the papers. But lately he has kept the most of them on his person, and a part might be useless, while if he missed those he leaves concealed, he would be sure to keep the others out of her reach."

"Use your own judgment, as to getting them," said Hazel-Eye. "I have ceased to feel the anxiety for their possession which I once felt. I know not what good they may do me, indeed, I do not care. I am contented here. The life of a free trapper suits me, as it suited my father when he turned away heart-sick from a world where he had known cruel wrong and harsh injustice."

"Gal, I shall get them papers! I've said it, and I'll do it!" said the hunter, impatient, as he ever was, if his will was crossed in the least. "Now, keep a sharp lookout here, for the old cuss or some of his gang may get here before you know it."

"Let them come!" said Rupert. "They will find us ready for defense."

The hunter now took his arms and departed in his usual way, with no word of farewell, no other statement as to when he would return.

"Ah, how dark it is growing," said Rupert, as he went to the cabin door. "It will be night before Cale can reach the trysting-place."

"It is the darkness of a rising storm," said Hazel-Eye, more experienced than he. "Do you not feel a deadly chill in the air? We will soon have one of those fearful storms of rain and wind which make us feel what God is in His anger—a storm which will tear huge trees from their strong fastenings in the earth, shake the mighty hills, and fill the ravines with resistless torrents. I wish Cale Durg had not gone. His is a perilous route over the mountains. He will be exposed to all the danger of the storm, while we, in this strong, well-sheltered cabin, will be comfortable and safe."

"Can I not call him back?"

"You might; yet I do not think he would return. He will not think of peril, but of her who waits to hear his signal cry."

"I will, at least, try to recall him; I am fleet of foot and know the trail—I was on it on my hunt but yesterday."

The young man seized his gun and sped away before Hazel-Eye could think whether it were best or not.

CHAPTER XXXII.
A Thrilling Shout.

Black clouds were sweeping swiftly through the air on the wings of a shrieking gale; the bending trees, the breaking limbs, told how strong it was, when Cale Durg reached the spot where he had promised to meet his blue-eyed love.

She was there, white-faced and trembling, for the shrieking gale, the pealing thunder, the almost night-like darkness, made more apparent by the oft-flashing lightning, was terrible to one so delicate as she.

"See! I have the papers! He has been away all day!" she cried.

"I knew it, for I saw him miles from here," was his answer, as he took a bundle from her hand, wrapped in oil-cloth. "Now, dear one, you will fly with me?"

"Oh, Caleb, my heart says yes—but—"

"Dearest, your heart is all goodness. Obey its voice. Come, darling, come—the storm will soon break out even more wildly than it rages now. When the rain comes, as it will in a deluge, the mountain will become impassable. Come, my sweet love, come while you can."

"Oh, Caleb there, there, do not frown on me. I will go my brave, true love—I will go."

"Bless you, darling, you shall never be sorry that you linked your fate with mine. Come, come, while we can! Cling to my hand, dear love!"

The hunter turned, and the young girl clasping his strong hand turned with him up the steep hill-side and through the forest now reeling with the wrathful tempest breath.

Oh, how the deep thunder rolled and rattled overhead. The fierce lightning seemed to spring and hiss like a serpent of fire as it tore through the cloud-swept air.

But on—on sped the hunter with his fair companion, though night was fast deepening the already darkness that enveloped them.

They were on the trail, but now only when the lightning flashed could it be seen. The hunter pressed slowly on, for a false step might lead them both to death.

They had stopped to breathe, when, even above the roar of the wind and the creaking of the trees, came another sound. It seemed like the baying of a hound.

"Is there a dog at the camp?" asked Cale, suddenly.

"Yes, a hound, brought from the plantation in Virginia."

"Then we are tracked—the papers have been missed—he has returned!" cried Cale. "Speed on, my love—if I can reach Roaring Brook we are safe. Hark! the rain—thank Heaven! the rain will soon come, and then the hound will lose the scent!"

The girl trembled, but she made no answer. She only pressed his hand with her soft fingers, and clung closer to his manly form.

Again they moved forward as fast as they could, but now their progress at the best was slow; for, except when the lightning flashed, they were wrapped in utter darkness, and the trail was old and hard to keep. Once lost, they could not find it again, and Cale Durg knew well what then would be the result if the hound kept on the trail. The bridge across the chasm passed, it could be destroyed, and then pursuit would be useless.

"Why, why does the rain keep back?" he cried, impatiently, as, half lifting Medora, he moved on more swiftly, while a prolonged flash of light showed him the path.

Closer and closer came the hound. It could be heard plainly now, and Medora trembled yet the more, for she thought she heard the shouts of the men urging it on.

Cale Durg did not merely think, he knew it was so.

Again in the dense darkness he had to pause. An obstruction was in his way. He stopped, and it seemed as if the hound was not a rifle-shot behind them.

"Darling, do not fear; I will slay the dog if we do not reach the bridged chasm in time," he said, as he felt her tremble.

"It is not for me—I can die. But, oh! it is hard to think that you, too, must perish, and all through me!" she sighed.

"Joy! joy!" he cried. "Do you hear the rain? It comes it comes!"

"Yes; but the hound is so close."

"Ah! Bless that lightning flash! This is the log I rolled into the path. A few steps more, my darling, and we are at the bridge. We will gain it, and we are safe. Once over it, and a few blows will bar our enemies from following. No man or beast can leap that fearful chasm."

It was so. Cale was within pistol-shot of safety. Even in the darkness he crept on over the log, and now he was at the tree-top, at the western end of the bridge, with his loved one drawn close to his side.

"Darling," said he, "I must lift you in my arms, and carry you across when the next friendly flash of lightning comes. You could never walk the slender pole, and even I must have light to do it. Ah! the rain, the blessed rain is falling now!"

"Yes; but the hound! Heavens, Caleb, it is here close, so close to us. And hear the men—his voice loud above the rest."

"No matter, love! Another minute, and we are safe! Were they within fifty feet, and we across, they could never reach us. They will have to pause in the tree-top, where we stopped a minute since; for it is thick, and in their way. Ah! the lightning. Now—Mercy!—*beset in front as well as rear.*"

The hunter spoke, alas! too truly. The red flash which lit the forest in his front, revealed the bridge, and there, close by foe stump of the new-fallen tree, an armed man, whose gun seemed, raised, as if ready to be used.

This, too, when the hound, tearing through the bushes in their rear, was baying with that eager cry which told his scent was fresh; while the cries of hoarse-throated men came all too plain, close, close behind him.

"Lost! lost!" moaned poor Medora, for she, too, had seen the man in front.

"The papers! They are gone! I have dropped them in our flight!" cried Cale Durg. "Oh, darling, fortune has deserted us in every way! We can die—thank Heaven—we can die together!"

And then, while again the lightning flashed over earth and, sky, he heard a shout which thrilled every nerve.

"Cale—Cale Durg! for heaven's sake, speak! Is it you?"

"Ay, boy—ay—it is I. Hold where you are, and I'll be with you in a minute!" cried the hunter, as he recognized the voice of Rupert Norcross. "Wait for another flash, and I'm there!"

Alas! at that instant in the darkness there was a flash—not from "Heaven's red artillery," but from a weapon in the fiendish hands of man, and as the flash lit up a face beside that of Cale Durg, Rupert Norcross screamed in agony. It was the face of his father, and as the report of a pistol sounded loud upon his ear, he heard the fearful scream of a heart-rent woman.

"Cale—Cale!" shouted the agonized young man.

There was no reply, but when a long, lurid flash of lightning came a moment later, Rupert saw the form of a woman borne struggling back between three or four men, and a man's body laying prone upon the ground just beyond the chasm.

"Cale—Cale!" he shouted once again.

"Ha! ha! Go look for him in another world!" came to him in a hoarse, mocking shout.

It was his own father's voice. He reeled in horror toward the fallen log and crept across it on his hands and knees.

All was darkness where he crossed, but he remembered where he had seen the body lying when the lightning revealed it to his view. Amid the pelting rain he crept on, until he felt it, and the instant he touched the garments and felt the hair of the panther-skin, he knew what he had dreaded all along. It was Cale Durg who had fallen; and too well he knew who had fired that shot.

"Cale—dear Cale!" he moaned, as he tried to raise the body in his arms. "Speak, if there is one spark of life left in you!"

There was no reply—not a moan or sigh to tell him to hope.

He tore open the panther-skin jacket—he opened the inner, shirt of soft tanned fawn-skin—he laid his cold hand upon the breast, yet warm, of the brave, true man.

Heaven's mercy! He felt a feeble beating of the heart. He lived—he lived!

But he was wounded—where or how badly Rupert could not tell. He must get him over that chasm—he must reach the cabin, where Hazel-Eye, with all her knowledge of wilderness surgery, could help him.

"Heaven and earth!" cried Rupert, as a blinding flash of light almost burned his eyes.

Then, so quick that flash and sound were mingled, came a deafening crash, and he fell to the earth, shocked and terror-stricken. The lightning had fallen almost on him—a bolt had struck the bridge—shivered and shattered it, and it was rent away.

Yes, the bridge was gone, and he on the western side, and now no chance for him to reach the cabin, even if he were alone.

In agony of mind, as he recovered in the cool rain from the dread electric shock which had almost palsied him, Rupert Norcross bethought him what to do. Something must be done soon for Cale Durg, or he would die, for he felt the heart-throbs grow more and more faint beneath his hand. Once more the lightning illuminated earth and sky, and threw up the rocks and trees to view. His eyes fell on a huge log, dry and old, hollow in the end toward him.

Toward it he dragged the fallen hunter, on until he was inside the rotted orifice, and out of the storm and rain. He had flint and steel, and now with eager haste from the dry punky wood, he managed by the aid of the first to start a light—first a feeble glimmer, then a blaze.

It enabled him to find where Cale Durg was wounded, and to check a hemorrhage which would have soon ended life for him. The ball had torn through the left breast of the brave man, above his heart, severing small arteries, but wounding no larger inner vessel.

He had no sooner checked the blood than he drew the hunter but so far that the cool rain would fall upon his face, and then while he chafed his cold hands, he watched eagerly for signs of returning life, watched by the fire which he had lighted, and so arranged it could not spread and so consume the temporary shelter.

It seemed very long to him, yet it was but a little while, before a faint moan broke from the hunter's lips, and his eyes, half-closed, began to wander as if in search of light.

"White Pine—Rupert—did I hear his voice?"

These were the first low, half-gasped words which left the lips of Cale Durg.

"Yes, yes, dear Cale Durg; I am with you, and will never leave you!" cried the youth.

"Ah, yes! Are we across the bridge—are we safe?"

"Alas! how can I tell him in his weak and dangerous state?" said poor Rupert to himself.

"Speak, boy—speak! Where are we, and where is she, the idol of my soul?" cried Cale, and with that vital force which only earth could all extinguish, he rose to a sitting posture.

"Be calm, brave Cale Durg—be calm, or your wound will bleed afresh, and I cannot stop it. You have bled terribly already."

"Ay, ay; I am sick with weakness. I will be calm, boy, but tell me all. Am I across, and is she left behind?"

"No; we are all on the western side of the chasm, and the tree bridge, where I waited for your coming, has been destroyed, by a thunderbolt."

"And Medora—where is she? Tell me, boy, or I will drag myself out into the storm to look for her."

"I do not know. When he shot you down, he and the villains with him tore her from your arms, and bore her back to the forest."

"Coward! Why are you here? Why are you not on her track, to rescue her or die?"

"Coward! This to me, Cale Durg?"

"Yes—to you or any man who'd let a helpless girl be dragged away by villain hands! Oh, Heaven! Why—why am I helpless?"

The hunter strove to raise himself, the blood gushed afresh from his wound, and he sank down fainting in the arms of Rupert.

"He will not call me coward if he only lives to see what I dare do to serve him," the young man said, in mortified agony. "Had I left him, he would have died! I could not have helped her with such odds against me!"

Again, with tender care, he stanched the flowing wound, and then, replenishing his little fire, he sat with the hunter's head upon his knees to wait for light, for in the storm yet raging, and in the darkness, he knew he could not do anything and be safe in the endeavor.

He sat through the weary hours of night, hearing the surging roar of the swollen stream, the pelting of the furious rain, and the shrieking of the winds among the withering trees. It was a fearful vigil, but manfully he kept it, till at last the gray glimmer of the coming day fell on his aching eyes.

CHAPTER XXXIII.
A Captive.

All night in agony Hazel-Eye paced to and fro in her cabin, while the wild storm raged as she had never heard it rage before in all her years of life in the wilderness. In agony, because one whom she had learned to love, in the full strength of a first fervent passion, was abroad in a forest in which he was a stranger, among a thousand perils which he was all unfit to meet, so little did he know of life in its rudeness there.

When day dawned, though the strength of the storm was gone, it still raged with violence, and the mountain torrents tore in awful channels through the old ravines, or made new courses over overflowing banks.

The girl trapper looked out upon the trees fallen in every direction; upon the great river swollen to thrice its usual size, bearing trees along as lightly as if they were straws in its turbid clasp, and she murmured: "If he did not overtake Cale Durg and go with him, Rupert is lost."

Hours went on, and though she watched—watched wearily, drearily, they did not come.

More and more anxious grew her sad heart, and at last, late in the afternoon, while Mad Eagle slept, she put on her belts, and took her rifle in her hand.

"I will go a little way—to the bridged chasm if I can," she murmured. "If I do not meet them, I may meet some sign—some smoke to show me they have camped until it is safe to travel through the hills."

And she placed food and drink where Mad Eagle could reach them should he wake, and with a piece of coal taken from the hearth, she drew two rude figures, one in a dress of skins, and the other in a fringed hunting shirt, and herself with an arrow in her hand. This rude sketch on a piece of white bark she knew Mad Eagle would understand as meaning she had gone in search of the missing men.

She placed it near his bed, then closed the cabin door behind her, and with a hurried step took a western course up the mountain.

Turning here and there, fording streams which would have daunted many a man, climbing over fallen trees, she pressed on, until at last, when it was almost night, she heard the hollow roar of the deep-gorged stream.

Thankful that she was close to a spot where she felt sure she would see a sign of their crossing, she hurried on, and in a few moments came to the new-made stump of pine, which Cale Durg had felled across the chasm.

Where was the trunk? A few splinters told its fate—lightning-riven, it had been hurled down into the depths below.

One instant she gazed at that, then her eyes fell on something laying on the ground close by—a rifle.

How quickly she sprang to pick it up, and then with a moan she recognized the weapon as that which Rupert Norcross carried, and near it lay his cap, with the white pine branch still in it.

Steps and the sound of a man's voice aroused her from her agony of grief.

"A gal cryin' here as if her heart was breakin'," said a man, and as she raised her eyes and grasped her rifle more firmly, she saw not one, but four men in the garb of hunters or trappers, armed with rifles, knives, and pistols, standing near her.

"She's lost her sweetheart, maybe, Will," said one of the men, taking up the rifle and cap of Rupert Norcross, which she had laid on the stump of the pine tree. "If so, she can find another in our crowd."

"Put that cap and rifle down! They do belong to a dear friend of mine. Put them down and go your way, while I go mine!" she cried.

"I reckon your way will be our way till we get better acquainted," said the man whom the other called Will. "At least till I change my mind, for I boss this crowd at present, the head boss bein' on his travels just now. Night is comin' on, and we shall camp, and as we've got grub on hand, you shan't go hungry."

"I shall return to my own cabin," she said, indignantly. "And woe to him who tries to stop me!"

Her hand was passing to her belt, where her revolver would in an instant more have been in her grasp, but one of the men who had stepped behind her caught both arms in his strong clutch, and the next instant she was disarmed.

"You use tools too handy to carry 'em round loose when you're mad," said the man who had first spoken.

"Cowards! Unmanly wretches! Have you no hearts?"

"Yes; rather too much to let a lone gal wander through the woods by herself, when there's an Injun war a-brewin'."

"The Indians would scorn to lay their hands upon a woman. Let me have my weapons, cowards—I can take care of myself."

"No doubt of it. gal; but we're goin' to help you do it. No fuss now, and you'll be treated all the better. Boys, we'll take the back track to the cave in the hill we was a-lookin' at."

Poor Hazel-Eye was helpless. She had no choice but to go where they lead her.

CHAPTER XXXIV.

In a Desperate Strait.

When light came, so that he could see the wan face of his wounded friend, Rupert Norcross was almost hopeless of ever getting him away from there. It was like the face of death—so white and cold. Again he strove to revive him. With a hunting-cup he went out, got water, and poured some between the lips of the hunter. He bathed his forehead, got him out into the air, and strove to chafe circulation in his stiffened limbs.

At last he succeeded in restoring consciousness, but that was all. The last struggle of the hunter, opening his wounds afresh, had caused a loss of blood which utterly prostrated him. He could see and recognize Rupert, but he could not speak above a whisper, and he was literally helpless.

What could Rupert do? He had no ax to cut another bridge. Not even a hatchet. Yet he must return to the cabin to get stimulants, and food and medicine for him, and then go to the Indians for help, to bear him back where he could be nursed into life, if that was possible.

He knew he must think quick, and act as quickly.

He asked Cale if there was not a route by which he could pass the chasm, and get back for help for him.

"Go save the gal—go save Medora, boy, and do not think of me," moaned poor Cale.

"We will together save her if you but let me save your life. I could never find her without your help. I will hunt for her with you, and die by your side or effect her rescue. But now, you must have help, or you will die!"

"You're right, boy," whispered Cale, and even that effort to talk exhausted him.

"You called me a coward last night—you did not mean it?"

"No, no; I must 'a been crazed!"

"Then lie here. I will leave water in your reach, and I will get help. I will bring back Hazel-Eye."

"No, she's a gal, and too weak. Go with your white pine branch in your cap to Howling Wolf, and he will give you a gang of stout warriors to carry me, and then with them you can go on her trail and bring her to nurse me."

"My cap is on the other side of the chasm," said Rupert. "I left it there with my rifle."

"Take my cap and rifle. 'Twill be all the better, for Howling Wolf will know 'em," gasped Cale, and his head fell back, he was so very weak.

Rupert obeyed, and took the panther-skin cap from the hunter's head, and placed in it a pine branch, as he was instructed.

"My rifle, too, lad, and the horn and bullet pouch; for you may need 'em, and I'm too weak to use 'em if need came. Take 'em and go, fast as you can, and get help, not so much for me as for her. It is gnawin' right into my heart that she is in his power, and he'll abuse her for what she has done for me!"

Cale Durg was so exhausted with this effort to speak that for several minutes he could not answer when Rupert asked him again if there was not a route by which he could reach the cabin without crossing the chasm of Roaring Brook.

At last, after Rupert had given him some water, he whispered directions which would lead him back by the route the hunter took when he first followed the trail that led with his meeting with Medora. Before it reached the river, Roaring Brook found a subterranean channel and was lost to sight entirely.

Rupert now placed Cale as comfortably as he could, where his eyes could look across to the stump of the tree he had cut for a bridge, and he said: "Watch for my coming, good Cale. I will be speedy as I can Keep up a good heart; the flow of blood is stopped entirely, and I feel sure you will recover."

"Ay, lad, I will. I can't die till I see her, and get her out of his clutches. So go on and don't fear for me."

Rupert pressed the cold hand of the brave man, and then, taking his heavy rifle in his hand and throwing his horn and bullet-pouch over his shoulder, he left the spot, bearing away to the south-west, to strike the route by the river which Cale had described to him.

CHAPTER XXXV.
A White Flag Waved.

The stockade, as I have termed it, in the Valley of Gold, was built after the usual pattern of frontier block-houses, out of hewn logs, surrounded by a fence of heavy posts, with two stories, the ground floor being used for eating, sleeping, and hospital room while the upper, pierced with small loop-holes for the rifles and ports at each corner for the howitzer, was left clear for action.

Up into the second story Garnier managed to get as soon as his wounds were dressed; for he had a detestation of the doctor and his pompous language, and he also wanted to talk with Major Whelpley.

The change in the air was one of the first things which attracted his notice when he reached there, and he spoke of it.

"Major, we're goin' to have a screechin' storm. I feel it all over me. You'll see afore long a black, murky wall of cloud rising in the west; it'll come slow at first, and you'll see lightnin' a playin' on it, and then the wind will sough over in gusts. After that look out—it'll just howl, and then the Indians will make their worst trial at you."

"What, attack us in a night-storm! I never heard of such a thing."

"I have, major, and I've been brought up to Indian fightin'. I've larnt of Ben McCullough, and old Aubrey, and Kit Carson, and some of the best that ever lifted hair, and I know the cusses from A to izzard.* They'll come on you in a storm like this, thinkin' you'll be all unprepared."

"Then they shall learn they are mistaken. I will double the guards out and in now, which will put over half our force on watch and under arms."

The major now went to attend to his duties, for he saw, as the scout had truly told him, that a fearful storm was indeed fast coming up. And, as with a glass he reconnoitered the hills in sight, he saw the Indians massing at different points, as if they were receiving orders from their head men.

Night set in, and with it came the storm. Only inside the strong inclosure could a fire be kept at all—the picket fires about the corral were blown away in an instant after being lighted.

It was late, fully midnight, and the guards had just been changed.

"What! watching yet?" said the major, as by the light of a lantern, set overhead, he saw Garnier kneeling by the howitzer and looking out.

"Yes, sir, now is the time to watch; from now till the break of day will be the time of greatest danger."

"Pshaw! Garnier, I know how faithful you are, and generally correct in all your judgment. But no Indian would face a storm like this to-night. The rain pours in torrents; the wind blows a hurricane, and—. Why do you start? That was a close flash, but the lightning struck in the hills beyond the river."

---

*Archaic substitute for the alphabetical letter Z. During this period, a common expression was "He doesn't know apple to izzard."

"Lightning'll strike us in a minute, sir. Alarm the guard at the corral; the Indians are at the gate—they are there by hundreds, sir. 'Tis as I expected—they've crept in on us unseen!"

The scout sprang to the lock-string of the howitzer, which had been pointed so as to sweep a range within a hundred yards, and without waiting for an order, fired the gun.

As it belched forth its thunder and its shower of grape, a sound louder than that of the tempest reached the ears of the astonished and suddenly-convinced major. It seemed as if demons filled the air, for piercing yells rose sharp on every side, while but a second later came the clattering of hoofs and the thundering sound of two hundred animals rushing over the plain. The corral gate was open, and now the shot and blow, the shout and whoop, as the surprised sentinels fighting hand to hand with the overwhelming mass of Indians told the unhappy officer how truly the scout had predicted this attack.

"Major, keep fast the entrance to the stockade!" cried Garnier. "If it is opened, we are whipped; they are all around us, the sentinels in the corral are lost. Hark! You'll not hear another shot or shout from them!"

Oh, Heaven! it was terrible! But now the garrison was all at work. The howitzer was belching death into the corral, and wherever, when it was loaded, it could best be brought to bear.

At every flash of lightning the men fired at the forms they saw rushing to and fro, while arrows whizzing through loop-holes lodged in the timbers and now and then hurt a man.

This could not, did not last long; the Indians had achieved a great result; the stock of the whites was all run off and many of their men had fallen, many scalps were in their belts. They could get no more scalps then, while they were losing warriors every time the lightning showed the white men where to fire.

Dragging away their wounded and some of their dead, they retreated, and soon the garrison had time to look to things inside, for no foe could be seen when the fire of Heaven made the earth visible.

The major detailed men to go and bury the dead. While this as being done, the Indians were seen dancing their fearful scalp dances on the hills far to the west, where even the howitzer could not disturb them in their cruel sports.

The garrison had at last laid all their dead beneath the earth, and the major, with some feeling of satisfaction, had counted over seventy dead Indians scattered around, which he could place against his loss, if he ever lived to reach the settlement to tell his story.

After the men had been refreshed with a noonday meal, he mustered the well ones in the upper room to inspect arms and look into the state of the ammunition yet on hand, and this duty done, he cheered them with a speech in which he applauded their past good behavior, and told them not to despair for the future. They were well provisioned, had ammunition enough to withstand the enemy in many a fierce attack, and Garnier, devoted and true, though wounded, had volunteered with a single man to go for help. That he would reach the forts below and return in time, the major assured the men he felt no doubt.

The scout told the men he would go when darkness once more set in, and as the river could be rafted below the great falls, he would build a raft for himself and companion, and soon reach a place whence help could be sent.

The men were less despondent when they heard this, and went to their duties cheerfully.

"What do you see, major, that makes your face flush?" asked Garnier, as he saw the major exhibit excitement while he gazed through his telescope upon the Indians grouped on one of the nearest hills.

"Captain Norcross, mounted, with arms in his hands, and seeming in friendly converse with the red fiends yonder! What can it mean?"

"I can't believe it, sir, after I heard that chief tell him he should die at the torture-post!" said Garnier, with an expression of wondering doubt.

"Look for yourself, my brave man, look for yourself!"

And the major handed his field-glass to Garnier.

"Do you believe it now?" he asked, as he saw the muscles of Garnier's mouth quiver and his thin nostrils dilate.

"Yes, curse him, yes! And there is a woman there—a woman dressed as women do in the settlements! Major, the first scout I make is over yonder, and if I don't make one traitor suffer there is no strength left in my well arm. Oh, that night was now upon us! But see, there is a white flag up, and they ride this way!"

CHAPTER XXXVI.
Finding the Marked Trail.

After leaving his friend the hunter, Rupert Norcross moved forward as fast as he could in the direction which the former had described, and, impeded as he was by uprooted trees and swollen water-courses, he yet made his way on until he reached the spot where the great basaltic cascades came in view.

At any other time his mind, so full of love for the grand and beautiful, would have been excited with the wonderful sight and he would have lingered long to gaze upon it. But now—he merely cast one lingering look that way, then turned along the marked trail which he had found where the hunter told him that he would.

It was narrow, made slippery by the recent rains, and thus doubly perilous, but it was evidently passable, for there were tracks fresh made upon it, going the very way which he had to take.

He did not ask himself who made these tracks, whether friend or foe. His only thought was to reach the cabin speedily, and after relieving the fears of Hazel-Eye, who he knew must feel anxious from his long absence, to get help for Cale Durg as soon as possible.

Swiftly, now that he felt sure of his course, he hurried on, and in a little while reached a turn where the trail trended away to the east, as he believed in the direction where the cabin stood. Here the track, which he had noticed, separated, one party going into the woods on his left, the other keeping on in the trail. This he barely noticed, for he felt as if he had no time to think or study tracks, and on he hurried.

In half an hour more the cabin was in sight, and now the tracks which he had seen were also lost. The parties making them had turned in some other way.

Hurrying to the cabin he entered, expecting to meet the glad cry of welcome from the lips of Hazel-Eye.

No one was there but Mad Eagle, who looked up eagerly and said: "White Pine is safe. Where is Red Panther and Hazel-Eye?"

"Red Panther is wounded, lying in the forest. I have come for help to bring him here. But Hazel-Eye—*you* ask for her. Has she been absent long?"

"Mad Eagle cannot say how long, for he was asleep when she left that sign, which says: 'I go to look for Red Panther and White Pine.' She left food and drink where I can reach them. Mad Eagle knows no more."

"She has taken her arms, she knows the forest well, and she will return. I will speed away to the camp of Howling Wolf, get help for Red Panther, and return," said Rupert, for he had no thought she had gone far. "If she comes back before I return, tell her the life of Red Panther is almost gone, and he will die if I do not get help to him quickly; for that reason I go on and do not turn to search for her."

"It is good. White Pine is true to Red Panther. Mad Eagle is pleased."

Rupert did not hear these words—night was coming fast and he hurried on.

CHAPTER XXXVII.
"He Yet Lives!"

Well for Rupert Norcross was it that Mad Eagle in council had told the Black-Feet he had adopted a pale-face son and named him White Pine, and told the sign by which he would be known. For when he was hurrying toward the camp of Howling Wolf, he found himself suddenly surrounded by a horde of painted, yelling savages, who, furious and wild, seemed determined to sacrifice his life instantly, but when the pine branch in his cap was seen their angry cries were hushed, their weapons lowered, and though none of those who met him could speak in the English tongue, he had only named their chief when by friendly signs they signified that he should be taken to his presence.

Rupert was then escorted on in honor toward a wigwam perched on a hill from which in the distance he could see the corral and stockade of the party to which he so lately belonged.

As the young man approached this wigwam, he saw near its open entrance a lovely creature, a white female, with golden hued hair hanging in glossy curls about a fair neck, her head bent forward, weeping pitifully.

He thought of the angel of whom Cale Durg had so often spoken; but this could not be she. Yet why was a white woman there, and what the terrible sorrow that made her weap so piteously? He had not time to think or ask, even had he the chance to ask her, for Howling Wolf, gorgeous in a scarlet blanket, a plume of lofty feathers, and hideous with war-paint, came forth.

"How!" he cried, speaking English well. "Is Red Panther dead? The young pale-face wears his cap and carries his long rifle in his hand! What has the young 'White Pine' to say?"

"This: that Red Panther, the friend of Howling Wolf and of Mad Eagle, lies helpless in the forest, where the hands of bad men laid him. White Pine is not strong enough to lift him, and he has come to Howling Wolf to get help to carry him to the cabin where Mad Eagle is being nursed to life by Hazel-Eye."

"Good! White Pine shall have as many of the strong men of the tribe as he calls for. They will follow where he goes. We have had a big battle. While the storm spirits swept the earth and shook the trees, the red men crept to the walls of the wooden fort, ran off all the horses of the pale-faces, and took twenty scalps. We lost many warriors, but the pale-faces all shall die."

"Who is the pale-face woman with the golden hair, that weeps in the wigwam of my great brother Howling Wolf?"

"She is to be the wife of Howling Wolf. He has bought her from the pale-face chief who rides with my braves to hold a talk with the pale-faces in the wooden fort."

And Howling Wolf pointed to a group of warriors riding slowly down the hill with a white flag in front of them.

Rupert Norcross shuddered. Was it not a form but too well known which he saw sitting erect upon a gray horse which had borne the same form over many a league in his company?

Yes; he shuddered, and could scarce repress a groan as he recognized, even in the distance, *his own father.*

Rupert heard the boom of the distant howitzer, and he saw the group about the white flag scattered and some of them falling. The gray horse and its rider, too, were down.

"Thank Heaven, his shame is ended! I will not mourn for him," the young man murmured to himself, and he turned quickly away, for now more than ever did he wish to reach the side of Cale Durg.

For if the latter lost the loved one of his heart, he knew it would be worse, far worse than death, and he believed that this was she who wept in the wigwam of the Black-Foot chief.

He did not even look at her again, nor cast a glance at the group which had been fired on from the fort; he bade brief adieu to Howling Wolf and, followed by the detailed warriors sent to aid him, hurried back toward the cabin on the hill.

Here, finding that Hazel-Eye was yet absent, he did not tarry long enough to more than breathe a message for Mad Eagle to give if she returned before he came back with Cale Durg.

Prepared to rebridge the chasm, and carrying food and drink to revive the invalid, Rupert now hurried on, and as night was close upon them they gathered torch-wood as they went to light them on the route.

They could not have gone without such aid, for soon darkness fell deep upon the tangled forest, and then with blazing torches they struggled slowly forward.

When at last they reached the chasm, he shouted out the hunter's name. A low, moaning cry came back.

"He yet lives!" cried Rupert, as he bade the Indians fell a tree.

CHAPTER XXXVIII.
Asleep at Last.

When Hazel-Eye, disarmed, helpless, found that resistance to the men who had thus surprised her would only cause more rude treatment, she resolved to go quietly on and trust to Heaven for protection and release, hoping, it is true, that

Heaven would put Cale Durg and Rupert on the track of the men who held her a prisoner, and enable them to rescue her.

For a time the party moved on in silence, as fast as they could walk, into a mountain range which she had often looked at, but never traversed. It was too far back from the running streams to be a haunt for fur-bearing animals; thus it had been out of her father's range.

Night was wrapping the earth in shadows dense and dark when they came to a lofty cliff, whose steep face barred their farther progress.

"Bring in plenty of wood, boys; we want light to study such a pretty picture by as this we brought along," said the leader, when they halted.

Then taking the arm of Hazel-Eye in his grasp, he said: "Come on, gal, and don't be afeard; it's rather damp in our cavern home, but fire will make it cozy."

He led the way into what seemed but a gorge at first, but soon, as a man followed with a torch of pine splinters set alight, she saw the rock overhead as well as on either side, and knew that she was in a great cave.

The walls were dripping with moisture, and the air was chilly, but as they passed on a little ways the cave was dryer, and when they stopped again it was in a spot almost free from wet.

Here the smoldering embers of a fire gave evidence of its previous occupation, and blankets, food, and other things which met her eye told that they had made it a dwelling at least for temporary use.

The other men now brought in huge bundles of wood, and in a short time a great fire crackled and blazed in the cavern, warming the air and lighting up its dark walls.

Hazel-Eye sat down on a projecting rock and, with folded arms, looking defiance from her haughty face, watched the men while one was preparing food and the other three were smoking and talking in a low tone.

That they conversed about her, she knew, though she could not hear their words, for she had drawn herself away as far as she could from contact with them, for their eyes were often turned toward her.

After all had supped, the leader left the rest smoking and approached Hazel-Eye.

Standing before her, he studied her face a little while, and then spoke abruptly.

"For a gal, you're about the bravest bit of flesh and blood I ever saw. You'd fight if you had the tools in hand. But we don't want fight just now. But there may be business 'twixt you and us which will pay. You know the chap it seems who heads our gang—for you say he killed your father, and I've heard him say as much."

"Yes; his name is Norcross, and he came from Virginia, where I, too, was born."

"Yes, gal, that's his name, dead sure, and he came from old Virginny, too. And if you had your rights, I reckon you'd be there runnin' a big plantation all to yourself, since your dad went under. That much I gathered from his talk when he was half drunk, boastin' of his deeds. Now what d'ye say? We un's are gittin' sick of playin' hide and seek, and follerin' his mad whims. If a chap took you back safe to old Virginny, and put you on your own, with the papers in your hands he took from the iron chest, what would be the reward?"

"I do not want to go. I am content in my cabin on the hill. Let me go back unharmed, and Heaven will bless you."

"Gal, you're foolish. In the world, with riches in your hand, you'd shine like a queen upon her throne. Now think of what I've told you. I'll have blankets spread for you, and you can sleep and dream, or wake and think till mornin'. Then you must decide. If so you say, we'll work our way back to Virginny after we've laid the 'old man' out, and got the papers. And if you don't say yes, then I reckon your doom is written out and ready to be published."

He turned and went back to the fire, for Hazel-Eye made no reply. But when blankets were brought and laid down near her, she wrapped herself in one and sat down, facing the men, who smoked a while, and then, with one exception, laid down to sleep.

That one, as sentinel, was left awake to watch her and to keep the fire supplied with fuel.

Hazel-Eye watched him long and earnestly, letting her own eyes appear closed, in hopes that he would fall asleep. She even lay down at last, and seemed to slumber, breathing long and regularly, but she was all nerved for instant motion, if his head drooped so that she could hope to pass him.

Alas, hour after hour went by, he showing not a drowsy sign, and by and by he woke another, who took his place. Unless her friends were on her trail, she felt that her case would, indeed, be desperate.

Hours passed, and she knew it must be near the dawn of another day. Must it dawn, and she yet remain helpless in the hands of those bad men? Ah, the sentinel at last, after replenishing the fire, sat down. Hitherto he, like his predecessor, had either walked to and fro, or stood where his eyes could fall on her.

There was hope—for if wearied with long watching while he stood, the ease of rest would surely lull his senses down.

She did not move, she only breathed, that he might think she slept, while her heart grew still in its throbbings, so anxious was she to see his eyes close.

The fire blazed up, and the heat served to strengthen hope in her bosom; so well she knew that it would produce drowsiness! She watched through drooping eyelids, and at last she saw his head begin to descend lower and lower toward his breast. Then, with an effort, it would be raised again, only to slowly droop once more.

Sleep was stealing softly on him now; no matter if he strove to shake it off, the warmth of the fire, his posture too, aided her every hope.

At last, *at last he slept!*

CHAPTER XXXIX.
Lost and Found.

The Indians, urged on by eager gestures from Rupert, soon had a tree across the chasm of Roaring Brook; and first of all the young man bounded over.

Cale was very weak, his exertion to cry out had taken all his strength, and he could only by a look of grateful pleasure show that he knew help had come.

With care Rupert had him lifted out into the open air, and while the Indians built a huge fire to warm him and themselves, Rupert administered the nourishment which he had brought. Not even this could bring back his voice to the hunter, so nearly was life gone, but a warrior, who saw his condition, took from his pouch some roots, pounded them between two stones, and taking water in Rupert's cup, placed the roots in it, and set it on some burning coals.

Soon it began to boil; then cooling it so it would not scald the hunter's lips, he raised the head of the latter and poured the draught down his throat.

The effect was almost instantaneous. The eyes of the hunter brightened, his muscles quivered, and a spasmodic action seemed to pervade his whole frame. In a few minutes he spoke, first in the Indian tongue to the warrior who had given him the draught, then to Rupert.

"You've done your part nobly, lad," said he. "Oh, that I had strength to aid you as much. I've got hard news for ye, boy. . . hard, bitter news."

"Oh, Heaven! It is from Hazel-Eye! In trying to reach you she has fallen into yonder fearful chasm, and she is dead!"

"She did not see me, I could not make her hear, and then *they* came!"

"Who? Speak quick, Cale—who came?"

"Some o' them same cusses that I fought with once before. Four of 'em in a gang, and they stole up before she knew it, took her arms, and marched her off."

"Oh? agony!"

"*Agony,* boy? Think you not 'twas agony for me to see it all, layin' here worse off than a suckin' babe for helplessness, when you know she was like a bit of my own heart to me—as dear as if she were my child."

"Yes, yes; you must have suffered. But I will get upon the trail and follow up the villains!"

"You'll not be able to follow it alone, my lad. I'll have to put some of the Injuns on it with you, and then you must wait till day; no trail can be kept in the night over land like that beyond the brook. By daylight I'll be better, for the Injuns know how to bring me up, at least for a time; and then while they tote me toward the cabin, where I've got to lay a while, you can go after her."

"It is hard to wait," said Rupert, sadly. "Every minute of delay is an hour of misery to me."

Cale grew a little stronger, and as the Indians made a litter and strengthened the bridge over which they would have to carry him, he gave a party, four in number, instructions to follow a trail they would find on the other side and to help White Pine, as they would have helped *him*, in such need.

He also strove to comfort Rupert, who in agony of mind saw Cale Durg moved on upon the litter toward the cabin, while he took up the trail which the Indians were not long in finding—the trail of the four men and their unwilling captive.

CHAPTER XL.
The Flag of Truce of No Avail.

"The fiends! Do they think that because our stock is gone and we have lost twenty men we'll receive a flag and perhaps listen to a proposal to surrender," cried Major Whelpley, as Garnier recognized Captain Norcross, mounted on his gray horse, riding with a band of painted warriors down the slope of a distant hill, with a white flag waving from a spear. "I would die before I would make any terms with them. Perhaps, with that lazy drunkard on their side, they think they can strike terror in our hearts, knowing just our strength from what he tells them. The howitzer shall cut short their expectations. You are a good gunner, Garnier. Be it yours to teach them how we will receive a flag from them, as soon as they are within range."

The eyes of the brave scout glittered as he turned to the gun and fixed the cap and laniard, for it was loaded when the major spoke.

"I'll make them less by half a dozen, I reckon. If the first shot misses, number two will not, for then I'll have their range," he said.

Waiting only till he felt assured the gun would carry to the slow-moving group, the scout, with a long and careful aim, fired.

"Norcross is down! The traitorous maniac has fallen!" was the major's cry, glancing through his glass. "And nearly half the party are down with him. But the others are speeding back. What does it mean? They must value *him* very much, for one warrior has lifted Norcross from the ground, and is bearing his body back before him on his horse. Perhaps he is only wounded. Quick! Load and fire again before they're out of range."

"We're too late. It won't carry to the spot where they are riding now. And see! They descend into a gulley as they go," said Garnier, sighing that he had not another chance. "One thing is sure: they know what good 'twill do to send a flag to us. Heavens! what is that?"

The major's eyes had fallen on an object crossing the plain, coming from the direction of the river, and going toward the hills on which the Indians were camped. It seemed to be a man or animal going at great speed.

"It looks like a man—dressed I cannot define how—look you, Garnier, and tell me what you think."

"It is a man, sir," said the scout, after a long, earnest use of the glass; "a man not dressed at all, for I see his white skin gleaming in the sunlight. He holds something bright in an upraised hand. It looks like a weapon. I cannot understand it, sir, can *you?*"

"A naked white man rushing past our fort toward the red fiends on yonder hills? No, no; it is too strange for all belief. Let me have the glass."

The major looked longer even than the scout had done.

"No horse could run faster, yet it *is* a naked man on foot, with some weapon brandished in his hand," cried the major. "He is running on right for the Indian lines. He is nearing them fast. They see him, and in groups gather as he gets nearer. More and more close; now they seem to stand, themselves surprised. On, he goes; he is almost to the nearest group. What can it mean? They scatter right and left as he speeds on, seeming to fly in terror from his presence. On, on he goes; and wherever the red men see him turn, they fly as if he was a demon grasping for their souls. Their camp is all in alarm. What can it mean? Can he be a *mortal man?*"

"No; sir. He has never slackened that bird-like flight, that headlong speed, since you first saw him near the river. No mortal man could run so swiftly and so long. Look, sir. He is running yet."

"Yes, on through the Indian camp, the warriors scattering as he runs. And now he is near the crest of the hill, near the last group which we can see. He does not pause. On, on he goes, and now I lose sight of him. He has passed beyond the hill. What can it mean?"

CHAPTER XLI.
Hurrying On.

Trembling now, Hazel-Eye watched the sentinel as the head, drooping on the breast, remained bent forward; though not a nerve had quivered when all their eyes had been fiercely bent upon her, now she shook from head to foot with mingled hope and fear.

Could she but reach her revolver, she did not, would not fear them all.

Oh, with what care she moved the blanket which she had wrapped about her form, so as not to make the slightest noise, while she freed herself from incumbrance so that she might move quickly and silently. Now did the early teachings of her life in the wilderness come well in play. She had been taught by her hunter father how to creep upon the feeding deer, the watchful antelope, the suspicious mountain sheep. To move without making a sound—to move and not yet make motion visible.

Freed from the covering she rose, stood for an instant watching the still sentinel, the reclining forms of the other men, and the arms all lying close together.

Then, as noiseless as her own shadow, she slipped forward, not quickly, but with slow, gliding steps, and in a few seconds she bent above the arms she sought.

Heavens! How calm she is now! No tremor in that little hand while she lifts and buckles on her own belt, seeing that her weapons are all right, and takes her own rifle, once her father's weapon, in her hand. She is armed once more, and fear is gone.

What will she do next? Fly in hot haste? No; with a hand which does not shake, she removes every cap from rifle and from pistol, thus for the time making useless the weapons which she cannot take away. Then bold, because they still sleep on so soundly, the sentinel and the three wrapped up by the fire, she takes a torch, lights it, and thus prepares to leave the cavern in the darkness by the route she came.

No delay now, but forward, with a swift, light step—forward through the great damp arches, formed by Nature's mighty hand—on over dripping rocks until she could hear the wind moaning through the branches of the trees. And yet no sound behind her—no sign that her flight was discovered.

A minute more and the cold wind fell blessedly on her hot brow; ah, she hears sounds now, or at least she *thinks* she does, and she casts the blazing torch down and springs out into the wilderness with the fleet bound of a frightened deer.

Away, away, she cares not whither, so she is free from them; she bounds, rejoicing as she hears the sound of running water close at hand, because in it she can walk and thus conceal her tracks and evade pursuit.

She hurried forward while the warm sun rose higher and higher, until it was fairly overhead, and then she saw that she was on rising ground—that she was near the hills and soon might gain a point which she might use to find her proper course.

On, as swiftly as she could go, that the day might not all be spent before she knew how to bend her steps, she hurried.

At last she reached a peak from which she got a view of the country for leagues below. Standing an instant to calm her mind, with closed eyes, she drew her breath, then looked eagerly down in front, and to the right and left.

Joy, joy! She saw smoke rising in a hundred spiral pillars far, far down below her; she saw hills of a reddish brown, to the right of these the volcanic bluffs upon the river below the falls. She knew now where she was. The smoke she saw rose from the camps of the assembled tribes of Indians under Howling Wolf.

She did not pause long to choose her course now. One glance at the sun far down on its western slope, and with her rifle on her shoulder, she stepped forward, not hesitating for a second how to go. No matter for a trail now, no matter for a compass. Had it been a hundred miles, instead of half a score, she would not now have lost her way.

The direction was taken; she could not, would not lose it.

"Night will fall before I can reach the cabin, but I will be there to-night," she murmured, as she hurried on.

CHAPTER XLII.
Rupert's Cry.

Swiftly and untiringly the Indians whom Cale had told to go with Rupert led the latter along the track of those who had captured Hazel-Eye. The track, often almost invisible, and at times lost, was always regained, and the day had not gone far when the party reached a pile of lofty rocks, a ledge where their passage seemed barred.

What is it which Rupert sees, and which, with a cry of joy, he lifts up?

The Indians look angry as they hear his cry, and putting their hands upon their mouths, by this sign tell him he must be silent. The men they seek are very near, without a doubt.

His cry, when he picked up a torch yet smoking, though the blaze was gone and only the remnant left unconsumed was in his hand, told them that the dark opening before them was a cavern, and in it, undoubtedly, would be found those they followed.

The Indians went in a little way, and then returned to prepare torches also, for they could not see where to go. Meantime Rupert looked for tracks in the wet sand by the cavern's mouth, and saw not only the tracks of the men, but the smaller pressure of her foot.

"She lives, thank Heaven, she lives!" he murmured, and he hurried to fix a torch for himself, such as the Indians were preparing.

It was soon done. Cautiously now, the party moved on into the gloomy passage-way. All was still. Not a sound reached their ears from within. In there it was always night, and perhaps the men they sought were sleeping now.

A minute more, and they saw that three men lay wrapped in blankets close by a fire, while a fourth sat with his back toward them. Beyond, near the farther wall, lay a pile of blankets, and there Rupert was sure Hazel-Eye was lying. So sure, indeed, that he could not restrain his impulses, but bounded forward to see and to assure her that help had come.

As he did this, his foot caught under a point of rock, and he stumbled. The sound woke the sleeping men, and though the sentinel was already in the grasp of the leading warrior, one of the others, the leader, snatched his rifle up, aimed at Rupert, and, thanks to the forethought of Hazel-Eye, *snapped* a useless lock, with an aim which, had the cap been in its place, would have sent him to instant death.

The Indians were not men used to trifling. Even while Rupert was lifting the blankets where Hazel-Eye had been, their hatchets were dealing swift death upon the surprised and now struggling men, and three were finished, when Rupert, failing to find the girl trapper, rushed up to save the fourth, that he might know from him where she was.

But the man knew nothing of her, except that she had escaped.

Giving the Indians the arms of the slain men, and such plunder as they could carry easily, he now showed them that the girl had escaped from her captors and was most likely in the forest. With the prisoner, they must hasten to find her track so as to guard her back to her home.

Well pleased with their scalps and trophies in the shape of serviceable arms, the red men hastened to carry out his wishes.

The sun was just going down when they reached the hill, and the Indians would have camped, but Rupert, eager to reach the side of Hazel-Eye, would not pause, and gave them to understand he would go on if he went alone, and they then took up the line of march again.

Her trail soon was lost, for twilight came, and then darkness, but there were stars overhead, and they kept going on—slowly, but surely, in the right direction.

CHAPTER XLIII.

The Papers Recovered and Lost.

Already had Cale Durg been carried on the litter some way along the trail by his Indian bearers, when the thought came into his mind that the package of papers which he had missed the instant before he was shot must have been dropped when he was groping his way through the tree-top to reach the log bridge, the night before, in the height of the storm.

He made the Indians put the litter down, described the bundle in oil-cloth, tied with a buckskin thong, and sent two of the warriors back to find it. While they were gone, the same Indian who had prepared medicine for him before built another fire, and again made him a strengthening drink.

This so revived him that he was able to remain in a sitting posture for nearly half an hour, when the Indians came back and with them brought the precious package.

He now told the Indians to move on for the cabin on the hill, which they reached with their burden in the afternoon.

Mad Eagle's eyes beamed with glad light when he saw Red Panther there, and he spoke such words of praise to the warriors who brought him as a chief seldom utters to those beneath him in rank.

Then he asked where White Pine and Hazel-Eye were, and why they did not came.

Weak as he was, Cale Durg told Mad Eagle all about the capture of the girl trapper, while he, too weak to raise voice or hand, was obliged to see it all.

The chief heard it all without a word until Cale had concluded the story; then he spoke:"The Great Spirit is good!" he said. "Hazel-Eye will not be left in the hands of bad men. She will escape, with His help, or stay unhurt until White Pine gets to her."

"I reckon you're right," said Cale, and as he felt faint and weak, he bade the Indians get food and eat, then go back to Howling Wolf and tell him Red Panther was safe, and thank him for his timely help. The one warrior who was so skilled in medicine he asked to stay until White Pine or Hazel-Eye—or, as he, hoped, both—came back to nurse him, as he knew he must be nursed.

The Indians obeyed his wishes, and ere night came on all but the one alluded to were gone. Still there came no sign of Hazel-Eye—no sound of the footsteps of White Pine or his little band of trailers.

Hour after hour passed, and the old hunter grew sad and dispirited, for he kept awake, urging the Indian to keep him up with strong herb-drink until they came, or he could hear from them.

Night was on the earth, and the hooting owl alone could be heard in its stillness. Suddenly there came another sound upon the listening ear of the wounded hunter. Mad Eagle heard it also, and the red attendant sprang to his feet, for it seemed like, the shriek of a maddened animal.

Nearer and nearer, louder and louder, until it seemed like, and yet unlike, a human voice, shouting out some wild cry.

The Indian rushed to the cabin door with his rifle in his hand, and as he opened it Cale Durg thought he heard, in a shrieking cry, the words:

"*My son—my son!*"

But the sound passed on and grew fainter until it was heard no more.

The Indian came back from the cabin door with a look of terror on his face.

"It was a spirit walking through the air—the spirit of a dead pale-face!" he said, and he sat down trembling.

A second later there was a shriek—a loud, piercing shriek—and Cale Durg tried to get upon his feet.

"It was the voice of Hazel-Eye—her cry for help which then rung in our ears!" he said, as he sank back helpless. "Go, Marten-Slayer, go!" he cried, to the Indian. "Go help her, if you have as much courage as a rabbit!"

"Marten-Slayer is not afraid of anything that lives!" said the Indian, gravely. "But spirits which walk on the clouds, which cry bad cries, and are in torment, fill the heart with fear. Marten-Slayer *dare not go out!*"

"*Coward!* Oh, that I could go!" moaned the helpless hunter. "I know it was her cry! The first sounds, too, came from some human voice, and the one who made them went past our cabin door."

"It was a spirit. I saw it in a cloud, like the mist of the storm which stands upon the mountain-top!" said Marten-Slayer. "I saw it, and my heart grew stiff, as if the hand of winter froze it."

"Spirits do not talk, though they may walk," said the hunter angrily. "It was no spirit-cry which last fell on our ears. I was a woman's call for help—I know it was."

"Hark! I hear footsteps now!" said the Indian. "I hear the tread of men."

"Yes; the voice of White Pine has reached my ear," said Mad Eagle.

"He comes—I hope that Hazel-Eye is with him," said the hunter, when he heard the voice of Rupert speaking to some one advancing with him.

The next second Rupert entered, with his prisoner by his side and the four Indians in his rear.

"Ah! you are here! I've recovered the *papers*, but where Hazel-Eye?" said Cale, as the young man hurried to his side.

"Is she not here? We have been on her trail all day. She escaped from her captors, of whom you see the only one that lives. The scalps of the others are in the belts of those braves. I expected to find her here."

"She has not come. But a little while ago I heard a scream, which I felt sure came from her lips. The minute before there was a wild, screaming sound, which Marten-Slayer says came from a spirit. There is some fearful mystery in this. She has not come; she must be near. Go, and with the Indians seek for her. Seek all around with blazing torches in your hands, and you will find her, or some trace, I know. It was her cry that heard. There is but one other voice like hers on earth."

Urged in their own tongue to hurry out and aid White Pine in the search by Cale and Mad Eagle also, every Indian hurried forth with him.

The prisoner, with his hands bound, was left in the presence of the two invalids, and, thoughtless act, without guard.

"We've met before. You were one of the gang who tried to put me under, a while ago down the hill," said Cale, faintly, as he glanced at the stranger.

"Ay, I was on your trail since, and I thought the old man did for you then. You've luck in livin', you have," said the man, gruffly.

"Yes, livin' as long as I can is a part of my nature. What are you doing there?" answered Cale, as the prisoner held his hands deliberately over the lighted lamp.

"Burnin' myself loose, my covey," said the man with calm composure, holding his wrists fairly in the blaze, though the skin cracked and shriveled with the heat which was burning into his flesh, while it was severing the bonds that held his arms together. "This is hot work, but I might be in hotter if I staid to see what you 'un's would do with me. So here goes. Ah! There's that cussed bundle o' papers; I've seen them before. Tell the gal I'll keep 'em for her."

The wretch was free, and while Cale, too weak to reach a weapon, and Mad Eagle in the same condition, could only cry feebly for those outside to return, the ruffian, who knew they were too far away to hear, snatched the bundle of papers and rushed from the cabin with a taunting laugh.

"Misery! the papers for which I've risked so much are gone again, and that wretch gone to laugh at us who could not stop him. Hazel-Eye and the boy will both blame me, and they've a right to do it."

This was the cry of Cale Durg as the ruffian rushed away.

"He will not go far. My braves are keen of scent, have bright eyes for the trail, and they shall go on it while it is fresh," said Mad Eagle. "Our limbs had no strength, he knew it, and he laughed at us. We will take him and hear him howl at the torture-stake."

"He'll not howl much, by the way he stood fire here," said Cale, dryly. "The cuss must have been burnt to the very bone before that buckskin parted."

"Rupert! Oh, where is Rupert? I saw him—*him*—the murderer of my father!"

It was Hazel-Eye who came rushing in, her eyes wildly glaring, her face white, as if she was in mortal fear. "Where—where is Rupert?"

"He's out lookin for you, gal; he'll soon be here. Sit down—sit down, for Heaven's sake! You surely are not goin' mad!"

"*He* looks for me? Ah! the torches from which I fled—were they alight to search for me?"

"I reckon so, gal—I reckon so; but sit ye down till he comes back. 'Twill not be long, I'm sure."

"No, no; he seeks for me, and he may see what I have seen—hear what I have heard! Oh, horror! I will go to him! *Rupert!* RUPERT!"

Cale called to her to stop, but she would not.

She rushed out, just as she had entered, in wild haste, and with a frantic look.

"Crazy—crazy, as sure as that I live!" moaned Cale; "and here we have to lay and see her go out, when she should wait for him."

"Rupert! Rupert!"

This cry came back twice or thrice, and then they heard no more in the cabin for a full hour or more.

Then Rupert came, bringing the rifle once owned by Trapper Guy, but carried lately by his daughter.

He had found it and her track not more than a quarter of a mile from the cabin, and close beside it the track of a man in bare feet. The Indians who followed Rupert in said that it was a white man's track.

"Boy, she has been here, all wild and crazy-like, hollerin' for you; and when she heard me say you were out lookin' for her, she fled out again, in spite of all my pleadin' she should stay and wait for you."

"Heavens! where can she be now? Out—out with me again, and look for her!" cried Rupert, almost wild.

"Hold on a second, lad. Your prisoner burned his wristlets loose, grabbed the papers, and run. Look for *him* while you're at it."

Rupert did not wait to hear these words; he was far away ere the last had left Cale Durg's lips.

Again the Indians were sent out to help him by Mad Eagle, while Cale murmured: "He has gone crazy, too, I reckon, or he will if he don't find her."

CHAPTER XLIV.

Moving Down Stream.

When night fell still and dark over the stockade, Garnier, the scout, and Dion, an old comrade and dear friend of his, well prepared, started from the post, amply provided with cooked provisions, arms, and ammunition for the perilous trip, which, if successful, would bring relief to the beleaguered garrison. Indeed, it was the only hope of the brave men whom they left behind.

Silently and cautiously the two men crept away, side by side, for Garnier knew Howling Wolf so well as a warrior that he expected lines of sentinels and watchful scouts were scattered all around the post to prevent just such an enterprise as that he now was starting on.

He was right. They had not gone five hundred yards from the fort when Garnier touched Dion's arm, and both dropped flat from their half-raised position.

Between them and the sky they now could see three forms—Indians mounted, in the very line they were pursuing. These sat still, as if they were listening for a repetition of some sound already heard.

The two men dared not move while the Indians were so near, for they were in easy pistol shot, and Garnier knew not how many more might be within their signal-call.

For a long time the men were forced to lie thus motionless, but at last the Indians rode slowly on, and Garnier heard one say: "We heard prairie-dogs in the grass; the pale-faces will not leave the fort."

Garnier touched Dion's arm when they could neither hear nor see an Indian, and they crept on again toward the river, whose rushing waters sounded plainly in their ears.

Precious as time was they dared not hurry, for again they almost came upon a party around a sunken fire in a hollow who were so still that, till he saw a glimmer of light, the scout had no idea of their presence. These were also within pistol-shot when he and Dion crept back and took another route to reach the river.

This time, though they saw and heard videttes*, they reached the water, and,

---

*Mounted sentries stationed in advance of pickets.

lashing their arms and their powder on their backs, they waded out as far as they could, and in a bent posture kept their footing, and then moved down the stream.

The ice-cold water, coming from the melting hills of snow not very far away, so chilled their limbs that they were forced to leave it in a little while or they would have been too much benumbed to move.

When they were a little rested both men took the stream again, and, wading where they could and swimming where they had to, they reached the island just before the dawn of day.

And well for them it was they reached it when they did, for now they could see that scouts were moving to and fro on every bluff as far as they could see below, and that, beside this, hunters were moving hither and thither whose watchful eyes it would have been next to impossible for them to escape had they tried to push on.

Even where they were ensconced in a dense grove of willows, they felt far from safe. They were chilled to the marrow bone, but did not dare to build a fire to dry or warm by, for even if the smoke was not seen, light as it would be from the small sticks they could have lighted, its scent would be borne toward the occupied shore, for the wind blew directly from them in that direction.

Hardy as they were, they suffered, but their blood was somewhat warmed by the fever of excitement; for before they were fairly settled in a hiding-place, they saw a group of mounted Indians, with some on foot, examining what they feared from all appearance of the ground must be the route they passed to reach the river.

"They've found our track, Dion," said Garnier. "I'm sure they have."

"If they have, two men about our size will not reach the settlements," replied Dion, coolly. "There's one thing sure, they'll not get my hair before it is paid for."

"Nor mine," said Garnier. "We may as well look to our tools. They're on some trail, and if it is not ours, we know not whose it can be."

"They are. We must slide out here, for they'll be sure to search this island. Can't we loosen a log or two from that drift there and throw some brush on them, and, clinging to them, float with the current out of reach?"

"We can try it, mate. It is our best and about our only chance. We can work under the cover of the willows, if we work quick before they get down to where we took water."

The two men hurried to carry out this plan, for three or four gangs of Indians had concentrated on the trail just found, and were hunting it out. They followed it to the water, and then came down along the bank to see if it came out again, or it could be discovered in the water where there was little current. And now some swam across the river on their ponies to scout the other side.

Just as they arrived, fully thirty or forty of them, where the scouts had rested on the shore, what seemed to be a part of an old raft of drift-wood, loose and disjointed, broke away from the island and went with the current down the stream.

Of this the Indians took no notice, for they had just discovered the fresh tracks again, seen where the men sat down to rest, and where they waded off toward the island.

In a second a dozen ponies, with an Indian clinging to the mane of each, were swimming toward the island; and twice the number of Indians, with guns ready to fire, watched the island to see the first sign of the discovered white men when they should show themselves.

The Indians were soon on the island, and there discovered where those they sought had been, and the next second found out how they got away.

In a second their yells and signals told those on shore where to look, and riding furiously down the stream, gathering numbers as they went, the red men pursued the drift.

The scouts were now literally helpless. Out of their depth they could not use their fire-arms, and when the Indians mounted and dismounted began to take to the water by scores to destroy or capture them, they knew the hour for death or captivity had surely come.

"It's precious little use to try to fight here," said Garnier. "If we were on dry land I'd never croak, but say fight to the death. If we give up and they don't put us under at once, we may get away. Shall we try it?"

"Ay, if you think best, mate," said the other.

Garnier now threw off all attempt to conceal himself, and, dropping his weapons in the water, raised himself on a log so his head could be seen, and held up his empty hands as a signal of surrender. Dion did the same.

With many a wild yell of triumph the Indians closed upon them, towed the drift to shore, surrounded the two men, and held a pow-wow. After a fierce argument, in which it was discussed which was best, to slay and scalp them there or to take them to Howling Wolf, that he might put them to the torture, the latter plan was decided on.

Then bound, they were led toward the camp upon the hillside, overlooking the stockade.

CHAPTER XLV.
"My Soul Is Lost!"

"Rupert! Rupert!" cried Hazel-Eye, when she fled from the cabin in her wild excitement to seek for him who was even then looking so anxiously for her.

"Here! here!" cried a voice, so far away that she only knew by the sound it came from riverward; and, supposing that none but he would answer thus, away in that direction she ran swiftly.

"*Rupert!* RUPERT!" she screamed again, as she ran on.

"Here, love—here!" came the voice once more, and now so near that she rushed on, reckless of where she went so that she met him quickly.

She ran on a little way, a hundred yards or more, and then stopped to hear the beating of her own throbbing heart, and to ask in a piteous tone:

"Oh, Rupert! I am here! Where—where are you?"

"Here, gal—here, with your dowry in my hand!" hissed a husky voice in her ears; and she felt a hand clutching her slender throat, while another grasped her arm with crushing force.

"Don't struggle, gal; it isn't wise," said the ruffian. "If I handle your slim throat with these raw hands of mine, I'll get so mad I'll squeeze the very life right out of ye. I'm wolfish with 'em hurtin' as they do, and uglier than the she-painter. 'Tis but a little way to the snuggest hidin' place you've ever seen; the old man fixed it up as snug as snug could be. I'll make you cozy there, and—Hark! Thunder, what a screech! That's some animal."

The sound which made the man start and shake was not an Indian yell; their yells he had heard not more than a second or two before. It was a wild, unearthly cry, as if a wild beast in fearful pain tried to make a human sound to speak its sufferings.

The unhappy girl felt herself lifted up in his brawny arms; she felt that he was bearing her along. The thorns in the thick chaparral through which he passed tore her tender flesh; she could not cry out, she could not move hand or foot. Oh! how fearful was her strait.

Again she heard, and he heard, that fearful shriek, that unearthly sound, and she felt the man tremble while he bore her on.

Nearer came the dreadful sound, and now she recognized it. She has heard it once that night before: she had caught a glimpse of some form in human shape, which seemed to rush by her, shrieking out a fearful cry, and she had fainted then.

She did not faint now; she joyed to hear it, and to feel that fast as the brute who carried her fled on, the pursuing voice came nearer every second.

"It gains! it gains! My soul is lost!" groaned the man, as he staggered on, still holding her in his desperate grasp.

CHAPTER XLVI.

A New Hope.

When Rupert Norcross, on that night of horrors, rushed from the trapper's cabin, crying that he heard Hazel-Eye—he was right. The listening ear of love was not deceived.

Nearly fainting, with blood on her face and hands, bespattering her dress, he met her staggering toward him.

"Saved—saved!" she murmured out, as she fell into his arms.

"Saved—dear one, saved!" he added, as he bore her in, to find her now unconscious.

"Look quick, lad, and see where she's hurt!" cried Cale Durg, himself unable to do as he directed. "Don't give way to feelin'; be a man and help the gal."

Rupert carried her in and laid her on her own bed, got water as hastily as possible and bathed her face, striving by his loving words, as well as by other methods, to bring back the sense of life to her.

At last he succeeded, and from her own lips, as well as by careful examination, found that she was not wounded, except by severe scratches from thorns as she had been carried through the thickets.

"Gal—gal—what's that in your belt?" asked the hunter, quickly. Then before she could reply, he cried: "'Tis the bundle o' papers, gal—your papers from the iron chest—how came they there?"

"I do not know—I suppose the wretch who carried me off put them there. I think that he is slain. I saw the gleam of a knife—I heard the shout of him who rushed to my rescue, while I screamed, and then I felt the gush of blood flying in my face, and hot upon my hands and arms. The wretch loosed his hold on me—I knew by the river close at hand where I was, and so ran back here as fast as I could. You know now as much as I."

Now, a fearful scream was heard outside.

"Ah—that shrieking cry?" cried Rupert. "Oh, Heaven! can it be my father's voice?"

"Go see, Rupert, go and see. If it be, he has saved my life, perhaps done more!" cried Hazel-Eye, as the wild cry came nearer than before.

Then, as a form appeared at the open door, she fled with a shriek into her own room, for it did not seem mortal.

Rupert shuddered, but as that form staggered feebly on, and fell to the floor, with one faint cry, he recognized it, and cast over the nude and lacerated frame a robe of furs, while he knelt down in agony and breathed out the word:

"Father!"

"Who speaks? Not he? My son is dead—dead when I can prove my innocence! Ha! ha! The waters gave up the dead. The elk with the knife—the knife—"

A gurgling sound, and a choking sob, and the man ceased to speak.

Rupert Norcross seemed stupefied. He could not understand these words.

There was the knife, or one exactly like it, which had given Guy Mauricenne his death-wound.

Yet there on the shelf, before them all, lay blade and hilt of the knife found in the neck of the good hound Rolla, when the iron chest was taken. Blade, and hilt, and handle, though apart, were precisely like that now held in the hand of him who lay upon the floor, and whom Rupert knew to be the wreck of his father, though he supposed he had been slain when fired upon from the stockade.

Cale Durg was the first to speak.

"The papers—you have 'em gal, read them and see what name is there!" cried the hunter.

Hazel-Eye unrolled the oil-cloth which covered them, and took out a package. At the first look, she recognized a name, and a cold chill ran through her frame when she saw it.

"If there is a name read it," said Rupert, quickly.

"No—no," she gasped. "I do not, will not believe it can be so!"

"The name—the name!" said Rupert. "Read it, even if it is my own."

She shuddered, but lifting a paper, she placed her finger beneath the title. Rupert saw it, and desperately read aloud: "*Deed of Warrantee, from Henry Norcross, unto Guy Mauricenne.*"

"*Henry* Norcross? Not my father *Robert*, but Henry, his twin brother who died or was killed when I was but a child!" he cried.

"Who calls for Robert Norcross?" said the ghastly wreck, the man so nearly worn to death.

"Henry—Henry, your brother, *father*, *where* is he!" screamed Rupert, wild with a new thought, a new hope.

"Henry—he was killed—and then they said he lived again—oh, that my son, my poor son lived!"

"Father! Father! I live and I believe you innocent," cried Rupert, now on his knees, by his father's side.

"Rupert—alive? My boy, and he says I'm innocent? This is enough—let me die now!" gasped the poor old man, and he fainted quite away, as he recognized his son.

Cale Durg, so excited that he sat up in spite of his weakness, looked at the man, and then spoke: "Rupert. All has been the darkest kind o' doubt in my mind about all this matter. If your father has a brother livin', that brother has been the cuss in buckskin, botherin' us all this time—'twas he who killed Trapper Guy, 'twas he whose name is on that deed—'twas Henry Norcross, and he had a knife just like your father's."

"Then it was he whom I saw in the camp of Howling Wolf, with the girl of the golden hair!" cried Rupert.

"Boy—what do you mean? Speak—or—or if I could I'd strike ye down."

"In my own trouble I forgot it all," cried Rupert. "Or else I dared not tell you, I've been so crazed I know not which. But in the camp of Howling Wolf, I saw a female with blue eyes and golden hair, and while she wept, I asked the chief who she was. His answer was, that she was to be his wife, he had made the alliance with her father."

"Heavens—it was Medora—my Medora!"

"Yes—I spoke the name—she started at the sound and I gave her a sign to hope."

"Oh, why—why did you not snatch her from his power and bring her here to me!"

"You must know how little power I had there. I went for help for you," said Rupert, reproachfully.

"Fly now—do not waste a second—and tell Howling Wolf she is mine— mine! I will die for her!"

Mad Eagle raised his thin, wasted hand—a sign that he would speak.

"White Pine could speak no word which Howling Wolf would listen to," said he. "What Red Panther said with his own lips the great war-chief might stop to hear. What Mad Eagle said he would give ear to. Let a swift runner bring in my warriors to carry Red Panther and Mad Eagle both to the Black-Foot camp. Then Mad Eagle knows Howling Wolf will hear our words and give back to Red Panther the angel of the golden hair, whom he loves with a single heart."

"Let it be so, if it must," groaned Cale. "But every minute of delay seems a year of life to me. I shall grow gray before the nightfall comes."

Mad Eagle made the first runner of his warriors hasten for litter bearers to the nearest line, and told the rest to make ready everything to move him and Red Panther to the camp of Howling Wolf.

While this was being done, Rupert, attending on his father, saw that reason was coming slowly back, though he was too weak to prove it much in conversation. Yet he could say enough to convince that son, if not all the rest, that he had been innocent of murder, innocent of treason to his comrades, and had never touched or seen the papers in the iron chest; that, when boys, he and his brother had everything alike, even to knives and guns.

"My Uncle Henry must be alive, and be the one who has wrought all this wickedness," said he, after he gathered from his father that his twin brother had been reported dead, and then alive; but if alive, would not be apt to be doing well, for he had been very wild and wicked in his younger days, had killed a friend in a duel, and been forced to fly his home.

"If it is he, then I fear he is the father of my lost Medora," said Cale Durg. "It is the only way I can account for seeing her with one whom I supposed to be your father. The two must look alike if they were twins. Oh, how can we unravel all this mystery?"

"Easily, if he yet lives. Never, if he was killed when the howitzer was fired— that is, completely, for the tongue which might confess will then be hushed forever."

"We will know when the camp of Howling Wolf is reached," said Cale.

"To know it is as important to me as it can be to you," said Rupert. "It will prove my father's utter innocence of crime. I will have him carried also to the Indian camp, and I and Hazel-Eye will keep him company."

"Yes, Rupert; for after the suffering I have endured, brave as I thought myself, I dare not stay alone," said Hazel-Eye.

"Darling, it shall not be my fault if you are ever left alone again. Get ready, the Indian litter-bearers will soon be here."

CHAPTER XLVII.
A Gallant Volunteer.

The night had been passed most anxiously by Major Whelpley in the stockade. He had not slept at all, for he knew how difficult it would be for Garnier and his mate to pass the cordon of sentinels which the Indians would keep out, and until he was sure they were beyond the peril of capture, he could not rest.

When the light of day came, from the top of the stockade, he scanned the river and the plains as far down as his eye could reach with his glass, to see if there was any sign of their having been killed or taken. For he knew the Indians would be apt to show their triumph in either case, and for that he scanned every group which he could see far or near.

Soon after sunrise, while he had a cup of coffee in his hands, brought there by his servant, the major was visited on the roof of the stockade by Dr. Bugle, who came to make his morning report.

The major was excited, and told the doctor to look through his glass.

The doctor took the glass and looked in the direction indicated by the words and motions of the major.

"Shades of misery!" he muttered. "The red devils have got the two scouts, Garnier and Dion, in their hands. They'll murder them by inches. What a shame. Two brave men, and such subjects as they would have made if they'd died here instead of there."

"Yes, our two messengers are captured, and my last hope goes with them. While food lasts, we can stay here, but when it is done, then we all go under. We might as well pitch out now and die fighting, as to linger on until we grow too weak to fight."

"Can't we work some way to rescue the poor fellows? Can't we buy their lives? I'd give all I have but my specimens and my antidotes to save 'em. Let's send a flag and try."

"I fired on the flag the Indians sent. They will retaliate, and not receive one from me even should I send it."

"May be not. I'll run the risk and carry it."

"Will you, doctor? Do you mean what you say?"

"I do, major. I generally say what I mean, and mean what I say. I'm willing to risk a little to save two such brave men—such splendid subjects. Were they to die with us I'd be paid tenfold for my trouble."

"Doctor, you're a strange subject yourself, but there is good in you. If you'll try to get to the chief of the Black-Feet with a flag, you can offer anything we have for the men but our arms and ammunition, and say we will leave this section at once, without delay, carrying nothing with us but our arms."

"I'll try it, major—that is I and my man. Jean Burte—*Jean Burte*, I say!"

"Yes, monsieur doctaire, I am here."

"Get ready to go with me to the Indian camp, sir!"

"To ze camp Indian, sare? To be murdered; to be roast alive and zen eat wizout salad? Ceil, doctare, you do not mean *zat*?"

"I do mean that. Get ready, or I'll roast you here and baste you with tincture of capsicum."

CHAPTER XLVIII.
"What Does It Mean?"

Howling Wolf stood in front of his wigwam. His face was dark with anger. He had sent food and drink to the girl with golden hair, and she had refused to touch it! She had not tasted meat, nor had her lips been moistened with drink, since he who called her his daughter brought her to the wigwam of the chief and offered her as a surety of his faith if the chief formed an alliance with him.

Suddenly a runner came from the plains toward the river, and when the chief heard his words—then his face was all aglow with ferocious gladness. The runner came to tell him that two pale-faces had been taken, while trying to escape down the river from the fort.

"Ho! Call all the chiefs and warriors together!" he shouted. "Let the Great Prophet's tom-tom sound. We will set the torture post and roast the pale-faces by a fire slower than the tortoise in its journey. Our young braves shall dance the scalp dance with warm scalps in their hands. Let the pale-face in his wooden fort shake now. He can send no runners past the watchers of my tribe."

Soon the long line of yelling savages came in sight with the two helpless prisoners.

Howling Wolf looked at the prisoners, and a sardonic smile again lit his demoniac features.

Two great posts, painted red, were now set in the ground in front of the wigwam of the chief, and the warriors by hundreds began to form the death-circle. Outside, with horrible screams of fiendish joy and rage, the squaws of the warriors lately slain danced in wild delight.

And while this was going on, runners came to tell the chief that two pale-faces, with a white flag in the hand of one, were coming from the fort.

"Ugh! It is well!" he cried. "Let them come and see these pale-faces suffer. Then we will keep one, and send the other back to tell what he has seen—to tell the pale-faces how they, too, shall eat fire and dance upon the path that leads to death. The heart of Howling Wolf is glad. Let the dying pale-face, the father of the maiden with the golden hair, be brought out here where he can see the men suffer who have made him sick."

Four stout warriors went in and brought out the wounded man, who was so like Captain Robert Norcross that both Garnier and Dion shook in anger on their feet, and muttered "traitor!"

He was placed in a sitting posture near the chief, and held up by a strong warrior, while drink was given him to infuse life enough in him to see the torture.

"Let the splinters be brought to stick into the flesh of the hated pale-faces, and the pine knots got ready for the fire," said Howling Wolf. "Then let the men who come with the flag be brought here."

"Dr. Bugle!" groaned Garnier, as the doctor and Jean Burte, the bearers of the flag, were led into the circle.

"Yes, man—yes, 'tis I. What do these *aborigines* intend to do?" exclaimed the doctor.

"To burn us—torture us to death. For heaven's sake kill us with your own hand!" cried the scout.

"No—no; I come to buy your lives. I've risked my own to do it. Where is the chief?"

"I am here," said Howling Wolf. "But the pale-face will waste his breath if he talks to Howling Wolf. He may fold his arms, and see the pale-faces burn."

"I will give blankets, beads, whisky, gold—all that we have in the fort, but our arms and powder, if the chief will spare those men, and let them go back with me, and we will leave the country of the aborigines forever!" said the doctor, eagerly, while poor Jean Burte stood and trembled.

"Ugh! Howling Wolf is not a woman. He is a brave. His lodge-pole is hung thick with scalps. See! the scars of a hundred battles mark his breast!"

The chief threw back his gorgeous robe of painted skins, revealing his giant form covered with scars.

A runner, forcing his way in, brought a message to the chief. The latter heard it, and raised his hand as a signal for those who were about to begin the torture to wait.

"Mad Eagle and Red Panther are here," he said. "They come with White Pine and Hazel-Eye to look upon the agony of the doomed! The pale-faces may be proud. They have many eyes to look upon them while they dance the dance of death. Ugh! we will wait."

At this moment, the surging crowd gave way, while the little column came forward—the warriors who carried Mad Eagle, Red Panther, and the form of Captain Robert Norcross, while by the side of the latter walked Rupert and Hazel-Eye.

The chief cast one wondering glance at the dying man, held up by the warrior at his side, and another at him who lay on the litter brought in and placed side by side with that of Mad Eagle and Cale Durg.

"Which is the spirit, which the real man?" he cried, for, white and ghastly, both men looked as much alike as like could be.

And their eyes met, for Rupert raised his father's head to give him drink from a flask which he carried.

"Henry!"

"Robert!"

The first spoke in a tone of wonder—the other gasped out his brother's name, for both recognized each other, though years had gone by since they met.

Even the prisoners trembled now, for this was wonderful to them; they could not understand it, and for a moment a superstitious fear made them think one must be a fiend assuming human form to mock the other.

"What does it mean? Has the Great Spirit made two men so alike that one can take the other's place and not be known?" asked Howling Wolf.

Mad Eagle spoke. He told Howling Wolf that the Great Spirit had made two beings just alike, and given one a heart of goodness, while He let the other spirit guide the other.

That the good man was the father of White Pine, on whom he had laid the symbol of protection when he named him. The other was he who was dying there before them.

Meantime, Henry Norcross, feeling death in his almost ice-cold heart, spoke in agony to Robert. "Brother, I am dying," he gasped out. "A life crime is at its end. I have prayed to meet you before I died, but little expected it here and now. Ah, where is my child, Medora, she is——"

"Where—where is my love, Medora?" cried Cale Durg, hearing the name from his lips.

A glad, wild cry broke from a woman's lips, within the wigwam, and it rang out on a hundred ears. While Howling Wolf turned his fierce eyes toward her, Medora rushed to the litter where Red Panther lay, and buried her weeping face from sight upon his bosom.

"My child! My child!" groaned Henry Norcross, in his dying agony. "I risked all for her, and have lost!"

"Murderer of Guy Mauricenne, what could you gain?" said Rupert, sternly, realizing as he looked upon that face and form, all that he had so unjustly charged upon his father.

"I tried to gain her fortune for my child!" gasped Henry, as his head drooped on his breast. "I have lost—I have lost! Heaven, how like her mother!" groaned the dying man, as he cast his eye over Hazel-Eye. "Girl, your father robbed me of a love which was more than life to me. I have sought a fearful vengeance—ah—I perish, and now my punishment will come."

A quivering gasp and he was gone.

"Why does she weep upon your breast?" asked Howling Wolf, as he bent over Cale Durg and pointed to Medora. "She is the promised wife of Howling Wolf."

"She is the wife of Red Panther now!" said Cale, and his eyes flashed as he spoke. "The Great Spirit has been witness to our vows. Before that man brought her before the chief, her heart was mine, and we had vowed to live for each other or to die together. Howling Wolf is great. He has many squaws of his own proud race. He would not tear from Red Panther's breast the lily which the Great Spirit planted there?"

The chief trembled with emotion, which he strove to hide.

Mad Eagle saw the act, and he spoke once more. "Howling Wolf is like the tallest pine upon the mountain top. All eyes look up and see him. Let him be good as well as great. Let Red Panther have his wife. See! her father's head is down; he will never lift it up again. He is dead. The Evil Spirit has passed away. Let Howling Wolf, in his might, show mercy, for it will be like the sun which the Great Spirit sends to make the ground bright, when He calls in the black spirits of the storm and shuts them in his caves."

"Mad Eagle is right! His words are words of wisdom. He is a true brother to Howling Wolf. I will listen to his counsel," said the chief.

"The heart of Mad Eagle is glad. We will grow strong, for the smile of the Great Spirit will warm our hearts. Let Howling Wolf tell his warriors to go to their camp-fires and cook meats for a great feast."

"But look! the torture-posts are up, and our enemies are bound!" said Howling Wolf.

"Mad Eagle sees. But let Howling Wolf yet listen to the words of counsel. Darken not an hour of gladness. Throw water on the fire and unbind the prisoners; we decide the fate in council. The Great Spirit shall tell us what to do."

"It is well," said Howling Wolf. "Again my ears open to the speech of Mad Eagle. I give to Red Panther the maiden with the golden hair, who sobs upon his breast. White Pine and Hazel-Eye stand hand-in-hand, and Howling Wolf will never part them. If it is the Great Spirit's will that the pale-faces he allowed to go in peace, the chief of the Black-Feet will bow his head and say, 'let His will be done!'"

Never were men more joyfully surprised than were Garnier and Dion, when they found themselves once more free and were told to go back with Dr. Bugle and Jean Burte to the fort, to tell Major Whelpley, Howling Wolf would hold a peace-talk, when the sun of another day stood midway in the heavens, and that to Captain Norcross, his son, and Cale Durg and Hazel-Eye, aided by Mad Eagle, they owed both life and liberty, as well as the probability that the whites would be allowed to go in peace from the hunting-grounds of the brave warriors in the great North-west.

Not until moving on toward the fort, unimpeded by the Indians, could they fully realize their miraculous escape.

Reader, I have almost finished.

Would you see a happy sight to-day?

Go where the Shenandoah heads in the Blue-Ridge Mountains of Virginia, and in a valley as lovely as can be found in all our broad land, you will find under one great roof, in one old-fashioned house that has stood a century as the old Norcross Plantation home to happy families.

Caleb Durg, and she who was Medora Norcross, and Rupert Norcross, with she who was Anna Mauricenne, have here united fortunes and settled down for life, while one gray-haired man wanders, sad and yet with a quiet pleasure in his sadness, over the broad ground where he and his twin brother played.

THE END.

ᖪᖷ III ᖷᖪ

The Miner Detective; or, The Ghost of the Gulch

Editor's Notes

Like *Hazel-Eye, the Girl Trapper, The Miner Detective; or, The Ghost of the Gulch* is unique among Ned Buntline westerns, and for some of the same reasons. The setting is compact, and the story is not bothered by a number of long-distance chases and hackneyed melodramatic devices. Additionally, the geographic background of the setting—the gold fields of Northern California—is confidently accurate and unencumbered by topographical impossibilities. The cast of characters is remarkably small for a Ned Buntline dime novel; there is only one villainous element for the hero, Melrose, to contend with. What's at stake is far more specific and, to some degree, more plausible than in most of Judson's other western adventures.

Another exceptional feature of *The Miner Detective* is the first-person point of view. In almost all of the other tales, the third-person omniscient is the point of view of choice, with dialogue and action taking responsibility for most of the exposition. The first person is reserved for the authorial voice in those cases, and it appears mostly as an intrusion or commentary on the characters or the situation. But in *The Miner Detective,* the narrator is an interacting character who becomes caught up in the plot and actually plays a key role in its resolution. Although never named, the narrator possesses most of the same qualities that Judson imagined himself to have.

The strange uniqueness of this novelette seems to suggest that this might not actually be a genuine Ned Buntline story; and since there is no known previous publication of it before the 1889 *Log Cabin Library* reprint reproduced here, such speculation finds traction. The heroes and villains of *The Miner Detective* seem to be better rounded and more realistically defined than average for a Ned Buntline dime novel, and the plot is more direct and unencumbered by intrusive comedy or authorial observation. Finally, it's more or less a ghost story, something else that sets it apart from the rest of the Ned Buntline canon.

At the same time, there are sufficient indicators that this is indeed a genuine Ned Buntline tale. Many of his linguistic trademarks appear in the text, especially his references to temperance, and elements of his style are clearly evident. Finally, it is one of only a few stories set in California and very likely reflects on his experience during his San Francisco stay between 1868–1869, during which time he is known to have visited the gold fields around Sacramento.

Of all the Ned Buntline westerns, *The Miner Detective* probably is one of the few that stands up today, almost without apology or excuse. There is far less of the farcical exaggeration and hyperbole that infects many of his other books. Here, the hero is quiet and deliberate, almost mysterious, and the solution of the ultimate crime, although telegraphed early on, remains a more important goal than any romance. In many ways, the story forecasts the sophistication of the detective story as it would be developed by Arthur Conan Doyle, and it demonstrates Edward Z. C. Judson's instincts for creating real suspense and keeping the reader in the dark while the mystery unfolds.

⋆ The ⋆
MINER
DETECTIVE

CHAPTER I.

The Apparition.

"Not for all the gold in the great 'Blue Lead'—not for all the coin your team could draw on a dead level, would I pass another night in the gulch down there, sir! If I haven't grown twenty years older in a single night, call me a tangle-necked liar, and I'll stand it without squirmin', and that's more'n I often take straight!"

There was a genuine look of horror in the honest face of the man who thus addressed me, and I ran my eyes over him from head to foot, with an interest heightened by the survey.

His dress, the pick, pan, and shovel which he carried, as well as the roll of blankets strapped to his back, and the knife and revolver in his belt, told that he was a miner on a prospecting tour.

"You look as if you'd been scared, my friend," said I, as I drew my horses in under the shade of an oak on a level spot in the grade, for I was ascending the mountain leading up from Yankee Jim's toward Wisconsin Diggings and Iowa Hill.

"*Scare* was no name for it, sir. If I hadn't got my full growth Barnum might have me for a dwarf. I know I've shriveled some, old as I am."

"You've seen a nest of grizzlies, I suppose," said I, carelessly.

"*Grizzlies!* Ha! ha! GRIZZLIES!"

He laughed scornfully. Then he stripped up the sleeve of his red shirt, revealing on his left arm a mass of scars, as if it had been crushed all to pieces.

"That's grizzly *chawin!*" said he.

Then he tore open his shirt bosom, and exhibited a breast in which great furrows had been torn.

"That's grizzly *clawin'*," he added; "and I killed the grizzly that did it, single-handed, with my knife, and I can prove it by Vessie Morrison over at the hill, for he got in and found me in a faint on top o' the dead bear. I'd rather see ten grizzlies all at once than see what I saw last night."

"You interest me strangely, friend," said I. "You have a face which speaks of more than usual intelligence, courage, and character. I'd like to know what could have *terrified* a man like you. I'll let my team rest till you tell me, and then we'll lunch, if you will, and go on. What did you see down there that has so sprung your nerves?"

"A *ghost*, sir—a GHOST! I never believed in such a thing before, but I do now."

Then, lowering his voice, and looking back, as if he expected to see something supernatural in the narrow trail by which he had reached the road, he said: "It was the ghost of a woman, calling on some name and crying out, oh, how piercingly: 'Vengeance, vengeance!' It was *terrible*, sir. My blood runs cold yet."

"You *heard* a voice, you could distinguish words, and yet you believe those words came from the mouth of a spirit? You don't look like a drinking man, or I'd think you were bordering on the shakes."

"I am a Son of Temperance, sir, and never use liquor."

"Then this hallucination of yours is indeed singular."

"It is *no* hallucination, sir. I saw what I *say* I did!" said the man, almost angrily. "You're bound for Iowa Hill, are you not?"

"Yes, there is where I expect to pass the night."

"Then when you get there ask any man you meet—miners, storekeepers, and all, if they know Ned Griffin. They'll tell you yes. Then ask 'em if they ever knew him to tell a lie. If they say yes, I'll cut my throat, for I'm Ned Griffin."

"My friend, I do not doubt that you believe you saw a ghost. Now tell me what it looked like, and where you saw it."

"I will, sir. Do you see that little valley down there, where a brook tumbles down the mountain and forms a little pond, and do you see an old cabin near it?"

"Yes. I see all you describe plainly, and it is as sweet a bit of scenery as ever human eyes rested on!"

"Well, sir, it was down there that I stopped last night; but I pray I may never stop there again. I was struck with the looks of the place, and water runnin' so handy if there was dirt rich enough to wash, so I went down there yesterday. I found rich dirt and panned out three or four ounces in the afternoon, and then went with my grub and blankets to the old cabin to stay for the night, calculatin' to pitch in and work the claim as long as it paid well. I built up a fire in the old stone fire-place, cooked some bacon, and ate supper. Then I fed the fire with some stout chunks to make it last, rolled up in my blankets, for I was tired, and went to sleep! How long I slept I don't know, but I was woke by a strange feeling. It seemed as if an ice-cold hand had been laid upon my face, and the freezing impress of each finger had left its mark where it had been laid. I sprang to my feet and spoke. The fire had burned out, and all was still and dark in the cabin. Yet an awful chill crept over me, and I felt as if some supernatural thing was there, close to me.

"All at once, outside the cabin, I heard a voice, shrill and clear like the tones of a woman—wild, too, as the scream of a frightened bird, cry out:

"'REVENGE! REVENGE! REVENGE!'

"I sprang to the door, which was partly open and saw, right before me, drifting like a cloud along the other side of the ravine, the form of a woman robed in white, or rather it looked like mist, showing the outlines of a shape as graceful as imagination could picture! Far off to show so plain, yet I could see that her eyes were as black as night, her features perfect, while her face was white as snow itself. Her long black hair floated loosely over her shoulders and far down her back.

"I thought in an instant that it was some poor crazed creature, lost here in the wild ravines, and rushing out I shouted aloud to call her attention, wishing to help her and prevent her from perishing in such a wild, dreary place.

"She stopped, turned full toward me, raised her right hand toward the sky, and shrieked out wilder than ever:

"'Revenge! *Revenge!* REVENGE!'

"I wasn't a bit frightened then, for I still thought her a living human, and I called out to her to hold on till I came, for I wanted to help her if I could be of use.

"She did not stop—she kept on, seeming to float rather than to walk over the ground, and every minute or so came back her wailing cry:

"'*Revenge—revenge!*'

"Thinking even yet that it was a live woman, gone crazy, I followed her as fast as I could over the rough ground, while she moved on up the gulch, till all of a sudden, with, that one word, shrieked out wilder than ever, she disappeared. She went as sudden as a flash of powder.

"I ran forward, thinkin' she had fallen down into some hole, and broke through the chaparral at the spot where I last saw her. I stopped, just in time, for I was on the edge of an old shaft, deep and dark, and nearly went into it. Had she gone there? No—it could not be, for over it, stretched in a hundred tiny threads, I saw the web of a spider and not a thread broken. I listened but I could hear no sound. I shouted out: 'Where are you?' and only the echoes of my own voice made answer.

"Then I realized that I *had* seen a spirit, felt that some fearful tragedy had happened in that gulch, and I felt worse scared than I've ever felt before in all my life, and I've fought the Apache and the Comanche, had some rough times on the borders, and as you see have had it rough and tumble with the grizzlies! I got back to the cabin just as quick as I could, built up my fire, and staid for daylight, without trying to sleep again. I tried to pan for a while after the sun rose, for gold is plenty down there where it has washed down from the hills, but I felt so uneasy I couldn't stay. Cold chills ran over me, no matter how hard I worked, and so I left off, climbed the hill, and here I am. That's all my story, sir!"

I looked long and earnestly in the miner's face.

He evidently believed that he *had* seen a spirit, and, brave in every other point, was now succumbing to a superstitious fear. The thought struck me that I would show him the fallacy of his belief, while perhaps I might locate a valuable claim. So I said to him: "Mr. Griffin, I've a proposition to make."

"What is it, sir? I'm open to a'most anything but goin' back down there. That I will not do. I forgot some o' my traps when I came away, but I wouldn't go after 'em for ten times their value."

"I'll get them for you, for I am going down there, and shall spend the coming night there. My proposition is this: That you take my team and carriage and drive on to Iowa Hill and have it put up at Madame Beausicon's tavern. I will take my rifle, revolvers, and blankets and go down into the gulch. Tomorrow I'll go there to meet you, and tell you what my experience is. Will you drive my team on?"

"Yes, sir, if you desire it; but you must write a line, as you seem acquainted at the Hill, telling Madame Beausicon what you have asked me to do, and where you intend to pass the night, so that if anything *should* happen to you, I'll not get blamed."

I wrote a few lines in my memorandum-book, tore out the leaf, and handed it to him.

"All right, sir," said he. "I'll drive the team to the Hill, and if you say so, drive down here in the morning for you."

"You can, if you like," I replied. "Good afternoon."

He returned my farewell salutation, and as I went down the hill drove on. But I noticed that he often looked back, perhaps to see whether I intended to keep on into the gulch or not. I hurried down all the faster for this, and was nearly down into the little valley before he was out of sight.

CHAPTER II.

A Dream.

I was rather tired when I reached the bottom of the steep hill and somewhat scratched with the chaparral thorns, but I felt all right after resting for a while on a mossy rock, spangled with beautiful flowers, especially after I had taken a drink from a clear spring which bubbled out from under the base of the same rock.

I now went along the little valley, passing some fresh dirtheaps where the miner had been panning, and reached the old cabin. I stood in front of it a moment to gaze in a thrill of admiration on the view which lay above and around me.

Up—up—went on every side those stupendous mountains, ragged with cliffs, but so dotted with the nut pine, the red-berried manzanita, and the magnificent mountain laurel, that only here and there could the black, volcanic rocks be seen in their awful grandeur. Flashing in the light of the lessening day I could see rivulets leaping here and there from their hidden sources in the hills, descending toward the small stream and lakelet at my feet, thence to journey by the middle fork of the American toward the Sacramento and the western sea. I thought I had never seen a lovelier scene.

I did not pause long, beautiful as the view was, but entered the cabin, its open door showing that the miner had left it in haste.

There was nothing peculiar in the cabin itself. It was just like hundreds to be seen in the deserted mining grounds of California. Built of logs, with a huge stone fire-place and chimney at one end, some bunks made of split slabs of cedar at the other, and one window without glass, but with a shutter hung on old boot soles for hinges: a slab floor, a roof of the same material, it was very lonely, but in foul weather with that fireplace all aglow it could be made quite comfortable.

Some old cards, broken bottles and pieces of crockery lay scattered around, evidently left there by the long-ago occupants, but what pleased me most just then—for I was very hungry—was a glimpse of the "traps" Griffin had said he left.

These were his coffee-pot and frying-pan, a side of bacon, some crackers, coffee and sugar.

None but a hungry man, used to roughing it in camp, can tell just how nice such things appear.

I was not long in taking advantage of the situation. I soon had a roaring fire going, the coffee-pot on, and a half-dozen slices of bacon in the frying-pan. Catching a couple of grasshoppers, I put one on a hook which I always carried, with its line, un-jointed my Japanese fishing-rod-cane and threw for a trout in the edge of the little lake. I had not a second to wait—a dozen jumped at the first cast, full two pounders at that, and two were all I wanted for supper and breakfast. I was back at my fire with the fish before the bacon was done brown, and then I soon forgot hunger in as good a supper as anybody could make for me, at any rate.

When this was over—as I never smoke tobacco or drink whisky—I had nothing to do but to get fuel for the night and prepare for the ghost, if ghost there was.

I found plenty of dry wood close at hand, and before the shades of night were fairly set, had enough in to keep a roaring fire all night. Then I arranged my blankets in a bunk, and taking a bench, drew it up before the fire and alongside of the slab table, and gave the reins to my imagination.

Who built this cabin, and where was the builder now? Was he one of the earnest, anxious workers who came in forty-nine, made his pile quickly and went back to enjoy it in comfort among his kindred, or was he one of those wild, drinking, fighting, wandering creatures who made a fortune but to spend it, knew no life but dissipation, and finally ended that in some mad debauch or red-handed broil? Had woman, frail and delicate, tender and loving, ever sat beneath that rugged roof? Had she smiled or wept while listening as I did now to the rippling streams and the mournful sound of the night birds? Had any one dwelt here who had a soul to appreciate the magnificence of the scenic surroundings, or had the dweller or dwellers been so absorbed in thoughts of gain as to see nothing but the auriferous dirt beneath their feet?

Thus I thought and mused as the evening wore on, and then I went to thinking of the ghost which Griffin was so sure he had seen.

This did not trouble me, for then, as I had been from my earliest childhood, I was a disbeliever in all supernatural appearances. A brave, sensible father, and a pious mother, had taught me to disregard all dangers which I could not distinctly see or feel.

Yet I went to wondering whether I should be honored with a visit, or be allowed to slumber quietly, for I now began to feel sleepy.

I went to the door and looked out. The moon had just risen above the mountain crest in front of me and threw down a flood of light into the valley, making the water glitter like liquid silver. I now closed the door, but as there was no inside bolt or bar, merely saw that the wooden latch fell securely into the notch where it belonged when the door was shut.

I then looked to the caps on my rifle and revolvers, put them all within reach of my hand, rolled up in my blanket, and lay down in the lower of the two bunks.

I fell asleep almost instantly, and probably was almost as soon dreaming.

And *such* a dream! It thrills me yet with unspeakable ecstasy to think of it.

I was wandering along in a grand forest by the side of a magnificent stream, and I was not alone. One whom I had looked up to as a subject looks to his queen, in reverent worship—one gifted with all choice gifts of genius, grace, and beauty—was walking by my side, drinking in with her dark-brown eyes the glorious beauties strewed about us by the hand of God. The music of rustling leaves, of rushing waters, and clear-toned birds, filled our ears. Beauty and love seemed to make the very air delicious.

We paused. It was by the water-side, beneath a grand old tree, whose gnarled roots had been washed bare by the rushing current, and there, as I looked into her glorious eyes, and on her face all full of intellect, forgetting everything but one thought, I poured forth my story of undying love. I trembled while I spoke, for each word went forth hopeless of a kind response.

It was over. The song of running waters, of bending branches, of happy birds, was heard again, while I tremblingly waited for my fate.

It came—came as the sun comes out of the ebon cloud—came as peace comes to weary minds—came as relief comes to him who is grappling with death.

Her eyes, so soft, so full of soulful love, of high-born truth; looked what her lips whispered:

"Thine!—forever thine!"

These were her words, and then our lips met in the holy purity of love which is, and must be, everlasting.

Then—at that instant, before I could dream of another look or word—I woke, woke to the cold touch of a hand upon my face. An icy chill seemed to stiffen the current in every vein. Yet I was conscious, and rose as quickly as I could—rose to see that the door which I had carefully closed before I lay down, was now wide open. I heard a sound as of light, receding footsteps, and grasping my rifle in one hand, with a revolver in the other, rushed to the door.

Instantly I saw, some distance away, just such a form and face as Griffin had described—that of a young female, very beautiful, robed in white, moving toward the upper end of the gulch.

"Halt!" I shouted. "If you are an angel from the upper air, for never was a fiend so fair, halt and speak to me!"

She made no reply, though her face was half-turned toward me, but seemed to glide away, rather than to walk. Leaving my rifle, but retaining my other arms, I rushed on up the gulch in pursuit of her. Over bowlders, through thickets of thorny chaparral, I went, and was so near her that I could see the flashing of her large black eyes as they were turned to me—realize that she was a living being—when I stumbled, and fell with violence against a rock, which for an instant shocked me beyond the power of motion.

Even as I fell, I heard, in a wild, shrieking tone, the cry: "Revenge! revenge!"

When I rose, perhaps a minute afterward, there was no one in sight. She had disappeared. I pressed on at once to the spot where I had last seen her, and there I found the old shaft of which Griffin had spoken. The spider-web was still over it, so she could not have fallen or descended into it.

I looked carefully around in every direction—looked in vain to find a sign that a human foot had pressed ground except on the old trail made by Griffin, and that now made by me.

It was strange. I had seen something which every sense but that of touch told me was a live, a real woman, crazed perhaps, but a woman who could move and talk—one, as we have said, beautiful withal. What had become of her? She had vanished like the mists of morning before the sun of summer.

Could it be a specter? No, no—I would not yield to such weakness. I would wait and investigate. Once before on the Cumberland, in Tennessee, I had broken the spell of a haunted house on the river-bank, which had terrified a neighborhood, and made the owner leave the house to ghostly intruders.

A revolver held the ghost at bay, and revealed the fact that a nest of counterfeiters and thieves had made it a rendezvous and workshop.

I did not, would not believe in ghosts; so back I went to the cabin, determined to freshen up my fire, and wait and watch for another visitation.

Just before I reached the old cabin, I crossed a strip of sand, three or four yards wide. I examined it, and found the distinct marks of a small, slender foot, which seemed fresh.

Now I was sure, for no spirit could leave a trail like that. The spirit of my dream—sweet spirit, so far, far away!—could have left just such an impress had she been there in reality; but none but a real foot, a lovely one at that, could have left its model in those glittering sands.

I re-entered the cabin, replenished the fuel in the fire-place, and then sat down. I looked at my watch to note the time. It was only one o'clock in the morning.

CHAPTER III.
Staking Off Claims.

I sat before the cheerful blaze, and went to dreaming out to romances again, as I am ever doing when awake, and to pondering over events in a stranger life than I would dare to delineate in a story, for fear of utter disbelief, occupying myself thus for an hour or more, I think, when all at once I heard the voice of a man speaking in an angry tone.

As I sprang to my feet, I heard another voice speaking a bitter curse, and then I heard the clash of steel meeting steel.

I was at the door in another second, and my eyes fell on two men engaged in deadly conflict on the hill-side beyond the little lake. Their clashing knives, their angry cries, and fearful curses came as distinctly to my ears as if I were within reaching distance; and so plainly did they stand out to view that I felt there was no illusion here. Though not disinclined as a general thing to take a hand in a free fight, I like peace when it can be had on honorable terms. And I thought I would hurry over and mediate if I could, before one or the other of the parties "went under."

I started with this thought, but before I had gone ten steps from the cabin, in the clear moonlight, both men vanished from my sight, and I heard no more sounds of strife.

"Both are down—dead most likely!" I cried, as I hurried around the head of the lakelet and rushed toward the rocky ledge where I had seen the men.

When I reached the spot I was dumb with surprise. Not only was I disappointed in not finding dead or wounded men, but I could not see a single sign or token of the presence of a human being there then, or at any previous period. The rock—gray granite, mixed with quartz—was unstained by blood; there was not a mark which I could see.

"Mystery on mystery!" I muttered. "I am awake—I surely saw and heard men, and they were here! The range was exact from the cabin to this spot. I marked the position of the blasted pine on the ledge above too carefully with my eye to be mistaken. I don't wonder that the miner was scared, for this beats all I've ever seen, and I've been through a good deal in my eventful life."

I looked around in every direction, but I did not see or hear anything that gave sign of life. Not even a bird was startled as I strode hither and thither from the ledge to the chaparral, and at last I went back to the cabin to study and wait for daylight.

I had not long to wait now. The greater part of the night was gone, and by the time the coffee-pot was boiling, the gray of dawn was upon the earth.

I made out some sort of a breakfast. My appetite was not strong, I know, but I was so nervous that I took an extra pot of coffee to calm myself.

By sunrise I was on my way up the hill toward the road, after having looked in vain for any sign or track except only the small footsteps in the sand before alluded to.

When I reached the road, Ned Griffin was there with my buggy and horses.

"You've seen it!" he cried, eagerly, as I came up to where he held my mustangs under the shade of an oak tree. "I know it by your white face and the dark circles under your eyes! You haven't slept a wink!"

"There you are mistaken. I had a good long nap before I was woke up by somebody or something!"

"The ice-cold hand, sir—the hand upon your face?"

"Well, yes—I may as well acknowledge I fancied that I was wakened by the touch of a cold hand, and after that my experience so far as the woman went was much like yours. But I had a ghostly tragedy to follow my opening piece."

And I described to Griffin the fighting scene and the sounds I had heard as well.

"Have you ever seen men like 'em before?"

"Not that I can remember. One was very large, with heavy black whiskers and long curling hair hanging over his shoulders. The other seemed to have light hair and no beard."

"Slighter in form, too?"

"Yes, a great deal."

"One was like Alf Dunning, who sneered at the idea of there being ghosts here, when I told my story on the Hill last night. The other was more like little Jerry Spindle, who looked as scared as if he had seen it himself. *Thunder*—look!"

"What is the matter—what surprises you?"

"You know the old saying, sir. Talk of the devil and he will surely appear. Do you see that party crossing the hill, and coming down this way by the trail?"

"Yes!"

"Well, sir, that big fellow who leads is Alf Dunning. There is a gang coming to stake off claims in the gulch, for I was fool enough to tell 'em there was rich dirt there."

"Then we will both hurry down ahead of them and stake claims for ourselves. If there should be a rush here, the claims alone will pay."

"That is true, sir. I'll unhitch the team, and hurry down after you. Go ahead. I'll be at the bottom as soon as you are."

CHAPTER IV.
Bill Tulip.

Ned Griffin, true to his promise, had the team put out of harness in a few seconds, and when I reached the bottom of the gulch he was by my side.

"You claim the old shaft," I said, hurriedly, "while I plant my stakes over on yonder ledge where I saw the fight going on."

"Why, sir, *pay* dirt is better right here in the middle of the gulch."

"I don't care. Something tells me the claims I name will pay better. Take my advice, and if you lose I'll bear the blame."

"Good—I'll do it. But first, before they get down, I'll put a padlock in the hasp of the cabin door. We'll claim that as the last occupants."

The miner suited his actions to his words, and put a lock on the cabin, and then, while I went to mark my intended claim, he hurried to do the same with his.

Meantime the party from Iowa Hill, with Alf Dunning, or Black Alf, as he was often called, was coming down the hill, a dozen or more in number, whooping like so many wild Piutes.

Griffin and I soon walked out and marked the two claims that we intended to hold, and then hurried to meet each other, as we had agreed, at the cabin.

When we got there Black Alf stood before the door, his dark, repulsive face wearing a most malignant expression.

He was the center of a group of rough and lawless-looking men, while close by him, timid and cowering, stood a woman, young and fair. In the whole crowd of men there was but one who did not look as bad, so far as character went, as Alf himself, and, to say the least, these looks were murderous.

This one man seemed to be quiet and of a rather better class than the rest, but he seemed to be with Alf in everything, for he never took his eyes off him or left his side while under my observation. I heard him called, by name, Bill Tulip.

"I'll like to know who put a lock on my cabin door?" cried Black Alf, as we came up.

"Your cabin? Who made it your cabin?" said Griffin, heedless of the frowning look and harsh tone of the other.

"That's cool. I've half a mind to put ahead on you first and answer afterward," said the fellow; confident in his size and the number of his followers.

"'T'would be rather unhandy work, Mr. Alf Dunning," said Griffin, as be revealed the butts of two revolvers, with a hand on each. "If this is your cabin, prove it."

"I built it in '49, and you'll find my name chipped on the hearth-stone, date and all. And that isn't all—you see this woman here? She was but a bit of a child then, but her mother lived here with me for nigh on two years, and me and three other chaps worked a rich claim up yonder way."

He pointed toward the place where the old shaft bad been dug.

"What became of my mother? I was so little I can only just remember," said the young woman, in a tremulous voice.

"She died—so did the rest. All took sick and went but you and me, gal—but ask no more. Stranger, will you take the lock off that door?"

"Yes; I'll resign the cabin since you say you built it. But the deserted claims here belong as much to one as another. No one has been here for years—so I've staked my claim and I'll hold it."

"And I will do the same," I added.

"Where's your claim?" asked Alf, turning to Griffin.

"Up under yonder ledge, where an old shaft has been sunk."

The face of Alf Dunning grew ghastly in an instant, at first. I thought, with passion, but when I saw his huge frame tremble I knew it came from another cause.

"I wish you joy of that claim," he said, with a forced laugh. "You'll find it worked clean as a baby's face. Where's yours?"

The last question was propounded to me.

"Over under that ledge."

I pointed in the direction.

Again he seemed strangely agitated, but, with another mocking laugh, he said: "You're smart, you are. You'll find rock over there—that's all."

"Red dirt, maybe!" I said, fixing my eyes on his.

"What do you mean, you interlopin' nobody? What do you mean?" he cried, furiously, adding oaths too vile and fearful for me to place before my readers.

And he sprang toward me as if he intended to attack me.

"Hold on, Alf—hold on! The stranger has done you no harm!" cried Bill Tulip, as he stepped between Alf and myself.

"Well, let him keep his free lip buttoned. I don't like Yanks, no way—they'd better give me elbow room."

Ned Griffin had unlocked the cabin door by this time, and, when we went in to remove what belonged to us, we saw, sure enough, the name of Alf Dunning chipped in the hearth-stone, and another name below it—MEDORA.

The young woman, who came in just after us, saw the name, and, turning to Alf, who was close behind her, asked: "Was that my mother's name?"

"Yes," said Alf, in a husky tone.

"Where is her grave?" continued the girl.

"I don't know. It wasn't me that buried her."

"Who did?"

"Gal, stop askin' questions; I'm not in humor to be bothered by your nonsense, or that of anybody. Set the cabin to rights; lay out your blankets, and get ready to cook our dinner after these strangers have vamoosed."

The girl, or woman, sighed, but with a submissive look obeyed his orders, while we went out with the few traps that we owned.

"Where will you camp?" asked the man known as Bill Tulip, in rather a friendly tone.

"Nowhere at present. Our claims are marked, and I think I'll go to the Hill, and get a tent to live in here."

"Do, and be sure to come back. I think your claims will pay," he said, in a quiet, but I thought in a meaning way.

"We shall come back; and it is likely, if you remain here tonight, you'll find more company than you dream of now."

"You believe in this ghost story, then? There may be something in it. Black Alf wouldn't come here alone, I know. Well, we will see what comes. Good-day, if you are going, sir."

"Good-day!"

Ned Griffin and myself now started up the hill toward the spot where the team was left, putting the things we did not wish to carry away in a crevice under a cliff to await our return, for I was determined now to see the thing through.

Looking back as we ascended the hill, we saw smoke rising from the cabin chimney, and the men of the party at work in the gulch where we knew "pay dirt" lay handy to the water.

"I reckon when night comes they'll know more of the gulch than they do now!" said Griffin, as we toiled up the hill.

"Yes, if they receive such experiences as we have," I replied. "What do you know of that ruffianly fellow, Black Alf?"

"Nothing to his good, and not a great deal, any way. He bears a hard name. He drinks hard, and is ugly when he drinks. It is said he has killed three or four men, managing to make them draw their tools first, so as to keep the law on his side."

"The girl, or woman, who is with him—who is she?"

"I do not know. You heard what he said. At the Hill she does not pass as his daughter, and you notice that he did not say her mother was his wife."

"True. There is a strange *mystery* to unravel, and I feel as if we were the men predestined to do it."

"Well, sir, what is to be will be. I'd like to see through that ghost matter, for I don't like to be scared without knowing what it is that scares me."

"Nor I. We will go to the Hill, buy a tent, more arms and ammunition, some provisions and tools, and come back and see it out."

"I am agreed, sir, if you take me as a partner."

"Of course I will. There is a pretty hard lot down there, but well-armed and watchful, I think we can hold our own."

"I reckon so, sir—but here we are—the horses look glad to see you."

"Yes—they know there's barley coming when they reach the stable."

CHAPTER V.

"No Dream."

We were soon at the Hill, and while I made arrangements to have my team kept till I wanted it, and engaged some Chinamen to pack down the things we purchased, on their donkeys, I made all the inquiry I could into the character of Black Alf and his gang.

He and the rest bore hard names, excepting the man Tulip, of whom nothing was known, as he had but recently come there and joined him.

Of the young woman little was known except that she was treated very harshly by Black Alf, of whom she seemed to be much afraid. His precise relation to her no one knew—one thing was certain, he never called her his daughter.

Both Griffin and myself were advised more than once in a friendly way to keep out of the gulch while Black Alf was there, but we had both set our minds upon seeing the adventure through, and we would not back out now.

The sun was well down its western slope, when, with a half-dozen donkey-loads of stuff, we got back to the gulch, finding Black Alf and his gang all at work in the pay dirt as merry as crickets.

Moving on up the gulch to where a stream gushed from the hill near the old shaft, we cleared a place for our tent, and, unloading the animals, began to pitch it. While doing this, Black Alf came up, and looking ferociously at the Chinamen whom we had brought to drive the donkeys, asked if we intended to work them pig-tailed heathen there.

Angered with his domineering manner, I replied that we had merely hired them to pack our things down, but if we found we needed their help we should not hesitate to hire them to stay.

"If you do, there'll be more ghosts in this gulch than there are now," he said, bitterly, garnishing his remark, as usual, with oaths.

"Perhaps the same hand would try to make them," I answered, in a sarcastic tone.

"What in thunder do you mean by that!" he cried, furiously. "If you don't button your lip I'll cleave you to the chine!"

He half-drew a huge bowie-knife as he spoke, but the man Tulip again interfered, and said in a low tone: "'Twill not do, Alf; there's too many people on the Hill who *know* they're here. Keep easy and let 'em work their claims."

"Ha! ha! Their claims will pay, in a horn," said the burly ruffian, with a sneering laugh. "But they musn't bring pigtails down here till I've quit; if they do there'll be *red* dirt, as the stranger there says, or I'm a liar and a coward!"

We had no need of the Chinamen just then, so our packers were sent back, and we soon had our tent erected and a fire in front of it by which to cook our supper.

We had everything snug before the night shadows deepened, and our arms all loaded and ready for use, so that duly prepared we could await what the night might produce in the way of peril or excitement.

We supped just after sunset, and then sat in front of our tent before a large and cheerful fire, talking on various subjects, and listening to rude bursts of song and hoarse laughter coming from the cabin below us.

"The whisky is passing, and they're having a lively time down there," said Griffin, as the sound came louder on our ears.

"Yes—*such* men only find life in the fiery aid of stimulating drink, or in the excitement of cards," said I. "Their lives are not human—they are more animal than the lives of animals themselves. For animals will not drink whisky."

The noise of carousal at last began to die away in the camp below, and by ten or eleven o'clock all was still.

Griffin and I had decided that while we remained in the gulch, one or the other would keep watch, and having decided on two-hour turns, he lay down to sleep while I took the first watch.

It was a little after midnight. No sound save that of falling water and of the wind among the trees had reached my ears for an hour at least, and I began to feel very drowsy. I looked at my watch and saw that an hour must pass before I could call my companion.

I knew I would sleep if I remained sitting near the fire, so I rose, threw on some fresh fuel, and then began a short walk to and fro in front of the tent. Pausing at the trunk of a beautiful manzanita tree close by, I took out my knife and amused myself by carving the initials of a dear and cherished name there, thinking that per-chance when I had passed away, it might meet the eye of one whom I might see no more, but never could forget. I had just finished the pleasant task when a shriek—wild, piercing, fearful—rang upon my ears, coming from the valley below.

First one, then another, and another, so loud that I sprang to the blanket where Griffin was lying and aroused him.

"Up—up!" I cried. "There is murder going on down there, sure!"

In a second he was on his feet, but the shrieks had died away, and all we now heard was the hoarse talk of excited men down at the cabin.

"Let's go down and see what the matter is," said Griffin, as he belted on his knife and pistols, and took up a loaded rifle—a repeater.

"I am ready," was my answer, and together we went down.

Every man was out in front of the cabin, and as the moon was now up, we could see their faces, and that all, with one exception, were dreadfully alarmed. The exception was Bill Tulip. He was perfectly calm.

Black Alf had his arm under the form of the girl, who had fainted.

Tulip was bathing her head with water, endeavoring to restore consciousness.

"What's the matter down here? D'ye want any help?" asked Griffin, as we came up.

"Neither your help nor your company is wanted," said Black Alf, savagely.

"Whose screams did we hear?" I asked, without paying any attention to him, but addressing myself to Tulip.

"Hers, I reckon," said he, pointing to the girl, who began to show signs of consciousness. "I was asleep when—the noise woke me. By that time she was in a dead faint."

"My mother—my *murdered* mother!" moaned the girl, as she gazed wildly about her. "Oh, Heaven—where—where is she now!"

"Hush, fool—you've been dreaming!" said Black Alf, with a scared look, as he too glanced around. It seemed as if he feared to see something—the *something* which had so frightened her.

"It was no dream. I saw her. She spoke to me. She called my name—plainly I heard it—*Eldiva*—ELDIVA—then came the word *Revenge!* REVENGE!"

"Hush, and go in!" said Black Alf, sternly. "The men must work to-morrow and need sleep. Hush—and go in to your bed!"

Look—LOOK!" screamed the girl, and she pointed to the opposite side of the ravine. "*Look*—LOOK—'tis not a dream—'tis not a dream!"

CHAPTER VI.
"He Is a Bad Man."

Instantly every eye was bent in the direction in which the hand of the girl Eldiva pointed; and, as if floating on the air, over against the very cliff near which I had seen the two men fighting, and where I had, for reasons of my own, located my claim, all saw the distinct figure of a woman, clad in white, with both arms up-lifted, as if imploring the aid of the Ruler of all, for her face was turned toward the sky. It was the same figure which I had seen before—the same face.

"*Vengeance!* Vengeance! VENGEANCE!"

Three times, in a tone low, mournful, and thrilling, did that word reach our ears. Then the figure vanished from view.

At the same instant, the girl Eldiva screamed out: "*Mother!* MOTHER!"

Then she fell, and fainted.

At this instant I noticed that there was a new face in the crowd of men—a face I felt sure that I had seen in San Francisco, though I could not distinctly localize it—and the eyes in the face of that man were bent with a searching, eager look on the countenance of Alf Dunning.

There was good reason for looking at him. There was an expression of blanched terror in his face, a wild look, which no one could mistake. He was fear-rooted to the spot, and did not speak or move till after Eldiva had fainted. Then he gasped out:

"It *was* the ghost of her mother, sure enough!"

"*How* did she die?"

That question came, in a low, stern tone, from the man whose face seemed strangely familiar to me—the new-comer in the crowd.

Alf Dunning trembled from head to foot; but only for a few seconds was he thus discomposed. He did not answer the question, but asked another: "Who are you, and how came you here?"

"I am a *man*, and walked here. I own a claim in this gulch," said the stranger. "Now answer my question—How did Medora Roget die?"

"Medora Roget! How knew you that name?" cried Dunning, and his face grew dark with passion.

"No matter. I have asked you twice—I now ask, for the third and last time— how did that woman die?"

"Go ask her ghost!" cried Dunning; "and, mark you, stranger, keep away from this cabin if you know when you are well off!"

The stranger laughed, and then I remembered where I had seen him. It was in the Chinese quarter, on Jackson street, between Kearney and Stockton, in a Chinese row, when he suddenly appeared, and the row was ended by the combatants flying away in apparent terror, as he uttered a cry in their own language. He seemed to me then to be a man of power and mystery. What he was now, or intended to do here, I could not divine, but I meant to learn.

Some of the party having carried the girl into the cabin, I glanced inside, and saw that she had recovered from her swoon, but sat near the fire, weeping, while Dunning, who went in also, stood near, with a scowl on his repulsive face, and his arms folded over his brawny breast.

"Rather hard cases, these, sir!" said I, approaching the stranger, who yet stood outside the cabin.

"You don't know them, sir, and you had best give them a wide berth, if you value property and life," was his reply. "You and your companion, Ned Griffin, are not liked by them."

"You appear to know who we are?"

"Perfectly well—as well as I know each and every one of that gang in there. Keep your eye skinned for them. It is a friendly warning, and you'll do well to take it. Good-morning."

The stranger strode away, and, bending his course down the gulch, was lost to our sight in a moment afterward, as suddenly almost as we lost sight of the ghostly visitant.

"Thundering strange, all this!" said Griffin, his voice and looks indicating surprise. "I'm half sorry I came back down here."

"Don't stay if you are afraid!" said I. "You need not feel delicate in leaving on my account. I shall stay and see the thing out."

"So will I, sir, no matter what comes of it. That's a sure thing. I'll show you whether fear is a part of my composition or not, if these devils give us a chance."

"I do not doubt your courage," was my answer. "I think we shall see this *mystery* solved before we leave. That there has been foul murder done in this vicinity I do not doubt. Nor do I doubt that Alf Dunning had a hand in it. And as the justice of Heaven is ever retributive, and not so partial as that of man, I feel sure that he will be punished for his crime through Heavenly aid and power!"

"Well, sir, I hope, if he *has* done a murder here, he'll have it brought home to him. He killed a good friend of mine over at Knight's Ferry, for next to no cause at all, but he managed to make him draw first, and so kept the law on his side. He is a bad, *bad* man!"

"I have no doubt of it. Let's get back to our quarters."

CHAPTER VII.
A Call Agreed Upon.

We returned to the tent, but neither Griffin nor myself slept again that night, but freshened our fire and sat before it, talking till the light of day once more revealed the scenery around us. He talking of the strange scenes through which he had passed since '49, when he first landed, and I adding scraps of history gleaned by me from time to time in regard to the country, which corroborated what he was telling me.

When day broke we prepared our breakfast, and ate with such appetite as one must get in that pure and high altitude, roughing it as we did, and then we began to lay plans for the day.

"I think I will explore my claim," said Griffin. "The way Black Alf sneered at the idea of there being any gold left in the old shaft makes me think there *is*."

"If not gold, there may be something else which he does not care to have you see. I noticed his *bitter* look and sneer also when you told him where you had located your claim. And I will aid you in the investigation."

"Thank you, sir. I will see what we need to work with, for it is a dark-looking hole, and must be deep."

An hour later Griffin and myself were standing by the side of the old shaft looking down into the gloomy depth, estimating whether a piece of rope which Griffin had brought would be long enough to reach the bottom, as he intended to use it for a descent.

Fastening a large stone to the rope, Griffin was about to lower it when the strange man who had attracted our attention down at the cabin, a little while before, hurried up to the spot.

"Hold on, my friend, hold on!" he cried, addressing Griffin. "I don't want my spider-web broken just yet."

"*Your* spider-web? What do you mean? Are you drunk or crazy?"

"Neither, I hope. I belong to Golden Gate Division of Sons of Temperance, and shall not disgrace it. And I am at work at a job which requires all my senses in a sound condition!"

"Then what do you mean?"

"Just what I say. I do not want *my* spider-web broken just now. Look here!"

And the stranger reached out his hand, took hold of what had *appeared* to Griffin and to me to be an ordinary spider's web, of the large net-like character seen frequently stretched over chaparral, or from rock to rock, in that region, and raised it from its attachment on the side of the shaft next to him.

We at once saw that it was an artificial net, of the finest silk, made in such exact imitation of the usual work of the large spider of the country that it would deceive any one unacquainted with its real nature.

"I know what is down that shaft," continued the stranger, "and I will inform you that it is *not* gold, but it will be worth more than gold in forwarding the ends of justice before I am done with the job I have in hand. For this reason I ask for a short time that you leave my web alone, while I unravel another web and finish what I have been some weeks about. If you are in a hurry, gentlemen, to find pay ground, you are welcome to use a claim which I squatted on six weeks ago in the lower part of this gulch, when I came here to begin the job I have alluded to. I keep the claim only to cover my other object."

"May I ask your name and business, sir?" I now said.

"You may call me Melrose for the present," said the stranger. "Yon shall know my business soon—that is, if you will aid me in my endeavor to reach proof of a great crime and to punish the perpetrator, as well as to find out the hiding-place of a vast amount of treasure belonging to penniless orphans."

"That aid you may depend upon, Mr. Melrose," was the reply made by me and joined in by Griffin.

"Then, if you please, act strictly under my advice, and, if we have any trouble, you will learn that I have help close at hand, and where it is least expected."

"All right, sir—you can depend on us. What do you desire us to do now?"

"You will see two new arrivals here about noon. A large, bony Irishman, with a pack-mule carrying his tools and camping fixings, will come, accompanied by his wife, a woman as big and strong as he, and two young children—a boy and girl—whom they will describe as having picked up on the road out of pity, because they had no money and no friends. Employ this man and his wife, and keep them with you, though they are really acting for me and under my instructions."

"Where would you advise us to work a claim?"

"Just below where Dunning and his gang are at work. But keep your tent where it is, and let Billy Flynn, as he will call himself, tent close to you. I shall have some fresh hands on my own claim in a day or two, and in the meantime keep your eyes and ears open, and do not be surprised at anything, for you'll see stranger sights yet than you have seen!"

"Will you please answer me one question, sir?" asked Griffin.

"As many as you like!" said Melrose, with a smile, "if they do not conflict with my plans."

"Did you ever see me before you saw me this morning?"

"Yes, and talked with you nearly a week ago about this very gulch at Wisconsin diggings."

"I was there a week ago, talking to an old Virginia negro, with white hair, but nearly double with age."

"All de way from de Rappahannock, marser!" said Melrose, in a tone so altered we could hardly realize it was the same speaker.

"Heavens—*you* were the old nigger I pitied so, and shared my dinner with, as well as supplying him with tobacco?"

"Yes, marser, dat for why I done tole you 'bout dem rich diggin' in Pigtail Bend. Yah—yah!"

The imitation was so perfect that even our astonishment could not check our laughter.

"Were you here when I arrived?" continued Griffin.

"I was not far away. Do you remember a man who had been in Australia playing draw-poker with Alf Dunning three weeks ago in the Empire saloon at Iowa Hill?"

"Yes—Alf cleaned him out, or at least he said so, and did it by cheating!"

"Well, I was that Australian, and I let him win, while I drew some information from him that was worth more to me than the money that I lost."

"Well, Mr. Melrose, you beat all creation in disguises!"

"It is a part of my trade, sir. Through my hints, conveyed in a mysterious letter, more than through your statements night before last, Black Alf and his murderous gang were induced to come down here, to a spot which he has for a long time dreaded more than any place on earth. Have you any more questions to ask?"

"Only this, sir. Who is the girl Eldiva, who is kept in the power of Alf Dunning either by fear or influence?"

"She is the daughter of *one* of his victims—not *his* daughter, however. Wretch that he is, he could hardly do what I am sure he intends to do, if that was the case. But when she claims it, she will find protection from *his* brutality!"

"Then she claims it *now!*" said a low, mournful voice close behind us.

The girl had approached noiselessly, for she was barefooted and walking on hard ground, while we were all so intent on the words of Mr. Melrose that we did not hear her. "Has he been renewing his abuse?" asked Melrose.

"Yes sir—he called me a whimpering coward—said I had seen nothing, and only fainted for effect—and he threatened—ah, I dare not tell you what!"

"I know, poor girl, without your telling. I said you should have protection, and you shall. But I am not ready to come out openly yet. I will tell you what to say the next time he gives you an angry look or word, and it will make him dumb, if I do not mistake the abject moral cowardice of the man. Tell him you had a dream, and dreamed *three names* were handed to you by a skeleton hand. I will whisper the names to you—let him only hear them. Tell him a voice told you to reveal those names to the nearest magistrate, coupled with his own. *Then* if he threatens, let me, or these friends, know instantly. Take this whistle, blow it, and we will come when the call is heard."

Mr. Melrose whispered the names in her ear, handed her a small ivory whistle, and bade her hurry back before her absence from the cabin was noticed by Alf or his men, who were at work in their sluices.

The girl, with a look of gratitude and thankful words, hastened to obey, evidently feeling that she would henceforth find some protection from a brutality that was wearing her young life away.

And now Mr. Melrose moved away from our vicinity, taking a route which would keep him out of sight of the party of Dunning, as indeed we were in our position, though we could see them by looking through openings in a thicket of trees between us and them.

The girl had already returned unseen to the cabin, when Griffin proposed that we should go down and locate a new claim, where we could work while we carried on our observations.

"Suppose that Black Alf objects to our changing base," said I, "what shall we say to avoid a quarrel?"

"That we locate a new claim for our man, Billy Flynn, and he and I will work that before we do the others."

"All right—the plan is good, and will work, that is if he comes to hand, as Mr. Melrose says he will, at twelve o'clock. I suppose you know what Melrose is?"

"I can guess, sir, and if he is what I think he is, it will be our duty to help him. Black Alf has long been a terror to good men, and if he can be brought to a fitting end, it will be the better for everybody but him."

"Yes, if that be the end of a rope, with him swinging at it. Buckle on your belt, get your mining tools and measuring tape, and let us be off for the new claim."

CHAPTER VIII.
"Murder Will Out."

We were not long in passing over the space between our tent and where Dunning and his gang were at work. As we passed the cabin, a look was exchanged between us and the girl Eldiva, which expressed returning courage on her part and hopefulness also, and then we kept on past the place where the other men were mining, cut some stakes from the chaparral near at hand, and commenced measuring and marking out a new claim just below the ground now being worked by Dunning and his gang.

We had got down the first corners, when Dunning sauntered up, and, in his usual insolent way, said: "I thought you chaps had taken your claims elsewhere. Mining law don't allow a feller to locate all over the diggins."

"We are locating this ground for a partner who will be here before dinnertime," I said, quietly.

"Yes; I suppose we'll have a colony before the week is out," said the ruffian, with an oath.

"It'll be all the better for as good a poker player as you are," said Griffin, striving to speak pleasantly.

"Yes; if all new-comers aren't as stingy in game as you be," growled Dunning. "But look here, men, if this talk about a *partner* is all sham, and none comes, curse me into heaps if you'll work this claim without a fight. Yon hear that, don't you?"

"Yes," said I, rather angrily; "and we don't care a button for your threats. There is our new partner and his family coming down the hill."

"A man, woman and two brats, eh!" said the ruffian, turning his eyes to the party, which, with a laden mule driven before them, were coming down the trail.

"The woman will seem like company to your gal," said Griffin, feeling his way to learn what Black Alf thought of the newcomers.

"Company be cussed! If my gal opens her lips to strangers I'll cut her tongue out. I've got her under *rule*—bet your bottom dollar on that."

And the fellow laughed—more like a hyena than a man.

He now turned to watch as we did, perhaps with even more interest than we, the approach of the new-comers.

A heavily laden pack-mule preceded the party, which consisted of a tall, stout-built man, with a ruddy, intelligent face and a pair of sharp gray eyes twinkling in it; a woman, very coarse in face and form, and two pale, lovely children, the eldest a boy of not less than fourteen or fifteen years, the next a girl, probably a couple of years younger, looking so much alike that they would at once be recognized as brother and sister.

The man and woman were coarsely but comfortably clothed, as were the children, though the clothes of the latter indicated poverty.

Yet, as we said above, they were both handsome in face, and too genteel in figure and bearing to be mistaken as the children of those they came with.

"How d'ye do, Mr. Ned Griffin, how d'ye do, sir?" cried the man to Griffin and myself, as he drew near, evidently tutored in the part he was to play.

"The top of the morning to you, Mr. Bill Flynn," said I. Then giving a name, haphazard, to his wife, I added: "How is Bridget this mornin'?"

"Long life to yer honor. She is well barrin' the *tire*, for it's a long walk, up and down, from the Auburn ravine, and that done since three o'clock this blessed mornin'."

"Well, you've made good time, my man—but whose children are these you've got along?"

"Sure, sir, it is orphans they are, widout father or mother, and me and the ould woman, havin' none and never like to, either, we thought we'd kape 'em wid us, rather than see 'em worriting along alone as they were below."

"It shows your good heart, Bill Flynn. We've just staked out this claim for you, and we'll all work it together after we've got your tent pitched."

All this time Alf Dunning had stood gazing at those children, who, with blue eyes and light-brown hair seemed so *unlike* those they came with. And while he looked, his face wore a strange expression—an inquiring, troubled look, as if he was trying to call up some memory.

"What's your name?" he asked, abruptly, of the boy at last, in a tone and with a look not calculated to make a favorable impression on a child.

The boy turned a quick, sharp look at him, and seemed to form an intuitive dislike to the man; for, with a glance which expressed his feelings, he turned toward his sister, and said: "Julia, darling, answer no questions asked by strangers. I shall not."

"We'll see, you brat, if you can't answer a civil question!" cried Black Alf, and he strode toward the boy as if he intended to inflict chastisement on him.

"Stand back there! Shame to yer mane sowl!" cried the woman Bridget Flynn, in a voice almost as masculine as that of her husband. "Lay but a finger's weight on the lad and I'll not lave a hair in yer head!"

"Then why don't he answer a civil question?"

"Civil, when the growl of a grizzly bear would be music to the way you spoke to the child!" cried Billy, advancing to the side of his irate wife. "Sure an' the boy is right to have nothin' to say to yez, and I'll uphould him in it!"

"Bully for you, Billy! It's yourself that is able to take a man's part ony day. Where shall we put the baste's load down, gintlemen?"

"Up on the hill, near our own tent," said I. "We will go up and help you to put up your canvas."

Alf Dunning glared fiercely at the whole party, and especially at the boy and girl, as we passed on, and I heard a muttered curse, and a threat, which I could not fully understand, leave his lips as he strode on even faster than we toward the cabin.

He saw that the girl Eldiva was standing in front of the cabin, and that we must, of course, pass close by her. His words expressed the cause of his haste as he hurried on.

"Into the cabin there, you gaping idiot!" he cried. "Into the cabin and attend to your work, or I'll cut the skin from your back with a raw-hide!"

The girl did not move, for we were now very close, and our looks told her she would be protected at all hazards.

"Don't you hear me, you putty-faced cat?"

"I hear you, Mr. Dunning; but a woman, where I am, is such a curiosity, and children, too, that I want to look at them," she replied, in a tone so fearless that his eyes dilated with wonder.

"You think you've got backers, I reckon!" he cried, adding a nameless epithet and a bitter curse as he spoke. "I'll show you better!"

Rushing on, he raised his hand to strike her.

"Hold, Alf Dunning, or I'll speak aloud three names given to me last night in a strange way, which other ears would take more note of than you like. Hold down your hands, and hear me whisper the names in your ear—then strike, if you want to."

The astonished man bent his head to hear the whispered names.

Strange indeed was the effect which instantly followed. He fairly sprang back, while his dark face blanched to a ghastly pallor.

"Has Satan himself been talking to you?" he cried.

"Yes; and revealed enough to hang you. Now will you strike me?" she cried, triumphant in her first success over the brutal tyrant.

"No, no, girl; let there be peace between us. I must know more of this," he said, as we passed on.

"Heaven bless your sweet faces, children. I'll come to see you by and by!" said the girl to the children, as they passed in our company.

"You'll look through dead eyes, then," I heard him mutter, in an undertone.

And if ever murder spoke in hateful, evil eyes, it did in his at that moment. I knew something must be done to protect her, and in an instant a thought flashed over my mind.

"There are others who know the names which were whispered to you just now!" I cried. "Let the least harm come to that girl from your hands or by your influence, and to your sorrow you will learn that *murder* will out!"

"*Murder?*" he gasped. "MURDER?" he cried, in a louder tone, and then he rushed into the cabin alone.

CHAPTER IX.

A Shriek and a Cry.

We were busy for the next hour in getting up the tent of Billy Flynn, and arranging in it two compartments, using blankets to partition the same, so that the children might be by themselves when they desired.

We now learned that their names were Julia and Jesse, though they did not for some reason reveal their last names, and though both seemed quiet and very sedate for their years, yet they were pleasant in their replies to our kindly meant advances.

We had got the tent fixed, and Bridget was very awkwardly trying to cook dinner, so awkwardly indeed that Billy apologised for her by saying that she was used to a stove and not to an outdoor fire, and Ned Griffin turned to work to help her, when Mr. Melrose suddenly appeared.

Both the children ran out to meet him with cries of pleasure on their lips, and he kissed them each on the forehead with a tenderness that seemed almost parental.

Then he took them one side and talked for a long time earnestly, as if he was instructing them in some plan which they must follow. After dismissing them and telling them to gather beautiful flowers if they chose, which grew plentifully all around, he came to where Billy Flynn, Bridget, and Ned Griffin and myself were seated on a large rock, and with a smile, addressed us: "I am glad to see you all take so kindly to each other," he said. "In a work like that before us, only unity of feeling can beget that union in action which will insure success."

"No fear, sir, but that we'll all work together," said Billy Flynn, and when he spoke now there was not the least sound of the brogue on his tongue, nor in his accent any sign that he had ever been nearer to Ireland than he was at that moment.

Griffin looked at him a moment, and then laughed outright.

"Couldn't you be a darkie from old Virginny, too?" he asked.

"Yes, marser—that is if 'twould *pay!* Dis chile am up to a'most any dodge dats got money behind it."

The reply of Billy Flynn was as much negro like in voice as had been that of Melrose when assuming the same character, and Griffin could hardly realize that he was the same man whose former brogue was Milesian enough to have deceived any one.

But so it was. His was an assumed character, and one he was well able to keep up when necessity demanded it.

"How did you know my name when you met me?" continued Griffin, addressing Billy Flynn.

"I had name and description both given me before my arrival," replied the latter. "There is but one of Dunning's party whom I have ever seen yet. I know the name and have a description of them all. The one I know is—"

"Hush—you need not explain," said Melrose, quickly. "Our friends here will learn all about him, as well as the rest, in the proper time. And now be lively in fixing up camp, and make yourselves as much like real miners as you can. I must keep in the shade and not seem to know you. Keep a close eye on the children, for were that wretch, Black Alf, to suspect who they are, their lives would be taken, if he could do it. All works well now; I hope it will soon work even better yet. Good-by till I come again. I will be with you when least expected. Three rapid shots at any time will draw me and more to your side. And now, again, good-by. Be vigilant while you appear careless—let one be awake and on watch at all hours!"

We all gave assent, and the next instant he was gone.

Not a moment too soon, either, for in less than three minutes afterward Black Alf was seen, coming toward the spot, accompanied by the girl, Eldiva. He had a kind of sickly smile on his face, a look of assumed friendliness which was not well calculated to deceive old students in face talk.

"Me and the gal thought we'd come up and see you," said Alf, in a drawling tone, "for it isn't in woman nature to be on-friendly with her kind, and the gal says she's took a reg'lar likin' to them children—which I don't see around, by the way."

"No, they're afther flowers, the swate crachures likes 'em so," said Bridget, with a smile that opened full six inches of mouth.

"And they're not like to be back soon, since they had dinner afore they went. But sit ye down. If it's civil you'd be wid us we'll meet you half way jist!" said Billy Flynn, with a droll twinkle in his sharp gray eyes.

"May I go and hunt them up? I like to gather flowers and wander over the hills when I have a chance," said Eldiva, with a sigh.

"Not without I'm along, gal, grizzlies are thick around here, and you might see another ghost," replied Alf.

"I pray Heaven that I may, if it only is the spirit of my dear mother."

"Gal, I told you not to talk of her."

"Well, sir, don't be angry; I'll try and not do it again."

"Will you have some o' this? It is prime whisky—none of your rot that will kill at eighty rods up hill!"And Black Alf produced a huge flask, tendering it first to me, then to Ned Griffin, and last to Billy Flynn.

Of course the first two declined; and even to our surprise, for he had a red face, Billy Flynn did the same.

"An Irishman, and go back on whisky!" exclaimed Black Alf. "Why, I never saw or heard of the like before. It's like mother's milk to three of 'em that I've got in my crowd."

"Bad 'cess to 'em, then, for it's not Father Mathew men they are!" cried Flynn. "That's what I am, sir, total abstinence from the crown of my feet to the sole of my head! Mind that, if ye please!"

"Then I'll drink a share for you all," said Alf, with an attempt at a laugh which distorted his face and made the girl shudder. "Maybe your woman will drink, though."

"Me touch the devil's broth!" cried Bridget, bitterly. "Niver the drop, while my seven sinses are about me. Sure it has pisoned my betters and I'm not goin' the way the drunkard travels."

Alf tried to laugh again, but he made a bad attempt and washed down the effort with a lengthy draught from his flask."Is there anything in the eatin' line we can help you with?" he asked. "We've lots of grub down at the cabin."

"We want nothing of you, Alf Dunning, but a clear coast and no favors!" said Ned Griffin, who was beginning to tire of the presence of the fellow.

"Well, that is easy given, but because I was a bit cross a while ago, when I felt out o' sorts, you needn't keep up the snarl when I want to be friendly. I came up here to please the gal, for I was rough on her, and felt sorry after 'twas over."

"It's all right," said Griffin, catching a cautionary glance from me. "I don't want to quarrel, but I'm not in the best humor myself. I'll take a walk and see if I don't feel better."

Alf made no reply, but he put away his flask, took out his pipe, filled and lighted it, and sat smoking for an hour almost, while Bridget and Eldiva chatted together. Bridget had so many droll things to say that Eldiva got to laughing as heartily as if she had never known care or sorrow.

Alf Dunning seemed lost in his own dark thoughts, for he did not speak for a long time, though Billy Flynn, Ned Griffin, and myself were talking about work, prospects, and many other things in which he had a chance to join.

At last, he said abruptly, addressing Griffin: "You've took the old shaft for your claim?"

"Yes," said Ned, "I have, and mean to work it by and by!"

"You'll find nothing but bad luck in it!" he said, gloomily. "That's what me and my partners found there. Not a bit o' color even in the dirt, and only a streak here and there of sulphate in the rock. It won't pay. If I was you I'd let it alone. There's rich ground down the gulch."

"I'll make the oldest shaft pay, I reckon," said Griffin, in a quiet way. "The ghost of that woman always disappears near there, and I reckon that means something."

"Lord, don't talk of it. See how white my gal turns. I guess I'll go back to the cabin—come gal, come!"

"May I not wait till the children come back?" she added, in a pleading tone.

"No—not now—we'll come back and see them to-morrow. I want to make friends with that bright-eyed boy. I spoke rough to him to-day, and scared him, but—"

"It is not so! You did not *scare* me! I'm not afraid of you, but I do not like you, and never will be your *friend!*"

It was the boy himself who spoke. Light of foot, he and his sister had come up the hill in a line with some bushes which hid them from view until they were within five or six yards of our group, and Jesse had heard every word spoken by Dunning when he rose to go.

"We'll see—we'll see when I send to town and get some nice things, such as boys and girls like!" said Alf, with a forced smile on his face.

"You'll be *my* friend, will you not?" asked Eldiva, as she advanced to the brother and sister, who stood hand in hand, and reached out her thin white palm.

"Yes," said both the children, simultaneously. "Yes, for you are not like him."

"Oh, thank you."

Tears were in her eyes when Eldiva kissed them, and she said: "I am going now, but to-morrow I will come and see you, and together we will go to pick flowers. I must go and get supper for the people at the cabin; it is late, and will be dark before I can get it ready."

"Take these flowers now," said Julia, and she reached out a bouquet which she had culled.

"And this wreath from me, too," said Jesse, in a warm, earnest tone.

Alf Dunning looked on and scowled, and then, in a low tone, muttered to himself: "To-morrow—yes, to-morrow, and the sooner the better—all three at once. For I know them—yes, I know them."

I heard his words, and I think Eldiva did also, for she started nervously, and as she moved down the path, looked back several times.

They had staid so long that twilight was already on us, as they moved away.

They had been gone perhaps a minute, or a little more, long enough to have gone a couple of hundred yards, when a wild shriek from the lips of Eldiva, a strange cry from the man, came back to us with a startling effect.

An instant after we heard the shrill sound of the ivory whistle which had been given to the girl by Melrose.

Clutching our weapons, we rushed down the hill.

CHAPTER X.
"What Is It That Speaks?"

When we reached the last range of thicket between our camping-place and the cabin below, we found the girl Eldiva standing, with her hands clasped in an attitude of terror, while prone at her feet lay the body of Black Alf, stretched across the trail.

"What is the matter here? Have you killed him?" I cried, for that was my first thought.

"No, sir—no! He has not been touched by mortal man, but here right where he fell, he was met by what seemed to be a man, bleeding from a horrible gash in his head. Alf Dunning sprang back against me in a dreadful fright, and as I screamed with terror, he uttered a name—one of the names whispered to me by Mr. Melrose—and sank as you see him to the ground. At the same instant the man seemed to vanish from sight, making no sound. I was so frightened that I blew my whistle. I hope I did not do wrong."

"No, you did right, my brave girl—perfectly right!" said Melrose himself, coming among us, we knew not from where, so sudden was his appearance.

"Now, men, we must arouse this cowardly murderer, and see him to his cabin, for he'll never get there without help. I dislike to use liquor, but if his flask is not empty, we had better pour some of its contents down his throat," said Melrose.

"Raise his head, and I'll do it, sir," said the girl.

"Thank you, that relieves my conscience a little, for I hate to even handle the poison. Alf got a pretty bad scare. His own guilt added to it. He hears on every breeze, in every rustling leaf, the charge of *murder!*"

"Who says—who says I did a murder? He killed himself—I didn't do it!" moaned the man, half-unconscious, but struggling with slow-returning consciousness.

"Liar! Murdering wretch!"

These words seemed to come from a voice above them all in the air—a voice so deep and hollow in its tone that the blood ran chill in all our veins when we heard it.

"Heaven's mercy! What is it that speaks?" cried Eldiva, in mortal fear.

"His accusers! Vengeance—*vengeance*—VENGEANCE!" cried a voice, this time shrill, even as it seemed unearthly—the voice of a woman.

Alf Dunning, who had been raised to his feet, and who now heard these words with a cry of horror, broke away from the sustaining arm of Melrose and rushed down toward the cabin at headlong speed.

We all followed him, not that we cared for his safety or his feelings, but to escort the poor girl Eldiva back to the shelter of the cabin.

When we reached the cabin, we found him surrounded by his rough gang, asking eagerly if he had been insulted or attacked by us.

"No—no—I met the devil himself in my road!" he groaned. "Give me whisky, give me drink to drown out accursed memories!"

In an instant a tin cup was filled to the brim with raw, fiery whisky, and he drained it to the last drop. Another, and then a third, before he gave the word to stop, followed the first. Soon the effect was visible in his face and manner, and he began laughing wildly at the fear which had overwhelmed him.

"Ha! ha!" he cried. "I don't believe I saw anything at all. It was all fancy. I've got dispepsy, or something like it, and fancy things which are not, cannot be. Ha! ha! The liquor drives away all such folly. Drink—drink, that's the order of the day. More whisky, boys—more whisky!"

Another tin cup was filled for him, and he drank it. It was more than enough to have deadened the senses of any other man in the cabin, but Black Alf was one of those few, peculiar men who never seem to get entirely or help-lessly drunk, and, to use a favorite phrase of theirs, "can carry all they can hold."

So the ruffian became more quiet under the influence of the drink, for his terror was passing away, and his nerves becoming more steady.

Seeing our party yet lingering at the door, and remembering where he had been so recently, the attempt on his part to get up a reconciliation, for his own purposes no doubt, and they could not be good, he now called on us to come in.

Three of us were about to decline, but the fourth, Melrose, for Bridget had staid with the children, gave us a nod to follow him, and, walking in, we took a seat near the fire on a bench.

"You're welcome, all, gentlemen—welcome, I say. It's a pity you don't drink, for I've got capital liquid lightnin'—hand me another cup, boys."

"Please, Mr. Dunning, don't drink any more till after supper. I'll soon have that ready. You'll spoil your appetite if you do."

"What's that to you, you infernal—"

"Stop, sir!" cried Eldiva, to whose expostulation he was replying, with a look of fearful anger. "Stop before you make me speak the name which I heard a second time to-night, and tell what I saw!"

The ruffian turned white, in spite of the strong drink he had taken, but he did not go on with his brutality—he lowered his voice, and said: "Well, don't make me mad; Get supper ready, for the boys are hungry enough to eat wild-cat. I know I am, and so must they be. We'll eat, and then make a night of it, singin' songs and tellin' stories. Maybe we'll get up a nice game of draw-poker, or a little old sledge, or euchre. I'm ripe for fun now, and I'll be riper when I get a couple of quarts more of corn-juice down. Ha! ha! This is a jolly old world, and lots of jolly folks in it. The only trouble is finding 'em out. Hurry up the grub, gal—hurry up the provender."

The ruffian laughed gleefully, for once more he was on an even keel, and thought he had plain sailing before him.

"Let us be going," I whispered to Melrose.

"No—not just yet. He proposed stories—I want to draw him out in that line. The work which I came here to do progresses nobly. We will stay for a while at any rate."

CHAPTER XI.
Black Alf's Story.

With a haste which showed that she had been inured to labor of that kind, the girl Eldiva prepared supper, and soon had the slab table covered with fried bacon and trout, and the almost universal dish among miners, pork and beans, while hot coffee was ready for those who desired it.

The most of Black Alf's gang, however, "went in," as he did, for whisky, even at meals, and this evening they did not vary their custom.

For the purpose of aiding to carry out the wishes of Melrose, and perhaps because the poor girl Eldiva looked so pleadingly at us, we all remained and made as hearty a supper as inclination would permit.

After the meal was over, and pipes were alight on every side, we huddled around the great fire-place, into which some huge dark logs had been cast, and while the blaze lessened the chilliness of the night air, prepared to listen to such stories as might be given.

"Let's have a story from the boss of the crowd," said Melrose, who was seated nearer the door than any of us.

"A story from Black Alf—a yarn from the boss!" came up on every side.

"Pshaw, boys! I'm not in a talking mood," said Alf, in a way which showed a little more coaxing would draw him out.

"You came here in '49, didn't you?" asked Melrose, quietly.

"Thunder! '49 wasn't born when I came here first. 'Twas in '45, just after that long-haired sojer, Fremont, came over the Sierras in the winter time. I'd got into a scrape up in the Nor'-west with the head agent of the fur tradin' company I trapped and hunted for, and had to leave, you see. I didn't come alone, neither. I was on my way down to Chili, or some other unknown region; but the devil or something else made me stop at the Mission down on the bay, and I was there when the 'gold fever' broke out, and I've been here ever since."

"Tell us about the scrape in the Nor'-west. You must have been as good-lookin' as they make folks about that time," said Melrose.

"You just bet your bottom dollar I was that!" said the ruffian, with a coarse laugh. "Give me another cup of whisky from that jug, Ben Keeno, and then I'll let out a part o' that scrape. Not all, though—not all!"

The whisky was handed to Alf, who drank, and then, settling back in his corner, he commenced his story:

"'Twas in '44—the spring-time o' that year, when the water was all over the banks from the melted snow—that about seventy of us all told, trappers, hunters, clerks, and the head agent or factor of the company, left Saint Louis, and headed up the river to reach as far up the Yellowstone as the stern-wheeler steamboat *Irene* could carry us. She was a smart little Pittsburg boat, with one Captain George running her; and she made good time—bet high on that—considering the drift that always comes down on a freshet. After we got settled aboard, knowing we had a long trip ahead, we all went to huntin' up something to do to pass time away—I among the rest. The old trappers looked to their traps, their hunting tools, and the presents they were takin' to the squaws they'd left behind when they came to the settlements. The new ones watched what the old ones did, looked to their arms, and did what you are all doing now—listened to yarns, spun by old cusses like me. Pass that cup again, Ben."

The speaker, having "freshened his nip," went on: "Some took to cards. I didn't care much for 'em then, and hadn't much with me to stake on 'em, for I was dead broke when the agent, who was aboard, met me in the city, lent me enough for a fit-out, and engaged me to come along. I was hard up, in fact, when he took me by the hand. He was a queer chap, that agent—looked as sour as crab-apples when he spoke, but had a heart as soft and sweet as a ripe peach. He was in luck afore he came away, for just the prettiest girl in all Saint Louis, one of the daughters of a rich old Frenchman, fell in love with him, and he with her, and they got married. How it was I couldn't tell, for he wasn't a bit under fifty, and maybe nearer to sixty, and she was only sixteen, and just as handsome as handsome could be. Tall for her age, slender-waisted, but plump otherwise, with jet-black eyes, and hair when shook out that almost hid her out of sight—she was enough to make any man shiver with joy just to look at her.

"Well, fool-like, for men in love are always foolish, the agent brought his bride along on this trip, and though there were a dozen women, all told, aboard, she was the only real pretty one there. He just worshiped her, and at first she seemed to think there was nobody like *him*. But after we got well up the river, he had to be in the pilot-house a great deal, for he knew more of the river than all the rest put together, he had been up and down so often, and so he couldn't see to her as he did at first, for the pilot-house wasn't as big as this fire-place, and no room for anybody except them that were at the wheel.

"So, to kill time, the best-looking chap there was aboard, and *he* was about *my* size, got in with her in the way of talk and playing crib and dominoes, and talking soft nonsense, and then it wasn't long before her laugh was just as cheery when her husband wasn't there as when we was, may be a little cheerier. The chap I alluded to *knew* he was good-lookin', and that he had the gift of gab pretty well developed, and he sailed in to make a conquest if he could. There's no use in tellin' exactly how he did it, or some of you might larn and try to git my gal away from me, but before that boat got up the Yellowstone to the last tradin' post, where we were all to leave her, the young bride cared a heap more for the young chap that had been such company on the voyage than she did for her husband. And the best of it was, the old man didn't dream of such a thing, but believed she was just the truest, lovingest bit of beauty that ever danced to music. And 'twould have been a long time before he would have found out any different, if it hadn't been for *her* foolishness. You see, a woman in love is like a man half drunk. She hasn't got a bit of prudence. She lets her heart run away with her brains. When the boat had landed the stores, took in the fur on hand and the men we came to relieve, the agent expected the young wife to go back to her folks, and stay until he went back the next spring. That was the understandin' when she came away, for it wasn't a nice place for a woman to winter in up there among the hostile Blackfeet. But her and the young chap made up she should stay, and when the husband wanted her to go, she flung her white arms around his neck, and cried and went on so, the old fool thought she'd die if he sent her back, so he consented she should stay, and he'd make her as comfortable as he could. So the boat went back without her.

"Then the trappin' parties were made up, going off in squads, as the agent arranged 'em to take ground where fur was plenty.

"The young chap was put into one of these parties, but he took sick all of a sudden, and couldn't go. He was just sick enough, too, to need a nurse, and you might know who nursed him. Oh, she was keen, that woman was. Her husband always took a hot whisky punch or toddy before he turned in of a night, and she got into the way of making 'em for him. The young man gave her a hint, and as she could get at all the medicines, she used to fix them toddies so *nice* that the old man couldn't wake up for four or five hours after he'd taken one, no matter what occurred, so she had plenty of time to nurse the young 'un, and no one to interfere.

"Well, this run for awhile, the young man keeping just sick enough to stay in the fort and be nursed, while love was having a high time. Bet your bottom dollar on that.

"Whatever put the old chap into suspicion I never knew, but he got suspicious, and one night he *pretended* to drink off the toddy which she had made and doctored, but he *didn't*. Instead of sleeping, as she thought, the old cuss kept awake, and watched her. And then he found out how *sick* the young chap was, and how much his nurse loved him, and he got into a big mad, and pitched in to *choke* her and larrup* *him*. You might know how that game would end. I had *to put a knife into him!*"

"*You?*" exclaimed several of the hearers.

"Well, yes. I may as well give in that the young chap was *me*, for it wasn't anybody else. I had to shove a knife hilt deep into him, and then of course I had to git up and git. The woman wouldn't let me come alone, you see—so taking arms and ammunition, and the old chap's watch and money, we slid. We had a hard time a getting over to this coast, and a rough one in getting down it to California, but we

---

* To beat, flog, or thrash.

got here at last, for she clung to me as tight as a burr to a sheep's wool all the time. She was just about the lovingest creature you ever saw or heard tell of."

"Where is she now?"

It was Melrose who asked the question, and his eyes fairly blazed while they looked the ruffian in the face.

Black Alf trembled but did not reply.

"Where now is poor Medora Roget?" cried Melrose a second time.

"Dead—*dead*, and you know it!" said the man, in a tremulous tone.

"How did she die?" asked Melrose, in the same stern tone.

"Yes—speak—how did my poor mother die, for now I know you have told her sad story," cried Eldiva.

"You'd better find out, if you can," said the ruffian, defiantly. "Ben, hand me another cup of whisky."

"We will, and you shall get hung over the bleached bones of your victims!" cried Melrose, rising to his feet and turning to the door.

Quick as a flash of lightning would break from a cloud, Black Alf drew a pistol and raised it, but the girl knocked the barrel up and the ball tore through the roof over our heads.

"Devil, there's another load for you!" cried the wretch, but with a sarcastic smile she spoke a name so quick and low that *he* only seemed to hear it.

With a groan, while a sickly pallor came over his face, he let the weapon fall from his hand and then sank back into the seat from which he had sprung.

"More whisky, Ben," he gasped. "More whisky! I'm getting to be the cussedest coward that ever whined. I'll not stay in this infernal gulch another night."

"Leave it, if you dare!" came in a sepulchral tone from some source. "Like thoughts of your hidden treasure, the spirits of your victims will haunt you awake or asleep, as well away as here. Murderer—there is no rest for you this side of the grave!"

The head of the ruffian was bowed between his clasped hands, he trembled with terror and unspeakable dread, and Ben had to shake him and speak several times before he would take the fiery drink he had called for.

While he drank, Ned Griffin, Billy Flynn and myself left the cabin.

CHAPTER XII.
Black Alf's Riches.

When we reached our tents on the hill-side, we found Melrose, and a female cloaked and masked, sitting near the campfire, talking in a low tone. Bridget we heard inside, singing an old-fashioned ballad all about Captain Kidd, in a very masculine tone of voice, to the children.

The female arose when our steps reached the ears of herself and Melrose and walked away, seemingly well acquainted with the ground, for she took a trail which led over toward the eastern side of the gulch, without any hesitation.

"Wait for me at the Dropping Spring," said Melrose, as she went off, and then he turned to us.

"How did you leave Black Alf?" he asked, as quietly as if his life had not been so recently endangered by the ruffian's merciless hand.

"So badly scared," said I, "that he knows not what to do. I think he will try to leave the gulch."

"If he does his way will be barred more strongly than he dreams. He will not go until we know where he has hidden an enormous amount of gold, which I know he once possessed, the result of robbery and murder, and which he has had no chance to take away. He has lingered around to let bad rumors die away, and suspicion subside, so that he might move it unobserved, or abstract portions unseen, and he has been too cunning, even in his drinking bouts, to reveal its vicinity to any one. At least that is my belief. But I know it is somewhere in the gulch."

"Perhaps in the old shaft," said Ned Griffin.

"No, I have searched every part of it. There is something else there, however, which in time will aid in fixing his just doom. He knows what is there, and for that reason wants to make you believe the place is not worth working. It is not very valuable perhaps, just now, but it was, for a vein of solid, virgin gold was struck by him and his former partners, of such astonishing richness that they took it out by pounds at a time. But it run out at last, and then with millions in their hands these men *might* have gone East, where they belonged, and enjoyed their wealth. That they did not was the fault of one man. Not satisfied with his share of this immense fortune, he craved it all. You may imagine the rest. These men disappeared suddenly. The ruffian, Black Alf, said they had gone East overland with a mule train of their own, and left him to work the claim alone. That was his first story, when, with the beautiful woman who followed his fortunes, he left his gulch and went to Iowa Hill to live. Since then he has varied in his stories. Sometimes he says his partners died of cholera, and he was afraid of dying too, and left them unburied. That the grizzlies ate up their bodies, bones and all."

"But the woman. Had she no story to tell? What has become of her?" I asked, eagerly, for my interest was all excited.

"She had frequent spells of melancholy and nervous fits, after she came to the Hill. So I learn from women who knew her slightly, for Black Alf would allow her to make no intimacies. She would weep for hours with her little daughter, Eldiva, in her arms—the child of her married love—and only cease when Alf with threats would make her join him and drink till she was unconscious of the cause of misery which was wearing her life away. At times she would say strange things, and talk wildly about murder, and then Black Alf would abuse her terribly. At last, she got so bad, he was afraid to keep her where folks could hear what she said, and he hired a man and came down to this gulch to live in the old cabin again. A few days after, he went back to the Hill and said the woman had run away with the hired man, and made a great fuss, swearing to kill them both if he could ever find them. He even went down to San Francisco in pretended search of them, and there he met a lady, the unhappy mother of the two children now in that tent, who came on from her Eastern home to join her husband, who had written to her nearly two years before of his success, and sent for her. She had come by the way of Panama, where she had been taken down with fever herself, lost one child, the other two narrowly escaping death. She had been detained by sickness, and the want of money to come on with, for over a year, and when she saw Black Alf, whose name she had heard of through her husband's letters, she eagerly asked after him.

"The wretch told her that her husband had started East overland and had with his companions been murdered and robbed by the Piute Indians on the great plains of Nevada. She was too weak and feeble to bear up under the terrible shock, for she believed it all, and finally died, leaving with her last breath those children to a friend who will never desert them!

"Black Alf did not stay to learn of her death, though he soon knew it through the papers. He came back to the Hill, where he has kept his headquarters for years, watched more closely than he dreams. Gradually there has been gathered about him a hedge of proof which soon will be sufficiently strong to hold him in the stern hands of justice and send him to the doom he merits. You heard his tale to-night—his confession or boast of what was probably his *first* murder. How many he has committed since, I do not know to a certainty, but one thing is sure, enough can be brought directly home to him to swing him from the gallows-tree, when the case is sprung. But I am not ready yet. These orphans must have the gold for which their unfortunate father toiled, and at last perished. And when that is found, the cry for 'vengeance' shall have its answer.

"His doom is not far off. But the hidden treasure must come to light. Coward like, the wretch has got a band of kindred spirits about him. He will soon be driven, I hope, to confide in them enough to ask aid to carry away his hidden store. When he does I shall know it. How, I cannot now explain, but he can do nothing without my knowledge. One thing is now especially required. That is watchfulness over the safety of these children, Julia and Jesse. He has recognized them, for in their faces the father's likeness is reproduced. He will murder them or have them murdered if it can possibly be done."

"They shall be watched over night and day," was my reply. "What do you think is the intention of the brutal wretch toward poor Eldiva?"

"His intention is to make her even more his slave than her poor mother was. But he has been foiled so far, and shall be, since she is under our eyes and a protection which will never leave her so far from sight that a cry for help will not carry swift assistance to her side."

"She does not seem bad for one brought up amid such wild and rough associations."

"She is not. She is yet pure in the sense to the world most essential, and with the favor of Providence and our aid, will so remain. Still more, she will, I hope, be an instrument to aid in forcing on him a fearful retribution for the murder of her father and the wrongs to her poor mother. But, gentlemen, I must leave you. I will go in and kiss the children good-night, then, leaving them to your vigilance to guard, hasten away to perform my work at another point. Get to work at your claim to-morrow, to keep down all suspicion."

Melrose now entered the tent, and when he did so Bridget Flynn came out. We could hear him speaking tenderly to the children, who seemed to love him so much, and then in a little while he came out.

"If the girl Eldiva comes up to walk with the children to-morrow, let them go, Bridget," said he. "They will have a protecting eye and hand near them, so you need not follow. But during the night a guard must be constantly kept. On their lives depend too much not to require all our vigilance, apart from the value of life as life. Good-night all."

The next moment he was gone, taking the same path by which the cloaked and masked female disappeared.

CHAPTER XIII.
Mr. Melrose's Vigilance.

I had the morning watch. Ned Griffin took the first—that from midnight to four was kept by Billy Flynn, and now with the morning star in full view over the snows of the Sierra Nevada, I paced my lonely beat in front of our two tents, and thought of one who in my loneliest hours comes ever as a bright and blessed memory to make me feel that though alone, I cannot be all lonely.

The moonlight fell bright on the rugged cliffs to my right and left, and the shadows lay black where it did not fall, while where water could be seen it shone like liquid silver to the vision.

Suddenly I saw a form coming swiftly, noiselessly, toward me. I was about to hail and order a halt, when I recognized the form and face of the girl Eldiva.

"Do not make a noise!" she said, "—oh, pray do not! for if my absence is discovered in the cabin I will be surely murdered. I left them all asleep, and I want to tell you something and then get back before they wake."

"Do so; I will listen," said I.

"And you will tell Mr. Melrose?"

"Yes, if you desire it."

"I do; he *must* know it. Black Alf has laid a plan to murder those sweet children, and he even meant without my knowing it to make me help in the dreadful work; but I will die first."

"Go on and tell me your story. It will soon be day, and then your absence will reveal all, for they will discover it."

"I will, I will, sir. After you went away last, Alf grew moody and thoughtful, and stopped drinking himself, but he plied all the rest with drink but the two worst men— Ben Keeno and Sam Reddy. When all but these were in drunken stupor, and I was asleep, as he thought, inside my curtained corner of the cabin, he commenced talking to these two men. He told them that he had more gold than anybody dreamed of, that it was hidden away, and that they should have a round sum if they would do his bidding fully and fearlessly. This they promised to do, no matter what it was.

"'Even if I ask you to kill somebody?' said he.

"'Not the girl Eldiva,' said Ben; 'she is too pretty to kill.'

"'No, not her; I've got something beside death for her at present,' said Alf. 'Them two children that are up yonder have got to be put out of the way. While they live I stand in fear of a discovery which might lift me higher than I want to go. They must be put out of the way.'

"'What'll you give if we *do* the kids?' asked Ben.

"'A hundred ounces of gold,' said Alf.

"'Make it a hundred apiece and we'll do it—won't we, Reddy?' said Ben.

"'Yes,' replied the other; 'I wouldn't touch the job for less.'

"'Then it is a bargain,' said Alf, 'and I'll hold you to it; and to help you, I'll lay the plan.'

"'Good! What is it?' cried Ben.

"'The girl Eldiva has taken a big liking to them, and they to her. To-morrow

I'll tell her, after her morning work is done, or, if it is any handier, after dinner, to go up and walk out with 'em. Then, when you see her go, you two can slip off through the bushes, follow her and them unseen until you get the chance, then do the job. Do it clean. Kill 'em, and bury 'em, too; but tear up their clothes into shreds, and bloody 'em, so it'll appear the lions or grizzlies did it and eat 'em clean up. Then, I reckon, the thing will look right.'

"'But the girl—she'll tell a different story if she is not killed too; and curse me if I'll lay a hand on her. She'd haunt me forever if I did,' said Ben.

"'It will be easy to fix the girl. She'll be just scared enough to do anything she's bid, and to do it natural, too. I'll be close at hand, and I'll make her swear to tell that she saw the children in the claws of the grizzlies and ran for help. If she should hesitate, I'll kill her with my own hand. She will not, for she is afraid of me when she has no one nigh to back her.'

"'Do you think the plan will work, Reddy?' said Ben.

"'Yes; but we'll not work in it till Alf gives us half pay down.'

"'Here it is, and if you do the job right, I'll double the amount,' said Alf, and he took a hundred ounces from his belt.

"You've got more?" said Ben, as Alf had nearly emptied his belt.

"'Yes—more than you and him could carry. Is this right now?"

"'Yes—we'll turn in and get rested for to-morrow.'

"They lay down, and then Alf came to my bed to see if I was asleep. Oh, I could hardly breathe when he bent over me, I was so terrified; for I knew he would, indeed, kill me if he thought I had overheard his plans.

"But I kept still, breathing regularly, and he went away in a minute or so, satisfied. He took a blanket and rolled up in it across the threshold of the door, which, fortunately, had been left open, it was so warm inside.

"I watched until I heard his heavy breathing and knew he was asleep, then I came out, and, stepping over him, hurried here. You know all now. I will not aid in the dreadful work—I will not leave the cabin at all to-morrow, and oh, do, do watch over those sweet creatures, for Heaven's sake!"

"You *will* walk out with them to-morrow!" said a quiet voice close to us, and Melrose came out from the shadow of the tent.

How he got there, unheard by one who has the quick sight and hearing of an old soldier, experienced in three hard wars, I could not imagine. But it was so.

"You will now hurry back to the cabin," he continued, "and sleep if you possibly can. At any rate, when all waken, do you make it necessary to be called as if from a sound slumber. And hide all appearances of agitation, for the least sign may put them on their guard. When Black Alf proposes to you to come up here and walk with the children, thank him and start. When you arrive, go with them, but be sure to take the route I shall now specify. Follow this trail to the left, go across the ravine and keep down among the ledges on the other side. When you get to a deep ravine which leads up near a waterfall, most likely those wretches will approach to carry out their plans. Do not fear, there will be help there, and if it should become necessary, they can be riddled with bullets before they can raise a murderous hand. Now, good girl, go, be fearless and trust me. You shall never lack aid and protection when you need it."

Eldiva bowed her lips to his hand, and without a reply darted away, and was in a moment lost to view.

"Mr. Melrose," said I, "I do not know whether you are Satan or not, you seem to be doing too good a work for that; but how a mortal man could get as near me as you did in the shadow of that tent, I cannot imagine, without the least sound reaching my ear!"

"I was there when you relieved Billy Flynn," he replied, "approaching at that moment, with my moccasined feet over the rocks in the rear. I was a partial witness to the conference in the cabin, and got a sign, too, that there was danger in this quarter from one who was believed to be in a drunken sleep by Black Alf. So I got up here, and was waiting when the girl came. I was near enough to hear her story. You know the rest. Now I must go to fix things to foil this new phase of villainy. When morning comes, you must all go down to work, in the manner proposed, on your claim, except Bridget, who will remain here with the children."

At this instant a low cry, like that of a whip-poor-will, was heard. I knew, however, that it came from human lips.

"I am wanted. Good-morning!" he said, and in an instant he was gone.

CHAPTER XIV.
Foiled.

When the day dawned, trusting entirely to the strange power and sagacity of Melrose, whose character I began both to understand and appreciate, though I woke Griffin and Billy Flynn, I did not tell them of my visitants, the incidents which had occurred during my watch, or even give a hint of the new peril in store for the children. I deemed it not only unnecessary, but imprudent, for by some look, some thoughtless word, one or the other might put Black Alf on his guard if we should meet him on our claim or elsewhere that morning.

So we got our breakfast early, armed, as we always did when we left our tent, and with pick, shovel, and pan, proceeded down to our claim.

When we passed the cabin I got a glimpse of the face of Eldiva and exchanged looks with her. Her expression satisfied me that she had got back undiscovered and was prepared to do her part in the day's programme according to the wishes of Melrose. I smiled encouragement and placed my hand on the butt of my revolver to signify that she would be protected under all circumstances, and kept on.

When we passed the spot where Alf and his gang were at work, the former stepped up, and not only spoke to us, but shook hands. I hated to touch the dirty fist of the wretch without gloves on, at any rate, but policy forbade a direct insult just then, so I endured the contact, though the pressure which I returned to his muscular grasp was very faint.

"You're out bright and early, friends," said he.

"Men who eat well, feel well, and sleep well, are able to do so," said I, carelessly.

"Where's that independent cuss that was with you last night, him that keeps a pickin' at me as if he was sure bent on a fight?"

"Mr. Melrose, you mean?"

"Yes; I heard one of you 'uns call him by that."

"He does not belong to our party—just drops in once in a while. I don't know where he is."

"Well, for his own sake, I hope he'll not drop in on me any more. I don't want to hurt him or any other man, but I can't stand everything. Have you got all the tools you want to work with? If you haven't we'll lend what we're not using any time."

"Thank you. We've got everything we need, and our tools are always in order," he replied, emphasizing the word which signified *weapons* as well as working implements in that section.

"That's a good thing," said he, "in a rough country, when you don't know who is around you. I'm always well fixed myself. How's them children to-day up there?"

"Well, I expect, though they were not up when we came down. The young need and take more sleep than we do."

"Yes, I s'pose so. Good mornin'. I'm going to work a while, and then I'll look up a deer or an antelope. If I'm lucky I'll send you some venison."

The man now turned away, having very cunningly covered a way to account for his leaving camp on an expedition the nature of which I understood but too well.

We went on to our claim and commenced work, seeming very busy, but my eyes did far more work than my hands, for I was watching all the time to see who left the other party, and when they left.

There was no change until after dinner, which they took at the cabin, while we ate the cold lunch we had brought with us.

Soon after dinner I saw two men of their party, the roughest, wildest-looking of the crowd, each take a pick and pan and slip away though the chaparral, as if going on a prospecting trip. At the same time I saw the girl, Eldiva, going up toward the tents, and a minute or two later I saw Black Alf himself, armed with a gun, start on the hunt he had spoken of to us. His course was the same taken by the two members of his gang just alluded to.

Generally calm—for from boyhood I have been placed in trying scenes, where self-possession was often essential to preservation—I thought I could obey the wishes of Melrose, and remain at our claim apparently engaged in my work. But I could not. A feverish fire ran through every vein—I feared something might deter Melrose from being able to protect those helpless little ones from the plot laid to destroy them; and at last, fully ten or fifteen minutes behind them, I, too, crept away, depending only on speed to overtake them, knowing also that I must move with the cunning and stealth of an Indian on the trail, or I would do far more harm than good.

I begged the rest—that is, Griffin and Flynn—to stay where they were, and, if asked about me, to say I was sick and had gone off into a shady spot to lie down; and then I started, making a bee-line for the ravine, which Melrose had described to Eldiva the night before.

I reached it, fortunately, before any one else, and, finding a clump of close-set dwarf pines, stepped in among them, where, hidden myself, I could command quite an extended view.

I had not been there five minutes before I got a glimpse of Black Alf on a knoll about three or four hundred yards away, where he rose from among some bushes, looked over into the ravine, and then squatted down out of sight. I did not see the other men, but I saw the bushes in the chaparral shaking, and by careful watching satisfied myself that they were agitated, not by the wind, but by persons creeping through them. And in a little while I could even see that instead of following each other in Indian file, there were two lines of march, one for each of the intended assassins.

These lines could be traced by the tremulous motion of the branches and tall shrubs from the spot where I had seen Alf Dunning raise up.

Suddenly my attention was called elsewhere. I heard the merry laugh of children—that music which will penetrate the hardest heart, soften the most obdurate soul, make even villainy pause ere it works its destiny.

A minute later I saw them coming hand-in-hand with Eldiva, who looked really beautiful; for they had placed a wreath of white flowers on her bare head, which, contrasting with her raven-black hair and the rich red of her rather brunette complexion, added greatly to her natural beauty.

How happy the two children seemed amid those flowers—the loveliest in the world, I care not where you go, surrounded by scenery *only* California can exhibit.

I almost forgot their peril, while I admired their beauty and listened to the music of their glad voices.

Nearer and nearer to me they came, and now I could see that Eldiva was nervous and anxious, in spite of her endeavor to seem composed. Her eyes wandered from point to point, she led the children in the most open ground, and would not let them rush to the thickets, where, on creeping vines, flowers the most gorgeous were to be seen, or approach the great rocks, covered with ferns and mosses.

Again I got a glimpse of Black Alf. He was much nearer now, and but a little way ahead of him the bushes shook where his two murderous minions crept.

I was calm now, not a tremor in my hand, while I looked once more at the caps of my two revolvers, and turned the chambers to see that they were in working order; for the children were close by me, passing on, and the men who followed them must pass or come under my range before they could harm them.

I looked around in every way for some sign of Melrose or those who he had said would be near when aid was required, but I saw no evidence of the vicinity of any one other than those already mentioned. I was thankful that impulse had brought me there. For impulse, especially first impulse, generally sends one in a right direction. Had I time for moralizing or argument I'd *prove* that. But I haven't.

Eldiva led the little ones a short way beyond me, to where the brook which headed in the ravine ran purling over a pebbly bed, and sat down on a log with her face toward the head of the ravine. She had an apron full of flowers, and I heard her tell the children that now she would help them to make wreaths and bouquets while they rested.

They sat down on the log, one on each side of her, and chatted away in happy glee, their voices rendered even more musical by the rippling accompaniments of running waters.

Why did she turn her face up the ravine, when she must have known that the danger was in her rear? That bothered me, for it was my first thought; then, when I saw how often and how nervously she looked up into the narrow, dark gorge, I thought that I might be mistaken, that she believed the assassins already hidden there, and feared they would dart down upon her and the children.

Again I saw Black Alf, his head just raised over a clump of bushes, not over sixty or seventy yards away, and a second later, creeping over the ground—their mining tools gone, but each with a huge bowie-knife in his hand—the two wretches came.

I almost held my breath, while I cocked the revolver clutched in my right hand and watched them as they crept on.

There was a low range of bushes between them and their intended victims, within about ten yards of the latter, and they crept along so as to keep that cover. When Black Alf got to another clump only a few yards farther back, he halted, put down his gun, beckoned them to his side, and whispered what I presumed were his last directions.

All this I saw, and yet no sign of Melrose, no evidence that there was any one but myself to meet and foil the horrible crime which those fiends meant to perpetrate.

The men conferred with their master but a few seconds, and then with hats and shoes off, their great knives drawn in their dirt-begrimed hands, they crept on.

Heavens! My heart stopped beating. They were within almost the distance they could leap at a single bound, and the girl and the children laughed on. They had not heard the tiger-step of the murderous enemy.

The men rose, looked at the children, then glanced at each other, as if to nerve each for the death-blow he was to make.

Never did my eye glance with such cool satisfaction over a pistol barrel as it did at that instant, for both men were in exact range, and so near of height, that I felt sure of sending one ball through both heads.

My finger was on the trigger, I waited only to see the drawing up of the muscles, which would indicate the intention to spring, when with one sound I saw two rings of smoke rise from a clump of cedar over beyond the children, and the wretches leap not forward, but up, with that strange, quivering bound which always follows a death shot in the heart.

Eldiva, with a wild scream, the children clinging to her, turned only in time to see them fall in the death agony so near, when Black Alf, with a fearful oath, broke from his cover and rushed toward them.

Before I could cover him as I meant to with my pistol, a woman with hair of jetty hue hanging loose over her shoulders, a face white except where a deep, livid, scarred gash crossed the white brow, stepped fairly between him and those he rushed to destroy.

With a yell of horror, he staggered back, pressed his hand over his eyes, and fell senseless to the ground.

At the same instant I saw the woman dart from sight into the bushes, while Melrose himself, coming from the clump of cedars, told Eldiva to hurry to the tent with the children and then go back to the cabin without fear.

"I will attend to *him*," he said, pointing to Black Alf, who lay yet senseless where he fell when the female form stood out before him.

Eldiva needed no second bidding to hurry from that fearful spot with her charges. With a shudder she passed the two men, whose eyes were unclosed and glared in the iciness of death upon her as she went by. And the children, speechless with wonder and affright, clung to her as she hurried on.

It was not until they were gone that I showed myself to Melrose, who was now approaching Black Alf.

A look of reproach expressed his feeling.

"Did I not tell you I would protect them?" he said. "There was no need of you coming here, or mixing up in this affair."

"I couldn't keep back," was my reply. "If a shot had failed, or any of *your* plans miscarried, you would not have regretted that I was here to lend you aid to save the helpless."

"My plans *never* miscarry," he said. "Now, get out of sight. He will soon recover his senses, and he must not see you. On second thought, he shall not even see me, but be more than ever mystified. Creep away quickly and get back to your work, unseen if you can. I will meet you at the tent at sunset, and tell you how he acts when he comes to. He will find no trace of me or mine, only the dead bodies there, which I will leave for him to bury. Go, and go at once. He will not long remain in a swoon."

I obeyed, and hurried from the spot. In twenty minutes I was at work in the claim with my two partners. I learned that no one had been there to note my absence.

I had been at work perhaps ten or fifteen minutes when Black Alf was seen rushing through the chaparral, bare-headed, and without even his gun, toward the place where his gang was at work.

Wishing to hear his report of what I had so plainly seen, I managed, by walking quickly up the stream on which our sluices were laid, to get there nearly as soon as he, in time to listen to his first words, for he could not speak for three or four minutes, he was so out of breath with running.

His clothes were torn and discolored, for he had rushed through the thorny chaparral and tumbled over knolls and rocks in his haste, and his face was white with fear, while his huge frame shook from head to foot.

CHAPTER XV.

Searching for the Reds.

Black Alf, surrounded by his gang, who wondered at his terrible state of excitement, did not see me approach, and I was glad of it, though I was satisfied he had not seen me on the spot where he had been so terrified.

"What is the matter, Alf—have you been chased by grizzlies?" exclaimed Bill Tulip. "You are all in tatters. Where's your gun?"

"I dropped it after I shot, for they were close upon me, so close that I couldn't wait to see if they scalped the others!"

"They—*who*—what do you mean? Have you gone crazy?" cried a half-dozen at once, amazed at his words and incoherent manner.

"If the Indians—Piutes, Walla Wallas, or whatever they are—get here and fire on you, as they did on me and Ben Keeno and Sam Reddy, I reckon you'll know what is what!" he gasped. "Them two are killed, I seen 'em layin' out stiff, and the reds were coming for me—so I had to git. I fired once, and then run. Didn't you hear my gun?"

"No," said several.

"I did, and when I saw you coming in just now, came in to hear what luck you'd had," said I, thinking this a good way to account now for my presence. "I heard a gun somewhere about half an hour ago, I thought."

"*One*? You most likely heard mine as I fired from the hill, running. They shot in a volley. How I got off is more than I can tell."

"What shall we do? If there is a big gang of Indians they'll come down here!" said several of the men.

"I don't think it can be a big gang," said Bill Tulip, who was the least excited of any man in his party, "because if it was they would have followed Alf up and be here now. Let us all arm and go and hunt for 'em."

"I don't want to—I am lame and tired," said Alf. "But I'll tell you uns where to go, and just where to find Sam and Ben."

"Oh, come along with us and show us," said Bill Tulip. "We'll go slow. In fact, we must, with scouts and flankers out to keep 'em from ambushing us."

"Yes, we'd never find 'em without you," said another.

"Our party isn't strong enough! I know there is a big crowd of 'em!" said Alf, trembling yet with excitement.

"I and my two partners will go with you. We are armed," said I.

"Well—if you insist, gentlemen—but I'm no ways fit to travel. Let's all go to the cabin and get some whisky and more weapons first, at any rate! Has any one seen the gal come back? I hope they haven't got her!"

"It don't look so, since I see her now on the hill there with the two children," said I, pointing to a knoll near the tents. "I'll go and warn her that there are Indians around while you get your drink and arms."

I saw that Alf did not like to have me communicate with her, but he was too much confused to form any plan to prevent it, and I went as fast as I could to tell her his tale, so she could invent one to tally with it enough to keep him from thinking she knew of his late murderous plot, and make our future work easier and safer so far as she was connected with it.

I did not take many minutes to carry out this plan, and I was back at the cabin by the time Alf and his gang were roused and fortified in courage by whisky, and ready to move.

"Had the gal seen 'em?" asked Alf, when I returned.

"No, but she was fired at in the bushes, and was so scared that she ran a mile or more right along the ledges in the bushes with the children to get away. She has seen nothing, but she heard the bullets whistle close by her."

An indescribable look of relief settled on Alf's face then. He seemed to be at once satisfied that his plan had not been discovered by the girl, and, as his two accomplices were dead, it would not be, and he could go on and plot again, next time, perhaps, more successfully.

He made no more objections to going to look for the bodies of the men, but seemed to wish to hurry so that night might not overtake the party in the place where he had left them, and where he had seen that which he had not now mentioned at all, the female apparition that terrified him into a swoon.

Bill Tulip was a volunteer scout, and with me and Ned Griffin kept in advance of the party, taking the route which Alf described, and which I knew well enough already.

As we marched rapidly, we were not over twenty minutes in reaching the spot where the bodies lay—a little pool of blood close by each.

As Alf Dunning gazed on them, a strange perplexity appeared on his face. I could not account for it at first, but when I remembered that I had seen them bare-headed, without shoes, knife in hand, creeping toward those whom they meant to murder, and saw how they were now arrayed, though laying just where they had fallen when shot, I saw reason for his wonder.

Their picks and pans were by their side, their hats and shoes on, and their knives were in the scabbards at their belts.

This was undoubtedly what bothered Alf, and something, too, which he could not speak of without bringing suspicion on himself in our presence, for that he would hide from Griffin, Flynn and I much that his gang might know for all *he* cared was evident.

"Let's search the woods and gulch for the reds!" said Bill Tulip.

"You'll not find 'em. If they'd meant to stay, they would have scalped and robbed these bodies. See—they haven't touched a tool or a weapon," said Alf. "I'll bet they chased me till they saw our camp, and then cleared. Let's carry the bodies back and bury 'em."

"Why not do it here?" asked Bill Tulip.

"'Cause we haven't got no tools but their two picks. They were only prospecting, and had no shovels."

"We can send and get shovels easier than we can lug them back," said one of the men.

"Yes; and 'twould be dark afore we'd get 'em under ground. I'll not stay out of sight of our cabin after dark for all the gold in the valley. It is *haunted*, and I know it," said Alf, with a shudder. "I'd rather let 'em lay here to be eat up by coyotes."

"That we will not do," said several of the men, indignantly. "They've worked, and eat, and drank with us, and we'll bury them, decently, if we can't do anything more."

"Bravo!" said I. "Make a couple of litters, and we'll help to carry them in."

There were hatchets in the belts of some of the party, and thongs and belts to bind the poles together, so it took but little time to make the litters and get them ready for use.

Though I hated the labor of moving such wretches from the spot where they had so nearly done a base and cruel murder, I could not but aid, so as to keep from Black Alf any thought that I had known all his plans and had been prepared to aid in thwarting them.

It was rather a weary job, and the sun was just over the western hills when we got to the cabin with the bodies.

Eldiva was there, completely collected in her manner now, engaged in preparing supper.

I saw that Black Alf studied her face very sharply when he arrived, but she bore his scrutiny bravely, not appearing even to see that he looked at her as she kept at her work, and he turned away with a look and a sigh of relief to refresh himself with a draught of his usual beverage.

Then he asked us three to stay to supper. We excused ourselves by saying that Bridget would be mad if we did, for she would have supper hot when we reached our tents.

"Then come back afterward," said Alf, "for I shall bury these poor fellows to-night. There is no use in keeping 'em above ground, and it makes me feel bad to look at 'em."

"What, bury 'em widout a wake, when you have whisky galore and pounds of terbaccy?" cried Billy Flynn, indignantly.

"Sure, 'twould be haythenish."

"I thought you were a Father Mathew man, Billy?" said I, in surprise.

"Sure, I am, sir; but don't they howld wakes over the dead?"

"I don't know," said I, "not belonging to the fraternity."

"They do, sir, and be this same token I know it, for I was at a broth of a wake on the Barbary coast not long ago."

"The Barbary coast in Africa?"

"The divil, no! Down in San Francisco, sure, where the nagers, and the sailors, and the longshoremen, and the short-shoremen, and the loveliest wimmen all congregate. 'Twas a high ould time intirely. And there'll be no wake, sir?"

The last question was asked of Black Alf.

"No!" said the latter, with a scowling look. "When ten o'clock comes their graves will be dug, and they'll go into 'em."

"Two hours before the moon rises," I said, as we turned to go.

"Yes," he answered; "but pine-knots will give us all the light we want."

CHAPTER XVI.
The Boy Armed.

When we reached the tents, Bridget indeed had a steaming supper ready for us; but I remarked that it was not cooked as well as women generally prepare food. The bacon was not half browned, while the trout were fried to a crisp, and some biscuits she had baked would have made better ballast than cobblestones. The coffee was muddy, too; but we were all too hungry to stand on trifles, though we grumbled some.

"Who the divil can cook widout a stove and cast-iron fryin'-pan?" retorted Bridget. "Sure, an' it's not meself. Wait till it comes to washin' for yez in cowld wather, and nothin' to bile the shirts in, and then see what ye'll say. Ah, there comes Mr. Melrose to see the children, poor dears—Heaven bless 'em and them that loves 'em."

Melrose, indeed, came up the trail leading from the east, not the one that passed the cabin, and joined our party. He paused until I related to him all that Black Alf said when he came in, and what had occurred when we went for the bodies. He listened attentively.

"Has he no suspicions that you saw him or his companions?" asked Melrose.

"No. I was not even missed from our claim by him or any of his gang."

"That is well. How about the girl? Has she kept up her part well?"

"No one could do it better. She shows no appearance of terror or suspicion; said to him she thought Indians or somebody fired at her, for she had heard guns and bullets, and ran as fast as she could with the children till she got back here. She is now attending to her work at the cabin in her usual way, and no one seems more composed there than she does."

"All goes well, then. Black Alf has failed in his first attempt, but I have no doubt that he will make another. We must be on the alert constantly. Have the children had supper?"

"Yes, sir, they have," said Bridget. "They were hungry when they came in from their long tramp, and I gave 'em supper before the sun set."

"Then I will go in and have a talk with them," said Melrose, "while you are eating, for I supped an hour ago myself."

We assented, and again turned to our rather unpalatable meal, with appetites too eager to refuse what lay before us.

Nearly, an hour passed, and we could hear the low murmur of childish voices, and the deeper tones of Melrose in earnest conversation all the time.

At last, when we were thinking it would soon be time to go and see the men buried if we intended to do so, Melrose came out, and with him came the girl and boy.

Both had evidently been weeping, and they were yet agitated. Their eyes were red and swollen.

The boy had a belt on, and in it were two richly mounted Derringer pistols and a long dagger. It was the first time we had seen him so armed.

"I have been telling these children the history of their father's death," said Melrose, "and I have armed the boy, so that he can help to take care of himself and his sister if peril comes near them when none of us are at hand."

"Yes, with these I will *kill* the murderer of my dear father—the man that broke poor mother's heart!" said the boy, his blue eyes flashing and his face flushing with color.

"Not until I say it is time, Jesse," said Melrose, calmly. "Remember your promise to me."

"Yes, sir, I will. I will always try to mind you, but it will be very hard to see him, and know he is where I can kill him, and feel I ought to do it, and not try."

"You *must* control yourself, my dear boy. Remember I have much yet to do for you and your sister—that I must find out where the wretch hides the treasure that is rightly your own, and so acquire all proofs that the law of man as well as that of

Heaven shall justify you in slaying him, before you can act. I will not say nay when the right time comes, though a death by slow torture—a hundred deaths, were such possible—would not be punishment enough for him, even in this world. I must go now. Stay in, and do not without my knowledge go even a hundred yards from the tents. Should Eldiva ever come to walk out with you, it will be with my knowledge and consent. That you can remember. Otherwise never go out of sight of this spot."

"We will not, best of friends, more than father to us!" said the boy, with deep feeling.

Melrose now left, for it was already dark. We lighted a lantern, and the three of us men prepared to go to the burial.

I noticed, looking at the boy with surprise, that a strange change had come over him. He seemed to have sprung into sudden manhood, ahead of his years and of his growth. His eyes were darkened with a stern, determined look, and, as he moved back into the tent, his arm around his sister's waist, it was with a heavier, firmer tread than I had noticed before.

CHAPTER XVII.
"Such a Sight!"

"I never saw a boy turn *man* so quickly as that child has," said Ned Griffin to me, as we moved on in single file down the trail after Billy Flynn, who kept ahead of us with the lantern.

"What could produce such a change?"

"The knowledge of the terrible wrong which has orphaned him and his sister," said I. "Great griefs either kill or *make* us. Great misfortunes overwhelm some men, while others, gathering all their mental strength, rise over the black waves, buffet the billows, and, scorning the storm, ride in triumph to a position which, with their energies dormant, could never have been reached. That boy will never be a *boy* again. He would stand fire now as steadily as you or I, who have both been where Death reaped his richest harvests on many a sanguinary field. He will raise his hand to kill without a shaking nerve, bear agony without a tear or murmur, endure hunger, thirst, or lack of sleep as well as we could."

"I believe you. Melrose must know human nature well."

"Yes; he is a man of power in every way. It requires such a man to be a good detective. Patience unlimited, courage undaunted, and cunning unequaled are all requisite to follow the track of villainy, arrest its perpetrators, and consign them to due punishment."

"They're getting ready down there," said Ned, pointing to torches ablaze in front of the cabin, and changing the theme of conversation as suddenly as it began.

"Yes; we must hurry up—double-quick there, Billy Flynn."

"Double quick, is it, sure? Suppose I hit a bowlder and broke my head and lantern at the same time?"

"Why, we'd patch up your head," said I, with a laugh. "But we'd have to send to the Hill for another lantern."

"Well, sir, I don't want to break either. They can see we're coming, and they'll be dacent to wait till we get there, I reckon."

They did. In fact, they were only digging the graves, and were not quite through when we reached the spot.

"Glad to see you, gentlemen—glad to see you. It looks friendly like," said Black Alf, again reaching out to shake hands. "I'm sorry you don't drink. The air is fogmatick to-night, and a drop of whisky takes the chill off. Glad to see you, though, for all that."

"The holes are dug, cap," said one of the men, approaching Alf at this moment.

"All right. Got the slabs too?"

"Yes; they're all ready."

"Then go ahead—bring 'em out. I suppose you 'uns haven't no prayer-books, have you? I know that dead folks generally has prayers said over 'em, but I reckon Ben and Sam wouldn't care about it if they had the say, for they did more swearin' than prayin', a thousand to one, while they lived. Bet your last dime on that."

Some of the men now brought a large bundle of newly split cedar slabs and laid a layer of them at the bottom of each grave.

"I should have thought one grave would have served for both men," I remarked to Alf.

"No, 'twouldn't do. They wouldn't sleep together livin', and I doubt if they'd lay quiet dead in the same hole. We've been bothered enough with ghosts around here to do all we can to keep from having more."

"Do you really believe in ghosts?" I asked, watching his face closely.

"*Believe?* I *know* there's such things, sir. Don't speak it, sir, for I don't want to scare all my men away, but I saw one today in broad daylight. The ghost of a *woman*, sir—yes, of a woman whom I knew better than I ever knew anybody on earth."

"*How did she die?*"

This came in a whisper only, but such a whisper! Cold, like an icy blast sweeping through a charnel-house, it reached his ears and mine.

"Oh, Heaven!" he groaned, and he shook from head to foot. "Who spoke—who spoke?"

There seemed to be no one so near us that a whisper could have reached us, for we stood back from the crowd, close to the trunk of a tree whose outer branches reached over the new-made graves.

No answer came, and trembling, gasping, Black Alf moved up into the crowd, who were now drawing close to the pit with the first body, that of Ben Keeno.

"Do you want to say anything, cap?" asked the man who had the lowering lines.

"No, no! put him in quick, and then bring Sam and put him in and cover him up. I'm sick—I'm not fit to be out here! 'Tis cold—awful cold!"

"In hell 'twill be warm enough for *you*! Ha! ha!"

It was a loud, mocking voice which spoke these words, and it seemed to be right in our midst.

"Thunder and fury! who is trying to scare *me*!" yelled Black Alf. "Give me some whisky, one of you—I'll not stand this. If I could see who spoke, I'd have his heart out!"

"Ha! ha! ha!"

This mocking laugh seemed to come from every point of the compass, and I do not think there was one man on the ground who did not feel the cold chills run over him. I know I did, and I would have very much liked to run if I could have got away without being called a coward.

A jug of whisky was brought to Alf a second later, and he drank a long, long draught.

Then he laughed wildly, and cried:"Go on with the funeral, boys, go on with the funeral, and then we'll go on the biggest jamboree you ever heard tell of!"

The bodies, wrapped in blankets, were now lowered into the graves, more slabs laid over them, in lieu of coffins, and then, without a word, the dirt was shoveled in and graves filled.

When the work was all done, and Black Alf had taken another heavy draught from the liquor jug, he cried:"Now come into the cabin, boys—come in and we'll make a night of it, such a high old night as will make the very devils laugh! Come on—come on—"

He stopped! His words froze on his lips, his eyes seemed to almost start from his head, his form to draw up in stature, as with upraised hands he started back from the sight which rose before him—before us all.

Such a sight—oh, horror—pen cannot describe it as it was! Even now my blood curdles with the terrible memory.

CHAPTER XVIII.

A Fearful Mystery.

Beyond the spot where the graves had been dug there was a tall group of madrona trees, whose bright red trunks glistened in the reflection of the torchlight like painted bodies. Just to the right of this there was a ledge which rose in a perpendicular wall, perhaps fifteen or twenty feet, of black volcanic rock, such as is seen in Table Mountain, on Feather River.

Directly in front of this rock we all saw the form of a gigantic man, the very counterpart, except in size, of Black Alf, clutching a beautiful woman by the throat, while she with clasped hands seemed to be on her knees pleading for life.

The expression on his face, more devilish than a *human* face could be, was distinctly visible, while his uplifted hand, clutching a huge bowie-knife, told that he meant to be as merciless as he looked.

A cry of horror broke from every lip but that of Alf himself.

He seemed frozen to the ground—rooted to the earth, in white, speechless terror.

Suddenly the figure of the woman vanished, and where she had knelt two men lay prone upon the ground, gashed, bleeding, yet motionless, while the same giant apparition of Black Alf, knife in hand, towered above them.

Again a cry, a wild cry of horror, broke from every one but *him*—from all but Alf Dunning. He stood with eyes set, his face a bluish white, looking at it all, but speechless, as if paralyzed.

The forms of the two men faded away in a mist-like atmosphere, and then the giant form seemed to be bending over a heap of nuggets of gold and glittering dust. As he did so, a woman, holding two little children, a boy and a girl, by the hand, was seen close in his foreground. His figure started up, with angry face and the clenched hand to strike. He struck.

The woman fell, and the children knelt weeping over her body.

Now, for the first time, Alf spoke.

"It's a cussed lie!" he gasped out, in a hoarse whisper, which yet reached every ear in the party. "I *didn't* kill her. She died nat'ral, and I can prove it!"

Then his strained nature seemed to give way, and he fell to the earth heavily, in a swoon so entire that we thought him dead at first.

"By thunder, I'm goin' to leave these diggins!" cried one of the men hitherto staunch to Alf in everything, as he helped to carry his senseless leader to the cabin. "I can meet anything but ghosts—they freeze the very life in me!"

"And I'll go too!" cried another. "All the gold in Californy wouldn't keep me here!"

"He who attempts to leave before the hand of Justice has its due shall die before he climbs to the mountain's crest!"

These words, in a tone so stern that it chilled our veins, seemed to come from a voice in the upper air, and while it sounded cold and hollow in our ears, another voice, that of a woman, low and musical, spoke these words:"It is written in the book of Fate, *and it shall be!*"

When Black Alf fell, every vestige of the objects we have described passed away, and the black rock alone met our eyes in that direction.

"What do you think of all this?" asked Ned Griffin of me, as we stood in front of the cabin, for we would not go in.

"I think that we have seen more than we can account for, for one thing. Next, that even on earth the sinner finds a foretaste of the punishment which we are told will come after death. I would not feel as that wretch will feel when life is brought back to him in there, for all the gold which Melrose says he has hidden away somewhere in this haunted valley."

"Were those spirits which we saw?" asked a low voice close to us.

It was Eldiva, and her face was whiter than the handkerchief upon her neck.

"What else could they be?" said Griffin. "It is a fearful mystery."

"One which I will stay to see revealed, if it takes the entire season," I added. "Come, Griffin, let us be going. Billy Flynn is waiting."

"That I am, and anxious to get out of this place," answered Billy. "Let's be off to our tents, gintlemen, for I am as tired as a penny postman wid his day's work just ended."

We were not sorry to leave the spot, for it seemed to us as if the very air breathed out in whispering voices telling us of crime. Silent and full of thought, we went back to our quarters to try to sleep, but sleep, with minds so excited as ours had been, would not come to our relief.

CHAPTER XIX.
The Haunted Gulch.

"Do you know where the diggings are which Melrose says he is working?" said I to Billy Flynn, when we were at the breakfast which Ned Griffin had cooked, for he was so much better over the frying-pan than Bridget that by unanimous consent he was appointed first assistant in that line, and, like most first assistants, he took the chief duty on himself.

"Faith, not exactly, sir; but I belave it's jist beyant the turn in the upper end of the valley. When I was on the mountain, a comin' down, I saw his signal there-away, for you see we've got signals in our business, so we can know where each other hangs out, whether we are near enough to spake or not. Do you want to see him, sir?"

"Yes, I would like to have him know what occurred down at the cabin last night."

Billy Flynn was taken with a sudden fit of laughing, which rather surprised me, as I had said nothing which would bring on a laugh that I was aware of.

"What are you laughing at?" I asked, half inclined to wrath at what seemed unnecessary, if not untimely, levity.

"The iday, sir, to think jist that you'd be afther takin' the trouble to let *him* know it!"

"Why, he is anxious to learn everything which will bring proof of guilt home against that man, and I am sure we all saw enough signs of guilt in his face last night, not to speak of the exclamation made just before he swooned away."

Again Billy Flynn burst out laughing.

"And you'd thravel all the way down there and hunt him up to tell him what we saw and heard last night!" he cried, as soon as he could stop laughing.

"Yes."

"Well, sir, you'd have all the throuble for nothin'. He knows more about what we saw last night than you or I, or all of 'em down below there in a hape. Why, sir, he is the smartest man jist on the coast. Go and see him if you like, but he'll tell you it isn't *news* you can carry to him."

And Billy turned away to speak to Bridget, who was bringing the children out to breakfast.

As they sat down, I saw Eldiva coming up the hill and went to meet her, for she seemed in haste, and I thought there might be trouble below.

"How is Mr. Dunning this morning?" I asked, noticing that she was excited.

"He seems to be well, sir; but I do not think he is quite right in his head. He spoke more kindly this morning to me than I ever knew him to do before, and told one of the men to help me in my work, so I could get through early and come up and see the children. Then he asked me some strange questions, and finally told me he intended soon to leave the mines and the country. He would buy a vessel in San Francisco, and sail away to a foreign land, where money could buy everything, and I should go with him and be a princess. I think he is going crazy, sir."

"And I think, my poor girl, that there is a good deal of 'method in his madness.' He undoubtedly would like to get away with a vast treasure which he has got hidden somewhere, and would carry you with him if he could."

"Oh, I would die first! It is terrible to be held under his control now as I am. I will get free from him, or I will kill myself!"

"Do not be rash. There are those close at hand who will protect you. As for him, I think his race is nearly run."

"Oh, I hope so, sir. Can I see those dear children now?"

"Of course. Did he say anything about your walking out with them any more?"

"Yes, sir—told me to go whenever I wanted to."

"Then he means mischief still to them. He will not learn prudence from his first failure. But go on; you will find the children at breakfast now."

Eldiva passed on to the tents, and, as I had put on my weapons when I rose, I kept on down the hill, intending to have an interview with Melrose before I went to our claim.

When I approached the cabin, for the trail ran right by it, Black Alf came out. His face wore a haggard look, his eyes were blood-shot and wild in expression.

"Good-morning, stranger!" said he. "Queer sights down here last night, wasn't they?"

"Rather singular. What did you think of them?"

"I was too bad scared last night to think, for I am skeery in things I can't put my hand on. But now, sober and candid, I believe there's a regular spirit-gang in this valley. It's a haunted gulch—that's what it is."

"Why *should* it be haunted?"

"Why, there must be a heap of treasure here. I heard a preacher chap say once that hell threw up gold in volcanoes, so as to make sin plenty and populate the regions below. We know well that gold makes a heap o' trouble."

"Yes, people are *murdered* because they possess it!" said I.

"Hush! Don't talk that way, or you'll bring them spirits up here in broad daylight. I'm not going to stay here long. I'd leave in an hour if I was ready. But the boys seem afeard to go. They heard something last night, which I can't remember hearing, and they say they'll stay and work now. They are in good pay-dirt, and taking out lots of dust; but if we're to have ghosts a hammerin' away at us every night, I reckon it will soon wear 'em out. Are you going to work alone this morning?"

"No, my partners will soon be here. I am taking a walk before they get down, to see how things look. I may strike a rich ledge accidentally, strolling around."

"There is no pay in the ledges around here," he muttered, as I moved on.

CHAPTER XX.

Balked.

I walked slowly on, making here and there a slight turn, so that I could look back, without appearing to do it intentionally, to see if he was watching me. I found that he was, and that he was playing the same game that I was, trying to avoid the appearance of it by doing some sort of work near the corner of the cabin.

I soon entered a clump of bushes which hid me from his view, while I, through the leafy screen, could see his actions, for I halted behind the first large bush that I passed.

He entered the cabin, took his gun, as he had done the day before, and in a few seconds came along, evidently on my trail. That he meant to see where I was going was sure, if he did not indeed intend something worse.

I made up my mind in an instant to foil him there. A long experience in Indian warfare among the Seminoles of Florida and the wily red men of the Western plains had taught me enough for that.

I turned up a dry, rocky opening, where there was no soil to leave a mark, and, careful to avoid breaking even a single twig, stepped lightly from stone to stone as I hurried to reach the rocky precipice, which loomed up to the west of me, along the base of which I meant to make my way toward the point where I hoped to find Melrose.

That I made good time may be inferred when I tell the reader that, halting almost a mile from where I entered the bushes, I saw Alf Dunning just trying at that point to find my trail.

He seemed to be completely confounded in his endeavor to trace me, for he wandered to and fro in different directions, and at last returned to the spot where he first entered the thicket, and where he had lost the last sight of my trail.

I supposed he would now give up his effort and return. But a new idea seemed to strike him, and he started off directly toward the point where I expected to find Melrose, or where he had said his claim lay, and he moved at a rapid pace.

Instantly the thought struck me that there might be a murderous intent in his bad heart, and I took a course which I thought would intercept his, enabling me unseen to either get ahead of him or be so close that I could watch every action.

To do this and keep concealed was not easy, but keeping the cover of rocks and trees, and once in a while stopping to get a glance at him, I managed the matter so well that I halted at last actually in sight of where Melrose was at his claim, not working himself, but with half a dozen stalwart miners hard at work, quietly overlooking them, while he sat smoking on a rock near a couple of log cabins.

I halted, because I knew from his position when I saw him last that Alf Dunning must go very near me if he kept on.

I had been hidden in a bunch of chaparral about five minutes when he reached an open spot near me, It was evident that he now could see the men at the diggings, and also could see Melrose, for his face grew darker than ever with hateful passion.

I saw him take the old caps from his gun and from his revolvers and put on fresh ones. I knew now that he meant mischief, and I resolved to thwart him.

He moved on very stealthily and cautiously, taking a course by which he could approach the place unseen where Melrose was seated.

I had to let him get quite a start before I could leave my place of concealment, but it gave me time to see that he had chosen a dry ravine for his route, which would lead him rather a circuitous course, though it would cover him until within pistol shot of Melrose. I also saw that I could get into the same ravine near where Melrose was ahead of him by taking a short cut, though I must go a little distance over a level place where there was a risk of his seeing me.

"Neck or nothing—I will try it," I muttered, and I sped on as fast as I could.

When I reached the open place, I lay down flat and crawled over it, a plan which I think saved me from discovery, for I saw him soon after, stealthily moving along the ravine, showing no sign of agitation, as he would have done had he seen me, most likely.

I now moved on, careful not to leave a track, until I found a good hiding-place where the villain must pass close to me, from which I could also see Melrose, though only him, for his party were at work in a ravine which ran parallel to the one in which I lay.

I had been snugly ensconced here for a few moments only when I saw him creeping along as slyly as an Indian approaching game. With bent form, his gun trailed, barefooted; his shoes hung to his belt, he moved slowly forward, pausing often to look around him, as if he feared detection from some prying eye, and at last he halted not more than fifteen or twenty yards in front of me.

Here where some stunted pines made a cover, he could evidently see Melrose, and here I learned his intention, and in a second after took hasty steps to thwart him.

For he stopped where only the branches of a clump of manzanita trees hid him from a clear view of the rock on which Melrose was sitting. He crept around until even that range of bushes was out of his view and then selected a branch to rest his gun upon, knelt down, and laid the barrel over it.

It was but a few yards, but never did I pass the distance more quickly or lightly, for I knew I must be quick and still, or he would hear and turn on me before I could foil him.

His gun was at his shoulder, his eye ranged along the barrel directly on the body of Melrose; even his finger was pressing trigger, when I reached my arm over his shoulder and knocked the barrel out of its range.

At the same instant it was discharged, but the bullet flew wide of its mark, near enough to warn Melrose, however, of his recent danger, for he came bounding toward the spot just as Black Alf turned with a fierce curse to grapple with me—so suddenly, indeed, that he overthrew me before I could use the weapon I had in my hand. His knees were on my breast and his clutch upon my throat, when a crushing blow from a pistol butt on his head deluged me with the ruffian's blood, while it relieved me from his attack, for Melrose had reached my side in time to give his aid in return for what I had done for him.

In a second I was on my feet, but even sooner, with professional skill, Melrose had slipped a pair of spring handcuffs over the wrists of the senseless villain, and, searching him for arms, disarmed him.

"He was creeping up to murder you!" I said, "and as I had been watching him for some time, I took the liberty of knocking his gun on one side just as he was in the act of firing!"

"Thank you!" said Melrose. "I shall not forget the kindness. He seems to have a good gun. I will take care of it and his other tools till he knows how to make a different use of them. But he is coming to. We'll hear some cursing now—he is good at that!"

Melrose was mistaken. The man glared out a sullen hate, looking like a wild beast just caged, and too much astonished to rage.

"Good fit, eh? Not very valuable, but very useful some times!" said Melrose, sarcastically, as Black Alf looked down at his iron wristlets.

"Take 'em off!" growled the ruffian.

"What for?"

"I'll fight you both! Cuss you, I'll fight you both!"

"It wouldn't pay. We would have to kill you, and that isn't the way you must die. You must choke with a rope around your neck. That is *decreed*—it is only a matter of time as to the when and where."

"If it hadn't been for him, you'd be past dyin' now."

And the wretch indicated me by a ferocious look.

"I know you meant to give me a dose of lead, but I've taken several, and survive them yet. Now, what will you do if I let you go?"

"Kill you the first chance I get."

"Good. That is a fair warning. Yet I *shall* let you go; for you cannot kill me, and I will hang *you!* That is as good as sworn to. I have got your tools, and shall keep them. After I release you, go back to your gang. I will not tell you how to behave for that will make no difference in the end. Go back and work your claim."

"I'll see you in Tophet first. I'll quit this cussed gulch this very day."

"No—you will not. If you go, you will not carry with you certain treasure which *you* fancy is safely hidden."

"I know it is."

"No, Alf Dunning, yon do *not* know it. When you are swinging from the limb of a *blasted* tree—you know where it is and what blasted it—your treasure will be in the possession of the orphans whose father you murdered."

"Devil—let me go!"

The ruffian, white-faced and trembling, seemed completely cowed, while with flashing eyes Melrose looked him in the face and spoke these words: "I will directly; but mark you, Alf Dunning, if you attempt to leave this gulch without my permission, you will be in irons before you go a mile. You are hedged in by men who know their business, and who will perform it. Take my advice and go back to work. If you act differently, you will only hasten your own doom."

As he said this, Melrose took a key from his pocket and unlocked the manacles.

Alf, when his wrists were free, looked as if he would like to turn on us; but he was disarmed, and we were both ready and well prepared for him.

"*You'd* better keep out of my way," he said to me, as he turned and stalked back over the route by which he had come.

"He is a coward at heart—you need not fear his threat; but it is well to be on your guard at all times and in all places," said Melrose to me.

"It is my nature never to be off my guard," was my reply. "From boyhood a life of constant change and adventure has inured me to this."

"I am glad to hear it. Now come to my quarters, please, and accept of such rude hospitality as I have to offer."

"Thank you. Is the claim yonder paying well?"

"Not very; but it serves to amuse and to some degree profitably occupy the time of men who are waiting for something else."

We passed on toward the largest of the two cabins. As we passed the smaller, I got a glimpse of a female moving back from the half-opened door—not of her face, but merely her form and dress.

CHAPTER XXI.
A Curious Bridge.

Questioning is often an impertinence, and I have in my lifetime been too much annoyed with it not to avoid its use on my own part, so when I sat down to a very nice cold lunch with Melrose in his cabin, though I would have been well pleased to know who the female was that seemed to occupy the lesser cabin alone, and what she was doing there, since he had a Chinaman cook for himself and party, I did not offer a single interrogation, but waited for him to tell me what he chose and retain what he preferred not to reveal.

"You are better fixed than miners generally are, Mr. Melrose," said I, glancing around at various comforts in the shape of dishes, cooking utensils, furniture, etc., seldom seen among such rude surroundings.

"It is a way I have, that of being comfortable in a place if I only intend to stay a week there. Yet I have been here or in the vicinity for over a year, intent upon but one object, which is, I now hope, in a fair way of speedy accomplishment. When I took the job in hand, I knew that I had a cunning villain to cope with, that I had to follow a trail well covered up, and that I must take time and nerve myself to a patient and discouraging labor. So I fixed up as comfortably as I could for myself and those who were from time to time called to assist me."

"Had you not visited the upper cabin, now occupied by Alf and his gang, before Griffin or I went there?"

"Yes, several times, but ever careful not to leave any trace of my visit, for I wished him to believe that the gulch was entirely deserted. As you have learned, this end of it is difficult of access, invisible from the road which winds along the hill, and I think was never visited, and I *know* it was never worked nor occupied till I came here. Therefore, this was a good place to wait and watch in. Now that Alf has found it out, it matters but little where I am, for I shall have to act more openly than ever."

"Suppose he tries to leave?"

"I would know it night or day, in less time than he would take to walk a half-mile. He dare not attempt it. He will stay, and try his best to take the lives he has already attempted, and now most likely yours will be included."

"Taking life is a game two can play at," said I, "and experience has taught me that the game generally stands best with him who on the defensive remains ready for resistance. The one who attacks is almost always nervous, frequently too hasty, and fails through these very faults."

"You are right, sir; and as the poet has it, I forget his words exactly; however, 'he who is right, is thrice armed for the fight.'"

"True, Mr. Melrose. And now, with thanks for your hospitable kindness, I think I will get back to my party. They will think I am lost or have been murdered if I do not rejoin them soon, for I said nothing of my intention to wander away when I left."

"All right, sir—I will not detain you longer. I shall be up to see the children by and by. Will you go by the route you came?"

"No, sir; not if there is one nearer, for I came in a very roundabout way."

"There is a direct path, but unless you know it, one obstacle would check you altogether, and an incident would occur which would alarm you with all your evident nerve. You can take the path on which I will leave you in a few moments and go—if you pace it out you would lessen the distance a few steps over a quarter of a mile. You will then come to a deep cut which will appear to be impassable to you, for you will see no way to bridge it, it is too wide to leap, and, being deep, has sides too steep to climb. But just to the left of the path you will observe the stump of a tree, which stands surrounded by moss and fern, the stump having been cut off nearly twenty feet from the ground; any one would be puzzled to think how or why, if he did not know the secret.

"You will reach up as high as you can on this side of that stump, and bear it over as if you would try to push it down. You will find by its yielding that it is set on springs and hinges, and it is, indeed, a cunningly contrived bridge, for it will bend over till, by your weight upon it, it reclines on the opposite side of the ravine. Pass over it, and when you have left it, it will spring back into its original position."

"Yes, sir; but in coming this way from our camp, how would you get your bridge over to you?"

"Easily. In the ledge to the left just off the path there is a dark niche. In that, under a flat stone, there is a lariat with the usual noose on it. A skillful hand can throw it over the stump, and thus make the bridge passable. This is one my inventions to prevent intrusion here. Another would warn me of an attempt to intrude, and that is the secret which would, I said, shake your nerves if you did not understand it, for you would believe an attempt was being made to assassinate you. When you leave the bridge, seeing it back in its position, walk one hundred regular paces—steps of about thirty inches. This will take you to a sharp turn in the path, angling around a rock. Bushes almost close overhead and make the pathway dark. Look close before you advance, and you will see at about two feet apart, stretched just clear of the ground, three pieces of copper wire. Were you to step on either one, or trip it with your feet, a gun, to the trigger of which it is attached, would be discharged, making a report which I, or those whom I leave on watch, would hear.

This is a trick invented originally by the great bandit Joaquin, and one which he made more terrible because the guns were heavily loaded, which he so placed, and so directed that those who sprung the triggers would receive the contents in their bodies. Mine are merely placed as alarms. Now, sir, trusting to secrecy on your part, I can safely direct you by the shorter route, and in a half hour you can be at your camp. In fact, as a surprise, I think you had better hurry on and arrive there before Black Alf can possibly do so, and then face him with a bold denial, if he should speak of it, of having met him down here. This, if well carried through, will make him believe you have a double, or that he has seen a spirit in your shape. I would like to so madden him with mystery that he will believe himself crazy or fully bewitched! Be careful as you pass the wires—a touch will discharge the guns."

"I will, Mr. Melrose. Good-by."

"Good-morning, sir. We will probably meet again in three or four hours."

He had, while conversing, led me to a narrow but distinct footpath, along which I now hurried as swiftly as I could go, for I was as anxious as he could be to reach our diggings ahead of Alf and unseen by him or his men, so as to tell my partners what to say, and then throw a complete mystification over him.

I soon found the cunningly contrived bridge, used it, and when I saw it spring back to its place, hurried on, not pausing to look for the lariat because it would take time, and I had none to spare.

I also reached the alarm trap, saw the wires, stepped carefully over them, and passed swiftly on. I only stopped once on my route, and that was when I reached an elevated spot on the trail, which wound along under the ledge on the eastern side of the valley, where I halted to look back and see if I could see Black Alf.

I *did* see him, and saw to my intense satisfaction that by keeping east of the little lake I could reach our claim and communicate with my partners at least fifteen or twenty minutes before he could get to the cabin or to his diggings.

I pushed on rapidly to accomplish this end, and soon was with Griffin and Billy Flynn, to whom I related a part of the events of the morning, telling them just what to say and how to act if Black Alf came over to us, as I felt sure he would if he saw me at work, whom he thought to be in the far end of the valley. I had got them thoroughly posted, and was myself hard at work in my shirt sleeves, with even the blood marks removed, when we saw him coming.

"Go over to the other diggings, getting there just as he gets in," said I to Ned Griffin, "and ask to borrow a pick. Tell them that I broke the handle of yours about an hour ago in prying at a rock, and you would like to borrow one till night, when you'll mend yours. That will start him, and if he isn't over here soon, I'm mightily mistaken."

"Good as wheat. I'm on hand," said Ned. "I'll break the pick-handle first, though, to keep up appearances."

And he did so before starting on his errand.

CHAPTER XXII.

A Threat.

I was not wrong in my prediction of the effect which a sight of me at work and the announcement that I had broken Griffin's pick an hour before would have on Black Alf. Ned afterward told me that when he arrived at the other diggings he met Alf, who was looking at me with a bewildered look, as if wondering how I had got there before him unseen.

When Ned asked for the loan of a pick, and said I had broken his while prying at a rock an hour before, Alf looked wilder than ever.

"Was he there an hour ago?" he asked, his face expressing disbelief before the question was answered.

"Yes; he has been there all the morning. He was gone a little while into the chaparral before we came on a short walk to prospect, but he was back and at work when we commenced."

"There an hour ago?" asked Alf again, in a tone and with a look of bewilderment.

"Yes; two, almost three hours ago. Why do you ask?"

"Blame me if I can understand *this*. I'll swear I saw him somewhere else an hour ago, or somebody so like him that he couldn't be known from him."

"You're crazy, I guess. You'd better come over and ask him yourself where he was an hour or two hours ago."

"Blasted if I don't!" said Alf.

And he started off to see me before Griffin could get the pick he wanted and return. He wanted to question me before Griffin could prompt me. This suited us exactly, for I well knew what Griffin had told him.

"Stranger, will you do me a favor?" he asked, when he arrived, eying me keenly while he spoke.

"Certainly, if it doesn't cost too much. 'What is it?" said I.

"Tell me if you've seen me before, to-day?"

"Yes, of course I have. You seem sober—why do you ask such a foolish question? Didn't I meet you in front of your cabin, and talk to you when I took a little prospecting walk before I came here to work?"

"Yes, I thought it was you; but now another question. Haven't you met me since?"

"Not till now," I said, coolly. "I went over as far as yonder bit of chaparral, turned off east toward my own claim on the ledge, skirted around the little lake, and got here to work just as the other two came down the hill."

"And have been here ever since?"

"To be sure. I've been trying to get out that flat rock up there, for I know there must be gold under it. I broke Griffin's pick, and I've weakened mine. I'll have to give it up as a bad job, I'm afraid."

"Stranger, you're going to die!" said he, earnestly.

"I expect I shall when my time comes!" said I, smilingly.

"Yes, but *soon*. For I have seen your double!"

"My double—what do you mean?"

"A man as like you as you are like yourself."

"Where?"

"No matter where, I've seen him, and it is a sign that you are going to die!"

"Well, sir, if death comes naturally, I hope I am ready for it. If it should come unnaturally, I don't think I shall die alone! As to doubles, I don't believe in them. But there are mysteries in this valley which I acknowledge I cannot understand."

"Neither you nor me, nor any one else can," said he, shuddering. "I believe the *devil* has a claim here."

"I have no doubt of it," said I, looking Alf squarely in the face when I spoke, for I was thinking of his claim at the moment.

"I wish I was out of the place," he said, and he glanced around uneasily.

"Why don't you go?" I responded.

"I dare not—I dare not now, at any rate," he muttered, looking up at Griffin, who returned with the pick at this moment.

"Well, are you satisfied that I'm not a liar?" asked the latter, addressing Alf.

"Yes, and I'm either crazy or bewitched. Thunder and Mars, where does *that* cuss come from?"

He pointed to Melrose, who was leisurely descending the path which led from our tents to the diggings.

"From our camp, where he passed the night with the children of whom he seems to think so much," said I.

"By thunder! I wish somebody would knock me down. I'd like to feel whether I am *myself* or not. I took one drink, and that a light one, when I got up, and haven't touched a drop since!" he cried.

"How did you get that bruise on the head?—it looks like a fresh cut. Did you fall down?" I asked, pointing to the mark which I so well knew how he got.

"By heavens! I know how I got it. It wasn't a dream that gave me *that*, anyway!" he cried, fiercely. "I'll know when that cuss gets here, if it costs me my life. I'd rather die at once, a cussed sight, than to live on to be hunted to death by ghosts and worried down to a shadow!"

"What is that over on yonder ledge, beneath that blasted tree?—look, Griffin, look!" I cried.

"A woman, dressed in white. Who can it be? Bridget is at the tent, this man's gal stands out in front of the cabin. Who can it be?" cried Griffin, in apparent astonishment.

"I know—yes, I know but too well—'tis no living creature!" gasped Black Alf, while a shudder convulsed his gigantic frame.

"By day and by night, I must see her—*her*—who would drag me with her down into that dreadful gloom! By Heaven! I'll *force* a fight, and die!"

CHAPTER XXIII.
A Good Shot.

The expression on the face of Black Alf while Melrose was approaching was fiendish to an indescribable degree. Hate and fear seemed to struggle for superiority, while the man tried to disguise the existence of both. The vision, or appearance, whatever it might be termed, which he had seen under the blasted tree, passed away out of sight as suddenly as it came, but Melrose, coming with a firm and resolute tread, was too real for any one to doubt *his* presence.

When he came up, Alf, who had watched his motions all the time, exclaimed, in a bitter tone:"Where's my gun? My pistols, too, and knife—where are they?"

"What is the fool talking about? Why do you ask me?" said Melrose, catching from a meaning look of mine that I had made the villain believe in "*my* double," and now coming in to try *his* luck on the same tack.

"You know well enough. Who hit me here over the head? Perhaps you'll deny doing that!" said Alf, angrily, pointing to his bruised head.

"You told me you got that by a fall!" said I, quickly, to aid Melrose in the mystification.

"I lied! *He* did it and he knows it!" said Alf, angrily.

"I know you are either drunk or crazy," said Melrose, contemptuously. "When I use violence toward you, it will be to lead you to the scaffold. Your doom is written, man, and you cannot avoid it!"

"I believe it is; but cuss me if I'm going to die for nothing!" said the man desperately. "I'll choke you, if I can't shoot you, you thief-catching cop!"

He sprang at Melrose with an angry bound, and I looked to a grapple which would require my interference, but Melrose was more than equal to the exigency.

He stepped a little to one side, reached out his foot, and tripped the excited man so easily that he plunged forward over one of our piles of pebbles, and plunged into a sluice of muddy water beyond, immersing his entire body.

"A good place to cool off in," cried Melrose, with a sarcastic laugh. "You should keep your temper, Mr. Dunning. It is unhealthy to get mad in this climate."

"I'll make it unhealthy for you," said Dunning, as he rose and shook the muddy water from his dripping form. "You'll not live long, for you've got a double as well as he."

And when he said this he dashed off toward his cabin, evidently feeling the need of "wet within" to balance the wet without.

I now had a chance to tell Melrose what had occurred between Dunning and me, and how completely I had made him think I had not been where he supposed he saw me.

"The man will go crazy, indeed," said he, when I concluded my statement. "My sudden appearance has confirmed your story in his eyes."

"Yes; and I am almost convinced of your being possessed of miraculous power, for I cannot imagine how you could follow me so quickly as to come from the direction of the tents so soon."

"I know every foot of the ground, followed you in a very short time, and walked fast," said he. "But look," he added, pointing to the girl, Eldiva, who came out of the cabin quickly, as if frightened or driven out. "There may be trouble up there."

"I'll walk that way and see," said I.

"Perhaps you had better not. He is desperate now, and where he can find arms to supply the place of those we took from him. If the girl needed help she would blow the whistle that I gave her."

"True; but she comes this way. Her face wears a look of alarm."

In a few seconds the girl came down to the spot where we stood.

"Oh, sir, I believe he has gone stark, raving mad," she said. "He came into the cabin just now and commenced drinking whisky, cup after cup. I did not dare to speak, he looked so wild and haggard.

"All at once he turned on me, and his eyes seemed to burn right into me with hate. Then he hissed out these words: 'Leave, gal, leave, or I'll murder you, too.'

"I dared not stay. Oh, what shall I do—where shall I go?"

"Go to the tent on the hill and tell Biddy Flynn I sent you there, and you are to remain and be protected. Let him dare to go there to harm you. He will then forfeit the little claim to forbearance which I yet allow."

"I must go without my clothing and some relics of my dear mother which are in the cabin, if I go now."

"They shall be sent to you if you say where they are."

"In a little trunk under the bunk in the end of the cabin, sir."

"All right, you shall have them. Go up the hill at once and remain with the children, out of sight. I will see you by and by. If he does not drink himself into a helpless stupor he will require looking to. You shall not be yielded again into his power."

"Oh, sir, if you can protect me from him I shall be too happy. But he is terrible when he gets mad."

"I know how to tame him," said Melrose, quietly. "Have no fear."

The girl turned away, her eyes glittering with emotion, and at once hastened up the hill, as we hoped, unobserved, for the men were all busy in the claim below, or at least seemed to be, and Alf kept inside the cabin.

Melrose now left us, going across the gulch in the direction of the blasted tree, and was soon out of sight. I did not feel like work, but made up my mind to remain at the claim until supper time, just for appearance sake, unless called away by some new exigency. But all three of us cast frequent glances toward the cabin, wondering what Alf would attempt when he had got a full head of steam on, if he was still pulling at his whisky jug.

Two hours, at least, passed, and it was well along in the afternoon when he came out. He did not stagger. It seemed as if drink could not affect his knees. But his face was purple, his eyes red and rolling, his utterance, as he tried to sing a verse of a bacchanalian song, thick.

"Eldiva!" he, shouted; "where in thunder are you, gal? Scared, maybe, to see me drink a few extra horns o' whisky. Gal, you'd better show up! Come out o' your hidin' place, or I'll hide *you* when I find you."

He got no answer. He strode to and fro around the cabin, looking behind the rocks and bushes near by, vainly, of course.

Then he went down to the diggings where his men were at work.

Here, though we could not hear him, we presumed he was making inquiries about the girl. We saw one of his men point up the hill toward our tents, and then we were sure she had been seen when we thought she had not.

He turned and walked swiftly up the hill, not even stopping at the cabin to take another drink.

I proposed that we should all follow him at once. But Billy Flynn coolly said: "My Biddy up there is more than a match for him, sir. Some of us must stay to watch these scalawags of his down here. If one goes it will be enough, at any rate."

"Then I will go," said I, "for he has undoubtedly armed himself again, and arms in the hands of a man wild with drink are bad playthings."

Suiting my actions to my words, I set off at a rapid gait to see what he was doing.

When I arrived at the tents, in truth before I got there, I heard him and Biddy in high altercation, and when in sight, saw her barring his way with a stout club, while he was cursing her fearfully, swearing he would pass into the tents which she guarded.

"I'll cleave you in two if you don't get out of the way," he said, as I was hurrying up, and I now saw that he had a large bowie-knife in his hand.

"Murdering dog! Advance one step, and you die! Biddy, stand aside. Boy as I am, I am too much for him."

It was the boy Jesse who spoke, and his revolver was raised in a line with the bad man's breast.

He had stepped out from the tent, and behind him, white with fear and trembling, stood the girl Eldiva, holding the hand of little Julia.

The ruffian did not seem to notice them. His eyes were fixed on the boy.

"His face! His face!" Alf groaned aloud.

And he shook from head to foot, while the boy, with close-set lips and eyes sternly fixed on him, stood, the embodiment of juvenile heroism, in front of his sister and her friend.

"The odds are altogether against you, Mr. Dunning; you had better retire!" said I, deeming it best to show that the boy and woman had backing.

The ruffian turned and saw that I, also, held a revolver in my hand.

"I'll go!" he said, in a voice husky with rage. "But I'll come again, and not alone. As for you, gal"—he turned to Eldiva—"I've spared you for a good while, for the sake of one I loved once as well as a cuss like me can love, but I'll do it no longer. Mine you are, and mine you shall be till I make you crawl in the dirt at my feet and make you beg for a kind word instead of a kick!"

He turned on his heel and strode away down the hill, without saying more.

"Oh, how I wanted to kill him!" said Jesse, as he lowered his pistol, let down the hammer, and replaced the weapon in his belt.

"Why did you not do it?" I asked, wondering at the great self-possession of the boy.

"Mr. Melrose said I must not, till he gave me permission, except in the last necessity of defense for sister and myself. I would have broken an arm first, and a leg afterward, but I wouldn't have killed him."

"You think you could hit just where you please?"

"I don't think it, sir, I *know* it. Mr. Melrose taught me how to shoot long ago. And I have practiced in our cottage garden down on the bay until I am a pretty good shot, I think. Do you see that pine burr hanging at the end of the branch, sir?"

He pointed to a burr and a nut-pine full forty yards from where he stood, and drew his pistol again.

"Yes, I see it. Could you hit that?"

"I could, sir, but I will only cut it from the limb, and then bring the burr to you to see that it is not injured."

He fired the instant he said this, with that suddenness of aim which good shots always possess. The burr dropped, and he ran to get it, and showed me that he had cut it clear from the branch with his bullet.

"I am satisfied," said I, "that you know how to handle weapons well enough to protect yourself and sister from such a wretch as he."

"I'm going to take care of *her* too, for she loves us, and we have never had any one to love us but Mr. Melrose!" said the boy, looking at Eldiva. "Never at least since our dear mother died."

Eldiva's sad face brightened when these words reached her ears, and she said: "Yes, I love you both so, so dearly. My heart went out to you the moment I saw you. I, too, have led an unloved, a wretched life. How it is to end, I dread to think, for that fearful man will carry out his threats if it be possible for him to do it!"

"Fear not! Protection is ever near you, and you will yet know a sheltering love which will repay you for all that you have suffered!" said Melrose, coming, as he so often did, suddenly and unobserved upon us.

"Jesse, my brave lad," he continued, "you showed all the nerve just now that I expected you would. Always obey my directions as you did to-day, and you will get through the trouble all safe, and go out of this gulch rich and happy too."

"If I am rich, you will be rich too," said the boy, pleasure beaming in his eyes.

For he was like all good boys, who delight in receiving praise when they know they are deserving of it.

"Do you not think that Black Alf will arm his party and come back here to try to remove Eldiva?" I asked now of Melrose.

"Most likely he will; but I shall be ready to aid you and the rest here in thwarting him. I hope that before another day dawns all my plans will culminate in success. He is now in a state of desperation which will cause him to forget the prudence which has foiled me for over a year in making discoveries that I desire. I will leave you now to hasten preparations. As soon as I have gone, fire three shots, with a one minute interval between each. Then, when your partners come up, they probably will at once see to all your arms, and be ready for any event which comes."

"Shall we open fire on him and his party if they approach us?" I asked, thinking it best to listen to his judgment at any rate.

"If they do not halt when you bid them. But do not let *him* fall by a bullet. The murderer must *hang!* He dreads the rope as much as an Indian would—who believes that a warrior, if shot, goes to the red man's heaven, but if hanged, is doomed to wander through all eternity among lost spirits."

Melrose said no more, but hurried away. I at once took the heaviest repeating rifle we had, and fired three shots, with the interval between each that he directed.

About a minute after my last shot had been fired, I heard three answering reports far down the valley, and from this concluded that the signal had been agreed upon and was understood by the men whom I had seen at work near the cabins in the early part of the day.

In a little while Ned Griffin and Billy Flynn came up from the claim, and reported that Black Alf had called all his men into the cabin, and when they came past it, the whole gang were holding a high carousal.

Their leader evidently intended to set them up with drink, to prime them for the work which he had in view.

We had supper at once, and while it was being got ready, looked to our weapons, and had every one made ready for instant use, for we expected that their use would be necessary, and that in a little time.

CHAPTER XXIV.

A Scene of Horror.

Night drew on, with us all on watch—no fire lighted now, to guide those who would only come as enemies. Darkness enveloped the scene, for the moon was not yet up, and there was a hazy fog rising from the stream below and from the little lake, which dimmed the starlight.

Just after dark we had a surprise, but it did not come from Alf Dunning's gang. Melrose came in on the trail which led from the east, bringing with him ten men, all armed, and a female wrapped in a black mantle, which fell from her head to her feet, while her face was hidden by a veil of the same somber hue.

"I am about to operate on your claim, Mr. Griffin," said Melrose, and, opening the slide of a dark lantern, he showed that one of his party carried a rope ladder, with some other implements. I also noticed by the same light that every man of the party carried two or three pairs of steel handcuffs slung at his belt, ready for use.

"Men, you will all take the post below, remembering your instructions to make prisoners of and secure all who approach, not using a weapon except when actual danger to your own lives demands it."

He gave this order to the silent group who were in his rear, and all, except the man who carried the rope ladder, moved silently down toward the cabin.

Then he turned to the female, approached her, and spoke in a low tone for several minutes. We could hear a soft, musical voice responding at times, but could not understand what either said.

After a few moments thus spent, he conducted the female into the smaller tent—not that in which the children were, but in the one erected by Griffin and myself for our own use. He returned, and then said: "The place is now well guarded. If you will visit the old shaft with me, we will learn some of its secrets—or rather *you* will, for I know them already."

Griffin and myself, being the ones he specially addressed, went with him and the man who carried the ladder to the shaft, which was about a hundred yards farther up the hill.

Arriving there, the artificial web was carefully removed by Melrose, with the remark that he might need it again some time, and would not injure a fiber if it could be helped.

This done, one end of the rope ladder was fixed to the trunk of a tree close by, and then it was lowered away into the dismal-looking hole.

Melrose, lantern in hand, was the first to descend, and then at his request Ned Griffin and I followed. The other man came last. The direct descent was at least thirty feet, and then we observed that a gallery led from the shaft, propped up by timbers. It looked rather unsafe, but Melrose boldly entered it, and we followed.

We only went a few yards—perhaps fifty or sixty feet—finding the passage singularly dry for an underground place, when both Griffin and myself started back with an, exclamation of horror.

For two bodies lay stretched out on the ground in their clothes, but with the evidence of a horrible death upon them. They seemed to have dried up, for the skin was dark and discolored, like parchment, and there were only hollow places where the eyes had been; but the dry atmosphere must have prevented the usual decay, for the shape of each was distinct, and the limbs, though shrunken, could be seen as the garments covered them.

"There," said Melrose, pointing to one form, "lies all that was mortal of the father of the two orphans who are in the tent below. And *here*"—his voice trembled with the intensity of his emotions—"here is all that is left of my *only* brother!

You need not wonder why I have followed the murderer as I have. But justice will soon reach him. I must now get these bodies into the upper air. They have been preserved by the strong arsenical atmosphere down here, and I fear will crumble away when we get them above. But he must look at them before he swings, as swing he shall before another day's sun goes down, for I shall not wait for the law's uncertain hand in this case."

"You will have them taken above?" asked Griffin.

"Yes; they will not be hard to move—they are dried up and light now. That wretch carried them hither from the spot where he killed them when they were full weight. A witness whom he does not dream of saw it, for he thought she was first destroyed. But we must to work, for I feel as if the end was near at hand."

We found, indeed, that the bodies were light, and to take them to the shaft was no trouble. There—two of us having gone up—they were raised by a rope, and then, when we all came up, they were carried down and placed near the tents in a position selected by Melrose.

We had just concluded this labor when the signal was heard between us and the cabin. It came clear and sharp, like the cry of a bittern startled from its nest.

"That is Bill Tulip. He has news for me," said Melrose. "Remain here till I return."

And he hurried off as fast as he could walk.

He was not gone over five minutes.

When he came back I could tell by his voice that he had heard good news.

"We have a tramp before us, gentlemen," said he; "that is, if you want to see this adventure through in all its phases."

"All right, sir, I am ready," said I.

"Me too. Count me as *one* in all you have to do," said Griffin.

"I will explain as we go," said Melrose. "Bill Tulip is one of my men, and has acted as a spy in the gang of Black Alf all the time, communicating with me by signal or otherwise whenever it was necessary. By my direction he has so acted as to urge the villain on in many things when prudence would keep him back, and to-night, when Alf was trying to urge his party to come up and attack us and take the girl, Eldiva, from us at once, he cunningly hinted that there would be risk of being punished for murder if the crowd remained, and all hands ought to leave with all the gold they could get, so as to get out of the country.

"Alf bit at the bait, and said he could give them all enough, and he would after the work was done.

"But Bill is an old hand at this kind of work, and persuaded several to say they would do nothing until they had the gold in hand.

"The result is that he and four more are to go with Black Alf in a few minutes to get the required treasure. This enables me to find what I have looked for a long time, his secret hiding-place, where the gold was carried after he murdered his partners. Bill Tulip made an excuse to come this way, to see if we were on the watch up here before the party starts, and that enabled him to let me know what I have told you, so that we may now follow and carry out the rest of my plan."

"How will you know the route they take?" I asked, as we hurried on, going over toward the blasted tree, of which mention has been made two or three times.

"Do you see that?" he asked, and we got a sudden glimpse of light, looking like a very bright star—saw it a second and it was gone.

"Yes; what is that?"

"A peculiar lantern, carried by Bill Tulip, who walks in the rear of his party. He has shown it to me three times now, at points where it would not be observed by those who are with him. See, I answer it now."

And a sudden flash, a single shooting ray of light flew out from a slide in his lantern, and then all was dark again.

I was satisfied, though surprised, and, as we hurried on, felt sure that a man who so thoroughly understood his business could not fail in carrying it to a successful termination.

We moved on as fast as we could, careful to step lightly, and soon were in hearing of the men before us. Drink made them noisy, and caused a lack of caution which was certainly serviceable to us.

We went on until we reached the spot where the blasted tree stood, passed it, while Melrose whispered:

"Here is where those two were murdered whose bodies you saw, while just beyond, where the ledge overhangs the lake, is the spot where another shrieking victim leaped to escape his murderous hand—leaped, as he supposed in his fiendish heart, to a death and a grave at the same dread instant.

"Ah, they halt. There is some entrance to the cliff, for they pause where I once before observed foot-marks, but could find nothing more. Come on, silent and fast—come on."

At the same instant we saw the flash of the light ahead, shown three times rapidly, and then it disappeared.

"It is the place—it is *the place*," said Melrose. "Now let every man be as silent as he can, for I do not wish him to dream that his secret is known beyond those he has trusted until all my hand is ready for exposure."

CHAPTER XXV.
Making Preparations.

No answer was necessary. With every nerve quivering, yet completely under control, we hurried on. We heard no sound now for a little time, but when we came close to the lofty ledge, we heard them talking again, and through a thick bunch of cedars, close beneath the cliff, got a glimpse of light.

Creeping up to the very edge of this thicket, we peered in among the branches, and saw where a rock had been rolled away from in front of a small cave, big enough for a good-sized grizzly bear's den—perhaps fifteen or twenty feet across in the interior, but not over three or four at the utmost at the opening.

Glancing in, we saw Black Alf, with the bull's-eye lantern wide open, overhauling a pile of canvas and buckskin bags, which lay in one corner.

"All's right. There has been no one here since I was, and that is over five years ago," said he. "And, boys, here is enough of the yellow stuff to satisfy any four or five men, but not enough for all our gang. Now I've trusted you four. I'm willing to do well by you, but I don't feel like giving up *all* this, share and share alike, to them that we've left over at the cabin. What do you say?"

"Honor among thieves!" said Bill Tulip, with a dry laugh, and a cough given to inquire if we were near.

An owl hooted just then outside, and his cough was answered.

"Yes, that's all well to *talk* about, but who ever knew it to be carried out in practice," said Alf. "Now what I propose is that we carry back each of us a couple of bags, and say it is all there is, though it will not be a quarter. Then when we're done our work, and are ready to go, we can all come back secretly without the other chaps knowing it, and get the rest. *You* are safe, you know, for now you know the hiding-place and how to get to it."

"That is so," said Bill Tulip. "I'm agreed."

"And I—and I," added the others.

Melrose now gave us the signal to move away, and we hastily got out of the range in which they must pass to return, so as to avoid the chance of a discovery which would ruin our hopes of keeping Black Alf in the dark about our movements until the trap was ready for springing.

They soon came out, evidently full of glee, and as Bill Tulip, who carried the lantern, stumbled and let the slide slip aside, on purpose, of course, we who were hidden saw them all plainly, and that each carried a couple of bags of treasure with him.

"Curse it—can't you keep from flashing that light!" cried Alf, angrily. "Some of them cusses on the hill will see us sure."

"It was an accident—I didn't mean to do it," said Bill, in an apologetic tone.

"Well, be careful. We can feel our way back as easy as we felt it here. We've been lucky not to see any ghosts to-night."

"We've all got too much whisky in to let 'em scare us if we do see 'em. That old tree looks ghost-like," said Bill.

"Hush—don't talk about that tree. 'Twas singed by the devil's own hand!" gasped Alf, as he hurried on.

They were now so far ahead of us that we could not hear any more of their conversation, and, taking a different course, Melrose led the way back to the tents as quickly as we could go.

On reaching them, he took Billy Flynn and the man who had been with us in our late adventures, and went down to communicate further orders to the men whom he had directed to take post between us and the cabin. Before going he gave us these directions:

"I wish, while I am gone," said he, "that you two would collect all the dry fuel you have and put on as many pine burrs and knots as you can collect, so that we can have plenty of light when it is needed. And I think it will soon be needed. I am in hopes of securing those who would attack us before they are ready to commence, for if Bill Tulip leads the way we can do it, and I hope to do it without any unnecessary effusion of blood, or peril to ourselves. All that will depend, as most successes do, on nerve and cool action. Remain where you are and wait for me. I will be here soon after they begin to approach, I think."

CHAPTER XXVI.
Illuminating the Show.

Few of my readers will understand the nervous feeling of watching and waiting, when unseen dangers are to your knowledge surely approaching. Only "trying it on" can teach that sensation.

Griffin and myself hastened to pile up the dry fuel, of which, thanks to the industry of Bridget Flynn, we had a large quantity on hand, and to so arrange it that in a few seconds a powerful blaze could be made. We were occupied at this for perhaps fifteen or twenty minutes, when, having finished, we paused to rest.

Just then I heard a sound which seemed to be like the fall of some body. Then all was still for a few moments. Again I heard it, and now I whispered to Griffin to learn if he heard the sound.

"Yes," said he; "it seems to me as if some one had been knocked down. Yet, if such was the case, others would be alarmed."

I thought so, too, but I heard the sound repeated several times before I heard any other noise, then all at once I heard a struggle, the sound of angry voices, and saw the light of two bull's-eye lanterns flashing upon struggling forms between us and the cabin down the hill.

Two pistol shots made us dread that serious damage was being done to our friends, but in a few seconds the struggle seemed to be over, for we heard nothing more except loud and angry talk.

In a few minutes we heard footsteps coming and saw Melrose with his lantern flashing on the path advancing toward us.

"Help me to make some arrangements for a final tableau," he said, as he came up. "I have succeeded beyond my hopes. Bill Tulip is worth his weight in gold. Every man of that party is a prisoner in irons. Help me with those bodies, and then we will interview the gentlemen who are cursing down there so bitterly."

We hastened now to place the bodies in an upright position against the tent in which the veiled woman remained. Melrose placed a white blanket over them, so that they would not be noticed while it remained.

This done, he went into the tent and spoke to the female for a few seconds, probably telling her what to do at the proper time.

He then came out and went into the other tent and brought the children and Eldiva out in front, and led them into the tent where the female was. I heard him say to all: "No one must speak until I utter the words, MONSTER, BEHOLD! Then you will all step out where you can be distinctly seen, every face turned toward Black Alf."

Having given these orders, Melrose now asked if we had the fuel ready to set on fire.

"In half a minute we can light a blaze which will illuminate the whole gulch!" was my answer.

"All right. Do not light it until I give the word!" said he.

He now threw the glare of his reflecting lantern down the trail and blew his whistle thrice.

In a moment we saw a column of men coming up toward the tents, and soon found that it was composed of those under command of Melrose, who were guarding the party of Black Alf, he being foremost of all, in the grasp of Billy Flynn, and each man of them ironed. They had all been disarmed, and some were bleeding from rather harsh bruises over their heads.

They were all halted in line just in front of the tents, and when all were up and the line complete, Melrose said: "Light up, gentlemen. We want to have this show illuminated!"

In less than three minutes a blaze flashed up twenty feet in the air, and you could have picked up a pin in every direction for a hundred yards around.

Melrose looked at the sullen, hate-speaking face of Black Alf, and, with a sarcastic smile, said: "You're not smart in surprises, Alf Dunning. When you work against a detective force you have no easy task."

"What'll you *make* by all *this?* That's what I'd like to know. We've done nothing to be arrested for," said Alf, spitefully.

"We will see, before this fire burns down, Mr. Dunning—we will see. In the first place, we shall make a pretty good sum in uncoined gold. Not the two bags apiece, which you five brought from the cave to fool your duped confederates with, but all the pile you left behind you. That will be something of a *make*, will it not?"

Alf groaned. His supposed *secret* was out. Gnashing his teeth, he turned to where Bill Tulip stood free, and shouted: "You're the cussed traitor that betrayed it all. I'd like to cut your throat."

"I've no doubt you would. But you are a bungler at concealing murder when you have done it," said Bill.

"*Murder?* Who says I ever did a murder?" cried the villain.

"I do! Not one, but many!" cried Melrose.

"Ha, ha! It is easy to say it. But *proving* comes next. You can't do that!"

"I can. I have witnesses, which you, brazen with effrontery, and brave with the rum in you, dare not face."

"You lie! I dare face *anything.* I've seen your ghosts. I'm not afraid of *them.* Go on and show your witnesses."

"MONSTER, BEHOLD!" cried Melrose, in a tone of stern solemnity.

At that instant, while Eldiva came from the tent, with Julia and Jesse on each side, holding her hand, the woman who had entered the tent, enveloped in black, stepped out clad in a robe of white, her hair streaming in glossy looks of ebon hue over her shoulders. Her face would have been very, very beautiful had not a red scar marred the upper part of it.

At the same time the blanket was drawn from in front of the two bodies.

Melrose pointed first to the woman, then to the bodies, and again repeated the words: "*Monster, behold!*"

Alf Dunning looked worse than I had seen him in any of the scenes of terror before described. His eyes fairly protruded in stony horror. He was frozen with fear. He could not even tremble.

His eyes were fixed on the face of the woman. He did not turn them toward the dead bodies until Melrose called two names—"Robert Duluke, Ebert Melrose"—and pointed to the bodies.

Then the eyes of the murderer glanced in the direction in which Melrose pointed.

The murderer trembled now, but he did not speak. Quaking from head to foot, he turned from the bodies to look once more at the woman.

"Medora Roget!" he gasped. "Spirit, why do *you* haunt me?"

Then she spoke, and the wretch learned that *one* whom he supposed to be beyond the call of mortal voice was there alive to testify to his guilt.

"I live, Alfred Dunning!" she said, in a voice that did not tremble. "I live to see you punished, not for what you did to me alone, but for the crimes you wrought on others; and, to punish you yet more than death, to tell you that the kind and indulgent husband, from whom you lured me away—your once bene-factor, whom you repaid with base ingratitude—took me back, unworthy as I was, after I escaped from your murderous hand by Providential aid, and, lately dying, left to me and to his child, who stands close by a mother who yearns for her caress, a fortune greater than you can dream of."

"Mother! mother!" screamed Eldiva, as she sprang to the arms opened to receive her.

"Yes, angel daughter—yes, I am your mother, who has been for a long year near to you, using means to aid this brave detective in carrying out the ends of justice."

For a moment all was still but the sobs of almost delirious joy which broke from mother and from daughter.

Then Melrose spoke: "Alf Dunning, you failed to kill her whose young life you clouded, though you supposed the blow which left that scar was fatal, and that the lake into which she plunged became her grave. But you *did* kill my brother, and you *did* kill the father of these two children."

"And now I will kill *him!*" cried the boy, and his revolver was out of his belt in a second.

Melrose stayed his hand, crying out:"No, no, Jesse! It must not be your hand which sends that man to death. You are young. I would not have the stain of blood upon your hand—its shadow on your soul—even though the murderer trembles before your eye. He does not deny his guilt. He will be punished when to-morrow's sun is but one hour high. He shall swing from the blasted tree beneath which his crime was done, and which withered from that dreadful hour, and Heaven have mercy on his soul!"

The murderer did not speak. He was dumb with conscious guilt. While the children and Medora Roget were removed from his sight, led into the tent by the hand of Melrose, he turned to gaze with a ghastly look into the flickering fire as if to read a thereafter in its blaze.

I do not like executions, nor to describe horrors.

But before I close this story, I must say that Alf Dunning was executed by men who, acting as a vigilance committee, believed they did right; that his gang scattered, glad to be allowed to go, as they did.

And now to all—especially to my boy readers, and girls as well—*don't* believe in ghosts. I do not now, nor did I ever.

How, then, came those strange apparitions which I have described, you ask.

They were made by the aid of what is termed a magic lantern from reflecting pictures, and those who were in the work, concealed in convenient places, spoke when voices reached the ears of those who wondered at the appearances. It was all managed by MELROSE THE DETECTIVE.

THE END.

∽ IV ∽
Wild Bill's Last Trail

Editor's Note:

Edward Z. C. Judson's attitude toward James Butler ("Wild Bill") Hickok is another of the many mysteries surrounding the author's life and career. In *The King of Border Men,* Judson extols Hickok's heroic traits, even attributing to him the honor of dispatching Jake M'Kandlas, Buffalo Bill's lifetime nemesis. In Judson's story, Wild Bill neatly acts as a foil to Buffalo Bill by behaving in almost precisely the same way as the plainsman hero, but he brings to his character a rougher edge, a background as a frontier lawman and gunfighter. Wild Bill is a heavy drinker who wants to reform but can't quite, a professional gambler and denizen of the lowest haunts of various towns. Wild Bill's name is as much associated with sin and dissipation as it is with honor and bravery in Judson's writing. Judson presents Hickok in all manifestations as a chivalrous gentleman, a civil if rough-spoken individual whose reliability is totally above question. In many ways, such contradictions and ambivalences reflect the true character of Hickok, who, in spite of his actual fame and almost legendary presence in American history and culture, remains in many ways a shadowy and obscure individual.

There is some question about just when or even *if* Judson ever met Hickok. He certainly knew of him because of William Cody's association with Hickok, dating back to the Civil War years. It's likely that Cody himself told Judson sufficient tales, sufficiently embellished, to stir Judson's imagination about the rascally fast-gun killer that Hickok was supposed to be. Moreover, Judson was eternally fascinated by the question of law and order on the frontier, something that he often mentions during his authorial intrusions. Only Texas Ranger Ben McCulloch and mythical mountain man Cale Durg are referred to as often as is Hickok in

Ned Buntline dime novels, and only Buffalo Bill is referred to more. Hickock is usually identified as the greatest of town marshals, not as a gunfighter or gambler, but always as a figure to be revered, even emulated, in all but his devotion to drink.

After Buffalo Bill and Judson parted ways over a monetary dispute with regard to *Scouts of the Plains,* Hickok joined the acting troupe, which was now under Cody's control. Hickok replaced the Cale Durg character that Judson had created for himself. Hickok's stint with the players was short-lived, though. He was disgusted to find that the "benzene" or whiskey he was given to drink on stage was actually tea, and when he discovered that the guns he was given to use carried blank loads, he delighted in firing them off near the legs of the other actors, burning them and making them jump, even after they were supposed to be lying dead. He refused to stick to the script, flirted shamelessly with the female members of the company, and soon left for the frontier, declaring that the theater wasn't for him.

Judson wrote nothing specifically about Hickok from 1873 through the rest of the decade*. When Hickok was murdered by John (Jack) McCall in Saloon #10 in Deadwood, Dakota Territory, on August 2, 1876, he was almost instantly turned into a legend, but Judson, who seldom let a sensational opportunity pass, did not deal with Hickok's murder until the publication of *On the Death Trail; or, The Last of Wild Bill,* in 1880.˙

Judson's version of events leading up to the Hickok's death are at considerable variance with the facts, even as they were well known and widely published at the time. Rather than deal with Wild Bill's reputed attempt to reform himself and his close association with Martha Jane ("Calamity Jane") Cannary, his recent marriage, or his vow to give up gambling and start mining for gold, Judson chose instead to seize on a fairly minor aspect of McCall's trial testimony and exploit it to the fullest. From the story's outset, Hickok is presented as a man tormented by his own misdeeds and haunted by a dream forecasting his own demise. At his historic trial, Jack McCall stated that his motivation for shooting Hickok was to take revenge for his brother, whom McCall claimed Hickok had gunned down in Abilene a year or two before. It was ultimately revealed that McCall had no brother, and so he was hanged. But Judson apparently found in the perjury the core of a story. This revenge motif essentially makes up the plot of *Wild Bill's Last Trail.*

As in so many of Buntline's dime novels, the plot follows a chase and rescue scenario, but in this case, villains such as Persimmon Bill are also opposed

---

* The exact date when Hickok left the play isn't known. Connelley reports that Helen Cody Wetmore recalled that he left the cast in only in the first season; however, he is listed as part of the cast on playbills in 1873. Connelley, 164.

by Hickok's boon companions, Captain Jack Crawford and California Joe. Addie Neidic, created from whole cloth, apparently, provides the love interest, and Cale Durg is referenced. Curiously, the villains who provide the conflicting action that moves the plot more or less walk away from the story after they've driven Hickok into Deadwood. Jack McCall figures prominently as a character. This version of Wild Bill is a far cry from the intrepid hero and close sidekick of Buffalo Bill who was displayed by Judson in *Buffalo Bill, the King of Border Men.*. In his later manifestation, Hickok has become a fatalist, a tortured man who is spooked by nightmares and visions, one who senses the proximity of his own death and is terrified to meet it.

Most curious, though, is that the circumstances of the actual shooting of Wild Bill—where it happened, how it happened, and the legendary detail of the "dead man's hand" (full house: aces and eights)—are totally ignored. For Judson, the famous Ned Buntline death scene required more drama than an ignominious assassination in a dirty mining camp saloon could provide. Judson provides a version of Wild Bill's actual nature that runs counter to both history and legend. One senses that there was more going on here than the usual Ned Buntline liberty with the facts in order to make a sensational story. There's a feeling that perhaps Judson was carrying some kind of grudge against the man who replaced his character Cale Durg on the Buffalo Bill stage, and he was determined to bring a man who was a legend in his own time down to earth.

The version here is taken from *The Nugget Library,* a Street & Smith publication dated 1890. It is a reprint of the original version that appeared in the *Street & Smith's New York Weekly* in 1880.

WILD BILL'S

LAST TRAIL

38 W.C.F

CHAPTER I.

The Avenger.

"Bill! *Wild* Bill! Is this you, or your ghost? What, in great Creation's name, are you doing here?"

"Gettin' toward sunset, old pard—gettin' toward sunset, before I pass in my checks!"

The first speaker was an old scout and plainsman, Sam Chichester by name, and he spoke to a passenger who had just left the westward-bound express train at Laramie, on the U.P.R.R.

That passenger was none other than J. B. Hickock, or "Wild Bill," one of the most noted shots, and certainly the most desperate man of his age and day, west of the Mississippi River.

"What do you mean, Bill, when you talk of passing in your checks? You're in the very prime of life, man, and—"

"Hush! Talk low! There are listening ears everywhere, Sam! I don't know why, but there is a chill at my heart, and I know my time has about run out. I've been on East with Buffalo Bill and Texas Jack, trying to show people what our plains life is. But I wasn't at home there. There were crowds on crowds that came to see us, and I couldn't stir on the streets of their big cities without having an army at my heels, and I got sick of it. But that wasn't all. There was a woman that fell in love with me, and made up her mind to marry me. I told her that I was no sort of a man to tie to—that I was likely to be wiped out any day 'twixt sunrise and sunset, for I had more enemies than a candidate for President; but she wouldn't listen to sense, and so—*we buckled!* Thank Heaven, I've coaxed her to stay East with friends while I've come out here; for, Sam, she'll be a widow inside of six weeks!"

"Bill, you've been hitting benzine heavy of late haven't you?"

"No; I never drank lighter in my life than I have for a year past. But there's a shadow cold as ice on my soul! I've never felt right since I pulled on that red-haired Texan at Abilene, in Kansas. You remember, for you was there. It was kill or get killed, you know, and when I let him have his ticket for a six-foot lot of ground he gave one shriek—it rings in my ears yet. He spoke but one word—'SISTER!' Yet that word has never left my ears, sleeping or waking, from that time to this. I had a sister once myself, Sam, and I loved her a thousand times more than I did life. In fact I never loved life after I lost her. And I can't tell you all about her—I'd choke if I tried. It is enough that she died, and the cause of her death died soon after, and I wasn't far away when—when he went under. But that isn't here nor there, Sam—let's go and warm up. Where do you hang out?"

"I'm in camp close by. I'm heading a party that is bound in for the Black Hills. Captain Jack Crawford is along. You know him. And California Joe, too."

"Good! It is the first streak of luck I've had in a year. I'll join your crowd, Sam, if you'll let me. Captain Jack and Joe are as good friends as I ever had—always barring one."

"And that is?"

"My old six-shooter here. Truth-Teller I call it. It never speaks without saying something. But come, old boy—I see a sign ahead. I must take in a little benzine to wash the car-dust out of my throat."

Bill pointed to a saloon near at hand, and the two old scouts and companions moved toward it.

As they did so, a young man, roughly dressed, with a face fair and smooth, though shadowed as if by exposure to sun and wind, stepped from behind a shade tree, where he had stood while these two talked, listening with breathless interest to every word. His hair, a deep, rich auburn, hung in curling masses clear to his shoulders, and his blue eyes seemed to burn with almost feverish fire as he gazed in the direction the scouts had taken.

"So! He remembers *Abilene*, does he?"

And the tone of the young man was low and fierce as an angered serpent's hiss.

"And he thinks his time is near. So do I. But he shall not die in a second, as his victim did. I would prolong his agonies for years, if every hour was like a living death; a speechless misery. Let him go with Sam Chichester and his crowd. The avenger will be close at hand! His Truth-Teller will lie when he most depends on it. For I—I have sworn that he shall go where he has sent so many victims; go, like them all, unprepared, but not unwarned. No, he thinks that death is near; I'll freeze the thought to his very soul! He is on the death-trail now. With me rests when and where it shall end."

The face of the young man was almost fiendish in its expression as he spoke. It seemed as if his heart was the concentration of hate and a fell desire for revenge.

He strode along the streets swiftly, and, glancing in at the saloon which the two men had entered, paused one second, with his right hand thrust within his vest, as if clutching a weapon, and debating in his mind whether or not to use it.

A second only he paused, and then muttering, "It is not time yet," he passed on.

He went a little way up the same street and entered a German restaurant. Throwing himself heavily on a seat, he said: "Give me a steak, quick. I'm hungry and dry. Give me a bottle of the best brandy in your house."

"We've got der steak, und pread, und peer, und Rhein wine, but no prandy," said the German, who kept the place.

"Cook the steak in a hurry, and send for some brandy then!" cried the young man, throwing down a golden eagle. "Your beer and wine are like dishwater to me. I want fire—fire in my veins now!"

"Dunder and blixen! I shouldn't dink as you wus want much more fire as dere is in your eyes, young fellow. But I send for your prandy."

The young man threw one glance around the room to see if he were the only occupant.

There was another person there, one who had evidently just come in, a traveler, judging by a good-sized valise that was on the floor beside his chair. This person looked young, for the face, or as much of it as was not hidden by a very full black beard, was fair and smooth as that of a woman, while the hair which shaded his white brow was dark as night, soft and glossy as silk, hanging in short, curling masses about his face and neck.

He was dressed rather better than the usual run of travelers; in a good black broad-cloth suit—wore a heavy gold watch-chain, had on a fine linen shirt with a diamond pin in the bosom, and appeared to feel quite satisfied with himself, from the cool and easy manner in which he gave his orders for a good, substantial meal, in a voice rather low and musical for one of his apparent age.

The last comer eyed this person very closely, and a smile almost like contempt rose on his face, when the dark-eyed stranger called for claret wine, or if they had not that, for a cup of tea.

But his own strong drink was now brought in, and pouring out a glassful of undiluted brandy, he drank it down and muttered: "That's the stuff! It will keep up the fire. My veins would stiffen without it. It has carried me so far, and it must to the end. Then—no matter!"

The stranger or traveler looked as if wondering that the young man could take such a fearful dose of fiery liquor, and the wonder must have increased when a second glassful was drained before the food was on the table.

But the latter came in now, and the traveler and the young man with auburn hair, at separate tables, were apparently too busy in disposing of the eatables to take any further notice of each other.

When the first had finished, he took a roll of cigarettes from one of his pockets, selected one, took a match from a silver box, drawn from the same pocket, and lighting his cigarette, threw a cloud of smoke above his head.

The second, pouring out his third glass of brandy, sipped it quietly—the first two glasses having evidently supplied the fire he craved so fiercely.

The traveler, as we may call him, for want of any other knowledge, now rose, and as if impelled by natural politeness, tendered a cigarette to the other.

The man with auburn hair looked surprised, and his fierce, wild face softened a little, as he said: "Thank you, no. I drink sometimes, like a fish, but I don't smoke. Tobacco shakes the nerves, they say, and I want my nerves steady."

"Strong drink will shake them more, I've heard," said the traveler, in his low, musical voice. "But you seem to have a steady hand, though you take brandy as if used to it."

"My hand is steady, stranger," was the reply. "There is not a man on the Rio Grande border, where I came from, that can strike a center at twenty paces with a revolver as often as I. And with a rifle at one hundred yards I can most generally drop a deer with a ball between his eyes, if he is looking at me, or take a wild turkey's head without hurting his body."

"Then, you are from Texas?"

"Yes, sir. And you?"

"From the East, sir. I have traveled in the South—all over, in fact—but my home is in the old Empire State."

"If it isn't impudent, which way are you bound now?"

"I haven't quite decided. I may go to the Black Hills—may remain around here awhile—it seems to be rather a pleasant place."

"Yes, fer them that like it. I'm off for the Black Hills, myself."

"Ah! with a company?"

"Not much! But there's a company going. I'm one of them that don't care much for company, and can take better care of myself alone than with a crowd about me."

"So! Well it is a good thing to be independent. Do you know the party that is going?"

"Some of 'em, by sight. The captain is Sam Chichester, and he has California Joe, Cap'n Jack, and about twenty more in his party. And Wild Bill has just come on the train, and I heard him say he was going with the crowd."

"Wild Bill!" cried the stranger, flushing up. "Did you say he was going?"

"Yes."

"Then I'd like to go, too—but I'd like to go with another party, either just before or behind that party. Do you know Wild Bill?"

"Know him! Who does not? Hasn't he killed more men than any other white man in the States and Territories—I'll not say *how*, but is he not a hyena, sopped in blood?"

"You do not like him?"

"Who says I don't?"

"*You* do! Your eyes flash hate while you speak of him."

"Do they? Well, maybe I don't like him as well as I do a glass of brandy— maybe I have lost some one I loved by his hand. It isn't at all unlikely."

The traveler sighed, and with an anxious look, said: "You don't bear him any grudge, do you? You wouldn't harm him?"

A strange look passed like a flash over the face of the other; he seemed to read the thoughts or wishes of the traveler in a glance.

"Oh, no," he said, with assumed carelessness. "Accidents will happen in the best families. It's not in me to bear a grudge, because Bill may have wiped out fifteen or twenty Texans, while they were foolin' around in his way. As to harm— he's too ready with his six-shooter, old Truth-Teller, he calls it, to stand in much danger. I'm quick, but he is quicker. You take a good deal of interest in him? Do *you* know him?"

"Yes; that is, I know him by sight. He is thought a great deal of by an intimate friend of mine, and that is why I feel an interest in him."

"And that friend is a woman?"

"Why do you think so?"

"It is a fancy of mine."

"Well, I will not contradict you. For her sake I would hate to see any evil befall him."

There was a cynical smile on the face of the young man with auburn hair.

"If a woman loved him, she ought not to leave him, for his life is mighty uncertain," said the latter. "I heard him say to Captain Chichester, not half an hour ago, that he didn't believe he would live long, and such a man as he is sure to die with his boots on!"

"Did he say that?" asked the traveler.

"Yes; and he seemed to feel it, too. He had to do as I do, fire up with something strong to get life into his veins."

"Poor fellow! He had better have staid East when he was there, away from this wild and lawless section."

"Stranger, there mayn't be much *law* out this way, but justice isn't always blind out here. If you stay long enough, you may learn that."

"Very likely; but you spoke of going to those Black Hills."

"Yes, I'm going."

"Will you let me go with you?"

"You don't look much like roughing it, and the trip is not only hard, but it may be dangerous. The redskins are beginning to act wolfish on the plains."

"I think I can stand as much hardship as you. You are light and slender."

"But tough as an old buffalo bull, for all that. I've been brought up in the saddle, with rifle and lasso in hand. I'm used to wind and weather, sunshine and storm—they're all alike to me."

"And Indians?"

"Yes—to Comanche, Kiowa, and Apache. But these Cheyennes and Sioux are a tougher breed, they tell me. I'll soon learn them too, I reckon. There's one thing sure, I don't go in no crowd of twenty or thirty, with wagons or pack mules along to tempt the cusses with, while they make the travel slow. You want either a big crowd or a very small one, if you travel in an Indian country."

"You have not answered my question yet. Will you let me go through to the Black Hills with you?"

"Why don't you go with the other party? They'll take you, I'll bet."

"I do not want to go where Wild Bill will see me. He may think his wife has sent me as a spy on his movements and actions."

"His *wife!* Is he married? It must be something new."

"It is. He was married only a short time ago to a woman who almost worships him. She did all she could to keep him from going out into his old life again, but she could not."

"You *can* go with me!" said the other, abruptly, after a keen and searching look in the traveler's face.

"What is your name?"

"Willie Pond."

"Rather a *deep* Pond, if I know what water is," said the auburn-haired man, to himself, and then he asked, in a louder tone, "Have you horse and arms?"

"No; I just came on the train from the East. But there is money—buy me a good horse, saddle, and bridle. I'll see to getting arms."

And Mr. Willie Pond handed the other a five-hundred dollar treasury note.

"You don't ask my name, and you trust me with money as if you knew I was honest."

"You'll tell me your name when you feel like it!" was the rejoinder. "As to your honesty, if I think you are safe to travel with, you're safe to trust my money with."

"You're right. Your money is safe. As to my name, call me Jack. It is short, if it isn't sweet. Some time I'll tell you the rest of it."

"All right, Jack. Take your own time. And now get all ready to start either ahead or just behind the other party."

"We'll not go ahead. Where will you stay to-night?"

"Wherever you think best."

"All right. This old Dutchman keeps rooms for lodgers. You'd better stay here, and if you don't want Bill to see you, keep pretty close in doors. He'll be out in the Black Hillers' camp, or in the saloons where they sell benzine and run faro banks. Bill is death on cards."

"So I've heard," said Mr. Pond, with a sigh.

Jack now went out, and Pond called the Dutch landlord to him and engaged a room.

CHAPTER II.
Persimmon Bill.

As soon as the auburn-haired man who called himself Jack had left the German restaurant, he went to a livery-stable near by, called for his own horse, which was kept there, and the instant it was saddled he mounted, and at a gallop rode westward from the town.

He did not draw rein for full an hour, and then he had covered somewhere between eight and ten miles of ground, following no course or trail, but riding in a course as straight as the flight of an arrow.

He halted then in a small ravine, nearly hidden by a growth of thick brush, and gave a peculiar whistle. Thrice had this sounded, when a man came cautiously out of the ravine, or rather out of its mouth. He was tall, slender, yet seemed to possess the bone and muscle of a giant. His eyes were jet black, fierce and flashing, and his face had a stern, almost classic beauty of feature, which would have made him a model in the ancient age of sculpture. He carried a repeating rifle, two revolvers, and a knife in his belt. His dress was buckskin, from head to foot.

"You are Persimmon Bill?" said Jack, in a tone of inquiry.

"Yes. Who are you, and how came you by the signal that called me out?"

"A woman in town gave it to me, knowing she could trust me."

"Was her first name Addie?"

"Her last name was Neidic."

"All right. I see she has trusted you. What do you want?"

"Help in a matter of revenge."

"Good! You can have it. How much help is wanted?"

"I want one man taken from a party, alive, when he gets beyond civilized help, so that I can see him tortured. I want him to die by inches."

"How large is his party, and where are they now?"

"The party numbers between twenty and thirty; they are in camp in the edge of Laramie, and will start for the Black Hills in a few days."

"If all the party are wiped out but the one you want, will it matter to you?"

"No; they are his friends, and as such I hate them!"

"All right. Get me a list of their numbers and names, how armed, what animals and stores they have, every fact, so I can be ready. They will never get more than half way to the Hills, and the one you want shall be delivered, bound, into your hands. All this, and more, will I do for her who sent you here!"

"You love her?"

"She loves me! I'm not one to waste much breath on talking love. My Ogallalla Sioux warriors know me as the soldier-killer. Be cautious when you go back, and give no hint to any one but Addie Neidic that there is a living being in Dead Man's Hollow, for so this ravine is called in there."

"Do not fear. I am safe, for I counsel with no one. I knew Addie Niedic before I came here, met her by accident, revealed myself and wants, and she sent me to you."

"It is right. Go back, and be cautious to give the signal if you seek me, or you might lose your scalp before you saw me."

"My scalp?"

"Yes; my guards are vigilant and rough."

"*Your guards?*"

Persimmon Bill laughed at the look of wonder in the face of his visitor, and with his hand to his mouth, gave a shrill, warbling cry.

In a second the mouth of the ravine was fairly blocked with armed and painted warriors—Sioux, of the Ogallalla tribe. There were not less than fifty of them.

"You see my guards—red devils, who will do my bidding at all times, and take a scalp on their own account every chance they get," said Persimmon Bill.

Then he took an eagle feather, with its tip dipped in crimson, from the coronet of the chief, and handed it, in the presence of all the Indians, to Jack.

"Keep this, and when out on the plains, wear it in your hat, where it can be seen, and the Sioux will ever pass you unharmed, and you can safely come and go among them. Now go back, get the list and all the news you can, and bring it here as soon as you can. Tell Addie to ride out with you when you come next."

Jack placed the feather in a safe place inside his vest, bowed his head, and, wheeling his horse, turned toward the town. Before he had ridden a hundred yards he looked back. Persimmon Bill had vanished, not an Indian was in sight, and no one unacquainted with their vicinity could have seen a sign to show that such dangerous beings were near.

No smoke rose above the trees, no horses were feeding around, nothing to break the apparent solitude of the scene.

"And that was Persimmon Bill?" muttered the auburn-haired rider, as he galloped back. "So handsome, it does not seem as if he could be the murderer they call him. And yet, if all is true, he has slain tens, where Wild Bill has killed one. No matter, he will be useful to me. That is all I care for now."

CHAPTER III.

A Warning.

When Wild Bill and Sam Chichester entered the saloon alluded to in our first chapter, they were hailed by several jovial-looking men, one of whom Wild Bill warmly responded to as California Joe, while he grasped the hand of another fine-looking young man whom he called Captain Jack.

"Come, Crawford," said he, addressing the last named, "let's wet up! I'm dry as an empty powder-horn!"

"No benzine for me, Bill," replied Crawford, or Captain Jack. "I've not touched a drop of the poison in six months."

"What? Quit drinking, Jack? Is the world coming to an end?"

"I suppose it will sometime. But that has nothing to do with my drinking. I promised old Cale Durg to quit, and I've done it. And I never took a better trail in my life. I'm fresh as a daisy, strong as a full-grown elk, and happy as an antelope on a wide range."

"All right, Jack. But I must drink. Come, boys—all that will—come up and wet down at my expense."

California Joe and most of the others joined in the invitation, and Captain Jack took a cigar rather than "lift a shingle from the roof," as he said.

"Where are you bound, Bill?" asked Captain Jack, as Bill placed his empty glass on the counter, and turned around.

"To the Black Hills with your crowd—that is if I live to get there."

"Live! You haven't any thought of dying, have you? I never saw you look better."

"Then I'll make a healthy-looking corpse, Jack. For I tell you my time is nearly up; I've felt it in my bones this six months. I've seen ghosts in my dreams, and felt as if they were around me when I was awake. It's no use, Jack, when a chap's time comes he has got to go."

"Nonsense, Bill; don't think of anything like that. A long life and a merry one—that's my motto. We'll go out to the Black Hills, dig out our fortunes, and then get out of the wilderness to enjoy life."

"Boy, I've never known the happiness outside of the wilderness that I have in it. What you kill there is what was made for killing—the food we need. What one kills among civilization is only too apt to be of his own kind."

And Bill shuddered as if he thought of the many he had sent into untimely graves.

"Stuff, Bill! You're half-crazed by your dramatic trip. You've acted so much that reality comes strange. Let's go out to camp and have a talk about what is ahead of us."

"Not till I buy a horse, Jack. I want a good horse under me once more; I've ridden on cars and steamboats till my legs ache for a change."

"There's a sales stable close by. Let's go and see what stock is there," said Sam Chichester.

"Agreed!" cried all hands, and soon Bill and his friends were at the stable, looking at some dozen or more horses which were for sale.

"There's the beauty I want," said Wild Bill, pointing to a black horse, full sixteen hands high, and evidently a thoroughbred. "Name your price, and he is my meat!"

"That horse isn't for sale now. He was spoken for an hour ago, or maybe less, by a cash customer of mine—a red-haired chap from Texas."

"Red-haired chap from Texas!" muttered Bill. "Red-haired cusses from Texas are always crossin' my trail. That chap from Abilene was a Texas cattle-man, with hair as red as fire. Where is your cash customer, Mr. Liveryman?"

"Gone out riding somewhere," replied the stable-keeper.

"When he comes back, tell him Wild Bill wants that horse, and I reckon he'll let Wild Bill buy him, if he knows when he is well off! I wouldn't give two cusses and an amen for all the rest of the horses in your stable; I want him!"

"I'll tell Jack," said the stableman; "but I don't think it will make much odds with him. He has as good as bought the horse, for he offered me the money on my price, but I couldn't change his five hundred-dollar treasury note. It'll take more than a name to scare him. He always goes fully armed."

"You tell him what I said, and that I'm a-coming here at sunset for that horse," said Bill, and he strode away, followed by his crowd.

An hour later the auburn-haired man from Texas reined in his own horse, a fiery mustang from his own native plains, in front of the stable.

Though the horse was all afoam with sweat, showing that it had been ridden far and fast, it did not pant or show a sign of weariness. It was of a stock which will run from rise of sun to its going down, and yet plunge forward in the chill of the coming night.

"You want the Black Hawk horse you spoke for this morning, don't you?" asked the stableman, as Jack dismounted.

"Of course I do. I've got the change; there is his price. Three hundred dollars you said?"

"Yes; but there's been a chap here looking at that horse who told me to tell you his name, and that he intended to take that horse. I told him a man had bought it, but he said: 'Tell him Wild Bill wants it, and that Wild Bill will come at sunset to take it.'"

"He will?"

It was hissed rather than spoken, while the young Texan's face grew white as snow, his blue eyes darkening till they seemed almost black.

"He will! Let him try it! A sudden death is too good for the blood-stained wretch! But if he will force it on, why let it come. The horse is bought: let him come at sunset if he dares!"

And the young man handed the stable-keeper three one hundred-dollar greenback notes.

CHAPTER IV.
"Give Up That Horse, or Die!"

Leaving the livery-stable, the young Texan went directly to the German restaurant, and asked for Willie Pond.

He was shown up to the room recently engaged by the traveler and found him engaged in cleaning a pair of fine, silver-mounted Remington revolvers.

"Getting ready, I see," said the Texan. "I have bought you a horse—the best in this whole section; I gave three hundred dollars. There is your change."

"Keep the two hundred to buy stores with for our trip," said Pond.

"No need of it. I've laid in all the stores we need. You can buy yourself a couple of blankets and an India-rubber for wet weather. A couple of tin cans of pepper and salt is all that I lay in when I'm going to rough it on the plains. The man that can't kill all the meat he needs isn't fit to go there."

"Maybe you're right. The less we are burdened, the better for our horses. Are we likely to meet Indians on the route?"

"None that will hurt *me*—or you, when you're in my company. The Sioux know me and will do me no harm."

"That is good. The Indians were my only dread."

"I've a favor to ask."

"It is granted before you ask it—what is it?"

"I want to break your horse to the saddle before you try it. You are not so used to the saddle, I reckon, as I am. I will take a ride at sunset, and bring him around here for you to look at."

"That is right. I am only thankful to have you ride him first, though you may find me a better rider than you think."

"Perhaps. But he looks wild, and I like to tame wild uns. I'll have him here between sundown and dark."

"All right. I told you I'd see to getting arms. I had these revolvers, and cartridges for them, but I want a light repeating rifle. Get me a good one, with as much ammunition as you think I'll need."

"All right. I'll get a new model Winchester. They rattle out lead faster than any other tool I ever carried."

The Texan now left. He had not spoken of Wild Bill's desire to possess that horse, because he had an idea that Mr. Willie Pond would weaken, and give up the horse, rather than risk bloodshed for its possession. And perhaps he had another idea—a mysterious one, which we do not care to expose at this stage of the story.

The young Texan hastened from the German restaurant to a small, neat house in the outskirts of the town. Knocking in a very peculiar manner, he was admitted at once by a tall and strikingly beautiful young woman, whom he addressed as if well acquainted with her.

"I'm here, Addie, and I've seen *him*."

"You found him all right, when you told him who sent you, did you not?" asked the lady, leading the way to a sitting-room in the rear of the cottage.

"Yes, ready to do anything for one you recommend."

"Poor Bill! A braver man and a truer friend never lived. He loves me, and I fear it will be his ruin, for he will too often come within the reach of those who would destroy him, if they only knew where and how to reach him. Persecution and cruelty placed him on the bloody path he has had to follow, and now—now he is an outlaw, beyond all chance for mercy, should he ever be taken."

"He never will be taken, guarded as he is."

"You saw his guards, then?"

"Yes, forty or fifty of them, and I would rather have them as friends than foes. He wants you to ride out with me to meet him when I go next with some information that he needs."

"When will that be?" asked the lady.

"In the early morning, or perhaps to-night, if nothing happens to me between now and sunset to make it unnecessary."

"Between now and sunset? That is within two hours. Do you anticipate any danger?"

"Not much. I have a little task before me. I have a horse to break, and a man known as Wild Bill to tame."

"Wild Bill!—the dead-shot, the desperado, who has killed at least one man for every year of his life?"

"Yes, the same. But ask me no more questions now. After I have tamed him I will report—or, if he has settled me, there will be no need of it."

"Do not run this risk."

"It must be done. He has, in a manner, defied me, and I accept his defiance."

"Surely he does not know—"

"No, he knows nothing of what you would say if I did not interrupt you. Nor do I intend he shall at present. It is enough that you know it, and will care for both my body and my good name, should I fall."

"You know I will. But you must not fall."

"I do not intend to. I think I can crush him by a look and a word. I shall try, at least. If all goes well, I will be here by eight to-night to arrange for our visit."

"I hope you will come, and safely."

"I will, Addie. Until the cup of vengeance is full, Heaven will surely spare me. But I must go. I have no time to spare."

The young Texan glanced at the chambers of a handsome six-shooter which he carried, to see if it was ready for use, replaced it in his belt, and then, with a cheerful smile, left the room and house.

Hastening to the stable, he selected a saddle, lengthened the stirrups to suit himself, took a stout bridle from among a lot hanging in the store-room, and accompanied by the stable-keeper, approached the newly purchased Black Hawk horse.

"I may as well have him ready," he said; "for if Wild Bill is to be here at sunset, that time is close at hand. You say the horse has not been ridden?"

"No," said the stable-keeper. "My regular breaker was not here when I bought him. Black Joe tried to mount him, but the horse scared him."

"Well, I'll soon see what he is made of, if I can get saddle and bridle on him," said the Texan.

They now together approached the large box stall in which the stallion was kept. The horse, almost perfect in symmetry, black as night, with a fierce, wild look, turned to front them as they approached the barred entrance.

"Steady, boy—steady!" cried the Texan, as he sprang lightly over the bars, and at once laid his hand on the arched neck of the horse.

To the wonder of the stableman, the horse, instead of rearing back or plunging at the intruder, turned his eyes upon him, and with a kind of tremor in his frame, seemed to wait to see what his visitor meant.

"So! Steady, Black Hawk! Steady, old boy!" continued the Texan, kindly passing his hand over the horse's neck and down his face.

The horse uttered a low neigh, and seemed by his looks pleased with his attentions.

"That beats me!" cried the stable-keeper. "Old Joe had to lasso him and draw him down to a ringbolt before he could rub him off."

"Hand me the saddle and bridle," said the Texan, still continuing to pet the beautiful and spirited animal.

In a few seconds, without difficulty, the same kind and skillful hands had the horse both saddled and bridled.

The Texan now led the horse out on the street, where quite a crowd seemed to be gathering, perhaps drawn there by some rumor of a fight in embryo.

And as he glanced up the street the Texan saw Wild Bill himself, with his six-shooters in his belt, come striding along, with California Joe and a dozen more at his heels.

In a second, the Texan vaulted upon the back of the horse, which made one wild leap that would have unseated most riders, and then reared on its hind legs as if it would fall back and crush its would-be master.

At this instant, Wild Bill rushing forward, pistol in hand, shouted: "Give up that horse, or die!"

CHAPTER V.

A Square Back-Down.

The Texan paid no heed to the words of the desperado, but bending forward on the horse with his full weight, drove his spurs deeply into its flanks. Startled and stung with pain, the noble animal, at one wild bound, leaped far beyond where Bill and his friends stood, and in a second more sped in terrific leaps along the street.

"The cowardly cuss is running away!" yelled Bill derisively.

"It is false! He is no coward! He will tame the horse first and then you!" cried a voice so close that Bill turned in amazement to see who dare thus to speak to *him*, the "Terror of the West."

"A woman!" he muttered, fiercely, as he saw a tall and queenly-looking girl standing there, with flashing eyes, which did not drop at his gaze.

"*Yes*—a woman, who has heard of Wild Bill, and neither fears nor admires him!" she said, undauntedly.

"Is the fellow that rode off on the horse your husband or lover that you take his part?" asked Bill, half angrily and half wondering at the temerity of the lovely girl who thus braved his anger.

"He is neither," she replied, scornfully.

"I'm glad of it. I shall not make you a widow or deprive you of a future husband when he comes under my fire, if he should be fool enough to come back."

"He comes now. See for yourself. He has tamed the horse—now comes your turn, coward and braggart!"

Bill was white with anger; but she was a woman, and no matter what he felt, too well he knew the chivalry of the far West to raise a hand or even speak a threatening word to her. But he heard men around him murmur her name.

It was Addie Neidic.

And then he turned his eyes upon the black horse and rider. The animal, completely under control, though flecked with foam, came down the street slowly and gently, bearing his rider with an air of pride rather than submission. As he passed the German restaurant, the rider raised his hat in salutation to Willie Pond, who stood in his window, and said, in a cheerful voice: "Remain in your room. I have news for you and will be there soon."

Without checking his horse, the rider kept on until he was within half a length of the horse of Wild Bill, then checking the animal, he said, in a mocking tone: "You spoke to me just as I rode away. I've come back to hear you out."

What was the matter with Wild Bill? He stood staring wildly at the Texan, his own face white as if a mortal fear had come upon him.

"Where have I seen that face before?" he gasped. "Can the dead come back to life?"

The Texan bent forward till his own face almost touched that of Wild Bill and hissed out one word in a shrill whisper: "*Sister!*"

It was all he said, but the instant Wild Bill heard it, he shrieked out: "'Tis him—*'tis him I shot at Abilene!*" and with a shuddering groan, he sank senseless to the pavement.

In an instant Bill's friends, who had looked in wonder at this strange scene, sprang to his aid and, lifting his unconscious form, carried it into the saloon where Bill had met California Joe, Captain Jack, and the rest of their crowd.

Left alone, the young Texan said a few words to Addie Neidic, then dismounted and told the stable-keeper to keep that horse saddled and bridled, and to get his own Texan mustang ready for use.

"I must be out of town before sunrise, or Wild Bill and his friends may have questions to ask that I don't want to answer just now," he said.

And then he walked a little way with Miss Neidic, talking earnestly. But soon he left her, and while she kept on in the direction of her own house, he turned and went to the German restaurant.

Entering the room of Willie Pond, he said, abruptly: "If you want to go to the Black Hills with me on your own horse we'll have to leave this section mighty sudden. Wild Bill has set his mind on having the horse I bought and broke for you, and he has a rough crowd to back him up."

"If I had known Bill wanted the horse so badly I could have got along with another," said Pond, rather quietly.

"What! let *him* have *that* horse? Why it hasn't its equal on the plains or in the mountains. It is a thoroughbred—a regular racer, which a sporting man was taking through to the Pacific coast on speculation. He played faro, lost, got broke, and put the horse up for a tenth of its value. I got him for almost nothing compared to his worth. On that horse you can keep out of the way of any red who scours the plains. If you don't want him I do, for Wild Bill shall never put a leg over his back!"

"I'll keep him. Don't get mad. I'll keep him and go whenever you are ready," said Pond, completely mastered by the excitement which the young Texan exhibited.

"Well, we'll get the horses out of town and in a safe place to-night. And for yourself, I'll take you to the house of a lady friend of mine to stay to-night and to-morrow, and by to-morrow night I'll know all I want to about the movements of the other party, and we can move so as to be just before or behind them, as you and I will decide best."

"All right, Jack. I leave it to you. Are you sure the horse will be safe for me to ride?"

"Yes. A horse like that once broken is broken for life. They never forget their first lesson. A mongrel breed, stupid, resentful, and tricky, is different. Be ready to mount when I lead him around. I will send for your traveling bag, and you will find it at the house where we stop."

"I will be ready," said Pond.

The Texan now left, and Pond watched him as he hurried off to the stable.

"The man hates Wild Bill with a deadly hatred!" he murmured. "I must learn the cause. Perhaps it is a providence that I have fallen in with him, and I have concluded to keep his company to the Black Hills. But I must call the landlord and close up my account before the other comes back with the horses."

The German was so put out by the sudden giving up of a room, which he hoped to make profitable, that he asked an extra day's rent, and to his surprise, got it.

CHAPTER VI.
Off to the Hills.

It was some time before Wild Bill became fully conscious after he was carried into the saloon, and when he did come to he raved wildly about the red-haired man he shot in Abilene, and insisted it was his ghost, and not a real man, he had seen.

Bill's friends tried to cheer and reassure him, and got several stiff draughts of liquor down his throat, which finally "set him up," as they said, till he began to look natural. But he still talked wildly and strangely.

"I told you, Joe," he said to his old friend; "I told you my time was nigh up. This hasn't been my first warning. That Abilene ghost has been before me a thousand times, and he has hissed that same word, 'sister,' in my ear."

"Bah! old boy. What's the use of your talking foolish. You've seen no ghost. That red-haired chap was as live as you are."

"He did have red hair and blue eyes, then?"

"Yes; but there are lots of such all over the world. Red hair and blue eyes generally travel in company. But he was nothing to scare you. You could have wiped him out with one backhanded blow of your fist, let alone usin' shootin' irons, of which there wasn't 'casion, seein' he didn't draw."

"Where is he now?"

"I'll go and see. I suppose he is over at the stable."

Joe went out, but soon returned to say that the Texan had just ridden off, after paying his bill; the stable-keeper did not know where.

"Let him go," murmured Bill. "If he is a man, and not a ghost, I wouldn't raise a hand to hurt him, not for all the gold in the Black Hills. He was so like—so like the chap I dropped in Abilene!"

Bill took another drink, but it seemed as if nothing could lift the gloom which weighed down his heart. Only once did his face brighten. That was when Sam Chichester said there was no use hanging on at Laramie any longer for a bigger crowd; they were strong enough now, and would start for the Hills inside of four-and-twenty hours.

"That's the talk for me!" cried Bill. "I want to get out of here as soon as I can, Joe, and pick me out some sort of a horse. I don't care what, so it'll carry me to the Hills. I can't breathe free any longer where there's such a lot of folks."

"I'll get you a first-chop horse, Bill," said Joe. "There's some half-breeds in a corral just out of town, as tough as grizzlies, and heavy enough for your weight or mine."

"I don't weigh down as I did," said Bill, with a sigh. "I've been losin' weight for six months back. No matter. It'll be less trouble to tote me when I go under. Remember, boys, when I do, bury me with my boots on, just as I die."

"Stop your clatter about dyin', Bill. I'm sick o' that kind of talk. It's time enough to talk of death when its clutch is on you."

"I can't help it, Joe, old pard. It keeps a stickin' in my throat, and if it didn't come out, I'd choke."

"Let's go to camp," said Chichester. "Can you walk now, Bill?"

"Yes."

And the party rose, took a parting drink with the landlord, and started for camp.

Outside, Bill gave a startled, wild glance toward the spot where he had seen the Texan; but no one was there now, and he moved on with his companions toward their camp, listening to, but not joining in their conversation.

On arriving at camp, Chichester, as captain, gave orders that each man should report on paper, or verbally, so it could be taken down, just how much ammunition he had, the number and kind of his arms, private stores, etc., so that if there was not enough to make the trip safely, more could be provided. The number and condition of horses, pack-mules, etc., was also to be given.

No man would be fitted to lead such a party did he not consider and post himself fully in all these particulars.

Quite a crowd of townspeople followed the party out, for the news soon spread that they intended to leave in a short time; so around their blazing camp-fire there were many visitors. Toward these Wild Bill cast many a stealthy glance, but he did not see the red-haired Texan there.

CHAPTER VII.
The Outlaw's Love.

Willie Pond was much surprised when he found that his ride only extended to a small but pretty cottage just on the outskirts of the town, where the young Texan, introducing him to Miss Neidic as his temporary hostess, left him while he took the horses to a safe place of concealment not far away.

Miss Neidic took her new visitor into the rear sitting-room and, while giving him a cordial welcome and passing the usual salutations, scanned him with a keen and critical eye. The impression left must have been rather favorable, for the lady seemed to feel none of the embarrassment usual when strangers hold a first interview, but talked on as easily and naturally as if she had known him half a lifetime.

"How long have you been in town, Mr. Pond?" was one of her many questions.

"Only a day. I arrived on the express, westward bound, which passed this morning," was the answer.

"Why, that was the same train the desperado, Wild Bill came on."

"Yes, he was pointed out to me by the conductor. But why do you call him a desperado?"

"Because that is his character."

"I thought none but outlaws were called desperadoes."

"There is where the mistake comes in. Most outlaws are desperadoes, but a man can be a desperado, and yet not an *outlaw*. If to be always ready to shoot for a look or a word—whether his opponent is ready or not—is not being a desperado, I do not know what is. But excuse me. He may be a friend of yours."

"Oh, no," said Pond, with some confusion in his manner. "But a very dear friend of mine married him not long since, and for *her* sake I feel a sort of interest in the man. I fancied that he was rather wild when under the influence of liquor, but for all, a brave and generous man, when truly himself."

"Brave, as brutes are, when he feels he has the power to *kill* in his hands; but generous? *Never!*" said Miss Neidic.

"You are his enemy."

"No; for he has never done me, personally, an injury; but he *has* injured friends of mine—sent more than one down to untimely graves."

"There, I said it—you are his enemy, because of what he has done to your friends."

"I am *not* his friend, nor do I wish to be the friend of such a man. But the enmity of a woman is nothing to him. He looks for friends among such men as he now consorts with—California Joe, Sam Chichester, and that crowd. I know but one real gentleman in the party, and that one is Jack Crawford."

"I know none of them."

"You lose nothing, then, for it is little honor one gains by such acquaintances. They suit Wild Bill, for they drink, gamble, and shoot on little cause; they are ready for any adventure, never stopping to count risks or look back when evil is commenced or ruin wrought, no matter what may be its nature."

The entrance of the young Texan now caused a change in the topic of conversation.

"I have learned when that party starts," he said. "They are making their final preparations to-night, and will break camp in the morning early enough to make Twenty-mile Creek for their first night's halt—probably about ten o'clock."

"Do you propose to go ahead of them?" asked Pond.

"No; it will be more easy and safe to follow their trail. They will not have over fifty animals all told, and there will be lots of feed left for us, even if we keep close by. And we can get as much game as we need any time, for we can use but little. One pack-horse will carry all our stuff and still be able to travel at speed, if need be."

"You understand it better than I," said Pond. "Arrange things to suit yourself, and I will conform to your plans."

"All right. You had better turn in early, so as to get a good rest. For after we are out, long rides and night-watches will tell on you, for you are not used to them."

"I will show you to a chamber. Your valise is already in it," said Miss Neidic.

Mr. Pond followed her, and the Texan was left alone to his thoughts, which he carelessly expressed aloud.

"So far all works well," he said. "Mr. Willie Pond is as soft as mush; but I've read him through and through. He wouldn't go with me if he didn't think he'd have a chance to serve Wild Bill, for, though he shuns Bill, he thinks more of Bill than he would have me think. I'll bet Addie has found that out."

"Found out what?" said the lady herself, who had returned so noiselessly that Jack had not heard her.

"That Mr. Pond, as he calls himself, is a friend of Wild Bill's."

"All of that, and maybe something more, as you may find out before you are through your trip."

"What do you mean?"

"Nothing but this—keep your eyes open, and study your Mr. Pond closely."

"There is nothing dangerous about him?"

Miss Neidic laughed heartily.

"Nothing very dangerous to *you*, at any rate," she said; "but if they all go in the morning, we must see Persimmon Bill to-night."

"That is so. Shall I bring the horses round?"

"No. We might be overheard. I will go to the stables. Get the horses ready. I have some things to put up for Bill, and I will come as soon as I pack them in a pair of saddle-bags."

Jack now left for the stable, and Miss Neidic, with a woman's forethought, began to gather up many little things which might be useful to her outlaw lover, who had little chance to procure articles of comfort, not to speak of luxury, except when on some raid in the settlements.

In ten minutes she was ready and on her way to the stables.

Jack had her own favorite horse saddled, while for himself he chose the Black Hawk beauty.

In a few seconds both were mounted, and in the darkness they sped away over the same route which Jack had taken when he went to visit Persimmon Bill.

Little was said as they rode on, for the horses were kept at a swift gallop, and before the hour was up they had approached the ravine as near as they deemed safe before giving the signal.

Scarcely was it given before it was answered, and a second later Persimmon Bill himself was by the side of Addie Neidic's horse, and she was pressed to the outlaw's bosom with a fervor that showed he had a heart more than half-human left in his breast.

"It's kind of you, Addie, to come out here in the chill of the night to see a wild cuss like me, outlawed by man, and forsaken by Heaven!"

"It's safer to come by night than by day, for you and for me, Bill," she said. "And I couldn't bear you should go away again till I had seen you. And I've brought you a lot of things I know you'll need."

"I shall not need much of anything, Addie, on the trail I'm soon to take. Your friend here I know is safe, or I wouldn't say so much. But the truth is, the reds are going to rise in a body all over the north and northwest, and we'll sweep the Black Hills, and clean out every 'blue-coat' that is sent to check the rising. The Sioux have made me a big chief, and I'll have my hands full. If you hear of the 'White Elk,' as second only to Sitting Bull himself, you'll know who it is."

"You, of course!"

"Yes, Addie; that is the name they have given me. And if the Sioux fight as I think they will, and all the northern tribes join, we'll force a treaty that will give us all the Black Hills and the Yellowstone, Powder River, and Big Horn Country for ourselves forever. Then, my girl, and not till then, can I make a safe home for you, and not till then will I ask you to be my wife. For then the outlaw will be safe, and can live in peace, and look for days of home and happiness."

"Bill, when you ask it, be it in peace or war, I am yours. You are brave as the bravest, and had you never been treated wrongfully, would not now be a hunted outlaw. I love you, and you know it."

"Yes, Addie, and I love you too well to ask you to share my lot till I can see some sunshine. But this stranger has news for me."

Persimmon Bill turned to the Texan, who had drawn his horse away a little, so as not to intrude on the conversation between the lovers.

"I have the news you asked for," said Jack. "The party, all told, who will start at nine or ten in the morning, and camp twenty miles out to-morrow, number twenty-nine men, all well armed, the most of them with repeating rifles and six-shooters. Half of them are old scouts, the rest are miners, gamblers, and a couple of them are traders. They have fifty animals, saddle and pack, and carry no wagons. The mules are loaded pretty heavy, at least them that belong to the traders, and are well worth capture."

"All right. And there is one of the party you don't want hurt until he is in your hands?"

"Yes, that man is Wild Bill. I want him in my power, so that I may see him die slowly, surely, awfully!"

"There is another man in that party, Bill, who mustn't be hurt. He did me a kindness once, down at Cheyenne—saved me from insult and wrong. His name is Crawford—Captain Jack, they call him."

"Yes, I know him. No harm shall befall him, if I can help it."

"Thank you, Bill; you needn't be jealous of him, for it is only what he did that makes me ask a favor for him."

"I know it, Addie."

"No woman on earth can make me jealous of you. I've too much confidence in your truth and love. But you'll not attack the party anywhere near here?"

"No, not till they are far beyond all the military posts. I want no pursuit when I do my work. Our animals are in good order for the war-path now, and I want to keep them so. I'm drilling my braves at every chance, so as to fit them to meet such men as Crook, Custer, and Carr. All they want is drill and discipline to make them the best soldiers in the world, and they're coming into it finely."

"Well, you were a soldier yourself long enough to know all that should be done."

"A soldier too long, girl—too long a slave to men who held authority only to abuse it," said Bill, in a bitter tone. "The cruelty exercised on me then turned my best blood to gall, and made me what I am. I hate the name, and my blood boils beyond all restraint when my eye falls upon a uniform. Rightly have the Sioux called me the 'Soldier Killer,' for never do I let one who wears the button escape if he comes within my reach. But you must not stay too long. Good-night—I will not say good-by, for we will meet again."

"Good-night Bill."

"One word to your friend here," added the outlaw. "Follow the trail of Chichester, about three hours back, whenever he moves. I will probably, for three or four days, be about as far behind you. On the night of the third or fourth day out, or, if it is bad weather for travel, a day or two later, I will surround you, and take you and your friend prisoners, to all appearances. But of course no harm will come to you, and you will be free when the other work is done. Then I will close up and wipe out Chichester's gang, saving the two who are to be spared. Then I will be ready for the war-path, for I need the arms and ammunition these people have to finish arming the drilled marines who are specially under me."

"All right, sir; we understand each other," said the Texan, wheeling his horse to take the back trail.

Addie Neidic, as if from some uncontrollable reason, turned once more toward her lover, and bending from her saddle, threw her arms about his tall and splendid form, and kissed him again and again with passionate tenderness.

"Do be careful of your life, dear Bill," she said. "You are all in all to me. If you perish, life will be valueless to me."

"Addie, I'll try to live for your sake, and work my uttermost to achieve what will give you and me peace and quiet in the end. Good-night, once more—good-night, my beautiful, my own."

"Good night, Bill—God bless you!" she sobbed, as she turned her horse and followed the Texan at a gallop.

CHAPTER VIII.
Foiled by a Woman.

It was their last night in town before breaking up camp, and the Black Hillers, as they already called themselves, under Chichester, were determined to have a lively time of it.

They commenced "wetting up," or pouring down liquid lightning in camp, but, being reminded that what they used there would be missed on their journey, they started to skin the saloons in town, and finish out their spree where it would not diminish their own stores.

As Wild Bill said, they were going where money would be of little account, if all the stories about the gold to be found were true; so what they spent now they wouldn't have to carry. And they went in, as such reckless men generally do, spending their money as freely as they could, and drinking with a "looseness" that promised headaches on the morrow, if nothing more.

Wild Bill went in on the spree with a rush, as if he wished to drown the remembrance of his late fright, and despite the cautions of his friend, Captain Jack, who strove hard to keep him within bounds.

California Joe of course was in his element, and in a little while all the party became so turbulent that Crawford left them in disgust. For, as Addie Neidic had said of him, despite his associations, he was a gentleman.

By midnight every saloon had been visited, and many of them pretty well cleaned out, and now Bill proposed to go and break a faro bank that some of the party spoke of.

"I have seven hundred dollars left out of a thousand my woman gave me before I started," said he. "I'll lose that, or break the bank; see if I don't."

All of the party who were sober enough went with Bill, and soon he was before the green board.

Without even waiting to get the run of the game, he planked a hundred dollars on the king, and lost. Without a word, he put two hundred dollars more on the same card, and won. He left the four hundred down, and in another turn he had eight hundred.

"Luck is with me, boys!" he shouted. "I'll break the bank! Let her swing for the king once more, Mr. Dealer!"

To the wonder of all, though it was the last turn of the cards, the king won, and Wild Bill picked up sixteen hundred dollars.

His friends now urged him to quit, but the demon of the game had entered his soul, and he swore, with a terrible oath, that he would play till he broke the bank, or was broke himself.

A new pack was now put in the box, and once more the dealer cried out:

"Make your bets, gentlemen—make your bets! The game is ready!"

Bill, with a reckless bravado, as much of rum as of his own nature, again laid all his winnings on one card—this time the queen. And with wonderful luck—it could be nothing else—he again doubled his pile, this time his gains being thirty-two hundred dollars.

"Stop now, Bill!" cried California Joe. "This can't last!"

"It shall last! The bank can't stand more than two more such pulls!" shouted Bill, wildly.

And again on the same card he staked his entire winnings.

The dealer and banker were one; he turned pale, but when all bets were down, he pulled his cards without a tremor in his hand. But a groan broke from his lips as the queen once more came out on the winning side.

Once more Bill's stakes were doubled, and this time he changed his card.

The banker hesitated. His capital would hardly cover the pile if Bill won again.

"Keep on," whispered a voice in his ear; "if he breaks you; I'll stake your bank."

The banker looked up and saw, though she was disguised in male attire, a face he well knew. It was that of Addie Neidic, and he knew she was able to keep her word.

Wild Bill had heard the whisper, and his face was white with rage, for he thought the bank would succumb before it would risk another chance with his wonderful luck.

But he let his money lay where he put it, and cried out to the banker to go on with his game if he dared.

The latter, with firm set lips, cried out: "Game ready, gentlemen—game ready."

The cards were drawn, and once more Wild Bill had won.

Coolly, as if money was no more than waste paper, Bill gathered up the pile, and began to thrust it away in his pockets, when the disguised woman, Addie Neidic, thrust a roll of thousand-dollar notes into the hands of the banker, and cried out: "This bank is good for fifty thousand dollars. Let no braggart go away and say he has bluffed the bank, till he breaks it!"

Wild Bill trembled from head to foot.

"I know you!" he hissed. "You are the woman who bluffed me at the livery-stable. I'll win your fifty thousand dollars, and then blow the top of any man's head off who'll take your part!"

"Play, don't boast; put up your money!" was the scornful reply.

In an instant Bill put every dollar he had won, every cent he had in the world, and a gold watch on top of that, on the Jack.

Not another man around the table made a bet. A pin could have been heard, had it fallen to the floor, so complete was the silence.

The banker cried out, "Game ready," and slowly drew the cards.

"Jack loses!" he cried, a second after, and Bill's pile, watch and all, was raked in.

"Devil! woman or not, you shall die for this!" he shouted, and his hand went to his belt.

But even as his hand touched his pistol, he heard that fearful whisper, "sister," and saw a white face, wreathed in auburn hair rise over Addie Neidic's shoulder, and with a groan, or a groaning cry of terror, he fell back insensible to the floor.

CHAPTER IX.
The Ghost Again Appears.

When Wild Bill fell, the banker declared his game closed for the night; and while Bill's friends gathered about him and sought to bring him to, the woman, Addie Neidic, took up her money and left by the rear entrance, and the banker, with two or three of his friends, escorted her home, fearing Bill and his gang might annoy her, if the latter came to before she reached her residence.

The auburn-haired Texan did not go with her, but with a slouched hat drawn over his head, and a Mexican blanket over his shoulders, stood back in a corner, unobserved, to hear Bill's words when he came to, and to see what next would appear on the desperado's programme.

"That ghost again! He came to break my luck."

These were the first words that Wild Bill spoke, when recovering his consciousness; he glared out upon the crowd with bloodshot eyes.

"It was a woman who broke your luck. Addie Neidic backed the bank, or 'twould have given in," cried another.

"Who is Addie Neidic?" asked Bill, with a wondering gaze. "Oh! I remember—the woman who called me a coward over at the livery-stable. Who is she? Where does she live?"

"In a cottage west of town. They say she's rich! Let's go and clean out her crib!" cried a ruffian who did not belong to Bill's party, but most likely held some spite against Miss Neidic.

"Ay! That's the word! Let's clean out the house and set fire to it!" cried another, a chum of the first speaker.

It required but a leader now to set the vile work going. And Wild Bill, gradually recovering his reason, but mad with drink, and just realizing that every dollar he had, and even his watch was gone, was just the man for such a leader.

"I'll go! Show me the house, and we'll teach her to wear her own clothes, and let men's games alone!" shouted Wild Bill.

In a moment fifty men were ready to go; but first they made an onslaught on the wines and liquors on the sideboard of the gambling-room.

While they were madly pouring these down, the auburn-haired Texan slipped from the room, and ran swiftly to the cottage of his fair friend.

"Addie," he cried, as she opened the door to his signal, "Wild Bill and a crowd of full fifty men are coming here to rob you and burn your house. They are mad with drink, and even if the stranger up stairs will fight, we three can hardly hold them at bay, no matter how well we are armed."

"We will not try it!" said Addie, calmly. "I had about made up my mind to go with Persimmon Bill. He loves me so well that I ought to be able and willing to bear hardship for his sake. I care little for the house and furniture, though they are mine, and cost me a large sum. I have money and jewelry that we can carry off. I will rouse my two servants while you call your friend, and we will all be out of the house before they come. No one but you knows where your horses are kept. Let that be the place of rendezvous, and before daylight we will be safe with my lover."

"No; I do not want to be with him yet, Addie. I will take this newly found friend and see you safely in reach of Bill, but we will make camp elsewhere till Bill's party starts. Then we'll be on his trail, and you on ours, as it was agreed upon."

"As you like, Jack. But we must hurry."

"All right—as soon as I bring my friend down, do you go with him and your servants to the stable, carrying off what you can. Leave me here, for I want to give Wild Bill one more good scare."

"As you please, but be careful he don't kill you while you scare him. Ah! I hear their yells. We must be quick."

Willie Pond had a white, scared face when he came from his chamber, for while the Texan told him of the danger, the yells and shouts of the drunken ruffians who were approaching could be plainly heard. It seemed as if a gang of demons from the lower regions had been let loose on earth.

"Come with me," cried Addie Neidic, as Mr. Pond came down with his valise in hand. "Be quick, or there will be murder under this roof."

Pond, seemingly dazed and bewildered, obeyed, and out by a rear door hastened the fair owner of the doomed house, with her maid, and man-servant, and Willie Pond, while the Texan, telling them he soon would follow, remained.

Plainly now the shouts and vile threats of the drunken marauders came to the ears of the single listener.

"I wish I had a barrel or two of gunpowder here," he muttered. "I'd make them sing another tune."

Nearer and nearer they came, and now the Texan extinguished every light but one, which he shaded with his hat. Then he looked to the front door and windows, and saw that they were all barred, except a single shutter, which he left so he could open it.

A minute later, and the tramp of a hundred hurrying feet came loudly on his ear. Then shouts: "Clean her out. Kill her and burn her crib!"

In a minute the crowd brought up before the closed doors.

"Open your doors, woman, or we'll shatter them!" cried Wild Bill.

"Open, or down goes everything!" shouted the crowd.

"Here, Bill; here is a shutter loose!" cried one.

Wild Bill sprang toward it, and as he did so the shutter flew open; he saw a white face surrounded by auburn hair; he heard one gasping cry—"*sister*"—and he fell back in terror, crying out: "The ghost! the ghost!"

But some one fired a shot, the light went out, and all was dark where the light had been.

Bill recovered from his shock almost as soon as he felt it, and joined with the shout:

"Down with the doors! Down with the doors."

The crash that followed told that the frail obstacles had given way, and Bill cried out: "In and clean the crib out. Ghost or no ghost, give us light, and clean the crib out!"

Cheer after cheer told that the house was entered, and a minute later, torches made from splintered doors and shutters blazed in a dozen hands as the ruffians ran to and fro in search of plunder.

"The ghost. Find the ghost, or the woman!" yelled Bill.

CHAPTER X.

A Mystery.

The excited and ruffianly crowd dashed to and fro, overturning the furniture, tearing aside curtains, and looking for plunder, but unable to find anything of value, beyond the furniture, or to see a single living person under the roof. Not a dollar in money, not a piece of plate rewarded their search.

"Fire the crib! fire the crib!" came from fifty throats, and almost as soon as spoken, the act was consummated.

Wild Bill, angered to find no one on whom to vent his wrath or slake his thirst for revenge, looked on the blaze as it rose with gloomy satisfaction, muttering that he only wished the witch of a woman was burning in it.

The crowd increased as the flames rose higher and higher, but no one tried to check them, and soon it was but a smoldering mass of ruins where the pretty cottage had stood.

But the late occupant, unharmed, was a mile away, and, having just paid off and discharged her faithful servants, was on the point of mounting to ride off with the Texan and Mr. Pond when the last shout of the dispersing crowd reached her ears.

She smiled when she heard it, and said: "I can afford all the harm they have done. I led but a lonesome life there. I feel that the change I am about to make will be for the better."

The three, with two loaded horses besides those they rode, now moved quietly but swiftly out of the suburbs of the town, where the horses had been stabled, and with the Texan leading the way, steered to the westward, having no compass but the stars.

For an hour the three rode on, and then, pointing to some timber ahead, the Texan said: "Addie, there is where you will find him whom you seek. Tell him I have not altered any of my plans, and that I shall lay in camp to-morrow at Lone-tree Spring, an hour's gallop south of the Twenty-mile Creek. The next morning I will follow the trail we spoke of. And now, Addie, good-by, and don't forget me."

"You know I will not. I hope yet to see you happy, and to be happier than I am now. We shall meet again, perhaps, Mr. Pond, but good-night for now."

And while the Texan and Mr. Pond remained still on their horses, she rode on, leading one pack-horse, toward a growth of trees seen dimly ahead.

The Texan remained where he was until he heard her give the signal and receive an answer, and then turning to Pond, he said: "She is safe; we may as well move on. We have a long ride to where I intend to camp."

"All right," said the other. "This night's work seems almost like a dream. I can hardly realize that Wild Bill would lead such a disgraceful crowd of ruffians and do such a dastardly act as to burn a woman out of house and home."

"Rum takes all the man out of those who use it," said the Texan. "I use it myself sometimes, I know, but it is when I feel as if I was all giving out, and couldn't go through what was before me. And I feel abashed when I think I need such a stimulant to fire up my flagging nature."

Pond made no reply, but rode on thoughtfully at the rapid pace which the other led, the pack-animal keeping close in the rear. At last he asked:"Who did Miss Niedic expect to meet where we left her?"

"A brave man who loves her dearly, but who has been driven in his desperation by cruel injustice to do some work which keeps him outside of towns and settlements for the present. His love is returned by her, and henceforth she will share his dangers and his hardships."

"None can tell but those who test it, how deeply, how entirely, and how lasting a true woman loves," said Pond, with a sigh.

"And none but a woman wronged can tell how bitterly she can hate!" said the other, as he dashed his spurs into his horse and galloped on.

Miles were swiftly passed over, and the gray of dawn was just beginning to soften night's darkness in the east, when the Texan exclaimed:"Here we are; now for a rest of one day, at least."

And as he spoke he drew up his horse by the side of a small pool of water, which trickled out from under the roots of a single large tree. For an acre or so around it there were bushes growing as high as the horses, but when light came, no other growth but that of short buffalo grass and prickly cactus could be seen.

The Texan unsaddled his horse and unloaded the pack animal before Pond could get his saddle ungirthed. Then the Texan sprang to his assistance, finished stripping the horse, and with a long lariat picketed it out in the best grass. His own horses he turned loose, saying they never would stray from camp.

Then, taking his rifle, he stepped out from camp, saying he was going after meat.

In fifteen or twenty minutes, Pond heard the crack of his rifle, and in less than half an hour the young man was back, with the fat saddle of a young antelope on his shoulder.

"Here is meat enough for to-day and to-morrow," he said. "Next day we will be on buffalo ground, and we'll have some hump ribs to roast."

Gathering a few dry, light sticks, he soon had a hot and almost smokeless fire ablaze. On the coals of this he set his coffee-pot, broiled some meat, and while Mr. Pond looked on in surprise, he quickly had a nice breakfast of antelope steak, coffee, and a few hard biscuits which were in the pack.

While Pond took hold and ate heartily, praising the food by his actions as much as his words, the Texan ate lightly, yet all that he wanted—not touching the bread, but using meat entirely.

"There'll be the more left for you," said he, when Pond noticed that he ate no bread. "I never care for anything but meat on the plains. It gives bone and muscle, and that is what we need here. The more simple the food, the better the health. We use ourselves to salt, but we would be just as well off without it. Eat hearty, and take a good nap. We have nothing to do to-day. The party whose trail will be our guide to the 'Hills' will not start till late. We shall not move until to-morrow morning, and then I'll show you the coals of the camp-fire which they'll light to-night. There will be no need for any shelter but this tree overhead. Everything looks clean and dry skyward—there's no better camping ground than this for a couple on the plains. The water is good, feed plenty, and we don't require much fire this time of year."

Pond, tired and sleepy, was only too glad to take the Texan's advice, so he spread his blanket, lay down, and soon was in the land of dreams.

Meantime the Texan, with a small field-glass in his hand, mounted the tree, and, from a perch on its uppermost limbs, scanned the prairie in all directions, but most often in the direction from which they had come.

Nothing was in sight but wild game, scattered here and there, and he soon came down and prepared to take a rest on his own account.

"They'll not pass till afternoon," he muttered, "and I may as well rest a few hours while I can in peace and safety."

He took a long and curious look at the form of his sleeping traveling companion, and a strange smile flitted over his face, as he muttered:"A mystery, but I can solve it."

CHAPTER XI.
In the Wilds.

If ever a man was astonished, when he responded to that after-midnight signal at the mouth of Dead Man's Hollow, it was the outlaw Persimmon Bill. He came from his place of concealment expecting to meet the Texan with news, and found instead Addie Neidic, and with her, on a pack horse, all the wealth and apparel she had in the world.

"Addie, love, what does this mean?" he cried, as she sprang from the horse and threw herself into his arms.

"It means this, Bill. I have come to stay with you, go where you go, live as you live, and die where you die!"

"Addie, dearest, did I not tell you to wait till I could give you a home in peace and quietness!"

"Yes, Bill, but there were those that would not let me wait. To-night, had it not been for my Texan friend, most likely I would have been murdered by a mob of drunken ruffians led on by Wild Bill. Warned in time, I escaped with all that I had worth saving, except my house and furniture. Those they burned; I saw the blaze from my stable, where I went to get my horses to come to you."

"By all that's fiendish, this is more than I can bear! I'll ride in with my Sioux and burn the cursed town!"

"No, Bill; for my sake, keep cool and hear me. I am glad it is done. I was wretched and lonely there—how lonely no words may tell. I was in constant anxiety on your account. I trembled daily, hourly, lest I should hear of your death or capture. Now I shall be with you, know of your safety, or if you are in peril, share the danger with you."

"But, Addie, you can never endure the privations and the fatigue of such a life as I must lead at present. Soon I must be on a bloody war-path. We will have regular troops to meet, great battles to fight."

"And it will be my glory and pride to be with you in all your perils—to show your red allies what a pale-faced woman dares and can do for him whom she loves."

"Dearest, I see not how it can be helped. But I grieve to see you suffer."

"Do not grieve, my love, while my face is bright with smiles. Do not let your heart be heavy while mine is full of joy. Think but this—I am thine until death. We will never part while life thrills our veins. Your triumphs shall be mine; I will glory in your courage, and in your enterprise. I have arms and well know their use. No warrior in all your following can ride better than I. That I am fearless I really believe, for twice inside of ten hours have I defied Wild Bill in his anger, and laughed when his hand was on his pistol. But take me to your camp. I am tired, and the night air is chilly; and take care of the pack horse. My silver and over one hundred thousand dollars in money is on his back, and what clothing I shall need for a time."

"You bring a rich dowry, Addie, but your love is worth more than all the treasures the world could show. Come, darling, I will take you as the most precious gift a wild, bad man ever received."

"You are not bad, Bill. You are my hero and my love!"

Bill could only press his answer on her lips, and then with the bridle of her horses in his hand, and her arm linked in his, he walked back up the winding bed of the ravine for near a quarter of a mile.

Then he emerged into an open space where there were full a hundred Indian ponies staked out, with their owners lying in groups about near small smoldering camp-fires. A few only were on guard, and these on seeing their white chief appear paid no apparent attention to the companion, though they doubtless saw her. It is the Indian's nature to be stoical, and never to manifest surprise, no matter what occurs.

Inside the line where the ponies were staked was a small brush house, and in front of this Bill halted with his led horses, with his own hands unsaddled one and unpacked the other, leaving packs and saddles in front of the house.

Well he knew they were as safe there as they would have been behind bolts and bars in the settlements—even more safe.

"Come in, my love," he said. "The Sioux will care for the horses. Come in and receive the best a fond heart can give in the way of shelter and comfort."

"It is all I ask," she murmured, as with him she entered the "Outlaw's Home."

CHAPTER XII.

On the Trail.

It was high noon when the young Texan woke up, and when he rose Pond still lay sleeping. The former laughed lightly, as he rose and bathed his face in the limpid water, for the beard of the sleeper had got all awry, showing that it was false.

"No need for a disguise here," said the Texan. "But let him keep it up. When the time comes I'll read him a lesson."

Cutting some antelope steaks, the Texan built up a smokeless fire, and had them nicely broiled when Willie Pond woke up.

"Mercy! How I have slept!" he said, as he looked at the sun, already fast declining toward the west.

"You are not used to passing sleepless nights," said the Texan. "When we are fairly launched into the Indian country you may not sleep so sound. Take hold and eat. A hearty eater on the plains generally stands travel best. To-morrow, it is likely, we'll have a fifty-mile ride or more, if those Black Hillers get sobered down to their work. They'll do well if they make their twenty to-day."

Pond went and bathed his face and hands in the limpid water before eating, and as he expressed it, "rubbed the sleep" out of his eyes; then he went at the toothsome steak with appetite not at all impaired by the pure open air he was breathing.

The meal, taken with comfort and deliberation, occupied a half hour or more, and as there were no dishes to wash, "clearing up things" only consisting in tossing the bones out of the way, wiping their knives on a bunch of grass, scouring them with a plunge or two in the dry sand, they were all ready for next meal-time.

"Your horse hears something, so does mine," said the Texan, pointing to the animals, which suddenly stopped feeding, and with their ears pricked forward, looked off to the east-ward.

"I can see nothing. What can alarm them?" said Pond.

"They hear the tramp of the Black Hills party, I think. Horses have far better hearing than we have, and will feel a jar of the ground that would not attract our attention. I want no better sentinel than my mustang, and your Black Hawk seems to take to the watch by instinct. I will go up on my look-out post and see if anything is in sight."

Slinging the strap of his field-glass over his shoulder, the Texan hurriedly climbed up the tree. Seated among the topmost limbs, he adjusted his glass and looked away to the north-east.

"There they are!" he cried.

"Who? What?" exclaimed Pond, rather nervously.

"The Black Hillers, straggling along mighty careless. Their route covers half a mile in length; when in good marching order it should not cover a hundred yards, with scouts in the rear, front, and on both flanks, at twice the distance. That is the way we travel in Texas."

"Wild Bill has been a scout so long I should think he would know all about it," said Pond.

"A heap them scouts know who travel with Uncle Sam's troops!" said the Texan, in a tone of contempt. "Let them ride with a gang of Texan Rangers a few months and they'd learn something. Your troops can't move, or stop to water, without sounding their bugles to tell the Indians where they are. In the morning, all day, and at night, it is toot, toot with their infernal horns, and the reds know just where to find 'em. One of our Texan Ranger bands will travel a hundred miles and you'll not hear noise enough to wake a coyote from them all. These Black Hillers travel slow to-day. They're sore-headed from their spree, I reckon."

"They deserve to be. Drunkenness always punishes the drunkard. I have no pity for them."

"Can you see any sign of them from where you stand?" asked the Texan.

Pond looked carefully off in the direction the other pointed, and replied:

"No. They do not even raise dust."

"Then we are safe here from observation. They go too slow to make dust, and they're moving over grass anyway. It will be dark before they reach their camping-ground. But to make the next, which is full fifty miles away, they'll have to start earlier. Ah! what does that mean?"

"What startles you?"

"Nothing startles me, but a couple of men from that party have dashed out from the line at a gallop, and they ride this way."

"Heaven! I hope Bill—Wild Bill—is not one of them!" cried Pond, greatly excited. "Are you sure they are coming here?"

"Riding *this* way does not assume that they're coming here!" said the Texan, coolly. "They may have flanked off to look for some fresh meat. Yes, that is it," he added. "They bear up to the north now; they want to go ahead of the party so as to kill something fresh for supper. Captain Jack kept sober when all the rest were drinking last night, and I'll wager he is one of the hunters, and most likely Sam Chichester is the other. We're safe from observation, Mr. Pond, so don't get nervous. We'll not see Wild Bill to-day."

Pond smiled, but there was a tremor about him that showed he was easy to take alarm and hard to get over it.

The Texan came down from the tree and busied himself in gathering some dry fuel—small sticks which would make a quick hot blaze and little or no smoke. Then he cut off some long thin flakes of antelope flesh from the saddle hanging on the tree, and half cooked, half dried it.

"Meat may be a little unhandy to get in the rear of that straggling band," he said. "If we have a little on hand, it will do no hurt."

"You are thoughtful," said Pond. "I would make a poor manager, I fear, on the plains. I should forget everything until it was needed."

"You are not too old to learn," said the Texan, laughing.

"Excuse my asking the question, but have you long been acquainted with that strange and beautiful woman, Addie Neidic?"

"Not very long, myself. But I had a brother who knew her very well, and loved her almost to madness. She was his true friend, but she did not love him."

"Is he living now?"

"Living? No! If ever you meet Wild Bill—but no, it is *my* secret. Ask me no more about him."

Every word just spoken flew from the Texan's lips like sheets of fire; his eyes flashed and his face flushed, while his form trembled from head to foot.

"Forgive me! I did not mean to wound your feelings!" said Pond, moved by the excitement of the other.

"No matter; I know you didn't. No matter. It will all come right one of these days. I wish my heart was stone!"

Pond was silent, for he saw the Texan's eyes fill with tears, and he seemed to know that nothing which he could say could soften a grief so deeply felt.

The Texan was the first to speak. "Addie Neidic is a strange, but a noble girl," he said. "Her father was a rough sporting man, but her mother was a lady born and bred. The mother lived long enough to educate Addie in her own ways, but she died just as Addie was budding into beauty. Addie met her lover when he was a soldier at Fort Russell, near Cheyenne. After he was driven to desertion by cruelty and injustice, she met him from time to time, and when her father died, leaving her all his fortune, she moved up to Laramie. I think I know now the reason why—she could meet him more often."

"You said that he was an outlaw."

"Yes; when he deserted he killed the two sentinels who were on guard over him, then killed a mounted officer and rode away on his horse. He was hunted for by whole companies as fast as they could be mounted, but he could not be taken. But after that, if a soldier or an officer rode alone a mile or more from the post, he seldom returned, but his body told that Persimmon Bill, the 'Soldier Killer,' as he was called, still lived around. Wild Bill has done bloody work—cruel work in his time, but Persimmon Bill has killed ten men to his one."

"It is strange that an intelligent woman like Addie Neidic should love such a man."

"No—he is both a martyr and a hero in her eyes. A more stately form, a nobler face, never met favor in the eyes of woman. To his foes fierce and relentless, to her he is gentle and kind. She will never meet aught but tenderness at his hands."

"I wish I could have seen him."

"You may yet see him, Mr. Pond. He travels the plains as free as the antelopes which bound from ridge to ridge. Adopted by the Sioux nation, known to them as the 'White Elk,' he has become a great chief, and their young braves follow in his lead with a confidence which makes them better than the soldiers sent to subdue them."

CHAPTER XIII.
The Black Hillers en Route.

The young Texan had judged rightly when he conjectured that it was Sam Chichester and Captain Jack that had ridden out from the straggling column of the Black Hillers, as he saw from his eyrie in the tree.

They had two objects in doing so. The ostensible object was to reach the camping-ground first with some game for supper, but another was to converse, unheard by the others, on the probable dangers of the trip, and means to meet and overcome such dangers.

"There is no doubt the Sioux are on the war-path," said Chichester to Captain Jack, as they rode on side by side.

"None in the world. They've taken a hundred scalps or more already on the Black Hills route. The troops have been ordered to move up the Missouri and Yellowstone, and that will make them worse than ever. We'll be lucky if we get through without a brush. That was a mean thing, the burning out of that Neidic girl last night, wasn't it?"

"Yes, Crawford, and if Persimmon Bill ever comes across Wild Bill, *his goose is cooked!* Mark that. There is not a surer shot, or a deadlier foe on earth than Persimmon Bill. He has defied the whole border for the past three years—ridden right into a military post and shot men down, and got away without a scratch. They say he has been adopted by the Sioux, and if he has, with such backing, he'll do more mischief than ever."

"I don't believe Bill would have injured the woman had he been sober. It was a mean thing to do any way, and I'm sorry any of our party had a hand in it."

"So am I. But look, Jack, you can see tree-tops ahead. That is the timber on Twenty-mile Creek. There we camp. We'll spread a little here, and the one who sees a fat elk first will drop him. We'll keep within sight and hearing of each other, and if one fires the other will close on him."

"All right, Sam."

And the brave young scout, all the better for being ever temperate and steady, gently diverged to the right, while Chichester bore off to the left.

Game in the shape of prairie hens rose right and left as they rode on, and every little while a band of antelopes, taking the alarm, would be seen bounding over the sandy ridges, while an elk farther off, startled by the antelope, would take fright and trot off in style.

The two hunters were now nearing the timber, and they rode more slowly and with greater caution.

Suddenly, as Chichester rose over a small ridge, he came upon a band of a dozen or more noble elk, which trotted swiftly off to the right, where Captain Jack, seeing them coming, had sprung from his horse and crouched low on the ridge.

Chichester saw his movement, and lowered the rifle which he had raised for a flying shot, for he knew by their course the elk would go so close to Crawford that he could take his pick among them and make a sure shot.

The result justified his movement, for the noble animals, seeing only a riderless horse, scented no danger, and kept on until they were within easy pistol-shot of the experienced hunter.

Crack went his rifle, and the largest, fattest elk of the band gave one mighty bound and fell, while the rest bounded away in another course, fully alarmed at the report of a gun so close and its effects so deadly to the leader of the band.

"You've got as nice a bit of meat here as ever was cut up," cried Chichester to Captain Jack, as he came in at a gallop, while Crawford was cutting the throat of the huge elk. "The boys will have enough to choke on when we get to camp."

"I reckon they'll not growl over this," said Jack, laughing. "I never had an easier shot. They came down from your wind, and never saw me till I raised with a bead on this one's heart."

The two hunters had their meat all cut up and in condition for packing to camp when the column came up.

One hour later, just as the sun began to dip beyond the trees on the creek side, the party went into camp, and soon, over huge and carelessly built camp-fires, slices of elk steak and elk ribs were roasting and steaming in a most appetizing way.

The party were hungry, and the hungriest among them were those who had drank the hardest the night before, for till now they had not been able to eat. But the day's travel had worked some of the poison rum out of them, and their empty stomachs craved something good and substantial, and they had it in the fresh, juicy elk meat.

It was a hard and unruly crowd to manage on the start. Chichester found it difficult to get men to act as sentinels, for they mostly declared that there was no danger of Indians and no need to set guards.

Little did they dream that even then, within three hours' ride, or even less, there were enough blood-thirsty Sioux to meet them in fair fight, and defeat them, too.

Only by standing a watch himself and putting Crawford on for the most dangerous hour, that of approaching dawn, did Captain Chichester manage to have his first night's camp properly guarded.

Wild Bill, gloomy and morose, said he didn't "care a cuss" if all the Indians of the Sioux nation pitched upon them. He knew his time was close at hand, and what did it matter to him whether a red wore his scalp at his belt or some white man gloried in having wiped him out.

But the night passed without disturbance, and a very early start was made next morning.

Chichester made the men all fill their canteens with water, and the animals were all led into the stream to drink their fill, for there was a long, dry march to the next camping-ground.

Chichester and Captain Jack both knew the route well, for they had both been over it in one of the first prospecting parties to the "Hills."

CHAPTER XIV.
Pond Seized with Terror.

Nothing of note occurred in the little camp at the Lone-tree Spring that first night. Just before sunset the young Texan and Willie Pond took a gallop of four or five miles to exercise their horses and use themselves to the saddle, and when they came back with freshened appetites, ate heartily, and afterward slept soundly.

The next morning both woke with the sun, and after a hearty meal the pack-horse was loaded, the other animals saddled, and the route taken for the Hills.

A ride of six or seven miles brought them into the trail of the larger party, and at noon, or a little before, the Texan halted on the camping-ground occupied by that party the night before.

The embers of their fires were yet alive, and over them the Texan cooked dinner for himself and companion.

Pointing to the bones and scraps of meat thrown around, the Texan laughed, and said: "They've plenty now, but before they get through they'll be more careful, for if the Indians are thick, game will be hard to get; and I'm thinking they'll find Indians before they're three days out."

"You said the Sioux would be friendly to you?"

"Yes; I have a talisman. Did you not see me put this eagle feather, tipped with crimson, in my hat last night before I rode out?"

"Yes. Is that your talisman?"

"It is. It is from the coronet of a Sioux chief, and was given to me as a safeguard."

"I wish I had one."

"Keep with me and you will not need it."

"Do not fear that I will go far from you. Alone, I should feel utterly lost on these prairies. Where will we camp to-night?"

"Very close to the party that is ahead of us. They will go to a creek and a piece of timber that is fully fifty miles from here. About a mile from where I think they will camp there is a small ravine, in which we will find what grass and water we need. It will be near nightfall when we get there, if we do our best in travel. But if we ride hard, we'll take the longer rest. I do not care to keep too close to them as a general thing, but to-night we can't help it."

Their nooning was short, and taking the precaution to water their horses well, and fill their canteens, they rode forward over the well-defined trail quite swiftly.

Toward night they could see the trail freshened, but nothing was in sight except a distant mark when night fell, which the Texan said was the timber where the party ahead would camp. Just as the sun was setting, smoke was seen to rise in that direction, and the Texan spoke contemptuously of the carelessness which would thus expose a camping-place to those who were yet miles distant.

"If a captain of a ranger band would do such a thing in Texas," he said, "his men would reduce him to the ranks and put one in his place who knew how to be cautious."

"It surely is imprudent. But they are a large party to cook for, and must have large fires," said Pond.

The young Texan laughed scornfully."Let every man make his own fire, make such fires as you have seen me make, and the smoke could not be seen a rifle-shot away," was the answer. "That party will never reach the Hills. Mark that! If Indians are within twenty miles they'll see a smoke like that. But what is it to us? We're safe."

"I am not so selfish as to wish harm to reach them, even if we are safe!" said Pond, testily.

"That is as much as to say that I am selfish. Well, I acknowledge it. I go in for number one. If they can't take ordinary care of themselves, let them suffer."

Willie Pond made no answer, but rode on in silence. Night was now upon them, and all was still except the thud of the galloping hoofs upon the plain.

Suddenly a gleam of fire was seen far ahead. The Texan noted it, and swerved off to the left.

"There is the camp," he said. "I can easily find our resting-place now. I was afraid we would not see their fires until we were right up to the timber. But they are careless with their fire as they are with their smoke. We shall have moonlight in an hour, and in less time we'll be in camp."

He rode on now, more slowly, for the horses were tired, and he seemed to know so well where to go that there was no haste.

The moon was just above the trees when the Texan led the way into a narrow ravine, with heavy timber on either side. Up this, full ten minutes they rode, and then an exclamation of pleased wonder broke from the lips of Willie Pond. For they came out into an open circular plain or area of several acres in extent, covered with rich grass and centered by a bright, mirror-like lake.

"What a lovely spot!" cried Pond. "Who on earth would dream of finding such a paradise inside of gates so dark and rude."

"One who had been here before," said the Texan. "But speak low, for careless as they may be over there in camp, some one might be outside listening."

"Why, it is over a mile away, is it not?"

"Yes, along the line of the wood. But over this cliff, were it crossed, it is not a quarter of that distance."

And the Texan pointed to a rugged tree-crowned cliff on their right.

"I will be careful," said Pond. "My enthusiasm breaks out when I see beautiful things. I can hardly restrain myself."

"We will unsaddle and camp. Our horses are tired, and need food and drink," was all that the Texan said.

And he at once unloaded the pack-horse, and unsaddled his mustang.

Pond, become more handy, now did the same for Black Hawk, who seemed to take quite a fancy to his new master, curving his back proudly under this caressing touch.

"Shall I picket him, as we did at the last camp?" asked Pond, when he had unsaddled his horse.

"No, let him go with mine. They have been together long enough to mate, and they'll feed peaceably in company. Mine will never stray or stampede, and the other will not go off alone."

The simple camp was soon fixed; and as they had cooked meat left, and biscuit, with plenty of water to drink, both agreed that there was no necessity to build any fire.

"The smell of smoke might reach some sharp-nosed scout over there," said the Texan, "for the wind blows that way. We'll eat, and then turn in, for rest will come good to both of us."

The horses plunged off to the water and drank, and then went to cropping the luxuriant grass, while their masters ate their suppers with appetites strengthened by their long and wearying ride.

After they had supped, Willie Pond would, as usual, have enjoyed his dainty cigarette, had not the Texan warned him that tobacco smoke would scent farther than any other, and might be more dangerous in betraying their presence than anything else.

So Mr. Pond had to forego his smoke. He took a blanket, and moving up to a little mossy knoll just under the edge of the cliff, threw himself down to sleep.

The Texan also took his blanket, but he lay down near the saddles and packs.

Pond was so very weary that he soon fell asleep. How long he slept he did not know, but a strange, oppressive dream woke him, and with the moonlight shining full in the valley, while he lay shaded beneath a tree and the overhanging cliff, he saw a sight which froze his very heart with a mortal terror.

The ravine by which he and his companion had entered was filled with mounted Indians, who were riding silently into the little valley.

CHAPTER XV.
Cheated of Their Prey.

Literally dumb with terror, so weak that he could not rise, Pond saw this strange cavalcade moving up toward the little lake, and looked to the spot where the Texan had lain down to see if he had yet taken the alarm.

To his wonder and redoubled alarm, he saw the Texan not alone, but with a white man, dressed in buckskin, by his side, and a woman also, apparently in friendly converse, calmly waiting the Indian advance.

Recognizing at a glance the woman as Addie Neidic, Pond realized that the man must be no other than Persimmon Bill, and that his followers were the blood-thirsty Sioux whom he headed.

"Heaven help me! There is some fearful treachery here. Wild Bill and his companions are lost if they are not warned in time. How can it be done?"

How strangely, as if by intuition, strategy and cunning thought come to some when environed by unlooked-for danger.

Without a moment's hesitation, Pond so arranged his blanket that if glanced at it would appear he was yet sleeping under it, for he left his hat on the stone where his head had been, and his rifle leaning against the tree right over it.

Then, bare-headed, with no weapons but his pistols and knife in his belt, he crept off up the hill-side with the silence and stealth of a scout who had been a life-time in the business. He wondered at himself as he began to scale the mountain-side, not daring to look back, how he could creep up amid those fearful crags so noiselessly, and how he could have got away unseen, when the Texan and those who were with him were not a pistol shot away.

On, on he kept, ever seeking the shadowed spots, where no moonlight could reveal his form, until at last he was on the very crest of the hill. Look-ing down he plainly saw the camp-fires of the Black Hillers below. They were most likely buried in slumber, and, if they had sentinels out, his life would be endangered by a rapid approach. But of this he seemed not to think as he hurried almost recklessly down through thickets, over crags, and along rug-ged gulches.

How he got down he hardly knew, but he was down, and rushing toward the nearest fire, when he heard a stern, short summons close in his front:

"Halt! Who comes there?"

A man, armed with rifle and pistols, stepped from the shadow of a tree, and Pond gasped out: "A friend. A friend come to save all your lives. There are a hun-dred Indians within a mile of you, led by the desperado, Persimmon Bill."

"Who are you?" was the stern inquiry.

"Wild Bill will know me. Take me to him, quick!" was the response.

"To our captain first. Come along!" said the sentinel.

The next moment Willie Pond was in the presence of Sam Chichester and Captain Jack, telling his story.

"It looks like truth, and if it is, the quicker we get out of here the better. If we can get fifteen or twenty miles the start we may keep it," said Chichester.

"He says Wild Bill knows him. Where is Bill?" cried Jack. "Ah, there he comes."

Bill, awakened by hearing his name called, was rising, and now approached the party.

Pond sprang forward, and addressed him hurriedly in whispered tones.

Wild Bill for an instant seemed lost in astonishment, his first exclamation being, "Great Heaven! you here?"

But after he heard the whispered words he only added, addressing Chichester: "Captain, this friend of mine will not lie. We are in danger, and he has risked his life to save us. I want a spare horse for him, and the sooner we get from here, the better for our hair."

With as little noise as possible, the whole party were aroused, and the danger explained. Quickly the animals were saddled, and in less than twenty minutes the camp-ground was all deserted, though more fuel had been purposely heaped on the fires to keep up the appearance of occupation, if scouts should be sent to examine the camp.

"It lacks four hours yet to daylight!" said Chichester to Captain Jack. "We'll get just that much start, for they'll make no attack until just as day begins to break. I know the ways of them red cusses only too well."

"You haven't much the advantage of me in that kind of knowledge, Sam. But if that fellow was anywhere right as to their numbers, and the Sioux are well mounted, they'll bother us yet before we get to the hills, no matter if we do get eighteen or twenty miles the start!"

"We'll give 'em a long race and a tough tussle before they get our hair anyway!" said Chichester. "I wonder who that fellow is? Bill seems to like him right well, for they ride as close as their horses can move together. Bill has supplied him with a hat—he came in bare-headed, you know."

"Yes; he must have had a terrible climb to get over to us. The only wonder is he got away undiscovered."

"He said he left his blanket in a shape to make them think he was sleeping under it."

"He must be an old hand to fool them so nicely."

"He doesn't look like it. He doesn't ride like a scout or a plainsman—he sits his horse too gracefully."

"No matter; one thing is certain. Wild Bill knows him well, trusts him, and they stick as close together as twins."

"Yes. Captain Jack, I wish you'd take the rear and make those packers keep up. There must be no lagging. If a horse or mule fails they must be left. I'll keep the advance going."

Thus the Black Hillers swept on at a gallop, knowing that a merciless fate was theirs if overtaken by the Sioux.

CHAPTER XVI.

The Pursuit.

The young Texan had not dreamed of being followed so soon by Persimmon Bill and his Indians, and he had lain down to sleep as honestly and confidently as Willie Pond, when he dropped down by the saddles and pack.

He was aroused by a touch on his shoulder, when he awoke and was surprised to find Bill and Addie Neidic standing by this side.

"Where are your Indians?" was the first question the Texan asked, as Bill whispered, in a low tone: "I am here. I have followed the trail a little sooner than I thought I would. The Indians are in the ravine waiting for my signal to come in and let their horses feed and rest before we attack. Where is your friend?" continued Bill.

"Sound asleep under that tree up there. He sleeps like a log, and will not wake till I shake him up. I never saw such a sleeper. Yesterday he spent most of the day snoring."

"It is well. There is no use of alarming him before we are ready for work. I will give the signal, and let my warriors file in."

The outlaw waved a blanket in the air, and the Indians silently filed into the valley. At another signal they turned their horses loose to graze, and then gathered in groups out on the plain to take food and rest themselves while their leader conversed with the Texan, who, having seen him before, they knew as his friend.

Meantime, the Texan, motioning Addie Neidic and her lover to take seats on his blanket, conversed with the latter in a low tone on the plan of attack.

"I shall not make it until just as day dawns—for two reasons," said the outlaw. "First, then they will keep the most careless guard; second, when light is coming, we can see how to kill, and how to save the two whose lives are to be spared. We will do the work in a hurry when it is done. I have given my warriors their orders; most of them know Wild Bill and Captain Jack, for both have been on the reservations often when they have been in. For these reds can go where I cannot, and get arms and ammunition where I would not dare apply for them."

"Shall I not make you and Addie some coffee?" asked the Texan. "I can do it without danger, for I have a small alcohol lamp in my pack, which I had to keep for use when I could not get fuel."

"It will be refreshing, indeed, if there is no risk in making it," said Addie Neidic.

"There is none, and I will soon have it made," was the reply.

Shaded from even Indian observation by the blanket he raised on some bushes, the young Texan speedily made a quart cupful of strong coffee, and shared it between the lady and her outlaw lover. It and some cooked meat he had gave them strength, and then all three lay down like the others to rest for an hour or two, the outlaw bidding one of his warriors keep watch, and to wake him when the morning star was seen over the trees in the east.

And little dreaming that their intended victims were far away from their camp, the Indians and their leader took rest preparatory to their deadly work.

When his warrior sentinel awoke him, Persimmon Bill found that the morning star was well up, and it was full time to be moving toward the scene of action.

"You will stay here in the valley, dear Addie, till we come back," he said. "We will steal away quietly, and not wake that sleeping stranger if it can be helped, for he might, in his terror, fire his gun, or in some way give an alarm. Should he wake, hearing firing over there, keep him quiet with persuasion or your revolver until we return, and then—if he is obstreperous, I will quiet him."

"Let me go with you, Bill," she said. "I am not afraid."

"It must not be, dear Addie. There is no need of your being exposed [there,] and it is well to have *him* watched *here*. Our main certainty of complete success is in a surprise. The least alarm may prevent it."

"I will remain then," she said. "And you need not fear for any alarm from him—for I know I can keep him quiet should he wake. I have a keen persuader here, if I have to use it."

And she touched a poniard in her belt, which also contained two good revolvers.

"An outlaw's bride," she added, smiling, "must be prepared to take care of herself."

The Indians now began silently to form their march, as they saw their white leader mount and the young Texan also get his horse. The Black Hawk seemed uneasy that his master was not at hand, and the Texan was obliged to tie him by the side of the horse ridden by Addie Neidic before he would be quiet.

"It is strange that Mr. Pond does not wake with all this noise," said the Texan, as he rode off with Persimmon Bill. "But as I told you, he is the soundest sleeper I ever traveled with."

The Indians now filed away out of the valley as silently as they entered it, for, knowing the close vicinity of the other camp, they were aware how necessary it was to be cautious.

And now Addie Neidic stood alone, while the morning star rose higher and higher, gazing at what she supposed was the sleeping man on the knoll.

The moon had got so far around that she could see his hat, the rifle against the tree, and the outlines of his form, as she believed.

"I will move up and secure his rifle," she thought, after the band had been gone some time. "He might wake, and in his first alarm use it foolishly."

So she moved with a noiseless step within reach of the gun, and the next moment it was in her possession. Then she looked down, to see if he showed signs of waking. To her surprise, she saw no motion as of a breathing form under the blanket. A closer look told her that if a form had been beneath the blanket, or a head under that hat, it was gone. And, feeling with her hand under the blanket, she found it cold; no warm living form had been there for hours.

"He has been alarmed, seen us, and crept away—perhaps is hiding in terror in the brush," she muttered.

She did not even then realize that he might have fled away to alarm the other camp. She did not even understand several shrill yells, which reached her ear from over the hill. She had not been with the Sioux long enough to know their cries. These yells were the signal cries of scouts sent in, who had found a deserted camp. She only wondered, after hearing the yells, that she did not hear firing—the sounds of battle raging.

While she yet wondered, day dawned, finding her standing there by the empty blanket of Willie Pond, holding his rifle, and looking up the hill to see if he would not creep out, now that light had come and the Indians had gone.

A shrill neigh from the black horse called her attention toward the animal, and she saw the Texan riding into the valley on a keen run.

"Where is Bill?" she asked, as she ran to meet the rider, with Pond's blanket, hat, and rifle in her hand.

"Gone at full speed with his warriors on the trail of the Black Hillers, who have been alarmed in some way, and have got at least two hours' start. He sent me back to bring you and Pond along."

"Here is all of Mr. Pond that can be found," said Addie, holding up what she had found. "I went to the nest, the bird had flown, and the nest was cold."

The Texan rode quickly to the spot, and in a moment saw the trail over the ridge made by Pond when he had escaped.

"It was he who gave the alarm—him whom I believed so sleepy!" he muttered. "He must have seen Bill and the Indians when they first came, arranged his blanket and hat as you found it, and crept over the hill. When I cautioned him to keep quiet, I told him how near and in what direction they were. I see it all. Green as I took him to be, he has outwitted us all!"

"It is so. This is his horse—a noble animal, too. We will take that with us."

"Of course; and we must hurry on, for Bill is miles on the trail already. He will be even more surprised than we when he knows how the Black Hillers got warning. I'll not give much for Mr. Pond's hair," said the Texan.

In a few seconds, the horse which Addie had ridden was saddled and ready, and, leaving his pack-horse behind, but leading the Black Hawk, the young Texan, with Addie Neidic by his side, dashed at full speed over the valley, and out of the ravine.

Once out on the open plain, they could see far away to the west a cloud of dust. It was made by the Sioux under the White Elk, who were pushing the horses to their wildest speed on the trail of the fugitives. This trail the Texan and Addie Neidic followed at their utmost speed.

The double trail made by the Black Hillers and the pursuing Indians would have been plain indeed to follow had not the column of dust served as a guide.

With their horses at full speed, and better than the general run of Indian ponies, the Texan and his fair companion gained slowly but surely on the Indians, and within an hour had passed the rear of their column, and were pressing well to the front.

Yet it was noon when they ranged alongside of Persimmon Bill himself and reported the discovery Addie Neidic had made.

"One more scalp ahead of us," was all he said, when he heard the report.

And he pressed on still faster.

CHAPTER XVII.
Unlooked-for Aid.

With their heavily-laden pack-horses, lengthy as their start was, the party under Chichester saw their pursuers plainly in their rear before the day was two-thirds passed, and Captain Jack, hurrying up the rear all he could, sent word to Chichester that the reds were gaining rapidly.

Chichester sent word back to press the rear forward at its utmost speed. He could see timber ahead, and if they could only reach it, they might be able to make a stand. Satisfied, from the report of Willie Pond, that over one hundred well-armed and well-mounted Indians were on his trail, fearful that many of his men would flinch in battle, he dared not, with the few that were true, make a stand on the open plain.

Had all been like Wild Bill, California Joe, and Captain Jack, he would have halted, rested his horses, and given the reds battle rather than fly from even treble his number. But he knew well that a few cowards would weaken the rest, and he wanted to get some shelter before he met such odds.

The timber was yet fully two hours' ride distant, half of the pack-horses had given out and been left, and many of the mounted men complained that they could not keep their horses much longer in the column.

Sam Chichester had been obliged to slacken the pace in front, and the enemy were gaining so fast that the glitter of their arms could be seen even amid the dust-cloud that rose above them.

Suddenly another column of dust was seen, and this appeared to come from the direction of the timber, though south of the route the Black Hillers were taking.

"Men!" muttered Sam Chichester, "there's no use in our running much farther. If that new cloud of dust is made by Indians, all that we can do is to sell our lives as dearly as we can. We will soon know one thing or the other."

"They're not on the line we're taking. They can't be coming for us," said Captain Jack, who had ridden to the front. "They're coming in our flank."

"And night is coming, too," growled California Joe. "If we can keep on for two hours more, we'll have darkness to shield us, for no red will fight in the dark without he attacks, and has camp-fires to light up with."

"We'll keep them on while an animal will move, and when we must, turn and fight for life or vengeance, if we must go under," said Chichester. "Forward, men—forward once more!"

Again Captain Jack took the post of honor, for such indeed was the rear guard in this case. Suddenly, on looking back, he saw that the Indians, instead of gaining, had come to a halt.

"They've given it up! they've given it up!" he cried, sending a messenger forward to Captain Chichester to slacken the speed of the column.

It was now almost sundown, and the men in the column, choked and thirsty, weary beyond expression, could hardly believe the news was true. They were soon satisfied, though, that it was; but it was not for an hour yet, when twilight was beginning to gather, that they learned the real cause of their present safety.

The Indians would have been upon them before night set in, had they not first discovered the nature of the dust cloud to the south-west, or rather who it was raised by. The field-glass of the Texan, even miles and miles away, had detected the flutter of cavalry guidons amid the dust and showed that mounted troops were near enough to come to the aid of the Black Hills men before they could be crushed and their scalps taken.

So, much against his will, Persimmon Bill was obliged to slacken his pace, and soon to turn his course, so, as by a night march, to put his warriors beyond the reach of those who might turn on them.

When night fell, Chichester, joined by two companies of cavalry, bound for the Hills, under orders to join forces already on the way by another route, moved slowly to a camping-ground in the timber, for which he had been heading hours back.

The horses of the troops were weak from scant forage, and the commanding officer did not feel it his duty to wear them out chasing Indians, though he held himself ready to protect the mining party as long as they remained with him.

And they were just too willing to go on with such an escort, even with the loss of all the pack animals left on their trail; and had Persimmon Bill only halted, instead of falling back, he would have found that there was no danger of pursuit.

Chichester and Crawford, when they compared notes and found not a man of their party lost, though half its property was gone, felt satisfied that it was no worse, for at one time it seemed to both that nothing was left to them but to sell their lives as dearly as they could.

In a well-guarded camp all were settled before the moon rose, and never was rest more needed by animals and men.

CHAPTER XVIII.
On the Death-Trail.

Bivouacked on the treeless plain, so far from the old trail and from the timber ahead that they could see no sign of the Black Hillers or the troops, the next morning's sun rose on the band of Sioux led by Persimmon Bill. Used to all kinds of exigencies, the red men did not mind either a lack of food or of water for so short a time. They were only angered with the thought that those whom they had deemed an easy prey had escaped them.

As soon as it was light, Persimmon Bill had the captured pack-horses examined, and it was found that several of them were laden with provisions. Others had ammunition and stores, and on some of them were found kegs of liquor.

These the wary leader at once destroyed, telling his followers that there was no foe so deadly to the red man as this fire-water, and not one drop should pass his lips or theirs. The provisions were at once distributed among them, as also the stores, but the liquor was given to the thirsty sands, where at least it could do no harm.

Then a council was held by the leader with the chiefs and head warriors of the band, and it was decided that it would be foolish to pursue the Black Hills people farther, now that troops were with them, unless a large band of Sioux could be found. For it is not Indian policy to risk battle against odds, or where there is danger of great loss and little gain. To reach water and good hunting-grounds was their first necessity; after that they could consider where next to go. Sitting Bull was rallying all the tribes for war, and the "White Elk" had promised to join him.

Gloomily the young Texan heard all this talk, and at its close, when a decision had been arrived at, he said: "Here we must part. I follow the trail of Wild Bill, if I follow it alone. I had hoped to see him die a slow and cruel death, where I could have heard him plead, and plead in vain for mercy. But that hope is gone, if he reaches the Hills in safety. But he cannot live—he shall not! I have sworn to kill him, and I will! The spirit of him who fell at Abilene cries up from a bloody grave for vengeance, and the cry shall be answered. You have been kind to me, Addie Neidic, and so has he to whom your heart is given. I shall never forget it. But our courses now lie apart—I follow yonder trail, while you go I know not where. We may not meet again—if we do, I shall tell you Wild Bill is dead!"

"Stay with us. I will yet help you to your vengeance," said Persimmon Bill.

"No; it will be too long delayed. I am hot on the death-trail now, and I will not leave it. Fear not for me. I shall hover near them till they reach the Hills, and then I will not wait long to fulfill my work. When the deed is done, if I still think life is precious and his friends press me too hard, I may look for safety, as you have done, with the Sioux."

"Come, and you shall find in me a sister, and in him a brother," cried Addie Niedic.

"A *brother*? I had one once," came a low, sobbing cry from the young Texan's lips; then, with his head bowed and scalding tears rolling down his cheeks, he drove the spurs into his horse, and sped away swiftly in the direction of the old trail.

The Black Hawk horse, saddled and bridled, but riderless, galloped on by the side of the Texan's fleet mustang, with no wish to part from his company.

"He had death in his eye! He will kill Wild Bill, and we shall never see him again," said Persimmon Bill. "The miners are rough, and condemn before they try, and hang as soon as condemnation is spoken. I pity the boy—for he is but a boy."

Addie Neidic smiled."We shall see your boy again," she said. "Something seems to whisper to me that his fate is in some way linked with ours. I, too, feel sure that he will kill Wild Bill and then escape to join us. And you, my hero, will rise till all these Indian nations call you king. How these who follow you look up to you now, obeying every word or sign. And think, on these vast plains, and in the endless range of hills, valleys, and mountains, there must be countless thousands, who want but a daring, skillful leader to make them the best light troops in the world."

"You are ambitious for me, dearest," said Bill, with a strange, sad smile. "I hope to prove worthy of your aspirations. But we must move. I head now for the Big Horn Valley, to meet Sitting Bull."

CHAPTER XIX.
"Save, Oh, Save My Husband!"

"Safe and in port at last, as old Cale Durg used to say, when a scout was over and he was back in garrison."

This was the joyous exclamation of Captain Jack Crawford, as he turned to Sam Chichester, when their party rode into the settlement at the Deadwood Mines in the Black Hills. Escorted nearly all the way by the cavalry they had so providentially met, they had been troubled no more by the Indians, and excepting the loss of some horses, and a part of their "fit-out" and stores, had suffered nothing. Not a man had been hurt, and best of all, they came in sober, for the benzine had all gone with the lost packs, for it was heaviest on the mules, as it would have been on the men, had it not been lost.

"I'm glad the trip is over. My temper never has been more tried," said Chichester. "The most of the men have had their own way, though when we started they promised on honor to obey me as captain. But honor is a scarce article with the majority of them. Now they're here, they'll go it with a looseness."

"You bet," was Crawford's sententious remark. "Wild Bill will be in his element. Look at the signs. Rum, faro, monte, all have a swing here, you can swear."

"Men, into line one minute, and then we part!" shouted Captain Chichester to his party.

For a wonder, with temptation on every side, the weary riders obeyed, and drew up in a straggling line to hear their leader's parting speech.

"Men, I promised to bring you here safely if I could, but to get all of you here that I could, anyway. I've kept my promise, we're here."

"Ay! Three cheers for Sam Chichester!" shouted Wild Bill.

The cheers were given, and Chichester said: "Thank you, boys. Now do me one favor. You are here in a busy place, and I see by the signs that benzine is about as plenty as water. Touch it light, and do behave yourselves, that my name will not be disgraced by any of Sam Chichester's crowd. Every man is his own master now, and must look out for himself. I wish you all good luck, and shall work hard for it myself."

The speech was over, and in a second the line melted away and every man was seeking quarters or pitching into the benzine shops.

Wild Bill would have been the first to go there, had not his companion, Willie Pond, said, in a low tone:"Bill, please get quarters for you and me before you do anything else. You know what you have promised. Remember, if it had not been for me, neither you nor one of this party would ever have got here."

"You're right. But I'm so cussed dry!" muttered Bill. "You're right. I'll find housing for us two before a drop passes my lips."

And Bill rode on to the upper part of the town, as it might be called, where some men were putting up a new shanty, in fact, just putting the finishing touch on it by hanging a door.

"Will you sell that shebang?" asked Bill, of the man who seemed to be the head workman.

"Yes, if we get enough. We can build another. What will you give?"

"These two horses and a century," said Bill, pointing to the animals ridden by himself and companion, and holding up a hundred-dollar bill which Pond had furnished him.

"O.K. The house is yours!" said the man. "Boys, put for timber, and we'll have another up by sunset."

Bill and his companion dismounted, removed their blankets, arms, and saddle-bags into the house, gave up the horses, and were at home. It did not take long to settle there.

Night had fallen on the town of Deadwood, but not the calm which generally comes with night where the laborer is but too glad to greet the hour of rest. Lights flashing through chinks in rude cabins, lights shimmering through canvas walls, songs, shouts, laughter, curses, and drunken yells made the place seem like a pandemonium on earth.

Almost every other structure, either tent, cabin, or more pretentious framed house, was either a saloon or gambling-hall, or both combined. And all these seemed full. The gulches, sinks, and claims that had been the scene of busy labor all the day were now deserted, and the gold just wrenched from the bowels of the earth was scattered on the gambling table, or poured into the drawer of the busy rumseller.

At this same hour, a man rode into the edge of the town on a noble black horse, leading a tired mustang. Both of these animals he staked out in a patch of grass, leaving the saddle on, and the bridles hanging to the saddle-bow of each. Then he placed his rifle against a tree near by, took the old cartridges out of a six-shooter, and put in fresh ones. This done with the greatest deliberation, he pulled his slouch hat well over his face, entered the nearest saloon, threw down a silver dollar, and called for brandy.

A bottle and glass were set before him. He filled the glass to the brim, drank it off, and walked out.

"Here, you red-haired cuss, here!" cried the bar-keeper. "Here's a half comin' to you; we only charge half-price when it goes by wholesale!"

The joke fell useless, for the red-haired man had not remained to hear it.

In the largest hall in the place, a heavy gambling game was going on. There was roulette, faro, and monte, all at different points.

Before the faro-table there was the greatest gathering.

Wild Bill, furnished with money by the person known to us so far as Willie Pond, was "bucking against the bank" with his usual wonderful luck, and the crowd centered around him as a character more noted and better known than any other who had yet come to Deadwood.

"I'll bet my whole pile on the jack!" shouted Wild Bill, who had taken enough strong drink to fit him for anything.

"Do be careful, Bill—do be careful!" said a low, kind voice just behind him.

It was that of Willie Pond.

"Oh, go home and mind your business. I'll break this bank to-night, or die in the trial!" cried Bill, defiantly.

"You'll die before you break it!" shrieked out a shrill, sharp voice, and the red-haired Texan sprang forward with an uplifted bowie knife and lunged with deadly aim at Bill's heart, even as the person we have so long known as Willie Pond shrieked out: "Save, oh, save my husband!"

But another hand clutched the hilt of the descending knife, the hand of a short, thick-set, beetle-browed desperado, who shouted, as he drew a pistol with his other hand: "Wild Bill is *my* game. No one living shall cheat me of my revenge! Look at this scar, Bill—you marked me for *life*, and now I mark you for *death!*"

And even as he spoke, the man fired, and a death-shot pierced Wild Bill's heart.

The latter, who had risen to his feet, staggered toward the Texan, who struggled to free his knife-hand from the clutch of the real assassin, and with a wild laugh, tore the false hair from the Texan's head. As a roll of woman's hair came down in a flood of beauty over *her* shoulders, Bill gasped out: "Jack McCall, I'm thankful to you, even though you've killed me. Wild Bill does not die by the hand of a *woman!*"

A shudder, and all was over, so far as Wild Bill's life went.

His real and true wife wept in silence over his body, while sullen, and for a time silent, the supposed Texan stood and gazed at the dead body.

Then she spoke, addressing McCall: "Villain, you have robbed me of my revenge! For by my hand should that man have fallen. No wrong he could have done you can be more bitter than that which put me on his death-trail, and made me swear to take his life.

"Two years ago a young man left a ranch close to the Rio Grande border with a thousand head of cattle, which had been bought from him, to be paid for when delivered in Abilene, Kansas. He was noble, brave, handsome. He was good and true in all things. He was the only hope of a widowed mother, the very idol of a loving sister, whose life seemed linked with his. He promised when he left those he loved and who so loved him that he would hasten back with the proceeds of the sale, and then, with his mother and sister, he would return to the birthplace of the three, to the old Northern homestead where his father's remains were buried, buy the old estate, and settle down to a quiet and a happy life. Long, anxiously, and prayerfully did that mother and sister wait for his return. Did he come? No; but the soul-blighting news came, which, like a thunderbolt, struck that mother—my mother—dead! Wild and despairing, I heard it—heard *this*.

"The son, the brother, who never used a drop of strong drink in all his life, who never uttered an oath, or raised a hand in unkindness to man or woman, had been murdered—killed without provocation—no chance to defend his life, no warning to prepare for another world—shot down in mere wantonness. There lies the body of him who did it. Do you wonder that, over my dead mother's body, girl though I was, I swore to follow to the death him who killed my brother? It is not my fault that I have not kept my oath. I would have done it had I known that you, his friends, would have torn me limb from limb before his body was cold."

"And served him right!" said an old miner, whose eyes were dimmed with moisture while the Texan girl told her story.

"Where is McCall? His act was murder," cried Sam Chichester.

"He has sloped, but I'll take his trail, and if there is law in Montana he shall hang," said California Joe, who bounded from the house, when it was discovered that the murderer had slipped away in the moment of excitement.

How well California Joe kept his promise, history has already recorded. Followed over many a weary mile of hill and prairie, McCall was finally arrested, tried and convicted, as well by his own boast as the evidence of others, and he was hanged.

But one glance at our heroine, for such the red-haired Texan is. With a look of haughty defiance, she asked: "Have I done aught that requires my detention here?"

"No," said Captain Jack, "thank Heaven you have not. We'd make a poor fist at trying a woman by Lynch law, if you had done what you meant to."

"Then I go, and few will be the white faces I ever see again!" she cried.

The next moment she passed out, and as the crowd followed to see whither she went, she was seen to spring on a coal-black horse which stood unhitched before the door, and on it she rode at wild speed away toward the north-west, while a saddled but unridden mustang followed close behind her.

The course she took led toward the regions where Sitting Bull, in force, awaited the attack of the soldiers then on his trail.

THE END.

Endnotes

IX. **pointing to his $15,000 yearly income, derived from his pen**: The claim of $15,000 varied; often it was inflated to $20,000, although that claim seemed more likely about ten years later. In the post-Civil War years, Judson was writing for several publications, principally for *Street & Smith's New York Weekly*. He was also contributing stories directly to Beadle and Adams, originators and main purveyors of the dime novel, as part of their ten-cent novel series (see Edmund Pearson, *Dime Novels; or, Following an Old Trail in Popular Literature* [Port Washington, N.Y.: Kennikat Press. 1968], 83). In addition, he was writing hunting and fishing stories, travelogues, and articles on other subjects for a variety of other periodicals.

IX. **and one of the world's greatest liars did not come up in conversation**: Biographical details of Judson's life here and throughout are distilled from several sources, most especially from *The Great Rascal: The Life and Adventures of Ned Buntline,* by Jay Monaghan (New York: Bonanza Books, 1951). Monaghan's volume, which offers an extensive bibliography, is a curious blend of fact and supposition, actuality and speculation, a heady mixture of astonishment and admiration, and is heavily based on previously published sources, most especially *The House of Beadle & Adams and Its Dime and Nickel Novels: The Story of a Vanished Literature,* by Albert Johannsen (Norman: University of Oklahoma Press, Volumes 1 & 2, 1950, Volume 3, 1962) and on *Life and Adventures of Ned Buntline,* by Fred E. Pond (New York: The Cadmus Book Shop, 1919). Monaghan also relied on several other studies of period figures, in particular such works as *Wyatt Earp: Frontier Marshal,* by Stuart Lake (New York: Houghton Mifflin, 1931) as well as "The Life and Times of Ned Buntline," by Stewart H. Holbrook, in *Little Annie Oakley and Other Rugged People* (New York: Macmillan, 1948). Monaghan's dependence on these materials resulted in the propagation of a many erroneous statements, apocryphal anecdotes, and complete fabrications. His biography is further flawed by a genteel glossing over or blatant omission of details (often unsavory) about Judson's life, as well as by total ignorance of large time gaps and inexplicable connections in Judson's activities and associations. Pond, Monaghan's principal source, was supposedly a personal friend of Judson's, but his 1919 biography was published some thirty-three years after Judson died. It also is based on a number of Judson's personal testimonies and stories, many of which are outrageous fabrications that should have been apparent to Pond at the time. Lake's biography of Wyatt Earp has also been thoroughly discredited by William B. Shillingberg in his article, "Wyatt Earp and the 'Buntline Special' Myth," *Kansas Historical Quarterly* 42:2 (1976), 113-154; rpt. http://www.kancoll.org/khq/1976/76_2_shillingberg.htm#Ref139. The Holbrook chapter in *Little Annie Oakley and Other Rugged People,* which originally appeared in *The American Mercury* in 1947, is also filled with mistakes in fact and what appear to be almost ridiculous exaggerations about Judson's life, and it cites no available source. The Johannsen volumes were probably also based largely on Pond's account, although there is more effort made to be accurate in verifiable details and to qualify unsubstantiated statements, even though Johannsen acknowledges that the task approaches the impossible. He writes that the details of Judson's life "are so luried and varied . . . that it is impossible to write a fair account of him . . . A three volume biography would be none too large. . . The one biography that has been published [Pond's] is too fragmentary and incomplete, and the various notices in the biographical dictionaries are inaccurate and confusing. Even Judson's own accounts of his adventures are so conflicting that one must believe that he was sometimes amusing himself at his listener's expense" (Johannsen 167). It's noteworthy that Judson apparently kept no diary or journal. "I have little to write about myself," he once said. "I detest autobiography" (quoted in Monaghan, 283). Apparently very little personal correspondence survives—this is remarkable, given his profligacy and constant attention to his personal image. Curiously, also, very little was written about him by contemporary sources other than period newspapers and official documents, or if it was, it has not survived in known forms or locations. Since the 1950s, numerous small pieces have appeared in print and on Internet sites that not only compound the errors and mistakes and falsehoods initiated by Pond, Lake, Monaghan, and others, but which offer imaginative embellishments of their own. Because Judson was prone to exaggerate and enlarge on his own life and experiences so often, even under oath, separating the truth from the fiction in his biography is a frustrating prospect. Given the dearth of reliable and consistent period documentation, it may well be impossible. Allusions to and statements about his life in our present book are drawn from what might be called a "preponderance of the evidence," reconciled and collated for consistency, possibility, probability, and frequency of independent appearance.

X. **while trying (unsuccessfully) to escape a Nashville lynch mob:** Judson's near-death escapade in Nashville is well researched, and none of the particulars is in dispute. For the fullest discussion, see Monaghan,105–109.

X. **he was an unrivaled master:** So full of incredible experience was his youthful life that he felt confident enough in the sensationalism of his experience to write an autobiography, *Ned Buntline's Life-Yarn,* which was published in the *Knickerbocker* when he was only twenty-two.

X. **even the exact place of his birth isn't known for sure:** Over the years, he gave 1820, 1821, 1823, and 1824 as the year of his birth. It's generally accepted that he was born in Stamford, New York, where he eventually settled and which he claimed as home. The most widely credited birth date is May 20, 1823.

X. **and possibly seven wives and, allegedly, a dozen mistresses:** The tale of Judson's several marriages would make a better story than he ever wrote. His first wife, apparently, was Serebrina Martin, a mysterious woman no one seems ever to have met, and who he variously claimed to have met in Cuba or Florida. He installed her in Clarkesville, New York, and used her failing health as an excuse for resigning his naval commission. She died sometime around 1845, possibly in childbirth. In 1847, he lived briefly in New York with Mary Gordon, possibly a poet who wrote as Laura Lovell, whom he brought to the city from Boston and then shortly abandoned. Some sources claim Gordon filed charges of desertion and breach of contract, but no record of such has been discovered. In 1848, he married Annie Abigail Bennett, English-born daughter of a wealthy British immigrant, who provided Judson with funds for his publishing enterprises, especially a revival of his magazine, *Ned Buntline's Own.* Although Judson was accused of keeping as many as six mistresses at the time, including a notorious actress named Nora Jones, Annie was apparently devoted to him. They had one son. Annie finally divorced him on charges of desertion in 1849 while he was serving time in prison for inciting the Astor Place Riot. In 1853, he married Lovanche L. (Kelsey) Swart, widow of the foreman on a yacht, *Buntline's Own,* that he had purloined, quite literally, from under a judge's nose. That same year, Lovanche threw him out and brought charges of bigamy against him, claiming that he was already married to an actress named Josie Juda. He hired eighteen-year-old Eva Gardiner as housekeeper for his hunting cabin, Eagle's Nest, on Eagle Lake, New York, and married her in 1856, although he was still allegedly married to both Josie and definitely married to Lovanche. Eva died in childbirth on March 4, 1860. On November 2, 1860, he married Catherine (Kate) Myers and sent her to Eagle's Nest, hiding her shoes from her so she could not escape the loneliness and isolation of the remote cabin. She soon gave birth to a daughter, Mary Carolitta. In 1863, while on furlough from the army, he fell ill and was wandering the streets of New York when he ran into Lovanche, who took him in and nursed him back to health. They were married again—although they had never been officially divorced—on January 14, 1863 at St. Luke's Episcopal Church on Hudson Street. He departed from Lovanche and went to visit Kate Myers at Chappaqua, New York, where she had just given birth to a second daughter, Irene Elizabeth. When Lovanche heard of it, she turned him in to the army for desertion. While he was in the stockade at Fort Hamilton on charges of desertion, Lovanche brought him writing materials to produce a manuscript for her to sell, and she gave out abroad that Irene Elizabeth was not Judson's child. For a time in this period Lovanche and Kate both occupied the cabin at Eagle's Nest, each claiming that she was Judson's legal wife. What happed to Josie is not recorded.

After his military imprisonment ended and he was, inexplicably, given an honorable discharge, he returned to Kate, but sent Lovanche a Valentine's Day card in February, 1865. Kate gave birth to Edwardina in 1868. In May, 1871, Lovanche filed a complaint of divorce for desertion, but he talked her out of it. In the meantime, he married Anna Fuller, his "Hazel Eye," the daughter of a Stamford, New York, butcher. Kate, hearing of the marriage, divorced him on November 27, and Lovanche again filed divorce papers but agreed to a settlement of $50 per month; she did not obtain a final divorce decree until February 1874. Anna Fuller gave birth to Irene (his second daughter named Irene) in 1878 and to Edward Judson, Jr., in 1881. Lovanche continued to resurface, demanding money and payments she was owed throughout the period until 1881, when she was finally paid off by Street & Smith, Judson's publishers. She later published a letter stating that she and Judson had never been married, but still later, upon the death of Judson's daughter Irene (II), Lovanche wrote to local papers, averring that Judson had never been married to Kate. In addition to these liaisons, Judson was accused of having seduced and sired children by a farmer's daughter in upstate New York, to whom he may or may not have been married. He continued to stay in touch with Mary Porterfield of Nashville, the woman whose husband he shot and killed in 1846 in what may or may not have been in self-defense.

XI. **youngest commissioned midshipman in the U.S. Navy:** The commission was the result of an extraordinary piece of heroism that seems to be authentic, wherein Judson saved a boat's crew from an icy death in New York harbor following an accident (see Monaghan, 53–54).

XI. **the Mosquito Fleet patrolling the Mexican coast:** His experience in combat was, in the main, exaggerated. He apparently led a detail ashore into the Florida swamps in pursuit of Seminoles, whom they may or may not have actually seen. Hunger, thirst, oppressive heat, and hoards of mosquitoes were the chief enemies of the expedition (see Monaghan, 61–63).

XI. **a way with words that could provoke as often as they persuaded:** He apparently read widely as a child, both before and after he began his maritime career. He recalled that his reading *Three Spaniards,* a cheaply produced romance, inflamed his father, who expected him to read for the law. Later he read virtually all of James Fenimore Cooper, Washington Irving, and Sir Walter Scott, as well as Shakespeare and at least some classical literature (Monaghan, 38, 48).

XII. **seldom taking a break until the piece was done:** "I once wrote a book of 610 pages in sixty-two hours," he claimed. "During that time I never ate nor slept. I never lay out plots in advance. I wouldn't know how to do it, for how can I know what my people may take it into their heads to do? First I invent a title. When I hit a good one, I consider the story about half finished. After I begin, I push ahead as fast as I can write, never blotting out anything I have once written and never making a change or modification. If a book does not suit me when I have finished it, I simply throw it into the fire, forget it and start another." This quote appears in various forms in a number of sources, but it's cited most fully in *The Fiction Factory; or, From Pulp Row to Quality Street: The Story of 100 Years of Publishing at Street & Smith,* by Quentin Reynolds (New York, Random House, 1955), 46.

XII. **but only reluctantly spoke or wrote against slavery:** In 1854, he devoted a series of articles to try to separate Abolitionism from nativism as planks of the American or "Know-Nothing Party." He never showed any profound interest in abolishing slavery (Monaghan, 214).

XII. **held suffragists in nearly satiric contempt:** It wasn't until 1880 that Judson added women's suffrage to his list of reform causes, speaking on the topic of "Women in the Parlor and Over the Washtub" at a combined temperance and suffrage rally (Monaghan, 271).

XIII. **once tried to embrace spiritualism:** In 1854, when spiritualism threatened to split the newly formed Republican Party in two, Judson embraced the movement and attended some séances. He soon recanted, though, when he discovered that the spiritualists had no political agenda (Monaghan, 216).

XIII. **inciting a riot in St. Louis:** The Astor Place Riot of May 10, 1849, one of the worst civic disturbances in New York's antebellum history and possibly the only one in U. S. history involving the production of a play, is well chronicled. Monaghan's account of Judson's leadership role in the affair is about as full as anyone's and it jibes almost entirely with other published versions (Monaghan, 171–180). The St. Louis Riot is less well known and Judson's role in it is less well defined. Having to do with an 1851 electoral contest between Whigs and Democrats, confrontations between Irish and German immigrants, and involving the Know-Nothings in some ancillary role, it turned into little more than a street brawl that Judson had some hand in instigating (Monaghan, 200–205).

XIII. **left disgraced and bereft on the streets of Baltimore:** Monaghan, 247.

XIII. **adopted the honorific for the rest of his life:** Judson had actually used the title "Colonel" before. In 1851, billing himself as "Colonel Ned Buntline," he headed a troupe of players, including a singing quartet, and plied the Ohio and Mississippi rivers by boat. Dressed as a Cuban insurrectionist, he lectured on such topics as "Cuba and Her Martyrs," and, costumed as a Seminole chief, spoke on "Wrongs Done the Indians in America." He also lectured on nativism and tried to enlist new dues-paying members in the Patriotic and Benevolent Order of the Sons of America (Monaghan, 196–197). After having his portrait made in 1865, he added the subtitle: "Chief of Scouts" to his billing when he spoke.

XIV. **summer or early fall of 1868:** Why, precisely, Judson went to California or how, exactly, he got there is a matter of conjecture. On May 1, 1868, *The San Francisco Evening Bulletin* ran a front-page story announcing that he would be coming west at his first opportunity and reported that he would be taking a steamer and also had tickets on the Panama Rail Road, but no other details were offered or have survived. Travelling via steamship and railway across the isthmus of Panama was, actually, the most expedient of the three alternatives (overland across the continent, overland across Mexico, or around the southern tip of South America, all harrowing and extremely dangerous), and it was most likely the route he took.

XIV. **and by other ventures:** He may well have gone as far north as Oregon and as far southeast as Yosemite; both are referenced in work he later published.

XIV. **rough-and-tumble politics of San Francisco:** At this time, anti-Chinese sentiments were growing violent in the Bay Area. Chinese laborers, thrown out of work by the completion of the Transcontinental Railroad, had flooded the city. Their willingness to work long hours for low wages added to an already extant sinophobia and alarm about the growing presence of Chinese in the city, especially among Irish immigrants arriving in the West either in search of gold or of work in the wake of labor surpluses following the Civil War. Whereas Judson was well known to be a champion of xenophobia and nativism, he was not particularly sympathetic to the Irish, who themselves were immigrants, in favor of the Chinese, for whom he seemed not to hold a brief one way or another. His refusal to become involved in local politics cooled his popularity to some extent, particularly in San Francisco, a city where the temperance movement never did find a solid foothold and where his notions of other social reform fell on mostly deaf ears.

XIV. **possible brief detour into Colorado:** Despite several claims to the contrary by various sources, there is no evidence that Judson actually was ever in Colorado, apart from the brief leg of the railway route that took him through the northernmost part of the territory.

XIV. **wanted nothing to do with the brassy writer:** The implication is that North had nothing but contempt for Judson. Some years later, when William F. Cody's first child was born, he announced that he was going to name him "Elmo," for Judson. He had apparently misunderstood Judson's first name.

North reportedly talked him out of it and convinced Cody to name the boy for Kit Carson, instead. This is described in *Telling Western Stories: From Buffalo Bill to Larry McMurtry,* by Richard W. Etulain (Albuquerque: University of New Mexico Press, 1999),162.

XIV. **found asleep, and probably drunk, under a nearby wagon:** Details of the first meeting between Judson and Cody have been so often and so widely published that there is no need to repeat them here. What makes the story suspect is that in almost every instance, the specific details, right down to the North quote, are precisely the same, without variation. This suggests that they all stem from a scripted source rather than from actual events. The only variance in the tale comes from Judson himself, who later claimed that he first met Bill Cody when he was on a buffalo hunt (Holbrook, 86). However, Holbrook's piece on Ned Buntline is so full of misstatements, errors, and outright fabrications that little credibility can be given to anything he says.

XV. **"Buffalo Bill, the King of Border Men":** Cody was never called "Buffalo Bill" before Judson attributed the name to him. Frontiersman William Matthewson later claimed that he owned the name first, but initially gave it to Cody in 1860. Other sources indicate, though, that any number of men who hunted buffalo for a living or supplied buffalo meat to forts, railroad crews, or other parties owned the name, and that it was a generic title more than a sobriquet. To be called "Buffalo Bill" could also have been a satiric reference in the time, a point that would have utterly escaped Judson, an Easterner (Richard R. Walsh, *The Making of Buffalo Bill: A Study in Heroics,* Indianapolis: Bobs-Merrill, 1928), 126.

XV. **selling more than 300,000 copies:** The term "best seller" was not in use until 1910 (Frank Luther Mott, *Golden Multitudes: The Story of Best Sellers in the United States.* New York: Macmillan, 1947), 308.

XV. **Nathaniel Hawthorne complained of in 1855:** In 1855, Hawthorne wrote to his publisher, William D. Ticknor, "America is now given over to a damned mob of scribbling women, and I should have no chance of success while the public taste is occupied with their trash—and should be ashamed of myself if I did succeed" (quoted in Mott,122).

XV. **the dime novel as a form was successfully launched:** "They were small sextodecima booklets of approximately 100 pages, with clear type and with orange wrappers upon which was printed a stirring woodcut in black. They sold for ten cents" (Johannsen 1: 4).

XV. **first profitable production of literature in the country:** Christine Bold, *Selling the Wild West: Popular Western Fiction, 1860–1960.* Bloomington: Indiana University Press, 1987), xiii.

XV. **begun casting about for another successful venture:** Although by no means the only purveyors of dime novels, Beadle and Adams came to dominate the industry in name, if not in fact. Founded by Irwin P. Beadle and Erastus Flavel Beadle, they originally were I. P. Beadle and Company, but also published as Beadle and Company,and Beadle and Adams. Ultimately, they would produce such series as Pocket Novels, Beadle's Boy's Library, Boy's Library of Sport, Story and Adventure, The New Dime Novels, Beadle's Half-Dime Library, Beadle's Popular Library, American Tales, and Frank Starr's American Novels, all dime novel adventures. Others were the Pocket Library, Half-Dime Library, and Dime Library. Some series offered 1,000 titles or more (Pearson,50–52).

XVI. **with cash prizes to attract the best possible work:** Prizes ranged from around $75 to $150, depending on the length of the story. Judson's first story, *The Last Days of Calleo; or, The Doomed City of Sin,* brought him a $75 prize (Monaghan, 125).

XVI. **with Ned Buntline as one of their premiere authors:** Francis Scott Street and Francis Shubael Smith bought *The New York Weekly Dispatch* in 1858 and dropped the last word in the title. They were editors and owners of *The New York Weekly* until Smith's retirement and Street's death, both occurring in 1887. The firm developed a book publishing arm in the 1880s and by the mid-1930s was a principal purveyor of what came to be called "pulp fiction." They issued inexpensively produced paperbacks, digests, and comic books. Among their more sensational publications was *Astounding Stories,* which they acquired from Clayton Magazine in 1933 and continued publishing until 1961.

XVII. **less cumbersome method of collecting postage from the mail source:** Reynolds, 8.

XVII. **almost everyone read them:** Walsh notes (45), "They were not for persons of consequence to read in their libraries, but for boys, for travelers, for soldiers, for sailors, for brakemen on the railroads, and hunters in camps." But Johannsen claims, "They were read by everybody, except schoolma'ams, pedants, and the illiterate" (1: 9). That Mark Twain was familiar with them is evidenced by his reference to one of Ned Buntline's more famous tales, *The Red Revenger; or, the Pirate King of the Floridas: A Romance of the Gulf and its Islands,* mentioned in *The Adventures of Tom Sawyer.*

XVII. **sometimes under a different name:** Judson mostly stole from himself. In 1847 he sold "Race on the Bahamas" to *Star Spangled Banner,* but it was actually a retitled and slightly revised version of a story he previously had published in the *Knickerbocker.* His story *The Boy Gold Miner* also appeared twice. In 1893 it was published in *Good News,* a Beadle and Adams juvenile organ, and attributed to Edward Z. C. Judson; it had previously appeared, though, in *The New York Weekly* under the authorial name Edward Minturn, a known Judson pseudonym (Monaghan, 250). In another instance, a dime novel attributed to Ned Buntline, *Old Nick of the Swamp,* was reprinted several times, but was originally published in Munro's Ten-Cent Novels in 1867 and attributed to "An Old Hunter," a common pseudonym for Edward S. Ellis. In a Beadle's Frontier Series, a reprint issued after the turn of the century, Ned Buntline is listed as the author; it might have been an honest mistake, or it might have been that the publishers decided that Ned Buntline had more market value than Edward S. Ellis, whose popularity had faded by that point. Another publisher, Hartz and Sibley, on February 25, 1896 offered through their Gem Library (a nickel series) *The Banded Pards of Colorado; or, Steel Grip the Invincible* under the name of "Ned Buntling." There were apparently several "Ned Buntling" stories published around the same time, but who "Ned Buntling" may have been is lost to history. Judson was ten years dead by that date; as there is no record of a previous publication of these, and as the final "g" is printed in a fashion that makes it easy to read as an "e," it seems unlikely that these are by Judson.

XVII. **this inspired him:** Tracing and keeping straight the various literary journals Judson started is difficult. His first editorial effort was *Ned Buntline's,* which appeared in 1844; it was this one which received initial praise from Lewis Gaylord Clark, but Judson lacked funds to continue publication. That same year, he joined forces with Lucius A. Hine, son of a prosperous Ohio family, and they issued *Western Literary Journal and Monthly Review* in November. This also attracted Clark's attention, in spite of Judson's inflammatory editorials, most likely because he published work from such period literary luminaries as Albert Pike and C. B. Gillespie. The journal folded in 1845 and Judson launched *Ned Buntline's Own,* running tales from his own life and guides to travelers on how to avoid confidence games, thieves, and gambling pitfalls in the "West," principally southern Ohio, Illinois, Kentucky, and Tennessee. This effort again collapsed for lack of subscriptions. In 1847, after marrying Annie Abigail Bennett, he persuaded her father to use his own money to revive it and manage it. It was more or less a scandal sheet, preaching social reform and political agenda and launching scurrilous attacks on known individuals, which caused Judson to declare his life always to be in danger and to move about New York city in disguise. It continued to publish until 1849, when Judson and Annie divorced. His marriage to Lovanche in 1853 gave him an opportunity to revive his journal again with her money, but that project was short-lived.

XVIII. **"a literary man":** Monaghan, 125. Judson's first actual publication was "The Captain's Pig," an extended anecdote he unsuccessfully offered to Lewis Gaylord Clark, who rejected it. Judson had it printed himself and sold or distributed it on his own. No copy of the story has survived. One unverifiable source indicates that later in his career, he offered a reward of $1,000 to anyone who could produce a copy. None turned up.

XVIII. **out of reach of the average American:** Most quality romances and novels sold for about $1.50 at the least expensive; this was more than a day's wages for most people.

XVIII. **achieve some more respectable fame:** Over the span of his career, Judson would use a variety of pseudonyms for a variety of purposes. Some of these were Charlie Bowline, Jack Brace, Chaptain Cleighmore, Frank Clewline, Henry Edwards, Jiles (or Jules) Edwards, Clew Garnet, Edward J. C. Handleboe, Mad Jack, L. Augustus Jones, Edward Minturn, and Harrison Gray Buchanan. In addition, he wrote under female names from time to time, and some articles signed "By one who knows all about it," "By the Orderly," and "By the Recluse," are also attributed to him (Monaghan, 333).

XVIII. **seeking to make a few dollars:** One list of Beadle and Adams authors lists more than 250 names; a healthy majority of them have the words, "Dead" or "Dead/Suicide," or "Dead/Whiskey" noted after them (Pearson, 83).

XVIII. **first rank of American authors:** Judson's literary ambitions were most likely derived out of a life-long competitive relationship with his father, Levi. Levi Judson, a consummate Freemason, was also an aspiring writer. He ultimately did publish several tepid biographies of American historical figures, mostly rehashes of previously published material, and achieved a modest notoriety in the field. His son, though, seemed all his life determined to best his father and prove to him that Edward's childhood rejection of the law as a profession was a wise decision.

XVIII. **soldiers bound for Mexico and the Southwest:** The first novelette he sold, *The Last Days of Calleo; or, The Doomed City of Sin,* was extremely popular with soldiers bound for the war in Mexico. This would inspire him to write several similar tales of the Mexican War and later in life to falsely claim that he was a veteran of the fight. He wasn't (Monaghan, 125).

XIX. **believed Baker initially had plagiarized from him:** Baker neatly sidestepped the issue by responding to Judson's assertion that he had stolen material from him by saying that Judson claimed that all the stories in *Mysteries and Miseries* were true and all the characters were real, so it was no offense to merely reproduce that which was actual (Monaghan,147).

XIX. **his arrest for public brawling:** During the height of the *Mysteries and Miseries* period, a gambler named Samuel Suydam, who had refused to pay Judson's blackmail, showed up at the Bennett brown-stone and demanded that Judson come down and meet him. Armed with swords and pistols, Judson stormed into the street, while his young wife, Annie, went into labor. Police arrived and arrested both men, and Annie's father posted Judson's bail. When Judson arrived home, she was giving birth. The baby had a birthmark shaped like a dagger, a phenomenon that jarred Judson so badly that, at his father-in-law's insistence, he signed The Pledge (for temperance) immediately. Then he went out to a saloon to celebrate with a few "bracers" that led to a two-day binge (Monaghan, 166).

XX. **hungry for inexpensive reading matter:** Mott, 149.

XX. **was an opportunity:** The demand was immediate and huge. Individual title runs could top 80,000 copies, a phenomenal number for the time (Mott, 149).

XX. **would come to be sold by subscription:** One of the ironies of the term dime novel is that they only occasionally sold for 10¢. Actually, almost from the first, some sold for 25¢. "When is a dime novel not a dime novel? Using the term with customary meaning of the middle 1870s and thereafter, the Dime Novels were not sold for a dime, but the Nickel Libraries were! Popularly, the term had little reference to the price at which the booklets were sold, but it was applied especially to any sensational detective or blood-and-thunder novel in pamphlet form" (Johannsen, 1: 3). Over time, the price of these cheaply produced volumes would vary from a nickel to a quarter or even two for a quarter. Beadle and Adams were adamant about the price, however; they actually published a picture of a 10¢ piece on the cover to discourage newsstand operators from trying to charge more. In the decades following the Civil War, the dime novel form would also morph into an often confusing series of "library" editions, all effectively the same—paper-wrapped rather than perfect bound, cheaply printed on inexpensive foolscap paper, garishly illustrated, and brightly colored. Called "yellow-backs" by those who continued to deride them, they actually were more often orange in hue. For more on this, see Pearson, 150–151.

XX. ". . . was in White Plains, New York": Pearson, 105.

XXI. appears nowhere in the company's records: Monaghan, 77.

XXI. during an 1851 visit to New Orleans: Judson tried without success to repeat his *Mysteries and Miseries* gambit in the Crescent City. The initial volume of the publication was not well received, though, and it turned out that no one in New Orleans, no matter how nefarious, was interested in paying to keep his name out of print (Monaghan, 193).

XXI. fairly thoroughly discredited: For a thorough discussion of "the Buntline Special" as well as attendant myths regarding Judson and Buffalo Bill, see Shillingberg.

XXI. the Wild Wild West: The term "Wild West" was coined long before Judson or the dime novel came onto the scene, but its specific application to the land west of the Mississippi did not come into common use until after the Civil War (Etulain, xii). Previously the term "border" was used to denote the line between the United States and western regions, be they U. S. Territories or Spanish possessions. The term "frontier," previously used to denote a line of international demarcation (as it still does in Europe), gradually replaced "border" in meaning and expanded to become a generic synecdoche for the entire expanse of land acquired by the United States by both the Louisiana Purchase from France (1803), which covered all the land from the Mississippi River to the Rocky Mountains and from the Gulf of Mexico to British North America, and the Treaty of Guadalupe Hidalgo (1848) with Mexico, which ceded Texas, New Mexico, Arizona, and California to the United States. The area covered by the treaty also included all or part of present-day Nevada, Colorado, Wyoming, Utah, and Kansas.

XXI. national spirit than at this time: The quote is misattributed. The original author was John B. Soule, a Terre Haute, Indiana, newspaper editor who published it as a headline for an 1851 editorial. Greeley appropriated it, misquoted it, and used in in his famous 1865 editorial in the *New York Herald*. His timing was acute.

XXII. future of America would be found: Probably no historian has more fully captured the *mythos* of the American West as it was perceived in Judson's time than does Henry Nash Smith. For a full discussion of the American comprehension of the American West in the mid-nineteenth century, see Smith's *The Virgin Land: The American West as Symbol and Myth* (Cambridge, MA: Harvard University Press, 1950).

XXII. ". . . mixed into 25 cent novels": Coggeshall is quoted in *The Dime Novel Western*, by Daryl Jones (Bowling Green, OH: The Popular Press, 1978), 3.

XXIII. *The Virginian: A Horseman of the Plains (1902)*: Daryl Jones's assertion that the first dime novel cowboy was created by Prentiss Ingraham, who fictionalized the exploits of Buck Taylor, a star in Buffalo Bill's show, in his 1887 *Buck Taylor, King of the Cowboys*, and in *The Raiders and Rangers* for Beadle's Half-Dime Library, has credibility (Jones, 101). The general perception of the cowboy previous to that was of an itinerant herder and agrarian laborer, rather than the "knight of the plains" that would be evolved out of the cattle drive era, roughly 1879–1889. When the exploits of Billy the Kid appeared, also in the 1880s, the image of the cowboy began to evolve into a more romantic figure, something that would be thoroughly exploited for the next century and would be enhanced and formalized on the model of Teddy Blue Abbott, among others.

XXIII. ". . . the myth of the American West": Etulain, 2.

XXIII. "The Greatest Romance of Our Age": Monaghan, 18.

XXIII. settings west of Mississippi: Etulain, 17.

XXIII. up until the present day: Of all the series in all the dime novels, the western stories were the most popular. Some years, more than 100 different series would be introduced, all running between 50,000 and 80,000 copies (Jones, 8).

XXIV. in later volumes, he got it right: Why Judson would put Wild Bill and Buffalo Bill together in the same story is a mystery on the face of it. The key incident in the novelette is the battle against the McCanles gang, which took place in 1862; Hickok and Cody didn't even meet until 1864 and never had a particularly close association (Walsh, 79).

XXIV. ". . . fame of Cody made it appear": Monaghan, 256.

XXIV. exploiting a chance when it presented itself: Cody's canniness as a showman who could spot an opportunity is well documented. He seemed to have a knack for knowing just how to present himself or his enterprise to the best advantage. In that sense, he and Judson shared a sixth sense for knowing what the public wanted and having the ability to deliver it with just the right amount of stagecraft and sensation.

XXIV. *Scouts of the Plains*: In December, 1872, the show arrived in St. Louis, where Judson was arrested on an old charge of inciting a riot and attempting to interfere with an election and, not incidentally, of skipping bail back in 1851. Although speculation was that Judson staged the arrest as a publicity stunt, he was nevertheless hauled before a judge and recharged. Carol S. Greeley, Treasurer of the Kansas Pacific Railway and President of the Provident Savings Institution, posted $1,000 bond, but Judson promptly skipped town again. When pursuing detectives dispatched by the judge attempted to seize the troupe's cash box, he claimed that the proceeds were not from *Scouts of the Plains,* but from a new show, *Scouts of the Prairie,* which was truly the same play, retitled.

XXIV. had huge appeal: Details concerning *Scouts of the Plains* are widely and well recorded throughout material on Judson and Cody and are generally in agreement on particulars. The original stage version was written, apparently with Judson's permission, by Fred Meader, a production Cody was invited to see and was utterly charmed by. By then, he had gotten over his surprise in finding out from the novelette that he, not Frank North, had killed Tall Bull, that he charged into the Indians' camp (he actually arrived some four hours after the battle) and that he rescued the captive white woman from the clutches of an Indian who was about to kill her. When he attended the performance, his impromptu summons from the audience to the stage gave him a taste of show business he apparently liked, in spite of his stage fright and awkwardness, which the audience found genuine and charming. Such was the impact of the novelette and Meader play on Cody's reputation—combined with two sensational hunting trips, one with James Gordon Bennett and one with Crown Prince Alexis of Russia, that took place in the interim, that Cody was suddenly elevated to national hero status, a role that propelled him to the Nebraska state house. He was also awarded the Medal of Honor for his service against the Indians in 1872 (Monaghan, 16), although Captain Jack Crawford, Cody's close friend and fellow scout, later averred, "Cody never received a scratch or killed an Indian" (Walsh, 15). In 1872, though, Judson was busy building Eagle's Nest, his home in Stamford named for his old hunting lodge. He had delighted locals by appearing in his own theatrical effort in the buckskinned guise of a character he named Cale

Durg, a Rocky Mountain Trapper, and the reception he received, combined with Cody's rising popularity, gave him the idea for a wild west show, starring Cody and featuring other scouts and real Indians. Accordingly, he sent for Cody, who had become disillusioned with his fledgling political career, and they met in Chicago, where Judson staged the new play based on a script that was part declamation, part temperance lecture, and mostly ridiculous banter, featuring actors hired to play Indians, who Cody had failed to deliver. Judson claimed he wrote the show in four hours. One critic wondered why it took him so long; this opinion was generally shared by most reviewers, who found it appallingly bad (Monaghan, 27–28); regardless, audiences loved it.

XXIV. **a dispute over money**: At the end of the tour, Judson paid Cody $6,000, which Cody thought was all too little, since Judson was announcing more than $20,000 in profits, and they parted company. John B. "Texas Jack" Omohundro, a Virginian who had ridden with J. E. B. Stuart, and Mlle. Giuseppina Morlacchi, an actress who was either French or Italian but who, nevertheless, played an Indian maiden, went with Cody as they started a new show on their own, with Wild Bill Hickok, hired to substitute for Judson's character, Cale Durg (Monaghan, 24). Judson always spoke well of Cody and made him the hero of a total of six novelettes, but there is no evidence that they ever met again after 1873. His one claim of visiting him in the summer of 1876 is clearly bogus, as Cody was, at the time, in Wyoming and Montana, riding scout for the 5th Cavalry in pursuit of Sitting Bull, following Custer's debacle at the Little Bighorn River and, famously and supposedly, killing Yellow Hair (Shillingberg, 150).

XXIV. **not returning to him until 1881**: Monaghan, 271

XXV. **Edward Ellis, Edward Wheeler, and Prentiss Ingraham**: Edward Ellis, author of *Seth Jones*, the sensational bestselling novel of 1860, is regarded as the author who more than anyone set the formulaic pattern for the dime novel western in the latter half of the century and beyond. His introduction of the historical Indian fighter Lew Wetzel as a fictional character in an 1861 novel, *The Frontier Angel; A Romance of Kentucky Rangers' Life*, played on the "ugly white man Indian-hater" theme that would become a consistent convention in western fiction until it morphed into the more comical rustic buffoon/sidekick to the hero of later forms (Bold, 28). Ellis went on to write hundreds of dime novels and became highly popular. In 1877, Edward Wheeler introduced the outlaw hero in the character of Deadwood Dick, a road agent in disguise, starting a series that ran to ninety-seven titles and established the tradition of the anti-heroic protagonist in western fiction. Colonel Prentiss Ingraham, son of the much maligned (by Judson) Professor J. H. Ingraham, was a veteran of the Civil War and soldier of fortune who fought in a half-dozen other conflicts around the world. Some estimates are that Colonel Ingraham wrote an average of two novels a month for a total of more than 1,000 titles before his death in 1904 (Etulain, 20–21). Others pare the total down to a more believable 500 or 600 (Pearson, 114). Ingraham possibly was the most prolific single dime novelist of the era. His principal importance, though, was that he utterly took over the Buffalo Bill franchise after publishing *The Crimson Tail* in 1876. Traveling with Cody as he toured with *The Congress of Rough Riders and Wild West Show* from the 1880s, Colonel Ingraham may well have authored as many as 211 of the more than 500 titles based on or supposedly written by Buffalo Bill, only about 300 of which were formally dime novels. Others aver that Ingraham probably wrote no more than 121 of them, still an impressive number (Jones, 65). Still, it was principally Ingraham who credited Judson with having written 400 dime novels (Johannsen 1:174); Ingraham would also write novelettes featuring Texas Jack, and multiple other works. For all that, Judson never seems to have regarded him as a competitor or rival, and Ingraham seemed to share a mutual admiration: "Perhaps my chief inspiration," he said, toward the end of his life, "was old Ned Buntline, who was really the first to write 'penny dreadfuls' and the inventor of the 'dime novel'" (Pearson, 212).

XXX. **Nothing salacious or even suggestive was allowed**: Street & Smith were particularly fastidious about the content of the fiction they published, especially after Edward L. Wheeler launched his Deadwood Dick series in 1877 (Jones, 3). As Dick was an outlaw/hero, the editors were especially cautious about the way he was handled. In later years, some dime novels based on the life of Jesse James were held back for fear that they might encourage murder in young boys (Bold, 6).

XXXI. "The Sentimental Age": Reynolds, 23.

XXXV. alter-ego: Cale Durg seems to have been an accidental creation that he made up mostly to amuse children around his Stamford, New York, home. Incorporating him into the play with Buffalo Bill and Texas Jack was, in some ways, a personal indulgence. Cale Durg appeared as a fiercely brave mountain man, whose principal role was to provide temperance lectures, it seemed. After the show's tour ended and a year later, Judson tried to take another show on tour, this time featuring Dashing Charlie and other characters from his other stories; it never could find an audience and folded in Louisville, while still on tour (Monaghan, 29). He mentions Cale Durg in some stories and makes him the avuncular hero of *Hazel-Eye*.

XXXV. ". . . other conventions of the romantic hero.": Bold, 12.

XXXV. ". . . drawing room *savoir faire*, and marriageability.": Jones, 47.

XXXV. ". . . told a whopper that nobody could believe.": Monaghan, 142.

Selected Bibliography

Bold, Christine. *Selling the Wild West: Popular Western Fiction, 1860–1960*. Bloomington: Indiana University Press, 1987.

Buckley, Peter G. "The Case Against Ned Buntline: The 'Words, Signs, and Gestures' of Popular Authorship. *Prospects: An Annual of American Cultural Studies*, 13 (1988): 249–272.

Carter, Robert A. *Buffalo Bill Cody: The Man Behind the Legend*. New York: Wiley, 2002.

Connelley, William Esley. *Wild Bill and His Era: The Life & Adventures of James Butler Hickok*. New York: The Press of the Pioneers, 1933.

Cox, J. Randolph. "Bibliographical Notes: Ned Buntline's Buffalo Bill Stories." *Dime Novel Round-Up* 76 No.3 (June 2007): 77–87.

---"Bibliographical Notes: The 'Lost' Buffalo Bill Serial by Ned Buntline." *Dime Novel Round-Up* 76 No. 4 (August 2007): 120–121.

Cox, William R. *Luke Short and His Era*. Garden City, N.Y: Doubleday, 1961.

Etulain, Richard W. *Telling Western Stories: From Buffalo Bill to Larry McMurtry*. Albuquerque: University of New Mexico Press, 1999.

Holbrook, Stewart H. "The Life and Times of Ned Buntline." In *Little Annie Oakley and Other Rugged People*. New York: Macmillan, 1948.

Johannsen, Albert. *The House of Beadle & Adams and Its Dime and Nickel Novels: The Story of a Vanished Literature*. Norman: University of Oklahoma Press, Vols. 1 & 2, 1950, Vol. 3, 1962. Online at http://libws66.lib.niu.edu/badndp/contents.home

Jones, Daryl. *The Dime Novel Western*. Bowling Green, OH: The Popular Press, 1978.

Lake, Stuart. *Wyatt Earp: Frontier Marshal*. New York: Houghton Mifflin, Co., 1931.

LeBlanc, Edward T. *Street and Smith's New York Weekly, 1857–1915*. Suring, WI: F. Schott Pub. Co., 1981.

Mead, Leon. "How 'Ned Buntline' Turned from Runaway Boy to Writing Genius; His Relations with 'Buffalo Bill' and the 'Know-Nothings.'" *Dime Novel Round-Up* 9 No. 101 (1941): 1–9.

Monaghan, Jay. *The Great Rascal: The Life and Adventures of Ned Buntline*. New York: Bonanza Books, 1951.

Mott, Frank Luther. *Golden Multitudes: The Story of Best Sellers in the United States*. New York: Macmillan, 1947.

Pearson, Edmund. *Dime Novels; or, Following an Old Trail in Popular Literature*. Port Washington, NY: Kennikat Press, 1968.

Pond, Fred E. *Life and Adventures of Ned Buntline*. New York: The Cadmus Book Shop, 1919.

Reynolds, Quentin. *The Fiction Factory; or, From Pulp Row to Quality Street (The Story of 100 Years of Publishing at Street & Smith)*. New York: Random House, 1955.

Shillingberg, William B. "Wyatt Earp and the 'Buntline Special' Myth." *Kansas Historical Quarterly* 42 No. 2 (1976): 113 to 154; online at http://www.kshs..org/publicat/1976/76_2_shillingberg. htm#Ref139

Smith, Henry Nash. *Virgin Land: The American West as Symbol and Myth*. Cambridge, MA: Harvard University Press, 1950.

Walsh, Richard J. *The Making of Buffalo Bill: A Study in Heroics*. Indianapolis: Bobbs-Merrill Co., 1928.

Bibliography of Buntline Novels

THIS FOLLOWING LIST OF TWENTY-FIVE TITLES CONSTITUTES, insofar as can be reasonably established with certainty, a complete bibliography of western dime novels published under the name Ned Buntline, a pseudonym for Edward Z. C. Judson. Judson is variously credited with more than 1,000 total publications, at least 400 of which are dime novels, or novelettes published in periodical form. It is possible, even likely, that there are other titles with western settings or themes published either under his name or under any of nearly a dozen other pseudonyms he used during his lifetime.

In his biography of Judson, Jay Monaghan refers to at least three and possibly more collections of original publications of *Street & Smith's New York Weekly,* but the locations of the materials that he seems to have looked through in the late 1940s and early 1950s have apparently disappeared or are no longer accessible. The main sources for original publications of Street & Smith's story weekly or story paper, as it has come to be called, are specific libraries at Syracuse University and the University of Minnesota, and two or three others. Syracuse University indicates that it has a "complete run," but a close inspection reveals gaps and missing pages in its holdings. Other libraries, including the Library of Congress, have only partial runs. In response to query, the LOC was unable to certify that they could locate any specific issues. The New York Public Library did not respond to multiple queries.

For the most part, the available copies of these materials can be found in microfilm form at any of several libraries across the country; but almost invariably, they are not the original Street & Smith publications but are reprints that were subsequently published by the Beadle and Adams publishing firm, or by the book publishing arm of Street & Smith that emerged in the 1880s, or by other periodicals and publishing houses over the course of the last three decades of the nineteenth century. Some were reprinted under different titles, and from time to time, the author's name was either altered or a pseudonym used by the author might be revived for a reprinted story with a "house title." In some instances, the reprinted text was cut to fit length format or editorial requirements demanded by a later publisher; in one or two cases, the reprinted text was edited for content. But the full extent of such alterations or what they exactly were in subsequent reprints, is not always clear. Insofar as can be determined and only with noted exceptions, the text of the microfilmed reprints used in this volume precisely duplicates the original plates and text of the Street & Smith publications or the other original publications.

The condition of the original publications and many of the reprints that do exist ranges from brittle to fragile to nearly completely deteriorated. In some cases, the original is in such bad shape that merely handling it at all causes it to disintegrate. This means that some of this material cannot even be digitally scanned, let alone photocopied, as the original paper on which it was printed was of the cheapest variety, acidic, and subject to rapid decomposition. As these materials were regarded as ephemeral at the time they were published, and as their contents have long been denigrated as "literary rubbish" by academic scholars and literary historians, little or no effort was made to preserve them. Only recently have literary historians and philologists begun to acknowledge the vital importance these story weeklies and dime novels, shilling shockers, nickel libraries, and other inexpensively produced fictions had in the formation of the modern American novel and film. Apart from their worth as embryonic examples of the popular fiction and culture that form the foundation for future writing, they also provide a unique glimpse into the social, cultural, and attitudinal profile of the nineteenth-century American.

Without rapid and comprehensive action, though, many of these materials will soon be gone. The loss to our understanding of this period of time and the importance it has to our own world is immeasurable.

The Western Novels of Ned Buntline

Big Foot Wallace, the Giant Hero of the Border. A Tale of the Lone Star State. Street & Smith's New York Weekly 29, no. 37–49 (1874). Reprinted *Log Cabin Library 97*, New York: Street & Smith, 22 Jan. 1891.

The Border Rivals. A Hunting Story of the Big Rockies. Beadle's Weekly, no 231–233 (1887). Reprinted as *The Montana Rivals; or, Shooting for the Queen of the Ranch, Banner Weekly* 12, 1894.

The Boy Miner. A Tale of Feather River. Street & Smith's New York Weekly 26, no 29–35 (1891). *Reprinted as The Boy Gold Miner; or, Fighting the Table Mountain Band. Good News no. 163–174 (1893).*

Buckskin Sam, the Scalp Taker. orig. pub. *The Scalp Taker, Street & Smith's New York Weekly* 30, no. 33–46 (1875). Reprinted as *Buckskin Sam, the Scalp Taker, Log Cabin Library 119*, New York: Street & Smith, 25 June 1891.

Buffalo Bill, the King of Border Men. Street & Smith's New York Weekly 25, no. 6–17 (1869–70). Reprinted, *People's Library 40*, New York: J. S. Ogilvie, 1881. Reprinted, *Buffalo Bill.* New York: International Book Company, 1886. Reprinted as *Buffalo Bill: Adventures in the West. Western Star 1.* New York: J. S. Ogilvie, 1887. Reprinted Fireside Library. New York: P. O. Vickery, 1 June 1896. Reprinted *Railroad Series 13–?*, New York: J. S. Ogilvie, 1900. Reprinted *Oglivie's Popular 50 Cent Books 13*, New York: J. S. Oglivie, 1902. Reprinted, *Fascinating Sensational Books 3.* New York: J. S. Oglivie, 1910.

Buffalo Bill's Best Shot; or, The Heart of Spotted Tail. A Story of Life on the Plains. Street & Smith's New York Weekly 27, no. 20–32 (1872). Reprinted *Street & Smith's New York Weekly* 41 no. 47 (1885)-42 no. 5

(1886). Reprinted *Sea and Shore Series 23* (1890). Reprinted as *Buffalo Bill's Best Shot: The Original Buffalo Bill Story, in Far and Near Series 28.* New York: Street & Smith, 1891. Reprinted as *Buffalo Bill's Best Shot; or, The Heart of Spotted Tail, Log Cabin Library 127,* New York: Street & Smith, 1891. Reprinted *Log Cabin Library 384,* New York: Street & Smith, 1892. Reprinted *Log Cabin Library Pocket Edition 3,* New York: Street & Smith, 1897. Reprinted (abridged) as *Buffalo Bill Stories. Buffalo Bill Thick Books,* New York: Street & Smith, 1901. Reprinted *Far West Library 2,* New York: Street & Smith, 1907. Reprinted *Buffalo Bill Border Stories 39,* New York: Street & Smith, 1918. Reprinted *Great Western Library 27,* New York: Street & Smith, 1928. Reprinted *Buffalo Bill and his Adventures in the West,* New York: Arno Press, 1974. et al.

Buffalo Bill's Last Victory; or, Dove-Eye, the Lodge Queen. Street & Smith's New York Weekly 27, no. 35–49 (1872); *Street & Smith's New York Weekly* 42, no. 5–19 (1887). Reprinted *Sea and Shore Series 24,* New York: Street & Smith, 1890. Reprinted *Log Cabin Library 128,* New York: Street & Smith, 1891. Reprinted *Log Cabin Library 386,* New York: Street & Smith, 1898. Reprinted *New Edition 49,* New York: Street & Smith, 1898. Reprinted (abridged and expurgated, "by the Author of Buffalo Bill") as *Buffalo Bill's Victory. A Story of Tangled Tales,* in *Buffalo Bill Stories 3,* New York: Street & Smith, 1901; et al.

Dashing Charlie, the Texan Whirlwind, Street & Smith's New York Weekly 27, no. 16–30 (1872). Reprinted *Log Cabin Library 141,* New York: Street & Smith, 1891. Reprinted *Sea and Shore Series 25,* New York: Street & Smith, 1891. Reprinted *Log Cabin Library 400,* New York: Street & Smith, 1896. Reprinted *Log Cabin Library Pocket Edition 42,* New York: Street & Smith, 1898.

Hazel-Eye, the Girl Trapper. A Tale of Strange Young Life. Street & Smith's New York Weekly 26, no. 37–49 (1871). Reprinted *Log Cabin Library 75,* New York: Street & Smith, 1890. Reprinted *Street & Smith's New York Weekly* 51, no. 11–13 (1895).

Little Buckshot, the White Whirlwind of the Prairie. A Wild Story about the Far Northwest. Street & Smith's New York Weekly 25, no. 33–45 (1870). Reprinted *Street & Smith's New York Weekly 43,* no. 6–19 (1887–88). Reprinted *Log Cabin Library 136,* New York: Street & Smith, 1891.

Long Mike, the Oregon Hustler. Log Cabin Library 139, New York: Street & Smith, 1891. [No previous publication known.]

Merciless Ben, the Hair Lifter. A Story of the Far Southwest. Street & Smith's New York Weekly 37, no. 17–25 (1882). Reprinted *Log Cabin Library 109.* New York: Street & Smith, 1891.

The Miner Detective; or, the Ghost of the Gulch. Log Cabin Library 1, New York: Street & Smith, 1889. [No previous publication known.]

Mountain Tom. A Thrilling Story of the Diamond Fields. Street & Smith's New York Weekly 28, no. 7–20 (1872–73). Reprinted *Mountain Tom. A Story of the Diamond Fields, Log Cabin Library 45,* New York: Street & Smith, 1890.

Norwood, or, Life on the Prairie. New York: Garrett and Co., 1849. Reprinted New York: W. F. Burgess, 1850. Reprinted New York: Garrett, Dick, & Fitzgerald, 186?. Reprinted as *Sib Cone, the Mountain Trapper.* New York: Frank Starr, 1870. Reprinted as *Old Sib Cone, the Mountain Trapper, Beadle's New Dime Novels 356,* New York: Beadle and Adams, 1876. Reprinted *New Beadle's Dime Novels 588,* New York: Beadle and Adams, 1885. Reprinted as *Fritz's Old Score,* New York: Beadle and Adams, 1890.

Orthodox Jeems. A Tale of Wild Adventure in the Black Hills. Street & Smith's New York Weekly 40, no. 6–11 (1884–85). Reprinted *Orthodox Jeems, Log Cabin Library 58,* New York: Street & Smith, 1890.

Red Dick, the Tiger of California. A Robber Story of the Golden State. Street & Smith's New York Weekly 27, no. 31–44 (1872). Reprinted as *Mountain Tom. A Story of the Diamond Fields. Log Cabin Library 140,* New York: Street & Smith, 1891.

Sensation Sate, the Queen of the Wild Horse Range. Street & Smith's New York Weekly 39, no. 33–39 (1884). Reprinted *Log Cabin Library 80,* New York: Street & Smith, 1890.

Silver Wing! The Angel of the Tribes. Street & Smith's New York Weekly 30, no. 17–26 (1875). Reprinted *Silver Wing, the Angel of the Tribes, Log Cabin Library 112,* New York: Street & Smith, 1891.

Stella Delorme; or, The Comanche's Dream. New York Mercury 21, 1859. Reprinted as *The Red Warrior; or, Stella Delorme's Comanche Lover. A Romance of Savage Chivalry, American Tales 53,* New York: Beadle and Adams, 1869. Reprinted *Beadle's Dime Library 23.* New York: Beadle and Adams, 1877. Reprinted *Beadle's Dime Library 1038.* New York: Beadle and Adams, 1900; et al.

Texas Jack, the White King of the Pawnees. A Mate to Buffalo Bill. Street & Smith's New York Weekly 28, no. 20–33 (1873). Reprinted *Sea and Shore Series 28,* New York: Street & Smith, 1891. Reprinted *Log Cabin Library 132,* New York: Street & Smith, 1891. Reprinted *Log Cabin Library 399,* New York: Street & Smith, 1896. Reprinted *Log Cabin Library Pocket Edition 31,* New York: Street & Smith, 1898.

Tombstone Dick, the Train Pilot; or, the Traitor's Trail. A Story of the Arizonian Wilds. Beadle's Dime Library 361, New York: Beadle and Adams, 1885. [No previous publication known.]

Wild Bill's Last Trail. orig. pub. as *On the Death Trail; or, the Last of Wild Bill. Street & Smith's New York Weekly* 35, no. 15–19 (1880). Reprinted as *Wild Bill's Last Trail, Nugget Library 49,* New York: Street & Smith, 1890. Reprinted *Diamond Dick Library 192,* New York: Street & Smith, 1896.

Will Cody, the Pony Express Rider; or, Buffalo Bill's First Trail. Beadle's Weekly 3, no. 127–141 (1885). Reprinted *Buffalo Bill's First Trail; or, Will Cody, the Pony Express Rider, Beadle's Dime Library 517,* New York: Beadle and Adams, 1888.

Wrestling Joe, the Dandy of the Mines. Street & Smith's New York Weekly 26, no. 8–26 (1871). Reprinted (abridged) *People's Library 9.* New York: J. S. Ogilvie, 1878. Reprinted (abridged) as *Wrestling Joe, the Dandy of the Mines; or, the Crimson Trail of the Avenger. Log Cabin Library 158,* New York: Street & Smith, 1892. Reprinted (abridged) as *Wrestling Joe, the Dandy of the Mines; or, the Crimson Trail of the Avenger. Log Cabin Library 401.* New York: Street & Smith, 1896.

Acknowledgments

WHEN I UNDERTOOK THIS PROJECT, I had no inkling of the difficulties and obstacles that lay in the way of collecting not only usable and readable copies of the primary material but also in assembling a reasonably accurate and complete bibliography of secondary sources. This journey took more than a year, and even after as thorough an investigation as can be accomplished with limited funds and modern technology and old-fashioned library scouring, there is always the nagging feeling that something has been overlooked or omitted.

Nevertheless, no work of this kind can be accomplished without the able assistance and contributions of many other individuals. In this case, I would still be helplessly "afloat," to use a favorite Ned Buntline word, without the dedication, imaginative innovation, dogged determination, and scholastic excellence of my research assistant, Elizabeth Berrett. The many hours she spent standing over a hot scanner or squinting at microfilm or digital reproduction provided as firm a foundation as could be built. Her reliability and constancy as well as her patience in putting up with my frequent panics and poor memory have sustained me over the past year and given me confidence that the work here accomplished is as complete and thorough as is possible. I also must acknowledge the tireless and eye-straining efforts of Lauren Dixon, who ably "read behind" me to verify the text in the microfilmed reproductions of Ned Buntline's work. Her superlative efforts were invaluable in the collation of the texts, deciphering and filling in the original words and phrases that had been obliterated by damage and inferior technical reproductive techniques, and creating as accurate a representation of Ned Buntline's original words as is possible.

A similar note of gratitude must go to J. Randolph Cox, former research librarian at St. Olaf College and editor of the *Dime Novel Round-Up,* a publication of long standing that is devoted to the preservation and study of this uniquely American publishing phenomenon. Not only was Mr. Cox willing to answer dozens and dozens of questions that came up in the course of my research, almost always responding to e-mail queries instantly, he also was able to provide me with a good many leads and suggestions for secondary materials I might otherwise have overlooked. His corrections, emendations, and well-informed speculations about matters that cannot be established with certainty have added immeasurably to the overall picture of the dime novel and Ned Buntline's role in its production. Additionally, Mr. Cox was able to examine and report on some materials that are in too fragile a condition to be reproduced or lent for perusal. His uncompensated service to this project has been remarkable.

Additional special thanks needs to be given to Angie Schroder and Lynne Thomas at the University of Northern Illinois Rare Books and Special Collections Department.

In Ms. Berrett's words, "They've been AWESOME!" Meredith Gillis at the University of Minnesota also deserves a special nod of gratitude for her patience with our many inquiries, as does Nicholette A. Dubrowolski at Syracuse University. Other librarians and archivists who provided special help and were kind enough to make extra effort on our behalf were Stephen E. MacLeod at the University of California, Irvine, Marj Ochs at the University of Texas at Austin, the librarians at the University of North Dakota and Auraria Library in Denver, Colorado, and the curators and researchers at the Buffalo Bill Memorial Museum in Golden, Colorado. I would also like to thank Christine Bold, author of *Selling the Wild West: Popular Western Fiction, 1860 to 1960,* for responding so fully to my e-mails, to Larry McMurtry and his staff at The Blue Pig for his advice on my attempts to locate original publications of dime novels, and the Interlibrary Loan staff at the University of Texas at Dallas for their cooperation and reliability. Additional appreciation goes to Dennis Kratz, Dean of Arts & Humanities at the University of Texas at Dallas for providing me with a course release to free up time to complete this volume.

Finally, I need to thank Carlo DeVito, Director of Sterling Innovation, for his patience in waiting until the materials and composition of this project could be completed and for his sustained support of the integrity of this project, and also my long-suffering wife, Judy, who, after all these years, still keeps trying to understand why I do what I do.